CHARLIE'S REQUIEM: RESISTANCE

BOOK 3

A. AMERICAN AND WALT BROWNING

PREFACE

THE UNTHINKABLE HAPPENED. WHILE CHARLIE, a pharmaceutical sales representative, was visiting her favorite physician's office just a mile from Universal Studios, an EMP struck the nation. Without electricity, computers, or even modern automobiles, the city of Orlando rapidly deteriorated into chaos.

After surviving the first week, Charlie left Dr. Kramer's office behind to try to find safety outside the city. Travelling with Janice, a nurse, and local college student Garrett, they were set upon by a white supremacist gang that had struck a deal with the country's new leadership.

A new brand of fascism is taking hold, driven by a remarkably well-organized Department of Homeland Security. DHS is using prisoners and criminals to scare the population into reporting to government camps. There, undesirables such as constitutionalists and the helplessly disabled are rounded up...and never seen again.

While Charlie and her friends fight their way through the urban nightmare, Dr. Kramer has returned to his home in the Central Florida countryside. His family has fared well, thanks to their hurricane preparedness, though he fears for his daughter Claire, who is stranded in Nashville at Vanderbilt University. Their neighbors have taken care of each other, and their suffering has been minimal. But Dr. Kramer has seen the horror of the government's new agenda, as the elderly and chronically disabled mysteriously disappear. Following the buses bound for the nearby camp, Kramer discovers the terrible truth. The camp is not for interment but extermination.

Former police officers John, Beth and Big Mike joined DHS and are now an integral part of the corrupt regime. Their personal ethics have turned them against their new government masters, as they too discover the nefarious powers that are controlling the reins of power.

Charlie and her friends made their way to her father's abandoned home outside Orlando to regroup. They were saved by a young investment banker named Jorge and his girlfriend, Maria, who herself was rescued from a DHS camp. Along the way, they picked up an abused young man named Beker.

They have survived, so far, with minimal survival skills. And now they are getting ready to push through the rest of Orlando, having fought and killed to gain every inch of ground. This terrifying new world has placed each of them in situations they could never have imagined. Every step they take will put them in mortal danger and every decision they make could be their last.

Charlie's Requiem: Resistance shows the inhumanity of man and the forces that make people rise to the occasion, or sink into depravity. Our military men and women who swore an oath to fight all enemies, foreign and domestic, can be used in nefarious ways. And Charlie has to find a way through all that, while keeping her life and soul alive.

CHAPTER 1

MAITLAND, FL
MID-WINTER

"In ourselves our safety must be sought.
By our own right hand, it must be wrought."

— William Wordsworth

A BULLET EXPLODED THE WOOD FRAME of the door beside Jorge's head. Cursing, he jumped through the front door of the abandoned home and dove for the floor.

"I can't see where it's coming from!" he yelled to me.

I stayed quiet, not wanting to give my position away. I was squatting behind a knee wall that jutted from the side of the home we had just broken into. Just in front of the wall, a cluster of camellia bushes, heavy with dark red blooms, anchored the corner of the front garden bed. The wall, more decorative than functional, was little more than a single layer of concrete blocks slathered with stucco. The high-speed bullets from a battle rifle, traveling around three thousand feet per second, would make short work of both the wall and me if the shooter found where I had hidden.

I had approached this corner of the home from the rear of the house, having circled through the back yard in a vain attempt to gain access to the structure through a side or back door. I had heard Jorge pounding on the front door as I snuck through the back yard, announcing our intention to break in. I thought that defeated the purpose, but he wanted to make sure no one was inside. I didn't argue since his incessant knocking would draw any potential occupant to the front of the home, minimizing the chances that I would be noticed.

CRACK...CRACK!

Two more rounds hit the door frame in an attempt to end my friend's life.

I belly-crawled to the corner of the wall, peeking around its edge. The bushes were flanked by foot-high society garlic ground cover, which prevented me from seeing anything other than the rooftops of the houses across the road. The street to my left was empty, and I risked crawling into the bushes. A scan to the right showed no people in that direction.

The gunfire seemed like it was coming from across the street, but with the homes tightly packed together, the sound of the rifle echoed. The shots could be coming from anywhere. Each house had a driveway that went straight up to a double car garage. The homes, built less than 30 years ago, all sat within a 50 feet of the street. Mature oak trees, towering nearly a hundred feet high, were planted between the sidewalk and road. Several driveways had abandoned cars or SUVs snuggled up to their closed garage doors. I stayed still, searching for the most likely place the shooter could have set themselves up.

I brought my AR-15 up to a prone shooting position and scanned the scene in front of me through my red dot sight. I once again wished I had a magnified scope to look through. My Aimpoint red dot was delightfully light, which was why I chose it. But having magnified scope right now would have been wonderful, and I vowed to change my optics as soon as I found one worth the additional weight I would have to lug around.

CRACK!

There! One house to the right and across the street. The garage door had been lifted about two feet off the ground, and the flash of gunfire briefly illuminated the dark interior.

"Stop!" Jorge yelled from inside the house. "Stop shooting!"

CRACK! CRACK! CRACK! CRACK!

Round after round poured into the home, the flimsy wood frame and stucco construction doing little to stop the bullets. I could hear Jorge scrambling to the back of the house. Then came the thud of the rear glass door slamming. I hoped he'd made it into the back yard.

The shooting from across the street stopped. I estimated they'd fired about thirty rounds.

I kept watch for movement from within the darkened garage while Jorge crawled up behind me. His heavy breathing began to slow as his adrenalin dump subsided. Being on the receiving end of close to a full magazine would make anyone jumpy.

"You alright?" I whispered, keeping my eyes on the enemy's position.

"Shit," he gasped. "That was intense."

"I guess they didn't get the memo," I remarked drily. We'd gone to all the trouble of leaving a note at the neighboring houses, stating our intent to search for food and supplies, but apparently the shooter didn't read it or didn't care.

My group had made our way to my father's house after abandoning downtown Orlando. My father, an avid sportsman, had a nice stash of gear for us, including a few rifles and handguns. More importantly, this was home for me. Although I didn't live here after my parents divorced, I had spent many weekends with him and his second wife before I left for college. Even though it had been over ten years since I'd slept under this roof, I drew comfort from the familiarity of the house. I nearly cried when I saw the same bedspread and pillows I used back then. I guess I needed some normalcy more than I had thought. That night, I felt good for the first time since the lights went off.

That was almost four weeks ago. Since then, we had organized ourselves and canvassed the neighborhood.

My dad lived on the middle street of three identical circular roads, which looped around and reconnected to the common north/south street that ended at the lake. He lived on the "inside" of the circle, with the "outer" homes backing up to a similar cluster of homes to the north and south. The three circular street neighborhood was as isolated as you could find. The southern street ended on Lake Maitland, while the other two circular streets to the north were guarded by eight-foot-high block walls to the east and north, effectively creating an isolated nest. A decent situation given that we were still in the middle of one of the most densely populated parts of Central Florida.

A few days after arriving, we began to venture out, making contact with anyone that hadn't left. With three similar circular roads making up our new area of operation, and my father's place on the middle of the three circular streets, it wasn't long before we had surveyed our surroundings and we found only two houses still occupied. The first was around the bend from my dad's place. The owners, both retired, were at the end of their ability to survive here on their own. The day after we showed up, we saw them walking up to the main road. They had finally given up and put their lives in the hands of the new government.

The other house that we had found occupied was owned by a young couple, Harley and Ashley Riker. They didn't see any need to leave their house for the unknown future of a government camp, especially after they heard our story. With a backyard pool and plenty of propane tanks salvaged from neighbors, they were able to boil water and cook meals. We agreed to cooperate while we were in the neighborhood, but otherwise our group left the couple alone.

We were, essentially, on our own.

With the detailed maps provided by DHS agent John Drosky, we planned our burglaries before venturing out. About two weeks ago, we wrote a note for each home and taped them on every front door in the surrounding neighborhoods, telling any stragglers that we planned on scavenging for supplies. We had hoped to prevent the type of attack we had just survived. The note stated that we were looking for food, assuring any homeowner that we would respect their property and would leave them alone. We wanted to head off any confrontations like the one we had just experienced. Thus, my sarcastic remark about the homeowner "not getting the memo."

"What now?" I asked.

"Best way to survive a gunfight is to run away."

"Or not get into one to begin with," I added.

Jorge grunted in agreement as we darted behind the house and approached the wooden stockade fence. Our backpacks were nearly full of salvaged items, and they went over the barrier first.

We limited ourselves to gathering calorie dense food so the packs were heavy, but I was still a little disappointed with our haul. Packages of trail mix and canned meats were high on our list, but surprisingly few places were stocked with such things. Most pantries offered canned vegetables, soups, and a ton of pre-packaged coffee pods. I didn't want to carry any item that didn't give me a full meal's worth of calories. Dried or dehydrated was best, although I do have to admit that I made room for hot chocolate packages. Sometimes, chocolate is the only thing that helps.

We scaled the fence, and a few minutes later we were back to my dad's house. I sighed as we deposited our loot onto the growing pile of goods we had salvaged. Spam, instant rice, pasta, nuts, peanut butter, and trail mix were calorie-dense foods, but they didn't make for particularly delicious meals.

One of the things we'd really been looking for was Crisco shortening, and we'd struck yellow gold—or lard—on a previous trip. A few days after the EMP struck, Harley had taken the meat out of his garage freezer before it spoiled and made jerky. Over two hundred pounds of venison and beef had been stripped and dehydrated in his Magic Elite 50 outdoor grill.

We ground up the dried meat and combined it with Crisco in a two-to-one ratio by volume to make pemmican. In some of the batches, we added a couple of extra items to add variety. A tablespoon of honey along with dried fruits like raisins, dates or dried apples were added in an equal volume to the fat. The taste was divine, but Harley warned us that the shelf-life of these pemmican balls were a year or less, while the pulverized meat and fat balls could last years.

I didn't care about shelf-life since we had less than fifty miles to travel. I went with the ones with the fruit.

When we were done, we had over a hundred Ziploc bags full of pemmican in addition to our other calorie-dense food supplies. Now we just needed a way to filter water for the trip. We still hadn't run across any water purifying straws or camping filtration systems since we'd started our search, and I was starting to get anxious.

"You guys alright?" Harley Riker asked as he joined us.

His wife, who had been boiling water outside, followed a few moments later. "We heard gunfire," Ashley said.

"Yeah, we're fine," Jorge replied. "We were over in the King's Row neighborhood and ran into a little trouble."

"More than a little," I added. "I think some idiot did a magazine dump on us."

"Which house was it?" Harley asked. "Me and Ashley ran into a guy on the south loop of the neighborhood while we were scrounging for propane. The way that guy was talking to us, he sounded like some kind of loner. What was weird," Riker continued, after he'd finished stacking some of the canned soups in a cluster on the floor, "was that his garage was lined with old newspapers and phone books, all stacked up against the walls, and even across the door opening."

"Was it the faded yellow one-story with the dirt front yard?" Jorge asked.

"Yeah," Harley said. "That's him. He's been a problem for his neighbors for quite a while. Never kept up the yard and always had the HOA on his back about it. They claimed his house was lowering the property values. You know the type."

"Well, I don't think we need to bother him anymore," I said. "We have enough to get out of the city."

"Have you decided where to go?"

"Not yet," I replied. "Jorge and Maria are definitely heading to his brother's ranch. I don't know if I want to join them, but I really don't see any other viable option."

"Still thinking of getting to Dr. Kramer's place?" Ashley asked.

"Janice and I would like to go there," I replied. "But we don't know if he can handle the extra mouths to feed."

About a week after the EMP had darkened the nation, Jorge's entire family had left their south Orlando home and walked to one of the state's largest cattle ranches. Located about sixty miles south of the city, it covered nearly half of the east/west length of the state and was home to thousands of heads of Brahman and Angus cattle. Jorge's brother was employed there and assured his family that they would all be welcome and needed when they arrived.

"Pretty sure my brother has the resources to take us in" Jorge said. "They're hunkered down on a huge cattle ranch, and they could use more people to guard the property. You two should think about joining us."

***

"I wish we could talk to John," Janice absently stated as she began to break down our backpacks and separate our supplies from the stuff we would be leaving behind with Harley and Ashley. "I would love to find out what's going on out there."

"Yeah, well I wish for a lot of stuff too," I replied.

I stripped off my battle belt and dropped it onto the kitchen counter. I'd taken it from my dad's gun closet, and I had to say it was a nice addition to my gear. It was a simple 5-11 tan nylon belt with an adjustable buckle. It has three magazine pouches attached to the left side, an IFAK on the right back hip, and a tan dump pouch hooked to it at the small of my back. I also took a single-point sling from his stash, which I used to carry my rifle. It let me use both hands as the AR hung on my right side. During those long days of scavenging, it had saved my back and shoulders from untold wear and tear.

I also had my dad's Glock 19 in an outside waistband paddle holster. It never left my side, even staying under my pillow when I crashed for the night. The Glock had upgraded ghost ring night sights and an extended magazine and slide release. My father called it his "Frankenpistol." He thought of himself as a regular gunsmith because he bought and installed most of the parts himself. I later found out he had a professional put in the 4.5-pound trigger, but I never let on that I knew that little fact. Despite the extras, it was nearly half a pound lighter than my Hi Point 9 mm, had double the magazine capacity, and a far better trigger. I will always fondly remember the strength and security the Hi Point gave me those first weeks after the lights went out, but there was no doubt that I was going to be running the Glock from this point forward.

I sent a mental thank you out to my dad for providing me and my friends with food, safety, and defense. I pray he's safe at his cottage in North Carolina.

Ashley and Janice finished putting the things we weren't taking on our journey into a cardboard box. Ashley hefted her stash and carried it outside to her red wagon, taking these cans and bags of food items to add to their own growing pantry.

It has always been difficult for me to break into homes and take the food that had been left behind. We discussed this when we got to my dad's house, and all of us agreed to minimize any damage in entering the homes. We also decided to only take food and a limited amount of clothing. Even though the country had been turned upside down, my conscience struggled against our immediate needs when it came to scavenging from the houses nearby. I was glad to see that the group felt the same way.

The Rikers had a nice one-story home on a cul-de-sac one street over. The houses at the bottom of their street were lakefront, and made up the southern boundary of the three-road homeowner association. Their location gave them some security since no one would be passing through on their way to somewhere else. If someone came down to their part of the neighborhood, they were there on purpose—a purpose that was, at this point, likely nefarious.

Their concrete block home was well built with heavy hurricane shutters attached to the street-facing windows, which provided some safety from the average burglar. I thought it gave them a false sense of security, especially seeing what damage the AR-15 had done to the house we had just left.

Harley and Ashley have adamantly refused to join us when we leave. They are comfortable here—frankly, too comfortable given the chaos beyond the neighborhood. I hope they reconsider. With my first-hand knowledge of the evil that I know will someday visit itself on this neighborhood, I fear for their safety.

"Let's get together at our place for tonight for dinner," Ashley said as she came back to the kitchen. "I've got some canned meat I'm going to put on the grill, and I can whip up some pasta and make bread in our gas oven."

"I'm up for that," Jorge said. "When do you want us over there?"

"Come on a little before sundown," she replied. "That'll give me time to make the bread."

I smiled a little. With the power off, we were weaning ourselves from technology and using nature as our guide. Before, it would have been "seven o'clock," or "after work." Now, our lives were marked by the position of the sun.

It was still winter, but the days were slowly getting longer. Typical of Florida, it hadn't rained lately, and the clear afternoon sky promised more of the same. The daytime was very comfortable, but the night air was downright cold. Layering clothes was the norm this time of year, and tonight would be no exception. We would be eating on the patio using a gas heater for both warmth and light. Despite the promise of gas heat, I had some new Mechanix gloves that I kept in my emergency bug-out bag, and I'd be wearing them tonight.

We had learned to carry one of these "go bags" wherever we went, each of us keeping a minimal amount of survival necessities on us at all times in case we needed to make a sudden exit.

I had attached some MOLLE straps and carabiners to my dad's old Wolfman duffel bag. The clips let me attach the bug-out bag to any other backpack I was toting, or I could hook it directly to my battle belt at the small of my back next to my dump pouch.

Along with the Mechanix gloves, my bag held a fire starter kit—which included some cotton balls saturated with petroleum jelly and wrapped in aluminum foil—along with a pack of matches and a Bic lighter. I packed feminine products, a spare pair of socks, and a change of clothes in a large Ziploc bag. There was a basic first aid kit along with the narcotics that Dr. Kramer had given me and Janice the first days after the EMP attack. My food supply was minimal, with just a few energy bars, a couple balls of pemmican, and some chicken bouillon cubes and hot chocolate powder. A vial of unscented Clorox was there if I couldn't start a fire—just eight drops would sterilize a gallon of water. I had also packed one of the woven cotton blankets that my step-mom used to keep in a wicker basket by the family room couch.

The clothes, food, medicine, and toiletries were wrapped in couple of black, contractor-sized trash bags, which could double as a rain poncho or ground cover. I had a lightweight two-quart aluminum pot stuffed on top, straining the zipper of the bag that I could use to boil water or cook some broth. The aluminum was light weight and would heat quickly on an open flame. Finally, I carried a pocket knife and always had my handgun on my hip and my rifle at arm's length. If I had to, I could grab the bag and rifle and be out the door in less than thirty seconds. With these minimal items, I would be self-sufficient for days.

I was as prepared as I was going to be—and now I wasn't sure what to do. Janice was sitting at the large round table sewing one of Garrett's shirts, which he had torn a few days earlier. Garrett sat next to her as usual, his handgun disassembled as he cleaned and lubricated it. Their chairs had been scooted together so that their shoulders touched as they did their chores. I heard murmuring from the adjoining family room where Jorge and Maria were sitting on the couch, snuggled next to each other. I watched in silence as they spoke quietly, both smiling and gazing into each other's eyes.

For almost a minute, I stood there while the other two couples were immersed in each other, and I suddenly felt very alone. I didn't realize until just then how isolated I was. Janice had Garrett, while Maria had Jorge. Me, I had nothing but my rifle and the memories of an embarrassingly small number of guys that had passed through my life over the last few years.

Depressed, I went to my dad's study and plopped down in his leather chair. I gazed around the room and saw his life story played out in the many framed pictures he'd displayed throughout the room. Absent were any pictures of my mom, which I fully understood. Instead, over a dozen black and white prints were interspersed with smaller color pictures on the wall and in desktop frames.

On his desk were the photographs that he held dearest, the ones he looked at when he sat down to work. There were three pictures staring back at me from their brushed chrome frames. One was of him and his new wife on their wedding day. I remembered the ceremony and the mixed emotions I felt when they exchanged their vows. Over the years, my anxiousness has diminished to a point where I am happy that he found peace and joy in someone else. But if I had to be honest, I will always be a little jealous, wondering if he couldn't have done the same with my mom. But as the old Sheryl Crow song goes, it's not about getting what you want, it's about wanting what you've got.

The second frame held of my grandparents on their wedding day.

The last picture was my favorite photo from when he and I went fishing in Canada. In the photo, we were standing in front of our boat, holding up our stringers of fish. We both looked so happy, with not a care in the world. I was just eleven years old then, full of possibilities.

I stared at the picture, remembering the warm and happy feelings from that week in the Canadian wilderness. Our guide would take us out each day with a large cooler loaded with goodies to make a "shore" lunch. I remember the three of us pulling up to a small island in the middle of the largest, cleanest lake I had ever seen. We could see thirty feet below us, the glacial water was so clear.

I'll never forget the man that guided us, nor the train-in trip to the fishing lodge. He was a half white and half Indian, or as the Canadians called them, an Odawa First Nation tribesman. He reminded me of some of the passengers I'd seen on our train ride to the fishing camp in the Ontario outback. Several times during the journey, the train would stop in the middle of the wilderness, and I watched as one or two solitary figures would jump off their car carrying a large backpack and supplies. The stops were little more than a patch of cleared grass with a tall wooden pole as a marker. As the engine began to slowly take us away, I saw these lone figures disappear into the surrounding pine forest, melting into the shadows of the thick needle curtains that draped down from the trees. Within moments, they had blended into nature, swallowed by her magnificent embrace. These men were rugged and completely confident as they strode away from the modern iron horse that brought them home.

My only disappointment was when I found out that our guide's name was Bill. I expected something far more exotic, but I suppose his white mother or father got to pick the name.

A moment of self-pity floated to the surface as I remembered the sunny days on that northern Ontario lake. We cubed a slab of bacon, frying it up in the large iron skillet, making the grease that we would fry our potatoes and fish in. As we cooked the spuds and freshly caught walleye, we chewed on the bacon cubes while a large, open can of baked beans sat at the edge of the fire. We ate like kings while Bill and my dad downed a couple of Labatt's beers and I drank my Coke.

But now, the fishing isn't for fun but for survival. And sitting around a fire at night doesn't carry the same mystique when there's no electricity to return to. As much as the fondness of those early memories made me feel, it also triggers a sadness when I recognize that life will never be that innocent again.

I don't know how long I lingered in the room, lost in my memories, but after a bit I got up from the desk. I removed the fishing photo from its frame and put it into my "go" bag before returning to the kitchen.

Garrett and Janice hadn't moved, still busy with their personal chores. Jorge and Maria were napping on the couch, each with an arm draped over the other.

"I'm going to take a shower," I said. No one noticed.

Our shower was outside. We rigged up a couple of shower curtains surrounding a five-gallon bucket that was hanging from the roof's eaves. Jorge had cut a quarter-inch hole in the bottom and glued a PVC pipe fitting into it. The end of the pipe had a barbed adapter onto which we shoved a flexible hose. The other end had been fitted with shower head, using another quarter-inch threaded adapter that was glued to the hose's end. The hose and bucket complex hung from a hook on the wall. A spring clamp squeezed the hose, acting as an off switch.

I brought a change of clothes out to the makeshift shower and retrieved my towel from the clothes line. I set them on a table that sat within arm's length of the curtains. Nearby, almost forty clear two-liter plastic bottles were sitting in the Florida sun. Harley had told us about this disinfection method, which had the added benefit of providing hot water at the end of the day to scrub off our tired bodies. I dumped eight bottles into the hanging bucket and stripped off my clothes, tossing them through the shower curtain onto the table next to my Glock. I grabbed a bottle of body wash from the ground, a communal stash of the liquid soap sat on the brick patio at my feet. I briefly released the clamp and very warm water began to flow from the shower head, soaking my hair and then spraying my body. I re-clamped the hose to save the rest—four gallons didn't last long, as I'd quickly learned. I scrubbed myself with lavender soap, leaving the rest of the water in the bucket dangling above my head until I was thoroughly clean.

My hair was becoming a problem, it's length making personal hygiene a chore. It was taking longer and longer to wash it, and after spending more time on my hair than the rest of my body, I decided that it needed to be cut off when I had a chance. I used to keep my hair short during my high school and college swimming career because it would have to fit under my swim cap. Since then, I've grown it out and had pampered myself with endless hours in the hair salon. I really loved my longer hair. It gave me all kinds of options to match my outfit or even my mood. Now, it looked like I'd have to return to my school days and sport a short cut again. It was just another thing to remind me of the world I now had to live in.

I rinsed off slowly, trying to make the warm water last as long as possible. Finally, when the bucket was dry, I toweled myself off, changed into my clean clothes and refilled the shower jugs with pre-filtered water, then placing them back in the grass to disinfect. We were using the pool as our reservoir, which seemed to be fine even though it was turning a dark green color. The pool provided water right in our backyard and reduced our need for outside trips, minimizing our risks of encountering bad people. With Lake Maitland nearby, we could have lugged water back to the house, but draining the pool minimized that risky journey.

We had set up a second five-gallon food grade bucket on the patio table. The top was covered with several layers of cheesecloth. I poured the pool water through it. The clarified liquid was then transferred into clean, transparent 2-liter bottles—no colored or foggy bottles allowed. After completely filling each bottle, I screwed the top back on and then placed them in the sun to heat up and disinfect. Theoretically, we could also drink the water, as long as it had at least eight hours of non-stop, direct sun exposure. If the sky turned cloudy or the bottles were exposed to less than half the day of direct sunlight, we would have to leave the water to disinfect for at least 48 hours total. In the winter, cloud cover in Florida was minimal, so we hadn't run into any problems.

For consumption, we were still using either scavenged bottled water or water we boiled over the gas grill. But out of convenience, we drank the water we had found. In a few more weeks, the Zephyr Hills supply would be gone, but I wasn't planning on being around that long.

I went back into the house. Janet and Garrett had finished with their chores and were now sitting in the living room.

"You going to let your boyfriend know about dinner?" Janice jokingly asked.

Beker and I were now the unofficial fourth couple in our eight-person neighborhood. He had never joined us in my dad's house, preferring to live in a small one-story block home a few doors down. My lack of a significant other was fodder for their warped sense of humor, but I had convinced them to at least not say anything in front of the poor kid. He was acting strange enough and didn't need encouragement to slide further away from us—or his sanity.

"You're a regular cougar!" Garrett chimed in and then grimaced, instantly regretting his attempt at humor.

Janice smacked Garrett on the shoulder to shut him up, but it was too late.

"Oh, and Janice was your high school sweetheart?" I replied. "Talk about the pot calling the kettle black!"

Janice looked away, and Garrett turned beet red as I reminded him of their nine-year difference.

"I give up!" Garrett begged as Janice pinched him on the arm to further punish him for the faux pas.

I enjoyed that.

"Just don't say anything like that in front of him," I admonished. "He's already been through too much."

After rescuing Beker from two of the Latino gang members, he had shown himself to be rather tight lipped, declining to join in our conversations and deflecting any questions we asked about his past. I figured it was the trauma of the attack that made him so antisocial, along with witnessing the violent death of his tormentors when Jorge and I each put a bullet into the scumbags.

Janice got up from the couch, purposely punishing Garrett one last time by grinding the heel of her hand into his thigh as she leveraged herself up. She joined me at the table, where I had begun to field strip my own sidearm, using the gun cleaning kit from my dad's garage.

"Hey," she said quietly.

"Yeah?" My concentration was directed to my Glock, which I was breaking down for a good lube and cleaning.

"Seriously, about Beker," she began. "Have you spent any time talking to the kid?"

I stopped what I was doing and looked up at her. "No more than you guys."

"I caught a glimpse of him after his shower yesterday," she whispered. "He was changing his shirt, and his body was scared by burns and cuts."

"Burns? Like he was in a fire?"

"No, like he was abused. I worked the emergency room, and he has classic cigarette burns all over his stomach and back."

Just when I thought humanity had sunk to new lows, I was brutally reminded that we had always been evil to each other. It's just that I was experiencing it first-hand and for the first time. If Janice was right, Beker might not think the world we live in now was any worse that the one he left behind. The EMP turned off my world and destroyed it for me. For Beker, our new world wasn't worse that the old one, just different.

She and I sat quietly while I reassembled my Glock. After replacing the magazine and racking the slide to load a round into the handgun's chamber, I put the gun back in its holster and sighed.

"What should we do?" I asked.

"I don't know," Janice said. "I've been thinking about this since I saw his scars. In one sense, it's not our problem. Whoever did that to him isn't around now. But on the other hand…"

"He is part of our group, and that makes it our problem." I finished.

"For whatever reason, he seems to gravitate to you more than any of us," Janice said. "If he's going to be part of this group, then our lives depend on him. We need to know what makes Beker tick."

She was right. I needed to learn more about our newest group member. But would he want to talk to me?

CHAPTER 2

MAITLAND, FL
BEKER'S HOUSE

"One can learn from what is not said."

— **C. Kennedy, Slaying Isidore's Dragons**

BEKER LIVED IN A ONE-STORY concrete block home that had yet to see the contractor's wrecking ball. Surrounded by newer "McMansions," the house was an original Florida mid-century modern, with a sloping flat roof and large louver windows. As I approached the front door, the living room windows caught my attention. Shimmering in the setting sun, their original leaded glass inserts reflected an oily, rainbow color from the turquoise and orange sky.

The kid had done a nice job with the little home. He had scavenged a manual lawnmower and kept the grass cut and the flower beds in pristine shape. The adjoining yards were cluttered with debris and overgrown St. Augustine grass nearly a foot high. They were a glaring contrast to Beker's place, further enhancing the cleanliness of his little two-bedroom block home.

As I raised my hand to knock, the door swung open, revealing the young man and a remarkably clean and orderly living room.

"Hi," Beker meekly blurted, his head down and eyes darting at his feet.

I smiled. "Hi, just wanted to stop by and see how you're doing."

"Fine."

I hesitated for a moment, expecting some further reply. But typical of the last few weeks, Beker remained quiet, a mysterious Sphinx.

"Mind if I come in?"

Beker looked over his shoulder, his head darting back and forth as if searching for something.

"It's a little messy," he said as he scanned the room for anything out of place. "I haven't had a chance to clean this afternoon."

"Looks great to me," I said.

In truth, the room was immaculate. The furniture and the table tops gleamed with a waxy shine. Not a speck of dust was evident. Thinking of what Janice had told me about the burns and abuse, I thought I understood his need to control his environment. His inability to open up, even to spend a little time with the rest of us, now made much more sense. Beker needed to feel safe, and to regulate everything around him to alleviate his compulsions. People, even those that meant him well, were an unknown variable that he couldn't control.

"I like your place," I said. "You've really made this a nice home."

Beker's face relaxed, and a bit of a smile creased his lips.

"Thanks," he said. " But I haven't gotten it quite the way I want yet."

I walked to one of the two couches and noticed Beker's face contort as he struggled to stay calm and composed. I was obviously invading his space, and he didn't like it.

"Do you have a patio out back?" I asked. "Maybe we can sit out there."

"Yeah," he said, looking relieved. "You want something to drink?"

Before I could answer, he scrambled to the adjoining kitchen. I heard the clinking of glass and ceramic.

"I got some oranges from one of the back yards," he called out. "You want some fresh-squeezed juice?"

"That'd be awesome."

I strolled to the back door and stepped out into the small, immaculate yard. The stone patio was spotless and the flower beds free of weeds. The wrought iron table and chairs were perfectly aligned, and a potted Christmas cactus sat in the middle of the round table, its tips a blazing red.

"Oh gracious!" I pulled out one of the chairs and leaned my rifle against the table. "The cactus is blooming."

"Yeah," Beker said as he joined me. In one hand, he held a large plate with Velveeta cheese sliced into squares with some crackers arranged in a pinwheel around the edge of the dish. A glass of orange juice was in the other hand. He proudly set the feast on the table and went back into the house, returning with a can of warm Coke for himself.

"Don't you want some juice?" I took a sip, savoring the tart, sweet taste.

"Had some this morning. Besides, that's the last of the oranges."

I set down the glass. "Beker, you shouldn't have done that."

He smiled. It was cute. He was living on his own for the first time, and he was playing house with his first guest.

"That's alright. I'll scrounge up some more oranges. They'll be around for another month or two."

"Well, thank you. It's really—"

Without warning, he jumped out of his chair. "Be right back!"

I chewed on a cracker and cheese while he rummaged around in the house, finally returning a minute later with a brown bag tied with a ribbon.

"Merry Christmas!" he said, once again staring at the ground at my feet.

I became keenly unaware that I had no idea what the date was. "It's Christmas? I guess so, if the cactus is blooming."

"I don't really know," he said. "But it's close. Anyway, here's a present I got for you."

I was deeply touched and felt guilty for not reciprocating. As if he read my mind, he added, "Don't worry about a present. You've done so much for me already."

I stared at the brown bag like it was from another planet. I was so confused about this kid. He rarely talked, didn't open up and kept his distance. Yet here he was giving me a Christmas gift.

"Well..." He finally said after I failed to open the gift.

Tearing the top off of the stapled bag, I was shocked to see what he had found for me.

"Oh my God," I whispered. "I can't believe it."

In the world before the EMP, if a guy had bought me a pair of one carat diamond earrings or a bejeweled tennis bracelet, I couldn't have been more appreciative than I was right now. I pulled out the package and gently laid it on the table, caressing it.

"Well?" he asked. "Do you like it?"

"I love it!" I replied. "I never would have thought you'd do this for me."

Beker blushed.

"You're a life saver!" I stood up and hugged him. His small frame stiffened as I pulled him close. A moment later, I felt him relax, and his thin arms timidly found my shoulders as he briefly hugged me back.

Beker had stuck pure gold as far as I was concerned. With that little Christmas bag, he'd taken away one of my biggest fears about the coming journey. He'd given me a Life Straw, a portable water filter that would let me drink from any source of water. No boiling needed. No bleach.

"Really? They're just water filters."

"Beker, they're more than that. On our trip, they'll be life itself!"

Beker sat back with a grin on his face. I suddenly realized just how tense he had been as his shoulders relaxed and a smile creased his face.

I had come over to quiz him, to get a feel for his intentions and treat him like a suspect in a criminal investigation. Now, I knew I was his friend, and any doubt about his loyalty had been laid to rest.

"I found a few more! There are enough for all of you," he said with a conspiratorial smile.

It was strange, but in a way, I felt like I had found a little brother.

"Come on," I said. "Let's show the others! They'll be so proud of you."

He lit up. "You think?"

"Beker, you have no idea. Now go get the rest of these and let's show the group. We're having dinner at the Riker's house at sundown. They'll all be so happy."

"Can I give them out?" He timidly asked.

"You bet! In fact, do you have any more ribbons and bags? These will be the best presents they've ever had!"

"Let's finish the cheese and crackers," I said. "Dinner's at the Rikers' house tonight. I hope you'll come over this time and hand out the presents yourself."

Beker, who just moments ago had seemed happy to share his gifts with the others, turned away. A look of confusion, or maybe pain, washed across his face. The change was so sudden, it was almost spooky.

He slowly rose from his chair and walked over to the garden bed flanking the patio. He bent down, facing away from me, and almost absently began pulling up a few stray blades of grass that had found their way out of the mulch.

"I don't know," he muttered.

"Beker," I began, "I really would like you to come over."

For a moment, the young man continued to prune the society garlic that was just beginning to sprout its purple blooms.

"Why?" he finally asked as he stood up and turned toward me. "You don't know me from Adam. Why are you doing this for me?"

I was taken aback, and my mind swirled with thoughts of his past abuse and our present situation. Had he ever had a normal relationship? Had anyone treated him kindly without asking for anything in return? I didn't know what to say.

"Sure, I get it," he continued. "You think I'm helpless. You think I'm weird!"

"No!" I said. "I don't think that at all."

"Then why? Why do you want me to be part of your little group? Why do you care?"

"Because that's who I am!" I replied. "Why is it so hard for you to just let people be nice to you?"

I immediately regretted my harsh response, but I was exhausted to the bone. I had to try to make him understand.

"Beker, this world really sucks. It's full of danger and uncertainties. And when you find someone who you can lean on, someone you can trust, then you grab that person and hold on. The good people are few and far between."

I got up and slowly approached him. He backed up slightly as I got close.

"I don't have any family to depend on," I began. "Jorge and Maria are going to leave to find their own family, and that leaves Garrett and Janice. My last friends on earth."

I reached out and took his hand. He tried to pull away, but I held firm. I lifted his downcast face up with my other hand and looked him in the eyes.

"And I have you. We have *each other*, okay? I need you to understand that. We need to trust each other, otherwise..."

"I had a family once," he choked out. Tears welled in his eyes as he wiped them away with his free hand. "Didn't work out too well."

"I'm not like them."

"But how do I know that?"

"You can't. But I promise you I will work to earn your trust."

The tears fell in earnest now. I hugged him and let him sob. I don't know how long we stood there, Beker releasing all the shame and pain he had bottled up for years. Finally, exhausted and spent, Beker gently pushed away and looked at me. His gaze was searching. Seeking the truth behind my words—and more importantly, empathy. If the last few months had taught me anything, it was that compassion was in short supply, but I had plenty of it for this lonely boy who bore the scars of his abuse all over his skin and his psyche.

"I'll be there," he finally said.

"Good, we'll get together about sunset."

I turned back to the table of cheese and crackers. Sitting down, I motioned for him to join me.

"You know," I began, "my mom is somewhere in the Tampa area."

"I didn't know that. I thought your mom and dad lived in the house you guys are using."

"She's my step-mom. My real mother left town years ago."

"So your parents are divorced?"

I hesitated, not sure how much I should tell him. I hoped that if I shared something about my past, it would help him open to me. "My mom moved on, and my dad eventually remarried. It all worked out in the end, I guess."

"So you're okay with your step-mom?"

"Yeah, she's alright. I mean, we get along and she doesn't get in the way of me and my dad."

"My mom and dad couldn't stay in the same room for more than two minutes before things got bad. My dad was pretty cool, though. He taught me how to play chess one summer. He had to work a lot, but he made time for me, you know?"

The kid obviously cared for his father. I didn't push him for any more information than he was willing to give up. He had spoken more in the last ten minutes than the prior month.

Beker didn't mention his mother at all. I assumed that was where he found his personal hell on earth, so I let it go. I made a mental note to let the others know not to bring her up.

We finished our cheese and crackers, and I stood to leave. "Is your bathroom working?" I asked.

"Sure! It's in the hallway to the left. I have a bucket of water in there. Just pour it in the tank and flush."

"Thanks, and thank you for the juice!"

"No problem."

I walked into the house, leaving the kid at the wrought iron patio table, soaking up sun. I walked down the hallway and found the bathroom, but there was no bucket of water. I went into the next room, a master bedroom with an attached en-suite bathroom and found the bucket of water. As I started to close the door, I glanced back into the perfectly made up room and noticed a few purple velvet Crown Royal bags sitting on the bed. Curious, I went over to them and opened their golden yellow ties, accidently spilling some of the contents onto the queen-sized mattress. Jewelry and gold coins scattered onto the floral bedspread.

He was stealing from the neighborhood! That's why he had been disappearing during the day while we were scavenging for food. He joined us for our morning huddle, then looted homes for their left-behind treasures! I was shocked, and felt totally betrayed.

I gathered the items and put them back into their small sacks, replacing them where I had found them. I closed the door and looked at myself in the mirror.

What have I done? I asked myself. *We all agreed to only take the necessities from the neighboring houses, like food and a few pieces of clothing. He's a thief! And I just invited him into our lives.*

I shook my head. After I finished in the bathroom, I opened the door to find Beker standing in the bedroom. A quick glance at the bed showed that he had removed his stolen loot and stashed it away. I gathered myself, refusing to allow him to know that I had discovered his secret.

"Oh! You scared me. I hope you don't mind, but the bucket of water was in here so I decided to use this bathroom."

Beker's face relaxed as I glided passed him and down the hall. He was on my heels as I got to the front door. I spun around and gave him a grin.

"See you tonight! And don't forget your presents."

He smiled back, and I turned down the front walk and made my way home as quickly as possible without looking suspicious. I had a lot to discuss with Janice, and I couldn't wait to get it out.

CHAPTER 3

Watts Bar Nuclear Plant
Spring City, Tn

"Everything the State says is a lie, and everything it has it has stolen."

— Friedrich Nietzsche

As Charlie was walking back to her father's house, Brendon Davidson was struggling with his nuclear plant's impending demise. His white, short-sleeved button-down shirt was filthy from days of sweat and grime. As chief of maintenance for the plant, his job had taken a dramatic turn since the EMP had taken all of his computers off line. The electromagnetic surge had fried every one of their electronic systems, causing the facility's backup generators to kick in. The old diesel generators had been unaffected by the electric surge, but several things had conspired over the last couple of months to bring the plant and its skeleton crew to this critical and rapidly deteriorating situation.

A nuclear power plant is a controlled nuclear detonation. Enriched Uranium is pressed into 1-inch-long pellets, composed of Uranium 235 ore that has been concentrated to a more reactive level.

The U235 readily takes on stray neutrons, which cause it to split into Krypton 92 and Barium 141, along with more neutrons. As multiple neutrons are separated, they spread in the pile of Uranium and collide with more U235. This causes these atoms to split as well, creating even more neutrons that seek out more radioactive material. This cascading reaction generates heat, which is then used to boil water. The corresponding steam then drives the plant's turbines, creating electricity.

But Murphy's law dictated that if something can go wrong it would, and several months later, things finally went sideways in a big way.

Before the attack, the plant had been in the process of adding a second reactor, the first one to go online in almost twenty years. It was fully charged with uranium, but this second reactor hadn't had its emergency generators installed yet. Instead, the power company had been using the other reactor's electricity to run the new reactor's own cooling pumps.

Now the original backup diesel generators had to do double the work, driving two water pumping systems, and they weren't up to the task. The supply of diesel was being managed by DHS, but the engines themselves were beginning to fail. Once one of the generators went down, the others would be inadequate to keep both nuclear piles cool. They were going to have to shut down one of the two water pumps and sacrifice one of the reactors to a nuclear meltdown.

A "China Syndrome" situation would occur, where the pellets would melt and condense into a pile of radioactive slag. The pile of Uranium would melt its way through the containment metal and concrete, eventually making its way into the earth itself.

When the uranium finally condensed into a pile of radioactive slag, it wouldn't create a nuclear explosion. That was the good news. That took uranium-235 concentration levels over 80%, while the nuclear material they were using was much more dilute. But when the hot, radioactive material hit the surrounding water, plumes of deadly irradiated steam would be sent into the atmosphere, contaminating an area up to sixty miles downwind.

Over a million people had lived in this danger zone until two months ago. When the power went off, most people had abandoned their homes to seek shelter the nearby Knoxville or Chattanooga refugee centers. How may were left was unknown, but Davidson didn't have the manpower to warn them.

Single by divorce and childless by choice, Davidson was a devoted employee. Educated by the Navy, he was disciplined and precise, which added to his anger when he realized that The worst part was that all of this should have—and could have—been prevented.

According to Davidson's contact at DHS, a series of brand-new generators were supposed to have been delivered right after the EMP hit. Several prefabricated conduits had been established outside the pump house where concrete pads had been poured. Diesel generators were to have been delivered and set on these pads, the female conduits of the building matching the male conduits of the generators. A week after the EMP hit, his contact at DHS informed him that the generators designated for use at Watts Bar were not in the warehouse where they were supposed to be, and replacements could not be found. Davidson warned DHS of the situation, even screamed it out on the plant's now quiet floor, that the reactors could meltdown if their antiquated diesel generators failed. All it earned him was a shrug from the DHS man who simply spun on his heels and left, never to return.

Now, one of the three older generators was finally overheating. The ear-splitting sound of metal grinding on metal was unmistakable as the machine's increasing heat caused the its moving parts to swell. No matter how much oil he used nor how many prayers he said, nothing was going to keep the generator from a fiery and spectacular death.

Davidson watched as the generator's thermostat pushed into the red zone. The cacophony of noise assaulted his ears, and he could smell something burning. He resigned himself to the inevitable.

"Shut it down now!" Almost as an afterthought, he said, "She's got nothing left to prove."

"What now?" one of the half-dozen remaining workers asked. "Should we evacuate?"

"Not yet," Davidson replied. "There's still a chance these two will keep things under control."

The other engineers nodded, yet all of them knew that his statement was more of a wish than a fact. Science was a harsh taskmaster. Numbers didn't lie. There was no gray area when it came to equations and proven calculations. The flow of water wasn't equal to the amount of nuclear material that needed to be cooled. They all knew the calculations from endless brainstorming sessions that they had performed over the past two months. They all knew that, within the next three days, one of the two reactors was going to melt. And unless DHS showed up with another generator, there was nothing they could do about it.

"We need to get help," one of the other plant workers said as the remaining two machines struggled to compensate for their broken companion. "Maybe we can dig up another generator from somewhere else. They've got a large one at the police station."

"Good luck getting them to give it up," Davidson said.

"They find out we'll be melting down in the next two days, I don't think they'll argue too much."

"How will you get it here?"

"One mountain at a time," the man responded. "One mountain at a time."

"Take the minibus," Davidson said. "It's got enough gas to get you to town and back. And take everyone with you. You may need the manpower. I'll stay here and see what I can do to slow the reaction down."

The remaining six workers filed out of the room, leaving Davidson alone with the deteriorating pile of uranium. He adjusted the water flow to the newer reactor when he saw its temperature beginning to creep up. But that was a temporary fix. When the other reactor started to overheat an hour or so later, he switched the flow and put more output in that side. The problem was that as each reactor cooled, the other heated more quickly. At some point, the system would fail, but at least he could push it out for a few days. He hoped his staff would return with the miracle generator that they needed.

Outside, the six workers gathered a few items to take with them and drove the old diesel minibus down the long, asphalt road and through the abandoned guard gates. At the end of the access road, they veered around several abandoned vehicles and slowly drove toward the local police station, just five miles away. With the security of half a tank of gas and a full day to complete their mission, the crew chatted easily with each other.

A few miles away, as they took a particularly sharp turn, they came face to face with a blockade of abandoned vehicles. The driver of the minibus slammed on the brakes as four men with black assault rifles sprinted from behind the roadblock.

"Get out!" one of the armed men screamed.

The driver opened the swinging door, and the six scientists and technicians quickly ran down the steps and onto the road. One of the four carjackers directed them into the grass and lined them up.

"Put 'yer hands on 'yer head and turn around!" the man yelled, his voice thick with a rural Tennessee accent.

"Wait!" one of the scientists said. "We've got to get into town. There's an emergency—"

"SHUT 'YER MOUTH!" The vandal yelled. "'Jist Do What 'Yer Told!"

"Look at that there bus," one of the other men said. "That's nice."

"Told you I'd get us a ride," the leader said.

The grimy, bearded men smiled at each other, two of them high-fiving.

The scientist tried to protest again before the butt of a gun smashed him in the forehead, sending him tumbling into the overgrown grass. Blood gushed from his scalp as he laid silently on his side.

"Too bad 'thar ain't any women," the ugliest, dirtiest of the thugs grunted.

"Y'all turn around," the leader commanded the power plant crew.

The five remaining men slowly turned and faced the woods.

"Please, mister, you don't understand…"

The staccato of four semi-automatic rifles let loose, dozens of rounds shredding the helpless crew. Within seconds, they lay dead, bleeding from multiple bullet wounds. The leader walked up to each body and put a bullet into all six skulls with a handgun.

"Let's move," he said.

"Where to?"

"The nuclear plant," the leader replied. "Y'all saw the sign on the side of the bus. If they got this ride, what else they got?"

"I like the way you think, boss," said one of the thugs as he slouched into the driver's seat.

Back at the nuclear plant, Davidson began gathering his notes and logbooks to preserve his team's efforts. The Department of Energy would require this data for its post-disaster investigation, and the meticulous engineer was going to make sure that the blame fell squarely on the shoulders of the Department of Homeland Security. The loss of the backup generators for the second reactor was the result of Homeland's negligence, and he wasn't going to let Washington deflect the failure back onto the dedicated workers at the plant.

He had ten storage boxes full of papers, all documenting the demise of their nuclear generator. Handwritten notes meticulously documented the power plant's death spiral. Hopefully, their efforts would give the Department of Energy a clue on how to handle future emergencies and some good could come from the unfolding tragedy.

The rumble of the old diesel bus reverberated off the office window, breaking Davidson's concentration. He wrestled with the last box of papers, lifting it onto the top of the stack of evidence he'd assembled. As he glanced out the window, wondering why the bus had returned so soon, confusion quickly turned to fear as four armed men emerged from the bus's door. Davidson ducked down behind the desk, less than a hundred yards from the unwanted visitors, and peered out of the window.

Davidson was on the first level of the three-floor building. The thugs paired off, two of them moving toward the front door. They held their rifles up at low ready as they scanned the front of the concrete office block.

Davidson had no combat experience. But his years spent in the Navy and his daily work with deadly nuclear material, gave him the ability to think without panicking. By the way the men walked and carried their firearms, he saw that they weren't professionals. But they had guns, and he didn't. That made his decision very simple. Escape was his only option.

The grounds of the nuclear power plant were vast, and the building he was presently in covered at least twenty thousand square feet. Roughly an "L" shape, the office building had two entrances. The one on the north side was the main entrance where Nuclear Regulatory Commission employees as well as guests entered. That's where Davidson's office was. But on the south end of the structure, there was an employee entrance that was shielded by a large copse of trees. If he could get out that door and into the concealment of the stand of southern oaks, he would have a chance.

He looked at the stacks of journals and paperwork in front of him. What was the most important documentation to take? After a moment of consideration, he opened a box near his feet. Davidson grabbed two journals and a folder of reports and stuffed them in his leather messenger bag. He slung the bag around his neck and then sprinted down the hall and out the back door. Without missing a beat, he plunged into the oak trees and raced south. Through the leafless forest he flew, eventually breaking free of their cover at the southern end of the stand. He then cut west and began to jog up Morrison Lane, a two-lane road that led to the dirt field where the government kept surplus equipment and unused shipping containers.

His staff was dead. Davidson knew it in his heart. There was no way they would have relinquished the bus otherwise. He had to make sure that their names were cleared, which kept his feet moving away from the plant—and away from the men with guns. Two hours later, he was far away, leaving the four criminals to their fate with the rapidly deteriorating pile of nuclear material. Surrounded by miles of fallow farmland, Davidson was safe. Now he had to find his way to the next occupied town, but he had no idea where that could possibly be.

He was miles from any town, and all the neighboring farms had been evacuated over the last three months. So he kept jogging, clutching the leather satchel that he hoped would deliver redemption for him and his people, because the truth was all he had left.

CHAPTER 4

OFFICE OF MAJOR GENERAL LESTER
FORT KNOX, KY

*"When one gets in bed with government, one
must expect the diseases it spreads."*

— Ron Paul

A s Davidson escaped the impending meltdown at the Watts-Bar
plant, Major General Lester hung up the phone in his office at Fort
Knox. A call from Washington had just informed him that he was
assuming control of the United States Military, Southern Command. He
was now in charge of the reorganized southern branches of the service,
putting all military assets under one umbrella.

DHS had instituted this change after the EMP took out the grid and
most of the country's computers. Centralizing power would give them
more effective control of the recovery and the country's military assets.
More importantly—and unbeknownst to the general—he had been selected
because of his consistent and unwavering belief in the chain of command and
a history of following the rules. Furthermore, he wasn't overly ambitious, so
he wouldn't present a threat to DHS. He was a "yes" man and would take
orders from above without hesitation.

The general was surprised to get a promotion, although his resume
indicated that he was more than qualified for the job. Pushing sixty, all he
had wanted was a less demanding command as his final years in the military
came to a close. He had taken the ROTC billet because he felt he could

leave a lasting mark on his beloved country by improving the quality and quantity of new officers.

In his mind, strengthening the ROTC program, where college students were nurtured into officers, was just the way to do this.

Nicknamed "Saint Bart," for his almost fanatical dedication to Army doctrine and unwavering devotion to following the rules, he was a hard driving and by-the-book soldier. He never took a short cut and never strayed from his orders, demanding that all under him tow the same line.

When he had taken over from his predecessor, he had given himself three years to bring the ROTC program up to snuff. He'd been on track to accomplish this when the EMP took out power to the rest of the country.

Fort Knox fared better than most, with multiple redundant backup systems to keep the base and their precious gold reserves safe. Because of this, life carried on relatively normally. With the successful evacuation of non-military personnel from the adjacent town of Radcliff to the base, the general felt responsible for the surrounding countryside. Crime was non-existent under his watch, and he had commanded that the remaining personnel and their families move onto Fort Knox property with little disruption in the base's function.

And now, as the phone settled into its cradle, he realized that he was in charge of far more than a few square miles of Kentucky countryside. He had been made commander of all of the country's southern forces, reporting directly to Washington and the head of the Department of Homeland Security. It was an awesome responsibility at a time when the nation would need stability and strength.

Lester pressed a button on his Ethernet wired intercom box. "Welch, have Captain Kuris and Lieutenant Ferraro report to me at once."

As a major general, he was entitled to two aide-de-camps. Normally, Lester would give an order to the captain, who would then disseminate his demands down the line. But with such a tectonic shift in responsibilities, Lester wanted to speak to both his aides at once. Their lives would be changing dramatically. It would be especially difficult on Ferraro, given his lack of combat experience. Lester was going to have to reassign the lieutenant and wanted to give him the news personally.

Fifteen minutes later, Lester's intercom squawked.

"Sir, Captain Kuris and Lieutenant Ferraro are here."

"Have them report immediately."

The two men entered the office. Each wore their Class "B" Army standard uniform. Their blue trousers and white short-sleeved shirts were starched to precision, and their appropriate rank was pinned to the right side of their stiff collars. Both the double silver "railroad tracks" bars of Captain Kuris and the single brass "butter" bar of Lieutenant Ferraro were parallel with the floor, and each had the Branch of Service Aide-De-Camp pinned on the other lapel. Their left breast displayed the campaign ribbons each had been awarded, the colorful boards displaying a rainbow of vertical bands that had, over the years, earned the nickname "fruit salad." There was not a single hair out of place, and each crease was flawless. Perfect, just as the general demanded.

"At ease," Lester said after salutes were exchanged. "I just received new orders from Washington."

Both men shifted slightly, their only outward display of surprise.

"Please, sit down," the general said as he took his own seat, waving at the two leather chairs at the head of the desk.

"Washington's reorganized the military and I've been given its southern command." Lester began. "This is going to mean big changes for us all."

Turning to Ferraro, the general continued.

"Lieutenant, I'm reassigning you to Orlando. You'll need a combat billet to qualify for your next promotion, and I'm planning to make Orlando a hub for our recovery. Can you handle that?"

"Yes, sir."

"Good, then let's get down to the details." Lester said.

Almost an hour later, the two aides departed the general's office.

"Well," Kuris said. "I thought things had gotten strange before."

"At least you'll be staying with the general." Ferraro sighed.

He liked his job and Captain Kuris was an excellent teacher to work under. He had hoped to get his own senior aide position when he became a captain.

"Come on," Kuris chided. "You'll love it there."

"Maybe now," Ferraro replied. "I won't miss the snow. But wait till summer. It'll be brutal."

The men continued down the glossy linoleum floor, their perfectly shined shoes clicking with each step. Their gait was so well synchronized that it sounded as if only one person was marching down the empty hallway.

"You should have electricity in your apartment, so staying cool won't be a problem. But I do feel for you. Florida can be brutal in the summer."

"I can't wait to tell Stella," Ferraro said sarcastically. "She'll flip. The kids love it here, and it's safe."

"Hey," Kuris said as he stopped and turned to his friend. "You'll be alright. Besides, this is your chance to put 'combat experience' on your résumé. You'll need that to move forward."

"Just about anywhere in the country is considered a combat zone right now."

"Chin up," Kuris concluded. "You could have ended up in Chicago."

Ferraro shivered, thinking of the massive "Charlie Foxtrot" that was going on in the nation's third largest city. With no power and millions of citizens starving and freezing over the winter, it was a massive "no-go" land for the military where the strongest survived and the weak were killed or enslaved. An assignment to that part of the country meant constant strife and a high probability of being wounded or killed.

"I suppose I could do worse than Orlando," Ferraro agreed as they retrieved their Class "B" windbreakers. "But I haven't heard anything about the city. Have you?"

"No, but that's a good thing. At least it's not bad enough to show up on our radar."

"Plus, it mean that the general trusts you." Kuris continued. "Orlando will be the hub of recovery for the entire southeast, so I'm sure he wants someone there who will send him accurate and unvarnished reports. Just do your job and you'll move up quickly."

"I'll put a good spin on this with the wife," the lieutenant said. "And thanks, Captain."

"You're welcome," Kuris replied with a smile, holding out his hand.

Shaking hands, Ferraro said, "I owe you, sir. I'll keep in touch."

"The general and I are both counting on it." Kuris said as the two men stepped out into the cold Kentucky morning.

Back in his office, General Lester began the task of converting his headquarters from an administrative office to a combat command. He made a list of subordinates he would need to bring his staff to a proper level. As he scribbled down his notes, his intercom buzzed, interrupting his train of thought.

"Yes?" Lester barked. "I said I didn't want to be disturbed."

"I'm sorry, sir. But your wife is here."

Damn it, Lester thought to himself. *She'll be pushing me to go to the lake house with the grandkids.*

After taking a deep breath, Lester hit the intercom and had his assistant bring his wife into his office.

"Thank you, sergeant." Lester said to his assistant as his wife took a seat in one of the chairs that the Kuris and Ferraro had just been using.

"What can I do for you?" Lester said after kissing his wife on the cheek and then returning to his chair behind his desk. She sat across from him, her hands folded in her lap.

"Bart, the convoy's leaving this afternoon and you haven't given me an answer on the lake house."

"You know the rules. I can't make an exception for you just because you're my wife."

"Oh Bart, please. The children need to get out of here. It's stifling. Your son-in-law's off doing God knows what in Washington and our daughter needs to get out of the house. You know how she loves the lake house."

He leveled his gaze at her, trying to contain his frustration. He had work to do, damn it. "I said no, Ann. Don't ask again. The rules are the rules."

"You made the rules, Bart. Need I remind you?"

"I don't have time for this. I've just been given a huge assignment by Washington. They've made me commander of our southern forces."

"All the more reason to get me and the grandkids out of here. You'll be living in this office for the next week, so we should get out of your hair. Besides, Haylee could use the break. It'll be another month before her husband gets home from the Pentagon."

General Lester had to admit that his wife's logic was sound, but he wasn't eager to break the rules. He hadn't risen to this level of responsibility and rank by ignoring the manual. Letting his family vacation while the rest of the base was on lockdown went against every fiber in his body.

On the other hand, the next few weeks were likely to be hell. He'd be lucky to get six hours of sleep at night and probably wouldn't be home for meals.

His wife could see the gears moving in her husband's brain, and from experience, she knew that silence was the best path to get what she wanted.

Lester sighed. "You know this goes against everything I believe in."

"Bart, you know it's safe. The entire county surrounding the lake has been cleared and everyone's been relocated to a safe zone or camp. There's no one within miles of our house."

Lester smiled at his wife, and Ann knew that she'd won him over.

"Thank you, Bart!"

"Take a sat phone," Lester said. "And check in with the sheriff's office when you arrive. I want to talk to him directly before you go to the house."

"Yes sir!" Ann said, giving him a mock salute.

His wife left the room and waved to the sergeant as she closed the outer office door, feeling pleased with herself. Their daughter Haylee would be thrilled to get away from Fort Knox. The families that had been evacuated to the fort were not shy about venting their frustrations at leaving their off-base homes. And because of the forced relocation, her daughter Haylee had been the recipient of several rude comments made behind her back. Nothing serious nor threatening, but aggravating just the same.

Ann walked to her government vehicle, a Cummins diesel-powered 2001 Dodge pickup. The base's mechanics had brought the truck back to life after the EMP, and her husband had grabbed it for the family's use. All Ann knew was that it drove over just about anything and that it had leather seats. Its extended cab allowed for a comfortable second row of seating with enough room for the kids and her daughter. They'd take the truck to the lake house, a four-hour drive in normal times. She had plenty of fuel to make the trip there, and the convoy that was leaving for Knoxville later that afternoon had fuel trucks that could top her off during the trip.

Driving the pickup to the base's vehicle "barn," Ann saw the man she was looking for standing by a six-wheel truck that was already loaded with boxes and other supplies.

"Captain Herman," she called out to the harried Army officer with a little wave.

Herman was organizing the convoy, reviewing the supplies and readiness of the M49 fuel haulers, HUMVEEs and a dozen M939 6-wheeled trucks. Over 40 vehicles in all, the logistics were difficult enough to organize without the general's wife tagging along.

"Good morning, ma'am," Herman said, his eyes and concentration on the ledger and clipboard he was reviewing. "What can I do for you?"

"The general has given me permission to accompany you this afternoon."

Herman put his clipboard down and sighed deeply. Just what he needed, a VIP to deal with.

Sensing the growing frustration in the captain's attitude, Ann Lester put her well-honed social skills to work.

"Captain, I promise I won't be a burden. And the general will be so happy to know that you've worked me into your convoy."

Herman knew there was nothing he could do about it, other than accept the inconvenience of having a gaggle of civilians accompany them. *Make the best of it*, Herman thought.

"No problem, Mrs. Lester. We're assembling the vehicles at 12:30 and departing at 13:00 sharp. Please be here no later than 12:15."

Looking at her watch, Ann saw she had two hours to collect her daughter and grandkids, pack the pickup, and be back to get in line. Having already planned on departing this afternoon, that wouldn't be a problem.

"Where will you be leaving us, ma'am?"

"Crab Orchard, Tennessee."

The captain reviewed his map. It was about two hundred miles from Fort Knox to Crab Orchard. His HUMVEEs had a range of about two hundred fifty miles, that would actually be a good place to stop and refuel his convoy. Captain Herman smiled as he felt like he had been given a break.

"That'll work, Ma'am."

"Can you spare some fuel for us when we get there?"

"Actually, I was planning on refueling all our vehicles there, so that won't be a problem."

"Thank you, Captain. I'll be sure to tell my husband how co-operative you've been."

Ann gave the captain her patented general's wife smile and hopped into the Dodge. Driving to her daughter's house, she mentally reviewed her supply list and found all in order.

"Haylee!" Ann Lester called out as she entered her daughter's kitchen.

"Hi, Mom," Haylee Romine replied as two fast-moving children shot by their mother.

"Nana!" the little boy shouted. Four-year-old Bart flung himself into his grandmother's waiting arms. Right behind him, his younger sister, Maggie, fought for some space in her Nana's embrace.

Hugging her grandkids, Ann looked up at her daughter and grinned. "You packed? We're leaving in two hours."

"Are we going?" the young boy asked.

"Your Grandpa said it's okay."

Both children whooped in delight.

"Up to your rooms," their mother said. "Let's get a bath before we leave."

The kids scurried out of the kitchen, laughing and jostling each other as their little feet clomped up the stairs to their second-floor bedrooms.

"I really needed this," Haylee said to her mother. "Thanks, Mom."

"Thank your father," Ann replied. "Quite frankly, I'm surprised he said yes. Something big is happening, and I think he wants us out of his hair."

"Whatever it is, I'm just happy we get to go. I've even packed the kid's ice skates just in case the lake is frozen over."

"Good idea," Ann said, smiling. "I'll start loading up the truck. "

"Can't wait!" Haylee said.

As Ann Lester turned to leave, her daughter held out her open arms and gave her mother a hug.

"Thank you so much, mom. I really needed this."

Ann Lester smiled and replied. "Watts Bar Lake, here we come!"

— TWO DAYS LATER —
WATTS BARR NUCLEAR FACILITY

The generators had failed. The screeching of failing gears and metal-on-metal friction would have been deafening—if anyone had been there to hear it. The final death throes of the coolant system came and went without human witness as the water pumps went offline. The breakdown of the uranium inside the containment vessel accelerated and the rods began to glow, the heat of the now-unchecked radioactive reaction building. The rods began to melt, forming a glowing slag of heavy metal at the bottom of the concrete container.

The concentration of uranium was too low to lead to an explosion, but the heated material began to eat away at its containment vessel's wall. By the end of the day, it penetrated the concrete barrier and hit the earth, drilling into the ground, flowing along the path of least resistance.

At 11:00 am on the third day after Davidson had fled the facility, the radioactive slag reached the nearby pond, sending up radioactive steam. The hot gas was grabbed by the eddies of cold wind that were sweeping in from Canada. The swirling bands from the advancing front lifted the poisonous air up, carrying it several miles to the east.

As the hot gas began to cool a few miles downwind, it settled on the shores of nearby Watts Bar Lake, bringing an odorless and colorless radioactive poison to whomever was exposed to it.

It was especially damaging to the two little children who were preparing to ice skate on Watts Bar's frozen surface. The inhaled mixture of radioactive iodine, tellurium, cesium and strontium found its way into their lungs. Within minutes, the poisons had settled into various glands and fat deposits and began to release deadly protons. These radioactive particles smashed through cell walls and broke apart strands of DNA, doing massive—but unseen—damage to their bodies.

A bomb had been set inside General Lester's grandchildren, and the countdown was already ticking.

CHAPTER 5

MAITLAND, FLORIDA

"The truth of what one says, lies in what one does."

— **Bernhard Schlink**

I WAS WORRIED ABOUT BEKER. SINCE I had found his stash of stolen jewelry a week or so ago, I'd become more and more concerned about his motives. He seemed the same on the surface, but now I knew there was more to him than the sweet, shy kid.

We had hoped to leave by now, but the weather turned nasty and a couple of hard winter storms, along with an increase in gang activity, had kept us here a few weeks longer than we'd wanted. Jorge and Maria were chomping at the bit to start their journey, but we'd all agreed to hold out until the weather cleared. Today was that day.

I had decided to go with Garrett and Janice to find Dr. Kramer's place. We chose a route that will take us north and then west of the city. The indirect path would avoid ninety percent of the heavy population centers west of town, but it would also add a few days to the journey.

Jorge and Maria were going the opposite way, east then south. If they manage to make it to the cattle ranch, they should be in a safe place with plenty of food and shelter.

And Beker's plans? No one knew. All of us had asked him, in one way or another, but he refused to tell us who he wanted to accompany. He might even stay, and after having told others about Beker's burglaries, Harley and Ashley were less than thrilled at the prospect of having an unreliable and shady neighbor a block away.

"Well, I think we're ready," Jorge said after we all reviewed the contents of our backpacks and battle belts.

With the life straw water filtration kits provided by Beker, we could get by with carrying far less water. Three clear bottles each should cover us for at least a day's water needs, and the filtration system would give us an unending supply of drinkable H_2O. A week's worth of calories via our homemade pemmican, along with trail mix, candy bars, and peanut butter, added considerable weight, but we couldn't rely on scavenging along our journey. We could only count on the things we carried on our backs.

Even budgeting for a few delays during the fifty-mile trip, we should still be able to make it to Monteverde in eight or nine days.

I planned to load up on calories today so that I could keep a steady pace and bang out at least ten miles on our first day's travel without needing to stop to eat. Janice and Garrett were going to follow the same plan. I was feeling hopeful for the first time in a long while that everything would all work out.

Harley and Ashley were going to grill off some fish that we caught in nearby Lake Maitland during our last meal together. Janice, Garrett, and I were planning on leaving around dusk, reasoning that the night would reduce our profile and hopefully help us avoid conflict along the way.

I tightened a strap on my bugout bag and nodded at Jorge. "Agreed," I replied. "Ammunition looks good too. Everyone's rifles and pistols clean and lubed?"

All heads nodded as we broke up to spend the next few hours resting. The winter storm had been followed by clear, blue skies. The last couple of nights were nearly moonless, with the constellations a vibrant and shimmering roadmap that would help steer us in the correct direction. Each of us had a more mundane paper map marked with rally points along the way, places where we could meet up if we got separated. I could only hope that we wouldn't need to use them.

I went to my dad's study. My heart was heavy as I sat in his swiveling office chair, surveying his room for possibly the last time. His absence was palpable, with pictures and knickknacks all reminding me of him.

I caught my breath, holding back a sob. I felt so alone. I thought I had come to terms with my new life, but now I was overwhelmed, engulfed with grief. My breathing became shallow and my eyes watered, but I didn't cry. I wasn't sure I had any tears left. There was nothing left but anger at whoever had started this mess and regret at surviving this apocalypse when so many others had died.

I drank in the sights of the room and inhaled the familiar smell, a mix of cologne along with the musky, earthy scent of my dad. I would miss this room. I missed him. I missed the world the way it used to be.

I must have drifted off to sleep because the next thing I knew, the light filtering in from outside was the yellow of evening. I stood up and stretched, mentally preparing myself for the trip. I needed to put on my game face, which I had discovered was much more than mere bravado. It meant I was committed. It meant I was in a place that wouldn't allow for distraction. I was focused and ready. That's my game face.

I learned a trick in college when I swam competitively, a sort of self-hypnosis that focused my mind and pushed my emotions to the side. As I began the breathing exercise, I heard the distinct popping of gunfire. I grabbed my rifle and rushed out to the backyard, where I was joined by the others.

The shooting sounded like it was coming from close by, but the tree-lined streets tended to both amplify and distort loud sounds. The distinct crack of two or more AR-15 battles rifle was clear, mixed with the deeper bark of heavier rounds, likely hunting caliber bullets.

All of us had grabbed our weapons on the way out of the house, just as we've trained ourselves to do. We scurried out of the yard and took pre-planned defensive positions.

The distant battle intensified at a terrifying rate as the number of AR rifles entering the fight grew. I heard at least a dozen weapons, the shots so rapid they sounded like a movie theater's popcorn machine.

The sound of the heavier caliber rifle boomed in answer. Four, then five heavy rounds in rapid succession were followed by the cacophony of a dozen .556 magazines being emptied once again.

After a few minutes of this back and forth exchange, the neighborhood grew silent. A minute or so of quiet was followed by the unmistakable sound of a large diesel engine and then a loud boom that reminded me of a traffic accident. The ARs began popping again, but a few seconds later, it was all over. We each gave the others a confused, frightened look. All we could do was hunker down behind cover and wait for the coming storm.

***

Cory Flannigan wasn't going anywhere. Not too long ago, a man and woman had invaded his space. They had been looting the house across the street from his garage fortress. After emptying over twenty rounds from his Bushmaster MOE M4 AR-15 at the two thieves, he had decided to switch over to his more powerful AR-10. Trusting the heavier .308 bullets, he was determined not to let any more looters escape from his sights.

Cory wasn't worried about his fate. He had spent the first few weeks after the loss of power collecting newspapers and phone books. He lined his garage with them, double stacking the paper to create an almost impenetrable barrier against most any bullet that could be sent his way.

His house was booby-trapped as well, rigged with non-lethal alarms that would let him know if it had been invaded. He'd considered more deadly traps, but explosives tended to cause fires, and he didn't want to inadvertently burn his fortress to the ground. A bullet would have to do, as long as he had some warning that someone was trying to sneak up on him.

Like every other day since the lights went out, Cory sat in his garage, peering out of the bottom third of the open door. Since the last incursion into his kingdom by the two criminals, he hadn't seen a soul. But that all changed when he heard the sound of over a dozen men breaking into the houses farther down his street. More looters were coming, and Cory was the man to stop them.

His garage was a veritable warehouse of ammunition and weapons. He was one of the firearm "super-owners" that ATF had flagged. He had bought several AR-15s along with a couple of hunting rifles, a half-dozen handguns (all 9mm to avoid having to buy multiple caliber rounds) and, of course, his AR-10. All were pre-positioned at different shooting stations in his garage. One was by the back door, looking out over his backyard. He had another protected shooting position by the garage's side window, and a third by the door to the kitchen. The last one faced out of the partially raised garage door and down his tree-lined street. It was there that he saw the gang of skinheads making their way down the road directly toward his house.

As the thugs came closer, he could make out their tattoos through his magnifying rifle scope. Swastikas, knives, and eagles were plastered on every inch of their bodies. The men looted the neighborhood with brutal efficiency. A pair of hoodlums would kick in the front door and disappear into the darkness beyond while the others kept watch. Cory knew that knew there was nothing left to salvage. His neighbors had abandoned their homes, but not before consuming anything of value and taking anything worth stealing with them when they left. These criminals wouldn't find a thing.

Finally, the gang of thieves entered Cory's designated kill zone, an open area with no trees impeding his view. HIs training had been limited to targets, not real people. As he learned from his failure to drop the first pair of thieves, shooting at firing range targets was a lot easier than hitting a moving person. But the skinheads were walking at a steady pace, moving toward him head-on instead of at an angle. A .308 round would put down a three-hundred-pound black bear, so it would be more than enough to stop a more fragile human being even if his aim was a little off.

Cory lined up on the nearest man, a scrawny piece of crap if Cory had ever seen one. Shirtless and with a cigarette dangling from his lips, he was skeletal. He had the look of an addict that spent his money on drugs instead of food or was so high all the time that he simply forgot to eat. As the scrawny man turned to speak with one of his larger companions, Cory pulled the trigger and felt the satisfying jolt as his rifle's stock slammed into his shoulder.

Keeping his scope on his intended target, Cory watched as the blood exploded out of the man's back. A rookie mistake, watching his first victim fall rather than immediately moving to his next target. That tactical error gave the others a chance to sprint for safety.

Cursing himself, Cory continued to scan the road, finally finding a leg projecting from behind one of the neighborhood's many oak trees. he lined up his sights and fired, once again keeping his scope glued to his target. The shot went high, clipping the asphalt, and Cory quickly lowered his aim and put two more rounds downrange. The third bullet found its target, and the leg was shattered into two pieces. The man's knee and lower leg bounced almost a yard away from the rest of the stump.

A scream from behind the tree confirmed his success, and Cory grunted to himself in satisfaction. He saw another limb poking out from behind a second tree, and Cory blew that one off as well, which brought a smile to his face.

But his grin was short lived as several of his targets began to shoot back. The targets at the gun range never shot back. How a person reacted to return fire was the difference between a marksman and a shooter, between a soldier and civilian with a gun. Suddenly, with deadly .556 rounds peppering his garage door, Cory realized that his plan wasn't so good anymore. He pressed himself down and tried to become one with the concrete floor while over a hundred bullets shattered his walls and shredded his phone book and newspaper barrier. The minute or so of sustained gunfire seemed like an eternity. So when the shooting stopped, Cory didn't react immediately, but lay still on the cool concrete.

After thirty seconds of silence, Cory decided that his bunker wasn't the place to be. He jumped up from behind his newspaper wall and ran to the kitchen door. If he could get out of his bedroom window, he could jump over the next-door neighbor's fence and make a quick getaway. He hadn't planned to leave, so he had no bug-out bag ready. He had no rally points scouted and prepped, so he had no idea where to go. He just had to get out of there and put as much distance between himself and those guns.

Just as he flung the kitchen door open, he heard the crash of several pots from within. Someone had tripped his alarm. Cory brought up his rifle and let off six or seven rounds at the skinheads that had snuck inside. All found their marks and the two men hit the ground, blood squirting from several arterial hits. But before Cory could move, several more rifles opened up from the living room, punching through the walls of the kitchen and sending Cory scurrying back to his paper-lined fortress.

The bullets from the street began to fly again, the air filled with instant death. Cory laid back down behind his newspaper wall as more and more of his house was ventilated. Finally, one of his phonebooks took one too many rounds, and a fifty-five-grain slug shattered his right knee.

Cory lost his breath. It felt like being kicked by a mule at first, but the pain transformed into an intense burn that was nothing like he had ever felt before. He howled and brought his AR-10 over the barrier and indiscriminately fired at the street.

Cory looked at his mangled limb, his foot tilted at an impossible angle away from his body. He began to sob out of pain and fear. In the distance, he heard the deep-throated growl of a large diesel engine. From down the street, a dump truck came rumbling toward his house. Cory brought his

AR-10 up and aimed at the driver's side of the windshield. The pain in his leg pounded, throwing off his aim, and he fired futilely three times before his bolt locked back. He was out of bullets! He had forgotten that the AR-10 magazine, because of the larger size of the rounds, held only twenty shots instead of the thirty that his AR-15 carried.

He scrambled for a spare magazine, but the deafening sound of the rapidly accelerating truck forced his eyes up to the garage door. Cory knew he would never be able to reload in time as the truck rushed up his driveway. The last thing he would remember was the impossibly loud crash of metal on brick, and the momentary feeling that an elephant had landed on his back as the garage's walls collapsed on top of him.

The battle had been concluded. And although Cory had taken out almost half a dozen thugs, the lack of training and poor planning that marked his tactics had doomed him. In war, lessons were often brutal and unforgiving, and dead men could not learn from their mistakes.

***

We kept our positions behind cover, the four of us at strategic intervals to provide supporting crossfire. Harley and I were taking cover on one side of the street, while Jorge and Garrett were on the other. Backyard walls and well-placed hides minimized our exposure to a flanking attack, but we kept our heads on a swivel, checking side to side for any enemy movement.

Many minutes went by, and with the sounds of battle long nothing but a memory, I began to relax. I sat back, lowering my weapon, and grabbed a bottle of water. Adrenalin has a way of dehydrating your body, and I guzzled my water greedily.

As I put the nearly empty water bottle back in its pouch, a man began shouting.

"You're dead if you don't come out now," he bellowed. "Surrender, and I'll let you live. Fire on us and you're dead!"

I glanced at Jorge, who gave me a confused look. We held our positions as the man turned the corner of our street. He was tall and muscular, and tattoos covered his body. He held his battle rifle like a toy, waving it at the houses with one hand. He carried a fireman's axe in the other. On either side of him, at least a dozen men prowled. They displayed an amazing level of discipline as each house was penetrated and cleared while the rest of them kept watch outside. They were coming our way, and there was nothing we could do about that. I looked to Jorge, hoping he had a way to win the battle without committing suicide in the process.

"Retreat?" he asked, speaking low enough to not be heard by the oncoming gang.

I nodded and turned to run. I would go back to my dad's house and then down to the lake, where we had planned an escape route to the housing development to our west. Then I heard a voice calling out in answer to the gang of skinheads marching down the road.

"TAURUS!"

The gang dropped to the ground, scanning the homes in front of us. To my shock, Beker walked out onto the street, holding up both arms. He walked out onto the street in front of us, between our positions and the advancing gang.

"Taurus, it's me. Beker!"

"Beker?" asked the large man, whose name was apparently Taurus. "What the hell are you doing here?"

Beker slowly advanced toward the men. He was clutching several purple velvet Crown Royal bags filled with his looted booty. The gang advanced to meet him, standing close enough that I could hear them speak.

"I'm so happy to see you guys," Beker began. "I've been hiding here since we were ambushed at the racket club."

Taurus took the bags from him and opened one. A large smile broke across his face as he went through the pouch of gold and jewelry.

"I was trapped here," Beker continued. "Two of them almost got me, but I escaped. They've been all over the place, so I had to hide."

Taurus grinned and put his arm around Beker's shoulder. "This is my man! Pinned down by the Spics, he still manages to find us the goods." He dropped let go of Beker and yelled to his gang, "Let's keep moving!"

As one, they began to march toward us.

"No good," Beker said. "I've cleaned all these houses out already."

Taurus stopped and looked down at our former companion. "Nothing?"

"I've cleaned out all the houses in this subdivision and down the road toward the racket club. Didn't go into King's Row yet, though."

"Just left there. Lost five men," Taurus said. "Bastard in his garage got 'em."

"There's another subdivision next street over," Beker said, jerking his thumb toward the older houses to the west, where we had planned to escape. "A couple of lakefront mansions and a ton of older homes. I haven't hit it yet."

Taurus thought for a minute and agreed. On command, the gang turned and retraced their steps to the main road. Turning left, they disappeared from sight.

Beker had just saved our lives. The little creep did have a heart in him after all.

Jorge and Garrett ran to our position, sliding to their knees next to me and Harley. Jorge pointed up the road.

"I want to follow them. We need more intel. How many and what they're armed with."

"You looking for volunteers?" Harley asked.

"Just one," Jorge said. "More than two will increase the chances of getting caught."

"I'll go," I said.

"You just want to check up on your boyfriend, but I think Beker has a thing for that big guy." Harley joked.

"This is serious," Jorge said. "No fooling around."

"You should know us by now," I replied. "Humor is how me cope."

"Then let's go," he said as he stood up and peeked around the corner of the house we were hiding behind. In a flash, Jorge disappeared, forcing me to run to catch up.

We got to the end of the street and peered around the corner. The gang was up ahead, moving quickly toward the main road. Based on the conversation we'd overheard, I was expecting them to leave our development. Instead, they turned back onto King's Row.

We followed them from a distance as they met up with an even larger group of thugs outside a home that had been destroyed by heavy gunfire. Jorge and I looked knowingly at each other, recognizing the house where someone had taken shots at us. A large dump truck had taken out the side of the garage. It was wedged against the concrete block wall, engine off and doors open.

"You get that damn thing working?" Taurus yelled as he approached.

A thin, shirtless guy wormed his way out from under the belly of the truck, his upper body covered with brown fluid.

"Sorry, Taurus," he said. "Hydraulic line's shot. It's done."

"Damn it!" Taurus yelled as he strode up the driveway. He called into the house, "You get it all?"

Five more men came out, each carrying multiple rifles and metal boxes full of ammunition.

"Nice haul," one of the thugs said, smiling at the group's leader.

A sudden, violent slap from Taurus sent the man sprawling onto the lawn. The tattooed crook shook his head and scrambled to his feet.

"What the hell was that for?"

Taurus grabbed him by the hair and turned his head to the dead bodies that had been lined up on the grass.

"*Nice haul?* You think that those guns were worth THIS?"

Taurus pushed him, sending the man stumbling onto the corpses. He drew his handgun and pointed it at the prone man.

"I…I'm sorry," the skinny mechanic said.

"Show some damned respect for your brothers," Taurus replied, his handgun unmoving and pointed at the man's head.

Everyone froze, including Jorge and me. Seconds ticked by, no one seeming to breathe, until the big guy slowly lowered his weapon and replaced it in his holster. Taurus picked up a shovel leaning against a nearby tree. He threw it down next to the man.

"Start digging, maggot."

"Just me?"

"I'll help," one of the others said.

Taurus grunted his approval. "About time you acted like a team. Now find some more shovels and get our men in the ground."

Thirty minutes later, the graves had been dug. Taurus took a minute to say a prayer over the dead before leaving with their haul. We let them go. The group now numbered nearly forty, all armed and all united behind their leader. They moved with tactical awareness, including a point man and rear guard, without direct orders from Taurus to keep them in formation. Those that weren't overburdened with stolen goods were flanking their comrades, rifles at ready and scanning their surroundings as they moved.

"Someone in their group has some military experience," Jorge whispered.

"Yeah, these guys are dangerous."

Jorge broke cover and began to walk up to the destroyed house. We cautiously walked over to the dump truck, sidestepping the oily liquid that was running down the driveway. Jorge jumped up onto the driver's runner board. A moment later he hopped back down, a key dangling in his hand.

"This is a universal key for just about any piece of Caterpillar equipment. I hoped they had left it. You never know when this will come in handy."

"I'm impressed."

"Thank my brother. They have some Cats on their ranch. He carries the key around his neck." He pocketed the prize, and we walked back home.

We had found out who our enemy was, and he was deadly, organized and ruthless. And unfortunately, he was now our neighbor. After the gang left, they settled into the homes to our west, just on the other side of our subdivision's eight-foot concrete wall, while leaving some of their men to guard several intersections in the area. We were surrounded and any sound that carried outside our area could bring the gang back. In one short afternoon, our lives had gotten very complicated—and dangerous. We were supposed to be walking to Dr. Kramer's house, but now we were trapped in a three block subdivision. We quietly returned to our houses and began to plan our next move.

CHAPTER 6

*"Opportunities will come and go, but if you do
nothing about them, so will you."*

— **Richie Norton**

"**G**ERRY, WAKE UP," BARB KRAMER whispered as she gently shook her husband's sweat-soaked shoulder. "You're dreaming again."

Kramer slowly lifted his head from the pillow. The light from the crescent moon cast shadows of ghostly apparitions from the passing clouds onto the bedroom's wall. He squinted at the darkened silhouette of the ceiling fan, which had stood immobile since that November day when the EMP detonated somewhere over the North American continent. The cool evenings hadn't required its use, but he would miss it in the coming summer.

"You know," Kramer whispered back to his wife of over thirty years, "I never knew how precious light was until all of this happened."

The two of them stared at the phantoms, the vaulted ceiling creating a movie screen of dancing shadows.

"That one looks like your uncle Saul!" Kramer chuckled as he pointed to a silhouette.

"Oh, stop," she said.

"No really!" Kramer raised his arm and traced the outline of the shape in the air above them. "That's definitely your uncle's nose and chin."

Barb stared at the black outline as it disappeared, finally seeing what her husband's imagination had found. "Well, I'll be," she snickered.

They lay together, caressed by the spring breeze that brought the heavy fragrance of the nearby orange groves. Several weeks a year, the overpowering fragrance of tens of thousands of orange blossoms covered the area. Although the perfume of was most intense at dusk, the scent lingered most of the night, carried by the cool night breeze.

"I'm so sorry you haven't had a good night's sleep since you came back." Barb said, gripping her husband's hand.

Sorry couldn't begin to express her emotions. Fear, anger and disbelief all swirled in her mind as the specter of her husband's discovery always seemed to float just below her conscious thoughts. When he had returned from his horseback trip with Mr. Jacobson, what he told her was a story too unbelievable to be real. In fact, their best friend and neighbor, Ed Grafton, had to drive to Mr. Jacobson's home and verify the details of her husband's horrific report.

After her normally steady and indefatigable husband had stuttered and stumbled his way through the tale, she got Ed Grafton to drive his old stove bolt pickup to the Jacobson home. Ed brought the old guy and his dog back with him, explaining that he found the elderly man sitting in a rocker on his front porch, holding an old revolver and clutching his deceased wife's favorite shawl.

"He looked like he'd been crying," Ed said when he helped Jacobson out of the vehicle and into one of the Kramer's spare bedrooms.

When her husband found out they brought his travelling partner back to their house, Kramer joined Jacobson in the bedroom and closed the door. An hour later, both men came out, seemingly back to their old selves. With Will and Rob guarding the road to the house, the rest of the group had gathered in their living room to listen to his report of their travels to the Coventry power plant, where they had watched agents of the DHS incinerate the elderly, the infirm, and other people they deemed undesirable.

"Are you sure?" she had asked in disbelief, challenging her husband's story. "Maybe it was just garbage they were burning?"

"No," Gerry had quietly replied. "I know what I saw."

"We watched buses loaded with people driving to the plant," Jacobson said. "And they were empty when they left."

"But maybe they were being housed in the plant somewhere?"

"Barb," Gerry had replied. "These buses were transporting chronically ill people, folks that were infirmed and fragile. They needed medical supervision, and there were no medical facilities there."

"You mean they burned 'em alive?" Trey asked.

"I don't know," Kramer replied. "We never went inside the fence, but I didn't hear any gunshots."

"I don't imagine any of the residents from the nursing home could have put up a fight," Jacobson said. "And cutting a man's throat is a lot harder than you'd think."

"So is pushing a man into a furnace," Ed had said. "Who knows how they did it. They did it somehow. Let's just all get back to our jobs here, and we can talk about it some more at dinner tonight."

That was several weeks ago, but the memories haunted her. Barb slowly released her grasp on her husband's hand, realizing that Gerry was likely off in his own world as well since he had failed to complain about the death grip she had just released.

She draped her arm over him and began to caress his bare chest. Getting an approving grunt from her husband, Barb Kramer decided that both of them could use a release. She straddled him and kissed him deeply.

"I love you, Gerry Kramer. And nothing will ever change that."

"I love you too," he replied as he fumbled with the buttons on her silk nightgown.

As the garment slid down her back and the fragrant breeze danced in her hair, she gave herself up to him, grateful that neither of them would be thinking about the world. At least for the next hour or two, reality could be pushed back and they would find some peace with each other. While her husband explored her body, massaging her sore muscles and caressing her bare skin, the rest of the world could crash and burn. Because in this room, with the love of her life at her side, her world was just fine.

The next morning, Barb's eyes struggled to open. Her body had melted into the sheets. Reaching blindly to her left, she felt around for her husband, but found only a rumpled bedspread and a stray pillow. She sighed, hearing her husband's muffled conversation with Mr. Jacobson in the kitchen. She was suddenly sure their voices—and the other sounds they made—had found the ears of their guest last night. Then the thought of her daughter hearing the two of them in bed was enough to drive away any idea of further sleep, and she was up and dressed in record time.

Barb entered the kitchen to find the two men eating cereal and reconstituted milk. A cup of instant coffee with condensed cream and sugar rounded off their breakfast.

"So what are you two talking about?" Barb said as she rushed into the kitchen and began pouring hot water over her own cup of coffee crystals.

"What else?" Mr. Jacobson replied. "What do we do about that power plant."

Kramer nodded. "We're going over to Ed's later this afternoon and see if he'll drive us to Vernon Bragg's place. We need to find out if this is happening anywhere else. He's been in touch with the rest of the world on that HAM rig of his, and he'll know if others have reported this and if there are any other people planning to stop this massacre."

"Stop the massacre? Just what do you think you can do? You're just an old man with a medical degree," Barb scolded. "*And* you have a family to take care of."

"I just want to talk with him," Kramer replied. "I know my place."

"No you don't, Gerry Kramer!" Barbara shot back. "You've got a martyr complex, and I don't want that getting you killed."

"Barb, please! I'm not going to do anything stupid, but this cannot stand. I will not sit by and watch another Holocaust sweep over my people."

"It's not just 'our people.' It doesn't matter what your religion is. You can't take this so personally."

"And why not?" Kramer demanded. "If not me, then who?"

"Now wait a minute, you two!" Jacobson interjected. "Let's stop this right now. Just remember who the enemy is."

"I do know who they are." Barb said. "They are a big, powerful army that has guns and tanks. And what do we have? Some rifles and a few vehicles that actually work. Just how are you going to overcome that?"

The argument continued between the couple while Jacobson sat quietly, allowing both of them to vent their frustrations. It was a heck of a thing they were trying to come to grips with. Jacobson knew that their anger wasn't really with each other, but with the new life they were thrown into. With a daughter almost seven hundred miles away and nothing but death and uncertainty just beyond their front gate, there was no one to vent to other than each other.

"You're crazy!" Barb yelled at her husband. "You couldn't give a rat's ass about me and our daughters. Why else would you go out there and stir up trouble!"

Jacobson slammed his hand down onto the wooden kitchen table, sending a salt shaker tumbling onto the floor. Momentarily jolted out of their fight, Gerry and Barb turned to see the old man staring back at them.

"I never thought I'd see the two of you fighting like little kids," he said. "Now both of you just sit your butts down and stop this."

The couple meekly settled into their chairs, both embarrassed at their behavior.

"Now I understand why you're afraid." Jacobson said as he faced his friend's wife. "The two of us are too old to go out and pick up a rifle. But there are thousands of people being killed because they can't help themselves. Shame on you, Barbara, for being so selfish."

"But—" she began to protest.

"And you, Gerry! Shame on you for not understanding your wife's side of this. I haven't heard a single word come out of your mouth that would let her know that you heard what she was saying. She has every right to express herself, and frankly, you're being too pigheaded to listen. Now both of you just shut your mouths for a minute and catch your breath."

"I would," Barbara said, "but my husband can be so hard to communicate with. Sometimes…"

"You two were communicating just fine last night!" The old man replied.

Barbara's face turned turn beet red.

"Oh my God!" Gerry said, a huge grin on his face. "You were listening?"

"Heck, I wish I hadn't. But with the windows open and it being so quiet and all outside, I didn't have much of a choice."

Gerry's grin began to spread, especially as he saw his wife's face turning a darker shade of red. She was literally at a loss for words, as Jacobson's face finally began to crack into a wrinkly smiled.

"All that heavy racket made me miss my own wife," he said. "I remember a time when the two of us were down by our lake, and the moon was coming up over the water. She got this devilish look in her eyes and the next thing I know…"

"No!" Barbara wailed. "Too much information."

Jacobson tried to keep a straight face, but a flustered and embarrassed Barbara was just too fun to watch. He began to laugh, his old cheeks and craggy nose scrunching into a Jimmy Durante face that made Barb smile as well. And just like that, the fighting was done.

"What about Caroline?" Barb said, her laughter dying away. "She had to have heard us last night."

"I think the dead heard you two. But you never know. I haven't slept well since the horrors back at the power plant, so maybe it was just me being awake already." Jacobson said.

Barb was mortified at the thought of her youngest daughter exposed to her parent's bedroom behavior.

"I wouldn't worry about it too much," Jacobson said. "I can't think of anything more important that a child knowing that their parents still love each other."

Barb took some comfort in those words, at least until her husband got his last dig in.

"You know," Gerry deadpanned, "there are numerous studies about psychologically damaged children blaming their problems on some Freudian adult behavior they witnessed. Now, I don't know if hearing things is as bad seeing things, but..."

"I wouldn't push that line of thought too much," Jacobson interrupted, seeing Barbara's face begin to darken. The last thing he wanted was another fight.

Kramer grinned, knowing that his friend was correct to stop the joke then and there. Barbara got it too, but it didn't make her feel any better.

Kramer faced his wife and took her hands in his and said, "I'm sorry, babe, I get it. I promise to be careful. But please, you have to understand that we may be the only people outside of the government that have any idea what's going on out there. At the very least, I can warn others."

"I get it," Barb reluctantly replied. "I just don't have to like it."

"You alright?" Gerry asked.

"Yeah, as alright as I can be."

Gerry got up from his chair and moved behind his wife, hugging her shoulders as she sat in the wooden kitchen chair.

Barb began to feel better about it all—until Caroline strode from her bedroom and saw her parents embracing at the table.

"Seriously!" the teenager cried as she stormed out of the front door. "Do you two never take a break?"

"Oh my God!" Barb said, covering her face with both hands.

Gerry smirked. "I guess that answers that question."

Jacobson quietly excused himself from the table and ambled back to his bedroom, where he plopped down in the room's only chair. His faithful dog lay next to him on the wooden floor, the canine's tail flopping up and down as the old man rubbed his snout and ears. Then the octogenarian closed his tired eyes, leaned into the heavy cushions, and reminisced about the nights he and his wife had shared down by the lake. As the minutes passed by, his smile returned and he drifted off into a peaceful and much-needed slumber.

***

Later that afternoon, Kramer and Ed Grafton drove the old stovebolt pickup truck to Bragg's place, leaving old Mr. Jacobson in his room to rest. As they travelled down the winding dirt road that passed for a driveway to Bragg's military surplus Quonset hut, they could hear the sound of heavy equipment coming from the clearing ahead. Already half-buried in the Florida sand, the elongated semi-circular building was being reinforced with strategically placed sandbags. A new Hesco barrier now stood in front of the structure's front door, and the old NCO was using a small backhoe to fill the rectangular gabion with sand. As the pickup pulled up to the front of the structure, Bragg shut the Caterpillar down and hopped out of the machine's open cab.

"Well, if it ain't ol' doc and Fast Eddie," Bragg croaked, referring to Ed Grafton's former career as a local racing legend. "What can old Vernon do for ya?"

Kramer looked at Grafton and nodded. "Hiya, Mr. Bragg. We wanted to pick your brain."

"Well," Bragg replied. "Them's slim pickins."

"Can we speak inside?" Grafton asked. "It may take a few minutes."

Kramer held up a basket of food Barbara had prepared. Ever since the old guy had connected her with their daughter over his HAM radio, Vernon Bragg could do no wrong.

"Watcha got fer ole' Vernon?" He asked with a smile.

"Barbara wanted you to know she's still thankful," Kramer said, offering the basket.

"Well, don't go tellin' yer wife I woulda helped anyways. But I surely appreciate it."

The three men moved around the partially constructed Hesco barrier and into the cavernous corrugated building.

Being partially buried under the sand gave the building some natural insulation from the cold and heat. Both Kramer and Grafton once again marveled at the moderate temperature that hit them as they went inside.

The three sat down at a cluttered table. Bragg opened the picnic basket and let out a low whistle.

"Yer a lucky fella," Bragg said absently as he pulled out dried meat and some fresh-baked bread. A Ziploc bag of oatmeal cookies and a couple of beers rounded off the booty.

"How are ya keeping things cold?" Bragg asked as he twisted the cap off the beer bottle and took a long gulp.

"We each have enough solar power to run a refrigerator," Grafton replied.

"Both of ya?"

"Yes," Kramer answered. "It eats about a hundred and eighty watts a day so it's no problem, especially since we got those extra batteries you told us about from the cell tower. Thank you for that."

Bragg downed more of the cold brew and let out a burp. "Twernt' nothin'."

Bragg downed more of the cold brew and let out a burp.

"Now, what kin' ole' Vernon do fer ya?"

Kramer told Bragg about their trip to the Coventry Incinerator and its apparent use to eliminate those that the government deemed unfit or too difficult to manage. Kramer described the busloads of people going into the plant and the empty buses leaving. Finally, he pulled out the partially burnt Brightside nursing home nametag he found in the field outside the plant's fence.

Bragg, for his part, sat silently and showed little emotion as the horrific story unfolded. When Kramer finished, Bragg simply stood up and walked over to his HAM radio workbench. He retrieved a notebook and brought it back to the table where Kramer and Grafton sat. Throwing the binder down, he spat out a curse and sat.

"I been hearing things out there," he said. "Folks is coming up missing."

He flipped through several pages, listing off the HAM operator's handle and location along with the estimated number of people missing. After totaling his rough count, the three men sat in silence, trying to wrap their heads around the magnitude of the situation. Including the busloads of people that Kramer and Jacobson had seen, there were tens of thousands missing without a trace.

"Now we can't be sure of these numbers," Kramer said, his voice shaking. "This is second – and third-hand information."

"You're right," Bragg replied. "But it ain't no coincidence that you seen some real nasty shit. Most of them reports is of big groups of folks that was there one day and gone the next."

Bragg wrote down some notes in his binder as he questioned Kramer for several minutes, asking about the type of buses, uniform colors and unit patches on the DHS agents, as well as whether the vehicles had antennas or mounted weapons. Kramer was impressed with the debriefing. When they finished, Bragg had a pretty good start on cataloguing the armament, communication equipment, and number of DHS agents that had accompanied the doomed prisoners.

"I'll get this intel to everyone I can. We'll just see what our high 'n mighty government is doing out there."

"Will you please let my daughter know?" Kramer asked. "If she's at the hospital in Nashville, she's probably seen something. I don't want her getting caught up in this."

"Claire has a serious problem," Grafton added. "She's got her dad's moral compass, but she's not old enough to know when to shut it off. She just might say something that would make her disappear, too."

"That'll be my first call," Bragg said. "Now you leave this up to ol' Vernon."

"How long before we know if you got the message to her?" Kramer asked.

"A day or two. Now don't you worry none. I'll be in touch."

With that, Bragg stood and went to an old metal locker set against one of the walls. He reached behind it, into the space between the curved wall and the straight locker, and pulled out a duffle bag.

"Here," Bragg said as he handed Grafton what looked like a walkie talkie. "Take this Hytera. Gotta chip inside that works on a frequency that ain't used by no one else. Just turn it on like this," he said as he rotated a knob that brought the portable HAM radio to life.

"How'd these survive the EMP?" Grafton asked.

The old man jerked his thumb back to the wall, pointing out several galvanized steel garbage cans.

"Them cans. Picked 'em up at the hardware store for next ta nothin'. Line the opening with steel wool and snap the lid shut. Best Faraday cages you can get."

Kramer was impressed. Vernon Bragg might look and sound like a hillbilly, but he was a sharp and capable man.

"I've set 'em to a bunch a repeaters in this area that's still workin', but if ya turn it to the one marked 'PRIVATE,' then only you an me can talk. But be careful. Them DHS agents can triangulate the signal even if they can't understand what we're sayin'.'"

"Then we better plan on talking at a certain time," Grafton suggested.

"Yar' a far sight smarter then ya look," Bragg joked.

"Well, that's not too hard." Kramer said. "If he was as dumb as he was ugly, he'd have trouble breathing and walking at the same time."

Bragg roared a deep, raspy laugh, then began hacking and coughing as his cigarette-scarred lungs seized up. After nearly almost thirty seconds of coughing and gasping for air, the old retired sergeant wiped his spittle-coated lips on his tattered military blouse and pulled another Camel out of its pack. Lighting it with his military issued Zippo, he took a deep drag and blew the blueish grey smoke up toward the rounded roof of his Quonset building.

He sighed. "Lil' hair of the dog."

"Let's monitor the private channel at ten each night," Kramer suggested, ignoring the stupidity of Bragg's last statement. "Then listen in every two hours until two a.m."

"Naw," Bragg replied. "Every snot-nosed rookie monitorin' the HAM frequencies knows that's when to listen in. Everyone calls at the zeros and 30s."

Bragg reached into his duffle bag and pulled out a digital watch that matched the one on his own wrist. "This one's fixed to the same time as the one on my wrist. Y'all can take it."

"Keep those in the garbage can too?" Grafton asked.

"Nah, keep a few of these in a faraday bag I got from a company called SurviveTek," Bragg said. "Don't like moving electronics around without protecting 'em."

Bragg made sure the watches were synchronized and demonstrated how to reset the seconds to .00 and where the time adjustment button was.

"Now," Bragg continued, "we're gonna listen in at thirty-seven minutes after each even hour, startin' at 1837 and stoppin' at 0237. And we ain't listenin' for more than two minutes."

"Okay," Grafton said.

"If we talk, then the next time we listen is thirty-seven minutes after each even hour *plus* add the hour we spoke to the end."

Seeing their confusion, Bragg explained.

"Say we spoke at 2237—and make sure you use military time, boys. Ain't no such thing as p.m. in the military. So we speak at 2237, then the next window will be the next even hour. Thirty-seven plus twenty-two equals fifty-nine minutes. That way, anyone trying to listen in won't be able to sit on the thirty-seventh minute after the hour. We'd start listening at 00:59. Y'all got that?"

"Makes sense," Grafton said with some hesitation.

"I get it," Kramer said. "So if we speak a third time, let's say the next day at 1859, then the next window would be at 2017 hours. Take fifty-nine plus eighteen, and that's seventeen after the hour, since fifty-nine plus one goes back to the top of the hour, plus seventeen more."

Bragg slapped his thigh. "Hot damn! Ya would a made an alright officer, Doc!"

Grafton's eyes lit up with recognition as he finally grasped the way that they could set up a new time without broadcasting it over the open HAM wavelengths. Vernon Bragg was a wily old coot, and Grafton was glad the man had been willing to help.

"Then it's settled," Kramer said. "We'll begin tomorrow night."

Bragg reached into his duffle once again and brought out a printed piece of paper. Handing it to Grafton, he said, "This is directions on makinz an antenna for the Hytera. Follow the directions exactly on the lengths of copper wire. Set it up high, on a roof or in a tree. Ya should get forty or so miles out with it. If you're off by more than an inch, y'all gonna be boostin' the signal on a frequency we ain't usin'."

"Copy that, Sergeant. I'm impressed." Kramer swept his hand to indicate the cavernous space. "How come you have all this equipment? You seem to have multiple…well, everything."

"Doc, you should know. Two is one, and one is none. Simple as that. Ain't no surprise when somethin' don't work. It's just plain ignorant to expect that things ain't gonna fail."

"I'm glad you did," Kramer said.

"Time to go" Bragg said, shuffling toward the single door. "Don't want them satellites to wonderin' what y'all are doin' here."

Bragg ushered Kramer and Grafton outside and with a wave and closed the door behind them.

"Always an interesting place to visit," Grafton said as he pocketed the watch and held up the portable HAM radio.

CHAPTER 7

SMYRNA, TN
278ᵀᴴ TENNESSEE ARMY NATIONAL GUARD

"It is easier to forgive an enemy than to forgive a friend."

— **William Blake**

A s Bragg made his HAM radio call to warn Claire Kramer, Staff Sergeant Kevin Thomas Dixon strode towards a three-story brick building, ignoring the frigid early spring gusts battering his already wind-burned face. He spat a silent curse, thinking of the wasted months he had spent trying to make his Apache gunships fly again.

The AH-64 helicopter was the most advance attack helicopter on the planet. A monster in battle, it could carry up to sixteen radar-assisted Hellfire anti-tank or seventy-six unguided Hydra-70 missiles. The final talon on the flying tank's lethal claw was the 30mm cannon that had a "shoot where I look" aiming system. The cannon was controlled by a monocular worn by the helicopter's weapons system operator, which rotated and swiveled the barrel to wherever the operator was looking. While the pilot sat in the rear elevated seat of the craft, the co-pilot and gunner sat in the front of the Apache and operated the helicopter's weapons systems. The Apache could hunt and strike in any weather condition you threw at it. The twenty-million-dollar aircraft was the tip of the sword in the 278ᵗʰ Tennessee Armored National Guard's attack plan. The helicopters normally would be out in front of the advancing tank battalion, killing as many of the enemy's armored vehicles and tanks as it could find, softening up the enemy's line of defense for the hammer-like punch of Tennessee Cavalry's M1A1 Abrams tanks.

Unfortunately, after the EMP fried most of its computers, their Apaches were now worthless lumps of metal.

As a crew chief for the Tennessee National Guard, Dixon was tasked with fixing as many of these warfighting machines as he could. So far, months into what the civilians had begun to call "the darkness," he hadn't revived a single aircraft. Stripping the machines down to their basic flying frame and eliminating as many computer controllers as he could had not solved the issue. After multiple scans, he had found several small computers that were unaffected by the electromagnetic pulse. He had stripped the functional computers, sensors, relays and switches from the all the helicopters and put them into a single machine. The result was an Apache with a computer system that turned on...but only presented him with multiple emergency warning lights. Not a single sound from the engine. Not even a listless turn from its blades.

Finally, he had to concede that without the proper computer diagnostic system and more spare parts, the job was impossible. As he strode into the base commanding officer's building, the scowl on Crew Chief Dixon's face told the story of a man who didn't like to fail.

Colonel Preston Cooper was in charge of the Air National Guard at the Nashville Airport, but his C130 transport aircraft were grounded for the same reason as Dixon's Apache gunships. None of their electronics worked. The colonel had transferred his headquarters to Smyrna primarily because of the extensive on-base housing available for his men and women, along with their families. Also, a number of functional HUMVEE and tractor trailers used to haul the Tennessee Cavalry's M1A1 Abrams tanks were stationed at this base. Minimal computer components were installed in the vehicles, so the HUMVEEs and "toy haulers" (as they affectionately called truck-tractors) were unaffected by the electric pulse that had fried most of the country's electronics. Presently, only the HUMVEEs were being used. They'd been sent out to the various armories scattered around the state in an attempt to bring in any Guardsmen that were trying to report for duty.

Located about fifteen miles south of the Nashville airport, the Smyrna National Guard headquarters put Cooper's people out of a high-density population area. Surrounded by an eight-foot chain-linked fence topped with concertina wire, Cooper felt he could operate with some level of safety and free up his soldiers for tasks other than security.

Just as importantly, he could get away from the Feds and the DHS clowns who had control of the Nashville airport. Watching the erratic and wasteful conduct by Homeland filled the native Tennessean with a loathing that was hard to swallow. Further, being put under the command of Deputy Associate Administrator McCain was way over the line. While true that the military was controlled by civilian leadership, it was unheard of for civilian DHS administrators to have direct control in a military chain of command.

The friction between Cooper and McCain had become unbearable when the colonel challenged a number of McCain's nonsensical orders. As a result of the breakdown in confidence between the Guard and DHS, McCain had begun to inflict small, punitive punishments on the Guardsmen. As far as the Homeland administrator was concerned, Cooper and his men had nothing to offer other than bodies that needed to be fed and watered. In the end, it had been a simple thing to get Cooper and his men transferred to Smyrna, where the non-functional Apaches were stationed.

"The colonel will see you now," the new E-2 aid said to the waiting Sergeant Dixon.

Dixon stood up and straightened his uniform as he approached the commander's office door. Giving the wood a single, sharp rap, he opened the door and strode purposefully into the room. Stopping three paces in front of the seated commander's metal desk, he stood at attention with his heels together and feet flared at forty-five. Dixon's eyes were fixed at the wall above the colonel's head. Snapping a crisp salute, Dixon barked out, "Sir! Staff Sergeant Dixon reporting, sir!"

The colonel absently returned the sergeant's salute and cleared a space on his cluttered desk. "At ease," Cooper said.

Dixon moved to parade rest, his hands crossed behind his back and his feet shoulder's width apart. Copper noticed Dixon's stiff demeanor and knew, before his sergeant even opened his mouth, that he had failed to nurse any of his Apache gunships back to flying form.

"Relax," Cooper said. "I know."

Dixon dropped his gaze, anger and pain reflected in his eyes.

"Sir, I tried everything."

"I don't doubt it, K.T."

"My Herks," Cooper continued, using the nickname for his Hercules C-130 transport aircraft, "were as dead as doornails, and they have half the computers you deal with. I just hoped that you could cobble enough unaffected parts together to make one or two work."

Cooper's soft words did little to mollify the hard-driven crew chief. The colonel stood up and came around his desk.

"Sit down, K.T. Let's talk."

The two sat down in the chairs that faced the colonel's desk. They were now speaking as fellow warriors, not as commander to subordinate.

"Things are happening that I'm not too pleased with." Cooper began. "I've been in touch with some of my men who stayed behind in Nashville and it's a real Charlie Foxtrot. DHS has no clue what they are doing."

"How so?" Dixon asked. "I haven't seen daylight in weeks."

"I know, and I've noticed how much you put into trying to make our Apaches work. And more importantly, how close you are to the men. So I have to tell you that we might be evicted by DHS. They want this airport and its land to create a relocation camp."

"WHAT?" Dixon shouted, the weeks of hard work and lack of sleep catching up to him. "Sorry sir," he murmured as he caught himself. "I didn't mean to yell. It's just that I've been juggling my men's problems and with all the time under the cowling, I just..."

"Apology accepted." Cooper said. "You're close with your men while I sit here in this ivory tower," Cooper said with a smile, his hand waving towards the cream plaster walls of his office. "I want to know what's going on with you and your families. I know you're all safe, that's why I moved us here. But I can only imagine your fears and frustrations. Tell me, what can I do for you and your people?"

"I don't know if I can answer you right now," Dixon said. "I wasn't prepared to discuss that. But I can say that most everyone has a missing relative or two they're worried about. That's their number one concern. But they know there's nothing more that can be done about that."

"Are you still sending out teams to check on the remote armories?" Cooper asked.

"Not anymore. After we were skunked for two weeks in a row, I didn't see a need to keep going back. If they were going to report, it would have been in the first month or two."

"I haven't seen our latest roster," Cooper said. "But last time I looked we had almost thirty-eight percent reporting. That's pretty good. In fact, the only decent intelligence I got from Agent McCain was that our National Guard regiment was above the Army's own rate of retention. After the EMP, the Army has less than a thirty percent effective force because of desertion and dereliction of duty."

Dixon, a proud man from Tennessee, smiled for the first time in days. "Thirty-eight percent. Not bad."

"I'd expect nothing less from our state or my soldiers." Cooper said. "I'm thinking of relocating to Fort Campbell. I've already sent some men ahead and they've got the room and supplies for us."

"I can speak for the men," Dixon said. "They'll follow wherever you go."

Cooper's shoulders relaxed. He got up from the chair and opened a closet door that hid a refrigerator. He returned with a couple of cold beers. Handing one to Dixon they both twisted off the cap. The colonel gave the bottle a quick tip towards his sergeant, and they both pulled a long draw from the chilled glass bottles.

"Nothing better," Dixon said approvingly.

A knock on the door interrupted the two men, and Cooper called for the person to enter. A young boy, perhaps six years old, galloped into the room. His right leg was bracketed by a metal brace surrounding a plaster cast that ran from ankle to mid-thigh. The child had a big smile on his face as he flung himself into the colonel's lap. Colonel Cooper's grandson, who had Down's syndrome, was the most loving person Dixon had ever met.

"Hi, Papa!" the little boy squealed.

"Marky!" A voice yelled from the outer office.

The boy's father, a lieutenant in the guard's "Outrider" engineering squad followed behind the lad. Jeb Cooper led the regiment's engineers, who paved the way for the 278th's tanks. Clearing mines and creating roads were often required to go from point A to point B, and that was the job of the regimental engineers. Jeb called himself a glorified bus driver, but his men often found themselves under enemy fire or beset by landmines designed to kill man and machine alike. They were soldiers that fought with a shovel as well as a gun.

"Marky," the father admonished the boy. "That's not the way we report to our commanding officer."

"But he's my papa," Marky replied as he hugged the old colonel.

"It's alright, Jeb," Colonel Cooper said to his son. "This is the first time I've been happy all day."

"That's because I'm the happy boy," Marky said as he leaned back into his grandfather's chest.

Jeb, seeing his father relaxed and smiling for the first time in a while, relented as the colonel let his grandson examine the contents of his desk's drawers.

"Glad you're here," Jeb said to Dixon as they shook hands. "I heard about the Apaches. We sure could have used them, but I never thought you had a chance getting any of them to fly."

"Thanks L.T." Dixon said. "If anyone would get it, I knew you would. At least your vehicles survived the blast."

"Minimal computers, and we had a few backup parts that were shielded in their storage sheds. Pure luck."

A few moments later, the colonel's daughter-in-law glided into the room.

"Hi, Nan," Colonel Cooper said. "Come for your little monster?"

"I'm NOT a monster!"

"You're just like Sullivan," the colonel said to his grandson, referencing the boy's favorite movie, *Monsters, Inc.*

"Yeah! I'm Sullivan," Marky crowd as he jumped out of his grandfather's lap.

"What happened to your leg, Marky?" Dixon asked as the boy staggered into his mother's arms.

"I fell," he said.

"A little more than fell," Nan Cooper explained. "A greenstick fracture of his tibia and he tore up some ligaments in his knee."

"He'll mend soon enough," Jeb said. "Kids heal quick."

As Nan bent over and picked up the young boy, Dixon noticed the bump in her belly.

"What happened to you?" Dixon asked with a smile.

"Talk to your friend here." She beamed, pointing to her husband. "He's what happened."

"Almost thirty weeks along," Jeb said. "Marky's having a baby sister."

"Yay!" Marky said. "Her name is going to be Boo."

"Boo?" Dixon asked.

The colonel laughed. "Also from *Monsters, Inc.*"

"Well, that might be her nickname. But we haven't decided on her real name yet," Nan replied, brushing her son's hair from his eyes.

"But that is her name," Marky complained.

"You can call her Boo," Nan said. The boy gave a satisfied sigh as his mother led him out of the room. "See you boys at dinner?"

"Seventeen thirty!" Jeb replied with a smile.

After Nan and Marky walked out, Dixon watched the other two men's faces. It was plain as day that their world revolved around those two—soon to be three. Dixon had no doubt that either man would step in front of a train to protect Nan and Marky. It made Dixon a bit sad, knowing that he didn't have that kind of family to go home to. It had just never happened for him, but he was happy for the Coopers. In a way, he felt like a part of their family as well. That's just the way Colonel Cooper made you feel when you served under him. After all, the Tennessee Cavalry was all volunteer, and the men of the 278th were proud to be a member of the group that began in the Revolutionary war, landed at Normandy during World War II, fought under General Patton and conquered the deserts of Iraq in both the early 90's and Operation Iraqi Freedom just a few years past. For almost two hundred and fifty years, the men of Tennessee have voluntarily served their country, and that bond made them all brothers and sisters in Dixon's mind. Colonel Cooper and his clan were a part of that brotherhood. He was family.

"I have some sensitive information," Jeb Cooper began once his wife and son were out of earshot.

"Go ahead," the colonel said. "The sergeant's been with us for over a decade. He's clear."

"I've been getting some, how can I say it, *disturbing* reports from my Comspecs. I'm having a hard time believing what they're telling me."

"Sit," the colonel commanded. Dixon and Lieutenant Cooper sat in the two chairs facing the him.

"Sir," Jeb continued, "there are multiple reports that civilians are being herded into relocation camps and of families being separated."

"Have you confirmed this?" The colonel asked, his brow creased with deep wrinkles.

"To some degree," his son replied. "I sent a squad to a camp that DHS set up outside of Memphis. A couple of my soldiers had family there. They had to threaten to fire on the compound with their Ma Deuce if DHS didn't produce their people to bring back with them. The stories I heard from those that were rescued are nothing if not abhorrent."

The colonel's face flushed as his anger percolated. Family was the most important thing in the world, and the government had no right to get in the way of that.

"A couple of families talked about a forced farm labor camp in Fayette County," Jeb continued. "And my men found a facility guarded by DHS about forty miles from Memphis. They couldn't get access to the camp. There was a significant response from the camp to our presence, including several MRAPs and up-armored HUMVEEs. From a distance, our men could see almost a thousand people manually working in the fields. I just debriefed our soldiers and their families, and they all told the same story. I'm recommending that we send a recon team over there to verify the situation."

"My God," the colonel gasped. "What the hell is DHS doing?"

"I don't know, sir. But I mean to find out," Jeb said.

Dixon sat quietly as the two men talked, their voices raised as they discussed the possibility that the people of Tennessee were being enslaved by those in charge in Washington D.C. It was too fantastic to consider, but after a few minutes of debate, they all felt that further information needed to be obtained.

"I want your Comspecs to monitor the airwaves, especially the HAM frequencies. If anything's going on out there, that's where you'll get the unfiltered *but* unverified truth. We'll use that information to direct our next mission."

The colonel got up and began to pace behind his desk. As he spoke, it was almost as if he was talking to himself, rattling off a laundry list of things he had to get done. It was going to fall on his son and Dixon to complete that list.

"We need to build some QRTs to respond to anything that needs investigating. Dixon, with your birds down, your men have nothing to do right now. Organize at least three squads of your most trusted soldiers and begin training them on intel gathering techniques. You know the drill."

Who, what, where, when and how. Critical thinking in a formula that they could train the soldiers to use when gathering information.

"I want this on the QT. No hint to anyone that isn't fully cleared and trusted. This can't get back to DHS or FEMA."

"Understood," both men replied.

"Make it happen, men. This is not what we volunteered for, but if true, it's what we will fight against. I want a report tomorrow by 1400, and I want your QRT's organized and training by the weekend. Is that clear?"

"Yes sir!"

"Then dismissed," the colonel said. As the two men turned to leave, he called to his son, "1730 dinner?"

"Yes sir, Colonel, sir," Jeb replied with a smile.

"See you there. And make sure my grandson knows his Papa is coming."

After leaving the office, Dixon and Jeb each went their separate ways., mentally creating a list that had to be completed before 1400 tomorrow. Meanwhile, Cooper's new E-2 secretary, Wright, knocked on the colonel's door and stuck his head into the room.

"Colonel, is it alright if I use the head? I've been holding it for a while."

"No problem, Wright. I'm sure I can handle myself while you're gone."

"Thank you, sir," the young man replied.

Exiting the outer office, Wright walked passed the men's room and entered an empty office. Dusty furniture sat in the unused room as he strode to a locked metal cabinet. Producing a key, he quickly opened the cupboard doors and pulled out a nylon sack. Unzipping it, he produced a satellite phone. He punched a button on the keyboard to dial a preset number.

"Wright, here," Wright said. "You asked me to report anything out of the ordinary."

The young man repeated the conversation he'd overhead at his boss's door. He told of the failure to get any of the Apache helicopters functional as well as the plan to investigate the camps.

"I want to know what and when they are planning on sending out their men," the voice on the other end of the said once Wright was done. "I want to know everything."

"Will do," the young traitor replied. "You'll take care of me, then?"

"Like my own son," the voice said back. "Keep me informed."

Wright disconnected the call and hid the sat phone back in the nylon sack. He stepped into the men's room and relieved himself.

Stupid Guardsmen, he thought.

He hated Tennessee. His family had moved here from California when his father took a job at a bank in Nashville. Joining the Guard was his dad's idea of giving him some discipline—and as long as he had played that game, he was given access to his father's money.

When "the darkness" hit, money held no more sway. After befriending a DHS agent in Nashville, it was clear to Wright who had power in this new world. Wright was now in the secret employment of the men from Washington.

When he was asked to keep an eye on Colonel Cooper by his handler, the order came from DHS. Technically, he was just following his commanding officer's orders since DHS was now in charge of the Guard. What was it to him if there was intrigue in the castle, as long as he got his just dues in the end?

Back in Nashville, McCain put down his satellite phone and congratulated himself on seeing the potential of one E-2 Guardsman Wright. Having a direct backchannel into Colonel Cooper's headquarters was critical in keeping control of the area.

The poor colonel, McCain thought. *He really has no idea of the layers of deceit and misdirection in today's political world.*

"One can never have enough knowledge," McCain said to himself.

The DHS assistant director punched a button on his intercom system.

"Yes sir," a crackly reply came back over the ancient, but still functional, twentieth century device.

"Get me Washington," McCain demanded.

If Colonel Cooper was going to make trouble, he needed to let his superiors know about it. Letting the man command a regiment of functional and deadly Abrams tanks was a good way to lose control. And McCain, like his bosses at DHS, were all about control.

CHAPTER 8

Vanderbilt Medical Center
Nashville, Tn

"Common sense is instinct. Enough of it is genius."

— **George Bernard Shaw**

A FEW WEEKS AFTER K. T. DIXON gave his grim report to Colonel Cooper, Dr. Claire Kramer flopped onto an uncomfortable plastic couch and slowly closed her eyes for the first time in almost thirty hours. Since her chronic kidney patients had been moved out of her care late last year, she had become one of the few remaining emergency room physicians at the city of Nashville's only level 1 trauma center. In fact, with only six such centers in the state, Vanderbilt's medical center was the de facto destination for almost all life-threatening injuries in central Tennessee.

And boy, was there was a lot of trauma out there. Gangs had taken control of much of the area. The roaming bands of thugs were responsible for any multitude of criminal offenses. Murder, robbery, and rape were at epidemic levels. About the only thing that Claire could think of that hadn't become an item of value was gasoline, even as the older vehicles that still ran had become a prize that the criminals would kill for. There were plenty of idle vehicles with full tanks of gas that were easy pickings for anyone with a siphon or someone that could drive a pick into a tank and catch the fuel with a bucket.

Her first gun-shot wound patient had been from a local junk yard where spare parts for the older, computer-free automobiles could be had. Criminal chop shops were springing up all over the city as crime lords sought control of the streets, and with a minimal presence of either police or the military evident outside of the university grounds, the gangs had free reign throughout the city.

Reports of neighborhoods coming together to create safe zones were also filtering into the emergency room. Wounded civilians were occasionally brought in as fire fights between the gangs and the various clusters of citizens became more common. Supplies were rapidly dwindling, so food and ammunition were now at a premium in the metro area. This brought the innocent and the criminals together with more and more frequency.

With the Vanderbilt medical center providing both primary care and emergency services for the new government, Claire found herself in something of a gilded cage. She had all the luxuries that one could want during an apocalypse, yet she was also a prisoner to a system that seemed to be slowly losing the battle to provide for its citizens.

She lay quietly in the lounge, grateful for the lights that shone above her and the cool breeze that she felt on her cheeks. She didn't know the time because she had stopped checking her watch. All that mattered was being available when the need arose. It didn't really matter what time it was when a person was dying. She often didn't know whether it was day or night outside, so that knowing it was 3:30 meant nothing. She slept when she could and ate when she found herself in front of some food.

Claire had abandoned her apartment and now slept in the bunkroom attached to the lounge. The men and women "hot bunked," sleeping in whatever bed was available when exhaustion finally overwhelmed them. Bathrooms were attached to their sleeping quarters, giving the residents and nurses a place to shower and private toilets to use. She knew that the rest of the country was experiencing a much more perilous situation, but Claire still resented being stuck here.

At first, after she was pressed into service in the E.R., they would see maybe one or two patients a day. Most of the injuries were burns from fires made for heat and cooking. A few accidental lacerations or the occasional traumatic amputation showed up as people, used to pushing a pencil or working a cash register, were now trying to build shelters and perform other manual labor projects they had never tried before.

But now, with spring's arrival and the summer heat occasionally threatening to break through, fire injuries were less common. Instead, groups of survivors were bumping into each other as they sought out the ever-dwindling resources of a dying city. Knife wounds had replaced accidental lacerations, and gunshots had become the number one injury she treated.

As she began to sink into a light slumber, she felt the air move near her as one of her fellow workers walked by. Claire smelled the generic antiseptic odor of the person, giving her no clue whether it was a man or woman. She heard the distinctive clanging of a coffee mug and the ritualistic sounds of cream and sugar being added to the ceramic cup. Claire snuck a peek, lifting her heavy eyes just enough to recognize Rachael Mason, one of the best trauma nurses she had ever worked with. Rachael had taught Claire more than any of the emergency doctors she had shadowed. Given that the trauma nurses were often the first in the hospital to triage the patient and begin their care, Rachael was a wealth of life-saving information and critical care tips.

"Did I wake you?" Rachael asked with a distinctive lack of sympathy.

"Like you care," Claire mumbled to her friend.

"You need to ask?" the nurse replied with a smile.

Claire heaved herself up from the furniture and stumbled over to the coffee pot.

"Why is it so quiet out there?" Claire asked as she poured coffee into an old beige mug. "Did they finally run out of bullets?"

"No," Rachael said. "It's close to five."

"I'm assuming you mean morning and not dinner time."

"You assume correctly. Even the gangs need some sleep."

Claire sat down at the table with her friend, both women savoring the brief moment of calm as they sipped their whitened and sweetened coffee.

"How's your family doing?" Rachael asked, breaking their trance-like state.

"Fine, I guess. I haven't spoken directly with them in a while, although I still get updates from that HAM radio guy. He sends me notes occasionally with a message for me from my dad or mom."

"That sucks," Rachael said. "But I guess it's better than nothing."

Claire had no good reply to this line of conversation. She knew that Rachael's parents had been killed early on in "the darkness" when they were ambushed by escaped inmates while driving their old pickup truck from the farm they owned near Ashland City. With so much confusion in those early days, their bodies had been recovered and cremated before Rachael had heard they were dead. She hadn't been back to their farm since they were killed, which was now likely occupied by squatters or just falling into disrepair.

Hoping to deflect the conversation in a more positive direction, Claire asked, "How was your last visit to Smyrna?"

"Well," Rachael said with a sly grin. "It was very productive."

"Do tell! And don't leave out a single detail. How's your beau?"

Rachael took another sip of her coffee, primarily to hide the growing flush that was developing on her cheeks. Claire was enjoying her friend's discomfort as Rachael struggled to decide just how much to disclose.

"Billy's...fine. He's just fine."

"Just fine?"

"No, he's *quite* fine."

"Come on," Claire begged. "Details! You know I have no life. I need a good story to get me through."

"Oh, alright," Rachael said, and the two women began gossiping like two teenaged girls. Billy Sims was Rachael's boyfriend. A private pilot before "the darkness," he was now with the Tennessee National Guard. At first, Rachael had been upset when the Guardsmen were relocated from the nearby airport to Smyrna. It was only fifteen miles away, but it might as well have been a thousand with gangs and criminals a constant threat. Recently, a regular convoy was established between the Smyrna National Guard Base, the Nashville airport, and the hospital, moving supplies between those three key areas. Rachael could hop a ride with the supply convoy and get back to the hospital within twenty-four hours.

"So what does Billy have to say about all this?" Claire asked.

"He can't be specific, but I got the feeling that the Guard isn't too happy with how the government is handling the recovery."

"Heck, I could have told you that," Claire said. "Our government has no control at all."

"No, it's worse than that. Billy says that some of the officers are starting to think that what's going on is exactly what the government wants. They're sending out men to investigate some pretty crazy stuff they've heard about."

Rachael scooted herself closer to Claire and spoke in a whisper.

"Remember what you told your dad? How all your long-term patients just disappeared?"

"Yeah, of course," Claire murmured, troubled.

"Well, some of the Guardsmen that reported for duty are talking about work camps with forced labor. And a few survivors have said that there are a bunch of people unaccounted for after a visit from Homeland."

"You're kidding!"

"Nope. Two of the Guardsmen from the Memphis area had to threaten DHS with their machine guns to get family out of the Memphis relocation camp. The place is a jail, and a lot of the men and some of the women that check in often go missing after a while. There was even a farm set up by DHS outside Jackson that refused to let the Guardsmen in. Said they didn't have the security clearance."

Claire's brain was too tired to process the information, she decided to visit the local HAM radio operator named "Slack" and get in touch with her father. He'd know what to do.

"Hey," Rachael said after a long pause. "You're drifting off."

"Just thinking," Claire replied. "I need to talk with my dad about this."

"No, the first thing you need to do is get some rest. I came down here to let you know that you're officially on weekend leave and don't have to report for ER duty for forty-eight hours."

"How...?"

"They have an Army doc here for the weekend, getting some real-world trauma experience. You are officially not needed, so get some rest and have fun for the next two days."

Claire slowly got up from the table and stretched her back. "It's been so long since I've had a day off. I hardly know what to do with myself."

"Get some rest,," Rachael said, nodding to the bunkroom door.

"Thanks. Let's talk later."

"I'll be here, just get some rest. I have a feeling we're going to need it."

Claire took the bottom bed on the last of the five bunkbeds. Hanging her lab coat on the wall hook next to her, she fell on top of the covers, too tired to pull the cotton blanket and sheets back. The last thing that Claire remembered was the cold, stiff pillow hitting the back of her neck as she fell into the deep abyss of a sleep long past due.

Twelve hours later, Claire finally pulled herself out of the lower bunk and stood and stretched. She went to a rack of fresh scrubs and found a set that fit, then grabbed her flip flops from her locker. A long, hot shower left Claire invigorated.

Afterward, she went to the hospital's cafeteria and got in line with the rest of the staff. The sight of baked chicken and mashed potatoes set her empty stomach growling, and she loaded her plate with more food than she could ever remember eating. She also grabbed extra chicken for the HAM operator, remembering her mother's penchant for sending food as a token of thanks. Embarrassed at the heavy tray, she rushed past the empty cash register. At least she didn't have to pay for anything; since money wasn't around anymore, the food was a perk for the hospital workers. She found a table well away from prying eyes and began the assault on her meal.

As she attacked a particularly delicious bowl of carrots coated in brown sugar, Claire felt rather than saw someone sit down next to her.

"Rachael?" she guessed.

"Were you expecting someone else?" her friend asked.

"Prince Charming. Note the spare chicken I brought for him."

"Never met him, though he must be a big guy to need that much food."

Rachael reached her fork over to the still-overflowing plate in front of her friend but received a dog-like growl from Claire for her efforts.

"Really?" Rachael asked. "You have enough to kill a horse."

"Probably, but I haven't had a hot meal since…what day is it today?"

"Good Lord, woman. It's Saturday."

"Then I haven't had a hot meal since Wednesday's breakfast."

"Living on protein bars?"

"And coffee, lots of coffee." Claire took a big bite of chicken breast topped with cheese and gravy, wrapped in a slice of white bread.

"They had ham sandwiches," Rachael said, eyeing the strange concoction with curiosity.

"No pig products unless it's an emergency. One of the forbidden foods."

"Oh yeah, it's a Jewish thing. What else can't you eat?"

"Camels." Claire deadpanned as she put another big bite of food into her mouth. "I'll bet they're delicious."

Rachael snorted and began working on her salad. "So what are you planning on doing tonight and tomorrow?"

"I'm heading over to talk with the HAM guy."

"With all the shit that's going on out there! Are you kidding?"

"There is a convoy leaving at nine o'clock, and they can drop me off a couple of blocks from this guy's house. I know he'll be there on his radio. He said that Saturday nights were particularly busy. I just need to speak with my family. I miss them."

"What about getting back here?"

"The convoy will pick me up when they return tomorrow. The radio guy offered me a room for the night."

"I'm sure he would," Rachael said.

"I don't think I have a lot to worry about," Claire said as she put her fork down and brought out a plastic zip-lock bag. She stuffed the remaining chicken into the bag along with a second full bowl of carrots. She zipped the bag closed and put it in a brown paper bag along with a half-dozen cookies wrapped in a napkin.

"You think that food in the belly will prevent lust in the heart?" Rachael asked. "Here in the South, we know that a way to a man's heart is through his stomach."

Claire stood up from the table and grabbed her tray of dirty dishes.

"Well? You didn't answer my question. How's that food gonna keep his hands off you?"

"He's old," Claire said.

"A dirty old man!" Rachael shot back.

"He's in a wheelchair. He was exposed to Agent Orange in Vietnam. I'm not an idiot, Rach, and I can take care of myself."

Rachael's face fell as her teasing manner drained away. "I'm sorry. I just..."

"I know." Claire said. "But sometimes you treat me like I was so stupid that if I had an idea, it would die of loneliness."

"I've never thought of you as stupid. Naïve, but not stupid. I'm glad to know he's not a threat."

"Oh, so you're glad he's crippled with a neurologic disease?" Claire replied, refusing to let her friend out of the box she'd put herself into.

"I said I was sorry," Rachael protested.

Claire smiled. "What do you say we go get some ice cream. I hear they've got strawberry tonight."

"Sound great," Rachael replied, grateful that her friend had let up on her. But the nurse still wasn't all that pleased to see Claire go out at night, even with an army escort.

"Why won't you let the guys drop you off at Slack's house instead of a few blocks away?"

"He doesn't trust them. Doesn't want them to know where he lives."

"Well, if the stories Billy's telling are true, it's probably a good idea to stay off the radar. I just hope the neighborhood is safe."

"It is. They have a militia set up. They're on a dead-end road with a small river backing up to them. They've got things under control."

"Well, I still don't like it, but I guess that's something I can't help."

"I love you too," Claire replied with a smile. "Let's get some ice cream. I've got an hour to kill before I leave."

"Please," Rachael said, "don't use the work *kill*."

CHAPTER 9

LEBANON PIKE (SR 70)
NASHVILLE, TN

*"One life is all we have and we live it as we believe in living it.
But to sacrifice what you are and to live without belief,
that is a fate more terrible than dying."*

—Joan of Arc

THE UP-ARMORED HUMVEE SWERVED TO avoid a burned-out Suburban that had come to rest across the right lane of the road. The driver, E-4 Specialist Janice Castro had been quietly cursing under her breath, while her fellow soldier Darius Jackson sat on the passenger side of the four-door vehicle.

"Hold on!" SPC Castro yelled from the front seat.

"I don't get it," Jackson said. "This was clear last night. Now it looks like a war zone."

"What do you mean?" Claire Kramer asked from the rear seat. "I thought you told me this was going to be a milk run."

"It normally is, ma'am," Castro said as she accelerated away from the cluster of burned out vehicles she had just swerved through. "Been doing this run for a month, and we haven't had a problem yet."

The road seemed to open up as they shot toward the Nashville Airport. After a minute or two driving on a quiet and open road, Castro's shoulders relaxed.

"We're through," she said. "But I still don't like it."

"We haven't seen any problems on this route," Jackson said as he turned in his seat to face their lone passenger.

Around Claire were boxes of supplies destined for the Nashville airport. Claire was smashed against her door, having created a space in the back seat by moving and piling crates of medical supplies that were bound for the airport, where they would then be distributed to aid stations throughout the area.

Jackson, a young African-American man from northwest Nashville, had an easy smile on his face as he turned to Claire. "Don't worry, ma'am. We've seen a lot worse."

"You sure about this, Doc?" Castro asked as they took a final bend in the road and began to slow down in front of the subdivision where "Slack" lived.

"Yes, thank you," Claire said.

The giant military vehicle came to a stop in front of a street that had been blocked off by several SUVs and an old pickup truck.

"Don't see anyone," Jackson said.

"Go check it out," Castro said.

Jackson swung the door open and produced a Surefire G2X flashlight from his pocket. The beam swept across the cluster of vehicles guarding the entrance to the housing development.

"Stay here," Castro said to Claire as she dismounted from the HUMVEE. She produced her own flashlight and lit up the left side of the road while her partner scanned the area to their right. Satisfied the area was clear, she propped her battle rifle on top of the vehicle's hood to cover Jackson's advance.

"Looks good," Jackson called as he walked carefully toward the barricade. Claire and Castro watched his beam darting behind and under the trucks.

"All clear!" he yelled as he returned to the HUMVEE. "No brass or signs of a fight."

Both soldiers returned to the HUMVEE and shut their doors.

"This isn't right, Doc," Castro said. "The barricade's been manned every time we've gone by."

Jackson stared out at the empty vehicles. "They've waved at us every night for a month. No way they just abandoned their front line of defense."

Castro turned to Claire. "I can't make you stay with us, but this stinks.

I'm strongly recommending that you cancel your little trip. Nothing about this makes sense."

"You said there wasn't any sign of a fight," Claire said. "Wouldn't there be bullet holes, spent casings, or blood if something happened?"

"Yes…," Castro hesitantly replied. "But that's no guarantee that things didn't go south here."

"Even if there wasn't a fight," Jackson said, "they've abandoned their barricade. You don't do that unless you've left the area. The best you can hope for is that the houses are all empty. The worse you can expect is that bad guys have taken control."

Claire sat for a moment, processing the information. In the end, there was only one choice she could make.

"I'm going in," she said. "I have to try and contact my family. That HAM radio operator is my only link to home."

"He's probably gone," Jackson said as he stared into the quiet subdivision. "Moved on with everyone else."

"I don't think so," Claire said. "He's wheelchair-bound and in no shape to leave his house."

"Is that why you're here?" Castro asked. "You've never explained why you're making this trip. If you're worried about your friend, we can arrange to have him brought to the hospital."

"You don't know him," Claire replied. "Besides being stubborn, he's a retired Marine."

From the conversations she had overheard, the soldiers had a real love/hate relationship with the few Marines they had run across. *Stubborn, loyal,* and *dangerous* were the three most common adjectives she had heard.

"Copy that," Castro said. "No reasoning with a jarhead once they're set on their mission."

Jackson laughed, his infectious smile bringing a grin to the two women.

"Very well," Castro said. "This is your stop."

"Thanks," Claire said. "What time is my pickup tomorrow?"

"We'll be rolling back through from the airport about 1300."

"See you tomorrow." Claire replied as she slid out of the back. Grabbing a backpack filled with the food and a couple of Cokes, she slammed the door closed and picked her way through the vehicles. She turned to wave and was met with a flash of the headlights followed by the growl of the HUMVEE's diesel engine.

A nearly full moon bathed the road in the bluish glow of its light. The entrance road split, and Claire followed the street to the right. She had been driven here just once before, and that was a while ago. As she walked into the neighborhood, she reminisced about the time before "the darkness," when she could have driven here in under fifteen minutes. Now her beloved sedan was nothing more than a useless lump of plastic and metal, sitting in the medical center parking lot across the street from the University's emergency room entrance.

Mist clung to the open field to her right. A few cries from an owl somewhere in the fog-covered meadow gave life to the neighborhood, and the constant chirping of crickets comforted her as she walked.

They stop chirping when there's a problem, Claire reminded herself.

Even with the background noises, the dark windows of the abandoned one-story brick homes gave the sub-division a tomblike air that eroded Claire's resolve. The street was a large circle. Slack's place sat at the bottom of the loop, his backyard on the river that marked the southern boundary of the neighborhood.

Muted sounds were coming from the center cluster of homes. Claire ignored them, but she began to pick up the pace as she felt, rather than saw, that someone was nearby.

CRACK...WHIIIIING!

A bullet flew by her.

Claire sprinted toward the field to her right as several more shots pinged off the road and slapped the dirt at her feet.

"There's one!" called a voice from behind her as she disappeared into the mist.

Several people were chasing her. Adrenaline dumped into Claire's bloodstream, and she barely felt the ground as her feet seemed to have a mind of their own. Deep into the fog, she stopped to get her bearings. The sounds of leather rubbing against metal, along with the crushing sound of many feet in the dry grass, was rapidly approaching. She turned to her right and began running back up the field.

Running parallel to the main road, she prayed that the fog would stay thick enough to cover her escape. But as she began to run uphill, the mist rapidly thinned. Seeing her cover disappear, she hid herself among the tall weeds and listened for her pursuers.

Like a trapped animal, her breathing was heavy and rapid. She tried to force herself to calm down, drawing on her crisis management experience in the emergency room where seconds meant the difference between life and death. She brought her breathing under control just as four men crashed into the spot where the fog thinned out.

"Where'd she go?" one of the men huffed.

"I think she turned back there," another replied.

"No, she went this way," the first. "We need to spread out."

Each carried a battle rifle and had a military belt or bandolier with extra magazines of ammunition strapped to their bodies. They wore jeans and sneakers, so they definitely weren't military or government.

The first man pointed over Claire's head and sent two of his comrades in her direction, while he and the other man moved south. They brought their rifles up and surveyed the fog covered and moon-lit field. By Claire's estimate, they were about thirty yards away when they split up. Her hiding spot was far from perfect, and if they got much closer, she would be captured.

Reaching into her backpack, she pulled out the plastic bag of chicken. As the two men slowly advanced toward her, they were scanning with their eyes side to side. About twenty yards away, both men stopped and looked to their left, peering into the fog at a noise or movement that had caught their attention. Taking advantage of the distraction, she heaved the bag of food deep into the field.

The bag landed with a thud, crushing the dried grass.

"Over here!" one of her pursuers yelled as they ran towards the sound.

Dropping her backpack, Claire sprinted back toward the highway, quickly losing the cover of the low-lying fog. Her legs moved with a speed and purpose that she didn't know she had possessed.

"There she is!" Claire heard from the field behind her about thirty seconds later.

She continued running up the slight rise of the hill, using the maturing oaks as cover. Loaded down with guns and ammunition, her pursuers were having difficulty catching up to her. In fact, as she came to the end of the field, she glanced back to find the four men now about fifty yards behind.

As she broke out onto the open street, she heard the crack of a rifle, felt the air pop next to her ear, and heard the zing of a bullet as it passed within inches of her head.

Claire's only thought at this point was getting out of the neighborhood, but as she zigzagged up the road, she realized that she had no plan beyond that. She didn't know where to go once she escaped; she just knew she needed to get away from these four men.

Another bullet pinged off the asphalt at her feet, pushing away any thoughts. Her brain wasn't capable of higher level functions as she tried to get away. The sound of two more gunshots pushed her forward at an even more frantic pace.

She could see the silhouettes of the trucks and SUVs at the front entrance about a quarter mile ahead as she rounded the bend in the road. Her pursuers were now blocked from a direct line of fire by the house on the corner. As Claire turned to look back, she stepped off the asphalt, causing her to stumble and fall. Quickly getting back up, she ignored the pain from her skinned knee and bruised right hand, and took off in a final attempt to get to the temporary safety of the vehicle barricade.

"Got her!" one the men cried in triumph, the voice closer than she thought was possible. She glanced back and saw that the pursuers had cut across the corner house's front yard.

Claire cried out in fear and tripped again. Turning to face her executioners, she began crawling backwards through the grass on the side of the road as the four men slowed down to a walk, confident that they had cornered their prey. The men at last became more than dark specters in the night as the nearly full moon cast a pallid glow over their bearded faces.

"Got us a pretty one," one of them said.

"Glad you're such a shitty shot. Would have been a waste to kill her."

"Screw you," the first one said.

They lowered their rifles, and one of the men stepped forward with a sinister smirk on his face.

"Say there, honey, what's your name?" he said as he approached with his hand out.

As the thug reached to grab Claire, the world exploded.

CRACK! BWRATT! CRACK! BWRATT! BWRATT!

The man who was looming above Claire jolted back and landed with a thud on the dark street. Two of his companions were trying to bring their rifles up when their heads erupted like a firecracker exploding a ripe cantaloupe into pulpy fragments. Their deaths were instantaneous as their bodies simply dropped in place. The fourth man screamed as three shots punched through his abdomen and chest. Within seconds, the four men were down, three of them dead and the last writhing and moaning from the gunshot wounds to his torso.

"Advance!" someone called out behind Claire.

She turned to see Castro and Jackson jogging toward her. Each held their black rifle up, staring through their ACOG scopes as they scanned the area.

"Clear!" Castro yelled. She dropped her slung M-16 to her side. "You okay, ma'am?"

Claire struggled to speak as she let SPC Castro pull her to her feet.

"What...how?" Claire stammered.

"You can thank Jackson for the save," Castro said. "He made us come back for you."

"It was no problem, ma'am." Jackson said before Claire could respond. "Our C.O. would have thrown us in the stockade if we'd lost one of our only docs."

Claire threw her arms around the young man, hugging him hard for a few seconds before letting go and embracing Castro.

"I don't care why you came back. Thank you!"

"Just doing our job," Castro replied. "Now we need to get out of here."

As they turned to go back to the HUMVEE that was parked on the other side of the makeshift barrier, Claire stopped.

"I can't," she said. "I have find my friend."

"You're joking, right?" Castro asked.

"No, I'm not."

"I'm sorry, Doc. But you're coming with me."

"I have to find out what happened to him."

"That's what happened to him," Castro said, pointing at the downed thugs. She began to pull Claire toward the waiting military vehicle. "We have to move. There may be more."

Claire resisted, but the two soldiers hauled her to the other side of the barrier. The HUMVEE sat idling with its lights off. Around them, the fog began to settle on the moonlit road. Claire looked over her shoulder. What if Slack was hurt and needed her help?

"Stop!" Claire said. "I need to tell you why I'm here."

"Ma'am, you've already told us," Jackson said as he began to push Claire into the open rear door.

"No, I haven't."

Claire shook their hands off her arms and took one step back. Facing the two Guardsmen, she made a decision to trust them with the real reason she had risked her life tonight.

"I don't believe the two of you are involved. If you are, then I'm dead as we speak."

The two soldiers looked at each other, confusion on their faces.

"Where are you from? Where is your billet?"

"Smyrna." Castro hesitantly replied. "Why?"

Relief flooded Claire's voice as she asked, "Do you know Billy Sims?"

"Sure," Jackson replied. "He's a friend."

"Then I have a story to tell you, and I swear it's true. I just hope you believe me."

For the next five minutes, they stood in front of the HUMVEE while Claire told them about disappearing patients and the chaos her family was facing.

"And that's why I need to get to my friend's house. I have to talk to my dad. I need to know what to do."

Castro gave Jackson a look before replying. "Doc, I believe you. We've heard some nasty rumors, and what you're telling me jives with them."

Castro turned to Jackson and barked out a command. "NVG's Jackson. Take the deuce. We're going in there."

Jackson and Castro each retrieved a tube with a cantilevered arm from a pouch on their MOLLE belts. Snapping it onto a square mount on the front of their helmets, they both rotated the lens over their left eye and a green glow bathed their faces as the night vision monocular came to life.

"Front seat, Ma'am" Castro commanded, opening the passenger door for Claire.

Jackson moved to the back and stood up through a hatch in the metal roof of the HUMVEE. He took his place behind "Ma Deuce," the M-2 machine gun mounted to the top of their vehicle. Pulling back on a handle on the right side of the gun, he racked the slide, putting a live round into the firing chamber.

Jackson leaned down into the cab of the HUMVEE and yelled out, "Locked and loaded!" He pulled himself back into position behind the machine gun and slapped the metal roof three times, indicating that he was ready to go.

"Which way, ma'am?" Castro asked.

"Claire," she replied. "Please, call me Claire."

"Maybe after we get out of the hot zone."

"Go to the right and down the street to the end," Claire said.

The vehicle's huge, turbine V8 engine roared to life as Castro steered around the barrier's vehicles and made her way to the makeshift blockade The HUMVEE pushed one of the barricade's SUVs to the side.

With the lights out, and the moon shining down, they were still visible. But the NVG monocular that each of them wore, lit up the night in a bright green hue. As far as the two soldiers were concerned, it was mid-day when they looked through the light intensifiers that were over their left eyes.

"Fourth house on the right," Claire said, as they made the turn at the bottom of the hill.

"See anything?" Castro asked over her military headset.

Claire couldn't hear Jackson's response over the rumble of the HUMVEE's engine, but given that they continued down the road, she assumed that all was clear.

Claire touched Castro's right arm and pointed to the single-story home where she had last visited Slack. The tall evergreen bushes that flanked the front door hid the entrance from view. Castro she turned the big machine and drove up the curb and onto the front lawn, then stopped directly in front of the house.

"Doc, you stay here until I give you the green light," Castro said to Claire. "Jackson, cover me."

Castro brought her rifle up and walked heel to toe to the front porch, then disappeared into the shadows between the tall bushes. A moment later, Jackson dropped back into the cab and exited through the rear door. Claire sat in silence for what seemed an eternity before Jackson returned.

"This way, ma'am," he said as he opened her door.

"Is he in there?" Claire asked.

"I'm sorry, we were too late."

Jackson produced a flashlight and guided her through the darkened house. Claire saw light ahead and entered the room where Castro stood. A camping lantern glowed in the kitchen, and another lit up the back bedroom.

"Slack?" Claire asked, already knowing that her only contact with her parents was dead in the next room.

Castro just nodded toward the open door. Claire hesitated for a moment then walked into the room. Slack was still in his wheelchair, his head tilted back. Multiple bullet holes riddled his torso. His mouth was open and his lifeless eyes stared at the ceiling. Rigor had yet to set in as Claire examined his body, so his death had occurred no more than a few hours ago. She gently closed his eyes and then turned to examined the desk. The radio and various other electronic equipment had been destroyed by multiple bullets. The HAM setup, a vintage Hallicrafter SX-122 he had owned since the early 70's, was now a useless pile of wires and vacuum tubes.

Claire lifted the camp lantern from the floor, shining its light on the desktop. Papers were strewn haphazardly, and Claire began examining them to see if anything of value could be salvaged.

"Come on, Doc," Castro said. "We can't hang out here. There may be more of them."

"A moment," Claire said. "Let me at least gather these papers to bring with us."

"You've got sixty seconds," Castro replied. "Jackson, get back out front and set up overwatch."

"Yes, ma'am."

Claire was collecting the various papers when she caught her name written down with what looked like red marker. She brought the page close to the lantern.

Claire, don't forget to take my car.

"What the...?" Claire said loud enough for Castro to hear.

"Whatcha got?"

"That crazy Slack. He left me a note to take his car. But he doesn't have a car."

"What about that?" Castro said, pointing to a car fob that sat on a shelf above the destroyed radio.

"Why is it flashing?" Castro asked.

"I don't know," Claire said, as she examined the wireless car controller. "There's no car name or logo on it."

"Maybe it's a duplicate?"

"But he doesn't have a car. He told me that much when I was here last time. He sold it years ago to help pay for his motorized wheelchair."

Castro moved next to Claire and took the fob, using her flashlight to inspect it more closely.

"That's weird," Castro said. "It's got a smart card slot."

Castro pushed on the edge of the card, releasing the tiny memory chip from its slot. Examining the fob again, she smiled.

"I'll be damned. It's a video recorder."

Claire collected all the sheets of paper and stuffed them into a plastic grocery bag she found lying on the floor.

"I'm ready," Claire said.

Castro gave Claire the memory card. "Hold this and don't lose it. We'll have to use a computer back at Smyrna to see what's on that thing."

"Smyrna?" Claire asked. "I thought you were going to the Nashville airport?"

***

"Oh, we're going there to drop off the supplies, but we're heading on to Smyrna for the night," she said. "I know that our C.O. will want to hear your story."

They returned to the HUMVEE, and Castro ordered Jackson back to the machine gun. Claire sat in the front passenger seat, staring out of the window at the darkened city as they drove, wondering just what she had gotten herself into. The HUMVEE's dashboard gave off little light, so she had to wait before she could read Slack's notes.

The trip to the Nashville airport took less than ten minutes. There were no further incidents, and Claire began feeling much more at ease when she saw the airport's lights painting the dark Tennessee sky.

Approaching the northwest corner of the airport, Route 155 crossed over Interstate 40. As they crested the top of the overpass, Claire gave an audible gasp as she saw tens of thousands of people amassed on the flat, concrete grounds of the airport. Buses were leaving the facility, a seemingly endless line of yellow and grey metal boxes spewing diesel fumes. They passed at least a dozen Greyhounds and school buses that were merging onto the interstate, breaking east and west depending on their destination.

Castro turned into the airport's commercial loading area. A DHS agent, backed by a variety of manned assault vehicles, stood guard. After passing over their orders and identification cards, they quickly dispensed with their cargo and returned to the gate. When they stopped to pick up their ID cards, they watched as another dozen buses rumbled past them on their journey out of town. All the transports were full of people; Claire could see their silhouettes in the foggy windows. Who were they? And where were they being taken?

Once the road was clear, they were waved through and the three of them were off on the final leg of their trip to the Smyrna airport and the Air National Guard's relocated headquarters. The fifteen-mile trip took nearly forty-five minutes. After clearing security, Castro pulled up to a building about a quarter mile from the main gate near the runway. The concrete tarmac was littered with lifeless aircraft. Several more darkened administrative buildings sat just ahead, all as lifeless as the Guard's dead helicopters. To her right were multiple apartment-like structures, each with a few lit windows. No one was outside.

"This way, ma'am." Castro said as she hopped out of the driver's side door and began walking up the sidewalk.

Claire wearily grabbed her plastic bag of papers and unconsciously touched her front pocket where she felt the outline of the memory card. Just inside the front door, a guard sat at a metal desk. Castro reported to him, and after a minute or two in hushed conversation, the guard picked up an old push-button phone and made a call.

"Follow me, please," the soldier said. "Sully, take over."

Another soldier, this one armed with an M-16, appeared from an alcove to her left. Claire was amazed that she hadn't even noticed his presence until just then. Castro and Claire followed the first guard and were led into an office marked "Commanding Officer."

"Take a seat," the guard ordered. "The colonel will be here momentarily."

Castro sat stiffly in one of the room's chairs while Claire chose to stand instead. She was tired from riding in the HUMVEE; its thinly padded plastic seats transmitted every bump and pothole.

"How can you sit down after riding in that thing all day?" Claire asked.

"Those were my orders," Castro simply replied.

Claire roamed the room, looking at a wall display of plaques as well as the official picture of the president. Claire wasn't much for politics; her life had been too busy for it to be a concern for her. She looked at the picture but found it uninteresting. Other than skin color, this president's photograph presented the same sanguine smile as all the other ones she had seen. It was a look she had never cared for. Given the constant problems a president faced, the optimistic grin seemed fake and out of place. The one thing she knew was that if she was ever elected president, her photograph would reflect an expression of sheer terror. It amazed her than anyone would want the job.

The clicking sound of shoes on the linoleum hallway floor approached and then stopped just outside the room. On cue, the door opened and a smartly dressed man entered. Greying temples and eyebrows indicated he was likely in his late fifties, but his physique spoke of a disciplined man, with a tapered waist and wide shoulders.

Castro snapped to attention, presenting a crisp salute and barking out her name.

"Sir, Specialist Janice Castro reporting."

The officer gave her a gentle smile and returned the salute. "At ease, Castro. It's too late to be so damned energetic."

"Yes sir," she replied, but she continued to stand stiffly with arms behind her back.

The officer went to Claire and held out his hand. "I'm Colonel Cooper," he said as they shook hands. "Thank you for coming. Let's go to my office."

Three of them went through a second door and into his private office. After seating himself behind his desk, Cooper folded his hands on the desktop and looked up at Claire.

"Well, I've been told you have a story you'd like to tell me."

His eyes and smile gave her all the confidence she needed. After almost ten uninterrupted minutes, including a description of her missing renal patients and other rumors she had gleaned from people she had treated in her emergency room, she produced the memory card and handed it to the colonel.

"I haven't gone through the papers yet," Claire said. "But that shouldn't take much time."

"Go ahead and get started." Cooper punched some buttons on his phone and said, "Get I.T. over here right away with a secure laptop and memory card reader."

Claire began going through the papers, putting them in a neat pile as she pulled each one out of the stuffed plastic grocery bag. About half way through, she found a handwritten note.

It read:

Message from Cornbread as follows – For Lady Doc

Contact father as soon as possible. Everyone is safe and healthy but situation has become dangerous. Confirmed mass murders by DHS agents. Incinerator plant outside Leesburg being used as crematory for sick and other undesirables. Thousands dead. Don't tell anyone. Don't talk about missing patients. DO NOT TRUST HOMELAND SECURITY.

Claire began to tremble as she re-read the message. Tears rolled down her cheeks. Cooper saw her crying and came out of his chair.

"What is it?" He put his hand on her shoulder. The fatherly gesture set off a range of pent up emotions and, Claire let loose with a full throttled sob. As she fell again the kind, older man's chest, he put his arm around her and motioned for Castro to bring some Kleenex from his bathroom.

"Here," he said, handing her a tissue. "Now what's caused all those tears?"

Claire handed him the note.

"That's from my dad," she said. "If he says that DHS is committing genocide, I believe him."

Cooper re-read the note then put it down on his desk, his face tensed in anger. He sat heavily in his chair and was about to speak when there was a knock at the door.

"Enter!"

"Sir, Specialist Rooney from I.T., reporting as ordered."

After the specialist set up the laptop and attached the card reader, the colonel turned to him and asked, "Is this machine secured?"

"Yes sir, the computer was wiped clean and we are not on the network."

"What's that about?" Claire asked.

"Viruses," the colonel replied. "Without knowing the history and source of this memory card, we've isolated the computer from the rest of our network. Can't be too careful."

The tech inserted the card and once the computer recognized it, Rooney navigated to the appropriate dialog box.

"Sir, just double-click on the icon and you'll be able to see its contents."

"Go ahead, Rooney."

Specialist Rooney opened the card and found two large movie files.

"Shall I, sir?"

"Go ahead."

The first movie file showed the final moments of Slack's life. The old man stared straight into the camera, a look of weary resignation on his lined face, and began to speak:

This is first sergeant Michael R. Creighton, retired United States Marines. This is my final report. Doc Kramer, I hope it's you and that you've found my note from your father. From what I've been hearing these last few months, and from what ole' cornbread has been saying, we've got ourselves a mess. Lots of people disappearing once the government gets involved.

Just a few minutes ago, one of the neighbors came down and said that DHS is at our front gate with enough heavy firepower to wipe our neighborhood off the face of the earth. They want to take us all away to their relocation camp. I can hear heavy engines out there. Even if they spare the others, I'm one of the ones they don't have a use for. I hope you find me with an empty gun in my hand.

***

When the recording ended, the colonel sat back in his chair and began to rub his temples.

"My God," he finally said. "Can this really be happening?"

He double-clicked the second file. It was Slack once again, but the camera was tilted at a slight angle and he was facing away from the screen. Claire guessed he had placed the recording fob on the shelf where Castro had first noticed it.

Someone was pounding on the door of his home. Seconds later, a crash sounded as they broke down the door. A voice shouting orders was calling for the men to search the house. All the while Slack waited, facing his inevitable death.

The retired Marine brought up a .45 handgun and racked the slide. Pointing the pistol at the door, he called out to the men just outside.

"What the hell do you want? Just leave me alone."

"Come on out, old man. Your neighbors said you'd be in here."

"I can't come out," Slack yelled back. "My wheelchair's out of power."

"Oh, for Christ's sake," a man said as he opened the door.

BLAM! BLAM!

The 1911 handgun spoke twice, sending its 230-grain hollow point bullets into the head of the DHS agent. A stunned look flickered across the man's face as the back of his head exploded. His body landed on the kitchen's linoleum floor at the feet of two more agents.

Slack emptied his magazine at the men in the kitchen. When his slide stayed back after his last round had been spent, an agent with a DHS logo on his tactical vest stepped into the doorway and emptied his thirty-round magazine in full automatic mode.

It was over in less than three seconds. Slack was dead, the gun falling from his limp hand onto the floor, and his beloved HAM radio equipment had died with him.

"Son of a bitch!" the DHS agent shouted. The camera continued to record as men dragged the two downed Homeland agents out of the kitchen. The agents left, not bothering to search the house, but the video continued to record. After almost five more minutes of viewing an empty room, the colonel stopped the movie.

The four of them sat in silence as they tried to process what they had just seen.

"Well," the colonel said. "This looks bad, but it doesn't confirm the stories."

"What do you mean?" Claire asked. "You heard what he said. And those DHS agents murdered him!"

"He shot first," Cooper replied. "If they had gone in with guns blazing, I could say that at least this group of operators were murders. But I can't smear the entire government based on this video."

Claire sat down, exhausted, realizing that the Colonel was correct. The only incriminating evidence on the recording showed a retired Marine sergeant making the first kill.

"So if DHS forced all the residents out of their homes," Castro asked, "then who were the four we put down?"

"Probably looters," Cooper said. "Opportunistic criminals that worked the neighborhoods cleared by our Homeland friends."

"Makes sense," Castro added. "They didn't wear uniforms and definitely had evil on their minds."

"Doctor Kramer," Cooper said after a moment, "please don't think I'm whitewashing this. There was no reason for those agents to kick down his door or force someone to abandon his home. I know that something is going on out there. I believe your father and I believe the First Sergeant. Most importantly, I believe you."

"So what are you going to do about it?" Claire asked.

"Tonight? Nothing. It's late, and I need to get home." The colonel pushed some more buttons on his phone and spoke to the front guard. "Have Doctor Kramer taken to the VIP apartment and set her up for the night."

"I'm fine to go home," Claire protested.

"Just get some rest," he said. "You've been through a lot and it's showing. We'll continue this tomorrow morning with my XO and another team leader. In the meantime, if you need anything, just ask. Any of the guards know how to get me."

Claire suddenly felt exhausted. The adrenalin she'd been living off the last few hours had finally given out, and she almost collapsed as she stood up.

"Doctor Kramer!" Cooper yelled as Castro caught her.

"I'm alright," Claire replied weakly.

"Yeah, you look great," Cooper said. "Get her to the apartment and call Doc Adams to check her out."

"No, really," Claire said. "I'll be fine. I just need some rest."

Cooper shook his head. "Castro, go get Doc Adams. I'll have the front guard take her to the apartment."

"Yes sir!" Castro replied and spun on her heels to leave the room.

But before she was out the door, Claire felt a weakness fall over her and the room began to spin. A dark tunnel started to form in her peripheral vision. As the tunnel narrowed and her vision turned dark, she knew she was passing out. The last thing she remembered was floating toward the ground as two pairs of hands cushioned her from behind. She thought that it felt nice to let go. As her day came to an end, she smiled and closed her eyes, knowing that she was finally safe.

CHAPTER 10

DHS HEADQUARTERS
ORLANDO, FL

THE MORNING AFTER CLAIRE KRAMER arrived at the Smyrna airport, John Drosky, the special agent in charge of the personal protection detail for Undersecretary Bedford of the United States' Department of Homeland Security, was having one of those days where he wished he had just stayed in bed. As he stood guard outside the office door, he had nothing but time to think.

What had started as a means of staying close to Bedford had rapidly deteriorated into a babysitting job. While John "attended" every meeting, he was always outside the room and only heard the rare raised voice or gleaned the occasional parting comments as the door opened when the meeting concluded.

Any number of Washington dignitaries had been coming and going, enjoying the Central Florida winter weather. Bedford had even set up a helicopter shuttle service to take the visiting government bigwigs to one of two confiscated resorts. Both The Breakers in West Palm Beach and a gulf-front resort on Anna Maria island were now property of the U.S. government. In the Orlando area, the Hyatt at Grand Cypress had been the site of a couple of Washington powwows, and the golf course had been opened for the events. Bedford had attended both meetings, but John had not been privileged to enter the conference room, spoiling any opportunities for further intelligence gathering.

"Another exciting day planned?" asked Dixon Bruner as he approached.

"Bru, if life got any better, they'd make it illegal," Drosky deadpanned. "I assume that Mrs. Bedford is on premises."

Former Ocoee policeman Dixon Bruner had been assigned security for Tanya Bedford as she recovered from the gunshot wound suffered a few months earlier.

"Making her obligatory appearance at one of her husband's social gatherings. She's taken the kid down to the commissary for some ice cream. Any idea where we're going today?"

Drosky shifted his weight from one foot to the other. Standing guard outside the director's office at DHS headquarters had become both a frustrating waste of time and the fodder for any number of jokes from his friends. Nightly dinner with Bru and his fellow agent friends, Big Mike and Beth, inevitably brought out dark humor—and almost always at Drosky's expense. Just last night, the trio presented John with a roll of toilet paper in a gold-colored box. "For the most royal wiping anywhere" was written on the front of the box, along with directions on how to properly apply the "gift" to Director Bedford's backside.

"Probably another worthless planning session," Drosky replied. "No doubt Captain Carlson and his wife will be meeting with our newest dignitaries out at the Grand Cypress."

"Getting pretty dicey out there if Mike's even close to accurately describing what he's come across."

"The entire south side of the city is a no-go zone," John said. "Since they pulled Mike and the others out of the area, we've been knee-deep in refugees at the airport."

Bruner sat down in one of the many chairs that lined the wall outside Bedford's office. Leaning his rifle against the muted grey plaster, he adjusted his battle belt and pulled a pack of gum from his vest pocket. Throwing a couple of sticks into his mouth, he began contentedly chewing as he leaned his head back and stared at the ceiling.

"I feel worthless," Bru said absently. "Tanya's on the mend, and her daughter's got two nannies. It's a waste of time hovering over them. They never go outside the safe zone, so I'm nothing but a chauffeur, driving them around in a six-block radius. What a joke."

"How is Lillie doing?" Drosky asked. "She better with mommy out of the hospital?"

"Yeah," Bru replied, still staring up. "She's not having as many nightmares now. Most nights she sleeps with her mother, except when you guys show up with Bedford for his 'quiet time' with Tanya."

Drosky smiled, watching Bruner stew over the way Bedford treated his wife. The director barely tolerated Lillie, the woman's daughter, and only used Tanya as arm candy for social gatherings and for pleasure on the occasional conjugal visit. Other than that, she didn't exist in Bedford's world as far as Drosky could tell. But it was obvious to John that his partner had become smitten with the woman.

"Bru," Drosky said, "be careful."

"What do you mean?"

"Tanya. Keep your distance. There are no positive outcomes for anything other than staying clear of her."

Bruner's head snapped up and he stared back defiantly at his friend.

"Seriously," Drosky said, "she's toxic. Off limits. You'll disappear faster than a fat kid chasing the ice cream truck if you get between the director and his family."

Bruner snorted, shaking his head in disagreement. "What family? He's there when he has his needs, and nothing more."

Bru stood and began to pace back and forth. Until that point, Drosky had assumed that his friend had an infatuation on the director's exotic and beautiful wife. Now, it looked like the crush had developed into something much more. John put his hand out and gently grabbed his friend's arm.

"Don't tell me you've…"

"No! Of course not," Bruner replied. "But the way he treats her and Lillie. I mean it's enough to turn my stomach."

Drosky released his friend's arm as he looked into his partner's eyes. "She's got you," he said.

"I don't know, John." Bruner replied. "It's so confusing. Some days, I'm happy to be there and other days I resent the heck out of being her babysitter."

"What does she say?"

"Nothing really." Bruner said. "She thanks me, talks to me. And Lillie likes to climb all over me. But Tanya and I have never crossed any lines. As much as I want to sometimes, we haven't done anything even close to wrong."

"Hmm," Drosky mused. "Sounds like you're becoming the father and husband without the romance."

"The way the two of them look at me...I wish I was."

"She's in a precarious situation," Drosky said. "The kid can tell that Tanya looks to you for security. You're the man her husband isn't capable of being. But Tanya has to keep Bedford happy or else he might just get rid of her."

"Not while I'm around!"

The sound of approaching footsteps from within the director's office stopped further conversation. Bruner retrieved his rifle and both men stood at attention, flanking Bedford's door.

"Thanks Mr. Director," a voice said just as the door opened. Another new player from D.C. exited Bedford's door. Captain Carlson and Micah Bedford followed him out.

"See you tomorrow on the first tee," the fat little man shouted as the Washington bureaucrat strode away, disappearing down the long, dim hallway. Bedford then turned to the captain. "You up for eighteen in the morning?"

"Do we have a choice?" Carlson replied, acting as if they were being sentenced to hard labor at a federal prison.

"See you for dinner at six tonight. I'll drive." Bedford said, dismissing Carlson.

The captain nodded and left the three at Bedford's door.

"What are you doing here?" Bedford asked Bruner.

"Sir, just checking in with Agent Dixon."

"I like to get a daily report from the men guarding your family," Drosky stated. "They're in the commissary for some ice cream. With guards at the entrance to the building and several armed agents in the dining area, he felt it was safe to report to me."

"Getting ice cream?" the rotund man stated with disdain. "I hope she isn't down there getting fat."

"No sir," Bruner said. "It's for Lillie. Your wife's doctor wants her to eat more to help her heal, but she's hasn't been too compliant with his wishes."

"Good," Bedford said with relief.

Both men started contemptuously at their boss as Bedford turned to go back into his office.

"Sir, with your permission," Bruner said to Dixon, "I need to get back."

"Dismissed," John replied, returning Bruner's salute.

"Director, a word please." Drosky said before Bedford could close his door.

"Sure, come inside," he replied, waving Drosky into the room.

"I have a recommendation," Drosky said after the director had taken a seat at his vintage mahogany desk. Salvaged from a high-end antique store, the massive partner's desk was inlaid with ivory and decorated with gold leaf. The hundred-year-old brass hardware gave off a dusky gleam rather than the shine of new metal. The desk easily would have fetched five figures in the "before" economy. Now, months into the country's recovery, it was being used by his corpulent boss to impress the visiting dignitaries.

"Recommendation for what?"

"Your family," Drosky began, standing at parade rest in front of the desk. "I think we need to start the rotating agents guarding Mrs. Bedford and your daughter."

"Why?" Bedford asked, looking up from the paperwork he had been scanning. "Is there a problem?"

"No sir," Drosky replied. "But there is value in having fresh eyes on any situation, and I think that rotating agents would be of benefit."

"Agent Drosky," Bedford said, giving John his full attention, "My wife trusts Agent Bruner with her life. You two saved her from those MS-13 gang members. You'll have a hard time getting her to agree with this."

Bedford marched around the desk, his eyes almost a foot below Drosky's own, Glaring up at the agent, he poked John's chest rig and said, "Just what's going on? I know you two are friends, so don't bullshit me. Is there something here I need to know about?"

"No sir!" Drosky confidently replied. "But I worry that if you leave Bruner in his present assignment, he may become too attached to your family."

"What! Are you telling me that something is going on between them?" he hissed, venom in his words.

"Not at all, sir, at least not yet. Please let me explain."

"Please do!" Bedford shot back, his face still flush with anger.

"Sir, it is our responsibility to protect you. Not your wife. Not your daughter. You are the primary asset."

"Go on," Bedford said.

"If I may be blunt," Drosky said, "I don't want any of my men becoming more attached to your wife than they are to you. If we get into another situation like the one where MS-13 attacked our convoy, I need to know that the men I command will think of you first."

Slowly, the director's face began to return to its normal color. A slight smile twisted his lips.

"Yes," Bedford said. "I see your point."

The portly man returned to his leather chair. The springs that supported the antique groaned in complaint as the director leaned back and rubbed his chin.

"You're right, of course. But I want you to stay with me. We can rotate security for Tanya and her kid, but you are to stay by my side. Is that understood?"

"Yes sir, completely," Drosky replied crisply.

Bedford appraised John, nodding to himself. "I must say, I made the perfect choice putting you in charge of my security. You've just proven that again. I don't like worrying about the men watching over my wife, if you know what I mean."

"Completely, sir. Tanya is a beautiful woman, but the men respect you too much to take advantage of that. Besides, from what Agent Bruner tells me, she is completely devoted to you. I don't think you need to worry about that."

"True," the bombastic man said. "But still, one never knows."

"Might I suggest a solution?" Drosky asked. "I know someone that you could assign to your family who would never be a concern."

"I'm listening," Bedford said.

"Agent Beth Hildreth."

"The female agent that stopped those gangbangers last month?"

Beth had been walking back to her apartment a few weeks back, when she spotted a group of MS-13 gang members raiding some of the nearby homes. She had called in support and personally took out one of the thugs with a well-placed bullet to his head, sending the rest scurrying out of the neighborhood. Beth had been hailed as a hero and was an asset in the field, but Bedford was more concerned with his own personal safety and controlling the population rather than confronting the gangs that were roaming the city.

"Yes sir," Drosky said to his boss. "I can't think of anyone more qualified. No distractions, if you catch my drift."

"Is that all?" Bedford asked.

"I would still rotate a man from my command, giving your family a second person to guard your wife and child. But if you keep the men rotating through this assignment, they won't forget who they are protecting, and Agent Hildreth can be the constant that would keep your wife satisfied with her protection."

A smug look came over Bedford's face as he pondered Drosky's suggestion. "Agent Drosky, I want you to permanently re-assign Agent Hildreth to my wife. Commence with a rotation of your men as you deem appropriate."

"Very well, sir," Drosky said. "As you order."

"Dismissed. And have my vehicle ready to travel to the Grand Cypress tonight. We'll be leaving around six."

Drosky snapped a salute, and after receiving the director's typical limp-wristed reply, he spun on his heels and left the room. Calling a replacement to take over his overwatch duty, John was finally able to leave the director's office. Striding down the hallway, he couldn't help but smile at the way he had accomplished three goals in one stroke. The first was to get his partner away from Tanya and Lillie. The young man was smitten, and leaving him in that position was a recipe for disaster. The second goal was to get Beth closer to him. He was more and more convinced that things weren't going well for the government, given the increased levels of gang and citizen violence. If the whole thing collapsed, he wanted her close by so they could team up and escape. The third goal was to have Beth share in the babysitting responsibilities he had been enduring. No longer would he be the only butt of Big Mike jokes.

Now, if I could just get Michael James Jones reassigned to headquarters Drosky mused.

CHAPTER 11

DISNEYWORLD
ORLANDO, FL

"Whenever evil wins, it is only by default: by the moral failure of those who evade the fact that there can be no compromise on basic principles."

— **Ayn Rand**

A s John Drosky concluded his meeting with Undersecretary Bedford, "Utter exhaustion" were the only words "Big Mike" could use to describe his physical and mental state. After being pulled out of Orlando's south side, where he had been patrolling right after the EMP hit, he had been reassigned to a Rapid Reaction Group. The first few weeks of his new assignment were all training. He'd learned urban combat techniques including breaching and clearing buildings and other small unit tactics. The training period also gave him time to bond with the other members of his four-person squad.

Following completion of his training, the last months had been a blur of activity, each day bringing another dangerous situation that involved clearing a building or sweeping an abandoned neighborhood. Rarely did they come across criminal gangs. Rather, they were often confronted by families or groups of ordinary citizens scavenging for food, medicine, or other necessities.

In the early days of their mission, it was standard operating procedure to turn the looters over to DHS for processing. After a couple of firefights where wholly unprepared refugees were slaughtered, the four-man squad decided to let the perps go, along with their salvaged goods. They'd given the looters a stern warning in exchange for their promise that they wouldn't return to loot again.

Repeating their mission day after day was taking mental and physical toll on them all, but especially on Big Mike, who was the largest member of the squad and had to lug around at least fifty more pounds of muscle than his battle buddies.

The heaviest burden he had to bear was the knowledge that his mother and sister were still unaccounted for. They'd lived north of Orlando in the Sanford area, miles from Big Mike's area of operation. Mike saw the crime and disease that had enveloped the west side of town, and he worried that his family was in peril. But there was nothing he could do about it, other than have John's girlfriend, Natasha, check the roster of refugees in Florida. The raven haired, blue-eyed Natasha worked at DHS headquarters, processing the new agents as they arrived. But more importantly, she monitored the camps and their progress in processing the citizenry into the nation's new system of government. She had a line on the area's activities and promised to let Mike know if she ran across his family's location.

Big Mike's fireteam consisted of himself, two Marines, and a Navy Corpsman. The other three retired from active service and all had combat experience. Mike, though by far the youngest and largest, was the least experienced of the four. At 6'4" and over 260 pounds, Mike towered over Cynthia Terrones, who was the most qualified. The staff sergeant had retired a couple of years back to start a private security company, specializing in counter-terrorism and marketing herself to the many resorts in the area. She had begun her career in the Marine's Military Police but moved up to a Special Reaction Team. She then distinguished herself as a member of a Fleet Antiterrorism Security Team before retiring after twenty years in the Corps. Now pushing forty, she ran rings around the three men she had been teamed with. Mike quickly learned from Cyn that speed, agility, endurance, experience, and brains were far preferable to brawn. And if it weren't for the cocky and condescending attitude of their DHS bosses, she would be giving the orders rather than taking them.

"Come on, Mike," Cyn said in a low voice. "Keep your elbow in."

Big Mike was trying to hide behind a faux marble pillar on a concourse at Disney's Caribbean Beach Resort, aiming his M-4 toward a restaurant a few hundred feet ahead. Mike had a bad habit of aiming his battle rifle with a "chicken wing," his left arm flared at a ninety angle from his body. The appendage would stick out from behind cover, presenting his enemy with a target. Cyn liked to remind him that a bullet to the arm was just as likely to put him out of the fight as a gunshot to the gut.

Roving gangs had been pillaging Disney's stores, and their squad had been sent in after game trail cameras, which had been placed strategically throughout the theme park, confirmed that there was activity in this area.

Moving toward the sound of voices ahead, Cynthia and Mike were performing a bounding overwatch maneuver with the other two agents, Joey Phillips and Alan Taylor. As the other pair moved forward on their left, Cyn and Mike aimed down the alley, covering their squad mates' advance.

Mike tucked his left arm tightly against his body as Taylor and Phillips paused on the left side of the walkway. A hand signal from the pair indicated that they were in position, and Cyn moved up and put her left hand on Mike's right shoulder, initiating their move forward to their next area of cover. They walked heel to toe, both weapons aimed downrange at the threat, and took a position behind a large planter. Cyn left Mike and swung further to their right, advancing under an overhanging roof, passing several ransacked souvenir shops. She took a position about twenty feet ahead of Mike, behind another pillar and to the right of Mike's lane of fire. Waving her hand side to side, she signaled the other pair to advance as she and Mike covered their movement once again.

Within a few minutes, the four were positioned outside the entrance to a restaurant from which the sounds of crashing furniture and laughter emanated. Cyn gave hand signals initiating their final assault. Phillips and Taylor advanced to the left side of the entrance. Taking a mirror from his front shirt pocket, Phillips scanned inside the building without presenting himself as a target. After watching for over a minute, Phillips pulled the mirror back and gave Mike and Cyn a signal that there were four bingos inside, each with a weapon. His final signal was that they were gang members and not a desperate family.

Cynthia had come up with the novel signals for what they were facing. An open hand with wiggling fingers represented a family, while a fist violently thrust into the air was a group that needed to be taken down. Mike felt the adrenalin course through his system. He needed to kick some butt after several frustrating weeks. He smiled at Cyn and was surprised to see a sinister grin in return. It seemed that she needed to dole out some good old-fashioned ass whooping as well.

Cyn and Mike advanced to the right side of the entrance and stacked up against the wall. Cyn held up her hand and counted down from five to one. Making a fist at "one," she peeled into the room and turned to the right, while Phillips mirrored her movement on the left. Mike entered and took center right, finding cover behind a pillar and an overturned table. He saw Cyn advance and stop about ten feet ahead and to his right. Her hand signal initiated the others to move, and after two more leaps, Mike found himself less than twenty yards in front of the four thugs, while Phillips and Taylor were in a flanking and supporting position on the left wall of the large dining area.

"Do we give them a chance to surrender?" Taylor whispered into his neck mic, which broadcast to the other three team members.

"Negative," Cyn replied. "You see the five-point crown on their arms? They're Latin Kings. They won't give up."

She repositioned herself, leaning against the pillar, and took aim at the group.

"Taylor, take the left one. Phillips, you're on the one with the yellow shirt. Mike, you take the playboy, the one with that stupid fedora. I have the one on the right."

The four took careful aim as Cyn gave final instructions.

"Countdown from three," she commanded.

"Is that on one or after you say one?" Taylor joked.

Cyn had drilled into them on this a million times. Taylor and Phillips were constantly trying to get her goat by asking that same question, on and off, over the last few weeks. Mike, who had a deep respect for her as a retired Marine, decided not to join in. Even though he had at least a hundred pounds on Cyn, she was quick and knew just the right places to strike a man's body. He would give himself a fifty-fifty chance of surviving a fight with her. She wasn't to be messed with.

"Shut it, Phillips. On my mark."

The four took aim at the men, who stood by a table full of canned goods and other looted items from the adjacent stores.

"Three...two...one!"

At "one," four rifles spat out their 62-grain, green-tipped .556 bullets.

The penetrators roared out of their barrels and, like a scythe cutting down grain, put the gangbangers to the ground in one fell swoop. With the slugs moving at over three thousand feet per second, the four men were dead before the sound of the gunfire ever reached their ears.

Cyn advanced on the bodies, weapon up, and scanned the room.

"They're gone," she whispered. "Move up and clear the kitchen."

The portholes in the double door entrance were lit with a dim glow, indicating that there was a light source inside. Few of the Disney buildings had skylights. It was most likely a lantern or flashlight illuminating the room beyond.

"Assume hostiles," Cyn said. "On my mark."

Neither Phillips nor Taylor joked this time, not with potential armed gangbangers waiting on the other side. Cyn counted down again, and they rushed the room, each breaking into their assigned lanes of fire. The squad, pumped for another fight, was met with silence. Scanning the room, the four advanced into the large, L-shaped area. Pots and pans were scattered over the white tile floor, and the detritus of months of abandonment were strewn among the discarded utensils.

"Shit. Over here." Taylor said.

After ensuring that their side of the room was safe, Cyn and Big Mike quickly moved to the other men. The other two were standing with weapons slung down to their side, facing away from the corner of the room that they had been assigned to clear.

"Oh, no," Cyn groaned, as Big Mike followed closely behind.

Lying on the floor, tied down to the legs of a metal prep table, was a young girl, naked and very dead. Her blank eyes stared up in terror and her mouth stood agape in a silent scream. Taylor found a tablecloth and covered the nude corpse. He knelt next to the victim and, closing his eyes, began whispering a prayer.

"Glad you didn't give 'em a chance to give up." Big Mike said.

"With this corpse," Phillips added, nodding his head toward the covered body. "They'd never have let us take them alive."

"They were dead men walking," Cyn said. "They just didn't know it. Too bad they didn't suffer."

"I'll call it in," Phillips announced as he moved out of the kitchen to radio their findings back to headquarters.

Cyn and Mike followed Phillips back into the main dining hall. As their squad mate continued outside to send his report, they stopped by one of the four corpses. Cyn squatted next to the dead man and stared for nearly a minute at the lifeless body. Then, in one swift and nearly invisible move of her hands, she drew her Ka-Bar knife from its sheath, grabbed the corpse's hair, and removed the man's head.

Big Mike stood in stunned silence. She had decapitated the body in a little more than a second. As she threw the head to the tile floor and walked away, he recalculated his chances in a one-on-one fight with his battle buddy.

Nope, he thought. *I ain't messing with her...ever. 50/50 was a pipe dream. He now put his odds at less than one in four.*

CHAPTER 12

MAITLAND, FL

"The Chinese use two brush strokes to write the word 'crisis.' One brush stroke stands for danger; the other for opportunity. In a crisis, be aware of the danger—but recognize the opportunity."

— **John F. Kennedy**

ALMOST FOUR WEEKS HAD GONE by since Beker saved our butts. What I thought was going to be a day or two of laying low to avoid the white supremacist gang turned into weeks of lying low. It seemed that one of the mansions, just on the other side of the wall from us, caught Taurus's eye. Within an hour of leaving our street, dozens more of the Nazi gang members had arrived to join Taurus in the neighboring subdivision. With the wall preventing direct access from our street to theirs, we at least had a buffer.

However, as the battle between the various rival gangs encroached on our neighborhood, vehicles began driving up and down the main road, bringing men and supplies from the area where we first saved Beker. As Taurus consolidated power over the area, the distant sound of gunfire could be heard throughout the day, most of the battles coming from across the lake and occasionally from the north.

We were now relegated to sneaking about at night, walking the two blocks down to the lake to get water and fish in the pre-dawn hours. We didn't want to use up our valuable pemmican, and Harley had rigged up a solar oven using mirrors to cook what we caught. As long as we didn't burn the fish, there was no smell nor smoke that would give our position away. We also used the solar oven to boil and sterilize our water rather than burning the remaining propane supply. Harley and Ashley still held out hope that the thugs will move on so that they could stay with their house. But with the arrival of Taurus and his gang, they had at least prepared bug-out bags in case they needed to accompany us to Doc Kramer's house.

Tonight, I was going with Harley down to the lake. He'd rigged up a bunch of empty bleach and laundry detergent bottles as floats. We had tied off fishing lines to the handles with a rock wrapped to the line's end to create a small anchor. Harley had sprayed the floats with a black-matte paint, and our plan was to place them off shore as a primitive trotline. Hopefully, with multiple hooks attached to the ten-foot anchored wire, we could harvest more food and minimize the danger of exposing ourselves to unwanted eyes.

After dinner, I did my typical nightly field strip and reassembly of my trusty rifle and hit the sack. It was well into spring now, with the smell of orange blossom in the air fading and the nighttime temperatures starting to warm. By June, sleeping indoors would become impossible, so we had to be out of here by then.

The last thing I remembered as I drift off to sleep was the sound of Jarrett—my semi-affectionate nickname for Janice and Garrett, in the style of Brangelina—doing more than snoring. I frowned, wishing I had someone to make noise with too. The next morning, Janice woke me for the trip to the lake. She was on overwatch, obviously not too tired from her and Garrett's escapades just a few hours before. They tried to be quiet about it, but sound travels in a machine-free world.

I stretched and silently put on my boots and battle belt, the nylon strap snapping in place with its brass cobra buckle. I adjusted it slightly, trying to evenly spread the weight of my Glock and multiple spare magazines on my hips. It didn't take long since I've been wearing a gun on my waist since "the darkness" began. Grabbing my AR-15, I slung it over my shoulder and then slid out the door.

The walk to the Rikers' place was uneventful, and Harley and I were soon working our way along the shoreline, well away from our white gang neighbors. We had to go slowly even though we were sheltered in a cove. Homes on the lake could have become occupied since we last fished here, so stealth was needed.

I took the lead, my red-dot sight beginning to dim as its battery started to die. I had found a couple of spares, but they were hard to come by. It used one of those disc batteries like you find in a camera or car fob and not a standard AA or AAA battery. I kept those two little energy discs in my utility pouch attached to my battle belt. The red glowing dot was still bright enough to see at night, but the daytime washes most of its visibility away. In the daytime, I used my flip-up iron sights (even though they are made of plastic) to help me aim. Jorge said that the sights were "co-witnessed" with my red-dot. I had no idea what he meant until I turned on the Aimpoint and flipped up the front and back sights. There was my red dot, hovering above the front sight, right in the middle of the rear sight's frame. The red dot and front sight were perfectly aligned. I was "co-witnessed!" Now that made sense.

"Here's a good spot. We need to clear that house," Harley said, pointing with his rifle to the dark mansion ahead.

I slid along the side of the hedge that bordered the mansion's backyard. Most of the homes on the lake had been, at one point, manicured horticultural masterpieces. Now, the earth was reclaiming its own, as the St. Augustine grass had been overtaken by weeds and wild plants. Still, I didn't want to march right through the lawn since I would leave a trail of broken stems that would show our passing. Better to stay to the side, where overhanging branches would hide our movements.

"Shit!" Harley hissed.

I snickered. The only thing that set Harley off was spiders, and the webs of Florida's many eight-legged critters were everywhere in the overgrown trees and bushes.

"Screw this," he said as he strode out a few feet from the overhanging branches. "I'll lead."

Harley began walking up the side of the lawn, bypassing the tangled matt of wild vegetation and dreaded spider webs to our left. With no sound nor light coming from the house, it was a pretty safe bet that we were fine. We cleared the house anyway. Ten minutes later, we were pushing a small aluminum boat out of the weeds and into the lake. We quietly paddled out into the cove, and stopped thirty or so yards into the deeper water.

"This is about eight to ten feet deep. This should work."

We grabbed the floats and began to unwind the fifty-pound test line, tying off a baited leader about every two feet. Fish eyes from previous catches, as well as worms dug from our backyards, were speared onto the hooks. With four or five hooks attached to the main line and ten floats set, we had almost fifty chances of getting some fish.

As we turned and started paddling back toward shore, our boat was jarred, almost like we had run aground, except that we had barely started moving.

"What was that?" I asked.

"A gator!" Harley said with a level of glee that didn't seem to fit our situation.

"You're afraid of spiders but excited that an alligator almost tipped us over?"

"Gators have a lot of meat," Harley said. "And I'm tired of fish."

"And how're you supposed to get that meat? Jump in and spear it with your knife?"

"Same as with the fish, only a bigger hook."

"I can't wait," I replied sarcastically.

"Neither can I," Harley said—except he was serious.

"Your brain's not right," I replied, shaking my head.

Harley just chuckled, which was the creepiest thing he could have done.

The next evening, we re-traced our steps. This time we brought a bigger float and hook set-up. Harley had three, one-gallon plastic jugs tied together with the fifty-pound line, and about four or five yards of twelve-gauge stranded electric wire hanging from the bottom which he had salvaged from a convenience store. He had two hand-sharpened coat hooks attached to the main cable, about three feet apart from each other, down near the end of the industrial line.

"I hate to ask what's in the garbage bag," I said.

"Squirrel," Harley replied. "I'll bait each hook with half of the carcass."

"Then what? You'll reel him in?"

"Not quite. Tomorrow, we'll try to find the triple floats somewhere near shore. They'll mark where he is. If everything works out as planned, we'll grab floats, reel in the wire, pull him up to the boat, and then kill him."

"With what? Your knife?"

"No, this." He pointed to a long-barreled revolver inside the nylon gym bag he was carrying. "It's a .22 caliber magnum. Put the end of the barrel to its head, right between the eyes, and pull the trigger. I'm going to use this bottle as a homemade silencer," he said as he pulled a two-liter Coke bottle from his gym bag and shoved the barrel of the revolver inside its modified opening.

"Will those coat hooks be sharp enough to go through his snout when he bites down?"

"Nah, he'll swallow them whole. I'm going to hook him in his stomach."

I shook my head at his gleeful description while we pulled our boat out of the weeds once again and pushed ourselves into the shallow water just off shore. The moonless night made our work difficult, especially since we couldn't use any light source to locate the black floating plastic. But we did recover seven of the floats and a total of seventeen fish of various sizes. Not bad at all.

"Here, take these while I bait the wire." Harley said.

I gathered the trotlines onto the floor of the aluminum skiff while he pulled out the fresh carcass, cut the squirrel in half, and hooked the body parts with the sharpened hangers. He put the end of the electric wire into the water and began to slowly feed the line down to the bottom of the lake.

"You didn't paint those floats black," I said.

"He's going to swallow the line, and we need to find him afterwards. He'll run after he swallows the squirrels, and black floats will be tough to see."

He turned to me after releasing the trap . "This is a long shot. The gator could take the bait and end up on the other side of the lake, so don't get your hopes up. White floats are our best chance to find him, if we find him at all."

Six hours later, I was awakened by a sharp punch to the shoulder. Harley was hovering over me in the pre-dawn darkness, his smile a faint glow in the dim light. As usual, he was in all black.

"Come on, let's go look for our gator."

"It's isn't even dawn. I thought we were going to check tonight," I complained. "Besides, someone might see us."

"I was thinking about that and changed my mind. By now, the gator's going to have found a quiet spot to lay up for the day. By this evening, he'll be on the move, looking for prey in another part of the lake. It will only be harder to find him the longer we wait."

I was none too happy, having done overwatch from midnight to three.

"You know I just got to sleep," I complained.

"You'll get over it once we make a pot of my gator stew. Now hurry up!"

Sleeping in my clothing had its advantages, and I was ready to move within a minute. Outside, we were joined by an equally sleepy Garrett, who was holding a five-gallon bucket filled with water. Two more buckets were sitting at his feet. Harley handed me a container half-filled with soapy water and a heavy bristled brush.

"Here, I'll need this to scrub the gator clean."

The dead silence of the neighborhood was both a blessing and a curse. No sound meant no thugs, but it also meant any noise we made would carry a long way. With some luck, we made it to the cove without incident and found where we had set up our gator snare.

"Sun will be up soon," I said as the eastern sky began to lighten. Faded pink and orange streaked the vista over the water. Within a few minutes we would be able to see more than just shadows lining the lake's shore, but that meant others would be able to see us, too.

"I don't see the floats," Harley said with some pleasure. "That's good, because it means a gator took our bait."

"Yeah, but that won't put any meat in our bellies unless we find him before it gets too light out."

"Let's keep going," Garrett suggested. "Maybe we can spot it farther down."

We left our buckets by the hidden boat and moved quietly through the next few backyards. We were starting to get uncomfortably close to the end of the cove. Another half a mile would put us near the racket club where we had rescued Beker from the Latin gang.

"There!" Garrett whispered, pointing to a cluster of cattails and tape grass under a dock near the bend of the natural inlet.

"I think I can reach the floats from the dock." Harley said. "Come on."

We crept through knee-high grass and weeds, keeping our distance from each other so as not to create a common path. We slid under the yard's decaying ornamental bushes, and after a couple of minutes of motionless surveillance, we went out on the dock. Harley pulled gently on the line and had enough slack to wrap the electric wire around the dock's pylon.

"This could get noisy, so we need to be quick about it. After I put a couple of slugs in its head, hustle back to the bushes and hide."

Garrett braced himself, feet against the pylon as Harley produced his "silenced" revolver.

"I think I can see him in the weeds there!" I said, pointing down and out about eight feet away.

"Help Garrett pull," Harley said as he leaned over the edge of the wooden platform. "Give a hard, steady tug on three. Ready?"

I positioned myself, feet at the pylon next to Garrett's, and nodded. I bent out and grabbed the line and began to wrap it around my hand.

"Don't wrap it like that," Harley said. "He'll just as likely pull you in as you pull him up. If he's too big, let the line go."

I adjusted my grip, and Harley began his countdown. On three, we heaved with all our might and the water exploded as the hook, buried in the beast's belly, tore at his insides. A massive head erupted from the water as both Garrett and I pulled a second time, bringing the gator closer to us. The creature's tail whipped back and forth, sending the monster twisting in the air.

Harley leaned out from the dock and hovered over the water, frozen and ready to strike. The gator belched out a roar. The twelve-gauge electric line was just strong enough to keep from being bitten through. As we pulled on the line, I could feel the primal strength of an animal whose species had stopped evolving hundreds of millions of years ago. The gator was a perfect fresh-water killing machine and needed no more improvement. We were trying to kill a modern dinosaur with a coat hook and a .22 caliber bullet.

The silenced revolver coughed three times.

The line went slack, and an eerie silence came over the cove as the massive beast's carcass settled into the shallow lake. The maelstrom was over, leaving the three of us lying on the dock in shocked silence.

"Hurry!" Harley hissed as he grabbed his rifle and sprinted for cover in the tall grass.

Both Garrett and I were right behind him, our AR-15s clutched in our hands. The three of us went to ground, waiting for any response to the gator's final fight for life. We held our position for nearly five minutes before we dared to move.

"I'll stay here and keep watch." Harley said. "You two go to the boat and bring back the buckets. I'll make my way back if someone shows before you return."

By the time we returned, the sun had begun to break over the treetops on the eastern shore. We dragged the carcass to the edge of the water, using the dock as a shield from any observers further down the shoreline. The ten-foot-long creature had to weigh almost four hundred pounds, so we could only bring him partially out of the lake.

Harley began by scrubbing the gator's back with the soapy water. Dumping one of the two buckets of clean water over the lathered scales, he then removed the creature's dorsal scutes, peeling off the back of the monster's armor in one piece.

"We won't have time to get all the meat," Harley said. "But we'll get the good stuff."

He cut along the spine and removed the tenderloin from both sides of the gator's back and dumped the two pieces of meat into the third bucket, which was still partially filled with clean water. Continuing up to the head, he cut out the jowls—two giant pieces of white jaw meat that were each as big as a turkey's breast. Then he cut off the creature's legs and put them into a garbage bag he had brought along. Finally, he cut into the tail and quickly removed two straps of meat he called jelly rolls. They peeled out easily, almost without a cut from his knife.

Garrett retrieved the line and floats, ripping the hook from within the body, and then we pushed the carcass back into the water. We watched it sink into the tape grass where it had originally taken refuge, all signs of its death and our involvement now hidden under the lake.

Harley returned to his house with the meat we had ripped from the beast. Exhausted, I barely remember my head hitting the pillow. I didn't awaken for another six hours. That afternoon, after my shower and a change of clothes, Janice greeted me with a smile.

"You guys had a good haul! Ashley said she's dehydrating over forty pounds of meat. You should see what she did. It's amazing."

Janice pointed to a couple of Fords parked in a nearby driveway. Our neighbor's SUVs had been converted into dehydration machines. The sun heated the inside of the vehicles. Oven racks were lined up on the floor of their cargo areas over a bed of aluminum foil. The racks were layered with thin strips of marinated alligator meat. Salted and dried, they would be edible for months. An oven thermometer sat among the strips of meat, it read 135°.

Ashley waved me over from her front door, and as I joined her, I could smell the gator stew cooking. She had boiled the dark meat from the beast's legs and added vegetables and spices to the mixture after it cooked. Waiting to flavor the stew once it was inside her house prevented the aromatic smell of the herbs from spreading to our unwanted neighbors. She handed me a bowl of gator stew that made all the craziness from the night before worth it.

I sat down and greedily shoved the food into my mouth. It was the first cooked meat I had eaten in weeks, and it was heavenly. It almost made me forget what waited on the other side of our eight-foot wall.

CHAPTER 13

VANDERBILT MEDICAL CENTER
NASHVILLE, TN

"Tolerance becomes a crime when applied to evil."

— **Thomas Mann**

F OR WEEKS AFTER RETURNING FROM Smyrna, Claire Kramer had been
throwing herself into her work. There were more and more trauma
cases in the emergency room as gangs and armed citizens clashed over
the dwindling resources of the dying city. Over a dozen gunshot wounds
had already been admitted since midnight, and the day wasn't even half
over. Nine of the thirteen GSWs had come from a single encounter, when
a large gang invaded a subdivision being guarded by a local militia. Four of
the gang members and one of the militia had succumbed to their wounds,
but the other four were expected to survive, albeit two with limbs missing,
amputated to save their lives.

"Hey, Doc," one of the surviving militia patients croaked.

Claire had come to the intensive care ward to check on her handiwork,
having transferred the man here after removing a bullet from his neck and
a stitching up knife wound to his hand that had come perilously close to
removing his four fingers.

"Yes?" she replied absently, jotting down notes on the paper charting
that the hospital reverted to since the computer systems installed by DHS
didn't have any hospital software on it.

"The old man," he said, grimacing in pain. "How is he?"

"Didn't make it," she replied, scanning the chart to make sure the appropriate vital signs were being monitored and recorded.

Claire was becoming irritated at the inconsistency of the recovery room staff. Several of them had abandoned their shifts over the last week, never to return. Most had been working in the intensive care and step-down units, with whom Claire had had little interaction until recently. She'd had to treat four patients who had been returned to the emergency room for infections or re-opening of wounds while in recovery. The state of the chart, along with the disorganization she found at the nurse's station, reinforced her concerns that the hospital was dropping the ball.

Her work spent saving lives was being squandered by the lackadaisical care provided during the recovery phase. Claire, her head buried in the chart, finally became aware that the patient was sobbing.

"Hey," she said, focusing her attention on him. "What's wrong?"

"Did he say anything?" The man wiped his eyes with the corner of his hospital gown. "Did he suffer?"

"No, he never regained consciousness. I'm sorry."

The patient turned his head and stared out the window. Outside, a fine mist swirling under a cloudy, grey morning sky. Spring was here, promising new life, but death still reigned in the city.

"You know," he began, "the Vols should be having their spring football game about now. And the CMAs and Bonnaroo Festival wouldn't be far off."

Claire stopped scribbling notes. The realization of just how far society had fallen blindsided her, an emotional sucker punch. She looked at the man lying in bed, his far-off stare into a past that would never return. The hum of the overhead fluorescent light was the only sound in the sterile room as each of them became adrift in thoughts of what had been.

"He was my dad," the man said, turning his head back to Claire. "He was fighting to keep our family safe."

The patient's eyes begged to tell her more, but Claire turned away. Then she stopped in her tracks and looked into her own heart. She realized that she was fleeing the conversation because it frightened her. She also knew a good man, an ethical man, who was putting his life on the line to help others. She didn't want this conversation. She didn't want to think about her family. She didn't want to recognize that she was helpless. She just didn't want to think about any of it anymore.

A tear began to form in the corner of her eye, and she fought to keep it from dripping down her cheek. Her dad had drilled into her the need to control her emotions. She was taught to fight the fear and bury the despair. Her Jewish legacy was filled with a history of oppression and enslavement, and yet their heritage continued by pushing forward and never giving up. To learn from mistakes both past and present.

Claire batted away the tear and grabbed a chair. Pulling it to the side of her patient's bed, she sat down looked into his eyes. She saw both love and pain, as both emotions begged and deserved to be voiced.

"Tell me about your father."

Minutes flew by, and Claire found herself sharing memories of her own father. The conversation was therapeutic for both doctor and patient. Claire felt her emotional heaviness lifted away.

After a lull, the patient asked, "Why are you working for them?"

"What do you mean?" Claire asked.

"The DHS agents. They killed my dad. They brought that gang to our neighborhood and let them loose on us. Just because we wouldn't move to one of their camps."

"I know," Claire said. "But I am doing so much good here."

"You could do good out there, too."

"It's not that easy. Where would I get supplies? Where would I get clean water to sterilize my instruments and wash my hands before surgery?"

"You boil the water. You find the drugs and tools you need. You run a generator to power lights. You just do what you have to do."

Claire wrestled with her conscience. She stood up and stared out of the window. Most of the snow had melted and tulips were popping up in the trash-cluttered landscape beds that lined the multi-story concrete hospital buildings.

She sighed. "I guess I'm just doing my job."

"Sounds a lot like the excuses I read about when they asked the soldiers who guarded the prisoners at Auschwitz and Treblinka why they did it."

Claire gasped, and her hand flew to her mouth. "No," she said.

"Then why stay?"

"I have nowhere else to go," Claire tearfully admitted. "I have nothing else."

"You would have us," he said with more certainty than Claire would have thought. "You'd have a city full of patriots that won't back down from these goons. We'd take care of you. I promise."

A few hours later, Rachael walked into the break room and found Claire sitting in one of the lounge's chairs, staring at the wall, crumpled tissues clenched in her fist. Rachael quietly sat next to her friend. She said nothing; Claire would talk when she was ready.

Rachael and Claire had been working side by side for almost fourteen hours. Since just after midnight, they had successfully saved over a dozen people. What was becoming an issue was that gang members who had been successfully treated by them in the past were returning with fresh wounds from newly fought battles. DHS had been taking the thugs away once the hospital had repaired the trauma, but obviously the criminals weren't being put in prison. They were back on the street, continuing to create mayhem throughout the city. One of their "return customers" even recognized Rachael as she was treating him for a knife wound. Whether out of bravado or because he had a warped sense of timing, he had the audacity to ask her out on a date while she was suturing his laceration. The man had reacted badly when Rachael laughed in his face, and security had to intervene as the thug tried to assault her.

"I'm tired." Claire sighed. "I don't have anything left in the tank. I don't know how much longer I can do this."

"I know. Me too."

The two women sank further into the leather chairs, each drifting off into her own world, when the door to the lounge exploded open and Rachael's boyfriend rushed into the room.

Billy was in full battle rattle, and his combat uniform was streaked with dirt. His rifle was slung over his shoulder, and his battle belt was still bulging with a full complement of magazines. Whatever had happened, he hadn't fired a shot, but his appearance indicated that he's been through hell.

"What is it?" Rachael gasped, seeing her boyfriend's appearance.

"Come now! I've got some wounded men out back."

"Why are you here?" Rachael asked. "Take them to the emergency room!"

"I can't! You need to come now. I'll explain on the way."

"Stop," Rachael said. "I can't just run outside with you. I don't know what you need. I can't give them proper care without equipment. Just bring them into the hospital. What's wrong with you?"

"Oh jeez, Rach. Just trust me. I can't bring them in. You need to come with me."

"Billy, you're not making sense. Just tell me what's happening."

Billy glanced at Claire, checking her up and down like an animal assessing another creature's intent.

"She's cool!" Rachael said.

"Is she with DHS?" Billy asked.

"No. That's Dr. Kramer, the friend I've told you about."

"Good. Bring her with you too."

"Where are the injured men?" Rachael asked again.

"Out back, at the loading dock."

"Oh Christ, Billy. Bring them around to the DHS checkpoint and they'll escort you into the E.R."

"That's the problem. I can't take them through the checkpoint."

"Why the hell not?" Rachael asked.

"Because DHS just tried to kill us, that's why," Billy said. "The bastards tried to kill us all."

— 12 HOURS EARLIER —

SMYRNA NATIONAL GUARD BASE

Colonel Cooper sighed as he looked at his son. He couldn't believe things had come to this. "Are you sure?"

"Yes sir," Lt. Jeb Cooper replied. "We are to be disbanded and absorbed into the Army. No more National Guard. No more Tennessee Volunteers. They're making plans right now to take over the airport and turn it into another relocation camp."

Colonel Cooper's mind refused to believe what he was hearing. DHS was not in charge of his unit; the State of Tennessee was. The state had ultimate control of his men, and until he heard from the governor, he wasn't going to listen to some two-bit Washington bureaucrat who hadn't seen combat in his life.

Since his meeting with Dr. Claire Kramer and her subsequent departure almost a month ago, Colonel Cooper had been sending his men out to get more intel on the government's activities. What he found nearly sent him into a rage-filled trip to Nashville to confront Deputy McCain. DHS was indeed using citizens as forced labor at multiple farms throughout the state. Families were being separated, and people that put up resistance often disappeared.

Cooler heads had prevailed, and the colonel instead began to plan their exodus to Fort Campbell to join up with the 101st Airborne division, who they trained with on a regular basis.

"Sir, we're as ready as we can be." K.T. Dixon reported.

"Any indication that the feds know what we're up to?" Colonel Cooper asked.

"No sir," Dixon replied. "All's quiet."

"Good, then let's do this."

"But sir," the colonel's son said, "we aren't supposed to leave for another week."

"Is there any reason not to leave now?"

"I suppose not." The lieutenant replied. "It's just going to rush a lot of the families that were expecting a few more days."

"The longer we stay here, the more likely it is that DHS will get wind of our plans. We're a high speed unit, so let's act like one. I want all my soldiers and their families ready to bug out by 1600."

Dixon checked his watch. He had a little over nine hours to prepare and produce the vehicles needed to move a couple of thousand people across the state. The journey would take them around Nashville and up Route 41, then bypass the city and connect to Interstate 24. From there, it was a straight shot to Fort Campbell.

All three men rose and left the CO's office. But a fourth man followed closely behind the others. He ducked into an abandoned office where he made a final satellite phone call to Nashville, informing Director McCain of the impending move. As instructed at the end of his conversation, E-2 Guardsman Wright removed the phone's battery and grabbed the nylon gym bag that DHS had given him.

Wright left the building and walked to a nearby shed where he kept his 2006 Honda VTX 1300. He kick-started the carbureted motor and left the base as directed by his contact at Homeland. After giving up his unit, the young traitor was returning to his masters. He shed no tear and gave no further thought to the men and their families that he left behind.

After the phone call from his contact, McCain reached out to Washington, letting his boss know about the battalion's planned march to Fort Campbell. He reported the expected time of departure and route of travel that the unit was to take and disconnected the call.

McCain wanted to be back in Washington, and passing along that information would go a long way towards a promotion. In his mind, he was already planning on where he would move his family. There was an old Tuscan villa just west of Georgetown that backed up to Glover Park that had caught his eye. It was on a cul-de-sac and offered the privacy he so loved. If possible, he'd find a way to bring Wright with him. There were many divisions within his command where a properly placed mole could be of use.

McCain smiled to himself as the wheels of the government began to turn against Colonel Cooper and his men.

CHAPTER 14

*"Nothing in the world is more dangerous than sincere
ignorance and conscientious stupidity."*

— **Martin Luther King Jr.**

A BOUT TWO HOURS AFTER COLONEL Cooper decided to send the men of the 278th to their new home at Fort Campbell, Captain Clark "C-Mat" Mathers was sitting in the pilot seat of his B-52H bomber, waiting for the ground cart to spin up his two inboard engines. The massive aircraft, sporting eight Pratt & Whitney TF33 engines, required engines number 4 and 5 be started by an outside source. Once these two innermost engines were running, they could be used to start the other six.

His co-pilot was sitting next to Mathers, acting as a flight engineer as much as anything else. The pilot could fly the beast without help, but the flight crew consisted of five men. The other members of the Minot AFB crew, a gunner and the electronic warfare officer, sat facing backwards behind the pilot, while down a short ladder the navigator accepted instructions and flight patterns from the Air Force's Global Strike Command. Although now, with the military under the control of DHS, they would be getting their orders from Washington, D.C.

The B-52 "Stratofortress" was a big, ungainly machine. Its wings were long and thin compared to the thick aluminum and titanium tube they were attached to, sweeping back and slightly tilted upward to handle the massive weight of the jet. With 480,000 pounds of weight the beast was affectionately referred to as BUFF (for "big ugly fat fucker",) often took the entire length of the vast Air Force runways to make it into the air.

Sweat was puddling on Mathers' face. Most of the aircraft's cooling capacity was needed to refrigerate the electronics that were crammed into every spare inch of the cockpit. The crew would have to endure this inconvenience until they reached their cruising altitude, where the outside temperature would drop below zero. Lining up the nose down the North Dakota runway, Mathers began final preparations for take-off.

"Set dry thrust," he said.

His co-pilot adjusts the throttles, and the giant bomber begins to roll.

"Cleared for water," the co-pilot replied.

C-Mat checked the jet's water pumps. "Four good pumps," he said as water misted into the front of the jet engines.

It seemed counter intuitive to spray water into a combustion engine, but the water vapor made the incoming air denser and allowed for more fuel into the mixture and thus more thrust. It also caused the engines to eject thick, black smoke, a hallmark of the B-52.

"Seventy knots...now!" C-mat called out to his navigator.

The navigator checked the passing seconds, using his knowledge of the length of the runway and speed of the jet.

"S1 expires...now," the navigator barked.

The S1 was the point of commitment. Either the BUFF has the speed to make it off the runway, or it doesn't.

C-Mat checked his airspeed once more and whispered into his neck mic, uttering just a single word. "Committed."

As the Stratofortress passed seventy knots, the lift being generated started to raise the wings while the rest of the nearly half a million-ton airframe stayed glued to the ground. The wings were trying to fly, but the rest of the ship refused to lift. C-Mat fought with the yoke of the craft, keeping the rear wheels from prematurely lifting first. If they started to rise, it would send the aircraft toppling end over end, creating a very expensive fireball on end of the 13,000-foot runway.

C-Mat pulled the eight engine throttles back to the fire-wall and finally felt the bomber surrender, slowly lifting into the North Dakota air. Typical of the BUFF, it flew when it wanted to and not a second before.

"Our buddies with us?" C-Mat asked his co-pilot after achieving their cruising altitude.

"Affirmative. On our right," said the co-pilot as he looked out his window to confirm that the other B-52 was on their wing.

"Settle in," C-Mat said. "This may be a long flight."

Just ninety minutes before, two crews had been scrambled for a mission to strike back at the enemy. No destination was given in the briefing; that information would be relayed while in flight by the computers in Washington. With a generally eastward path in front of them, C-Mat assumed this was a trans-Atlantic flight to drop his payload on whatever piece of shit country had set off the EMP.

The Minot AFB 5th bomb wing had been devastated by the EMP, with twelve of its fifteen bombers disabled by the electronic blast. The other three survived only because they were not in the continental United States at the time. C-Mat was flying one of these BUFFs that had been on a training mission to Elmendorf Air Base in Alaska.

Previously, the B-52s had been used for conventional strikes, dropping non-nuclear bombs and firing conventional cruise missiles in far-off places like the Middle East and Afghanistan. But with the loss of the B-1 and B-2 bombers to the EMP weapon, along with many of the nuclear missile sites, the remaining three BUFFs were once again being used to carry nukes. At any time of the day or night, one of them was flying with a payload of nuclear cruise missiles. Mutually assured destruction, a doctrine invented in the last century, would deter any Russian or Chinese attacks while the country recovered. Knowing that America's submarines and remaining bombers were out there, ready to strike back with a fatal nuclear blow, kept the enemy at bay.

Today's payload was conventional. Their partner's Stratofortress, which has survived the EMP attack while flying over Canada, had been upgraded and was now carrying sixteen CBU-105 cluster bombs on its wings. Each thousand-pound bomb contained forty individual bomblets, giving the beast six hundred forty chances to destroy the enemy. Meanwhile, C-Mat's own bomber was loaded down with fifty-one 500-pound and thirty 1000-pound gravity bombs.

"Sir, coordinates received," The navigator said.

"Where're we taking our little friends?" C-Mat asked.

There was a pause before the navigator answered. "We're going to Tennessee."

"What? Are you sure?"

"Affirmative," the navigator replied. "We'll receive final instructions when we are on station."

"What the hell. Have we been invaded?" the copilot asked.

"Must be," C-Mat replied. "The bastards are on our soil."

The five men sat silently, each slowly burning with growing anger.

"We're going to kill those SOBs," C-Mat said, his jaw set and fire in his eyes. "Let's burn 'em down."

"Damn right!" and "Hell yeah!" the others grunted.

No one was going to screw with the good old U.S. of A, C-Mat thought. *Absolutely no one!*

CHAPTER 15

278TH ARMORED CAVALRY REGIMENT
SMYRNA, TENNESSEE
1200 HOURS

ABOUT THE TIME THAT CAPTAIN Mathers and his B-52 crew learned of their destination, the men of the 278th had mustered along the camp's main road. Over a thousand soldiers waited by their assigned vehicles. Over a hundred HUMVEEs, along with dozens of M977A4 cargo haulers and even more decommissioned but functional M35 deuce-and-a-half trucks, were lining the road for as far as Dixon could see. The vehicles were stacked nuts to butts, with little room to pass between them.

"The soldiers are ready," SSgt. Dixon said to Lieutenant Cooper.

"As always, it's the families that are holding things up."

"We could send most of the soldiers up to Campbell now. It would let them get their quarters assigned by the time the families arrived."

"That's not a bad idea," Cooper replied. "If they leave now, that'll give Campbell four hours to square them away. It's make it a lot easier on the spouses and kids not having to wait around."

Sarcasm dripped from Dixon's words. "You mean no standby to standby? They'd never know they were in the Army."

"I know," Cooper said. "They'd be lost, wouldn't they!"

The two were standing outside of the colonel's headquarters, raised above the ground level by a flight of stairs and a concrete landing. The main doors were propped open behind them, while Guardsman lugged papers and boxes of non-essential "essentials" out and into an awaiting HUMVEE.

"A lot of crap," Dixon observed.

"Yet here we are, hauling it to another camp." Cooper replied, shaking his head in frustration.

"I'll talk with the colonel," Cooper said, watching the never-ending line of junk being hauled out of the building. "There's no reason for our soldiers to wait around."

"I'll reassign the equipment and vehicles," Dixon replied. "I'll make sure to hold back enough HUMVEEs to guard the second convoy. I've got a bunch of school buses that I'm using to move the civilians, and getting these vehicles out of the way will help me process the families."

"Go ahead," Cooper said. "I'll let my dad know."

"Yes sir," Dixon replied, and after exchanging salutes with the lieutenant, he spun around and strode to his vehicle.

"Gringold! Forester! On me," Dixon barked. "We've got a lot to do and no time to do it."

"What a surprise," Forester replied.

***

At sixteen hundred hours, the line of school buses with up-armored HUMVEEs interspersed between them were positioned on the camp's main road, right where the military convoy had been just four hours earlier.

"Good idea on splitting us up," Colonel Cooper said to Dixon.

"We'd never have had the room to pull it off if we hadn't."

The two men watched as the spouses and children of the Guardsmen loaded their belongings into the eight-wheeled Oshkosh cargo haulers and then took their places in the many school buses that the Guard had borrowed.

"Papa!" a little voice squealed.

"Marky!" the colonel replied as the young boy lumbered up the steps and into his grandfather's arms.

The colonel's daughter-in-law was lugging a large suitcase in one hand as she dragged another wheeled one behind her. Dixon shot off the landing and took both pieces of luggage from the pregnant woman.

"Thanks, K.T."

"You're lucky Jeb didn't see you doing that," the colonel admonished.

"Well, what he doesn't know..."

"Papa, are you coming too?" the little boy asked.

"Of course, I'll be in the car right in front of you," the colonel said, pointing to a HUMVEE laden with multiple whip antennas. "Now, off to your school bus."

"Give Sullivan a hug first," the boy said, holding the bluish green doll up to his grandfather.

"Marky! Not now. Papa has a lot to do."

"Okay," Marky replied good-naturedly as he hobbled down the stairs and limped onto the school bus, his leg brace making the steps a challenge.

"See you there!" Nan waved and then followed her son up the bus's steps.

"Where will you be?" the colonel asked Dixon.

"I'll be at the end in the recovery vehicle. Anyone breaks down, I'll be there to sweep up the mess."

"Makes sense. Keep in touch while we're moving."

"Of course, sir," Dixon replied.

"Everyone's ready," Jeb Cooper said as left the building and bounded down the stairs. "This went remarkably well."

"Don't jinx it," his father replied as he scanned the row of buses and military vehicles that were now idling in the street. "Let's move out. The fumes are going to kill me if we don't get going."

Soldiers attached to the multiple HUMVEEs guarding the convoy stood on the sidewalk next to the idling buses and trucks. Each waved, indicating that their assigned vehicles were loaded, running, and ready to move.

"Let's go! We're burning daylight," the colonel said over his headset, sending the massive convoy out the gate. With a little more good luck, Cooper hoped to be passing through Fort Campbell's perimeter by eighteen hundred hours.

"Looks like we did it," Dixon said to Sims as the two of them jumped into the cab of their giant tow truck. Both a mobile repair shop and towing vehicle, they would service and repair anyone that broke down on the trip.

"Copy that," Sims replied as he turned on the diesel's warming elements. When the glow point lights on the dash turned red, he engaged the ignition switch and the engine rumbled to life.

Normally, they would have traveled in a military open convoy pattern, with three hundred feet between vehicles. But the trucks, buses, and HUMVEEs were already bunching up. Many had less than a vehicle's length between them.

Colonel Cooper was about to admonish the drivers but realized that many of the school buses were being driven by civilians with CDL permits. They simply didn't know any better, and expecting military discipline from them was unfair.

What the heck, it's only for a couple of hours, he thought to himself as the suburban Nashville countryside began to roll by. The colonel let himself take a break and sat heavily back in his seat. Each bump reminded him of his age.

It will all be over soon enough, he thought with a grateful sigh.

CHAPTER 16

SCOTT AIR FORCE BASE
SOUTHERN ILLINOIS
502D AIR WING

WHILE COLONEL COOPER WAS PULLING out of the Smyrna National Guard front gates, a pair of Air Force officers sat at their respective terminals in one of six mobile ground control stations at Scott Air Force base in southern Illinois. The GCS looked like a metal refrigeration unit you might find attached to the back of a restaurant, only these containers were covered in duct work and electronic cabling. Umbilical cords connected each unit to a fiber optic cable where instant communications with their Washington controllers was performed at the speed of light. Almost two hundred gigabits of data per second were now bouncing between the GCS and the Pentagon's war room.

Flying the Predator, a remote piloted aircraft, requires the work of two airmen. One to pilot the craft, using controls not unlike game console paddles and sticks, while the other operates the craft's various cameras and sensors, helping the pilot designate their target.

"Vector south, cross winds at eleven knots," the sensor operator barked. "Holding pattern in two mikes."

"Two mikes, roger that," the pilot confirmed.

The sensor operator monitored multiple consoles, swinging the on-board cameras left and right, then switching to infrared and back to visible light. Tapping a keyboard mounted vertically on the wall next to his right shoulder, the drone received data and instructions for the final leg of their mission.

"All systems nominal," he reported to his superiors over his headset.

"Proceed to target," came the cryptic command.

Although the pilot and sensor operator has mirror image screens, the pilot was concentrating on flying the unmanned craft while the sensor operator fiddled and adjusted the flight controllers like a kid with ADHD playing with a Gameboy. While one was steady and deliberate, the other was a blur of motion.

"Approaching designated coordinates," the sensor operator announced.

"Put the bird in a holding configuration. Five-mile racetrack pattern."

"Roger that," the sensor operator said.

"Roger," the Air Force pilot replied as he tapped on his console, putting the Predator into a five-mile-wide circular flight pattern over the northwest Tennessee countryside.

A set of computer commands appeared on their monitors. They were temporarily relieved of their duties and would be replaced by DHS agents.

Both of the officers took off their headsets, exited the large metal box, and walked away.

"Damn spooks," the sensor operator mumbled. "Just once I'd like to know what they're doing."

"It's getting old. I'm tired of this Bravo Sierra."

"Let's quit and go to fly drones for Amazon, delivering dog food and cookies," the sensor operator said sarcastically.

"Point taken."

Once they had exited the large hanger where the multiple control stations were situated, two more officers, this time from DHS, entered and took their places in front of the screens.

"Matterhorn on station," one of the men said into his headphone.

"Good to hear from you," the Pentagon replied. "We're about an hour from contact."

"Roger that. Standing by."

Over the next hour, the two agents flew the Predator across the Nashville metropolitan area. Finally, the sensor operator spoke into his headset and microphone unit.

"Target identified. Travelling on Highway 24. Coordinates are as follows."

The DHS agent typed the information into his keyboard and sent it to

Washington. With the speed and location of the convoy confirmed, their job was done.

"Good job, Matterhorn. Return the bird to its nest."

"Returning to base, confirmed. Matterhorn, out."

The pilot hit a switch, sending the UAV a command to return to "home."

The unmanned craft slowly turned toward Scott Field, automatically following its designated flight path back to its southern Illinois base.

CHAPTER 17

HIGHWAY 24
21 MILES NORTHWEST OF NASHVILLE

DIXON PULLED OFF ONTO THE berm of the two-lane highway. One of the HUMVEEs had broken down and been moved to the side of the road. Dixon, pulling rear guard duty, stopped to repair the vehicle.

"Karma! What a bitch," Dixon said laughingly as he came up to a frustrated Lieutenant Cooper. The driver for the lieutenant had already opened the front hood, staring at the engine like he was studying an alien lifeform for the first time.

"Figures," Cooper said. "The day was going way too well."

"So what happened?" Dixon asked the driver.

"It just died."

"Let me take a look."

Cooper stared down the highway and watched the last of the vehicles disappeared over the crest of a hill. Almost a hundred buses, trucks, and HUMVEEs had made it to within thirty miles of their destination, and his vehicle had to be the one to break down.

Noticing the lieutenant's gaze, Dixon put his head back under the hood and commented. "Don't worry, L.T. The colonel will take care of your family."

Cooper grunted and craned his neck to stare over the sergeant's shoulders. "So, what's wrong?"

"Don't know yet, Lieutenant. It could be electric short, or possibly a clogged fuel line. When one of these beasts just quits, you look at what feeds it," Dixon said as he lifted some tubes and cords. Searching through the HUMVEE's wiring, he gave a grunt. "Looks like a loose cable. Let me tighten it a bit."

"Will that fix it?" the impatient lieutenant asked.

"I'll know in just a...hey! What's that sound?"

A low rumble, almost imperceptible at first but rapidly building in volume, was coming from behind them. All four men turned and stared.

Sims pointed into the sky and gasped. "Is that a BUFF?"

"That's an affirmative," Cooper replied as all four men stood and stared at the giant flying fortress.

Hugging the rolling terrain, the bomber jumped up and down, its frame buffeted by thermal drafts. Sims was fascinated by the wings as they flexed up and down with the shifts in the atmosphere while the aircraft's tubular body held a steadier course. It almost looked like the wings were flapping, just like a flying bird.

A growing sense of unease hit Dixon, and he turned to look at Cooper. Seeing a similar look of dread, they wordlessly scrambled into wrecker's cabin.

As Dixon started the repair vehicle, Sims and Cooper's driver stood frozen. They were snapped out of their trance when multiple explosions sounded up the road. The ground began to shake—the mammoth bomber was actually moving the earth under their feet. The sound of the engines pushing the B-52 through the air was deafening as it passed overhead, forcing the two men to cover their ears. Crossing in front of the late afternoon sun, an elongated shadow fell over the men, casting them into a temporary twilight.

The experience of being under the wings of a low-level B-52 flight would stay with the men for the rest of their lives. But what happened next would scar them forever.

B-52H

NORTHWEST TENNESSEE

As the Predator returned home, C-Mat received a final computer message. The onboard system updated the BUFF's flight path, sending the bomber toward the outskirts of Nashville.

"Twenty minutes to target," the weapon's control officer said.

The bomber began to descend, its speed automatically decreasing and its altitude dropping as the computer determined their proper flight path.

"Looks like we'll be making a low-level run," the navigator said.

"Love those," C-Mat said. "Make sure you're strapped in."

"One minute to target," the weapon's officer said.

"Thirty seconds to release." He stated as they approached their target.

The on-board computer sent a message back to base asking for any changes in their orders. An instant later, the mission was confirmed.

Meanwhile, their companion bomber was ahead of them and at a higher altitude. C-Mat watched as that Stratofortress released its sixteen cluster bombs from four hard points on their bomber's wings. The CBU-105 Sensor Fuzed Weapons dropped free, and parachutes deployed from each one, bringing the bombs into a nose-down position. As they approached the ground, C-Mat lost sight of them. Even without seeing the explosives' final moments, he knew that right now the enemy convoy was being riddled with death and destruction.

It was time for the coup de grace.

Less than a minute behind the first Stratofortress, C-Mat's bomber was now flying at five hundred feet, well below normal altitude. The ship was on autopilot and bouncing up and down like some demented carnival ride. Riding thermal waves of air, sometimes jumping almost ten feet at a time, caused the crew's safety harnesses to dig into their groins and legs.

About a mile from their target, the convoy of vehicles disappeared under the front nose of the jet. C-Mat struggled to see what and who he was killing, but the turbulence from the low-level run wouldn't allow him to sit high enough to see down to the ground.

"Command confirmed." C-Mat said to his weapon's officer. "On my mark."

Staring at the computer, the Captain Mathers finally saw the green words flash on his screen, confirming the crew's final orders.

"Release! Release! Release!" he barked.

All of their ordinance spilled out of the machine's belly. Travelling at almost four hundred knots, the bombs were spread down a line of destruction over a mile in length. The enemy convoy was going to feel the wrath of the United States Air Force as over fifty thousand pounds of explosives landed on their heads, effectively pulverizing the enemy vehicles that the first bomber had disabled as well as vaporizing the enemy soldiers that had dared to set foot on this great nation's soil.

As the Stratofortress lifted with the abrupt loss of all of their bombs' weight, C-Mat smiled and took control of the BUFF once again, steering their enormous aircraft back home.

He crowed into his headset, "Great job, boys. I'm buying the first round tonight!"

278ᵀᴴ Armored Regiment—Family Convoy
Highway 24
22 Miles Northwest Of Nashville

Nan Cooper sat in the back of the bus while her son settled into the window seat to her left. Marky had been amazingly quiet during the ride, and she was grateful for that. Several other families had lost control of their own children. She couldn't really blame the kids—their world had been torn from them months ago, and now they were being hauled off to yet another new home.

Their bus suddenly slowed down, and then it picked up speed once again. A few moments later, Nan saw her husband's HUMVEE, which had pulled off to the side of the road, and felt a pang of concern. He saw her and waved, a grumpy expression on his face. It must not be anything too bad—just a delay.

"That's Daddy!"

"Yes, it is daddy," she said with a smile. "And daddy's not going to be too happy when we get to our new home before him."

Marky, clutching his blue doll, smiled back at his mother. All was quiet. The only sound they heard was the low growl of the school bus's diesel engine. Then the little boy pointed up in the sky and gasped.

"Look, Mommy! Balloons!"

Nan Cooper leaned over her son and stared up into the afternoon sky.

"Those aren't balloons," she said. "They look like parachutes!"

She made out a tubular shape dangling underneath the half-deployed nylon chutes. Suddenly, the tubes dropped free, and a small explosion erupted inside of them. The tube fragmented into multiple smaller shapes, and each one of the ejected alien objects began to spin as tiny jets ignited, scattering them into the clear blue sky. Then, without warning, the hockey puck-like discs stopped their climb, and thrusters pushed the canisters straight down into the mass of vehicles below.

Nan realized what the objects must be, but her brain couldn't accept the information her eyes were relaying. "Oh no!" was all that the pregnant mother could say, as the first explosions detonated.

The line of vehicles was decimated as molten copper thrust through every engine—as well as many of the convoy's passenger compartments. Those skeets that couldn't find a target exploded in a final failsafe, sending shrapnel into their surroundings. It was like a fourth of July fireworks finale', only this one destroyed nearly everything it touched.

Nan quickly regained her senses, only to find the front of her bus ripped open, its engine torn and burning. She searched for her son, grateful to find him alive under the seat in front of her. Marky was beginning to cry. The sound of people calling for help began to filter through the ringing in her ears. Through the front of the now-destroyed bus, she watched her father-in-law crawl out of the back of his decimated HUMVEE. She waved to him as he frantically scanned her vehicle, a momentary look of relief coming to his face. But then the rumbling began, and Nan's heart dropped.

She struggled out of her seat, ignoring the pleas of a family behind her, and looked through the rear door's window, back down the road. The frame of the destroyed bus began to shake and the pained screams of the people around her quickly became shouts of fear as a massive jet rumbled towards them.

"Don't look, baby," she said, holding her son tight. "Mommy loves you."

As Nan clenched her boy against her swollen belly, the shadow of jet passed overhead, blocking out the sun. She turned her head and locked eyes with Colonel Cooper, who was on his knees, an expression of horror and sorrow on his face.

She gave him one final sorrowful look and received a regretful stare back from the defeated man. Then, in a flash of light, over a thousand souls disappeared from the earth as over a mile of road became a pulverized piece of hell. Within just a few seconds, the families of the Tennessee Cavalry's 278th Armored Regiment were gone.

142

***

Sims was sprawled on the pavement, the wrecker he had been clinging to smashed against a tree in the median between the north and southbound lanes. He staggered to the vehicle, looking for the lieutenant and SSgt. Dixon, when he noticed the lieutenant's driver crushed under one of the wheels. A quick check for a pulse confirmed the man's death.

Hearing movement in the cab, he rushed to the driver's side door and flung it open. The windshield of the wrecker had been blown into the cab. Its bulletproof glass prevented it from shattering, but the entire window slammed into both Dixon and Cooper, stunning them into semi-consciousness.

Sims pushed the shattered windshield up and out of the front of the truck and helped Dixon stagger to the ground. He jumped back up to retrieve Lt. Cooper, but the man pushed him away, staring up the road. Sims followed his gaze and saw the plumes of smoke rising over the crest of a hill about a half a mile ahead.

With a savage cry, the lieutenant kicked his door open and jumped down. As soon as his boots hit the dirt, he began to sprint up the road towards the devastation.

Sims began to triage SSgt. Dixon. He checked for breathing, bleeding and shock. Finding Dixon free of these immediate life-threatening symptoms, he helped the man get to his feet.

"You alright, Sarge?"

"Shit," Dixon replied, wiping his face and shaking his head. "What the hell happened?"

"We were bombed."

They heard Cooper yelling as he ran, drawing the two men's attention up the road where the lieutenant disappeared over the crest of the ridge.

"Let's move." Dixon stumbled, and Sims grabbed him around the waist, bringing him down on the ground.

"Not yet, sir. You need to rest."

"Just give me a minute." Dixon put his head between his legs, then rolled over and vomited. "My head. It feels like it's gonna explode."

Dixon sat back and took a deep breath. Looking over, he saw the driver's legs under the wrecker.

"Did you check him?"

"Yes sir. He's gone."

Sims left Dixon on the berm and checked the wrecker. The engine was still running, but it refused to shift into gear. The transmission was shot. After about five minutes, Dixon was able to get up and they began walking up the slope toward the smoke. With each stride, Dixon took control of his body, and by the time they made it to the top of the rise, he was walking strongly on his own. That is, until they made it over the crest of the hill and saw the devastation below.

Neither man had family in the convoy, but that didn't lessen the horror. The scene could only be described as apocalyptic. Massive craters, some over thirty feet deep and a hundred feet across, marred the highway. In fact, there was no more highway. Any sign of asphalt, signs or guardrails were gone. The convoy, for all intents and purposes, was nowhere to be seen. The field of devastation looked like the moon, other than the massive trees upended with their root balls sticking up in the air. A couple of HUMVEEs were still standing, their windows blown in and the metal frames compressed like someone had taken a vice and squeezed the jaws together.

Sims saw movement ahead, bringing fleeting hope that someone had survived, but it turned out to be Lieutenant Cooper. Scurrying out of one of the massive holes, he ran and called out his wife's name over and over again.

"Come on," Dixon sighed. "Let's help the lieutenant find his family."

The look on the sergeant's face told Sims that he didn't expect to find anyone alive, but they crawled down into the first crater anyway. Their brother needed them, and that was all the reason they needed to enter hell.

Ten minutes of crawling up and down the cratered road brought them within sight of the lieutenant, who was standing in the middle of the devastated highway. As they approached him, Dixon pointed to the side of the road where a HUMVEE had been flung against the trees. Two soldiers were lying on the grass outside the vehicle, while a dead man hung from the driver's side window.

"Over here!" Dixon shouted to Sims.

They rushed over to the injured men and examined them.

"This one has a pulse!" Sims said.

"Mine does too." Dixon replied, checking the other man.

Sims looked at the name patch on the fallen soldier's uniform as he assessed the damage.

"Kerns," he said to the man. "Hey, Kerns, can you hear me?"

The soldier groaned and gazed up at Sims without focusing. His breathing was rapid and shallow, likely from shock.

A scream came from the man Dixon was examining, followed by a string of curses.

"Got a broken leg here," Dixon shouted.

"No shit, Sherlock!" the injured soldier shouted back.

Dixon called out for Cooper. "LT, we have two injured here!"

Cooper ignored him, and after trying to get his attention three more times, Dixon ordered Sims to stay with the two injured soldiers as he jogged up the road.

"Lieutenant! We need your help to get the wounded to safety."

"Where are they?" Cooper's eyes darted back and forth across the devastated landscape. "This is the middle of the convoy. That's the safest spot to be. They should be here."

Dixon let the man rant. The lieutenant was losing it. His family was gone, and the man's mind couldn't allow himself to grasp that fact.

"Lieutenant, I have two injured men that need treatment."

"What?" Cooper said.

"I said, Sims and I have two injured soldiers."

"Then get them treated." Cooper said, as if he was telling Dixon to go to the corner store to get more milk.

"Sir, you need to come with me."

"I'm not leaving until I find them. Marky must be so scared. He hates loud noises."

"Sir, I don't think that's a good idea. You really need to come with me." Dixon gently grabbed Cooper's sleeve.

The lieutenant drew his handgun and pulled his arm away from the sergeant. Waving the Berretta in front of him, Cooper began to rave.

"Damn it, you're not listening. I have to find them. Marky needs a bath before he goes to bed. And if Marky doesn't get to bed on time, he's a basketcase. It's our first night at the new apartment, and I want everything to be perfect for Nan."

Cooper's eyes, wild with fear and anger, stared into Dixon's.

"You understand, don't you? I'm not leaving here until I find my family."

Dixon backed up a step and nodded. "Yes sir. I understand. Why don't you put the gun down, and we'll go look together?"

"I'm fine," Cooper snapped. "Go help Sims."

Cooper watched Dixon jog back to the side of the road where the injured soldiers lay on the grass. Then the lieutenant began to search the other side of the highway. The grassy median was littered with shredded clothing and metal fragments.

He tried to ignore the detritus, but one shiny object kept catching his eye. In the back of Cooper's mind, he knew what it was. But hope kept him from examining it and without hope, he had nothing at all.

Finally, after frantically searching every other spot, he turned to the shiny metallic frame that lay bent in the bushes. As he slowly moved closer, he recognized the hinges and straps that used to hold his son's leg together. It was Marky's brace, but there was no Marky.

The weight of it dropped the man to his knees. He had nothing left, no tears to shed and no hope to cling to. He bowed his head and said a prayer. Then, after hugging the cold metal brace to his chest, he pulled out his handgun and put the barrel into his mouth.

As he pressed his eyelids together, Nan's image floated in front of him.

Cooper smiled and pulled the trigger.

***

Dixon left the lieutenant and jogged back to Sims and the fallen men.

"Sergeant, my guy's in shock. He needs help right now," Sims said.

Dixon went to the damaged HUMVEE and pulled the corpse from the vehicle. Gently placing the dead man to the side, he jumped in and grinned savagely when the diesel engine fired up.

Dixon and Sims picked up the man with the broken leg and positioned him in the front passenger's seat. Kearns was placed on a tarp and they dragged him to the vehicle, loading him into passenger's rear side.

"Hop in back and keep this guy alive," Dixon said.

"What about the LT?" Sims asked, climbing behind the driver's side seat.

Dixon hesitated for just a moment. "He's staying."

Just then, they heard the muted crack of a gun.

"What was that?" Sims asked.

"The lieutenant," Dixon sighed. "He wanted to be with his family."

CHAPTER 18

VANDERBILT MEDICAL CENTER
NASHVILLE, TN

"The price of apathy towards public affairs is to be ruled by evil men"

—Plato

JOGGING DOWN THE SERVICE HALLWAYS of the Vanderbilt Medical center, Rachael and Claire had heard only the briefest explanation on how Billy Sims had come to the hospital. All they knew was that the convoy had been bombed by their own air force, and that the only four survivors of the attack were Sims and the three men at the loading dock.

"This way," Rachael said, pointing down a corridor that her boyfriend had accidentally bypassed.

"Sorry," Sims replied. "First time coming this way."

The hallway opened onto a giant, elevated platform. The HUMVEE had been pulled through one of the three roll-up garage doors and was the lone vehicle in the bay. A soldier stood next to it, his right hand resting on a holstered sidearm, while two hospital employees sat nearby on the metal stairs that fed the top platform down to ground level.

Rachael and Claire rushed down the metal steps and assessed the injured soldiers.

"This man is in shock," Claire pronounced. "He's needs an abdominal and chest x-ray, stat. Probable internal injuries."

She looked at Dixon and shook her head. "He's got to go through the ER right now or he'll be dead in hours."

"Compound fracture here," Rachael said, pointing at a piece of white bone that had pierced the man's skin. "He's got to go through the ER as well. Surgery and antibiotics, or he's going to lose the leg."

"What do we do?" Dixon asked. "We could be arrested if we bring them in through the DHS checkpoint."

Claire thought for a moment and made a decision. "Rachael, come with me."

"What are you two doing?" Sims asked.

"Yeah, what are we doing?"

"We'll take them directly to a triage room from here. Get them in the system and bypass the guards at the front door."

"Dr. Kramer, if we do that, we'll be arrested. You know the rules." Rachael said.

"They can't arrest us if we aren't here." Claire turned to Dixon. "I assume you're not turning yourself in."

"No ma'am. We're heading to Fort Campbell. They don't know what happened yet."

"Can you take another passenger? I can be useful," Claire said.

"And how about a trauma nurse?" Rachael added.

"You both would be most welcome!" Dixon eagerly replied.

Claire and Rachael sped into the hospital and retrieved a gurney and wheelchair. With the help of the two employees and the loading dock's hydraulic lift, they had both injured soldiers up on the platform and into the hospital.

They took the men to the admitting desk where they processed into the system. Within minutes, they taken to surgery where a ruptured spleen was to be removed in one man while the other had his fractured leg reset.

"Wow, that was quite a turnaround," Rachael said as the two women hustled back to the resident's quarters. "What made you decide to leave so suddenly?"

"I'm done helping the enemy," Claire replied.

Arriving at their communal sleeping quarters, Claire scooped her clothing up and piled it into a pillow case.

"What about your stuff?" Claire asked.

"Billy brought my clothes from his place, but they're in the wrecker back on the highway, so I'm wearing what I own now."

"Grab some scrubs. Grab everything useful you can find."

"There'll be stuff at the base's PX. Don't worry about packing. We need to leave now."

The two women rushed back to the loading bay, where they found the HUMVEE idling and facing the exit. The two employees, having helped move the wounded soldiers, were nowhere to be found. After they jumped in the back, the vehicle's diesel engine roared and they sped out of the garage, leaving the medical center and the city of Nashville behind.

A fog lifted from Claire's soul. She hadn't recognized the stress and self-disgust she had felt working with DHS until she broke free from the hospital.

Sims drove west at first, but once they hit Highway 24, he headed north. Then he suddenly cut across the grass and tree-lined median. They were now going north in the southbound lane. Claire was going to ask him why when they crested a hill and saw the devastation on the other side of the highway.

"There it is," Dixon said as they pulled over. The mile-long trail of destruction was not navigable, even with the four-wheel-drive of their HUMVEE. They had to skirt along the side of the carnage, stopping occasionally to call out for survivors. There were none.

The HUMVEE's mounted spotlight swept over body parts and charred vehicles. Dixon spotted Lieutenant Dixon lying on the ground, his eyes gazing up at nothing as he clutched his son's mangled leg brace in his hands.

Finally, they moved forward, speeding to Fort Campbell. Part of him didn't want to reach their destination. He'd be forced to tell the Guardsmen what had happened, and that was a conversation he never wanted to have.

They need to know. The thought drove Dixon onward. *They all need to hear how the government killed their families.*

CHAPTER 19

SOUTHERN COMMAND
FORT KNOX, KY

EVER SINCE THEIR RETURN FROM the lake several months ago, General Lester's two grandchildren had been sick. At first, their little bodies had been racked by vomiting and nausea. Initially, his wife thought that they had eaten something foul. Her diagnosis seemed correct because after the digestive problems went away, the kids returned to normal. Then about a month ago, they became lethargic, their symptoms much like a viral mononucleosis infection. That's when the medical mystery began. For many more weeks, the children had endured batteries of tests while their condition slowly deteriorated.

Finally, as their white blood cell counts began to drop, radiation sickness was the diagnosis.

"Sir, it's the only thing that makes sense. Nothing else could be causing their immune systems to shut down like that. We tested for autoimmune diseases, chemical poisoning, and anything that could affect their bone marrow. By our best estimates, your grandchildren were exposed to a high dose of radiation," the doctor reported to the distraught grandfather.

"Watts Bar," Lester said. "We haven't heard from the plant in months."

"If the nuclear piles went critical, the fallout could have caused these symptoms," the doctor said.

"Does that mean they're going to die?" The general's eyes begged for hope.

"It all depends on the amount of radiation they were exposed to."

"Well, they were never at the plant. They were at least two miles away at all times."

The doctor scratched his chin. "Then we're looking at fallout. That's trickier to diagnose because there are several radioactive isotopes they may have been exposed to."

"How can I help? Tell me what to do."

"You need to send a CBRN team to the plant and take some readings. That would be a great start."

General Lester's next five minutes left no person on the base with any doubt as to what their jobs were. A CBRN team was dispatched by the end of the day and was told that he expected them to report back their findings without delay. After the doctor was dismissed, General Lester commanded his aide to hold all further calls and meetings. He sat down in one of his office's high-backed leather chairs and began to rub his temples.

He never should have let his wife take the family to that damned lake house. No one was supposed to leave the base for any reason other than mission-related travel.

He never thought about blaming his wife, who had pressured him into the journey. Nor did he blame his daughter, who had made it clear that she needed the time away for herself. He didn't blame the nuclear plant for spewing its poison over the land. He didn't even blame the EMP that started the whole thing. No, he blamed himself. He had broken his own rules, and like any good leader, the buck stopped with him.

WATTS BAR NUCLEAR POWER PLANT
SPRING CITY, TENNESSEE

The M1135 Stryker Nuclear, Biological, and Chemical Reconnaissance Vehicle rolled into the front gate of the Watts Bar nuclear facility. The eight-wheel NBCRV was equipped with sensors mounted on the outside of the metal monster. Its four-man crew sat safely inside the over-pressured compartment as it rumbled down the dead plant's access road.

The capabilities of this vehicle were too numerous to list—at least before the EMP took out most of its sensor computers. But some of its systems were hardened against an EMP, given that its purpose was to check for fallout after a nuclear attack, and the radiation detection system was one of the ones that still worked.

The readings spiked as they approached the twin towers of the plant, so much so that any exposure outside the Stryker's protective armor would be limited to just a few minutes.

"Jesus, I've got almost four hundred rems," one of the technicians reported as they drove nearer to the protective dome.

"If Fukushima is any guide," another responded, "it could get worse if the rods have melted together."

"It's too hot to enter the containment dome," the squad leader said as he unfolded a diagram of the plant. Finding what he wanted, he barked orders to his men. "Cut across the parking lot and head toward that L-shaped building."

The driver rolled through the large parking area and over several grassy strips of land, ending up at the front of the administrative building.

"Radiation down considerably," the technician said. "Under ten rems."

"Let's look for some papers," the group leader said. "The more we know about the plant and the nuclear material it stored, the better."

Two soldiers exited the safety of their Stryker, the positive pressure chamber spewing sterile air out of the door as they left. Helmet-mounted cameras let the squad leader and driver see their teammates' point of view. As they worked their way into the building, the flashlights mounted to their rifles shone tight beams of light into the dark rooms.

The leader pointed at the screen. "Hold there! Carter, scan back to your left. I saw something against the left wall."

The television monitor displayed the office, a large square space with row upon row of cubicles running the length of it.

"There! Back to your right just a bit."

"I see it," Carter said. "Nichols, on me."

The other television monitor showed specialist Nichols sprinting down an aisle, joining his partner as they slowly made their way further into the room.

"I have bodies," Carter said, his flashlight playing over three corpses that were in the advanced stages of decomposition. "Glad I'm on oxygen."

"I've got a fourth," Nichols said, moving to an adjacent cubicle.

"Carter," the squad leader said into his microphone, "what's that to your left. That puddle by the wall."

"God, I don't know," Carter replied. "It's dried out. I don't have a clue."

"Well, shit. Look at that," Nichols said, pointing his light at the floor. Dozens of dead flies were littered on the industrial carpet.

"They're flies," Carter said. "And they're on that pile as well."

"Radiation." The squad leader said. "These four died of radiation. Are they carrying any identification?" The two rifled through the dead men's clothing, coming up empty.

"Over here," Nichols said. "I've got three ARs and an AK."

"I'd guess looters," Carter said. "I found canned food, some ammo and porn magazines."

"They picked the wrong place to loot," the team commander said. "Keep moving. The plant manager's office is just through those far doors. First office on the right."

"Copy that, we're moving." Carter replied.

Carter and Nichols scoured the administration building. After an hour of searching, the team gathered the papers they had found and returned to the radiation-protected vehicle. A spray of liquid doused their suits before they entered the Stryker.

"It was a bust," Carter said. "All the reports we needed were already gone. Someone must have taken them when they abandoned this place."

"Let's head back," the team leader said as he looked at a map of the area. "The rear exit will take us away from the containment dome and cut off a few miles on the way to our rally point."

The eight-wheeled vehicle easily maneuvered down the dirt road. After some off-road travel, they hit the highway that was to take them back to their rally point. With some luck, they'd be out of their monkey suits and in open air within the next thirty minutes.

About five miles away, they were startled to see a man running out of a local farmhouse, waving his hands over his head.

"Stay back!" the commander shouted over the vehicle's loudspeakers. "This vehicle has been contaminated with radiation. It is not safe to approach. Stay back."

"Please help me," the man cried.

"I'm sorry, sir. This is a military mission. Please report to your local camp for help. DHS has a facility about thirty miles from here."

"I can't! I won't live a day there."

"What the hell is he talking about?" Carter asked.

"No clue. Maybe he's gone insane. Wouldn't be the first time."

The commander returned to his microphone. "Sir, we'll alert DHS and have them come pick you up."

"No!" the man shouted. "They'll kill me."

"Sir, please get off the road and let us pass. We've been exposed to radioactive material and need to return to our base."

"Were you at the plant?"

After a moment, the team leader replied. "Yes. That's where we were exposed."

The man took a step closer. "I can help. I used to work there."

Nichols frowned. "Maybe he knows what happened."

"State your name and position at the plant," the leader demanded.

"I'm Brendon Davidson, chief of maintenance at Watts Bar!"

"Holy crap, Sergeant," Nichols said. "He'll *definitely* know what happened."

"Mr. Davidson, please stay here. I'll send a vehicle to pick you up within the hour."

"Good! Just don't tell DHS," Davidson shouted back as he moved off the street and into the front yard of the farmhouse.

"We won't. We're just trying to find out what happened at the plant."

"Hell, I can tell you exactly what happened!" Davidson shouted. "DHS happened. And I have the paperwork to prove it!"

An hour later A HUMVEE pulled up to the temporary rally point, carrying a civilian and a backpack full of documents. The Stryker had been already been decontaminated, a water truck dousing it for several minute to wash away any radioactive particles. The vehicle now sat on a trailer, and the crew was eating a hot MRE and drinking orange powder that had been added to a one liter bottle of water.

"You Davidson?" the team leader asked as the former plant maintenance manager climbed into the MRAP with the crew.

"Yes sir." His eyes were focused on the food.

"Hungry?" Carter asked.

"That's an understatement."

"Must be if you're salivating over this crap."

Nichols grabbed an MRE and tossed it to the man. He tore into the packaging, ripping open the pouch of the box's main entrée and shoveling in mouthfuls of a rubbery yellow substance studded with vegetables.

"Is that the omelet?" Carter asked with disgust. "You really should put some hot sauce on that."

"I haven't eaten anything for days," Davidson said between bites. "This is great."

"You really are starving." Nichols. "Here, try a this one."

Davidson finished the omelet and tore open a second box, this one a package of chili mac. He was about to bite into the entrée when Nichols took the bag of food and put it into its heating pouch.

Nichols handed him a package of marbled pound cake instead. "Chew on this until it's heated."

Carter mixed the enclosed lemon-lime electrolyte powder into a bottle of water and gave it to Davidson. Within a couple of minutes, the poor man had eaten the two entrees and was now contentedly chewing on a handful of Skittles that had been a part of his second meal. As he finished his candy, the MRAP rumbled to life and they began the trip back to Fort Knox.

"Well, tell me a story," the team leader said. "And don't leave out any details."

The former Watts Barr plant director told the team about the failure of the old generators and the mysterious disappearance of the promised replacements from DHS, along with the death of his loyal crew at the hands of the raiders. When Davidson had finished, producing documents to back up his tale, the four CBRN technicians grimly looked at each other. There was only one conclusion to be drawn. DHS was culpable in the plant's meltdown and therefore the radiation poisoning of the general's grandkids.

Later that day, Davidson finished his debriefing at the commander's office. Davidson had watched the general's expression throughout his interrogation. Earlier, on their ride back to Fort Knox, the Hazmat team had filled him in on the details of the general's family and their apparent exposure to the radioactive fallout. As Davidson's story unfolded, General Lester's face went from neutral to ashen and finally to a dull red.

"Thank you, Mr. Davidson. You've done your country a great service," one of the aides said, indicating that the debriefing was over.

As the door closed, Davidson could hear a muted scream of anger coming from the commander's office.

"God help whoever took those generators," Davidson said under his breath.

The NCO escorting him slowed his stride, and in a grim voice said, "You have no God damned idea how true that is."

***

"Traitors!" General Lester hissed. "Who would steal from a nuclear plant? What kind of sick bastard puts *millions of people* at risk?"

The general's aide, Captain Kuris, held his tongue. He'd never seen the man so out of control as his commander ranted on about sedition and incompetence.

"That's it. I've had enough. It's time to take control."

"Sir?" Kuris asked, barely hearing the general's last words.

"Nothing, Captain."

Lester began paging through the mountain of papers that Davidson had retrieved from the power plant.

"Here!" Lester said triumphantly. "Get these numbers out to every post we can contact. Do it now."

Kuris took the sheet of paper with the serial numbers of the missing generators that had been assigned to the failed nuclear plant.

"Sir, what do you want me to tell them?"

"Tell them to find those generators! When you know where they are, let me know right away. Is that so hard, Captain?"

Kuris studied his commanding officer. Lester's voice was steady and firm, but his eyes were off, sort of glazed and dilated. Definitely not right.

"Yes sir," Kuris said. "I'll see to it."

As Kuris left the general's office, an uneasy feeling started to settle into his gut. General Lester had displayed no emotion since their diagnosis of radiation poisoning. But now, with a target on the table, someone could be held accountable. This was personal for his commander—they'd hurt his family, poisoned innocent children.

When Kuris got to his own office, he handed his aide the list and gave the soldier instructions to broadcast the serial numbers to every station and fort under their command.

"Sergeant, don't put any more information into that memo. Just the numbers and where to report."

"Understood, sir."

Kuris didn't want any rumors or innuendos associated with the search, nothing to warn the potential perpetrator. If this was personal for the general, it would be personal for all the men under Lester's command. They all felt his pain, even though St. Bart never showed his emotions. Never that is, until just a few moments ago, when Kuris saw the hurt in the man's eyes. It seemed that Lester felt emotions after all, and that pissed Kuris off more than anyone could ever know.

CHAPTER 20

ORLANDO, FL

"We all make choices, but in the end our choices make us."

— Ken Levine

SEVERAL WEEKS AFTER DAVIDSON'S RESCUE, Drosky rolled out of bed, a low murmur of protest coming from under the sheets.

"It's not even dawn," Natasha groaned, the bedspread dropping back as she reached out to reveal her female curves. "Come back here."

Drosky hesitated for a moment. His first impulse was to follow her seductive voice back to bed, but he'd promised to meet Beth and Mike early at the mess hall.

"Babe, I've got to go. But I'll be back tonight."

"You could be a little late," she whispered sensually.

Drosky went to her side of the bed and sat down. Natasha rolled over and brought her left arm around his waist, pulling him against her body.

"Tonight. Can you keep those thoughts till then?" John softly asked.

"All day, mister. I'll be thinking of you all day."

Drosky leaned over and kissed his girlfriend. She leaned up into him, pressing her body through the sheets, practically begging him to give in to her desires.

He pulled away and smiled. "I'll be thinking of you too."

Drosky hurriedly dressed and left their quarters, jogging toward the mess hall. Beth and Mike were already there.

***

"Well well," Mike deadpanned. "Look who managed to show up."

"I'm exactly on time," Drosky said.

"No thanks to a certain dark-haired woman who will remain nameless."

"She's hard to leave," he admitted with a grin, sitting down with his plate of eggs.

Beth ignored the male banter, concentrating on her own breakfast and reading some papers. When she had been reassigned to guard Bedford's wife, she had been none too pleased about it. But a friendship was blossoming between the two women. Beth provided Tanya with another woman with whom she could confide—and now Tanya was providing Beth with stolen memos and other secrets.

"What do you have?" Drosky asked her, ignoring Mike's further attempts to goad him about his private life.

"Deployment schedule," Beth replied. "Timetable and strengths."

It was a bit risky meeting in DHS headquarters' mess hall, but at 0530, they were the only people in the dining area other than the kitchen staff. John figured that the best place to exchange secrets was in the open and at a place where they normally would meet anyway. They were known friends and ate breakfast together every day. It would be a lot more suspicious if they got together at a more secluded spot, and it wasn't every day that they exchanged information.

"Cyn's gonna like this." Mike said, looking at the spreadsheet.

"Seems Tanya's becoming quite the fountain of information," Drosky added, looking at another page from the stack that contained more details of the upcoming deployment.

Cynthia Terrones had been contacted by a growing opposition to the new government. Her years in the Marines and time spent doing security work for the theme parks gave her an interesting and varied list of associates. One of them reached out to her a two months ago, and she'd become part of that group of patriots. Four weeks ago, she brought Mike on board, who in turn brought in Drosky and Beth.

Now Beth's relationship with Bedford's wife was paying dividends because she had access to her husband's private files. In just a few short weeks, they had been overwhelmed by the amount and quality of the information Tanya had stolen. It was fitting that the woman Bedford had turned into his personal plaything was now stabbing him in the back.

The results of their efforts had been both immediate and remarkable. Two convoys of DHS agents had been ambushed by a growing rebel force, resulting in the loss of nearly a hundred men and truckloads of supplies, including small arms, explosives and anti-material weapons. Bedford had been livid after hearing of the second ambush, convinced that the civilians still left in the city were responsible, and not an organized resistance.

"I'll get these to Cyn," Mike said as he slid the papers into his messenger bag. "They'll be in our friend's hands by tonight."

None of them knew who Cynthia was communicating with, and if OPSEC was being followed, she likely didn't know who she was interfacing with either.

Someday this will make a great story, Drosky thought. *Too bad I can't keep notes.*

Later that morning, Drosky was in Bedford's office, reviewing the day's agenda.

"I'll need another vehicle," he said as he glanced at the day's calendar. "The trip to the airport is getting more problematic. I'll need to add two more vehicles for security."

"That's fine," the director said absently.

"Sir, I'll need to pull them from the city. Our fleet of up-armored HUMVEEs is dangerously low since the two ambushes. Do you have any recommendations on which units we should re-task?"

Bedford sat silently for a moment, then slammed his fist onto the table. "Damn it! I'm tired of fighting these ungrateful bastards."

He stood up and began pacing the floor in front of his desk. Drosky sat calmly, a blank expression on his face. It was good to see the stress their efforts were causing DHS. Drosky thought about the spreadsheets he had seen that morning and suppressed a grin. More agents were going to die, and that was just fine with him. Almost to a man, the agents that stayed with DHS were cowards, exchanging their souls for air conditioning and a hot meal. His efforts to stop the new government had allowed him to sleep well once again.

Bedford stopped his pacing, his expression suddenly changing from anger to calm.

"Get me Nixon," Bedford commanded. "Now."

"What for, sir?"

"Not your concern," Bedford replied with a nasty smile. "Just get him for me."

Drosky sent one of his agents to get the evil man. Ever since he had witnessed Travis Nixon shoot an unarmed father and burn two families this past winter, he had been searching for an opportunity to pay the bastard back. But Nixon and Drosky's paths hadn't crossed since. Nixon had been mostly absent since then, sometimes not showing up at the tower apartment for weeks on end. Finally, after a few months without running into him, Drosky's intense anger had subsided into a slow, simmering burn. Revenge and retribution would come soon enough, but not at the expense of ruining his budding career as a spy. Taking down Nixon was now secondary to providing the resistance with information.

A half an hour later, Nixon smugly strode into Bedford's office.

"You're dismissed," Bedford said to Drosky.

He reluctantly closed the director's door behind him and stood nearby. There was nothing he could do to overhear their conversation, and he vowed to somehow rectify that problem. *Perhaps a hidden mic?* he thought as Bedford and Nixon conspired in the room just a few feet away.

Behind the closed door, the director greeted Nixon warmly. "Travis!" Bedford said, clapping him on the shoulder. "How was your assignment?"

Nixon had been in Miami, where his men had crushed pockets of resistance on the island of Key Biscayne. The waterfront mansions were going to be prized pieces of real estate when the dust settled, and Bedford was bound and determined to be the owner of those lots. Nixon had performed with increasing efficiency as he learned what would drive the remaining groups of non-compliant citizens into the DHS camps.

"It's been a ton of fun," Nixon said.

Bedford let out a deep belly laugh, his stomach flab rippling up and down through his too tight white button-down shirt. It was late spring, and even with the air conditioning, the man was sweating through his clothes.

"I brought you here to solve another problem. This one is local."

"I thought we had this town under control?" Nixon asked, taking a seat across from the director's desk.

"We did, but things are starting to turn in the wrong direction."

Bedford handed Nixon a folder. The agent opened began reviewing the papers within. Settling himself in his chair with an audible grunt, Bedford opened his own folder and turned to the first page.

"On page one, you can see the damage we've suffered since the beginning of the month."

Nixon whistled as he reviewed the battle damage report. "A hundred and six dead?"

"Actually, it's up to one hundred thirteen. Seven of the critically wounded died since that report."

"And the material. Was that destroyed or captured?"

"Captured. Including over a dozen AT4s"

"Jesus," Nixon said. "That can do some damage."

"Exactly. That's why I need your men to get this under control right now. I can't have these ungrateful morons running around with shoulder rockets, blowing up my MRAPs and HUMVEEs."

"It's solvable. I just need a few weeks to weed out the rats."

"Whatever you need, it's yours." Bedford replied, handing the man a laminated card. "This is your 'God Card.' It will get you anything you want."

Nixon looked at the piece of plastic. It was roughly the size of a credit card, but it was so much better. Bedford's signature was on the bottom, and it authorized the holder to have full access to whatever he would need. With a smile, he put it in his shirt pocket.

"I'll be out there in the morning." Nixon said. He was already planning where to move his team and their entourage of female companions. The men had collected a virtual harem that he needed to keep housed and fed. This card would allow him to do just that.

"Any suggestions where we can base the men?" Nixon asked.

"Grand Cypress," Bedford immediately replied. "I've got a gas station out there, plenty of rooms for you and your boys, as well as a twenty-four-hour restaurant on site. There's even a spa for some of your tagalong guests."

Nixon's surprised look pleased Bedford. The man needed to know that Bedford was on top of everything around him, including the lifestyles and predilections of his agents.

"Oh don't be surprised, Travis. I know about the girls."

"And you don't have a problem with that?" Nixon asked.

"Problem? I'm looking forward to a visit."

"They're all yours, sir. Any girl you want."

"You mean *girls*, don't you?" Bedford deadpanned.

Both men laughed as Nixon rose to leave.

"You're my kind of boss, sir." Nixon said, shaking the director's hand.

"And you're my kind of soldier."

"Thank you, sir." Nixon saluted.

"Now get out of here and fix my problem," Bedford said as he returned the agent's salute.

Nixon exchanged a menacing glance with John Drosky as he strode past. Leaving Drosky behind to guard Bedford's door gave Nixon a level of satisfaction that he could barely contain. Since their days at the Orlando Police Department together, Nixon had held a grudge against him. Drosky had been a Marine, serving tours in Iraq, while Nixon had washed out after his three-year term had expired and been told not to re-enlist. Drosky reminded Nixon of the injustices that the military had heaped on him. And now Drosky was nothing more than a glorified guard while he was the Bedford's counter-insurgency man.

Maybe there is some justice in this world, Nixon thought as he patted the God Card in his pocket.

CHAPTER 21

ORLANDO, FL

"That's just the way: a person does a low-down thing, and then he don't want to take no consequences of it. Thinks as long as he can hide it, it ain't no disgrace."

— **Mark Twain, The Adventures of Huckleberry Finn**

A S THE NEXT FEW WEEKS rolled by, several convoys had been destroyed and scores of agents had been killed. Nixon's attempts to catch the elusive rebels had been an utter failure. Hitting the insurgent's camps only worked when they stayed still, but they were constantly moving. Whenever Nixon's men raided a suspected site, they found it abandoned and often booby-trapped. He'd lost four men so far to sophisticated explosives, and he'd failed to kill more than a handful of the enemy. Now, Nixon was in Bedford's office, trying to explain his lack of success. Drosky was stationed by the director's door and had the satisfaction of listening to Bedford's screams and roars of fury at Nixon'failures.

Drosky looked over at a pretty secretary who now occupied a desk in Bedford's waiting area. She was a young, well-endowed Latina from Miami who barely spoke English. Her only responsibility seemed to be occasional private visits to Bedford's office where he would "dictate memos," although these supposed directives never seemed to materialize to the rest of the world.

As one particularly vile curse found its way through the thick walls, Drosky nodded to the girl, getting a seductive smile in reply.

A moment later, the director's door was flung open as Bedford threw a final, profanity laced command at the cowering agent.

"You get this under control, Nixon. If you don't, I'll have you buried so deep you'll be fertilizing the rice paddies in China. Do you understand me?"

"Yes sir. I'll get it done."

Bedford slammed the door, leaving Nixon at the mercy of Drosky's sharp tongue.

"That went well," Drosky deadpanned. "You guys having a beer after work?"

Nixon's eyes flared, his fists clenching as he attempted to control his rage. The agent placed his beret back on his head, completing his self-created uniform. The black ninja outfit would have been comical if it weren't for the fact that Nixon had earned the right to wear it. His counter-insurgency efforts had resulted in hundreds of deaths in Miami, although his efforts so far in Orlando had been less than stellar.

"Just warming up", Nixon said as he brushed past.

Their eyes locked, neither man backing down.

As the agent passed Drosky, he turned and made a gun out of his thumb and fingers. Pointing it as John, he depressed his thumb like a pistol hammer strike.

"Bang! See you next time, Drosky." Nixon said with a smile, before turning to leave the director's reception room.

As he opened the room's outer door, something thudded into the wall next to his head. Turning to his right, the smug agent staggered back as he saw the blade of a Ka-Bar knife buried in the drywall about a foot away.

Drosky approached the trembling man, grabbed the knife's handle, and pulled. He removed the blade from the wall and sheathed it in one smooth motion. He returned to his post and stood calmly by the door. Out of the corner of his eyes, he watched Nixon gather himself and quickly leave the room. A smile creased Drosky's face as he noticed a wet stain on the front of Nixon's pants.

"I think he is going to change his clothes," the secretary said with a grin, in broken English.

"Yeah, I think he is."

Just then, the speaker on the woman's desk came alive. "Lucia, please come in here. And bring your pen and pad."

They both knew what that meant, another "private" session with the fat DHS director.

With a sigh, the girl got up from her chair and adjusted her form-fitting pencil skirt. She primped her white silk blouse and checked her face with a compact makeup mirror. She looked up at John with a brave but defeated smile and walked to the closed door.

"I'm sorry," Drosky murmured.

The girl stopped and gave Drosky a look. "I'm free tonight," she said.

"I'm not." John simply replied.

The secretary took a breath and entered the room. If experience was any guide, she'd be back soon. Their boss wasn't one to take long at anything he did.

***

Nixon scurried out of the director's office. The knife had been inches from punching through the back of his head. More than the act itself, it frightened him that he hadn't seen Drosky as such a threat. He'd have to re-evaluate the situation and determine the best way to get rid of him.

Nixon put that problem away because he had bigger fish to fry. Bedford had put him in charge of crushing the budding insurgency, but his efforts had been a total failure so far. What had started out as a twenty-five-man strike force had been reduced to nineteen by the insurgents. The tactics he had used in Miami were inadequate in this city. The insurgents were more organized, better trained, and seemed to anticipate his moves. His efforts so far had been a failure.

To make matters worse, another column of supplies had been raided, leaving Bedford with a shortage of both men and machines. The AT4s stolen in the first raids were being used with great effect when the rebels took out the lead and rear elements of the convoy, trapping the remaining vehicles in between. Crossing lanes of fire from pre-placed firing positions had decimated the column, resulting in the deaths over fifty more agents and loss or theft of tons of food and weapons. If this continued, it wouldn't be long before the insurgents would be better armed than the government.

"Take us home," Nixon said to his driver.

He leaned back in his seat and tried to come up with a plan. He had to think out of the box, and he had to do it quickly. Nixon had no doubt that if he didn't produce results soon, he would not live to see end of summer.

When they arrived at the hotel, Nixon walked into the wing of the resort that his group had occupied. Doors were left open and the sounds of video games and movies were flooding the hall. Even the moans of passion from one of the rooms failed to distract the agent as he walked down the hallway, pondering his next move. Approaching his own suite, he noted the sound of a movie he had seen before. It was a science-fiction flick about an interstellar crew of rebels that were fighting a future government. In an attempt to capture the rebels, the government killed all the people that had worked with them over the years.

He suddenly remembered a line from the movie, and his next move crystalized in his brain.

"That's it!" Nixon said, remembering the quote. "If your quarry goes to ground, leave no ground to go to!"

***

Lieutenant Ferraro was tired of the heat. Since moving to Orlando from Fort Knox, he'd been doing nothing but putting out fires between the military and their DHS friends.

Now, a third column of supplies had been destroyed and Bedford was complaining that it would be almost a month before another shipment could be arranged. The DHS director was infuriating—and more importantly, he was a corrupt and incompetent man. Rumors of graft and prostitution were rampant, and the airport was awash with "dignitaries" from Washington, D.C., as they brought their families and mistresses to the costal resorts DHS had impounded.

Ferraro's family was quartered in one of the city's central apartment buildings. They occupied a two-bedroom unit on the top floor of one of three federally built, four-story buildings. The square structures were painted in muted pastels and reeked of government design, with no esthetic qualities to the complex.

His wife had been reluctant to move, but his position as liaison put him at the top of Orlando's military food chain. The perks of command were now available for his family, which changed his wife's attitude about the move. At least that problem had been solved as she flitted about with visiting high-ranking official's spouses, enjoying the Grand Cypress resort and even taking the kids to West Palm Beach for a weekend.

But for Ferraro, the problems of command never ended, so he decided to wander about in thought, clearing his mind in anticipation of the coming day. Walking in the early morning heat was oppressive, especially compared to the cool, fresh summer air he'd left back in Kentucky. But the eighty-degree morning temperature was downright frigid compared to the expected afternoon high of ninety-six. And he didn't even want to think about the humidity, the kind that made his uniform damp and thick with hot, sticky moisture. So walking now was about the only time he'd be able to enjoy a quiet stroll, even though he'd likely be drenched in sweat by the time he got to his office.

Ferraro passed by the tower where many of the DHS agents lived. The front of the structure was always a beehive of activity as the men and women scurried back and forth between their new home and DHS headquarters just a few blocks away. He stopped and watched as people in uniform entered and left the building. Groups stood in the plaza in front of the building, and the roads were devoid of vehicles, used now as pedestrian walkways. In fact, several square blocks of the area were free of any traffic other than foot. It was nice to see people engaging in normal activities even though they were all federal agents and not average citizens.

Well, it's a start, he thought.

Instead of taking his normal morning path, Ferraro decided to continue down the road, moving beyond the tall building. The center of the city was returning to normal, at least in this limited area.

Generators weren't needed in town other than as backups now that the area was being fed by the Stanton Energy Center. The electric plant east of town was getting limited a limited supply of coal that was being brought in by train from West Virginia. After losing several shipments to bandits, DHS had begun providing on-board security for the trip. The reliable deliveries allowed a steady stream of electricity to be generated.

To bring power back to the center of town, the feeder lines into the city had to be verified as safe, and all power to uninspected buildings had to be cut off. If they had simply pulled the switch to feed the entire area, a deteriorating electric box or simply an oven or stove that had been left on could ignite a house fire that would rage out of control. It took months for the technicians to clear and certify the buildings before power could be reinstituted.

Suddenly, the nearby generators to the tower kicked in, deafening the lieutenant and forcing him to cover his ears.

Damn, he thought. *Someone must have taken out another transformer.*

One of their biggest problems now was the citizens of the city that hadn't complied with the government's orders to report to a relocation camp. These survivors lived on the scraps in the areas outside of downtown, and their wrath at the government seemed to know no bounds. Since the electricity was reestablished a few weeks ago, power interruptions had become a daily part of their lives. Ferraro didn't have a problem with people choosing to stay home and make a go of it. In some ways, he was impressed with those that had survived so far. But their vindictiveness in shooting out the newly installed transformers, just to make the government center lose power, angered him. If they chose to live like that, fine. But don't hurt those that are here to help. At least, that's the way he thought of it.

"I need some help here!" Ferraro heard someone shouting from behind one of the generators that were attached to the tower.

The lieutenant jogged toward the sound of the voice and found a technician struggling with an access panel that was askew and in danger of falling. The man was holding the massive plate of metal as diesel squirted out of a hose that ran from an adjacent fuel truck.

"Grab this while I shut off the pump!"

Ferraro took the technician's place and kept the panel from twisting free. One of the hinges had broken when the mechanic had opened it, and it was in danger of ripping the other hinge off if he let it drop. Moments later, the generator shut down, and the fuel stopped hemorrhaging onto the concrete pad.

"Thanks," the man said. "Ever since we got electric, these engines have been turned on and off almost every day."

The two men positioned the metal plate back in place and twisted the access panel's handle to lock it.

"These things were made to run without shutting down," he continued. "Every time we have to restart them, there's a specific procedure that needs to be followed. If I'm not here, the idiots inside just come out and flip the switch. Next thing you know, something goes wrong and I'm out here fixing their stupidity."

"I know the feeling," Ferraro said with a smile. "If people just followed the rules, we'd have a lot fewer problems."

"Amen, brother."

The technician grabbed his toolbox and hustled back into the bowels of the building, leaving Ferraro next to the silent machine. As the lieutenant turned to leave, he glanced at the panel one more time and something caught his eye. He leaned in and examined the writing on the side of the generator. Specifically, at its serial number: MAR49304Y.

Jesus! Could it be?

Several weeks ago, he'd received a memo from Kuris with a list of generator serial numbers and a command to report back to the captain if they were found. Ferraro had handed the order off to DHS. Since they installed the generators and did maintenance on all their equipment, he had asked them to check their records and let him know if these units were here. They never got back to him.

Without any explanation as to why those generators were to be found, Ferraro had let the matter go and went on with his assigned duties. Now, looking at the serial number, he got a sinking feeling that DHS might have let him down. He'd remembered the code because his daughter's name was Mary, and those letters were in several of the serial numbers. Ferraro wrote the number down and retreated to his office.

"Sergeant," he said as he entered. "Where is that list of serial numbers from Fort Knox?"

The aide opened a cabinet and retrieved the list. Ferraro took the paper and sat at his desk. It didn't take him long to discover that the number on the list and the one on the generator downtown were the same.

"Get Captain Kuris on the satellite phone," Ferraro commanded.

A few moments later, his aide brought the phone into Ferraro's office and handed it to the lieutenant.

"Ferraro, here," he said into the device.

"Hi, Lieutenant. How's Orlando treating you and your family?"

"Very good, sir. Thank you for asking."

"That's good. What can I do for you?"

"Sir, it's about that list of generators you were asking about."

The phone went silent, and Ferraro thought they'd lost their connection.

"Sir, are you still there?"

"Yes. Yes, Lieutenant. I'm here."

"I found one of the generators. I don't know if there are any more here. I directed DHS to review their records and report back to me if they found any of the serial numbers in their files. They hadn't reported back, but I ran across one of them attached to a high-rise here in town."

There was another long pause. "Lieutenant, I'm going to get back to you. Does anyone else know what you've found?"

"Just my aide, sir."

"You two keep this quiet. That's an order. I'll get back to you by the end of the day to give you further orders."

"Yes sir," Ferraro said with hesitation. "Can I ask, is this important? If I can be blunt, sir, you sound a bit off."

"Yeah, Lieutenant. I'm a bit *off*," Kuris replied. "I'm going to tell you a story, and you will not repeat it unless I say so. Is that understood?"

"Yes sir," Ferraro replied. "I understand."

Ten minutes later, Ferraro handed the phone back to his aide in the office's reception room.

"Sergeant, you are not to mention anything about this serial number or my phone call to anyone. Is that understood?"

"Yes sir," the sergeant said, but there was doubt in his eyes. "Is there something going on?"

Ferraro smiled grimly. "The wrath of God himself is coming to Orlando, and we're about to see it for ourselves."

CHAPTER 22

ORLANDO, FL

A FEW WEEKS LATER, THE GULFSTREAM C-20b rolled to a stop outside the maintenance hangar. Lieutenant Ferraro stood attentively outside the aircraft along with four armed soldiers as the door to the jet dropped down, allowing a ten-step ladder to extend to the ground.

Captain Kuris stood in the opening and nodded to the lieutenant. Moments later, General Lester appeared and strode down the extended stairs.

The four guards turned away from the arriving dignitaries, their battle rifles at low ready as they scanned their designated fields of fire for signs of danger. Lieutenant Ferraro approached the steps and stopped ten feet short. Snapping to attention, he threw up his best salute.

Lester, recognizing his former aide, returned the salute. Ferraro dropped his arm to his side, but before he could say a word of welcome, Lester reached out and shook his hand.

"Ferraro, good to see you."

"Y-yes sir," Ferraro stammered. "Thank you."

"You've done a great job here. I won't forget it."

"Thank you, sir. But I would recommend we get moving as soon as possible. It's dangerous to linger here."

"Lead the way, Lieutenant."

The general, Kuris, and Ferraro strode to a waiting Stryker, its outer hull reinforced by sandbags. A 50-caliber M2 was manned on the top. The rear door was down, creating a ramp, and the men walked at a hunch and then took seats along the mobile infantry carrier's bench seats. As the armored eight-wheeled vehicle began to roll, the general turned to Ferraro.

"A Stryker? Is it that bad?"

"It can be, sir. DHS has lost control of parts of the city. It's in my report."

"Yes, I read it. I thought that the route from the airport was secure?"

"It used to be, sir. Two nights ago, we lost three unarmored vehicles to an ambush. Since then, I'm not taking any chances."

Lester sat back, satisfied with the explanation. Kuris caught Ferraro's eyes and nodded with a slight smile. Ferraro nodded back, pleased at the acknowledgement he'd just received form his former mentor.

"He knows I'm coming?" Lester asked.

"Yes sir. I didn't tell him when you were landing, though. Said it was operational security. He accepted that. He has arranged a formal reception tonight, including dinner and a social. I don't think he has any idea why you came."

"Good, Lieutenant. You did the right thing."

"Did you locate the remaining stolen generators?" Kuris asked.

"All of them, sir. Every one of them is attached to apartments in the city, including the director's own building where he had a custom penthouse built."

Lester's face remained stoic. Only his eyes gave away the anger.

The ride to the former Orlando Police Department headquarters building was uneventful. No one there knew that the general was arriving, so he received a less-than-formal greeting when he strode in the front door. In fact, no one greeted him at all.

The general did not look impressed. "I like the formality." The general said sarcastically. "Is this the way DHS always operates?"

"Yes sir," Ferraro replied. "Most of the agents are former police or retired federal workers. They don't adhere to protocol. It's rather sloppy."

"That's going to change," Lester said as he scanned the chaos in the hallway. "I've seen enough. Take me to Bedford."

Not a word was spoken during the five-minute drive to the plush apartment building. Kuris and Ferraro exchanged worried glances as they watched the general, his left foot drumming up and down on the Stryker's floor.

A pair of guards posted at the entrance to the apartment snapped to attention when Lester exited the vehicle, earning an approving nod from Kuris.

At least someone's been trained properly, he thought.

At the top of the building, the elevator doors opened onto a long, lushly furnished hallway. Antique lawyer's bookcases, their original leaded glass windows shimmering, lined one wall. The cases were filled with a potpourri of Tiffany stained glass, exquisite porcelain, and fine crystal. The spoils of power on display to every visitor that came down the long hallway. Paintings hung on the opposite wall, including several original masterpieces that must have been pilfered from the Dali museum near Tampa. The only unifying theme to the treasures seemed to be a certain erotic aspect to the art.

They entered the director's waiting room and stopped in front of an unoccupied secretary's desk. Another guard was standing watch. The man glanced at Lester's collar, and seeing the stars attached he snapped to attention.

"I'm here to see director Bedford," Lester said calmly.

"Yes sir. He's...indisposed at the moment."

"What, may I ask, is keeping him so occupied?"

"Sir, he's in his office with his secretary," the agent replied, his eyes downcast as a flush crept in his cheeks. "She's...uh...taking dictation, sir."

Lester's eyes flared. "Well, make him available," he said. "Make it happen right now! Am I clear?"

The black-clad man turned and pounded on the director's office door. "Director Bedford? You're needed immediately!"

A muffled shout came from behind the heavy oak door. It sounded like a woman, but it was impossible to tell whether the cry was from pleasure or pain.

"Open the damned door now!" Lester hissed.

"I can't, sir," the distraught agent said. "It's locked from the inside."

"Go down the hall and guard the elevator," Ferraro commanded. The man nodded gratefully and trotted away.

Lester moved back, turned to Kuris, and nodded. The captain, a tall and fit man, stepped up to the door.

"On my mark," Kuris commanded to the four guards that had accompanied them.

"Three, two, one..." Raising his boot, he kicked the door near its ornate brass handle, sending the wooden plank crashing into the room.

The four soldiers rushed into the dusky room and set up a semi-circular perimeter. Their M4 rifles were up to their eyes as they scanned the room for threats.

Kuris followed through next with his M-9 handgun drawn while Ferraro drew his service weapon and held rear watch behind the general.

A woman screamed again as the armed men rushed the room.

Lester stormed into the office and found the woman, whom he assumed was the secretary, laying back on the director's desk, with her legs in the air and Bedford between them. Kuris looked at the corpulent man, his pants around his ankles and a look of fury and terror on the director's face, and almost shot him right then and there.

"Clear!" Kuris yelled after scanning the room.

The four guards brought their weapons down to low ready, and held their positions.

Lester strode to the desk and stared at Bedford. The man was too stunned to move, his eyes bulging. The general looked down on the woman, who covered her face in embarrassment.

"At least one of you has some shame," he said. "Get out of here and clean yourself up."

Ferraro led her out of the room. Before letting her go, he got her name and billet address, knowing that the general would want her interviewed later.

Bedford had backed away from the desk to allow his secretary to follow the general's instructions. With his pants still down, Kuris looked at his naked lower half and smirked. If the shrunken muscle was any indication, Bedford was far more afraid than he was angry.

"Please collect yourself, Director. I have time," Lester said, his voice deadly calm.

The Bedford pulled up his pants and scurried into his private bathroom. Lester scanned the office, noting the opulent and erotic nature of the decorations. He shook his head.

"Take photographs, lots of them," Lester told Kuris. "I want all the evidence I can muster."

Bedford returned, his thinning hair combed back and a fresh shirt hastily buttoned over his sweaty body.

"Uh, General. I wasn't expecting you until this evening."

"Obviously. Was this an inopportune time?"

The director frowned, his rodent-like eyes darting back and forth as he tried to come up with a response.

"Never mind," Lester continued. "We heard a scream from the room, didn't we captain?"

"Yes sir. Definitely a scream."

"Sorry about your door, Director. We were... concerned," Lester added.

"Uh, oh. That's quite alright. I can have it fixed."

The two men stared at each other. Bedford shrank before the battle-hardened soldier.

"We're taking a survey of all the assets under my command," Lester said. "Would you be kind enough to share that information with my captain?"

"Oh! Of course, General. I'll assign a team to assist you any way I can."

"Very good. Then I'll see you tonight at dinner?"

"Oh indeed. I'm sure you will enjoy what we have planned."

"I'm sure. Until then."

"Uh, yes. Until then," Bedford practically sighed.

The general and his entourage left the office and waited silently at the elevator door. The guard Ferraro had deployed to this spot stood nervously, unsure whether to salute or stay silent. The frozen look of fear on the man's face explained his lack of military decorum.

After the doors slid shut and the lift began to descend, Kuris said, "I assumed you were going to arrest him."

"Not yet," Lester said. "This is a den of rats, and I want to clean it out. I want everyone responsible for the deplorable state of this command removed."

Kuris nodded and glanced at Ferraro.

"Sir," Kuris began. "Lieutenant Ferraro's report on the state of the city includes some unedited after-action reports. I think this will give you a head start on the personnel responsible."

"Bring them to me as soon as I settle into my room, Lieutenant."

"Yes sir" Ferraro replied.

"And Ferraro, well done back there." Kuris added. "Glad you remembered your room-clearing techniques."

"I'm not soft yet, Captain. Thank you, sir."

CHAPTER 23

ORLANDO, FL

WHILE BEDFORD WAS PULLING UP his pants, Drosky and Bru were in the cafeteria of the newly recommissioned Orlando Regional Hospital, waiting for the director's wife to finish her final medical examination.

"She's recovered well," Drosky said.

"I think Beth had a lot to do with that," Bru replied. "Tanya seems to enjoy her company."

Bruner hadn't been let into the loop about Tanya's clandestine activities. It was agreed in the beginning that the fewer people that knew about their insurgent activities, the better. Besides, Drosky was concerned that Bru's increasingly protective behavior would lead him to dissuade Tanya from spying. After all, a spy only had two paths forward. Either their side won… or else they were caught and executed. Both scenarios were fraught with danger, and Bru had lost his ability to be reasonable after being reassigned from Bedford's family to another high value subject. He seemed more possessed by the director's wife since Beth took his spot and found any opportunity to be near her in his free time.

Today was one of those off days when he had magically appeared on the sidewalk of the medical office, receiving a warm smile and a wave from Tanya as Drosky escorted the woman inside. Beth was back at the director's apartment watching Tanya's young daughter.

Drosky checked his watch and noted that the thirty-minute examination was almost up. "I've got to go. Why don't you get back to your room and relax?"

"I'm not tired," Bru replied. "And I haven't had a chance to say hello."

"Dammit, Bru. Let it go. She's married. To the director!"

Bru dropped his head, acknowledging that fact. "I can't help it, John. She's in my head."

"Then get her out," Drosky replied to the twenty-two-year-old agent. "Move on, and if I see you trying to hang around her again, you're out. Do you understand me?"

"I can't John," he whispered. "I'm in love."

"Come on, you're being stupid. You don't even know her."

"We slept together," Bru finally admitted. "Twice. I love her."

"Crap," Drosky said.

Bru shook his head. "What can I say?"

"Report to personnel tomorrow. I'm reassigning you. Now get out of here."

Bru slammed his hand on the table, garnering stares from the other people nearby. The young man stomped away, leaving Drosky with a potential mess on his hands.

***

Later that afternoon, Ferraro and Kuris got together at a local pub that had recently opened. Sitting in a darkened corner booth, they had both privacy and a view of the clientele that came and went. If they didn't know any better, the normalcy of the situation would have made them think that the EMP never went off.

"So, what do you have so far?" Kuris asked after the waitress dropped off two locally produced draft beers.

"It'll be a couple of days before we have reviewed all the documents, but I did confirm the orders to steal the generators and bring them to the city. In fact, eight of the generators were pilfered from a warehouse immediately after the EMP went off. Not only did they take Watts Bar's backup generators, but they also redirected the other four from one of the plants here in Florida."

"Which one? Did it melt down too?"

"Turkey Point, down south. It's fine for now. Their existing generators are keeping the nuclear pile under control. Problem is, if two of the four go down, it'll go China Syndrome just like Watts Bar."

"Shit," Kuris muttered.

"Don't worry. I've redirected two of the machines down there."

"Where did you find them?"

Ferraro grinned. "Behind the director's apartment building."

Kuris smiled in reply and took a long draw from his chilled glass. "This isn't half bad!"

"Yeah, I could get used to it."

"What else do you have?"

"I have a flow chart of leadership. I figure the general would want to vet them, or at least know who the potential problem people are."

Kuris took the sheet of paper and nodded. "He'll like this. You've done a great job, Lieutenant."

"Thank you, sir. I don't like this, though. I just find the timing of the generator theft to be too convenient."

Kuris got a questioning look on his face. "How so?"

"I mean, it's almost as if Bedford knew he'd need the generators before everything went down. They were transported here within a week of the EMP, to an apartment building that had already been half modified into his private suite."

"You're saying that DHS had knowledge of the EMP before it struck?"

"Who knows," Ferraro said. "I'm just speculating here. But there are too many circumstances where just the right supplies were in just the right place."

"That could be coincidence," Kuris said. "The government has a ton of supplies all over the country. Probably two or three times what they really need. I can think of plenty of places we found food and ammunition after the electric grid went down."

"I know," Ferraro said. "But it took us months to figure all that out. DHS was up and running way too fast. They knew where to go and had it together inside a week. When's the last time you knew the government to be that efficient?"

"I don't think the general needs to hear that right now," Kuris replied after a few moments.

Just then, his satellite phone began to vibrate. "Kuris here."

Several moments went by before the captain replied. "When are they going into do that?"

A pause, and the, "Okay, thanks for the heads-up."

Kuris disconnected the call.

"Well?" Ferraro asked.

"It's the general's grandson," he began. "His white blood cell count was going down. Well, a week ago, the count started to rise rapidly."

"That's good, right?"

"No. It's leukemia. The kid's bone marrow is screwed up. That was the hospital. They're going to start him on chemotherapy. His grandmother is a match, and they're going to do a transplant."

"Will that cure him?"

"If he gets through the procedure, there's a good chance he'll recover. But he will still be living with impaired DNA and several organs have been permanently damaged. They've already removed both of the grandkids' thyroid glands. They've got a tough road ahead of them."

The two men finished their beers and went back to the general's temporary quarters. Kuris knocked on his office door and entered when invited.

"Sir, Lieutenant Ferraro just gave me a report on command structure as well as confirmation on the theft of the generators."

Lester was behind his desk, rubbing his temples, both elbows on the writing pad.

"Thank you, Captain. That will be all."

Kuris hesitated. "Sir, if you need to talk…"

"I'm fine. I suppose one of your moles let you know about the situation at the hospital."

"No good ADC would be without them, sir."

"I know. I feel so helpless sitting here."

"Well, this wasn't expected, but there's good news about the bone marrow match."

"I wish they had waited until I returned."

"I know they would have, if it had been possible. But they know what they're doing, sir. You have to count on that."

"Thank you, Captain."

"Sir, I'd understand if you didn't attend the dinner tonight. Should I tell Bedford not to expect you?"

"No, let's go. I need to get my mind on something else now. Besides, the director doesn't know how little time he has."

"You ready to pull the plug?"

"Soon, Captain. I've been in touch with Homeland in Washington and appraised them of the situation. They're sending a replacement. That person should be here within the week."

"Any names I'd know?"

"Ramona Qualls."

"Wow. The dragon lady from NSA?"

"The one and only. She's spoken with me already and told me to do what I want with Bedford."

"She'll whip this area in shape."

"True. I don't think we'll need to worry about Florida now that she's coming. She'll bust balls as well as any man I know," the general concluded.

CHAPTER 24

THE KRAMER HOUSE
MONTEVERDE, FL

"Older men start wars, but younger men fight them. "

— **Albert Einstein**

THE DAY FOLLOWING THE FORMAL dinner party for General Lester, Gerry Kramer was finishing his examination of one of the local high school kids. Over the last few months, the population of the academy dorms had dwindled to just a few dozen youngsters. Any students under sixteen had been turned over to DHS at one of their many bus stops to the east of town. Any of the others that wanted to go did so as well. So far, the remaining live-ins hadn't run across any federal agents. As long as they stayed away from the road to the power plant, they were left alone.

And as far as those buses went, the numbers had decreased exponentially following Dr. Kramer's return. In fact, they hadn't seen any of them in over a month. That just meant that they'd already eliminated most of the undesirables. The very sick had already died, and any political threats had been identified and terminated.

Their part of the world was calm, and Dr. Kramer liked that just fine.

"Well, Drake, the infection is under control. Next time, wear your shoes when you're outside."

The teenager nodded somberly. He'd been out on the overgrown lawn next to his dorm playing catch. His friend had passed the football to him, but it sailed over his head and tumbled into a higher patch of weeds. He had ripped his heel open on a piece of rebar while retrieving the ball.

The boy's school records showed that he had been given a tetanus booster shot just two years ago, so that wasn't a problem. But the kid hadn't reported the wound for almost a week, and by that time, the foot was swollen and the cut was draining pus. Debridement, antibiotics, and a few heartfelt prayers had saved his foot.

"Yes sir," the kid replied. "Can I start back with my training?"

Kramer smiled. "One more week, Drake."

Chris Newsome, the feed store owner, had a prepper group south of Winter Garden. A couple of months ago, he'd contacted Dr. Kramer and asked for some medical help for one of the people in his group. Afterwards, Newsome stopped by with some fresh beef from his ranch as a payment for Kramer's help. On the way, he'd run across the school full of kids.

Newsome and his ex-military friends presented themselves as larger-than-life characters to the impressionable students. Jack Cunningham, the owner of a local gun store and a former Ranger, was downright intimidating. His arms were as thick as a small tree trunk, and with the warrior tattoos, heavy beard, and wraparound sun glasses, he looked like he'd just stepped out of a Hollywood casting call.

Of the remaining kids left at the school, all but four had begun firearm training. Cunningham stopped by on an almost daily basis and had eventually armed all the young men and women with a black rifle of some sort.

"I'm a squad leader, you know," Drake said with pride. "My team needs me."

Kramer smiled grimly and dismissed the young man.

"It's sad," he said to his wife later. "They're too young to be doing this."

Barb put her arm around her husband and gave him a squeeze. "Old people like us have been saying that for thousands of years. It's always the young ones that pay the price for old people's follies."

Kramer began to clean the room, preparing to disinfect the counters and change the sheet on the exam table.

"Let Caroline do that. I have a surprise for you."

He stopped and gave his wife a questioning look.

"Sergeant Bragg contacted Ed and has some information on Claire!"

"What? He got in touch with her?"

"Yep!" Barb said with glee. "Months of nothing, then Ed says that Bragg is going to relay some news to us tonight after dark."

"Well, I'll be," Kramer replied. "Thank God."

Barb wrapped her arms around her husband's neck. She looked up him and wondered if her face was beaming as brightly as her husband's was. A tear formed in Gerry's eye and his lip began to quiver. He looked down, and she could see his joy.

"I've been so worried." He sighed. "I hope she's alright."

"Me too, babe. Me too."

The rest of the day dragged by; the minutes seemed like hours. But eventually, dusk settle and after dinner the three of them sat in the darkening living room, watching the kaleidoscope of colors from the rays of the setting Florida sun paint themselves on their living room wall.

"You know, I read once that the Florida sunsets get their colors from sand that is kicked up in Africa?".

Barb, lost in thought, turned to her husband and gave him the "I'm calling B.S." look.

"No, really. Claire told me, and I looked it up. The University of Florida did an upper atmosphere study above the peninsula and found sand particles from the Sahara Desert in the stratosphere. They think the sand from desert storms is carried across the Atlantic Ocean."

"Hmm. Fascinating. Any other tidbits of useless information, Mr. Holmes?"

Kramer scoffed. But his wife did have a point; he was full of trivial information. It was a byproduct of his medical training, where even the most insignificant fact or minute anatomic structure had to be memorized. The best physicians tended to be good at remembering unimportant or useless information, so any Trivial Pursuit team needed a Gerry Kramer.

Barb saw her husband's slightly hurt look and jumped up out of her chair. She plopped onto the couch next to him and nestled her head against his shoulder. The early summer heat was becoming oppressive, and their thermometer read ninety-five degrees in the shade earlier that day. The nights were still cool enough to endure, but in a few more weeks, that would change as well.

Barb sighed happily and saw her daughter's disapproving look. She and Gerry had tried to nip Caroline's budding relationship with the young boy next door in the bud, but the young people seemed to find alone time no matter what she did, and Barb was forced to accept the fact that she couldn't watch her youngest daughter every hour of every day. Both her husband and Ed Grafton had given the young man "the talk" about the dangers of childbirth in this environment. Rob knew, in no uncertain terms, that crossing the line would earn him repercussions far greater than a scolding or extra chores. She'd just have to trust Caroline and Rob. There was nothing else she could do.

"Hey Caroline," Barb said, "why don't you go see if Rob wants some dessert? We have fresh strawberries, and I made some cake."

The young girl got a questioning look on her face. "Okay, what's the catch?"

"Yeah, what's the catch?" her husband parroted.

"Nothing. You're old enough to make your own decisions. You know the consequences of your actions."

"What brought this about?" Gerry asked in total confusion.

"Claire. She's alone, far away from us. She always restricted herself. Always studying. She never let herself enjoy life. And I don't want Caroline to suffer too. If Rob makes her happy, then go for it. Just be careful!"

Caroline jumped up and rushed over to her parents. Hugging them both, she thanked them and dashed out into the dusky evening.

"That was quite an about-face," Gerry said, stroking her wife's hair.

"Well, it just seems right."

"I'll never understand you."

"Good. I'm the only one that needs to understand me. You just need to listen and do what I say."

Kramer grunted and patted her head. "Yes ma'am. I live to serve."

They both smiled and watched the deep orange light of sunset morph into a wash of blues and purples.

"I love that African sand," Barb said. "It's like a prism, dancing light on our wall."

"And I love you," Kramer said. "You're my prism, bringing color to my world. Thank you."

Barb smiled. So sweet and sincere. Although she didn't think it was possible until that moment, she fell even more deeply in love with her man. She closed her eyes and sighed.

Time slid by, and they drifted off to sleep. A knock on the door awoke them both some time later, and Barb bolted upright as the light from a half-moon filtered into the room.

"What time is it?" she asked, shaking the cobwebs from her brain. "And where's Caroline? I told her to come back here."

Kramer checked the watch Bragg had given him and was surprised to see that it was after nine p.m. Caroline had left over two hours ago.

Another knock brought them both off the couch. Gerry grabbed a candle from the coffee table, and they both went to answer the door. Barb opened it and saw Ed Grafton and Vernon Bragg standing on the front stoop.

"Mr. Bragg! What a surprise. I thought you were just sending a message."

"Ah, Mrs. Kramer. I thought ya might have some more of that cake you make. I figured I'd bring the message myself and score some of yer cookin'."

Both men had big grins plastered on their faces. Then Barb noticed all the other members of their group crowded on the stoop as well.

"Caroline!" Barb admonished. "I told you to come back home with Rob, not stay there."

"Sorry, Mom," Caroline said with a stupid grin on her face as well.

"What's going on? It must be good news if you're all here. Or is it bad?" Barb asked as her emotions ran the gamut from hope to fear.

"It's good news, Mrs. Kramer." Bragg said as he stepped back, creating a tunnel between all their friend.

Barb struggled to see into the crowd. As she peered into the night, two military men dressed in camouflage fatigues strode forward. Each had a black rifle slung across their chest and were decked out in full battle gear.

"Who are you?" Barb asked.

"Just friends, delivering a message." one of them said. He was smiling too. They stepped apart revealing a thin, muscular woman dressed in military clothes.

"Mom!" Barb heard an achingly familiar voice cry out as her lost daughter materialized from the shadows of the night. "I'm home."

***

Four hours later, after the tears and a well-deserved party concluded, the

Kramers sat in their giant common room with the French doors open, a gentle breeze wafting in from the surrounding countryside.

Caroline and Rob sat on the living room couch, holding hands under a pillow that they had place between them. Barb smiled at their incompetent attempts to hide their PDA while Rachael, a nurse that had accompanied Claire on her trip, dozed off in one of the family room's oversized chairs. Gerry and Claire were seated at the dining room table with Grafton and his men along with Bragg and the two soldiers that brought Claire home. Her tale of their escape from Tennessee was nothing less than remarkable.

After the bombing of the Guardsmen's families, the men of the 278th and the Screaming Eagles of the 101st had decided to break up into small groups. Clustering together would have just invited more airstrikes, and with most of their comrades stranded in Afghanistan when the EMP went off, they were not even close to full strength.

Their new mission, as directed by their acting commanding officer, was to set up insurgent groups throughout the south and east. Claire had joined one such group on their trip from Fort Campbell to central Florida.

The two men who accompanied her were from the remnants of the Tennessee Armored National Guard unit. Other soldiers were nearby, scouring the state in search of patriots that wanted to fight back.

"The kids at the academy are raw," Kramer was saying, "but they're in shape and have had some basic tactical training."

"And they're armed," Grafton added.

"That's a start." Sergeant Dixon said. "I'm not the one to train them, per se, but I'm going to add them to the list of potential recruits. I'll turn them over to the special ops guys that brought us here."

"So Newsome will be by here in six hours?" Specialist Sims asked.

"That's what he said," Bragg replied. "He wants ta talk with you about cordinatin' yer two groups."

The old sergeant had been communicating with Chris's group since the beginning. But like any well-trained forward observer, he never let one group know about the other unless appropriate. It seemed that Bragg had given them a portable Hytera ham radio, just like the one he'd given Kramer only with a different chip that didn't communicate on the same secure frequencies.

"I'll get the Airborne boys here as well. Let them coordinate their own training," Dixon said.

"So, what are your plans?" Ed asked the two military men.

"I guess we'll see if Newsome's group will take us in," Dixon said.

"We sort of feel like a fifth wheel," Sims added. "We're not special ops by any means, but I suppose they could use some more bodies."

"I've been thinking about that," Grafton replied. "With the maintenance experience you boys have, and my equipment and experienced mechanics, we could provide and repair vehicles for the resistance."

Everyone at the table sat silently. It was the first time anyone had said that word out loud. Resistance.

It was one thing to survive, to fight to keep your home and family safe. What Grafton had said crossed the Rubicon. Fighting their own government was treason no matter how corrupt it had become. The unspoken truth was finally out on the table. It was time to fight back.

"Wow. That sounded strange." Grafton admitted after nearly a minute of silence.

"We could provide medical support," Claire added, trying to move the conversation forward. "Rachael and I have treated plenty of trauma cases. With the right equipment and supplies, we could save a lot of lives."

Kramer's face was grim. He was elated to have his daughter back, and the thought of putting her into harm's way once again was unpleasant to say the least. Constant worry had left Kramer tired, a kind of exhaustion that sleep couldn't fix. When he saw his daughter just a few hours ago, a weight he'd been trying to ignore lifted. Now, he felt it starting to settle into place once again.

"How about you, Doc?" Dixon asked Kramer. "You up for the fight?"

Kramer looked at the people surrounding him. Their voices were full of patriotic energy, but he could see a tinge of uncertainty in their eyes. They wanted to believe, but they were waiting for his approval. Even Claire stared at him with anticipation.

"Well," Kramer deadpanned, "It sounds so exciting, doesn't it?"

The others sat back and glanced at each other. This wasn't the answer they'd expected or maybe hoped for. But Gerry Kramer wasn't one to sugarcoat a problem, nor give false hope for a solution. He'd learned that lesson years ago when he had almost given up medicine. Then, he had been saved through counseling and prayer. It was recognizing his limitations that made him the accomplished and revered doctor he'd become. He wasn't about to change that now.

"I know you want to do something," he began, "but I'm not sure you understand what that truly means."

Kramer slowly rose from the table, leaving the others to watch him pace back and forth.

"We've been put into a terrible situation, by an event we had no control over. Now, our own government has gone rogue, crushing our rights and holding our countrymen hostage for some food and a dry place to sleep. We've had our rights taken away, all for a little security."

Several of the others started nodding, and Dixon opened his mouth as if to speak.

"But does that mean we should fight them?" Kramer continued. "Is their way better? If we resist, many of you will end up dead."

Kramer stopped pacing and gazed at each of them in turn. All of them looked shocked, but they still waited for his answer.

"I'm a proud Jew. And we, as Jewish people, know the consequences of a rogue government."

He continued. "Think of it, over a million Armenians in Turkey suffered a similar fate at the hands of the Muslim government there. Many of you are Christians, and tens of millions of your faith were slaughtered under the Communists in Russia and China. And all of these acts of democide were committed in the last hundred years. By some accounts, over one hundred fifty million people were killed by their own government."

He stood over his daughter and put his hands on her shoulders.

"What is the common denominator in all of these atrocities? An all-powerful government, unaccountable to the people. And what is the difference now? We have a Constitution that our military swore an oath to uphold. Not a king nor a president, but the Constitution. I, for one, am not planning on giving that up."

Kramer looked at Dixon and Sims as he finished his speech.

"So my answer is the same as the one I gave when I was commissioned in the Air Force decades ago: I, Gerry Kramer do solemnly swear that I will support and defend the Constitution of the United States against all enemies, foreign and domestic; that I will bear true faith and allegiance to the same; That I make this obligation freely, and without any mental reservations or purpose of evasion, So help me God!"

The table erupted in cheers. All of them leapt up and began to hug and slap each other's backs as they pledged to do the same.

Gerry looked into the living room and saw his wife and youngest daughter standing next to each other, his wife's arm around Caroline's waist. Barbara was smiling and nodding her head, tears streaming down her cheeks. Kramer grinned back. It would have been a lot harder if she hadn't been on board, but thank God she'd seen it his way.

There was no more government of the people. It had become a sick shadow of its former self. Greedy and corrupt men were now in charge, and the blood of tyrants and patriots was about to be spilled. Kramer wasn't going to sit by and let his Constitution be taken away. He'd put up a fight.

The second American civil war was about to begin. However, this time it was without state boundaries. This was going to be a very dirty war. Neighbors would be killing neighbors, and Kramer suspected that assassinations were going to be as much of this war's tactics as frontal assaults and flanking maneuvers.

"We've got a lot to do," Dixon said after the cacophony had died down. "We'll start tomorrow."

"Then let's get some sleep," Kramer said, seeing the sky beginning to lighten as the night gave way to the coming day. "We'd better enjoy our quiet time now while it lasts."

It was going to be a long and brutal war. But what was there else to live or die for but their fellow patriots and a Constitution that reminded them all that they were born a free people, and that no government could take that natural right away.

CHAPTER 25

ORLANDO, FL

*"Justice will not be served until those who are
unaffected are as outraged as those who are."*

— **Benjamin Franklin**

A FEW DAYS FOLLOWING HIS ARRIVAL in Orlando, General Lester received a call from the hospital in Kentucky. His grandson had taken a turn for the worse, his body rejecting his grandmother's marrow. Having intentionally killed off the young boy's own deteriorating immune system in preparation for the transplant, young Bart Lester was living in a sterile tent with no way to fight an infection should he be exposed to one. Somehow, he had still caught a cold. With no white blood cells to battle the relatively mild virus, he was slipping away. Kuris stayed behind to continue their work as the general flew back to be with his family.

"Keep me posted," Kuris barked into the phone at his aide back in Fort Knox. "I want to know everything as it happens. Day or night, you call me. Understood?"

Ferraro felt helpless. Not only did he hurt for his general, but watching the captain struggle with his own impotence over the situation just added to Ferraro's own grief.

"Is there anything I can do, Captain?"

Kuris shrugged. "Not unless you can cure cancer."

"Why don't you come by my apartment tonight? My wife will make you her famous Pernil."

Kuris looked up. The Puerto Rican pork dish held a special place in his heart.

"I have some Medalla on ice," Ferraro added.

The island beer went especially well with the spiced pig. His wife also made a mean black bean and rice combo, and usually topped it off with fried sweet plantains.

"Hell, Ferraro. You had me at Pernil," Kuris quipped.

The lieutenant smiled. "I'll see you at 1800, and bring your appetite."

Ferraro saluted and left to finish his day, leaving Kuris to ruminate about his lack of control over the general's problems. Later, when the long afternoon finally ended, the captain was an emotional wreck. When he showed up for dinner at Ferraro's apartment, he was both troubled and exhausted.

"Captain, you don't look too good," Ferraro said.

"Oh my," Ferraro's wife, Stella, said. "You need to sit down."

"I'm fine," Kuris replied. "But I could use some of that beer."

"The place smells fantastic." Kuris noted as Ferraro's wife came back with a cold beer and a plate of Croquetas de Jamón, a fried ham appetizer.

"Thank you, Captain. Please take a seat," Stella replied.

Kuris and Ferraro sat in the living room. Their top-floor apartment overlooked a local lake. The sun was starting to set in the summer sky, and their west facing apartment's picture window benefitted from its tinted glass.

"It's a beautiful view," Kuris said as they gazed out toward the theme parks.

"The balcony is even better, and with no traffic noise to spoil the experience, we often eat dinner out there. But it's too darned hot now. We probably won't use our outdoor space until November."

"Shame," Kuris replied. "That's another five months."

They both were taking a long draw from their beer bottles when Stella announced that dinner was ready.

"Where are the kids?" Kuris asked.

"Stella's mom's apartment." Ferraro replied. "She lives three floors down. They're spending the night, so we won't have to rush our meal."

Kuris lifted his beer bottle and nodded. "Thanks guys."

The three of them attacked the food, and it was everything Kuris remembered from the last time Ferraro's wife had cooked for him. That had been over a half a year ago, back in Kentucky.

They made small talk, and Kuris slowly began to emerge from his bubble of depression. An hour later, their meal finished and Ferraro's wife busy cleaning her kitchen, the two men hazarded a visit to the apartment's balcony. Sliding the tempered glass door open, a hot rush of humid air hit them. They quickly closed the slider, and sat down in a couple of Rattan patio chairs. Ferraro produced a couple of cigars, and the two men soon were contentedly puffing on the fine Cuban tobacco.

Stella appeared a few minutes later with a couple of snifters of Cognac. Kuris sniffed the inside of the glass after having swirled the amber liquid a few times to admire its legs. The faint smell of orange met his nose.

"Grand Marnier?" Kuris asked as he took a sip of the warm liquid.

"Yeah," Ferraro confirmed. "Nothing like orange in Florida."

"To Florida!" Kuris said as he raised his glass in a toast.

"And the general," Ferraro added, earning him a nod from Kuris.

The two men began conversing as men often do. They bantered about friends, sports, and humorous stories about times long past. It was therapeutic for them both, at least until Stella opened the sliding glass doors.

"It's for you," she quietly said, handing the satellite phone to Kuris.

With a grim nod, the captain put the phone to his ear. "Kuris here."

The captain listened quietly for a moment, then hit a button to disconnect the call. He wandered over to the balcony's wall and stared out at the dark cityscape.

"Captain?" Ferraro asked.

"He's dead," Kuris simply stated. "The general's grandson just died."

Ferraro, unsure what to do, simply put his hand on Kuris' shoulder and held it there. Kuris, for his part, didn't move. Even after the others went back into their apartment, the captain stood immobile, lost in the frustration of not being able to do anything for his general. It was his job to fix things, and he was helpless to make things right.

Eventually, Kuris went back inside. Ferraro and his wife were in the kitchen, holding hands. Kuris shook hands with the lieutenant and gave his wife an appreciative peck on the cheek. And without a word, Kuris left the building and returned to his assigned quarters. He laid in bed and stared all night at the ceiling, planning his revenge on Director Bedford. It was going to be a long and painful day for the DHS administrator when Kuris finally got his hands on the man. He planned to extract justice, and it wasn't going to be swift, nor would it be painless. It would be just what the sniveling coward deserved.

CHAPTER 26

ORLANDO, FL

"There is a tyranny in the womb of every Utopia."

— Bertrand De Jouvenel

THE DAY AFTER THE DEATH of the general's grandson, Nixon hovered over a drone sensor operator as the technician fiddled with the controls of the LoJack GPS locator.

"Well, have you got its position?" Nixon asked.

"It's not steady. The signal is transmitting, but it's shutting itself on and off. Mostly off. I need at least twenty seconds of steady signal to triangulate the source."

Nixon scowled. The Latin gangs they had been using to scare the population into the relocation camps were becoming a liability. They were disobeying or ignoring almost every order they were given. Instead, they were fighting with other gangs over territory or attacking DHS convoys and stealing supplies.

Bedford had ordered their termination, and Nixon had been tasked with executing the plan. The problem was that the gangs knew this territory better than Homeland. They'd also been recruiting at a rapid pace, swelling their ranks even as Nixon tried to hunt them down. They would soon be big enough to challenge DHS's control over the city.

As far as he could tell, the city was being controlled by two factions. The first, an offshoot of the Latin Kings, dominated the southern part of the city, where they ambushed vehicles traveling to and from the airport. Their rival was a white supremacist group based northeast of town. Nixon had been inclined to let the two of them wipe each other out, but recently, the gangs had agreed to an uneasy truce. At least, that's what their DHS G-2 had informed him.

"There!" The technician said. "I've got them."

"Are they moving?" Nixon asked.

"No, they're stationary. Just give it a minute to make sure."

Nixon pressed the send button on his radio microphone, informing his counterpart in Operation Purgatory that they'd be receiving coordinates from the location of the LoJack he'd put among the supplies of a "broken down" truck. The Trojan Horse had been left on the side of the road, a few miles south of the airport.

"No movement. I'm sending the co-ordinates to the drone now."

"Where are they? Give me a cross street," Nixon demanded. "I'm sending my men in to finish the job."

"I doubt there'll be much left to finish," the technician said. "Both Reaper's are carrying two GBU-12s."

"In English, please."

"The two drones are going to hit their target with both of their five-hundred-pound, laser-guided bombs. That's literally a half a ton of explosives. The crater will be the size of a football field."

Nixon still wanted his men to check it out. He wasn't going to risk missing something because he didn't put eyes on the target. An after-action report delivered to Bedford would go a long way towards bringing him and his men back into the director's good graces.

After weeks of unsuccessful missions and mounting supply losses, Bedford had pulled Nixon's men from the Grand Cypress, shunting all of them into a reclaimed Best Western. It was not in a safe zone, forcing Nixon to run a guard schedule to prevent the theft of their vehicles. Bedford had even made them to give up their women, leaving the girls at the Grand Cypress for the director's occasional visit.

Bedford did promise to reconsider the move if Nixon produced results. This was the agent's best shot to do so.

Nixon had matured into the position, at least that's what he told himself. Traditional hit and run tactics that worked on Key Biscayne were a total failure here in Orlando, so he changed tactics

"The signal is coming from a storage facility on Highway 15, about two hundred meters north of Lee Vista Road."

"How long before the bombs hit?"

"They're two minutes out."

Nixon nodded. "This is Reaper," he said to his team. "Coordinates are on Narcoossee Road, two hundred meters north of Lee Vista. Initiate now."

Nixon's team was holding on top of a downtown parking garage, their Blackhawk awaiting the order to take off. The flight time would be about five minutes from his command until they arrived on station.

"Spinning up now, Reaper," the team leader reported.

"Good luck." Nixon said as he terminated the call.

Narcoossee Storage And Rental
Orlando, Fl

Julio Arnal had become the leader of the local Latin Kings after negotiating a deal with DHS to get their brothers out of prison. It didn't hurt that his primary rival had been found shot and disemboweled a day later in an MS-13 style gangland killing. The message had been sent, and so far, no one had challenged his reign.

Over the last six months, he had found that the key to keeping power wasn't through brute force. Anyone could do that. The real key was providing food, comfort, drugs, and women. It was his men's loyalty that kept him in power, and as long as everyone under him was satisfied, he had little to fear.

"Open them!" Julio commanded to his men, who were crowded around the crates they had salvaged a few miles south of the airport. Several of the polyethylene cargo containers and modular storage boxes had some interesting logos painted on their fronts. One of them, the crate he was standing next to, was marked as having liquor and beer inside. Others had manifests stapled to their lids listing hygiene items such as toilet paper and feminine products. There was even a medical supply box.

"*Meira!*" One of the men said, holding up bottle of whiskey.

"See if there is any tequila!" Julio yelled.

As the men tore open the individual cardboard boxes that were stored inside the polyurethane crates, they announced their new treasures. Every member of his ruling council and most of his fighting men were present. It had been a lean few weeks, and this booty was needed badly.

"*Jefe?*" one man called out. "What is this?"

The man held up two small metal boxes with multiple wires running between them. A hole began to form in Julio's stomach as the man brought the thing over to him. He recognized the GPS transmitter, having made his early mark with the Latin Kings stealing cars.

"*Chingado,*" he spat. Turning to his men, he yelled out, "RUN!"

The gangbangers barely had time to hear their leader's warning before the bombs struck. The four GBU-12s struck the ground just yards from the gang leader, effectively disintegrating Julio and his men.

In one stroke, Nixon had effectively decapitated the Latin Kings. Fifteen minutes later, he received confirmation from his men of the mission's success. There had been two survivors, and per Nixon's orders, the DHS team was bringing them to the hospital.

"Get video and gather as much evidence as you can," Nixon commanded the leader of his strike force. "Then bring it to me."

"Copy that, Reaper," the man replied as Nixon terminated the call.

"Perfect!" Nixon said to the drone operators after hearing the report. "I've got some live ones coming in."

Nixon had been studying military torture techniques, including waterboarding and sleep deprivation. Once the two of the prisoners were well enough to take it, Nixon planned on using some enhanced interrogation techniques to gather more intelligence and plan his next move.

Nixon left the ground control station that had recently been installed on the DHS headquarters' grounds and, after meeting his strike team to collect the videos and some key evidence, he reported to Director Bedford's office.

There was a new secretary at the desk. The blonde girl smiled as she escorted the agent into the director's room.

"She's a keeper," Nixon said, as he turned to stare at the secretary's swaying hips.

Bedford gave a frustrated grunt. Since his unfortunate first meeting with the general a few days ago, Bedford had kept his libido in check while at work. The last girl, a spicy Columbian teenager, had been reassigned. *It was a shame*, he thought. *She was rather enjoyable.*

"Yes," Bedford finally replied. "Now what do you want?"

Nixon held up the video camera, displaying the recorder like a kid showing off his Little League trophy. "I think you'll like this."

Bedford took the device and played the recording on the attached LCD screen. The leader of Nixon's crew was narrating as he scanned the devastation, adding his body count estimates to the grisly home movie.

"A little optimistic, isn't he?" Bedford said.

"Maybe, sir." Nixon replied. "But we have two survivors, and one of them confirmed that their leader and his top men were all in the building when it was hit."

Bedford nodded slightly, and Nixon continued. "Also, if you fast forward the recording, you'll see the number of vehicles parked nearby is consistent with the after-action report. We may be off by ten or twenty percent, but the evidence suggests that I—I mean, *we*—took out over a hundred of them."

"This is a good start," Bedford said. "But until I see evidence of your success, you're still at the Best Western."

The agent looked crestfallen. Nixon had thought that this would be good enough to return to the comforts of the resort hotel.

"Look, Travis," Bedford said. "You did great. You're thinking outside the box. Just give it another week, and keep doing what you're doing. You can do this."

"Yes sir."

"Now, get out of here and tell your men that they did a good job."

As Nixon turned to leave, Bedford raised his voice and called a last command. "Travis, why don't you and your men take the day off and head over to the Grand Cypress? You guys could use some R and R. But! It's just for today."

Nixon stopped and turned. "Thanks. The men will appreciate it."

As he turned to leave, the office door opened without an announcement and a squad of soldiers barged into the room. Two of the men grabbed Nixon and pulled him to the side. They frisked him and then shoved him in the corner of the room, holding their M4 rifles on him.

Bedford stood up from the desk. His body immediately began to shake from fear, his eyes wide and mouth open. Two more soldiers grabbed the director, spun him around, and put him against the wall. After checking him for weapons, a sergeant from the group called out the all-clear.

Captain Kuris entered, followed by NSA Assistant director Qualls. She strode confidently into the room and assessed the situation.

"Director Bedford. Or should I say former Director Bedford. I'm here to relieve you of your duties."

"I...I don't understand." Bedford looked at Kuris with wide, pleading eyes. "That was just a misunderstanding the other day. It was a one-off. It'll never happen again."

Kuris looked at the new director and received a "go ahead" nod from her.

"I know it won't happen again," Kuris said. "I'm here to place you under arrest for gross negligence...and murder."

Bedford's eyes bulged. "Murder? Are you talking about those gang-bangers? This is ridiculous!"

"Explain." Qualls said.

Bedford struggled out of the guard's grasp and retrieved the video camera from his desk. "I just ran an operation that eliminated the leadership of the Latin Kings," he said. "Here's the evidence."

Qualls took the camera and looked at Nixon. "Did you have anything to do with this?"

Nixon nodded. "I ran the operation."

"Who planned it?"

Nixon, sensing the shifting power, said, "I did, at the request of Director Bedford."

Qualls nodded. "Good answer. What's your name?"

"Agent Travis Nixon, ma'am."

"Agent Nixon, report back to me in two hours."

"Yes ma'am. Where is your office?"

"You're in it, agent Nixon."

Without missing a beat, Nixon saluted. "Yes ma'am."

Qualls returned his salute and Nixon, aware that he had just dodged a bullet, hurried from the room.

"Captain Kuris, Bedford is all yours," Qualls said.

Two guards grabbed the sniveling man and pulled him out of the room. Kuris followed and closed the door behind him.

Ramona Qualls looked around the room, noticing the obscene artwork and pornographic sculptures, and shook her head.

"Sergeant. I'll be back in ninety minutes. I want this room cleared of all this...," she waved a hand, "...*artwork*."

"Yes ma'am," the former marine replied.

In the hall, a defeated and mortified Bedford could barely stand. Incoherent babbling and the occasional curse were all he could manage.

A short ride later, Kuris placed Bedford in a basement room under one of the high-rise buildings nearby. Once a maintenance room, it was now a holding cell with bare block walls and hanging light bulbs illuminating the dank space. A single chair and table were in the middle of the room, and the guards shoved the obese man into the lone metal chair.

"Bedford," Kuris said. "Look at me."

The former director fought back tears. Snot ran from his nose, and his breathing was shallow with gasps and fits.

"The general gave me control of your fate. Your failures as director and, more importantly, your negligent behavior before the EMP event have brought you here. I am officially charging you with murder for causing a meltdown at the Watts Bar nuclear power plant, which led to the contamination of millions of acres in Tennessee and the death of the general's grandson."

Bedford couldn't understand what Kuris had just told him. "What meltdown? I've never been to Tennessee. You've got the wrong man!"

Kuris didn't react. He didn't even flinch. The captain pulled out a thick file from his leather messenger bag and threw it on the table. Pulling out a set of stapled papers from the file, he laid them on the table and spun them toward Bedford.

"These are orders for the transfer of generators to Orlando from their storage units in Virginia. Are those your signatures?"

Bedford saw the orders and recognized his handwriting on the papers.

"Uh, yeah. That's my signature. But what does that have to do with murder?"

Kuris explained the catastrophic events that came from his illegal reassignment of the equipment, leading to the nuclear disaster that poisoned the general's family.

"General Lester's grandson died because of you. He was only four years old."

"But—"

"We also found four more bodies at the plant. That's FIVE dead because of you."

"I didn't—"

Before Bedford could say more, Kuris grabbed him by the neck and lifted him from the chair.

"You son of a bitch!" Kuris hissed. "You may well have condemned thousands by giving them cancer."

Kuris flung Bedford back in his chair, sending him toppling backward onto the floor. Bedford' sniveling returned as he struggled to stand back up.

"You...you can't do this to me! I know people. I demand you give me a sat phone, now! I have rights!"

"Under the Patriot Act, and with the president initiating martial law, you have no rights. You've been classified as an enemy combatant and an environmental terrorist. Bedford, I own you." Kuris slammed his fist on the table. "I OWN YOU!"

A knock on the door interrupted Kuris' tirade.

"ENTER!" Kuris commanded.

One of the guards came in and handed the captain a satellite phone. Kuris took it, and both he and the guard left the room, leaving Bedford in an expanding puddle of his own urine.

Ten minutes went by before the door opened once again. Kuris strode into the room, his face pale and eyes burning with anger.

"Well, Bedford. You seem to have another problem. I just received word that the general's other grandchild, his last one, is in a coma. Her immune system is shutting down, and they don't have a match for a bone marrow transplant."

Bedford whimpered and shook his head. "I didn't mean it. I didn't know. You have to believe me."

Kuris walked up to the broken man and grabbed Bedford's chin, lifting his face so he could look into the man's eyes.

"You are vermin. You are scum. And you are a dead man."

Kuris slapped Bedford's face and spun out of the room. Bedford sat, his brain frozen in fear as spittle dripped from his forehead and down his puffy, red face. The condemned former DHS director didn't move even as the overhead lights were extinguished, leaving him in total darkness.

***

Ramona Qualls returned to her new office precisely two hours later. The room, which had felt dirty and seedy when she had first entered it, was now bright and clean. The heavy curtains that had covered the room's picture windows were gone, letting in the afternoon sunlight. The pictures and sculptures had been removed, along with the heavy furniture that the former director had stolen.

Qualls sat in the standard-issue government chair and scanned her new metal desk. The room was cold, sterile and functional. She liked it. There was nothing to distract her from the job at hand.

She had heard herself referred to as the "dragon lady." She had to admit it applied to her. Qualls was the daughter of an Army colonel and his Vietnamese wife. If you asked her to describe herself, she'd say that she was strong woman who used any means necessary to get what she wanted. Deceit, domination and an easy willingness to use her power dovetailed with the legend of the dragon lady. Her ebony skin, combined with Asian eyes, gave her the exotic look that had attracted the right men in her early years of her ascension to power. A few nights under the sheets with a couple of married supervisors gave her the leverage to advance quickly. After that, she'd done it on her own by using her power without hesitation and with brutal efficiency.

Orlando was a step in the right direction for her. Leaving the secret world of the NSA and joining the political realm would allow her to advance toward her ultimate goal. She wanted to be a United States Senator and, depending on her luck, she'd run for president. At forty years of age, it was all within her reach. She was attractive, smart, and ruthless. Nothing was going to stop her now.

Nixon arrived to see her right on time. He advanced to her desk and saluted with precision and style. Qualls studied the tall young man and admired his physique. *Not bad*, she thought, as she returned his salute.

"Agent Nixon reporting, ma'am."

"Take a seat, Agent," Qualls said as she produced the video recorder from a drawer in her desk. "So, tell me about Purgatory."

Nixon reviewed the after-action report and detailed the operation. When he was finished, Qualls nodded.

"So, Agent Nixon. Who was responsible for Operation Purgatory?"

"Ma'am. Director... I mean former Director Bedford gave me the green light."

"That's not what I'm asking. Who came up with this idea? Who planned the job?"

"I did, Ma'am."

"Bedford doesn't have the imagination for anything like this. His brains were between his legs."

Nixon sat stoically, earning more points from the new director.

"I like you, Agent Nixon. You're creative and ruthless. Qualities I need for the job."

"Yes ma'am."

"And you know when to talk and when not to. That's a rare quality, to be able to know when to shut up."

Nixon nodded but said nothing. Qualls looked him over once again. It was nice to see someone else that could do what they needed to, apparently without hesitation and with no moral fences. She'd read about the harem he'd kept at a local resort. That didn't bother her too much. He didn't flaunt it like Bedford had. Nixon just took what he wanted and didn't feel the need to show it off to the rest of the world. He'd followed vague orders from Bedford and, through guile and imagination, he'd managed to eliminate a huge threat to her rule.

Qualls began to feel a stirring that she hadn't felt in a long time. The new assignment had put her on a path to the ultimate position of power, and it excited her. She could smell the agent's earthy sweat and fell his animalistic aura. He was a kindred soul and she liked it.

"How about dinner tonight? I'd like your input on staff changes. You could help me weed out any undesirables."

Nixon had already been struck by the new director's beauty. She was older than any woman he'd been attracted to before, but her eyes and skin were oddly erotic. But it was her powerful presence that had really gotten his attention. She was dangerous as well as beautiful, and that excited Nixon as well. He would have to be careful with this one. Ultimately, the challenge to mix it up with the new director was too powerful to ignore.

"I'd be honored, Director Qualls."

"Eight o'clock, then. You are dismissed, Agent Nixon."

With that, Nixon rose and snapped a crisp salute. He left the room, well aware that she was watching him leave. After closing the door, he felt his face flush when he realized that he now knew how women felt as he leered at them from behind. Strangely, it felt both exciting and demeaning at the same time.

Later that evening, as the moon rose over the city, Nixon stared out of the living room panoramic windows of Quall's apartment. Servants had just removed the last of the dishes, and he was enjoying a snifter of brandy while the director freshened up in the bedroom.

The blue-tinted moonlight bathed the tops of the buildings but created purplish black shadows that enveloped the lower floors and street. It almost looked like the top halves of the buildings were floating in a dark ocean.

"Do you like the view?" Qualls asked as she returned, now dressed in a black maxi dress. Its neckline and spaghetti straps exposed her shoulders.

"The view is incredible," he replied with a smile. "And the city skyline is nice as well."

Qualls smiled back at him, and Nixon thought she may have just blushed a bit. But by the time she retrieved her own snifter, she had returned to the in-control woman that he'd been watching all night. She sat down on the couch and invited Nixon to join her.

She handed him a folder. "Look over these names and give me your opinion."

So, it's business, he thought as he took a seat next to Qualls and opened the folder.

She had a remarkably accurate package of the top thirty or so agents that had worked under Bedford. Nixon saw that his own file was missing but didn't let on that he had noticed that omission.

The files were broken down into three groups. A green sticker indicated a positive review and likely retention. The red group were those who she was going to let go or, in some cases, have arrested for gross negligence or theft. The third group, marked in yellow, caught Nixon's eye. He immediately recognized one name in particular.

"I agree on almost all of these assessments," Nixon said after looking over the files for the better part of fifteen minutes. "You have two files I'd reclassify. The first is Schneiderman. You have him in the red stack. I'd take into account the trouble he'd had with Bedford. Most of the poor reports are from the director himself because Schneiderman objected to the former director's predilection for young girls. Bedford took every opportunity to bury the man."

"I hadn't heard that," Qualls said. "I appreciate your input."

"The second person is John Drosky," Nixon said as he appraised Qualls for a reaction.

Without his own folder present, Nixon had no idea if the Qualls knew about their feud. He needed to tread lightly here, because if he unfairly condemned Drosky, it would look like an act of vengeance. On the other hand, Drosky was a jerk, and having him removed would be deliciously sweet.

"Agent Drosky had been in charge of Bedford's personal protection detail," Nixon began. "Now, I don't know if you are aware of it, but he and I have had problems in the past."

Nixon saw a flash of something briefly pass over Qualls face. *She knew. I'm glad I brought it up and got ahead of it.*

"Some of that goes back to our OPD days. I was on the SWAT team and he was a patrolman. For some reason, we never got along."

Nixon put the file down on the coffee table and sat back as if pondering how to proceed. The self-reflection was all an act, given that he had been planning on stabbing Drosky in the back since she had invited him to dinner. After a heavy sigh, Nixon spoke.

"The thing is, all those girls that Bedford assaulted? Drosky sat back and let it happen."

Qualls remained quiet, her demeanor calm and face stoic.

"You see," Nixon continued, "my men and I have women we live with. Those ladies are there by choice, not by force."

"That's debatable," Qualls replied.

"I know how it looks," Nixon said. "But it's true. Ask any of them. They are free to go as they please. We don't force them to do anything they don't want to."

"In exchange for food and a safe place to live?"

"Was it any different before the darkness?" Nixon argued. "How many women do you know that slept their way into money or status?"

Qualls briefly looked unsure of herself as Nixon made that point. He instinctively picked up on her reaction. It meant that she had engaged in some tit for tat in her rapid rise to power. Nixon sensed an opening and stood up as well. Sliding behind the new director, he gently placed his large hand on her smooth, bare shoulder. He felt her quiver at his touch.

"Power and money are as attractive to most women as beauty is to most men. It's just the way it is. Anyone, man or woman, that is open to that truth will live a happy and prosperous life."

He'd just given the director absolution for being attracted to the power and doing what she had to in her pursuit of it.

He put his left hand on her hip and stared over her head and out onto the night skyline. She drew in her breath at his touch, and he knew he had her.

"Drosky should be removed. I have it on good authority that he helped procure under-aged girls for the director to molest. No one should be allowed to turn a blind eye to that."

Qualls turned and faced the tall man. Her breathing was rapid, and her eyes told Nixon that he'd won. He pulled her to him and sealed the deal with a long, passionate kiss.

Drosky's finally out of my life, he thought with a smile. *And tonight is going to be a great night!*

CHAPTER 27

ORLANDO, FL

"You only have power over people as long as you don't take everything away from them. But when you've robbed a man of everything, he's no longer in your power—he's free again."

— Aleksandr Solzhenitsyn

TWO DAYS AFTER HER LIAISON with Nixon, Qualls signed the order to have Agent Drosky arrested. He'd been transferred to patrol following Bedford's arrest, and he and Bru were halfway through their shift when the radio came to life.

"What do they want?" Bru said as he picked up the radio. "Agent 437, receiving."

"Agent 437, is Agent 283 with you?"

"Yes, we're both here."

"Agent 283, return to headquarters immediately and report to your shift sergeant."

"Copy that. Returning at once."

Bru put the transmitter back in its cradle and gave Drosky a questioning look.

"Don't look at me," he said with a shrug.

The men drove their M-ATV back to DHS headquarters and parked just a few spaces down from where Drosky had left little Bree's body those many months ago. He glanced at the spot where he'd deposited the tiny corpse and shivered.

"I'll meet you in the cafeteria," Bru said. "It's almost four, so I doubt we'll be sent back out."

"Sure," Drosky replied. "See you there."

Drosky turned in his weapons and spare ammunition to the armory and went directly to the shift sergeant's office. After a quick knock on the door, he walked into the crowded room. The moment he did so, two pairs of hands grabbed his arms and pinned them behind his back. He felt zip-ties cinch around his wrists.

"Agent John Drosky," said the shift sergeant. "You are under arrest for gross negligence and conduct unbecoming of a federal employee."

He'd heard perps complain that they were in pain as they were handcuffed. Now, being on the receiving end of an arrest, he could literally feel their pain. His shoulders felt like they were a half an inch from being dislocated, and his hands were already going numb.

He wasn't read his rights. With martial law in effect, the rules had been thrown out the window. He said nothing as he was dragged out of the room and taken to the building's holding cells. The only saving grace was that most of his friends were out on patrol, so there wasn't anyone else being held at the time to see his shame.

The agents that escorted him to the cell cut his wrists free and backed out of the room. As the metal door clicked shut and the electronic lock bolted in place, Drosky rubbed his wrists and sat down on the padded bench. Confused and a bit frightened, he sat back and tried to think of what he could have done to deserve his incarceration. After a few minutes, he figured out why he was sitting in the old OPD holding cell: Travis Nixon.

It was just gossip at first, but Natasha confirmed that Nixon had spent the night with the new director. And now that Bedford had been arrested, there was no more intelligence to gather, so Drosky's purpose with DHS was gone. Unfortunately, he'd underestimated the speed of Nixon's influence and now he sat in a holding cell because of that miscalculation.

Yesterday, he had told Bru everything about their espionage ring. The new director was thinking of arresting Bedford's wife. There was no way that Bru would allow that to happen, and if they didn't take Bru and Tanya with them, his partner would likely end up dead.

They had all been planning on bugging out that weekend, which was just a few days away, but it was obviously a few days too late. They were supposed to travel north to Mike's family's home in Sanford. But now fate would send him to wherever it wanted, and Drosky had little hope that his final destination was going to be a good one.

CHAPTER 28

"Revenge, the sweetest morsel to the mouth that ever was cooked in hell."

— **Walter Scott**

As Drosky sat in the holding cell, Captain Kuris was entering former director Bedford's basement prison cell. For two days, he'd been grilling the man about the charges that had been levied against him. Beyond his culpability in the radiation poisoning of the general's family and the radioactive poisoning of hundreds of miles of Tennessee countryside, charges of rape and graft were being added.

The first day, Bedford had denied his culpability, but now he was in the bargaining stage.

"Captain Kuris, please listen," he begged. "I've got treasures stashed away that the government will never find."

"I'm not interested in your bribes," Kuris said.

"Why not? This won't last forever and the rest of the world is untouched and waiting for us. I've got enough gold hidden away to buy a small country and everyone in it. We could be kings!"

"Bedford, I'm tired of this. Now about this woman." Kuris brought out a picture of a young Latino girl that had been plucked out of the Fairground's female population. She'd been missing for four months and last seen being taken to Bedford's office.

"Damn it! Why won't you listen to me?" Bedford yelled. He calmed himself and continued, "Who cares about a little slut like that? We could have any woman we want with my gold. Our gold, Captain."

Kuris's anger almost got the best of him. He clenched his fists under the table.

"Yes!" Bedford said, mistaking Kuris' silence for thoughtful consideration. "I have a boat. A yacht, really, and we can be in South America within the week."

Kuris was about to beat the man down when there was a knock on the door. As Kuris stepped outside to talk, Bedford sat up hopefully. The young captain was considering the bribe! He started planning their route to Florida's west coast, where his gold and catamaran yacht waited.

Captain Kuris left the prisoner's room and took that satellite phone from the DHS agent.

"Captain Kuris, this is Captain Ferrant," said the voice on the other end of the line.

Kuris got a sinking feeling in his stomach. Ferrant was the general's aide while he was still stuck here in Orlando. The call couldn't be good if the general wasn't the one to reach out.

"Yes?" Kuris hesitantly replied.

"I regret to inform you that the general's granddaughter passed away just an hour ago."

Kuris almost dropped to the ground. The general's whole life had been tied up in those kids.

"There's more," the major said. "The general's wife had an *accidental* overdose of sleeping pills. She's in a coma now herself. They don't know if she's going to make it."

Almost ten seconds went by without a response.

"Kuris, are you there?"

"Yes, I'm here." Kuris replied, his mind reeling and emotions boiling.

"Are you alright?"

"No, I'm not alright. The son of a bitch that did this is getting three meals a day while he tries to bribe me to let him go. I'm having trouble holding back."

After a pause, the captain replied, "Kuris, I don't know if the general can go through a trial. Reliving the deaths of his grandkids and his wife's overdose are going to tear him up."

"What are you saying?"

"It's up to you how to handle Bedford, Captain Kuris. His fate is totally in your hands."

Kuris understood, and was glad that he had been freed from his leash.

"I'll take care of it. You can count on me."

"I know, Kuris. You are family as far as the general is concerned. Do the right thing."

The captain disconnected the call, and Kuris turned the phone back over to the agent.

"Go get Bedford's dinner," he told the guard at the door. "Make it something good. I'm going to try to bribe that fat man."

The agent nodded and left Kuris alone in the basement.

Twenty minutes later, the guard returned with a plastic tray. A dinner of flank steak and baked potato sat under a cloche, steam venting through the single hole in its top. It smelled divine.

As he stepped off the last of the stairs, a single gunshot rang out from the prisoner's room. The guard pitched the tray onto a nearby table and, with rifle up at ready, he flung open the door.

Captain Kuris stood in the room, his service pistol drawn and smoke wafting from the barrel.

Bedford was on the ground. The former director stared lifelessly at the ceiling, a perfect hole in the middle of his forehead. His brains were plastered across the beige concrete wall behind him. Blood and chunks of tissue were slowly dripping down to the ground, mixing with the hairy fragments of the man's skull.

"What happened?" the guard asked, lowering his rifle.

Kuris holstered his .45 caliber handgun. "He tried to escape."

He stalked out of the room and picked up the tray from the table where the guard had dropped it. Steam was slowly rising from the dead man's dinner. He lifted the lid and picked up a perfectly cooked slice of meat. Taking a bite, he nodded his approval.

"That's good," he said. Kuris turned to the stunned guard. "Have that cleaned up. I'll have a report for you to sign in the morning. Make sure you are at my office tomorrow at 0800."

The guard stared at the captain, then turned to stare at the dead man's corpse once again.

"Do you understand?" Kuris barked.

"Yes sir!" the guard said as he recovered enough to reply. As Kuris turned to leave, he asked, "Sir, what do I do with his body?"

"Send it to the dump," Kuris replied. "There's no one who'll want to claim it."

And with that, Kuris turned and left the basement, taking the plate of food with him. It would be a shame to let it go to waste.

CHAPTER 29

HOLDING CELL, DHS HEADQUARTERS
ORLANDO, FL

THE NEXT DAY, DROSKY SAT in his cell, waiting for his captors to take him away. The night had been miserable, with no bed to sleep in. He had a toilet and sink, and at least the bastards were feeding him. But they weren't making his stay pleasant.

As he lay back on the thinly padded bench he'd been provided in lieu of a cot, he heard a sound outside his door. He rose and crept to the wire-reinforced glass window and peered out.

Bru's smiling face appeared on the other side. The bolt clicked open and the metal door swung open. His partner stood there, holding Drosky's tactical gear.

"Room service," Bru deadpanned.

Drosky stepped into the hallway as his partner helped him into his plate carrier and battle belt.

"It's good to see you," Drosky said as he clipped his belt around his waist.

Bru handed Drosky his Glock with a grin. He started down the hall toward an open door made of metal bars. Drosky jogged to catch up. As they went through another security door, Drosky saw a body on the floor of a small room where security monitors showed a now empty cell.

"Is he..." Drosky started to ask.

"No, *she's* not dead," Bru said looking at the downed agent. "But she's hogtied and ready for the market."

Drosky grunted out a laugh as they exited the area, leaving the penal part of the building behind. The two men stopped at an intersection where the main corridor met their hallway. It was mid-morning, and there were a few agents going about their business. He was a known prisoner, and being recognized now would be a fatal problem for them both.

As Drosky and Bru hovered in a recessed doorway, waiting for the hallway to clear, an agent looked up from her desk in a nearby office and saw the two men across from her. As a good agent should do, she picked up her house phone and dialed the main desk.

"This is Agent Avella in room 142. I want to report that a prisoner has escaped."

Unaware of the impending disaster, Bru leaned out and after about a minute, saw that the hallway was finally clear.

"Let's go," he said, and the two men beat feet down the corridor toward the side entrance where Bru had left their M-ATV. The pair rushed through the double doors and out onto the short sidewalk.

"STOP RIGHT THERE!" a voice called out.

Bru and Drosky froze. Not twenty yards away, a HUMVEE was surrounded by four soldiers armed with M4 rifles.

"Shit, I'm sorry John," Bru said as he put his hands on his head and dropped to his knees. Drosky followed suit, and the four men advanced on them, rifles drawn down on them and fingers on triggers.

"Well! What do we have here?"

Drosky recognized that voice. Travis Nixon stood up from behind the HUMVEE. The cocky agent slowly strode up to the pair, savoring each step as it brought him closer to his enemy.

"Armed escape? That's a capital offense, Agent Drosky," He crowed.

"Blow me, asswipe," Bru shouted.

Nixon snickered and cuffed Bru across the face. The agent bent but didn't break.

"You still hit like a girl," Bru taunted. "You always were a pussy."

Nixon's rage flared, but as he went to swing again, Bru dropped to his side and brought his right leg up and kicked Nixon in the groin.

The bully dropped to his knees as his stomach muscles spasmed and the wind left his lungs. One of the four guards clocked Bru with the butt of his rifle a moment later, sending him to the ground. To Bru's credit, he made no sound while Nixon whined and choked on his own spittle.

When he was able to stand, Nixon brushed off his clothing and walked back toward the building. He paused at the double doors that led inside.

"As soon as I'm gone, shoot them." The four men gave him a confused look, and Nixon sighed. "They're trying to escape. Just shoot them!"

"Uh, yes sir," one of them replied.

A few seconds after the double doors closed, Nixon heard over twenty rounds being fired. With the pain in his groin slowly receding, he began to walk with more authority. Several agents rushed by him in response to the gunfire.

Perfect. He thought to himself. *Witnesses saw me inside the building when those two were shot. Can't blame me for that.*

Nixon strolled down towards the cafeteria and grabbed a coffee. Sitting by himself at one of the many tables, he heard some of the agents talking as they entered the room.

"That was crazy," one of them said. "They never had a chance."

Nixon smiled. It was finally over.

"I'm freaked," the other one said. "They were shot right outside the building! I mean, that's where we park."

"Who could get that close?"

Nixon was confused. Why would the death two escaped prisoners elicit this kind of response?

"Excuse me," he said. "What just happened?"

"Four agents were just killed. Shot in the parking lot!"

"Four?" Nixon asked. "Not two?"

"That's what I said," the man replied.

Nixon leapt from his chair and sprinted down the hall. He pushed his way through the throng of agents near the double doors. Once outside, he couldn't believe what he saw. His men were lying in a pool of their own blood, each with multiple bullet wounds including at least one head shot.

He staggered back to the cafeteria to collect himself. *If I blame the men for acting without him, that may work*, he thought.

"Crap. Drosky has more lives than a cat," he said to no one in particular.

***

Five minutes earlier, as Bru and Drosky waited for the bullets to strike, they heard the distinctive high-pitched crack of a .556 round. The both tensed, waiting for the lead to tear into them, when the fusillade of fire suddenly stopped. Bru glanced at his friend and found him staring back, both of them alive and uninjured.

"Move it!" someone shouted.

Drosky looked down the road and saw Big Mike and his battle buddy Cynthia, both with smoking rifles in their hands.

He and Bru ran to the waiting HUMVEE. Within seconds, the beast was off, careening down Hughey Street. Turning west, they drove along streets that were littered with abandoned cars and the street garbage of a dead city.

"How?" Drosky yelled over the roaring engine.

"How do you think?" Mike replied from the passenger's seat.

Drosky smiled. "Natasha?"

"Hell, John, she knows everything."

"What about you?" Drosky asked their driver. Cynthia tore through the city streets, expertly weaving around the obstacles.

"I'm done," Cyn replied. "We're getting help now from outside the city. Things are going kinetic. I'll explain later."

"We're heading to Sanford," Mike said with a grin.

"About time," Bru called out from the back seat. "What about Tanya?"

"She's safe for now. Beth will have to get her out when she can."

They rumbled up Route 441. The wide road was a major artery that fed the city from the north. There were no trees or roadside structures tall enough to hide their progress from any overhead eyes.

"Hold on!" Cynthia shouted as she careened their vehicle onto a side street. The street, also called Orange Blossom Trail, ran parallel to a commuter and freight train tracks.

"Up there!" Mike yelled, pointing to a two-lane street that cut into an older residential neighborhood. Taking the turn too fast, they jumped over the elevated tracks and briefly went airborne.

Mike grabbed onto his seat as if he might fall out of the HUMVEE. "Woah! This ain't a Blackhawk!"

"What's the rush? We're at least a couple of miles from HQ," Bru said.

"We need to put some space between us and them," Cyn said as she spun the steering wheel and ran through two front yards to avoid a series of stalled vehicles that were blocking the road. "They've got eyes in the sky now."

The HUMVEE slammed over a small retaining wall as they swerved back onto the pavement.

"How do you know that?" Drosky asked as they cut across another yard and onto a different side street. The zigzag pattern was moving them steadily north and east. Eventually, they would have to cross the interstate. With almost a half a mile of open space from one side of the expressway to the other, it would be their area of greatest vulnerability.

"You aren't our only asset inside DHS," Cyn replied as she spun onto a brick street that was lined by ancient oak trees. She slowed down near an intersection. With a confused look, she turned to the others.

"I need some help here. John, you were a beat cop. Which way do we go?"

Drosky hadn't been keeping up with the street signs as his body was used as a pinball by their aggressive driver. "What's that cross street?" he asked.

"We're on Westmoreland and that's, uh, Yale."

"Let's use Par Street to cut under I-4. There's plenty of cover getting there, and that way we'd be going under the interstate instead of over it," Drosky said.

He directed Cyn, leading her through the old neighborhoods and keeping their vehicle on as many tree-lined streets as possible. With the cluttered and blocked roads, it took about fifteen minutes to make it to the Par Street underpass.

They waited nearby under an old gas station's overhang, not a hundred meters from the interstate. They were hidden from above, giving them some time to plan their journey. After everyone had put in their two cents, they decided to follow Drosky's suggestion to cut through Winter Park and Maitland, then use the neighborhoods beyond to wind their way north of town. It was going to be an arduous trip, with white supremacist gangs standing in their way. But being discovered by DHS carried a far grimmer fate. They could shoot back at the gangs, but they were helpless against the missiles from a helicopter or drone.

Cyn accelerated out from under the cantilevered roof and turned left on Par Street. Less than a minute later, they were driving through an older residential neighborhood with streets named after various mid-western states.

"Get us to Minnesota Avenue, just up there at the stop sign, and stop under that oak tree," Drosky said, pointing up the street.

Cyn pulled up to the shaded area and turned to the other three. "This is where it gets dicey," she said. "From here on out, it's very commercial and very wide open. We have to decide right now: Do we weave through Winter Park or blast up 17/92 and take our chances?"

Mike frowned. "I saw the latest intel map of the area, and it's all gangs through Winter Park. I don't see us driving through there without taking some serious gunfire."

"I agree. But all of us need to make this decision," Cynthia replied.

"I trust Mike," Drosky said.

"You guys just saved our asses back there. You got my vote," Bru added.

"Alright, then. Orlando Avenue it is," Cyn said.

"I've got the turret," Bru said as he started to climb through the portal above them.

"I wish we had a 50," Cyn added, decrying the lack of a mounted machine gun. "I'd feel a lot better about this run."

"Hold up for a sec," Drosky said, pointing across the street to a fenced-in industrial park. "Pull in over there behind the pet care store."

Cynthia gave him a strange look but accelerated into the abandoned parking lot. Drosky jumped out of the HUMVEE, jogged over to the building, and found an open door. A minute later, a metal garage door lifted on the side of the building and Drosky waved his friends over. Cyn pulled up and into the open bay, where he was holding a big sack of sand.

"My parents boarded our dog here once, and I remembered that they had a sandy play area in the back parking lot. They used to let the animals poop and pee in it."

"Yeah?" Bru said. "What of it?"

Cyn chuckled and grabbed a fifty-pound sack. She heaved it over to the side of the vehicle. "No way to strap these on the outside, is there?"

"I don't think so," Drosky replied. "I doubt there's netting here, but we can put them inside. It'll give us some ballistic protection. A hell of a lot better than these flimsy doors."

Within minutes, the inside of the HUMVEE was stacked with bags of sand. It made the already uncomfortable ride even more so, but it was a good trade-off. The sandbags would stop just about any bullet. Other than a 50-caliber strike, they'd be safe.

"Well, that was special!" Cynthia muttered after having to crawl across the rear storage area and through the back window of the vehicle and then over two sets of sharp-edged military seats. It was impossible to open any of the front passenger doors without having the stacks fall out.

"Is there a problem, ma'am?" Mike sarcastically replied.

"Not my problem you're a freak." she shot back, making fun of Mike's giant frame.

Mike grunted as he squeezed into the back seat.

"Need help?" Drosky asked his friend.

"Nah. This ain't nothin'." Mike effortlessly pulled the remaining fifty-pound bags of sand up against the back seat area, finishing their bulletproof barrier.

"Everyone locked and loaded?" Cyn called out.

Receiving three positive replies, she hit the starter and backed the HUMVEE out of the loading dock. With her elbows hitting the bags of sand to her left and Drosky to her right, Cynthia spat multiple curses as she awkwardly spun the steering wheel to navigate them back onto the main road.

Finally, they broke out of the residential area and turned onto the main northbound artery. State highway 17/92 ran from Orlando all the way north to Sanford. In the time before "the darkness," it would have been a congested—but direct—drive to get to Mike's stomping grounds. But today, it was nothing more than a trash-littered slice of asphalt, with burned out and looted vehicles peppering the road. There were no straight lines anymore, the EMP had seen to that.

DHS Headquarters
Ground Control Station

"Dammit!" Nixon yelled at the sensor control officer. "Why can't you find them?"

"They're out there. It's only been ten minutes since we got on station."

After finding his men shot dead instead of Drosky and his worthless partner, Nixon sprinted to the drone's control station. With a fiber optic umbilical cord snaking its way into the building's core, it provided instant communication to one of the city's two Predator remote vehicles. A quick call to Ramona Qualls confirmed his request, and then the remote-controlled flying tank turned gracefully in the west Orlando sky fifteen minutes after Drosky and Bru had hopped into the waiting HUMVEE.

"What do you have on board?" Nixon asked.

"Two five-hundred-pound Mark 92s," the sensor control officer said as he continued to manipulate the drone's cameras.

"That should do it," Nixon said. "But what's taking so long?"

"Sir, we aren't even sure they went north."

"Yes, we are. They have enough information about our troop deployment to know that the north is their best bet. It's a no-man's land. They'll take their chances with the gangs before they try and run a DHS roadblock."

"Then they know we'll be looking for them with the drone." The pilot said.

"Of course, but they don't have a choice. They have to keep moving, at least if they want to live. They know that the countryside is their safest bet, and north is the most secure route. Just keep looking."

"Hey, to the left" the sensor operator yelled. "Vector north 20."

The pilot banked the drone, now at an altitude of over three thousand feet, and levelled out parallel with Interstate 4.

"There. Got 'em!" The sensor operator pointed at a moving HUMVEE careening up 17/92.

"They're all over the place," the pilot noted as the HUMVEE swerved at high speeds around the stalled vehicles.

"We'll have to do a low-level run," the pilot said. "Let's set it up."

The sensor control officer began to tap commands into his keyboard, and information streamed back at them, providing the crew the necessary calculations to align their craft for the kill.

The pilot turned and banked, bleeding off airspeed to allow the giant craft to slowly descend. As their drone settled into a straight northern track up Route 17/92, their target shot past Lee Road, just at the southern border of Maitland.

"Ten seconds!" the pilot said.

As they began their final run, the drone's computer received confirmation of its release order, freeing the crew to drop its ordinance.

"On my mark. Three. Two. One. Release!"

The aircraft, flying at five hundred feet, dropped its bombs toward the fleeing vehicle. Just one of those bombs would be enough to obliterate their target, but two was always better than one, at least when it came to blowing things up.

The Nixon and the RPA crew watched excitedly as the onboard cameras recorded their bombs' flight. It took less than two seconds before two bright plumes ignited, temporarily washing out the video feed.

"BAM!" Nixon shouted, pumping his fist into the air.

Highway 17/92

"There's Lee Road," Drosky announced. They swerved around a bunch of cars that had been abandoned in the intersection, several of them having smashed into each other, creating a twisted mass of plastic and metal.

"There we are! And no shots fired," Bru shouted from the turret, pointing at a train trestle that passed over the highway. "That's the city of Maitland just on the other side of the overpass."

"We'll get off this road and cut north through the neighborhoods." Cyn said, smiling. "I can't believe we've made it."

Bru was leaning down into the cab to say something, when their world exploded. The light and noise were unbearable, but nothing compared to the compressive wave of energy that threw the five-thousand-pound vehicle end over end, punching the four occupants with a concussive force that sent several tons of dirt, wood, and iron into the air.

By the time the mangled HUMVEE had settled on the ground, it had cartwheeled three times and ended upside down, surrounded by hundreds of pounds of mangled train trestle and earth. Shrapnel peppered its thin walls, while the top of the heavy machine had been crushed a foot or more into the cab. No sound came from the four-wheel drive transport, other than the squeaking of tires as they slowly rotated to a stop.

CHAPTER 30

DHS HEADQUARTERS

"People generally see what they look for, and hear what they listen for."

— Harper Lee, To Kill a Mockingbird

NIXON LEFT THE GROUND CONTROL station with a smile on his face. Not only had he finally gotten rid of Drosky, but leaving the claustrophobic room for the summer air felt oddly invigorating.

"Sir, Director Qualls asked that you report to her office immediately," one of the female agents said.

"Thank you, but I need a ride over."

"I'll take care of it for you," The young woman said, practically purring as she spoke.

"Very good, Agent…"

"Vicanti. Mia Vicanti." She smiled.

"I would appreciate it, Mia."

"Anytime, Agent Nixon. I've seen you before at the tower. I live on the twelfth floor."

"I have an apartment there, but I've not been by in a while. I'll look you up, next time I'm there."

"Your ride will be waiting at the front door in five minutes." She sashayed away, her hips continuing their conversation with an obvious sway and slight shake.

After grabbing a coffee in the cafeteria, Nixon found his driver and was at Qualls' office within a few minutes.

"Success?" she asked after Nixon reported and gave his required salute.

"Absolutely. We got them. Drosky, his partner, and whoever killed our men."

Nixon noticed that the director still looked pensive, her lips tightly pressed together, as she began to scan papers on her desk. Breaking protocol, he walked around her workstation and squatted down next to his new lover.

"What's wrong, Ramona? You don't look too happy."

"How's your anti-gang work going up north?"

"Fine. But it's only been about a week."

Nixon looked at the papers and saw AARs from Atlanta. "What's going on in Georgia?" he asked after Qualls failed to respond to his presence.

"It seems some Marines are mounting an offensive against the government."

"What? Marines follow orders. How is this possible?"

Qualls looked up at Nixon, a hint of fear in her eyes. That, more than any words she could have said, told him all he needed to know.

"Seems they don't like what our president is demanding of them. They've pushed into Buckhead and took out a company of agents. It was a slaughter."

"My God," was all that Nixon could say. "What does that mean for us?"

"We have to prepare for an insurgency," Qualls replied. "This may just be the start."

"How can I help?"

Qualls just sat there, uncharacteristically silent, tapping her fingers on her desk.

"I don't know," she finally said. "But the first thing we need to do is take care of the immediate problem. We need to get the white supremacists out of the city."

"Well, I'll need more people to make that happen. I've baited a bunch of traps in Winter Park and Maitland. I'll have to get further north into Casselberry and Altamonte Springs to cover their entire area."

Qualls sighed. "Whatever you need."

"Trust me," Nixon said as he put his hand on her back. "We'll own this city within the month."

MAITLAND, FL

Although I couldn't have known it, John's HUMMER lay smoldering just few miles away while I dozed in my father's study. The midday heat was becoming a problem. Now that the obscenely hot days were back, any movement or activity became a miserable chore. All I wanted was to be comfortable once again. Air conditioning was a fantasy, and a washing machine, hot shower and fresh food were pipe dreams. Life had become a dreary passing of time, and I'd been worn down. I didn't want to think anymore because there was no way out of our predicament. The gang activity had grown overwhelming, with even night journeys becoming a challenge.

"Hey Charlie," Janice said in a low voice, rousing me from my half-sleep. "I thought you might be in here."

"Not for long. I can barely stay in the house at night, let alone deal with this during the day. It's beginning to feel like a sauna."

"I know," Janice replied.

She stood there in front of me, a stupid look on her face. It was like she was stuck between coming and going, frozen by her indecisiveness.

"Here," she said as she handed me a paper bag.

Inside, there was an open box of feminine products as well as a partially filled bottle of pills.

"I know you're almost out, so I brought you these."

Feminine products were one of the two items were in very short supply. If I had a franchise of tampons and toilet paper, I'd have made a fortune.

"Janice! Where did you get these? And what's in the bottle?"

"Birth control pills," she replied.

"Pills? Why don't you use them? I'm not the one with a twenty-year-old boyfriend."

"He's twenty-one," she replied. "We figured out that his birthday was a month or so ago, but we forgot."

I thought about it and realized that my birthday was coming up sometime soon. But without knowing what day it was, birthdays were no longer a concern.

"But why don't you use the pills? You and G-man fighting?" I asked with mock concern.

Janice gave me a frightened look, and I knew instantly why she was here.

"Don't tell me," I began.

"Yeah," she replied, interrupting me before I could continue. "I'm pregnant."

"But, you're on the pill."

"That didn't seem to make a difference. And I don't know whether to be happy or scared out of my mind."

"I'd be both," I said sympathetically.

"Oh Charlie, what am I going to do?"

I stood there, not knowing how to help, when she moved forward and put her arms around me. I hugged her, as she quietly sobbed. After a while, she pulled back. Her eyes were swollen and red, but she had a smile on her face.

"I'm pregnant," she whispered with a grin, then her face dropped and she said it one more time. "Oh, God! I'm pregnant." And she began to weep once again.

"It's alright," I said, trying to mollify her. "It'll be alright."

"How am I going to do this? I can't have a baby out here. Pregnant or not, if the gangs get me, I'm dead. And so is my baby."

"How far along are you?"

"I've missed my period by over four weeks."

Janice's condition meant we needed to take action. We had to make the push to Dr. Kramer's place. We were living in a war zone, and within a few months, Janice wouldn't be able to walk herself out of here. We had to leave, and it had to be soon.

CHAPTER 31

MAITLAND, FL

"Opportunities multiply as they are seized."

— Sun Tzu

ROSKY BEGAN TO STIR. LIKE an old computer that had suffered from a power surge, his mind started back up in fits and stages.

First, it was the ears. A constant, high-pitched noise that diminished to a lower frequency as his awareness increased.

Next, it was his sight. It sluggishly returned, starting with a small circle of light that eventually widened into a tunnel. Batting his eyelids to clear the scratchiness, he tried to focus on the shafts of light that danced around the inside of their HUMVEE. The inside of the crushed vehicle was a jumble of sand, dirt, and broken electronics. He realized that the vehicle was upside down and adjusted his brain accordingly.

After that, it was the pain. His head pounded like the worst hangover he'd ever experienced, only times ten. The pressure lanced through his neck and spread out evenly across his entire skull.

Then, it was the pressure. His legs wouldn't move, sending adrenalin coursing through his system as fears of paralysis or amputation caused his nervous system to react. Pushing aside the pain and dizziness, Drosky frantically began patting himself down. Starting at his chest, he squeezed and probed his body until he eventually ran into a heavy object covering his lower torso.

Sandbags, he thought with relief. He reached down and pulled the first one off, but after shoving it to the side, he saw why his legs still wouldn't move.

Drosky cried out as he jerked his legs out from under his partner's body. Bru wasn't moving, his shoulders and head obscured by debris from their crash. John frantically tried to uncover his friend, but he soon ran into the roof of their overturned HUMVEE. Bru's body stopped there, his head and upper torso crushed under the two-and-a-half-ton truck.

Drosky gasped and sat back, striking his head on an upside-down metal bar. The blow sent pain shooting down his spine, overwhelming the shock from the vision of his friend's headless torso. He realized Bru must have been caught outside the vehicle when it flipped.

"Shit," he said, unable to think of a more eloquent response.

His mind cleared at the sound of someone else stirring inside the vehicle. Drosky abandoned thoughts of his former partner for now and crawled toward the noise.

"Hello?" Drosky shouted as he pulled himself to the front of the wreck, shoving aside sand that had ruptured from the paper bags. Using his arms like a trowel, he scooped the sand behind him, creating a path to the front seat.

He found the other two people dangling upside-down from their seats. Mike wasn't moving, but Cyn was rolling her head as she began to regain her senses. He felt Mike's neck and was rewarded with a fairly strong pulse.

"I'm stuck," Cyn gasped as she struggled with her safety harness.

"Can you move your legs? Is there any pain?"

"Yes, I'm in pain. And yes, I can move my legs. Now get me the hell out of this thing."

Drosky got his folding Spyderco knife from his pocket and quickly cut the polyester webbing and gradually lowered Cynthia to the roof of the four-door cab.

Mike groaned. "What happened?"

"We were hit," Cyn said as she righted herself. "Can you unlock your harness?"

"I'll try."

"Hold on for a sec," Cyn replied. "John, I'll need your help."

Drosky wormed his way up next to her, and the two of them braced Mike's shoulders.

"Go ahead and release the belt."

Mike reached down with his left arm and pressed against the roof.

The click of the belt releasing was followed by a less than graceful tumble, earning the three of them several more bruises.

"Where are we?" Mike croaked.

"Maitland," Cyn replied.

"We need to move," I said. "They'll be back, either with a drone or a couple of squads."

Mike craned his neck and looked at the crushed front doors. "How are we gettin' out of this thing? There's dirt everywhere."

"I've got sunlight back here. And...something else," Drosky replied, earning a look from the other two.

"Oh My God!" Mike gasped when he saw Bru's body trapped out of the turret. "He's dead?"

Drosky solemnly nodded.

"I'm sorry, John," Cynthia said. "We can mourn him later, but right now we need to get clear of the wreck. Grab whatever gear you can and let's go."

After retrieving their rifles and one of their "go" bags, John kicked out the rear driver's side door and crawled out onto the street. The HUMVEE was partially buried by debris and the dirt from the elevated railroad trestle.

"That's what saved us," Drosky said, pointing back at the crater. "The bomb hit the berm."

"That, and the bags of sand absorbed enough of the blast to keep us alive," Cyn replied.

"Yeah, but they'll know we made it when they get here and only find one body," Mike added.

The big guy unfastened a dented jerry can from the bed of the HUMVEE. It was leaking diesel fuel from a couple of pinholes where shrapnel had penetrated it.

"We need to burn it," Mike said. "I hate to do that to Bru, but it may buy us some time."

Drosky hesitated, until Cynthia chimed in. "He's right, John. We should burn it."

He at last nodded. It made sense tactically. But it still didn't feel right.

Mike splashed the heavy fuel onto the overturned vehicle while Cyn added a second can. Then Mike lit a gas-soaked chunk of debris and tossed it into the HUMVEE's interior. Within a minute, the truck was engulfed in flames, the cab becoming a funeral pyre for their dead comrade. The three survivors moved with a purpose and disappeared on foot into the abandoned Maitland subdivision. Once again, they were in enemy territory and had miles to go before they could rest.

The rest of the day, the three slowly moved north before stopping on the southern shores of Lake Maitland. John had little first-hand knowledge of the area, given that he never patrolled these streets. But growing up in the city had given him some experience in driving the roads and streets, so the trip to Sanford wouldn't be totally blind. Unfortunately, the lake extended all the way east to Winter Park. If they pushed to much farther in that direction, they would run into gangs, so sneaking along 17/92 was their best option. Running that mile-long gauntlet would best be done at night, so they found an abandoned mansion and took refuge on its second floor. The back of the house stared across the huge lake, where they could see other empty mansions sitting on the water, all of them falling into disrepair.

As the late afternoon began to give way to night, the three sat on a second-floor balcony outside the massive master bedroom. The home had been closed up fairly tightly, so no unwanted creatures were inside. They each took the opportunity to wash up using the home's oversized water heater tank. The pool out back was green with algae, but was more than adequate for filling the toilets. MREs from the salvaged "go" bag provided meals for them all, and they ate greedily as the evening sky turned an azure blue.

They spoke with muted voices, keeping their conversation to a minimum as they finished their dinners. Sound traveled on water, and normal speech could be heard over a mile away. Even a muted burp from Big Mike created enough noise to bring a disapproving look from Cyn.

As darkness blotted out the setting sunlight, a few pinpoints of lights began to show up across the lake.

Pointing to the lights dancing in the distance, Drosky whispered, "Gangs."

"We goin' that way?" Mike asked quietly.

"Yeah," Drosky said. "They're a block or two down from the main road."

"No other way out?"

"Nope, not without totally exposing ourselves. There's a bike trail that starts north of her and winds all the way up to Sanford. We have to go through Maitland to get to it. Otherwise, we'll be walking up a six-lane road with no cover."

"Damn," Mike murmured.

"Don't worry," Cyn said. "Even scum sleep. John, zero dark thirty?"

"Yeah, sounds about right."

"Okay," Mike said, "you two stop with the military crap. What are you talking about?"

"Just some slang. It means 'late at night,' but I'm thinking that we should move through that neighborhood an hour or two before dawn. That's when everyone is tired, especially anyone pulling watch for the night."

"Hmmph," Mike replied. "So we have a few hours before we leave?"

"At least four or five hours," Drosky said.

"Then I'm hitting the sack." The big guy moved with a grace that belied his size and rolled into the master bed. "Leave the sliders open; it's hotter than hell in here."

"I'll take first watch." Cyn said to Drosky. "You need some rest."

"Yeah," he sighed. "It's been a crappy day."

LATER THAT NIGHT

Mike felt someone shaking his shoulder and sat upright, his Berretta clutched in his right hand. The pistol never made it all the way around as his wrist was grasped and twisted back. The handgun was stripped away, and before he could move, a knee to his chest jolted him back onto the bed.

"You never learn," Cyn hissed as she placed Mike's gun onto the side table next to the bed. "You don't sleep with a gun in your bed. You'll just as likely shoot someone you don't mean to. Especially yourself."

Mike grunted and stood up. "Sorry."

"Yeah, I know, ya big dope. Next time, leave it in your holster."

The three met at the sliding glass doors that led out to the back yard.

"Everyone all fresh and clean?" Drosky deadpanned.

All three had taken the time to use the toilets and check their firearms. Cyn wasn't sure if any of their rifles had been bent or disabled by the blast, and without any tools, they were limited to a visual inspection of their assembled M4s. Separating the upper from the lower receiver, they could dry fire the empty gun and at least see if the hammer struck forward when they pulled the trigger. But if the barrel had been warped, it could be catastrophic. Hopefully, they could move without being seen. The last thing they wanted was to get into a firefight with unreliable weapons against an unknown number of gang members.

Drosky checked his watch and saw that it was just past two in the morning. A good time to be out and about without being seen. They moved in a staggered line, leapfrogging each other from one position of cover to another. The mile-long trip took the better part of an hour before they at last came to the first road that crossed north of the lake.

Cutting behind a burned-out McDonalds, they crouched in an alley that fed onto the road they needed to take. Moving to the east would bring them near to the gang members that they had seen from the balcony, but there was no way to avoid that unless they wanted to continue north and through an even more industrial area. Concealment was their friend, and so they pushed east.

About another mile in—and another hour later—the three of them stopped again. Cyn was in the lead, and she held up her hand and spun it in a circle, indicating that they needed to rally to her position. When they joined her, she pointed to the south side of the four-lane street. As they stared into the shadows of a subdivision entrance, Drosky saw slight movement near the base of an oak tree.

"Got him," he whispered.

"Just wait," Cyn replied.

Sure enough, a second person moved a moment later.

"How do we get by?" Drosky asked.

"Don't know. But we need to get closer before we decide."

About twenty minutes later, they lay prone behind a line of bushes. A parking lot for a recreation area sat on the other side of the street from the gang members. Crawling behind the hedge, the trio found themselves directly across from the two thugs. There was a three-foot median in the road as well as ground cover and an occasional crepe myrtle tree giving further concealment.

"We can't keep going," Cyn said. "We'll be exposed as we cross the street in front of them."

"Agreed," Mike said. "But we can't just stay here."

Drosky stared across the street. "We have to take them."

"If we cut back a bit, the median has some thicker bushes. We come up on their side and try to take them quietly."

They backtracked to the spot Cyn had mentioned. After crossing the road without being discovered, they moved up the opposite side of the street. Soon, they could hear the two men talking in low voices. There wasn't much cover for the next twenty yards; the houses were flanked by tall concrete walls and little vegetation stood between the two men and their three silent stalkers.

"I need a smoke," one of them said.

"Taurus will kill ya! He told us not to light up. Said you could see it a mile away."

The first man pointed across the street. "Hell, let's just smoke in there. No one can see us in the trees."

"Dude, we can't leave our post."

"We'll be right across the street," the first one said. "No one's gonna know. We've been out here for hours and ain't seen shit."

The man pulled out a pack of cigarettes and held it out.

"They smell right good," the second thug said. "Let's go."

The two men began to walk across the street, and Drosky turned back to his friends. "Follow me when they light their cigarettes. They'll have night blindness for a few seconds."

"Where are we going after that?" Mike asked.

"The next opening up there," Drosky said and pointed.

The three crouched down and moved to the last tree on their side of the road. After a moment of waiting, they were rewarded with the flare of a match.

"Now!" Drosky hissed.

The three of them walked heel to toe, their rifles pointed across the street at the dying flame. Within seconds, they had crossed the intersection the two men had just left. They were halfway to the next entrance when they heard laughter coming from further down the street.

All three went prone on the sidewalk as a group of armed men approached, pulling a couple of wagons full of items down the street's north side.

As the new group approached the woods where the two guards had taken refuge, one of the men in the party called out, "Who the hell is smoking?"

The two guards slowly walked out of the trees.

"You dumb bastards. What the hell do you think you're doing?"

All of them circled around the guards as their leader slapped and berated them for their stupidity.

Drosky nodded at Mike and Cyn, and they sprinted the last hundred yards to the next subdivision. An eight-foot-high concrete wall faced the road, and after turning right, they were hidden from view.

"Hasty ambush," Mike whispered, and the three set up behind cover, rifles pointed in the direction they'd come from.

After two minutes with no pursuit, they moved further away from the road toward the lake down at the end of the street.

"Let's keep going down and then turn left," Drosky said. "That should take us out of range of the guards. Then we can head back out and find that bike trail."

They hugged the left side of the two-lane street, keeping in the shadows of the trees and homes. It was a modest neighborhood with single-story homes built forty or fifty years ago. At the end of the road, mansions stood on the lake's shore. Typical of any area where lakefront property could be found, multi-million-dollar estates sat on a piece of waterfront property with smaller homes right across the street.

Drosky signaled to their left, and he and the others darted around the corner of a house and into its open garage. They removed their ballistic vests and sat down on the cool concrete floor for a few minutes, taking a much-needed rest.

"Let's keep moving. We can take this street a few blocks further, then cut back to the main road. I think we're about a mile from the bike trail," Drosky said.

"Everyone hydrate," Cyn said, and they each took a pull from the camelback bladder that Mike carried in the group's "go" bag.

"We'll need some more water soon," Mike said as he took a draw from the bladder's straw.

"Yeah," Cyn said. "I've got some purification tablets. Love that chlorine taste."

"Better than dysentery," Drosky said. "Lots of bad stuff out here now."

The three stood up and hoisted their ballistic vests back over their shoulders. As they slung their rifles over their necks, Cyn stopped and held up her hand.

"Someone's out there," she hissed.

The three of them moved back into the shadows of the garage. Drosky found the door into the house and opened it. A quick glance inside showed that it was empty. They moved into the home and took a position where they could look out front.

"There!" Cyn said as she pointed across the street. Her sensitive ears were always the first to pick out sounds.

Two people were slowly walking out of the gates of the mansion across from them. One was casually carrying a rifle, its barrel pointed forward and down. The other was walking with a five-gallon plastic bucket in one hand and a rifle casually slung over a shoulder. They were moving without caution, even giggling with the muted conversation. Drosky could pick up some of the words coming through his broken front window.

"Holy shit," he said as he stood up and moved to the garage.

The other two followed, confused at his sudden move. Before they could ask him questions, he was out the door and positioned at the corner of the garage, staring out onto the now-empty street.

As Cyn reached out to tap him on the shoulder, Drosky spun out of the garage and glanced back up the road. He ran across the street to the corner of the waterfront mansion's wall. After ensuring that the gang had moved on, he signaled for Mike and Cyn to follow and then slipped around the corner.

Cyn and Mike could barely keep up as he disappeared up the side road across the street. They ran to the intersection where Drosky had just been and looked up the road, just catching a glimpse of him disappearing between two-single story houses.

"What the hell?" Cyn said as the two of them hauled butt to catch up with their friend.

As they turned between the two homes, they saw Drosky open a wooden door that led to the back of the house. They sprinted forward, rifles up and ready, and ran into the backyard. Drosky had finally caught up with his quarry. The people, a man and a woman, were facing away from them. The man was pulling a stringer of fish out of the bucket.

Drosky snuck up behind them and stopped just a few feet back.

"Freeze," he said in a low voice.

The woman squealed in fear. Drosky approached her and, putting his hand on her shoulder, slowly turned her toward him. She gasped when she saw his face and flung her arms around his neck.

"JOHN?" she cried.

"Hello, Charlie. What the hell are you still doing here?"

CHAPTER 32

MAITLAND, FL

"The true soldier fights not because he hates what is in front of him, but because he loves what is behind him."

— G.K. Chesterton

W HEN JOHN SNUCK UP ON me and Mike, I about had a heart attack. But afterward, I was beyond happy. His story about their flight from town and their escape from the gangs left us all breathless. It was so good to see him. He had brought us hope once again.

"So, Charlie," Cynthia said. "Why are you guys still here?"

We were in Harley and Ashley's house having a breakfast of diluted condensed milk and stale cereal. As long as we let the milk stand in the old Frosted Flakes for a while, they became mushy enough to eat.

"We've been trapped here by a gang of skinheads," I said. "They set up headquarters next door."

Cynthia looked at John and shook her head. "I suppose I can't fault you too much," she said. "But you've become frozen, and that'll get you killed."

"We can't get by them," I said. "There are too many."

Cynthia shrugged. "We made it. But don't take it too badly. Most people lose their energy after a while. You get a little comfort or a bit of security, and you settle for that rather than pushing forward."

"I don't think that's fair," I began to say.

"Just look at what you have here," she continued over my protests. "Food, shelter, and friends. The problem is that you don't want to look too far ahead."

Cynthia got up and began pacing in front of everyone, taking on the role a professor explaining truths to her pupils.

"I saw this all the time when I would train my Marines on CQB," she said.

"What's that?" Maria asked.

"Close quarter battle. It's part of learning how to fight through an enemy inside a house or on a city street. We had "kill houses" set up like a small town and taught the recruits how to fight in close quarters. One of the drills involved clearing a house that had no lights. You had to go in and using a flashlight to find the bad guys."

She stared off into the back yard, lost momentarily in thought.

"We videotaped the Marines with night vision cameras, and the men and women could be categorized into one of two groups: Victims and Predators. The hunted and the hunters. Most of the hunted would freeze. A rare few relished the drill. They were predators who sought the fight."

Cynthia stopped moving and stopped to stare at us all.

"You guys have let yourself become the prey. You need to change your attitudes because in this world, only the hunters survive."

Later that day, we agreed that it was time to leave. Jorge and Maria were going to move east and then try and hook up with his family. We would join Cynthia, Mike, and John on their journey north to Sanford. From there, we'd decide on our best path to Monteverde and the hopeful safety of Dr. Kramer's home. Harley and Ashley were staying put. Tomorrow, most of us would finally leave Maitland for good.

EAST OF CHARLIE'S HOUSE
MAITLAND, FL

That night, three dark figures prowled the abandoned streets of Maitland. Moving silently among the empty homes and overgrown yards, they pushed east into unexplored territory.

"Looks good so far," Jorge whispered as the three crouched down in a wooded area across from an abandoned convenience store. Behind them was a pond, it's stagnant water emanating a sewage smell that all but guaranteed the area was safe. No one would willingly stay here for long if they had to breath the acrid sulfur stench.

Across the street, the front of the 7/11 was gone. Its glass façade long ago smashed, the shards of the broken windows were now a fine powder on the building's concrete slab. Abandoned gasoline pumps were entwined with creeping vines. The metal plate access to the store's underground fuel tanks had been removed and a make-shift tent had been erected over the open hole. A hand pump lay on the ground near-by, with a hose snaked into the in-ground fuel tank.

"Looks like they're still pulling gas out of the ground," Garrett observed. "That's probably where they're refueling before heading out for the day."

The moonlight was bright enough to see into the inside the store. It appeared empty, which was no surprise.

"Let's keep moving," Garrett said. "I don't think we should waste our time here."

"Agreed," Jorge replied. The convenience store would have been torn apart within the first week of the crisis, and nothing of value would remain.

They crept further east to the edge of the trees and came to an intersection. To their right, the crossroad pushed south back into Winter Park.

"Hey, this building looks intact," Janice observed.

She pointed down the street to a glass and brick house that had been turned into a personal trainer's business. Janice snuck up to the front of the converted house and looked into the window. Dirt and grime streaked the glass, but she didn't risk wiping them clean so as not to leave evidence of their passing.

"I want to check the back door," Janice said.

"Sure, I'm with you," Garrett said.

The three snuck around the corner of the building, keeping the trees between them and the convenience store. They found the back door ajar. The door creaked on its hinges when Janice pushed it open, bringing shushes and complaints from both of the men.

Janice slipped into the back room. Jorge produced a small tactical flashlight. He had scribbled green magic marker onto the lens, and the dim, green hue would be hard to see just a few hundred feet away.

"Here," Jorge whispered, handing her the flashlight. "Be quick about it. I want to keep moving east before we have to turn back."

Janice took the flashlight and found the door to the hallway. Beyond was a large room, likely used for aerobics or some other group exercise. Weight machines lined the sides of the space. Janice stood in the doorway, scanning the muted beam around the room.

"Oh my God," she said. "Look!"

In the far corner of the room, a pile of open boxes was stacked nearly five feet high. The top one had tilted over, and packages of toilet paper and a large, unopened box of feminine products had dumped out onto the floor.

"Charlie will love me for this," she said over her shoulder. "She's almost out of tampons."

Jorge made it to the door just as Janice began running into the room. She was closely followed by Garrett.

"Hey! Slow down," Jorge called out.

Janice never answered.

The explosion was deafening, sending Jorge flying back through the door and onto the floor. He struggled to lift himself, using his elbows to elevate his head to look into the exercise room.

Dust and debris filled the air. The room's left wall had a massive hole punched through it, and dozens if not hundreds of pockmarks had peppered the building's ceiling and walls. Weight machines were bent, and toppled over. Hundreds of pounds of iron and stainless steel had been tossed about like a kite in the wind. The strength of the explosion was beyond anything he had ever seen.

Jorge staggered into the room used his backup flashlight to search frantically for his friends. The noise of the explosion would attract the gang, and in desperation, he called out for Janice and Garrett.

As he stepped further into the destruction, he stumbled over something. Looking down, he recognized that it was the bottom of a leg. Charred and amputated below the knee, Garrett's shoe was nevertheless still neatly tied over the foot.

Cursing, Jorge turned and left. His friends had been effectively vaporized by the explosion. They were gone, and nothing remained of them but a bloody stump.

CHARLIE

Janice had been killed while she was trying to help me.

Every time I thought I was cried out, I somehow found more tears to shed. When Jorge came back and told us what had happened, I broke down and had to be carried into my dad's office, which had become my refuge over these past months.

Maria had stopped in once or twice during the morning and finally got me to leave with a promise of fresh outside air and a glass of sweet tea. I couldn't choke down the sugary liquid, but having people around me, offering support, lightened my load just a bit.

"She didn't feel a thing," Cynthia said. "I know that doesn't help now, but later on when you're thinking about last night, it will."

I looked up at her, a confused and angry look on my face.

"I know," she said. "I've been there before."

I filed her advice away. She seemed to know what she was talking about. Even John and Mike deferred to her. That says a lot.

"She died for me," I said. "Damn it, she died for a box of tampons."

"Yeah," Jorge said, shaking his head. "I never thought how important that is."

"Men," Cynthia said. "Don't think beyond what's right in front of them."

"It's my fault," I said. Cynthia turned to me. "Charlie, Janice and Maria needed those things too."

"Maybe Maria, but not Janice."

Cynthia looked confused.

"She was pregnant," I said.

The group deflated. Maria began to cry.

"Janice told me the other day. She knew I was low on feminine products, and she said she wouldn't need them for a while. That's why I thought we should move soon. Janice was freaked about it."

I left them after that and retreated into my dad's office. The others stayed gathered in the kitchen, discussing their next move. As I sat there, I ruminated about our time in Maitland. We had wasted months here in relative security, happy to survive but afraid to live.

We should have moved on. We had talked a lot about it but always found an excuse to stay.

I thought of the times when I had been the deciding vote, when Maria and Jorge wanted to leave but Garrett and Janice wanted to stay. I realized that I should have been the one to push us forward. I had been afraid to make the call that would send us out face possible death, never thinking that staying could be just as bad.

If I had been more forceful. If I had been more brave. If I had been more of a leader, Janice and Garrett might be alive. I was responsible for their deaths. I was the one that kept us here.

I fell into a deep depression as the night came and slipped away.

The next morning, with no sleep and a suffocating fog of angst clouding my mind, I left the office. I stumbled into the kitchen and found Cynthia sitting at the table, a lone witness to my self-pity.

I sat down and refused to meet her gaze.

"You blame yourself." She simply stated the fact as if she could read my mind.

"The truth is, it probably is your fault. At least in part."

My eyes flared, and I looked at her with an anger that would kill if it could.

"Ah. There is life in there."

"Screw you!" I spat.

She got up and poured herself a cup of hot water and added instant coffee crystals and sugar, stirring slowly so as not to clink on the sides of the cup. I found her anal-retentive motions infuriating. She sat back down and took a sip, staring over the lip of the mug at me.

"I told you earlier. You can either be the hunter or the hunted. It's as simple as that."

"I don't like your attitude," I shot back. "How dare you blame me?"

"Why not? You blame yourself. I'm just agreeing with you."

I had no good reply to that. It was true. She must have seen the look on my face and smirked.

"Look, Charlie. I don't want to pile on. You're in a bad place. I've been there before. But you need to put that aside so you can put the blame on where it belongs. That bomb was set by DHS. From Jorge's description of the explosion, it was probably a Claymore mine. Only the government has those."

I tried to process what she was telling me, but I was so tired that my brain took a moment to catch up.

"Yes, the government killed your friends," she said after seeing the confused look in my eyes. "You didn't see that coming, did you?"

I had nothing to say. In one sense, I felt relieved that the gangs hadn't done this. They were the enemy, and continuing to live close to them was our poor decision. But wasn't them. It was tyrants that were trying to rule the country. They were everywhere.

"Think about what I said. But think fast, because at nightfall, we're leaving. With or without you."

Cynthia stood up and left me alone at the table. I got up as well and went to my father's study. I closed the door and didn't come out again until sun had begun to drop below the horizon.

I walked into the kitchen and found the group gathered together. They fell silent when they saw me. Fully decked out with my battle gear, my rifle cleaned and slung over my shoulder, I went to the patio and stooped down beside a pile of charcoal we were using to help purify our water supply. Reaching in, I grabbed a piece of the charred oak. I stood with my back to them as I smeared my face with its dark, oily residue.

"Charlie, are you alright?" Maria asked.

I turned around and looked at them, my face painted with black streaks and a fire in my eyes that hadn't been there before.

"Charlie?" John asked. "What are you doing?"

"It's time to hunt, John," I replied. "It's time to hunt."

***

I used a number of sources in creating this book. The dialog in chapter 14 was heavily influenced by an article in the Daily Koss by author Major Kong titled "Flying the B-52." All of the remaining research was done through public websites with no particular source providing the bulk of the information.

I am very impressed with the Tennessee 278th Armored Cavalry. I researched their facilities in Nashville, paying a personal visit to several armories. Their history of service is unmatched and their performance in both kinetic actions and war games is on par with their peers, even though they are "part-time" National Guard. They drill with the 101st Airborne and are often the first to be called in all our major conflicts. Their pride in state and service is unrivaled.

A special thanks to a few important people. First, to my editor Erin. She's more than patient as my documents were returned with more "red" than "black" on the manuscript. Other writers will appreciate that. She's a saint.

Second, to Mark Phillips, his military experience was valuable in keeping me on the straight and narrow regarding the equipment in this book.

Third, to Angery American. He's the man. His knowledge in survival techniques is unsurpassed. He is a gem.

Fourth, to my wife. She's patient beyond words given that I have a full-time job and write on the side. I think she still likes me. I'm still in the house.

Finally, my thanks to several of the readers that helped me with the Air Force 5th wing and Tennessee 278th armored cavalry. They are vets who served in these units and gave me enough knowledge to sound intelligent.

I've started the next book in this series, Charlie's Requiem: Retribution. It will be available next summer and will sync this series with the Going Home series time line.

Thank you all for supporting Chris and me. It's been an amazing ride so far and I'll keep writing as long as you all keep reading.

SCALIA

THE FIRST DAY OF THE REST OF MY LIFE

A MEMOIR

PRISCILLA NYSTROM

The First Day of the Rest of My Life
A Memoir
Priscilla Nystrom

Dedications

*Long ago I overheard you say to your family, "She is a very strong woman".
And I believed you. A loving thank you, Carl E. for your belief in me.*

*To Brenda, my darling daughter who is now "Forever Young", I love you,
Bren.*

LISTEN TO YOUR CHILDREN

Listen to your children
Hear their anxious cries
Listen to their silence
Save their precious lives
Their dreams may be destroyed
Lest you miss one single clue.

Composed by the author of:
The First Day of the Rest of My Life
Priscilla Nystrom

ABOUT THE STORY

An intense and informative account of life seen from a four year old's perspective; she tries to understand her parents' abuse. Later on through grammar school her abuse grows more unavoidable and frightening. As a teenager, home-bound, sheltered from her peers, her anxiety grows as she tries to escape the open, hostile advances of her father.

Coming of age at twenty-one she makes a bold move to distance herself from her father. She is so successful, it seems, he consequently dies of heart disease. Relieved and grieved, conflicting emotions leave her feeling guilty, ashamed, over-whelmed with anxiety. She cannot explain her withdrawal from life.

Her mother who always left her misinformed and unpro-tected is lost to alcoholism. It is only with the help of her second husband who pronounces her, "a very strong woman," and the persistence of a caring therapist who relentlessly listens to her harrowing accounts of anguish; she finds relief. She relies on her

religious beliefs; a gracious quiet acceptance belies her fierce spir-it's quest for revenge.

Then comes the most painful loss of all, a tragedy that leaves her twisting in the wind.

CHAPTER 1

THE START OF THE FARM

$\mathcal{T}$his candid complex story began long before I was born. The facts originated from tales of long ago as emanated by the ancestors of my grandfather, Charles E. Dufour.

In 1918, a dangerous epidemic of influenza swept through the homes of the people in the city of Cambridge, Massachusetts. One particularly vulnerable family of French descent was compelled to move away from this industrial city, with hopes of saving their four young children from the dread disease. My ancestral family nervously anticipated a timely escape north to New Hampshire.

My grandfather, after much searching and speculating, finally located a fine tract of prime forest land. As a wool sorter by trade, he was most pleased to find clear open fields bordered by two rivers and 160 acres of gently rolling hills. Located in the small, beautiful township of Wentworth, New Hampshire, the "Smart Farm" as it was then referred to, later became the home and refuge for three generations of Dufours.

1

My grandfather, Charles Dufour, and my grandmother, his wife, Roseanna, raised their four children on the Dufour Farm. The oldest was Francis, next came Fitzpatrick and then Rose. My own father, Charles, was the baby, born in 1913.

The four siblings grew up to be strong, independent citizens. Each had his own ideas and concepts as to how the world should be run. This was an important aspect, for whenever the family gathered together, arguments broke out. The individual who could best boast his knowledge of politics with the loudest gusto became the winner of the "laughing crowd award." These discussions included a large dose of satirical humor. My father, the youngest, could always make his voice boom over the din of arguments that ensued.

At the gatherings, as a side amusement, the siblings would be laughing, coughing, stomping their feet, and pounding fists on the kitchen table. Only when each one began muttering in French did red faces begin to glow. Sensing the change, my father would finally stand up and start laughing at the sight. And soon they were all guffawing with him. He was once again pronounced the winner of the laughing crowd award.

The tenacious Dufour family had not only survived the deadly diseases of Cambridge; they had flourished on the farm. Each one of them moved on to other venues, always with farm values in their hearts. One by one they would return for a visit to recall simpler days. Many years later, I too returned, not just to recall memories, but to feel finally a veil of peacefulness drift over the rolling hills of the Dufour Farm.

CHAPTER 2

MY PARENTS

I shall endeavor to recount their individual histories, gathered from various family members over a span of many years.

My mother's life began in the year 1927 in Laconia, New Hampshire. She was one of the youngest born to a family of ten children. Her father, a seasoned railroad man, was constantly away from home. Her mother was confined to her bed—apparently from bearing too many children—and inevitably died, leaving only the father. My mother's father rose to the occasion and found a new wife who would watch over the many young children while he was away. He unexpectedly arrived home one fateful day to find his new bride in the arms of another man. The story goes that he took his own life in a vehicle on a lonely back road. My mother told us many years later that the story had been all over the newspapers about the poor little children being left homeless. A few families responded by offering foster homes to some of them.

My mother's horror stories of cruel foster homes was heart-

3

breaking. She kept running away from them, until one day she landed in the hospital with a ruptured appendix. While my mother was at death's door with infection and pain, a miracle happened. An elderly woman who incidentally was her grandmother, had heard of the family's earlier plight. She took an interest in my mother, and worked hard to form a bond of trust between them. My mother then lived with her grandmother. She brought my mother back to life, and they became inseparable friends.

After my mother was old enough to enter high school, she soon developed a talent for fine art and singing classical music. Her beautiful four-octave voice brought promises of valuable scholarships to places of higher education. Mother later noted that in collaboration with her slightly younger brother, she pushed aside the importance of her talents. They sang cowboy songs together, complete with yodeling, which punished her delicate high range of voice. Her teachers, concerned with her rebellious yodeling, tried their best to save her with responsible voice training. The hopes of higher education flew out the window, especially after she met my father, an older man of 31 years, who swept her off her teenage feet. At sixteen, she was a ravishing beauty with a dusky brown complexion, snapping black eyes and a perfectly proportioned body. She stood five feet two inches tall with a mane of raven black hair pulled back from her small face; her high-bridged straight nose was complimented by the highest of cheek bones. Her rosebud shaped mouth was full of large white teeth set in a pronounced overbite, which only served to widen her smile. Perky, flirty and mature in her street manners at sixteen—my father found her irresistible. Looking for a home and security, she left high school, and promptly married my father.

* * *

MY FATHER WAS BORN in Cambridge, Massachusetts in 1913, the youngest of five children born to the Dufour family. At that time, the influenza epidemic was raging throughout that area, causing concern for the very young. Father's parents were informed of the risks to their young ones and were encouraged to move north as soon as possible.

His father found a new home for them, a fine tract of prime forest land up north in the township of Wentworth, N.H. One hundred and sixty acres of rolling hills bordered on two sides by rivers, including a large barn one hundred feet long. A three-story house of a dozen rooms was ready to be occupied. For maintaining the farm, there was a blacksmith shop, a shingle mill, a corn shed and a tool barn—perfect lodgings for the fleeing family.

The French speaking family soon settled into their new home. The young people walked a mile each day to a one-room school. From the books the children brought home, their Canadian-born mother, Roseanna, learned words and phrases of English. Their father raised prize-winning sheep, cows who gave the richest milk, and large quantities of vegetables for the table and storage. My grandfather, unfortunately, died of a major stroke when he was just forty-five years old, during the flood of 1927. The two rivers flooded the farm; the buildings were narrowly spared as they were built on slightly higher ground. The family now depended on their mother to bring order to the chaos of their sudden loss.

My father, Charles, the youngest of the Dufour siblings was a tall young man at five feet eleven inches, with a long shock of dark hair that always fell loosely over one eye. Thick black eyebrows, hazel eyes and tanned French skin complimented his

large face and the pronounced long nose. His closed lip smile hid a mixture of two sets of small teeth. His body was erect, square shouldered and long legged, which made him a fine athletic skier, hockey skater and motorcyclist. He always wore glasses to correct an astigmatism over his otherwise lifelong perfect eye sight. During the grammar school era of my father's life, he seemed to be staying after school a great deal. He helped clean blackboards with two other boys while working to impress their new, very young lady teacher. Darkness fell early in the wintertime after a long day of school, so the fellows left for home on their skis as soon as the chores were completed. One evening, my father was held back to be alone with the new teacher. She taught him lessons of what it was like for her, a lonely woman in a small school of mostly young boys. He later learned that his comrades had been through the same ritual. The word spread and she was relieved of her duties. A man teacher was moved in to uphold a more scrupulous set of rules for the school.

CHAPTER 3

KEEPING THE FARM GOING

*M*y grandmother, Roseanna Dufour, then living on the farm, found herself raising her four children alone, after my grandfather had died previously of a stroke during the epic flood of 1927. Their children, now teenagers, were devastated by the loss of their father and the unexpected flood waters that surrounded the farm.

Roseanna held her ground, encouraging strong help from her sons and her daughter. She also took in boarders, who, for a good meal would help with the hard work of haying and wood splitting. Her infinite resolve kept her family together until they were of age.

Eventually the first son married and moved to Colebrook, N.H., where he became a well-known barber and respected Boy Scout leader. The next son moved to Laconia, N.H., where he excelled as a fine machinist in a prominent machine shop. Her daughter, after some time alone at the farm, took a job at a nearby shoe factory. She met her new husband-to-be and moved to Laconia, N.H. And then my father left the farm, to work in

Laconia, N.H. As an expert machinist, he became a foreman, and soon purchased an impressive home in the city near his work. He met the young girl who later became my mother, and they married.

All the siblings were contributing money toward my grand-mother's attempt to hold on to the farm. After a year or so, she had a mild stroke, which gave her cause to move in with her children. One by one, they took turns caring for her until the time came when my father could no longer withstand the stress of working for the machine shop. It was time to move back to the farm. He, with his young wife—my mother, and new baby—me, and my grandmother all headed for the peaceful hills of Wentworth, N.H.

I WAS NEARLY two years old. I remember well the ride to the farm. I recall sitting high on a special pillow my mother had designed so I could see out of the clouded windshield of the 1939 Desoto Sedan. Wearing a maroon wool coat and bonnet trimmed with white fur my mother had sewn for me, I was ready for adventure.

CHAPTER 4

REMEMBERING

*I*t's humiliating to remember painful situations caused by my family. I am grimly reminded that my childhood was darkened by hidden abuse. Each time I try to recall any happy occasion from that early time of growing up, only one memory comes back to me.

The incident happened long ago when I was only two years old. I recall a long steep stairway that led to cozy rooms upstairs in our farmhouse home. I'd enjoyed a young toddler's afternoon nap in one of those sunny peaceful rooms. Undisturbed by kitchen noises, I usually woke up by my own accord after a lovely rest. Then, of course, I'd squall loudly for my Mama. She'd promptly arrive at my crib, scoop me up and ride me down the steep stairs on her hip.

One memorable day she called my name from the bottom of the stairs. The side was down on my crib, since I was a big girl now. I clamored out of my bed, still hazy from the delicious nap. I found the stairs and sat down cautiously on the very top and peered down at my mother. She began to beckon me down the

stairs, which I took step by step on my bottom. It was a slow process; I soon began to lose interest in this new game. But then she held out her closed hand and with enticing words suggested she held a surprise for me. So I bumped just a little more until I began to slide from step to step until I finally reached her smiling face.

She held out her closed hand and slowly opened it to disclose my reward. There lay a tiny pink, rubbery baby doll with outstretched arms. Staring at the treasure with disbelief, I was reluctant to reach for it. "Go ahead take it, it's yours!" She exclaimed and with that I made a grab for it. I squeezed the rubbery little doll, rolled it over and over in my hands and then popped it into my mouth for a good chew. It was a two year old's delight. I have always remembered that one loving episode with my mother smiling at my enjoyment. After that, my father's covert actions kept my mother and me at odds with each other for a lifetime of pain and terrible hurtful memories.

CHAPTER 5

FOUR YEARS OLD

*a*t four years of age I was the center of my own universe. There existed no bad guys to contend with in my games of make believe. I usually played the role of mommy with my homespun cloth doll aptly named "Girl Doll." I sang and talked alone all day long, which gave my Mother much relief. I liked being very busy. As long as Mama could hear me, she surmised that all was well.

My favorite play area was located under the corn shed. This old wooden building in its day had been a sturdy crib where ears of corn had been laid up for the winter months. It stood on thick wooden posts four feet high off the ground allowing ventilation for the drying process.

I really was not concerned at four years old about the corn drying process. I had happily discovered the soft, slightly damp soil under the corn shed that emitted a sweet inviting aroma for play. A veritable treat for a little girl, who, with a flat piece of wood in her hands could bulldoze, mound, and scoop tunnels

through the soft soil. It was here in my world under the corn shed where my mother could find her very dirty little girl, happily playing and singing all the day long.

CHAPTER 6

BLANKED OUT

*F*all was arriving, evening was coming earlier in the house. Supper had been announced so I was washing my hands in the bathroom located next to the kitchen. Voices caught my attention over the running water in the sink. I turned off the faucet to listen, then walked to the open doorway and stood very still.

"I'm sick and tired of all the incessant work around here. You can keep this place all to yourself, along with your four-year-old brat. You and your mother can do it all. I'm leaving. You can take care of the kid for a change. See how you like it. I'm leaving!"

I had never heard such a harried voice. It was my mother's! *Mama's leaving me all alone? How can she do that?* Trying not to cry, I gritted my teeth and chewed my lip. I immediately changed the whole scene in my mind, blocking out the part of her leaving me all alone forever. This had not happened. No, I wanted my mother; she certainly was not leaving. A moment passed before I strolled out into the kitchen mildly aloof.

"Did you wash your hands?" she asked as usual.

"Yes Mama," I replied calmly as I walked to the table wiping my wet hands on my shirt front. Supper was served. I was safe.

CHAPTER 7

BUDDING ARTIST

In the kitchen of the old homestead, on an unusually quiet October evening, my father and grandmother, relaxing in their respective rocking chairs were conversing softly in French. My mother was at the hospital. She was about to deliver a new baby girl to the family. My new baby sister would be arriving very soon on the day after my own birthday only two days away.

At this tender age of four, unaware of the dangers of child-birth, I sat contentedly on the floor next to Grammie's rocking chair. After flipping through the pages of a brand new coloring book, I decided upon coloring a little lamb. Grammie watched while I arduously colored the page.

She suddenly stopped her side of the conversation with Father to exclaim in English, "Look at the nice job she's doing." Grammie was the silent type, so this occasion was a lovely surprise. "Stand up here, show me what you're doing so nice."

Slowly I stood up, leaving my warm spot on the floor, and after handing her my precious book, waited patiently. She held

the book tenderly in her work-worn hands. Smiling, her twinkling eyes gazed with pride at the yellow crayoned little lamb.

"The lines, she works so nice staying in the lines." As she spoke, Father leaned slightly forward in his chair.

She offered him the book to hold, but he mumbled "No, no."

Grammie gently squeezed my shoulder, offered a sad little grin and returned the book to me. I promptly dropped down onto my warm spot on the floor. For a moment I carefully studied the little lamb's yellow splendor. A sense of self was emerging, hope surfaced, I might one day become an artist!

Because of that tiny fulfilling encouragement, I later, in my teen years, pursued art classes with a purpose. I took a commercial-art course at home, and learned the basics of portraiture, lettering and advertising. Then I took private lessons with other artists to learn the art of painting. So I really did become an accomplished artist, selling my works in galleries, and at huge art-show events; and was commissioned to produce paintings for many private patrons. I still recall the uplifting feeling of hope from my Grandmother's tender encouraging words of praise.

CHAPTER 8

THE FIRST DAY OF THE REST OF MY LIFE

*O*ne sunny morning in the fall of the year, cool and breezy, I was heading out to play in my favorite sandy area under the corn shed. Wearing a little navy blue corduroy jacket Mama had sewn for me, I felt cozy and warm. I was ready to have fun. At four years old, there was much anticipation over new road grading and house building in my sand piles.

While cultivating my sandy road and humming a little tune, I paused for a moment and looked up. My enjoyment was interrupted by my Father's stealthy stride as he slipped by me. He seemed to be headed out to the big barn located nearby. I watched him with a curious new interest; he was in many ways a stranger to me. I had hardly existed in his grownup manly world.

His head turned ever so slightly as he walked by uttering something secretive through closed lips. "Well, come on," I watched his eyes black as thunderclouds.

Surprised, with my head held high in indignation, I replied in my bravest voice, "Mama said I can't go into the barn alone."

With what seemed a pained expression, he in turn replied,

"Well, I'm boss around here too, ya' know. And I say you can go into the barn with me."

My childish mind was spinning with uncertainty. Mama had said in a very important voice that I was not to go into the barn alone. Here was a grownup, my father, pressing me to go against Mama's wishes. My feet began shuffling from side to side, my hands felt cold. I tried to stuff them into my new jacket pockets but they didn't seem to fit. My tongue was dry, and now my hair seemed to be standing up funny. Tormented, I asked myself, what did he want me to go into that old barn for anyway? He had never, ever asked me to do anything with him before.

Now his eyes were becoming softer, almost smiling he gently presented, "Want to show you something."

I gingerly took an uncertain step forward. My feet had never felt so heavy. Show me something? Maybe he wants to be my father after all. Maybe he's going to show me how important I am. So, maybe it's okay to go into that old barn with him.

Reluctance turned into hope as I slowly approached him. He opened the huge barn door wide and stepped aside into a polite pose. My heart began to pound in my chest. What was there to be afraid of? He is my father. Mama won't be mad. I won't be in the barn alone.

Then a moment of cold fear gripped me as he pushed me through the open door ahead of him. Dust rose from the old barn floor. I blinked to adjust my eyes to the darkness ahead; I moved two steps forward. The huge barn door swung closed behind us. His hand now held my shoulder firmly, I dared not move again. What was he going to show me in this dark place? As if he read my thoughts, he released the grip on my shoulder and hurriedly moved ahead to face me. My stomach began to ache as waves of sickening fear washed over me. There was nothing here for me to see after all.

Father fell to his knees directly in front of my face. His large hands roughly lifted my new coat and felt for the elastic of my blue trousers. Grasping the pants he pulled them straight down, bringing my underwear down with them. I shivered with the cold air and the intense fear. What kind of punishment is this? My horrified mind was spinning. Groaning and gripping me with both hands, he pulled me to him and pushed his cold wet nose into my soft young belly. I was shivering violently, but his vise-like hands held me fast. He murmured, sniffed some more and grinned, "There's no hair on you yet, this is nice." He tried invading my private place with his cold finger, "You're going to be my girl now aren't you?"

I shook more and more, whimpering, crying, trying to pull away, large tears rolled down my cheeks. "OK, OK, there's nothin' to bawl that hard about." And with that statement, he roughly yanked my pants up, underwear and all, in one swift motion that lifted my feet up off the floor.

Freed at last. I turned blindly in the darkness, ran to the closed barn door and with my small fists pounded on the unrelenting door, until it swung open as if by magic. There stood my shocked and worried mother with anguished eyes. "What are you doing in this barn? What have I told you? You can't reach the latch, how did you get in here anyway?" Her voice trailed off as she squinted into the gloom and caught a glimpse of my father.

Scooting around her, I ran as fast as my little short legs would go. Now I knew Mama was mad at me. Still I ran to the house for safety. I decided to hide on the floor in the pantry. There were stacks of kettles that I could hide behind. Once settled into a good hiding place, with my heart pounding, the shivering lessened. *What on earth had just happened to me?* I couldn't seem to make sense of it.

I had no idea how much time passed. My hiding place

became cold and uncomfortable. I couldn't hear any sounds from the kitchen, so I decided to move out of the pantry. Surely now would be my chance to make a dash for safer ground. I clamored out from behind a huge kettle, softly lifted the pantry door latch, and peered out directly into my mother's accusing face. "I've been looking all over for you, how long have you been in there?"

Shocked and terrified, I knew she was going to hate me forever. I started to weep in shame, huge tears rolled down my cheeks and splashed onto the kitchen floor. She began her tirade. "What are you bawling for? All you had to do was mind me, couldn't you do that?" Her face now had become a blur as she pried me again and again, "Why did you go into that barn?" Choking, gasping for air, and stuttering, words would not fall out of my mouth. Desperate to defend my actions, I finally exclaimed, "He said I could go into the barn to see something."

Sarcastically she retorted, "And did you see something?"

"No," was my sheepish answer.

Her face took on a different shade of red as she peered at my sorry countenance. "Then what were you doing out there? What did your father do?"

Miraculously I could answer that question, I couldn't wait to blurt out, "He pulled my pants down."

Astonished and paled, her whole demeanor changed. Wringing her hands and screaming, "What?"

I started to cry again.

"I asked you, what did you say?" Storming and fuming into my face," are you lying to me young lady?"

I couldn't have spoken if I tried.

"All right then, I will ask your father, he'll tell me what's going on."

The kitchen door slammed louder and harder than ever before when she stormed outside to confront my father. I stood

for a while frozen dizzy with fear. *Oh, what have I done?* I overheard angry words being hurled back and forth between them.

The evening of that same day crawled slowly by, with no meal put on the family table. The whole house seemed to be in a wretched gloom. Much later, I was tucked silently into my bed, with no words to console me, lost and forgotten, I cried myself to sleep.

There is really no recollection of the time that must have passed before civility returned to our home. Perhaps a truce had occurred when my fifth birthday rolled around. Aunts and uncles of mine were due to appear for a celebration in late October with a cake and gifts. Usually when relatives arrived, friendly arguments and loud laughter were expected.

Conversations might lead into how young I would be when it was time for me to start school. Later, my mother had decided to announce to everyone at the party, "She needs to go to school to keep her out of trouble."

Eye brows raised, the relatives all smiled at my innocent birthday-girl self. During that uncomfortable moment, my father, ever the man of the hour, directed me toward a well-rehearsed challenge. "How much is twelve times twelve?"

I shyly answered, " One hundred and forty-four, " though I hardly knew what I was saying. The entertained folks smiled at him and clapped loudly. He had trained me well. Trumpeting his pride in himself, he finally nodded and grinned at me.

Mother's distaste for the incident was evident. I had hoped for a fleeting moment that she might understand my embarrassment or come to my aid. But instead there came a booming voice from my father, announcing, "That's my girl."

Totally alarmed at the vile insinuation, my heart sank into despair. This was not to be the last time that both my parents reduced me to numbness.

CHAPTER 9

THE FIRST DAY OF SCHOOL

*M*y father, mother and I rode together in the family car to the start of my first day of school. Without the slightest idea of what I was getting into, I hoped school was going to be a grand new adventure. When we arrived at the school building, the driveway was filled with emptying vehicles. I spied children running helter-skelter, laughing and chasing each other around the playground.

Mother and I approached the building walking slowly hand in hand. We walked through the wide entrance door, followed a line of children and found ourselves in a very large bustling classroom. The high windows in the room intrigued me; they seemed to reach to the ceiling. I could hear the children playing outside. Then I noticed the windows were covered on the outside with heavy wire mesh. Had some of the children tried to escape from this place? Maybe something out there wanted to crash in and grab everybody. This whole school idea began to give me the willies.

After a hurried introduction, I met Mrs. Corbett, an older

experienced first grade teacher. She immediately recognized my reluctance. I peered up at her to check her face for moral support. She smiled down at me with eyes warm and comforting. My mother, standing close by, grimaced and turned away from me. Without a word of goodbye she began threading her way back out of the room, leaving me feeling alone and forlorn.

I noticed many other little children wailing and clinging to their mothers. Such a noise they were making. I would never have been allowed to act like that. Mrs. Corbett began gathering all her new charges into a group around her. With a slight sweep of her hand, the mothers began to disperse quietly, stepping softly as they left their dear little children behind to enjoy their first day of school.

At long last that first day of school had come to an end and it was time to run across the yard to the waiting school bus. There it sat, rumbling and huffing smoky breath filling the air around it. After one look at all that, I decided to linger on the playground awhile. Ida, my new comrade who was several years older, in the seventh grade came running over to me, grabbed my hand and pulled me up over the slick metal steps of the waiting bus. The dingy bus door slammed behind us and we rolled away.

On the noisy trip, Ida sat with angel-warmth in her eyes and gently held my hand in hers. All too soon the old wretched machine began to slow down. It ground to a shuddering halt. The door screeched a protest as it was opened. I sat still as a mouse. The driver, also wretched, hating his job, barked fiercely and howled like a wolf, which sent the kids who were sitting behind me into raucous laughter.

Ida and I finally exited the bus together. She kept a tight grip on my shaking hand while we crossed the road in front of the groaning bus. She kept talking constantly to me about the rules of the road. "The road means danger! Always keep your eyes on

the lookout for cars coming and going. Specially watch out for big log trucks coming fast; they can't stop. Don't just watch the front of the bus. Sometimes wise guys will drive out around the bus, see you, and won't stop. Got it?"

I nodded my reply. Ida waved to the bus driver to continue on without her. We were left standing in the wake of heavy smoke and loud grindings of the machine. We walked together slowly down the hill, toward home, while she admonished me more about the dangers of the road. We finally reached the old iron bridge which led to the homestead, paused and smiled at each other. And for the first time that day Ida and I felt a quiet relief.

She turned, headed back up the hill and walked home to her house which was a mile away. There didn't seem to be any reason to unhinge my parents over my rescue. I knew there would come a time when I would handle all of this school bus business alone, thanks to my dear friend Ida.

AFTER A FEW MORE WEEKS OF school, I settled into a routine. Grammar school seemed to have become much more fun. I enjoyed learning new things such as *The Lord's Prayer* and the *Pledge of Allegiance* to the flag of our country. None of this important business had ever been discussed at home. Indeed I felt it was all fitting and proper for my school life.

The rides to and from school had now changed significantly. Our old huff-and-puff monster bus was finally safely put away. The replacement in the form of an old rusted and dilapidated station wagon was much smaller. But we were not without our usual acrid smoke which we had grown accustomed to. The engine labored loudly as we crawled slowly away from each stop.

Lately I had become the only girl to ride in the station wagon

bus. I did not see Ida anymore. I supposed she had moved away. The rear seats were filled to the brim with noisy roughneck boys. The torn front passenger seat was my throne. The driver, with the butt of a cigarette forever stuck to his lower lip, would cast a searing glance into the cloudy rear view mirror. His look would cause more snickering and jostling of each other from the noisy boys. Now and then I'd accidentally, of course, get a swat to the back of my head from a boy's misplaced rap. I was disturbed by this and thereby looked directly at the driver's profile to spot if he had noticed. His contribution to my defense was usually a loud, "Hey!" But one rainy day, he'd had enough of the boys and their swearing, raging commotion. The bus ground to a stop. The angry bus driver with his drooping cigarette butt, turned around, reached into the backseat, pulled out a victim, gave him a shake and stuffed him back into place. For a moment the silence was deafening. After the lesson on bus etiquette the boys were slightly quieter. Certainly all too soon the wrestling in the back seat resumed, and we were on our noisy merry way again.

One afternoon the lumbering crate of a school bus had finally once again reached my destined stop. I left my safe, tattered front seat midst howling and hissing from the backseat gang. I was ready for my peaceful walk home. Ambling along down the hill, lunchbox swinging, and day dreaming with my three invisible friends finally caused me to smile. I had invented these friends to accompany me on my way home each day.

Later that week after one of my most challenging school days was finally over, I slowly scuffed along the familiar dusty road toward home. It seemed that one of my invisible friends was in an argumentative mood. My voice soon rose unexpectedly as I lashed out with an angry retort.

Then, of all people in the world, my father, suddenly appeared on the road in front of me. He stopped and looked

around the area in disbelief. There was no one in sight but me. He fumed his displeasure, "I could hear you talking to somebody! You'd better stop that! Somebody's going to hear you and think you're crazy!"

His words hurt. I said nothing at all in defense of myself. He strode away annoyed and left me to ponder the consequences of my actions. Subsequently on the next day's walk home, my little invisible friends accompanied me as usual. We decided to whisper our anxious questions to one another so as not to be disturbed while we discussed the school day.

* * *

I LEARNED how to do many new things at school, but eating my lunch was not one of them as my stomach was perpetually in knots; I always felt nauseated by the mention of food. Eating at school became a challenge between Mother and me. She wrote notes to my first-grade teacher, "Watch her, don't let her throw her lunch away." So I disposed of sandwiches in pieces, for birds to enjoy on my walk home alone. In the winter time life became more difficult. Sandwiches were frozen too hard for me to break, so the whole sandwich wrapper and all flew up over the snow-banks along the road. During the springtime melt, my father spotted sandwiches all along the roadside.

My frustrated mother growled her displeasure at Father. His answer was, "Give her what she will eat." Soon a lovely peanut butter and jelly sandwich, banana, and two Oreo cookies landed in my lunchbox one day a week. It worked. I ate lunch once a week.

My father decided to become watchman over me as I walked home no longer alone. After two afternoons his companionship changed. He pulled me behind him by the

hand out into the swampy field along the roadway. Wet hay grew wild and tall there. I began to sneeze and squirm helplessly as he lifted my now wet school dress up over my face. I shivered with fear when he sniffed my belly and slid lower to explore my little girl's smoothness. Insects began buzzing around my dizzy head as I tried to squirm away. But since he wasn't going to be interrupted groaning, breathing, and saying silly words, I felt myself become numb. Comforting thoughts came to mind such as, he won't be tattling to Mama about my lunch disposals anymore.

Much later when I finally walked into the kitchen wet to my waist and met Mother with her crossed arms and pointed look, I waited for the questions to begin. Arms definitely tightly crossed and eyes glaring, she looked me up and down and did not utter a word. She just turned away; my usual clue to vanish to my room until supper time.

Shortly after that incident, my father no longer accompanied me on my walk home. Indeed, he disguised himself as a caring parent: thus he began hammering on hot metal in his blacksmith shop adjacent to the garage. On one previous occasion he had demonstrated this fascinating art to my mother while I watched from a safe distance away. Today he was beckoning me with a friendly wave of his hand to stand by and watch the magical proceedings. Hesitation gave way to curiosity while I ran to the tiny door of the shop.

He began his speech about molding metal into fine farm tools while he walked backwards into the darker depths of the shed. Then he reached for my clothes with his sooty blackened gloves. My heart was racing, "Lift your dress for me," he ordered in a raspy whisper.

"What are you doing in here?" It was my mother's voice from behind me. Father began mumbling about teaching black-

27

smithing or something. But Mama seemed to be most annoyed at me. "Come with me young lady, your dress is a mess."

I followed close behind her, leaving the teacher to himself. She lectured to me about coming straight home. "And don't stop at the garage."

I moaned a response, "What if he wants me to go over to watch him?"

She snapped, "I just told you, ignore him and get your little ass into the house."

I sighed, knowing that was easier said than done when it came to my father.

As expected later, Father pulled me aside, grumbling and groaning his displeasure. He attempted to fill my head with plans for sneaking around to see him. Most avidly he spelled out, "And keep your mouth shut."

Too young to understand anything about them, I felt anguished, guilty and cornered by both of my parents.

CHAPTER 10

THIRD GRADE

*G*oing into the third grade meant that I would move to another room to be with a new teacher. Classrooms at our small elementary school now held three grades. My newly assigned room had the first, second and third grades together. Of course those of us who were the oldest grade in the room, had privileges over the younger children. We had special times set aside for our own chosen activities. For many of my classmates standing at an easel with a long handled paintbrush and brightly colored pots of paint was a popular pastime.

I was not inclined to include myself in such a messy project. The teacher tried coaxing me, patiently providing an apron to wear. She placed newspapers on the floor around the easel to catch random splashes. Finally, one day, with much trepidation, I slowly approached the easel in front of me.

Staring at the large piece of blank paper before me, the brush heavy in my hand, I stopped to catch the teacher's smile of assurance. Solemnly I plunged the brush to the bottom of a jar of black paint. Onto the paper I outlined a form of my house with

chimneys growing sideways out of the roof. I gently put the brush back into the jar of black, and stepped away, I was finished. Understandably the teacher seemed unnerved, so I tried the whole process another day. Black was my color and my house continued to be my only subject.

In due time, tiny pencil drawings sketched on small pieces of paper interested me. One day I was challenged by a little boy to draw something especially for him. He said he would draw what a girl's private place looked like if I would do the same. I promptly refused. So he said he would do a drawing first just to show me what he knew about such things. To which I replied, "OK."

His rendition amounted to a wild scribbling, and we both giggled enormously when he retorted, "That's hair."

Surely I had to set him straight with my firm exclamation, "I don't have any hair!"

It was my turn to challenge his manly art work. So we agreed to swap pictures of the male species. We exchanged drawings, the little boy blanched in horror and unabashedly exclaimed, "I don't look like that!"

Too much for the eavesdropping teacher to bear, she rushed over to us and rudely grabbed our little pieces of paper. Mortified, she stared at the clearly aroused form I'd drawn. After gulping down her embarrassment she asked me calmly, "Where have you seen this?"

Proudly I knew the answer and I wanted to please my new teacher, so I calmly answered, "My Father."

Our teacher, keeping her calm demeanor, reported that she would like to come to my house for a little visit with my parents. She further explained that after her school chores were done this evening she would be right down.

True to her word she did drive right up into the dooryard of

the farm house. As she left the car, I watched her turn and give me a slight smile before she entered through the door to the kitchen. I heard a display of hearty greetings and then a quiet meeting must have taken place. I was not invited.

But I surmised that all was well when my mother burst out of the house with my teacher following close behind. They headed to the vegetable garden which was filled with a surplus of tomatoes. Soon I heard talk of gardens, canning and green beans. My teacher finally exited the garden smiling and headed for her car with a box of vegetables tucked under her arm. Without a look in my direction she jumped into her car and drove away from the homestead in a cloud of dust.

CHAPTER 11

RELIGION

One school day brought forth a surprising visit from a religious lady. We were enchanted by her divine love for our third grade class. She distributed colored pictures of Jesus's face and crosses that glowed in the dark. We were thrilled to receive such lovely gifts and listened intently to her soothing words of wisdom.

Of course my parents were appalled at the glaringly flagrant approach of her religious speech at my school. I was only allowed to hang the glowing cross on my bedroom wall for a short time. One day it mysteriously disappeared while I was at school. Broken hearted, I tried feverishly to appeal to my mother for its return. But there was no sympathy for my anguished cries.

Years later, in the sixth grade classroom at the same school, we had a curiously lenient teacher. He allowed his students to help themselves to classroom supplies from the school's stockroom. Each lesson required a specific type and color of paper, so we willingly left our seats to dip into the treasure trove of paper.

One·day as we stood lined up in the stockroom doorway, I

watched a student take a one inch thick packet of math paper. With a smirky smile he tucked it up under his shirt. I had always loved the smooth quality of clean white math paper. I, too, would help myself to an inch thick stack of that lovely paper. I quietly transferred most of it to my lunchbox left nearby in the cloakroom. I even added a few new yellow pencils to my private stash.

At home in the evening, whenever my mother opened my lunchbox, she took a very dim view of this new habit I was forming.

My mother decided I needed a dose of the Holy Bible. She emphatically pointed out to me, the phrase plainly written, "Thou shalt not steal." She included another line for good measure, "Honor thy Mother and thy Father."

I was distressed and then relieved to learn about such a book. Religion had finally come to light for me. I eventually acquired my very own Holy Bible and began with anxious fervor to study its contents. Hard-to-understand words and meanings slowed me down. But I got the gist that there was a loving God and He did not like badness.

I also learned the Golden Rule, which was a great start for a sixth grader. The religion I'd searched for had found me. Inadvertently my mother had set me up for a moralistic lifestyle which she herself could not maintain. But to this day I am thankful for her insight and timing of her gift to me, religion.

CHAPTER 12

GREAT EXPECTATIONS

"*Y*ou expect too much from people" my mother said as she turned her back to me.

But why do people say things if they don't mean it? I had just turned seven years old and was becoming disappointed with my school chums; I wanted answers. Surely my mother would enlighten my fevered mind and explain their careless actions. But as I attempted to form the question again, she simply repeated her pat answer. *Somehow life was all my own fault. My expectations were too high, yes, that's what it was. It hadn't occurred to me before; she was probably right.*

Even today, so many years later, her words ring in my ears. *Is it my fault that someone doesn't call when they promised they would? Why would they say they would if they didn't mean it? I guess I still expect too much. So I am angry with people. How dare they take my feelings so lightly? It hurts to feel so let down. Well, feelings be damned; let people say and do as they please. I won't let myself be affected anymore. I'll become numb to those ups and downs. By now, as an adult I'm old enough to know better.*

Admitting to myself that something my mother said sixty-five

years ago still affects my confidence—I wonder if she was just trying to teach me life's lessons? Not being one for flourishes or explanations, perhaps she just didn't want to notice her child's cry for help. Maybe she enjoyed watching my childish frustrated anger push me down. Maybe she was cramped with her own anger and enjoyed my anguish. Somehow I don't think she enjoyed me at all.

I was always searching for answers to questions that my mother would not hear. Especially when I asked her why my father was so intent on forcing me to touch him in private places. He was always trying to find a spot to be alone with me when I was only seven years old. She wouldn't answer me when I cried out to her my fears and helplessness.

"Tell him, NO!" she would finally say with a look of glowering impatience.

Frantically I continued to cry out to her, "He won't listen to me!"

The answer was always the same; she'd turn away and busy herself with something more important, which was my cue that the conversation was over.

Now, in my Golden Years, my eyes still sting with angry tears for that poor anguished child's cry for help. But even then, I would not relinquish my hold on her. I would continue to ply her with intimidating questions about my Father's actions.

Consequently one day I decided to try her idea of Just *tell him no*. One fall day my Father and I were going for a ride in his old fifties-era automobile. He always told Mother that I'd begged to go on outings with him, which was a blatant lie. Here I was, seven years old, caring nothing about a ride in his car, feeling car sick, and now alone again with him. He was enjoying his slick plan as he drove, smiling he reached over to touch me, as I cowered close to the passenger door. "We're

going to a lake up there on that dirt road that turns right at the stop sign."

My stomach dropped to the floor. My heart was beating loudly in my ears. *This was it, my chance to say no.* My face burned, my ears rang even louder as I squirmed in the seat. After a long moment I managed to muster a soft reply, "I don't want to go."

He was so taken aback his foot automatically slammed on the brakes. The car weaved and jerked its way up to the stop sign. Screaming his resentment toward me, "What's the matter with you? I came all the way out here just to make you happy!"

"I don't think it's a good thing," I cried out hopefully.

"And where did you hear that? Why are you being so miserable to me? I think you are being a piece of shit for hurting me this way."

Stunned at hearing his harsh words, I knew it would be only a matter of minutes before he attempted to do something rash. I could barely breathe. All my hopes slid away. I waited for a moment before moaning sadly, "I just don't think it's right."

His flushed red face said it all. He whipped the car roughly around into a U-turn and headed us back the way we had come.

The only recourse I had left; I tried to explain further, "Mama said I should tell you no."

"Oh she did, and you believed her. You're a piece of shit for telling her about our special secret. I told you never to tell anybody. And of course you opened your stupid mouth, now you've spoiled our whole day."

Disappointment and confusion sent me into a tailspin. I started shaking and crying miserably. He watched me squirm and finally slump with despair into the seat, hugging the car door. After a while he must have thought better of his little speech and tried soothing me with mushy words of endearment. He reached

over and touched my face. I shook more and cried harder. *What had just happened? What did I think would happen when I said no?*

I crawled deep into myself and my mind quieted, I had entered into my safe place.

"There that's better," he admonished with relief. "We don't want Mama to see you've been crying. She won't let you come with me anymore. And we don't want that, do we? Next time I'll find us a place closer to home so you won't have to get upset. OK?"

Defeated, I nodded my assent to his new plan. *And now what was I going to tell Mama?*

CHAPTER 13

MY LITTLE SISTER

With a sigh of relief, Father and I finally arrived home that fateful day. And I didn't have to tell my mother anything. When we walked through the front door and into the kitchen she was busily feeding my baby sister in the old wooden highchair. She merely cast a glance my way, immediately took in my red rimmed eyes, calculated my sad walk toward my bedroom and knew I'd said "no" to my father.

My little sister, then about a year old, squirmed impatiently in the highchair. Mother sat and shoveled food into the child's gaping mouth repeatedly, until the baby gave up her lunch all over the place.

Mother, expecting this maneuver, cleaned her up and began shoveling another fresh dish of food into her. Thus went the drill for feeding my allergy-ridden little sister. Weakened by mysterious multiple allergies and a vicious dose of asthma, she would frequently have seizures. Mother would breathe life back into her little blue-baby many times. Lack of oxygen to the poor baby's newly forming brain left her at times unresponsive and quiet. As

she grew, I became aware of her as a toddler who never seemed to play.

"What's the matter with her?" I questioned.

"Never mind, she just has asthma. She's allergic to food and plants. You just watch that she doesn't eat bad stuff and get into my flowers in front of the house."

Explanation over, I was to get on with my own little life. Did I know that she was not healthy? No, I expected her to laugh and play like other little children. When I was six, I'd shake her just to get a loud response, and slap her to make her cry. But Mother slapped me in return, so I'd know how it felt. So I cried but my sister wouldn't.

I was almost twelve before a family member, my aunt, informed me that my little sister had been through a difficult birth and a terrible beginning. She was not a normal healthy child. I needed to be more sympathetic and helpful toward her. Stricken with guilt over how I'd hurt my very own little sister, I vowed to be more understanding towards her in the future.

How long do you think that patient, understanding plan lasted? When I became thirteen, she was eight and in grammar school. I felt it was time for her to wake up and become a normal child.

I still found myself fighting her battles for her. I remember the day her second grade teacher took me aside to inform me that my sister was suffering from a terrible headache. I thought to myself, with all those allergies, when did she not have a headache? So the concerned teacher offered to give her some aspirin.

Then I went into tirades over her lack of knowledge and informed her that my sister was deathly allergic to aspirin.

"But she asked for aspirin" was the teacher's defense.

To which I responded disrespectfully that she had no idea

what she was doing, meaning my sister, of course. A note from the teacher went home in my lunchbox, expounding on my behavior. So my mother wrote a long note back to her explaining my sister's health condition for future reference.

After that incident I was portrayed as a meany by my peers. Still, when my sister became obstinate I would simply grab her behind the collar and drag her unceremoniously behind me until she got the point. Usually that happened when it was time to climb into the school bus to go home. She probably didn't like going home after school any more than I did.

We walked down the hill together at the end of the school day. We were each other's sounding board for dealing with friends and foes. She had her own outlook on life, with surprising intuitions for one so young. My father never abused her; he must have sensed a formidable outcome. She never knew he abused me. I spoke of it to her in later years; she would not hear of it.

CHAPTER 14

BLUEBERRY BUCKLE

One morning, I overheard my father emphatically explaining to my mother, "Blueberries everywhere, just hanging on bushes in clumps. I'll bring her along and she can pick a whole pail-full while I get some work done down in the mine. We'll bring a lunch, we'll stay all day, weather's going to be nice. She'll be fine."

"Hey, hey wait a minute! I don't know how to pick blueberries!" I admonished under my breath, "where are we going anyway, you mean I'm going to be alone with him all day?" *Mother must really hate me.*

I was seven years old, did I know what they were talking about? How could my mother set me up for this intimidation, especially when she knew how my father was when he was alone with me? He sold her the idea, that's what it was. Thoughts of all those pails of blueberries must have clouded her judgment. I was stuck.

We left the farm early in the fog the next morning. We drove up the steep winding paved road twenty miles to the little town of

Canaan, N.H. This road was renowned for dumping logging trucks over on their sides as they lost their brakes coming down the long treacherous hills. Over the cliffs they would go, logs rolling everywhere, trucks crushed along with the driver. Oh, I was scared all right. I'd never been on this nightmare of a road before. Those blueberries had better be good. This was only the beginning of the trip.

My father had leased the mineral rights to a mica mine on the site of Mt. Cardigan State Park. It wasn't meant for tourists; there was a fire access road that led to the fire tower atop the mountain. The mica mine was a hole in the ground that plunged six hundred feet down through granite ledges. Water was constantly pouring into the hole via springs that would fill the mine up overnight. In the morning, Father would fire up the water pumps and empty the mine to expose the valuable minerals at the bottom of the deep fault. Ladders led down the steep sides to landings built at safe levels and continued on down to veins of valuable mica. There were beautiful gems and minerals down there also. He was captivated by sparkling precious stones and paid no attention to the dangers of mining.

But first there was to be the trip up the fire road via the four wheel drive Army issue Jeep. The *Power Wagon* was famous for slowly clamoring up over mountainsides otherwise viewed as inaccessible. I sat gingerly in the torn passenger seat on exposed wire springs. I clung to the door handle as we rode, slamming from side to side, the vehicle growling and grinding down across holes and up over boulders.

There really was no actual road, just a hint of a path that wound endlessly through brush and downed trees. Large boulders loomed ahead; we clambered up and over them. Deep holes filled with mysterious ingredients awaited us. We dipped deep down into them, splashing water and brown stuff over the hood

and cracked windshield. It was not long before I was mortally ill, green with motion sickness, aching with pains from head to toe. Rocking and slamming, bouncing and sliding, my aching head surely was going to fall off. Maybe we could stop so I might relieve my stomach of its rattled contents?

But no, there was no mercy for me. On we went, sometimes backward, when we mired in the mud. Back up and slam forward again. Brutal body slams until I could no longer hold on to the door and slid to the floor. I crunched down and covered my head waiting for the end to come.

Finally, after what seemed an eternity, the Jeep's punishment stopped with an unceremonious bang. I carefully extricated myself out from under the dash. Slowly focusing my eyes on the strangely sparse surroundings, I didn't see blueberries dripping off tall healthy plants. I spotted scrubby little bushes sporadically growing out of rock crevices. And to make matters worse, many of the blueberries were mixed with prickly juniper bushes. I knew what they were like. We had them growing on the farm. Their needles stung and their blue-colored berries were bitter.

I turned my heavy head around to check Father's view of all this. He had already exited the cab and without a look back trudged off down a narrow, slippery trail to the mine. Shaking with every conceivable emotion, including bitterness, my body refused to move. Perplexed and wounded, I just sat very still for a long time, waiting for the inevitable outcome. Sure enough, he popped out of the dense woods, impatiently searching for me. Father's eyes squinted disgustedly at me sitting motionless in the cab of the jeep.

"What's the matter with you? Can't you take care of yourself? I looked all over for you, I thought you were going to follow me."

His gruff voice brought me out of my stupor. I began to

squirm on the scratchy seat. He opened the door beside me with a mighty racking motion meant to express his anger at my frailness. I slid slowly, carefully, delicately out on to the ground. Gagging and choking began; soon there was no stopping the mighty upheaval of what seemed to be everything I'd ever eaten in my lifetime. I knew I was going to die.

Father lost no time in taking over the situation. He began dragging me by the hand down the narrow trail heading to the mine. After we arrived he produced a filthy old blanket full of holes and spread it on the ground. Pointing at it and nodding was my clue to sit down. But not before he roughly pulled off my soggy clothes. Standing there naked set my teeth chattering even though the air was warm. He spoke softly, uttering words I did not understand while he pushed me over backwards down onto the grimy blanket.

Mournful sounds escaped him. His nose rubbed my tender stomach. Then his hands kept moving all over me. Time for me to enter into my quiet place; as this action of his was overwhelming my senses. I just wanted to feel numb. The only recollection of the rest of that day was of him raking blueberries quickly into a pail just before we left for home. I'd been sick and couldn't pick very many. I could hear the story he'd be telling Mama. Back into my quiet place I went. And there I stayed. The next day I went to school and felt nothing. There was no fear to deal with, no lies to tell, no anger to bear. I eventually emerged from my stupor, but now I knew I could slip into my own world easily whenever I needed an escape. This was my way of coping.

CHAPTER 15

REVELATION

I now realize that my father assumed that I owed him my very existence. Yes, I was owned by him. He took all he could from me as long as he lived. Though disheartened, I accepted my duty of giving him all that he thought he deserved. But one fine day he went too far in his quest for ownership of my soul.

From age twelve to eighteen, I had traveled extensively with my family across the United States. East to the west, and back again we journeyed to satisfy my father's wandering search for gold.

One hot summer in August the family holed up for a short while in the desert hills of Nevada. In a very rundown structure, aptly called the *cow camp* meant for desert rats and other vermin, we set up a home of sorts. Indescribable conditions, dirt floor, no windows, not for human habitation.

My mother was sickly, six months pregnant with my youngest sister to be. The family, comprised of my nine year old sister, sickly mother, gold miner father and me, was in dire need of a

month's supply of groceries. The nearest store was a long drive over mountain passes into California at least a hundred or more miles away.

Leaving my mother behind in that horrible hut, six months pregnant and with my nine year old sister, in the desert with no food or medicines seemed unholy to me. We left her and my sister sitting on the edge of a rusty iron bed frame with a filthy lump for a mattress. Reluctantly, upon my father's insistence, I was to accompany him on the journey. I was fourteen years old, so I was handed the responsibility of finding groceries and supplies for the family to last a month. Mother gave me a list of sundries written in smudged pencil on a piece of brown paper, and fervently asked that I choose only the most necessary items.

Early in the morning I climbed into the rickety pickup truck with my father. The old truck ground its way slowly across the valley and finally began to climb upward over the first mountain pass. Travel was slow and tedious; I rode in silence. Finally Father decided to stop on the summit to cool the hissing, rumbling radiator that was pouring out its steamy reluctance from under the hood.

We pulled over onto a rough side road that was obscured by stunted gnarly trees, the kind that try to grow only in the highest mountain elevations. Relieved to be rid of the heat and noise of the engine's roar, we sat outside on the truck's open tailgate to rest. As my head cleared, in my peripheral vision I caught sight of my father staring intently at my bosom. I ignored his vile attention, but soon he took matters into his own hands.

Roughly grabbing my upper arms and trying to force me to attend to him was frightening. His intentions had never been this wild before. He pushed me over backwards further into the back of the truck. Bumping my head during that move only accelerated his anger. I was frantic, by now my pants had been removed;

thankfully, my body would not respond to his harried attempts to penetrate me. After his audacity sent my mind into a quiet place, I calmly set aside my initial fright. Thoughts of his indecent imposition on my will gave me more strength to withhold my body from him. He, becoming more and more upset, called me filthy names that only added to my determination. Ultimately his strength and lust waned, leaving him exhausted with his own pants down. He had lost his frenzied battle with me. Finally the harsh reality of my father's lack of love and respect for me had hit home.

So we continued on our harsh journey up and down more mountain passes, to finally reach our destination in a town where I could shop for the much needed supplies. After two hours of decisions made solely by myself, for the welfare of the family, we headed back to the *cow camp*. On the trip back, he rambled on and on about his fatherly duties, expecting words of sympathy from me, of which there were none.

We finally landed at the camp, off-loaded the goods into a nearby shed and approached the dark room where the rest of the family waited. Mother instantly recognized seething anger on my face. She seemed to suddenly recover her diminished strength, and boldly asked me, "What happened?"

With a shake of my head there were no words to be said. I could never have explained my crushing disappointment to her. What if she collapsed in anguish and lost the baby? No, this lesson was all mine to savor until my indentured time was over.

CHAPTER 16

GOLD MINER'S DAUGHTER

*M*y father had taken up prospecting for the elusive gold to satisfy his lust for unusual adventure. Friends would gather around him to listen to his boastful stories of the riches that were hidden in the old abandoned mines of the Nevada high desert.

Thoughts of what the circumstances might do to my mother and me never entered his mind. We were just along for the ride, or for the work as he saw it. My mother was in it for the dollars and I was just in it because he liked to watch my body work.

Our family had traveled from state to state for years searching for the best gold prospects. We had camped in the hills of Arizona, Colorado, and California in old forgotten shanties left over from the gold strike days of the 1800s.

Schooling was a nightmare for me as a teenager, in and out of a new town every month, had left no time to make acquaintances or learn basic studies.

Nevada proved to have the most promising holes already dug

into the hills. Desert canyons rolled out the gold carpet for the believers. Settling down in Nevada, I could finally make myself known in a high school. While it was over a hundred miles away from where we lived, the school could give me what I needed for an education. Teachers and friends enjoyed my sense of humor and capacity for learning.

Our most recent prospecting encampment had a wooden floor, a cold water faucet, a propane cook stove and a tiny old wood stove. Two whole rooms gave the family the privacy they sorely needed. I preferred getting dressed without Father's lustful eyes upon me.

Five miles up the canyon road from the cabin lay the riches to be garnered for other miners to usurp. Father had deduced from his testing procedures that a certain old tunnel previously dug twenty feet into the hill was where the vein of rich ore would soon be discovered by him. Located high up at the top rim of the canyon, this mine would be "The Mother Lode."

Father laid out a compressor, a jack hammer and a broken wheelbarrow to begin work inside the tunnel. His expertise had been drilling and blasting granite back east in the deep mica mines. Here, the rock was limestone that crumbled at the slightest provocation. But still the urge to drill had to be met.

He finally found a solid vein of gray quartz inside the mine. Soon the drilling began. While the jackhammer shook my body, I tried to hold it in position on the hard quartz. He had to help me hold it in place of course as the jackhammer rattled me from top to bottom. Satisfied with the holes spaced strategically, it was time to load them with sticks of dynamite. A stick would be cut in half, a whole stick would cause too much damage to the cave walls. The half stick was carefully pushed down into a freshly drilled hole, followed by a "dummy." This was a tube of rolled news-

paper filled with sand to be inserted into each hole on top of the dynamite. Each charge needed to be held in its proper place. A blasting cap was then inserted into the "dummy" including a length of black fuse wire. Wires now hung from the charged holes in a neat row along the cavern wall.

Hang-fires, as they were called, when one fuse took a long time to detonate, was a disaster waiting to happen. Old fuse wire, slow blasting caps and especially old dynamite were a constant concern for miners, so they counted each detonated blast meticulously. My father concluded that he wanted to boast of his wealth later after all the dust had settled.

My mother and I took our places a safe distance away from the intended explosion. After lighting each fuse, Father took stock of the impending blast, looking around the area for loose miner's critters while he listened for approaching rattletrap pickups. Finally, he gravely announced in a booming voice that echoed around the hills of the canyon, "Fire in the Hole!"

OUT OF THE rough outline of the limestone tunnel entrance, blue acrid smoke escaped like a roaring freight train. Roiling plumes seemed to blast pieces of dusty particles high into the air overhead, floating, until at last debris began to settle to the ground. The landscape changed from stunted green pine trees and thick sagebrush into a gray world covered with the finest alkali dust and fine limestone powder.

Three people stood by waiting for the smoky conditions to clear away from the tunnel's entrance. The old man, my father, waited alone behind a pile of crumbled rocks. My mother and I were huddled behind a huge boulder, with our hands held over our heads for protection from falling rocks. Father surveyed the

situation with an air of excitement. He liked looking at those girls as they began to emerge from their cover. My mother looked good, petite, tanned and energetic for her 32 years. I was 15, young and strong.

The tunnel lead to a gold mine hidden deep in the hillside of a well forested canyon wall. "Probably the Mother Lode" he surmised to himself that supplied the lower land of the canyon with riches. Up here in the hills lay the hard gray quartz in veins of bedrock, laced with lead that signaled the possibility of impressive gold specimens. Prospecting and testing every rock of interest in this canyon had finally lead to this moment. Blasting out the inside of the tunnel could reveal a new vein of gold that might shine in the light of the miner's carbide lamp.

Impatient to catch a glimpse of his dream gold, he began to walk toward the blue smoky depths of the mine entrance. We watched his progress, then decided to try to change his mind. The fumes from exploded dynamite were toxic to his heart condition. His heart would thump and his breath shorten as soon as he inhaled the smoke. Sliding a hand down my young girl's shiny, tanned arms produced the same effect. My mother tossed her black hair off her face and smiled as she watched him head for the mine.

Always, after the initial blasted material was settled, there remained the job of removing the muck from the tunnel floor. Shoveling wheelbarrow loads of gritty, cobbled limestone and chunks of bedrock off the ground inside the smoky tunnel was a loathsome chore. Fill the rusted, sadly in-need-of-repair iron wheelbarrow, roll it outside, down a plank board to the edge of the dumpsite. Grip the dry cracked handles and lift the load of rocks up on end and watch them tumble down the mountainside. Again and again, I rolled the wobbly iron wheelbarrow back and forth from the tunnel to the dump. My father kept a

watchful eye on me, his hands always ready to keep me in motion. A nudge here and a squeeze there on my unwilling body and soon the floor of the goldmine was made ready for more prospecting.

Deep inside the mine, Mother was already chipping at the walls of the cave with a small pick hammer. She pulled pieces of new quartz specimens down onto the cleaned floor to be inspected more carefully later. Meanwhile a skirmish was taking place outside of the tunnel.

Grabbed from behind, my father had his arm wound tightly around my neck, his "reward" for my hard work. We were hidden behind a very large sagebrush where the wheelbarrow was usually stashed. Roughly he squeezed my ample breasts and tried to pull me closer to himself. The stench of his unwashed body and nervous sweat sent my head into a spin. Leaning forward desperately, I wound my fingers around the woody stems of the old sagebrush and managed to twist myself free of his grasp. Then I ran for the safety of the cool dark cave.

The mine was still laden with heavy residual smoke; I plunged into it blindly, stumbling and falling. Sitting among the debris with my arms wrapped around my knees, heart pounding, breath rasping, I thought I might cry. Deeper inside this dark, damp world came the intermittent sound of a small pick hammer loosening bits of ore, followed by the hollow clank of rocks falling into a tin can. As usual the only source of light, a dented carbide lamp, spluttered and finally blew its tiny flame out.

"Damn that stinkin' thing" growled my mother. She made a quick grab for it in the dark, slammed it back to life for a mere moment's light, then tucked her rusty can of treasures under her arm. With the can of quartz rocks secured she turned and began stumbling toward the sunlit opening of the mine's entrance. Clamoring and swearing over the obstruction of my body sitting

in her path, and with one more gasp for fresh air she finally reached the bright opening.

I remained sitting on the floor of the now quiet peaceful cave, alone at last. Sniffling, shaking and almost crying, I finally leaned back to rest against the cool damp wall. Random thoughts of scorpions, snakes and lizards began to take shape in my scrambled mind. The twenty foot length of tunnel completely dark seemed less safe now.

"Git out here", came a shout from someone blocking the light at the end of the tunnel. "C'mon out right NOW!"

The fierce command jolted my heart-racing, head-aching, dizzying thoughts as I asked myself, "what was worse, the inside or the outside of this awful place?"

After trying to stand on my wobbly legs I fell to the floor, crawling slowly on all fours toward the light. My worn out flip flops and ragged cut-off shorts, weren't much protection from the harshness of the cave's floor, now freshly scattered with broken stones. Finally when I could crawl no more someone roughly tugged me out by my arm. Mother was awash in anger and excitement about her find. "Git up, look at this, it's a real specimen, could be worth a hundred dollars easy, git up, look!"

Too much noise for my aching head. Young and strong with a will to survive, I gathered all my strength, jumped up from the ground and directly met her face. Grimacing, I brushed past both of my parents without a word. I usually walked the desert hills of Nevada when my tormented heart could take no more of the everyday frustrations that seemed to plague my life. Alone I sought answers from the canyons of the Nevada high desert. I found my much needed solace from nature's dependable beauty.

On a few rare occasions when my younger sister was out of grammar school, we would set out for a day of exploration together. Usually our little border-collie dog came along with us.

His job was to flush out the rattlesnakes that might be hidden in the sagebrush near us. Their warning buzzes always sent us on detours to avoid any contact. We never actually saw any of those bad guys, our trusty protector was always on point, and was never bitten.

CHAPTER 17

THE LIVING END

We were finally back home again on the farm in New Hampshire, after another stint of gold mining in the Nevada desert. It seemed good to be back; but here I was, twenty-one years old, contemplating spinsterhood while feeling the sad effects of another autumn approaching. Leaves were flying away and so were my hopes of ever living a normal life. I stepped sullenly out through the door of the farmhouse, while preparing myself for another dreary day. Upon looking up, I perceived my father's blurred image as he stood motionless beside the old family car, a dark green Cadillac. Tilting his head provocatively toward the car door, he silently invited me to accompany him. As usual, I felt trapped with nowhere to turn for help. After years of his bullying, conjuring and tantrums, he had crushed my will. After a short while, I reluctantly climbed into the passenger seat with much trepidation; by now I knew the drill.

He drove silently out of the dooryard and stopped the car next to the mailbox on top of the hill. He climbed out of the car

while issuing his usual orders for me to get into the backseat with him. Once settled into position, he began adjusting himself, pulling his trousers down around his ankles, struggling with a condom and finally growling at me to undress.

I slowly exited the front seat. While I leaned toward the car's open back door, he reached across the backseat, ruthlessly grabbed me by my hair and began shouting orders, "Get in here bitch, get up on my lap, spread yourself across me."

As I attempted to climb over him; he set to work tearing at my clothes. Shaking anxiously he began gripping my hips tightly while he squirmed crazily under me. Though I could see the situation escalating; my mind calmly cleared a path to a better place. My hands found his neck as his back arched, I began squeezing mightily, my thumbs tried to crush his windpipe. I was not afraid, I knew I could shut him down at last.

I began slamming my still-clothed lower body roughly into his exposed naked lap. Slam, slam, fierce angry cries rose up from my throat.

He squealed in pain, "Get off me! That hurts, stop it!"

His protests drove me wilder while I slammed him more and more. Flailing his arms, alarmed now at the ferocity of my attack, he tried to shove me away from him. My hands were still trying to squeeze his throat, I would not let go.

He wriggled and wormed, red faced and panting, he managed to open the car door and spill out onto the ground. I stayed inside, watched and waited. He tried to stand while pulling up his tangled garments, the condom thrown clear. His startled eyes now wide with fear as he expounded tersely, "You shouldn't do that, you could have torn the condom, that's dangerous and I know what can happen." His face blanched.

The truth was out. Now I knew for certain how I had come to be.

Pale and flustered, he managed a shaking form of control. "You need a boyfriend. I can't take care of you anymore."

My anger still fresh, burst forth with biting accusation. "A boyfriend? You nearly killed me with a punch to my head over a damned boyfriend."

Sniffing his reply, "That was only because I thought that boy was bad for you."

I screamed in rage, "But now you say I can have boyfriends just to keep me satisfied!" Seeing him trying to twist his own words, I removed myself purposefully from the car's backseat. I slammed the car door with the mighty strength of my convictions. He backed slowly away from me while reaching for the driver's door. Slipping behind the steering wheel he pulled the door closed, lowered his head for a moment, then dumbly drove away. I stood transfixed, alone at the mailbox, seething with anger and relief.

Yes, I was finally liberated. I'd beaten him at his own game. And now I could finally have a boyfriend. Words now were echoing in my head, he said he couldn't satisfy me anymore. Just as he had tried to satisfy me when I was four years old? What? I snickered to myself. The idea of being set free was slowly penetrating my fevered mind. I turned and walked triumphantly down the familiar hill toward home, my feet seemingly never touched the ground.

CHAPTER 18

MEETING OF THE STRANGER

t was October, the month of bright changing colors, harvesting, preserving, and my 21st birthday. After the incident with my father, I bravely decided to set up an art gallery to display and sell my own art work.

I chose a sunny upstairs room in the spacious farm house that would be my studio gallery. Watercolors, chalk, charcoal drawings and pencil art were framed and hung neatly in rows around the walls of a reclaimed bedroom.

The distinctive front door of the massive farm house was made ready to welcome all manner of curious art patrons. Some visitors took one look at the old unpainted home and drove out of the dooryard in a rush. Then occasionally there were brave guests, who once inside the house, managed to climb the steep stairway that lead directly to my art room.

These folks glanced nervously around the room, at once not seeing anything that impressed them; they made a hasty exit with a sigh of relief. Thankfully other people came in, lingered, asked pointed questions, offered advice and finally bought some of my

precious work. At twenty one years of age, I was beginning to look forward to my future as an artist.

Then, on the most memorable fall day, I watched as a prospective customer drove into the dooryard in a faded blue Ford Falcon. A man of stolid stature removed himself from the vehicle and looked around the yard apprehensively. I ran down the stairs to the outside, hoping he would not leave too soon and began walking toward him. As he approached me, his outstretched hand reached mine for an introduction. His demeanor was immensely sad. So was mine; I felt an immediate attraction. We seemingly walked into each other as if in a spiritual dream. After spending two hours together upstairs in my gallery, discussing our lives and comparing our views of the world, he purchased a small token of my art. This meeting began a gateway to changes that would begin my new life. Two more subsequent visits from the welcomed stranger raised my hopes for a glorious new beginning of a life I had longed for.

My father, viewing the whole scenario with jaundiced eye, began to assume the worst. His world was dissolving. No longer would I be his life's purpose. Even though he had set me free to choose a boyfriend, he still tried to exert power over my thoughts.

His prying questions soon proved the point, "You like that guy don't you?"

I answered with a firm "YES."

"You're going to marry him aren't you?"

That was not necessarily a question, but I answered without hesitation, "Yes." This was my exit scene. I played it with surety and belief in myself, as I watched my father's haggard face slowly age in front of my eyes. My heart's pain eased while I dreamed of a new life of painting, traveling and most of all real companionship. No longer would I be the victim of my parents' abusive regimen.

CHAPTER 19

PAINFUL THOUGHTS

*A*fter leaving the farm at twenty two years of age to be with my new husband, I was an emotional disaster. I had lost my father to his final stroke in January and now it was June. Grief and loss overshadowed my world, even though I had recently moved into a wonderful new environment. I was trying to adjust to a life of freedom from a long tedious imprisonment. My father had constantly monitored my every thought and move for over seventeen years.

Starting from when I was four until I overtook him at twenty one, there was the constant strain of watchfulness. Looking for safe places to hide from him, listening for creeping foot-steps approaching from behind always caused anxious fear. Sometimes when I was reading, he would surprise me with a surreptitious pinch. The most terrifying of experiences was being forced to ride with him alone in the car, the perfect place to be held captive to his unwanted attentions.

All of my young grammar school years were tainted by fright-

ening rides, with stops at remote places on our way home from my friend's house. My young body's rejection of his rough handling had left blood stains in my homemade underpants. Mother was chagrined to find such spots surfacing at my tender age of seven. She once questioned me about it, to which I calmly answered, "It was Dad's long fingernails; he scratched me there and I cried." I guess she never confronted him about it; the painful activity continued and I still cried.

Here I am now, years later pouring over my emotions of relief, relishing the freedom from horrors of long ago. So many memories that may never let me move forward.

I am sad that I never had a father who loved and protected me from life's ups and downs. My teen years were a sorry nightmare. I developed into an attractive young woman with dreams of being with a young man who would cherish my being. But consequently, "victim" was written all over me. The only boys I attracted were unclean in mind and tried to manhandle me. How would I ever know who to trust? Father had decided that no boy was ever going to be good enough for me. For my own safety, there were no proms or teen activities for me.

On unusual occasions I managed to spend some time with a girlfriend who lived within walking distance of the farm. We usually did our homework together. Then, one day after some clever maneuvering she set up blind dates for us. We all went to the movies together and later one young man walked me home by the light of the moon. We stopped on the bridge just out of sight of the house. I sighed as he took me gently into his arms to kiss me good night. His lips were huge, wet and sloppy and sucked my breath away, not at all what I had imagined.

"Good night," I proclaimed abruptly while stepping away. I wiped off my wet face with the back of my hand.

He hesitantly implored, "Do you think I could see you again?"

Without pause I pronounced a firm "No."

He sighed, "I figured as much." He turned, shoved his hands into his jeans pockets and strode away into the night. I decided there would be no more blind dates for me.

CHAPTER 20

GOOD MORNING

*N*ow, after thirteen years of marriage, an eight year old daughter, and a new beginning in a rustic country home, I groaned, "I don't feel like getting out of bed."

My husband admonished, "Why not?" His eyes drooped with morning sleepiness; his demeanor obviously saddened by my lament.

We had just finished moving ourselves to New Hampshire, only a day ago. Our long-standing dream had finally come true. After thirteen years of traveling around this U.S.A., job changes, and then the lovely addition of our sweet girl child, at last we had landed. However, I awoke feeling lost, overwhelmed with the task of organizing a whole new plan of living here in the North Country.

Count your blessings, I thought. *An old metal faucet perched atop the end of a black plastic hose clamped on the rim of a black kitchen sink provided the cold spring water. A two-burner electric hot-plate sat atop a wooden hand-made cupboard with room enough to spare for a pot-holder and*

a spoon. A wobbly table complete with three oddly- repaired mismatched wooden *chairs sat beneath the sagging ceiling of falling debris in the kitchen. I had better stop counting, things were adding up badly.*

The atmosphere of this pending project seemed daunting indeed. Now I remembered, I had readily agreed to this, our dream. My retirement savings-fund from the state of Massachusetts had paid for all this, after working five years at the women's prison in Framingham. Ten acres of forested hillside land, one acre of open field, a very rundown dwelling, with a dirt cellar and a cold-water faucet was now ours.

Our eight-year-old daughter began stirring in the next room. She was preparing herself for the beginning of her fourth-grade day at the local grammar school. The school bus would soon be stopping in the road that ran by our house. Count this bus stop as much better blessing.

I finally sat up on the edge of the bed, feet dangling, not quite ready to feel the frosty floor yet. Our daughter popped into the room, beaming. She entertained us, chattering and challenging me to hurry and make her breakfast. How could I not smile-- she made my day so happy! I didn't even feel the floor under my bare feet as I rose to meet the day.

Soon breakfast aromas filled the rundown kitchen. My kiss and a hug sent her outside with her father to wait for the pending school bus. I smiled and tears came as I watched them standing in the cool morning mist together, father and daughter. Relief washed over me. We had made the right decision to come here.

I had wished for our daughter to become a country girl, to grow up learning basic country values. Hard work, respect for nature's unpredictable ways, and most of all looking out for one another. Simpler activities that built strength and pride, chores done to benefit the whole family. I knew firsthand how respect for

oneself could expand horizons and grow a fine character. I'd had to learn these valuable lessons much later in life, so she was going to learn hers starting now!

CHAPTER 21

TIME

*Y*ou can just imagine how fast ten years fly by when you are bringing up an energetic, talented young lady. During her senior year in high school she decided to attend a vocational school in order to learn commercial art and printing. This along with her regular everyday classes. Meanwhile a variety of colleges and the military were competing for her scholarly attentions. She wanted no part of the college life.

While she studied at vocational school, she met a boy who was also taking art training. One morning she asked our permission to bring him home to meet her family. Without apprehension, we readily agreed to meet him.

Later that day when he walked in through our front door and met my eyes and said "Hello," I thought, *Oh no!*

I pictured them together forever; he was so right for her. It also crossed my mind that neither one of them was of age to become betrothed. Time settled that process. In March they announced their plans to be married in June. She would become

eighteen on the twenty-third, and the nuptials were set for the twenty -fourth.

Soon the young man's mother called me, frantic with misgivings. "Can't you talk them out of this? They're so young. My son won't be old enough to marry, I'll have to give him my permission in writing. Can't you change her mind? She's the one pushing for this!"

Change my daughter's mind? What reason would I give her to wait at least a year before plunging into a complex new life? So I said I would try to get her to consider a waiting period. The boy's mother and I both cried, our wisdom united.

My husband leaned on me to make a decision, "Are you going to let her get married?"

In a moment of enlightenment I could visualize them as partners for life. "Yes," was my bold and final answer.

The planning and the scrambling began. With the help of a dear friend we managed to put together their marriage ceremony. The church offered an in-depth marriage course for newlyweds, which they took with hopeful hearts. They designed and printed their own wedding invitations at school, and proudly distributed them.

Soon the month of June arrived. On senior graduation day, the young man's mother gave a party for my daughter, her son and their friends. The next day, my daughter's eighteenth birthday, his mother again gave a party at her house, which then also included the rehearsal dinner. Then the very next day would be the wedding.

That day arrived beautiful and sunny. I had planned every detail from family to food. Now it was time for me to openly cry, through the complete and perfect walk down the aisle, the singing and vows; all went well. We all ate and danced to the DJ's music

until my daughter and her husband rode off into the sunset. A happier couple you will never see.

Four years of marriage passed quickly for them; I never regretted my decision. They worked hard together, flourishing in each other's potentials, growing as a team. I found it only natural that she would eventually distance herself from me.

By now I had divorced her father, left home and moved in with another man. She came to our apartment and met the new man. She liked him, which pleased me greatly. She stopped by to see me on Mother's Day with a gift. It was a cement urn. We placed it on the step outside next to the apartment door. I watched her nimble hands place new plants carefully into the pot, then tenderly water them in.

With an expression I had never seen before, she exclaimed fervently, "One of these days you'll be planting this pot on my grave." So completely taken aback and chilled by this remark, I needed to take a deeper look at this beloved young woman. What would prompt her to say such a thing on Mother's Day? She, a no-nonsense person whose ideals never let her hurt anyone— what was this about? I finally found my voice to ask, "Why are you saying that?"

To add to my chagrin she replied, "Well, also one of these days when you look up at the night sky you'll be seeing me."

I began to tremble, the world blurred around me. I remembered that even as a young child she was always right. Nothing in life escaped her careful scrutiny. I shuddered to think that this life of hers had been planned; was this the reason for her rush through life? I had to push these thoughts down and away from me.

Silently, we hugged each other and she left. I watched her driving away, confident with her own purpose. My arms felt so empty suddenly. My darling daughter was going away.

CHAPTER 22

INEVITABLY

Once something is said there is no taking it back. I waited for the inevitable, day by day, unconsciously expecting the worse to happen. The very whisper of a thought that I might lose my daughter was incorrigible. How could I love someone so much and then lose her?

Before I left to spend a warm winter in Florida with my new family, I called my daughter. "Could we meet for lunch and visit for a while before I have to leave?"

I heard the silence on her end of the line, then bravely in a tearful voice she answered, "No, you go on and have fun, I love you Mom"

These words haunted me forever, as did the silence when she hung up.

While we were in Florida, the fateful day did come on a weekend in January. While driving, doing her usual Saturday morning errands, her car began sliding into a sharp curve on sheer black ice. Her smaller car was struck head-on by the much heavier van who was sliding sideways across the whole width of

the road. There was no escape. Instantly she was gone. The passenger side of the van was crunched, injuring the occupants, but not severely. They were very upset, distraught by our loss at their hands, and asked for our forgiveness. They must have felt uneasy about the strength of my forgiveness; but after all, I knew it was coming.

Now, years later, on Memorial Day, I fill my Mother's Day urn with lovely little flowers that will bloom throughout the summer. We place the urn reverently by the headstone of her grave. Standing quietly, we choke down tears as we again feel our loss.

She has been my guardian angel happy in her new role. I feel her saying *if it wasn't for you I wouldn't be here. I've ascended to full angel status because of you. I'm very happy here, Mom, I love you!*

If it wasn't for her "angel status" I would have jumped off the nearest bridge long ago. How empty my arms felt, how broken was my already wounded heart. But my strong spirit stepped up again to guide me to see the truth of her ultimate destiny.

CHAPTER 23

THERAPY

*I*t is with a terrible kind of joy that I have worked hard to present this true account of my life to you.

Years ago, as a young girl, I read intense novels recounting other families' lives; I concluded that mine was unusually sad, even though to the outside world, we seemed happy and normal. I finally discovered self-help books, and even tried hypnosis designed to lift my spirits, all to no avail.

Ten years went by. One day while visiting my doctor/ rheumatologist who had long been treating my painful arthritis condition, he voiced his exasperation plaintively, "You are very much depressed and you must see a therapist."

This led to various appointments for brain exercises, many visits to psychiatrists and ultimately a collection of experimental dosages of relaxants. All this while therapists were consistently being suggested to me.

I finally mustered the courage to call upon a therapist who lived only a few minutes away from me. I thought this would be an easy commute. I shakily rang the doorbell. A tiny woman

welcomed me warmly into the entryway. And soon I found myself sitting across from her on a deeply comfortable couch. The room seemed like a cozy place to sit and visit.

Since that day, I have trusted my therapist implicitly. She's heard my accounts of victimization and abuse. The more I opened up my mind to that lady, the more relaxed I became. She listened intently to the many horrid realities I'd buried from my early childhood.

After at least ten years of sessions together, through relaxing-therapy lessons, innovative books, soothing music, gentle hypnosis, touch-field therapy, and many cups of tea, I have finally reached a new level of acceptance.

I have never regretted knocking on her door that first time, so many years ago. Her patient, persistent search for the person she thought I could be has finally come full circle. I'm finally a talented artist again, a singer, gardener, crafty creative seamstress, cook, writer, twice a wife, and once a mother. I am the most thankful to God, by His Grace, I truly believed I could become my four-year-old confident self once again.

The power is in the balance:
We are our injuries as much as we are our successes.
Words taken from a book entitled the Poisonwood Bible

CHAPTER 24

SPIRITUALITY

I have a very strong spirit. I have found its very essence is composed of many factual conclusions. These spiritually-based conclusions were my strongest allies in a world of inconceivable physical and mental sufferings. The more I listened to my spirituality, the more empowered I became. I would like to suggest listening intently while your spirit weighs options, consequences and outcomes for you. Strive to listen without doubt (a tall order). We have only to fortify our beliefs in the spiritual realm to realize our quests for answers will be acknowledged.- Comprehension comes when we are in harmony with our inner spirituality. This empowerment has kept me strong through a lifetime of undercurrent that threatened the very core of my existence. I am here today because my fiercely loyal spirit has kept me safe for a purpose.

CHAPTER 25

THE END

*H*ow can I forgive these parents who hurt me so deeply? Sorrowfully how can I not forgive them? Their agenda was different from mine. They sought only to protect themselves from each other. Guilt and shame drove them over the edge, each in their own way, blaming one another for their individual plights of anguish.

Let them go, I think to myself, they are already dead. My father died when he was fifty-four and my mother died six years later, at age forty-six. What more tribulation can I possibly inflict on each one of them? I cannot forget them or disown them. My own true lesson is to forgive their transgressions, no matter how deep my pain. Let them go to their prospective rewards and or punishments. My fate is sealed with their release into another realm; relief becomes my peace.

ACKNOWLEDGMENTS

And to All My Five-Star Friends:

To Sylvia Field, my editor-extraordinaire, thank you for your patient advice, corrections and subtle rewrites!

To Jessica Aiken-Hall, who instigated the writing of this memoir, answered all manner of book publishing questions and formatted the final product. Thanks for your kindness and special interest in my project!

To Anna-Lisa Pruitt, my long-time therapist and dear friend, I will forever be indebted to you for saving my life!

And thank you for the work from Kimberley Grenier, for a beautiful, well executed cover design!

CPSIA information can be obtained
at www.ICGtesting.com
Printed in the USA
BVHW032344160919
558630BV00001B/35/P

9 780578 562650

Made in the USA
Lexington, KY
11 March 2018

SCALIA

Rise to Greatness |1936–1986

James Rosen

Regnery Publishing
WASHINGTON, D.C.

Regnery® is a registered trademark and its colophon is a trademark of Salem Communications Holding Corporation

ISBN: 978-1-68451-227-0
eISBN: 978-1-68451-232-4

Library of Congress Control Number: 2022921515

Published in the United States by
Regnery Publishing
A Division of Salem Media Group
Washington, D.C.
www.Regnery.com

Manufactured in the United States of America

10 9 8 7 6 5 4 3 2 1

Books are available in quantity for promotional or premium use. For information on discounts and terms, please visit our website: www.Regnery.com.

For Lorraine and Joe Durkin,

Jenn Barron, Ryan Durkin,

and Quinn Durkin

MEG SCALIA BRYCE: After his death, when people described him as larger than life, he was. And he was that way to us.

ROSEN: And he was cognizant that he was that way, right?

MEG SCALIA BRYCE: Oh, yes. Oh, yeah. I mean, he was putting on a show—but it was a great show.

—Interview by the author, August 2, 2017

CONTENTS

Book One

I WILL RISE

CHAPTER I

Little Nino

*It is good to know where you came from. It is
even better to know where you are going.*

—*Antonin Scalia, 1999*

On the evening of September 17, 1986, Constitution Day, the
United States Senate voted unanimously—ninety-eight to zero,
with two senators absent—to confirm Antonin Scalia, a judge on the
United States Court of Appeals for the District of Columbia Circuit
nominated by President Reagan as associate justice of the Supreme
Court.

That the nation's highest court, America's most powerful symbol of
freedoms guaranteed, would soon be seating its first Italian-American
justice, a landmark event, was largely overshadowed in the news. For on
that same day, despite a ferocious opposition campaign mounted by Senate
Democrats, the chamber had also voted to approve the elevation of
Associate Justice William H. Rehnquist, seated on the Court since 1971,
to chief justice. Scalia would assume Rehnquist's old seat.

The bitter confirmation of the chief justice—by a final vote of sixty-five
to thirty-three, the largest opposition tally ever sustained by a confirmed

nominee to that point—meant that Rehnquist, a demure, dry-witted Wisconsinite and a poker buddy of Scalia's, would succeed stately Warren Burger, chief justice since 1969, now retiring. The Democrats' assaults on Rehnquist—on his veracity, integrity, and racial sensitivity—were accompanied, *de rigueur*, by the exhumation of documents and witnesses from a quarter-century earlier, most of them familiar from Rehnquist's 1971 confirmation hearings. Conservatives called it "the Rehnquisition."[1]

Against this backdrop, Scalia's swift, effortless confirmation drew little attention; the assessment of the news media was that Scalia's ascension would not alter the ideological balance of the Court. Some observers, however, understood immediately that Scalia's personal characteristics—his unique combination of intellect, literary skill, and affability—would make him "a major force on the Supreme Court," as the *Christian Science Monitor* reported.

> Through his considerable powers of persuasion . . . Judge Scalia may wind up altering the balance—and thus the outcome of close decisions. In reaching court decisions he is widely viewed as repeatedly seeking to "try to find a middle ground," in the phrase of Judge Abner Mikva, a liberal colleague for four years on the Court of Appeals. He calls Scalia's approach "collegial," and says the appointment "is going to be good for the institution" of the Supreme Court.[2]

For the newly minted justice, a self-described Italian boy from Queens, the unanimous Senate confirmation marked a moment few men experience: supreme vindication, unopposed ascendance to the pinnacle of his profession. He would shape American law for the twenty-first century.

The one problem at the moment was: *getting ahold of him.* "Nino," as family and friends called him, was a social beast. On the evening of the vote he was out on the town, attending yet another of the suffocating black-tie events that pass for nightlife in official Washington. This one celebrated the forthcoming bicentennial of the Constitution.

What?

In the White House and the Department of Justice, where Scalia's nomination was being managed by a small team of Reagan administration officials already frazzled from "the Rehnquisition," having to worry about the judge's whereabouts was enough to stir unease. At the time of the vote, the president's men liked high-profile nominees to stay close at hand, twiddling their thumbs with their spouses in some designated hotel room or someone's ceremonial office, ready at any moment to receive, with suitable gratitude to the President of the United States, the call that would change their lives forever.

Scalia blew all that off.

Despite regular jogging and tennis, the judge was stocky. Thinning black hair retreated straight back over his head, leaving behind dark eyebrows and eyes. Despite his forbidding mien, Nino was almost unanimously well-liked in Washington. He was delightful company, often amusing, combining outer-borough Italian-American charm with Ivy League sophistication and self-deprecating wit. At any moment he was liable, with shameless and endearing grandeur, to commandeer a piano in someone's house and burst into show tunes or Christmas carols.

Now Reagan's men had to track the judge down on the rubber chicken circuit. The constitutional bicentennial dinner was at the Willard InterContinental Hotel downtown. An idea popped into the head of the assistant attorney general for the Justice Department's Office of Legislative Affairs, a mustachioed thirty-seven-year-old lawyer and former think tank colleague of Scalia's named John R. Bolton. In the kitchen at the Willard, Bolton established a dedicated phone line and enlisted hotel staff to corral Scalia at the appointed hour.

Earlier that summer Bolton had been one of the few officials present for Scalia's "murder board" sessions: a mock grilling ahead of the Senate confirmation hearings. The "murderers" peppered Scalia with the toughest, nastiest questions they could devise; he aced the test. No member of the Senate Judiciary Committee could remotely match Scalia's mastery of the law and debate. "He didn't do anything to prepare for the meetings [with senators] or the murder boards," recalled a law clerk. "He didn't find them very helpful. I think he was doing them mostly to make the White House comfortable, not because he thought he needed them."[3]

When the vote came Scalia was blithely puffing on his pipe, sipping champagne, mingling, and playing it cool at the Willard. Since 1982 he had been a judge on the D.C. Circuit Court of Appeals, often described as the second-most important court in America. Scalia moved with ease, confidence: the kid from Queens, a self-made man who had vaulted to Harvard Law and the federal bench. His confidence in himself and his own story, in the story of his immigrant father—in the American Dream—created a fierce independence in the man: *no one intimidated him.*

A Willard employee leaned into his ear—something about a telephone call. The judge followed him to the hotel's kitchen and a waiting receiver.

Scalia knew. This was it. Bolton's account of the critical phone call, when Scalia learned he had achieved the dream, is previously unreported:

> **BOLTON:** I said, "Nino, congratulations, you've been confirmed! Congratulations!" "Oh, that's great," he said. "That's great." I said, "Yeah, that's fantastic. The vote was ninety-eight to nothing." And I'm still going, "It's great, it's fantastic." There's silence on the other end of the phone. And he said:

"Who were the two who didn't vote?" And I said, "Oh, it was Goldwater and Garn. But it's fantastic, you were confirmed unanimously." And there's another long pause, and he said: "Do you mean to tell me we didn't get Goldwater and Garn?" And I said finally—at this point, I was a little irritated. Having just gone through Rehnquist with a much closer vote, I thought ninety-eight to nothing looked pretty good. I said, "Garn is in the hospital.... Barry we just couldn't find. Nino, concentrate: We, we just won ninety-eight to nothing." He said, "Yeah, you're right. That's great. It's great." He was happy and he left and he went back to his dinner. But that—that was the conversation.

ROSEN: What did you take away from that exchange?

BOLTON: Nino never missed a trick, that he wanted a hundred to nothing.[4]

This uncompromising commitment to perfection was a hallmark of the judge's since his earliest days. A reporter who profiled Scalia in November 1985, eight months before his nomination to the Supreme Court, wrote: "Scalia is seen as a man who has excelled at everything he has tried."

"He was gifted," Scalia's father said. "He was good at anything he did."

"When Christ said, 'Be ye perfect, as your heavenly Father is perfect,'" Justice Scalia once said, "I think he meant perfect in all things, including that very important thing, the practice of one's life work."[5]

❋   ❋   ❋

Antonin Scalia was born at Mercer Hospital in Trenton, New Jersey, on March 11, 1936, the only child of Salvatore Eugene Scalia, an Italian immigrant, and Catherine Panaro Scalia, whose parents had also emigrated from Italy. The future justice was, by his very existence, a miracle: the *only* child produced by a generation that extended, on both sides, Scalias and Panaros, to a total of *nine* brothers and sisters.

The boy, named after his grandfather, Antonino Scalia, a mechanical engineer in the sulfur mines of Italy, was called "Nino." "Antonin was a made-up name," the justice's son Gene told me. "My grandfather decided to Americanize his name; he didn't want him to have such an Italian name."

Nino was instantly doted upon and endlessly scrutinized by his parents and a large rotating cast of aunts and uncles. "Spoiled rotten," he would say. "There's a reason why I am the way I am."

> It's probably a lot easier to raise an only child with high expectations. He always feels he's the center of the universe and has a good deal of security. I think it must be harder to be with brothers and sisters competing for parental attention. That was never an issue in my life. I was the apple of my parents' eye.... Which is not to say I wouldn't have preferred to have brothers and sisters; I very much would have. I have no cousins. My mother was one of five sisters and two brothers...and my father was one of two children. He has a sister and I am the only offspring from that side, too. So I am really the last of the Mohicans.[6]

Scalia's father, Salvatore Eugene Scalia, was born December 1, 1903, in Sommatino, a province of Caltanissetta, Italy. Salvatore's mother, Maria, was a seamstress. She and her husband, Antonino, the mine worker, brought Salvatore and his younger sister, Carmela, to America. The family sailed aboard the *Duca d'Aosta* with nearly 2000 other immigrants, passing through Ellis Island in December 1920. "Sam," as the immigration authorities renamed Salvatore, was freshly seventeen and stood, according to immigration documents, four-foot-ten. The family had $400; Sam spoke no English. But he spoke French and Spanish fluently and possessed the four traits the justice later identified as characteristic of Italian Americans of the era: devout Catholicism; love of family; a capacity for hard work; and a taste for the "simple physical pleasures" of food, wine, and song.[7]

In the existing biographical literature, the reason behind the Scalia family's emigration—why they set out for America when they did—is nowhere addressed. Yet the justice's eldest son, Eugene Scalia, named after his grandfather and an accomplished attorney who served as secretary of labor, recalled Justice Scalia's citing a number of motivations for the move. "The family was going anyway," Gene told me, but "I remember being told that my grandfather [Sam] was a troublemaker in Sicily, a socialist agitator when he was young, and that actually he might have even spent a night or two in jail.... One of the many good reasons for my grandfather to get out of Sicily was that he was getting in trouble."

Fortunately for Sam, no trace of his socialist fervor followed him to America; at least no such information made it into the secret files of J. Edgar Hoover, the longtime FBI director who compiled data on all suspected socialists in the United States. In later years, when the Scalias' only child, Nino, would undergo four FBI background checks in fourteen years, the bureau would search "data banks" for his parents and dispatch agents to Trenton to interview their neighbors. The searches produced no results, and the agents found three families who attested that "the Scalias are dedicated, loyal Americans...an elderly quiet couple, of excellent reputation."[8]

Pasquale and Maria Panaro, the justice's maternal grandparents, had emigrated earlier from Naples. They married in New York in 1904 before moving to Trenton, New Jersey. The state capital was then a thriving industrial town. At the time of the justice's birth, it was home to 25,000 Italian Americans, more than 20 percent of the city's population.[9]

Pasquale was a tailor and *bon vivant*, an ebullient reveler active in *L'Ordine Figli d'Italia*. Despite his broken English, he loved to watch a lawyer friend perform at the local courthouse. Maria, described by Scalia's first biographer, Joan Biskupic, as "a short, sturdy woman who loved hats and carried herself with poise," presided over a modest two-story home that also served, on occasion, as a saloon. The eldest of the Panaros' seven children, born in Little Italy, New York, on November 7, 1905, was Catherine: mother-to-be of the justice. The few photographs of her reveal, as Biskupic wrote, "a serious and pretty girl who kept her dark hair pinned off her face." From a young age, she played the piano. Newspaper articles from the years before World War I, unmentioned by previous Scalia biographers, reported steadily on the progress of the precocious girl, alternately identified as Catherine and "Katie": her performance, at age eight, of "How Santa Comes" in the Monument School Christmas program; her repeat appearances, the following year, on the honors list.[10]

Four sisters and two brothers would follow, including Grace, developmentally disabled, scarcely capable of speech, who spent six decades in the Panaros' care. Vincent Panaro, Nino's uncle, became a lawyer and ultimately a local mayor and state assemblyman (as a Democrat). The youngest Panaro child, nicknamed "Babe," was Lenora, thirteen at Nino's birth and the aunt who most frequently looked after him.[11]

On June 26, 1926, five and a half years after the Scalia family emigrated from Italy, Salvatore entered the New Jersey Court of Common Pleas and became, on his receipt of Certificate No. 2290037M, a naturalized American citizen. His father, Antonino, also became a U.S. citizen. These were landmarks on the family's journey to the American

Dream. Assimilation was not resented; to the contrary, immigrants saw it as essential. "It should be noted," the FBI would later record in its background check for Nino's nomination to the federal bench, "that the applicant's father came into this country with the name Salvatore Scalia but was naturalized as Samuel Eugene Scalia."[12]

Possessed of what his son once described as "a nice tenor voice," Salvatore enrolled (as "Samuel Scalia") in the Eastman School of Music in Rochester, New York, for the 1926–27 academic year. Family lore records that illness forced him to abandon singing, but he passed on to little Nino a lifelong love of opera, along with a sizable collection of sheet music, and taught the boy to play piano. Sam's costliest purchase indulged his love for language: he bought, and briefly ran, an Italian-language newspaper in Scranton, Pennsylvania, named *Il Minatore* (*The Miner*). By 1931, Sam had earned not only his bachelor's degree from Rutgers but also a master's degree and doctorate in romance languages from Columbia University.[13]

Sam married Catherine, a first-generation Italian American who was teaching elementary school in Trenton, in August 1929. In the early days the couple lived with Catherine's family. Five years into the marriage, Sam, then a teaching assistant at Columbia, secured a study fellowship that took the couple to Rome and Florence; it was in Italy, in the summer of 1935, that they conceived their only child. By 1939, when Nino turned three, Sam joined the faculty of Brooklyn College. His professorship in romance languages employed him—*with only one day of recorded absence*—until his retirement in 1969. "He was a great American success story in his own right," said Gene Scalia. "What he did with his life and career—in a certain way it's even more impressive than what my father did." The justice agreed:

I am sometimes regarded as the son of an immigrant [who] made it to the Supreme Court; what a guy. But in fact...I am not the member of my family who made the family fortune, so to speak. It was really my father.... His father was not illiterate, but [was] essentially a blue-collar worker. And my father, just by dint of his own brains and effort became a doctor of philosophy and professor of romance languages. So, you know, I [was] sort of riding on his accomplishment, and what he wanted and obtained for his child: a good education.[14]

"My father," Justice Scalia said on another occasion, was "committed to the life of the mind—much more of an intellectual than I ever was." Into the twenty-first century, former students from Brooklyn College would approach the justice to say "what a terrific teacher" his father had been, how he had affected their lives. Yet Sam's accomplishments came at a cost to those around him, paid in time and mood. "As my mother described it," the justice said, "he always had a book in front of his face."[15]

A classmate of Scalia's who visited the home recalled Sam as "strong willed," with "strong opinions." Visitors were instructed that Dante's *Inferno* must only be read in Italian. "The father spoke with a heavy accent, but he wanted to be completely American," a neighbor recalled. "Yes, he was severe," the justice said. "He was demanding." Asked once what kind of father Antonin Scalia had been, one of the justice's sons said that he had been "stern" and "as needed, the disciplinarian, but not mean or forbidding in the way that I think *his* father probably was.... [Sam] did not have the sunny side to his personality that my Dad did."

If Nino came home with an A, his father would inquire, with a frown, why it wasn't an A+. All it took was a look, a raise of the eyebrow, a return to the foreign-language book beneath his nose, for Sam to convey his disappointment. Indeed, Scalia told Biskupic he thought he had disappointed his father: "I wasn't all that I could have been." The justice would term it "the shame of my life" that, despite a classical education that included six years of Latin and five of Greek, he never learned Italian as his father wished.

Even after Scalia ascended to the federal bench, he would send his published opinions to Sam, only to see them returned, marked up with edits.

Letters from grandchildren got the same working-over. The youngest, Meg Scalia Bryce, remembered her grandfather as "incredibly critical" of her father. "My dad used to read the comics every night before dinner," she told me.

> He'd stand at the kitchen counter and read the comics. After getting back from work, he'd kind of unwind before sitting down to dinner. They'd call them "the funny pages"—and my grandfather would say, like, "Look at you—what kind of man reads the funny pages?" He said something like that, just criticizing my dad for reading the comics. At this point, he was already on the [appellate] court.... So my grandfather was hard. He was difficult. And from what I understand from others, my grandmother was softer and sweeter.

Father Paul Scalia, another of the justice's sons, recalled that when he was a boy, the elderly Sam could display kindliness, as when he taught the lad how to twirl pasta with a fork and spoon, "a distinctly Sicilian way." But Father Scalia also sensed Sam had been "pretty demanding, pretty strict" with little Nino. After the old man died, teenaged Paul accompanied his father to Sam's house to dispose of his effects. In the basement, the future priest was staggered by the enormous library, divided not by subject but by *language*: Italian, Spanish, French, German, Portuguese, and English. "That sort of sets a tone, I think, in the family," Father Scalia said, "the seriousness of his work...this intellectual labor."

Another factor beyond dour perfectionism also contributed to the hard time the old man gave his son, the big-shot federal judge: *Sam didn't like his son's politics.* "He was a liberal man," a neighbor from Queens recalled in 1986. "The son turned out conservative, but the father wasn't."[16]

*   *   *

It was Nino's mother, "a kinder, gentler, and sweeter personality," who was more active in the boy's life. "She was the prototypical Italian mother," Scalia wrote. In 2008, C-SPAN's Brian Lamb, a longtime friend, asked the justice to describe "Catherine L. Scalia."

> **SCALIA:** That was my mother, who I only realized later devoted her life to making sure I did the right things, hung out with the right people, joined the right organizations.
> **LAMB:** What do you mean by "right"?
> **SCALIA:** I mean associated with young people that would not get me into trouble but rather would make me a better person.
> **LAMB:** How did she know that?
> **SCALIA:** Well, she made it her job to know who I was hanging out with. We'd have them over to my house, and she was a den mother for the Cub Scouts, things of that sort. She was a teacher, a grammar school teacher, and a very good one. When they died, I got some of the letters that she had kept [from] parents of children that she had taught.[17]

The little family of three was close-knit. "They were my only parents," Scalia would joke. Though dour by nature, Sam had many admirable qualities. These included his deep Catholic faith and what his son described as "an almost quaint, Old World courtliness.... He spoke softly and almost deferentially, listened attentively, and took an interest (as a good man should) in the lives and the doings of his friends." *A good man:* moral character was king in Sam's eyes, prized more than intellect or wealth. "Son," he would tell Nino, "brains are like muscles. You can rent them by the hour. The only thing that's not for sale is character."[18]

Above all, Salvatore's life and work represented the essence, the full power, of the American Dream, and the younger Scalia internalized this early on; indeed, it later informed the justice's jurisprudence. The son's accomplishments were made possible by the father's striving and assimilation—hallmarks of the dream that weighed most heavily on Justice Scalia's contemplation of one particular area of law: affirmative action.

"My father came to this country when he was a teenager," Scalia wrote in 1979, when he was still a professor. "Not only had he never profited from the sweat of any black man's brow, I don't think he had ever seen a black man."

I owe no man anything, nor he me, because of the blood that flows in our veins.... This is not to say that I have no obligation to my fellow citizens who are black. I assuredly do—not because of their race or because of any special debt that my bloodline owes to theirs, but because they have (many of them) special needs, and they are (all of them) my countrymen and (as I believe) my brothers. This means that I am entirely in favor of according the poor inner-city child, who happens to be black, advantages and preferences not given to my own children because they don't need them. But I am not willing to prefer the son of a prosperous and well-educated black doctor or lawyer—solely because of his race—to the son of a recent refugee from Eastern Europe who is working as a manual laborer to get his family ahead.

Moreover, Scalia sensed hypocrisy in those justices quickest to dabble in the social engineering of affirmative action, with its elaborately constructed racial quota systems. "I certainly felt that the Lewis Powells of the world were not going to bear the burden they were creating," Scalia told Biskupic. "It wasn't their kids. It was the Polish factory worker's kid who was going to be out of a job."[19]

Or the Italian immigrant's kid.

*   *   *

At the Cathedral of St. Mary of the Assumption, a Gothic fortress of a parish erected on the site of the Battle of Trenton in the Revolutionary War, little Nino was baptized.

"He asked me such questions!" recalled his Aunt Eva. "He'd ask about the universe, about everything.... He floored me many times." "He was bull-headed," said his Aunt Lenora. "We call it in Italian a *capo tosta*.... He knew what he wanted—even when he was little." A neighbor recalled that the boy "knew his place...never had a word out of turn."[20]

"The closeness of the Italian family is legendary," Scalia said later. The time he spent with his extended family, Lenora in particular, made a lifelong impression. Invited to lunch by a group of conservative Capitol Hill staffers in the early 1990s, the justice lectured them in the Senate Dining Room, the host recalled, not on the law but on the value of extended family.

He told very important stories about the impact of feeling a sense of confidence...that came from his family...that this was very instrumental [in attaining] all the things that he wanted in his own life. And he stressed that those began for him as a boy with his extended family, that these people were not just figures in his past.... He recognized both from his own Catholicism and just in the formation of his worldview how important these people were, but specifically this aunt [Lenora].... He spent at least a quarter of the luncheon speaking about his aunt.[21]

For two years, Scalia and his mother remained in the Panaros' home in Trenton while Sam, ensconced at Brooklyn College, took up residence in the Elmhurst section of Queens and visited them on weekends. In 1941, when Nino turned five, he and Catherine moved to Elmhurst to join Sam. The father had purchased a two-story brick row house with a small awning and front garden at 48-22 O'Connell Court, located on an L-shaped street named for the real estate developer who had built the homes the year before. The lot measured twenty-three by ninety-four; the front yard was too small for child's play. Still, it was *theirs*: for the first time, the Scalias lived in their own home (Sam's parents, Antonino and Maria, had earlier moved to Queens to be near Sam's sister, Carmela, and her family).

Justice Scalia told Biskupic, without elaboration, that he "hated" Trenton; Queens he *loved*. "It was a wonderful place," he would recall seventy years later. "There were Greeks...Irish, German, Jewish, Italian...It was the face of New York City." Unfortunately, New York's school system required little Nino to complete kindergarten a second time. "I'm a two-time loser in kindergarten," the justice later quipped. First grade brought him to the Lower School of Villa Victoria Academy, a private academy in Ewing Township founded by the Religious Teachers Filippini, a Catholic institute.[22]

When he looked back on his 1940s youth in Queens, which he did frequently, Scalia marveled at how differently children were being raised in the late twentieth and early twenty-first centuries, with play dates and soccer schedules. "Most of the sports I did were in the neighborhood—*and they were not organized!*" he would say. "My mother didn't drive me anywhere—we didn't have a *car!*" Entertainment, to little Nino, was watching the family that *had* a car, a Packard, *wash* the thing on weekends. "She would say, 'Go out and play,' and you had to find a game somewhere."

> So long as you did your homework, kept your grades up, stayed out of trouble—and in my case practiced the piano, which was a form of self-discipline and penance—parents did not care how you spent your leisure time. Much less did they feel any obligation to arrange it for you.... Family life did not revolve about the child's extracurricular activities.... Kids were left pretty much to decide for themselves what games they would play.... Nobody worried about kids carrying knives.... Nobody ever heard of a bicycle helmet.... You would go over to the field on a Saturday morning or Sunday afternoon and choose up sides. No adult supervision. No conceivable financial liability.[23]

Baseball, basketball, football, roller hockey, marbles, pen-knife games, War, Ringolevio, and "the quintessential game of my youth," stickball: Nino played them all *con vigore* in the streets, schoolyards, and gymnasia of New York, "morning to night on the weekends." His rat pack realized they could play basketball at night if they attached the hoop to the telephone pole, already equipped with a street lamp. He was "a little bit short, a little stocky," a classmate recalled when asked about Scalia's athleticism. He "liked to fool around with the basketball...to be one of the guys, somehow. He wasn't, physically." Nino rooted for the Yankees of DiMaggio and Rizzuto, and his beloved Popeye.

The earliest schooling had been in Trenton but Scalia's real education, he always said, came in New York: "We learned in Queens that the world ain't always fair." Scalia's Boy Scout Troop 17 gathered at the First Methodist Church at 91st Place and 50th Avenue—reportedly because the local Catholic pastor, opposed to the admission of Protestants and Jews to his church, refused to host Scout meetings. "I knew he was going to be an intellectual," Scalia's troop leader recalled, "because he wasn't a tree climber."

In sixth grade, a "roly-poly, jovial, Italian-American kid," as one neighbor remembered him, Nino developed his first unrequited crush, on a tall brunette named Theresa. ("She's good-looking," the justice mused, reviewing the class photo decades later. "I always had good taste.") In the neighborhood's abundant vacant lots, the boys lit fires and camped out. Winters brought sledding down a cemetery slope called Dead Man's Hill; summers flew by at Boy Scouts and in rabbit hunts with his grandfather, Antonino, out in *the country*: Woodbury, Long Island. "It was," the justice said, "a wonderful way to grow up."[24]

It never dawned on Nino that he, or the class cut-up, Hugh McGee, belonged to *ethnic groups*; but it did strike him that being a Catholic, or an observant one, set him apart. "Even in areas with large Catholic populations," he told a prayer breakfast in 1992, "it was a little bit strange to be a Catholic." That Catholic students were discharged from P.S. 13 an hour early every Wednesday, the "release time" set aside for religious instruction, was but one manifestation of this *apartness*. Nino's devout, disciplined parents inculcated in him that Christ "makes some special demands upon" Catholics, such as eating fish on Fridays, when other kids enjoyed hot dogs, "that occasionally require us to be out of step."

Whenever I wanted to go to a certain movie, or a certain place, that my parents disapproved of, I would say, of course, as children always do, that *everybody else* was going. My parents' invariable and unanswerable response was: "You're not everybody else." It is enormously important, I think, for Christians to learn early and remember long that lesson of "differentness"; to recognize that what is perfectly lawful, and perfectly permissible, for everyone else—even our very close non-Christian friends—is not necessarily lawful and permissible for us.

That Scalia carried these beliefs into adulthood, and impressed them on his own nine children, is evident from the recollection of his youngest, Meg, who said she and her siblings were made to understand they would observe "different rules, different standards" than other families. "You're not like everybody else," they were told. "You're a Scalia."[25]

✳   ✳   ✳

Nino graduated from P.S. 13 with straight As.

As a Supreme Court justice he would look back with fondness and admiration for the principal, Lillian Eschenbecker, and the other women who educated him. These memories leapt to mind when he considered gender discrimination. "Every cloud has a silver lining," he said. "I had really wonderful, accomplished, disciplined women as grade teachers in P.S. 13. Perhaps, maybe the same women today would not be teaching grammar school, they would be on the board, something like that. That was what that particular evil produced."[26]

His spiritual education also progressed. In the Catholic Church, the sacrament of Confirmation is administered to seal a baptized person with the Holy Spirit, thereby strengthening the young man's service to the Body of Christ. For his Confirmation name, Nino chose "Gregory," after the patron saint of musicians, students, and teachers.

This would lead to Scalia's being misidentified for the rest of his life as "Antonin Gregory Scalia," or "Antonin G. Scalia." Nowhere are Scalia's views on the matter set forth more explicitly than in his FBI files, declassified after his death. Interviewed by agents of the Washington Field Office in April 1982 as part of the vetting process for his nomination to the Court of Appeals, Scalia stated, "He has no middle name, however, at the time of his confirmation in the Catholic Church, he selected the confirmation name of 'Gregory.' He has never otherwise used this name, although, it may appear on some school records. He does not considered [sic] it to be part of his legal name."[27]

It was in Nino's Catholic education that he encountered, for the first time, a setback: he failed the entrance exam for Regis, the prestigious Catholic high school in Manhattan he was eyeing. A classmate from this period, who had also failed the Regis exam, told me the sting from this episode, this tiny mark of imperfection, stayed with Scalia for years: "He was loathe to admit that." About this lapse in his studious son, however, Scalia's unforgiving father, Sam, proved uncharacteristically gentle; maybe it was best, he allowed, if Nino attended a Catholic school with a more diverse student body.[28]

Under a full scholarship, Nino enrolled at St. Francis Xavier High School on Manhattan's West 16th Street. Xavier was a unique hybrid: a Jesuit-run Catholic school that was also a military academy, in which all students, or cadets, wore dress-blue uniforms, saluted upperclassmen and robed faculty, participated in junior ROTC training known as the Regiment, practiced rifle marksmanship, and marched in drills and parades. (Nino commuted twice daily on the subway, rifle slung over his shoulder.) The cadets' classical education began with morning prayers and included courses in Latin, Greek, rhetoric, and theology.

"Xavier High School was the most formative institution in my life," Scalia said upon his return to the school in 2011. "The Regiment's most important legacy, of course, was not pageantry; it was discipline, and duty, and sacrifice."[29]

On his first day at Xavier, in September 1949, Nino navigated a new and tougher environment. A survey of the classroom revealed, as he later put it, "a substantially Irish world," starting with his homeroom teacher, Father Thomas Matthews, "a crusty no-nonsense New England Jesuit" from the era when "Jesuits were allowed to be crusty and no-nonsense." Matthews opened the class with roll call. When the white-haired, bushy-browed, bespectacled Irishman came to "Antonin," he stumbled and asked Nino in a sharp Boston brogue, "Who's your patron saint?"[30] Father Robert A. Connor, one of the last surviving graduates from Scalia's class at Xavier, recalled another incident. "Scalia was maybe three seats behind me.... Tom Matthews was going through the names of us in the classroom...and he got to Scalia and he says, 'Goombah!'"[31]

Father Matthews was "a wonderful man, of considerable influence on me," Scalia said. The venerable Jesuit delivered another zinger that stayed with Scalia forever. The class was reading *Hamlet* when a "smart aleck" piped up with sophomoric criticisms. Matthews looked down at the young man and, summoning the brogue, admonished him: "Mistah, when you read Shakespeah, Shakespeah's not on trial; you ah."[32]

Reverence for text! Matthews's comment was not about the passive business of watching a play but about the active engagement inherent in *reading a text*; the admonition registered with young Nino. He would forever refer to it as the Shakespeare Principle: a solemn reminder that certain texts, unlike their readers, are eternally enduring, immutable, inviolable. Nino was imbibing the same strong stuff at home. An indelible image from his youth in Queens was the sight of his father, Salvatore

Eugene, hunched over a desk in the basement, toiling over his work, surrounded by foreign-language books: *the almighty texts.*

In his master's thesis, a work of literary criticism focused on Giosuè Carducci, the Italian poet and Nobel laureate, Sam pressed his theory of "literalness" in translation. "Literalness is, for us, one of the chief merits of a translation," Sam wrote. The translator's highest calling, he argued, was "reproducing the lyric vision of a poet...to transfer bodily the image from one language into another without sacrifice of glow or warmth, and not attempt to reconstruct it with dictionary in hand." Or as he put it elsewhere: "A poem is a poem, not this plus that." An Italian aphorism the Scalias passed down was: *traduttore, traditore,* the translator is a traitor.[33]

These cues that Nino took from Salvatore and Father Matthews, at home and in school, only reinforced what the young man was absorbing in the Catholic Church. Like all major religions, Catholicism, particularly before the Second Vatican Council, was *all about* sacred texts: the New Testament, the Old Testament, the catechisms, papal bulls, edicts.... The power of the liturgy rested on the church's fidelity, across the millennia, to sacred rituals developed from foundational texts. God's word was enduring, immutable, inviolable—particularly in Latin. As Father Paul Scalia noted in his homily for his father's funeral in 2016: "Scripture says Jesus Christ is the same yesterday, today, and forever."[34]

Given all the textualist fervor in Scalia's early life, it is easy to see how he became driven, made it his life's mission, to restore textualism to prominence in American jurisprudence: the belief that judges, in the business of interpreting the meaning of statutes, should be guided chiefly by fidelity to *the text* of the law, not expand the meaning beyond what the law was widely understood to have meant at enactment. "If you're growing up in the home of a man who teaches language for a living," said Father Scalia, "you're not going to monkey with the translation quite as much."

But the justice often bristled at the diligent efforts by reporters and scholars to pinpoint the origins of his textualism, to identify the early life experience, or set of experiences, that spawned his unswerving fealty to text. In an oral history he conducted with attorney Judith Richards Hope in Supreme Court chambers in December 1992—unsealed in 2018, its contents reported here for the first time—Justice Scalia was reluctant to ascribe to the Jesuits any particular influence on his legal philosophy.

> **HOPE:** Do you think that the Jesuit training and the classical training had any impact on the way you approach statutory analysis and interpretation?
> **JUSTICE SCALIA:** I don't know. I can't say that. Perhaps. I might have been the same without it.... Perhaps I have more regard for language and what it says, what it suggests, what it connotes, simply because I have had so much exposure to language in my life—not just English but French, German and Latin, Greek. So I guess you get to feel comfortable with interpreting words and seeing their relationship with one another. I would not attribute it to the Jesuits in particular.[35]

Appearing at the University of Michigan Law School in 2004, he quipped, "People ask me, 'When did you first become an *originalist*?' like they're saying, 'When did you first start eating human flesh?'" His answer tended to change over time. Even before his nomination to the Supreme Court, Scalia said he held a "strong view on the relative role of courts in our particular government," adding, "I suppose I came to that view, oh, sometime after I grew up, maybe when I was forty years old or so."

In his final years, however, the justice recognized originalism as a kind of lifelong obsession. Asked in 2013 if he had "already arrived at originalism as a philosophy" by the time of Watergate, when Scalia was in his late thirties, he said he didn't know, then added: "I've always had it, as far as I know. Words have meaning. And their meaning doesn't change."[36]

*　　*　　*

Nino thrived at Xavier. He was first in his class—straight As—and joined a slew of groups and societies, pursuing each *con vigore*. "Scalia was in all the activities in the school," a classmate recalled. "He was a favorite of the Jesuits... because he was bright and he was involved."

Prodded by his father, Nino took piano lessons; but not just any teacher was good enough for Sam. The school was in Manhattan. "That started young," the justice recalled. "At least until I was a junior or so in high school, I used to practice very faithfully and consistently, at least an hour a day, and got to be pretty good. Then, as other demands crept in on my time, I got a little worse every year, until I have fallen into the state of pianistic decrepitude that I am now in."[37]

He was class president his freshman and junior years. In the Catholic Forensic League, he excelled at debate ("Sparked by Nino Scalia," the Xavier yearbook exulted, "our team won about half of their hundred-odd debates"). He was president of the drama society and earned rave reviews as a supporting player in *The Green Pastures* ("sterling performance") and for his lead role ("extraordinary ability") in *Macbeth*. ("Probably the most significant thing I've done," he joked later, adding, "You know how many lines there are in *Macbeth*?")

He participated in two championship rifle teams while serving as prefect, then treasurer, of Sodality, the Catholic volunteer group (Sodality also organized the school dances, which Nino attended). He contributed to *Xavier Magazine*. He joined the French Club. He played the French horn in the marching band, and became its commanding officer as a lieutenant colonel—*unheard of!*—before rising to major. (This last feat was a triumph of will, not skill, as classmates recalled Scalia's playing the instrument "not that well.") He loved marching with the Regiment down Xavier's stately front steps, accompanied by the sound of the drum-and-bugle corps, before heading into the Church of St. Francis Xavier to attend Mass. There the cadets unsheathed their swords before the altar under its spectacular arched apse. He participated in the St. Patrick's Day Parade, marched behind the Fighting 69th of Irish lore, and in the ticker-tape shower for General MacArthur.[38]

Contemplating how Xavier shaped his father's life, Father Scalia, a vicar in the Arlington archdiocese, cited the school's high standards.

> The Jesuits today are sort of perceived as a great liberal force in the church.... But back then they were known for their precision, for their spit-and-polish, their rigor of thought.... And my dad loved that. He told me about the sixty-second verb. I studied Latin and Greek in college, and my dad's Latin, I think, was always better than mine, even though he didn't study it in college. But the Jesuits were just so tough. And so the sixty-second verb was [where] the teacher would give you a verb to conjugate in its entirety and you had to do so in sixty seconds. And he would stand there with a stopwatch.[39]

The fearsome Jesuit in charge of this was Father Morton Hill. Though Hill was by all accounts a kind soul, his terrifying Latin drills stayed with Scalia, and the other survivors, forever. Scalia's classmate Tom Campion said Hill was "a dominant figure." "Morton Hill," Father Robert Connor recalled, "was by far the Jesuit who was most demanding."

> In our junior year [he] drove us relentlessly through the five declensions of nouns and four conjugations of verbs under

pressure of a stopwatch. We were marked on speed and accuracy every morning. This was followed by approximately thirty lines of Cicero's *Catiline Orations* to translate, then turning an English sentence into Latin, with all the pitfalls of verb complexities. Daunting work. Every day. Through the misery, [Scalia and I] got to be good friends.[40]

Here the world started taking notice of Nino's sharpness, his instinct for the rhetorical jugular. In autumn 1951 he was selected to appear with other students on a Sunday morning television program called *Mind Your Manners*. No recording or transcript survives, but Scalia's performance impressed his classmates and friends, their parents, and his teachers.

Writing in *Xavier Review*, classmate Thomas Campion—a friend of Scalia for the rest of his life, and of Maureen after that—published the first newspaper profile of the future justice. An accompanying photograph showed "Nino Scalia": a proud cadet in honors uniform with a head of black hair and a broad smile across his chiseled face. "When we speak of Antonin Scalia," Campion wrote, "we naturally think of First Honor Cords, of the Debate Hall, of the Xavier Theatre, and of television."

For the past three years he has compiled one of the most enviable records at Xavier. To date, nineteen First Honor awards, one for each marking period, have been won by him.... He has also received each year the Gold Medal for class excellence. In short his name has become synonymous with exceptional accomplishment in the field of studies.

With him we associate skill in the science of debating and the art of dramatics. Nino has excelled in these activities.... Antonin is no stranger to the bright world of television. Last year he was a panel member of the popular Sunday show *Mind Your Manners*, where he displayed to the best his fine traits of character. His keen sensible answers, well seasoned with a bit of humor, stole the show again and again.[41]

Around this time Nino was selected to appear on a radio broadcast sponsored by the *New York Times*. The program featured three boys arguing for Dwight Eisenhower against three girls supporting Adlai Stevenson. Nino's thrust—ingenious for a sixteen-year-old—was to tie Stevenson to the foreign policy failures of the Truman administration.

But Scalia was incredulous at the judging by Averell Harriman, a Democrat. Harriman awarded victory to the girls. Scalia recalled that Harriman's performance "made him realize for the first time that a person of national stature and good reputation could be...a dolt." Even before the quiz show scandals of the era, young Nino Scalia had observed the potential for corruption in television: a jaundiced view of mass media that would reappear in his academic writing, executive branch service, judicial opinions, and interaction with the press.

Still, he had fun: the producers gave Nino fifty dollars cash and put him up at the Algonquin. Through these appearances on TV and radio as a teenager—the first time the broader public was exposed to Antonin Scalia's penetrating and amusing mind—the boy attracted his earliest fans. One of them was James Connor, father of Scalia's classmate Bob, who recalled that his dad "loved to watch Scalia take apart some politician...on the tube." *Oh,* the father would say, *Scalia really gave it to 'em this week!*[42]

The strength of Nino's Catholicism was also drawing notice by this point. *Xavier Review* reported him "continually strong in his faith," the product of a "fine Catholic education" provided by his parents and the Jesuits. Simply recounting all the faith-based activities Nino participated in would not, Campion cautioned, "tell the full story of his association with God.... Antonin in short has been leading among us a full Catholic life and we know him as a man who can truly be called an 'exemplary Catholic.'"

Though he would later describe himself as "a greasy grind" at Xavier, young Nino was also blessed with personal charm. His affable persona inoculated him from the social isolation that his relentless pursuit of Perfection in All Things might otherwise have visited upon him. "He is well liked by his school mates and acquaintances," the *Review* reported. "You might think he is living up in the clouds with Zeus and Venus, but his feet are firmly planted on the ground."[43]

Nor was Nino a stranger to hijinks, occasional descents into the kind of fun that gets a kid into trouble; but only his closest intimates would know it. In the late 1970s, when Scalia was teaching at the University of Chicago Law School, one of his sons, then in high school, joined a bunch of friends firing bottle rockets at an apartment building. "The cops showed up," Gene Scalia recalled. "We ran but they picked me up."

> It was the University of Chicago cops and I overheard a radio communication they were having [about how] the suspect believed to have provided the bottle rockets was wearing a light blue shirt. I looked down: I'm wearing a light blue shirt. So I immediately start explaining to them, "You know, look, I just stumbled across these guys...check me for powder or whatever." I didn't even personally shoot anything.... They said, "We're going to have to take you home. You're going to need to go talk to your parents about this."... So I went in, and I had to tell my Dad.... He looked at me and said, "Do you appreciate that that's serious?" And I said, "I do. I know it's wrong and I'm sorry." And he said, "That's *nothing!* When I was a kid, we used to have these M-80s!"... It was a

very funny moment where he stepped out of role and, rather than reprimanding me, he started telling about some of the stuff he'd done as a kid in Queens with fireworks.[44]

In his graduation photo in the 1953 edition of the Xavier yearbook, Scalia looked the best he ever would: trim and handsome; slick black hair flowing from a widow's peak, perfectly parted; an easy, winning smile flashed above the crossed-sword medals and Honor Cord on his chest. Bob Connor remembered Scalia's bringing girls to school dances, and even arranging a date for Connor on one occasion; but romance was difficult under the circumstances. "There was no time for girl friends at Xavier," observed classmate William Stern. "You were expected to do three or four hours of homework a night and if you were involved in activities, you went to school, came home, studied, and went to bed." He said of Scalia: "This kid was a conservative when he was seventeen...an archconservative Catholic. He could have been a member of the Curia."[45]

For Scalia the defining feature of his time at Xavier was the school's dedication to honing the quality his father had already taught him to value above all else: *moral character*. "The habit of courage is not acquired by study; it is forged by practice," Scalia would say. "And there is no better practice than the Regiment."

> By demanding obedience to duty, manly honor and discipline, frank and forthright acknowledgment of error, respect for ranks above and solicitude for ranks below, assumption of responsibility including the responsibility of command willingness to sacrifice for the good of the Corps—by demanding all those difficult things the Regiment develops *moral courage*, which, in the Last Accounting we must give, is the kind that matters.[46]

Scalia left Xavier on top, as valedictorian. "The gold medal winner," his faculty adviser declared. "By far the best in his class in every way."[47]

*   *   *

Two friends from Xavier would still be Nino's friends the day he died: Tom Campion and Bob Connor. Connor's parents, who had marveled at Nino's television appearances, saw him as an extraordinary friend: wise beyond his years, a good influence. Connor kept in touch with Scalia even after abruptly dropping out of medical school, in the summer of 1959, and moving to Rome to study under the founder of Opus Dei, Josemaría Escrivá: a priest trained in law. Two years later, trekking across Europe with Maureen as newlyweds, Scalia brought her to meet Connor. The three rendezvoused at the Opus Dei center on Bruno Buozzi Street, in the Parioli section of Rome, then repaired to a nearby restaurant. There an embarrassed Scalia, untutored in Italian, had to defer to the Irishman to order their meal—a moment savored by Maureen McCarthy Scalia.

Thereafter, the friendship with Connor lapsed. Ordained as a priest in 1964, Connor threw himself into religion, Scalia into law and family life. For reasons neither man could appreciate until they were much older, it turned out that Connor, and Scalia—*back in 1959, when Nino was still at Harvard Law*—had in fact played critical roles in each other's lives. Each was present, as interlocutor and witness, as the other charted his life course. None of that became clear to them, however, until much later: September 26, 1986, the day Scalia joined the Supreme Court.

By then, four years had passed since Scalia had been nominated to the appellate bench by President Reagan and Father Connor, seeing the news, had sent his old classmate a congratulatory letter: their first contact in two decades. Only then did Judge Scalia learn that Bob Connor—*the trumpeter at Xavier basketball games, popular with girls*—had become a priest. They remained close for the rest of Scalia's life: another thirty-three years.

"He had great respect for me as a priest," Connor told me. When Scalia held a reception at the Washington Golf Club, in northern Virginia, to celebrate his son Father Paul Scalia's first Mass, the justice invited Father Connor and proudly introduced him to Justice Clarence Thomas. *You're my oldest friend!* Scalia would say. "He was always loyal to the friendship," Connor said. "He had that Italian loyalty." Nino and Maureen hosted him for dinner half a dozen times. On these vinous evenings, the lifelong friends from Queens would speak of many things—and argue over faith and law.

But after a hug upon greeting each other, the first order of business for the old Xaverians was always the same: a sixty-second competition, Father Morton Hill–style, in the conjugation of Latin verbs.[48]

CHAPTER II

The Incarnation

Things do not work out the way you want,
but the way God wants.

—Antonin Scalia, 1998

In costume as Macbeth, Nino sported a dark cape decorated with lightning bolts, the profile of a wild boar emblazoned across his chest, and a flimsy fake mustache, clumsily applied, which scarcely aged him in the eyes of the audience. Lady Macbeth, at all-male Xavier, was played by John Gallagher, a younger student whose wig, shawl, and dress exposed him to ceaseless ridicule from the rifle-toting cadets. Gallagher looked up to Nino, who was older and a star student, as "an awesome figure." Scalia took the younger boy aside, urged him to ignore the taunts. Gallagher recalled years later how "kind-hearted" Scalia was about it.[1]

Nino's academic excellence and extracurricular zeal were stellar, but there was something else, the third leg of the stool that completed his greatness: the caliber of his *moral character*. He considered joining the priesthood. Nino wrestled with "the big decision" as a senior, during Xavier's annual retreat in spring 1953. Scalia loved retreats, made them a lifelong practice. "Any person who believes in the transcendental has to go on a retreat periodically," he said. "You will lose your soul (that is to say, forget who and what you are) if you do not get away from the noise now and then to think about the First Things."

A life devoted exclusively to God would have meant enrolling in St. Andrew's on the Hudson, the Jesuit seminary for the New York Province. "I might have made a heck of a Jesuit," Scalia later joked, averring to the leftward drift of the Society of Jesus in the late twentieth century. Ultimately, as the justice told CBS News, he concluded the priesthood was not what God wanted for him: "He was not calling me." The young man believed his gifts better suited to—*what?* He didn't know; something else, not the Church, not in that way.

The end of the Scalia-Panaro bloodline also weighed heavily on him. "I was an only child," the justice told Biskupic. "That was part of it."[2]

*   *   *

Nino's triumphs at the Xavier graduation ceremony drew the attention of a Brooklyn newspaper: "Mr. Scalia, son of Dr. and Mrs. S. Eugene Scalia...earned a 97.5 average [and] medals for general excellence, English, Latin, Greek, modern languages, religion, debating, and dramatics, a silver key for speech and a gold medal for participation in the Glee Club. He also participated on the junior varsity rifle team."[3]

College admissions officers took note: Here was a valedictorian, a handsome extrovert skilled at an array of extracurricular activities, with military training and the highest morals: an "exemplary Catholic." What college or university would reject him?

Top of Nino's list was Princeton, which offered a Naval ROTC program matched to his scholarship. Meeting the Naval ROTC academic requirements proved challenging even for the Xavier valedictorian. "It wasn't an achievement exam, it was an intelligence exam: spatial relations and that sort of stuff," he said. "I recall thinking it was the hardest exam I'd ever taken in my life—and I had taken a lot of exams."

A Scalia goes to Princeton—the American Dream! "I really wanted to go to Princeton," the justice recalled in 1992. There were practical reasons, such as the scholarship, but in his heart, he was pursuing the dream. "My mother's family was from New Jersey—from Trenton. And, gee, for Italian-Americans living in Trenton—Princetonians. God! That was really making it—to have one of your kids go to Princeton."

Yet in his formal interview with the school, young Nino detected a disturbing factor present in the room—prejudice—and his application to the university was rejected. In his recollections of this central event of his early years—*the dream denied*—Scalia always indicated that prejudice played a decisive role but always demonstrated reluctance to say so. "That was the only instance," he told Judith Richards Hope, "where I thought my background—I wouldn't say it was discrimination against Italians in particular. But I remember having the interview with a Princeton alumnus and I sort of had the feeling [that] he thought I was just not the Princeton kind of a person."

> HOPE: What does that mean?
> JUSTICE SCALIA: And he was probably right. At least at that time. Not from the right school, the right family, good club, not WASPish enough. That may be unfair. It was a long time ago, but I did have that feeling, and I must say that's the only time I have ever had the feeling…that being an Italian-American made any difference to my detriment in my life.[4]

Not the Princeton kind! It was code for all the hurtful words Italian kids in New York in the fifties heard early in life and trained themselves to transcend: *guinea, goombah, greaseball, dago, wop.*

Now Nino Scalia understood as never before: Sometimes it won't matter that you're valedictorian, that you excel at sports and societies and demonstrate unimpeachable moral rectitude. You can still find yourself defined by some innate characteristic, or applied label, some powerful and pernicious idea you cannot transcend by dint of piety, hard work, and ingenuity. The rejection was, he said, a "crushing disappointment."

As Nino came of age, the episode provided a painful reminder of a lesson he had first learned as a boy on the streets of Queens: *the world ain't always fair.*[5]

*   *   *

Justice Scalia never portrayed himself as someone whose rise to greatness represented a triumph over ethnic prejudice. "He didn't talk about it," Gene Scalia said. "I think he certainly would have admitted that ultimately [his ethnicity] helped him.... I mean, it was, I think, a factor in his being nominated to the Supreme Court."

> I heard more about [ethnic prejudice] from my mom, who grew up Irish in the Boston area.... I think he might have been more cognizant of being treated differently because of his religion than being Italian. Certainly, when you read his speeches...he talks about how it's necessary for Christians in today's world, and really always has been, to accept condemnation from civilized society for believing something that a lot of people will see as fantastical.... So he certainly believed that there was a bias in certain circles against Catholics, and there was.[6]

Wounded but unbowed, Nino chose a setting similar to Xavier: Georgetown University, the oldest Catholic and Jesuit institution in the United States—and a guarantee, for stellar Nino, of a full scholarship.

The kid from Queens moved to Washington at the height of the Cold War: the era of nuclear anxiety, McCarthyism, and civil rights. For a student of exceptional intellectual curiosity, steeped in the power of foundational texts and historical tradition, the atmosphere of the capital was intoxicating. *A Scalia goes to Washington!* Without knowing it, Nino had arrived at the place where he would spend the majority of his life.[7]

Georgetown then was a much different institution. Each school year kicked off with the Mass of the Holy Ghost, for which students gathered on an esplanade beneath the soaring spires of White-Gravenor Hall to watch a procession of Jesuit faculty in white robes. While not a military academy, Georgetown emphasized an educational mission equally focused, like Xavier's, on academics and the formation of moral character. In an age when "it was generally acknowledged that the Jesuits were among the finest educators in the world," Georgetown gentlemen were expected to acquire not only "mere skills" for careers but a grasp of "life's value" and powers of judgment that would serve them, as the college's president, the Very Reverend Edward B. Bunn, told them, "in all the problems and exigencies of life as a husband and father of a family, a member of your local and national community, and a devoted Christian."[8]

Once again, Nino's introduction to the new environment was bracing. He was seated in Intermediate Greek with twenty other students when a knock at the door brought a messenger from the front office bearing the news that six of them, including Scalia, were in the wrong class; they belonged in Advanced Greek. After a short walk, Scalia and the other expatriates arrived to find their new classmates translating Sophocles' *Oedipus Tyrannus*. Nino had four years of Latin, and three of ancient Greek, under his belt—but this new class was way beyond his level. That night, with classmate Dick Coleman, a fellow expatriate, Scalia huddled over the translation, struggling. In three hours, they managed seven lines.

"But we got it right," Coleman recalled. "That was my first experience with Nino's laser-like focus on getting a job done."[9]

*   *   *

Young Nino knew his presence on the Georgetown campus embodied the American Dream. He also understood it as a decisive moment in the development of his personal character. Graduation from high school meant "the departure from home...a time to let go," he recalled. "You have been living up to now in a moral environment that could be closely supervised by the people who love you most in the world, your parents. They got to know your friends, your teachers, your school—and did what they could to change or improve them when they thought that was for your good.... Your moral formation...is now pretty much up to you."[10]

Scalia was caught short when his English composition professor, a Canadian and "damned hard grader" named P. A. Orr, returned his papers. "I was not accustomed to getting the B minuses that I received on my first few assignments, and as a consequence every weekend of my first semester I devoted many nervous hours to writing and rewriting," the justice said. "I am grateful to this day." At the time, however, Orr's disapproval brought "so much angst...to my freshman year."[11]

A history major with a minor in a philosophy, Scalia bore down. He and Dick Coleman shared a suite as sophomores; they remained friends for the rest of Scalia's life. Their excellent grades and combined class ranking afforded them first choice of room in the sophomore dormitory. They selected a fourth-floor suite overlooking the nursing school.

As a sophomore, Scalia was elected president of the White Debating Society. The society was named for Edward Douglass White, the senator from Louisiana who later served as chief justice of the United States Supreme Court: Georgetown's only graduate, at that point, to ascend to the Court. Nino "pressured" Coleman, who had never debated, to join the society. This enterprise, atop an already formidable workload, plunged the pair into "craziness...a whirlwind of debate trips." They traveled as far as Vermont and Indiana. One match, at Dartmouth, saw Scalia, Coleman, two teammates, and their faculty advisor driving a thousand miles round trip (naturally, their car broke down on the return).

Scalia, Coleman, and a brilliant classmate named Peter G. Schmidt formed the nucleus of the varsity debate team and won the Hall of Fame intercollegiate tournament held at New York University. The future justice's debating style took shape in those matches. "Nino gave no quarter and asked for none," Coleman said. "He was not interested in making a point more palatable to others." Once, a teammate blanched at Scalia's assertiveness: "Can't you say, 'I think' or 'I believe this is so'?" "What does that add?" Scalia said. "Of *course* I think and believe it or I wouldn't have said it!"[12]

With his hangdog eyes and toothy smile, Schmidt was Scalia's principal partner on a winning team. "They were terrific together," Coleman said. "They won a lot of tournaments."

"Peter wasn't handsome," a colleague later said, "but you felt he was because there was an aura around him. He made everyone feel you were his closest friend."

"Peter Schmidt could sell ice to Eskimos," Coleman recalled. "But we knew then that he was not to be relied upon."

Schmidt became a prominent Manhattan attorney. Then—amid a tangle of multimillion-dollar fraud charges—he disappeared. "He has simply vanished, leaving behind his livelihood, his family, federal investigators, chagrined bar officials, a host of embittered friends and clients and a Federal judge who wrote that he was a 'fraudsman extraordinaire,'" the *New York Times* reported in 1989.[13] "His victims include foreign businessmen, European nobility and some of his closest friends."

Stunned but not surprised, Justice Scalia, from his Court chambers, alerted Dick Coleman to the scandal. "It just absolutely blew our minds," said Coleman. "And we just sort of talked about it on the phone and kind of chuckled that we could see it happening."[14]

*   *   *

Nino was also president of the Mask and Bauble Society, Georgetown's theater club; as a supporting player in *Heaven Can Wait*, he performed "ably," a critic said. (Co-starring with Scalia was future Academy Award nominee Eileen Brennan, of *The Sting* and *Private Benjamin*.) The yearbook further listed "Tony Scalia" as a participant in student council. He also joined the Earthangels, Georgetown's intramural basketball team. "Nino played a guard slot," Coleman recalled. "He had a deadly long-range two-hand set shot now known as obsolete."[15]

Nino's maturation in this period included learning how to work smarter, cutting down on preparation time. Once, after a debate tournament kept them out late on the eve of an early-morning exam, Scalia grew panicky. "Nino was distressed that we had not studied...and we would do terribly," Coleman recalled. "I pointed out it was 11:00. The exam was not until 9:00 a.m., which gave us ten hours and we could learn *anything* in ten hours." Scalia burst out laughing. "We studied, we did get some sleep," Coleman noted, "and we did do well on the test.... Many years later Nino told an audience that I had ruined him for life, that by nature he had been a plan-ahead, methodical guy but that I had inculcated cramming methods into him.... Nino told the group: 'Dick firmly believed that the sooner one started a job the longer it would take.'"[16]

Junior year brought Nino's first foreign travel: a study-abroad program at the Jesuit-run University of Fribourg, Switzerland's only Catholic university. "We both came out of Jesuit high schools, we're at a Jesuit university," recalled Coleman, "the education is definitely European-based."[17]

Nino and fifteen classmates sailed an Italian ocean liner, the *Conte Biancamano*, across the Atlantic, with stops in Spain, Portugal, and Gibraltar. The Georgetown *Hoya* newspaper charted their progress, including their bus trips to the great cities of Italy—Nino's first visit to his ancestral homeland—as well as train trips to Spain, Austria, and Germany. They visited England before the voyage back home.[18]

The classes at Fribourg were taught in French, which Nino spoke fluently. But the phrase that the Swiss professors used with Scalia and the other native speakers of English who hailed from the United States, Canada, and Australia—*les pays anglo-saxes*, or the Anglo-Saxon countries—"deeply offended" the *paisan* from Queens. The visit to England, however, brought him around. He felt more at home and realized, as he told an audience at Catholic University decades later, it wasn't just the language but also the inherited patrimony of religion, political traditions, literature, and culture.

> You are not just the child of your parents.... Physically you are totally theirs, to be sure. But intellectually, attitudinally, culturally, you are a child of the West, and of that particular *part* of the West that is the United States—which is close to, but not quite the same as, the part that is England.... You

are, to mention only a few of your forebears, a child of
Homer and Alcibiades, Cicero and Caesar, Dante and the
Medici, Alfred and Chaucer, Joan of Arc and Louis XIV,
Elizabeth and Shakespeare, Milton and Cromwell, Carlisle
and Edmund Burke, Hamilton and Jefferson, Nathaniel
Hawthorne, Abraham Lincoln and Mark Twain.

Scalia's travels through Europe, his acquaintanceship with the different histories and forms of government, deepened his gratitude for American law and society. "Frenchmen were Frenchmen before there was a French constitution," the justice would say. "Italians were Italians. Germans were Germans. But we were not Americans, we were not a nation, until that document was adopted.... It's really what made a country out of us."

Exposure to the art, architecture, and landscapes of the Continent also deepened Scalia's appreciation for all he had yet to learn. "One of the values of college education," he said later, "is to make the mind aware of the immeasurable immensity of human knowledge, and the even greater immensity of things still unknown.... This attitude of humility before the breadth of knowledge mankind has accumulated, and before the even greater breadth of the unknown, is the beginning of wisdom."[19]

*   *   *

Senior year, back at Georgetown, brought more debate trips, more trophies; indeed, Scalia and his three partners in the Philodemic Society formed "the best collegiate debating team in the nation that fall," capturing the Hall of Fame championship a second time. But when administrators unexpectedly moved up that year's oral examinations, the

Scalia team pulled out of the Cherry Blossom Tournament, hosted by Georgetown. The school fielded a less accomplished team, and victory eluded them.[20]

But Scalia had made the right call. In his case, the oral exam was not only a prerequisite for graduation but an event that left a lifelong mark. Facing a panel of three professors, Scalia was on his game—at first. "It was like Babe Ruth brought his bat that day," he remembered. Near the end, history professor Walter Wilkinson, round-faced and balding, posed what struck Nino as a "softball" The professor asked him which, of all the historical events he had studied, had had the most impact on the world.

How could he possibly get this wrong?

There was obviously no single correct answer. The only issue was what *good* answer I should choose. The French Revolution perhaps? Or the Battle of Thermopylae—or of Lepanto? Or the American Revolution? I forget what I picked, because it was all driven out of my mind when Dr. Wilkinson informed me of the *right* answer—or at least the right answer if I really believed what he and I thought I believed. Of course it was the Incarnation.

And the *way* Wilkinson had said it, with a sad shake of the head: "No, Mr. Scalia. The Incarnation, Mr. Scalia."

The Incarnation! How could he have been so foolish? Of course Christ is above all things!

For Scalia the lesson was that his Christian faith, nurtured by the Jesuits at Xavier and Georgetown, and the career he would soon choose, the means by which he would nourish his physical being, were not "two separate operations"; rather, he was expected, properly, to approach all his earthly endeavors from the perspective of devout Catholicism.[21]

Once again, as at Xavier, Scalia graduated as valedictorian. In his Cohonguroton Address, on June 9, 1957, he urged his fellow Hoyas to absorb the lesson from Wilkinson: "If we will not be leaders of a real, a true, a Catholic intellectual life, no one will."

> The intellectual life, which is essentially the never-ending search for truth.... does not belong to the college and the university.... It should stretch far beyond, to wherever there is a man to think. It is our task to carry and advance into all sections of our society this distinctively human life, of reason learned and faith believed. If we fail to do this, if we allow the cares of wealth or fame or specialized career, to stifle our spirit of wonder, to turn us from the hunt, to kill in us what was most human.[22]

If anyone had told Scalia at this point that he would someday sit on the Supreme Court, he would have found the notion preposterous. Asked in 2008 what inspired him to study the law, Justice Scalia answered with the French expression *faute de mieux*: the absence of anything better. "When I got out of college, I didn't have the slightest idea what I wanted to do with my life," the justice said. "I knew I wanted to go to graduate school. I had an Uncle Vince [Panaro], okay? Most Italians have an Uncle Vince. Vince was a lawyer and I used to visit his law offices in downtown Trenton now and then, and he seemed to have a good life. So [I thought] I'll give it a shot. And as it turned out, it was what I love."[23]

Undaunted by the experience with Princeton, Scalia aimed again for the Ivy League. Asked if there was some reason he chose Harvard Law School, he said: "I thought it was the best. It had the reputation at that time as being number one. I got admitted there and thought I ought to go there."

This time, the elites had welcomed the Italian kid from Queens.[24]

A Scalia goes to Harvard.

CHAPTER III

All Seasons

*You can't tell the story of Nino Scalia
without Maureen.*

—Brian Lamb, 2017

Georgetown classmates found Nino's driving "scary." Dick Coleman dreaded out-of-town debate matches. "We were taking turns driving and everybody was chatting away until [Scalia] took the wheel—and everybody eventually grew silent," Coleman laughed. "He would get interested in talking and not watching the road. I said, 'We're going to relieve you now, Nino.'"

Deficiency as a driver dogged Scalia the rest of his life. "God help you," a former clerk said when a reporter once mentioned having been a passenger in the justice's BMW. Everyone who knew the man, it seemed, had a horror story about his driving.[1]

It made for the one time in his life when he found himself on the wrong side of the law. On September 3, 1955, Nino, nineteen, was driving up Route 1 from Trenton to Manhattan to catch the *Conte Biancamano*, the ocean liner that would take him and his classmates to Europe. A state trooper pulled him over. "I received a traffic ticket for speeding," Scalia later told the FBI, "which required my personal appearance some weeks later in East Brunswick, N.J., municipal court. My parents tried to get a waiver of this appearance in my absence—which they ultimately did, but not before an arrest warrant had issued." The episode dragged on for nearly a year—and made the papers. Magistrate Adele Watson slapped contempt-of-court fees on three lead-footed drivers who had missed court appearances: Edwin Rosen of Newark, Thomas Summers of Trenton, and "Antonin G. Scalia," AWOL Hoya. All paid their fines.[2]

Friends recalled Nino's dating but didn't remember any specific women. "Extracurricular activities plus my studies," Scalia told an interviewer in 1975, "left me with little time for anything else."[3]

Soon, however, a woman was in the picture—and there to stay.

*   *   *

Scalia's tour of the American Dream brought him to Cambridge, Massachusetts, and the Ivy League in the autumn of 1957. Such blessings were not simply to be enjoyed, they were to be *honored*: with more worship of God, hard work, discipline, perfection. "The first year in an American law school," Justice Scalia remarked a half-century later, "is a life-changing experience."[4]

An early account of Scalia at Harvard depicted him as having "an almost comical intensity." "People just competed for second," a friend recalled, "he was just so superior academically." "I was a good scholar," Scalia recalled. "All my life I had been good in academics.... I kept my nose to the grindstone."

At the same time, he was affable, quick-witted and self-deprecating, with a genuine interest in others' stories and problems. He played piano and led sing-alongs. "Classmates were intrigued by Scalia's personality," an early profile reported, "a combination of scholarly seriousness and life-of-the-party gregariousness."

Scalia himself said, "I really think that to try to identify what particular talent you have that helped you to advance in your profession, I think perhaps mine was the ability to interest myself in whatever problem happens to be the one that is set before me at the time, even relatively dull and even relatively inconsequential problems. I have always had the ability to get enjoyment out of that."[5]

No one, outside of Maureen, knew Scalia better than Judge Laurence Silberman: the justice's closest friend and *consigliere*. Larry graduated Harvard Law behind Scalia in the 1960s, hired him at DOJ in the 1970s, sat on the Court of Appeals with him in the 1980s, and served as his counsel when Scalia was nominated to the Supreme Court. Silberman told me Scalia's originalism dated to his law school years: "Harvard used to stand, however imperfectly, for the proposition that judges should never make policy.... There was a judicial activism in the '20s on the conservative side. And in the '50s, when Nino and I were going to law school, there was a counter-reaction against judicial activism. Nino and I took it beyond what our teachers had taught us, or the justices on the Court had done with it."[6]

Another Harvard classmate, Daniel Mayers, agreed the faculty emphasized judicial restraint: "We all were very struck by this argument that there were neutral principles of law which, if you really disciplined yourself, you could apply without regard to your own political preferences."[7]

The main event during Scalia's time at Harvard came in April 1959, when Herbert Wechsler, a law professor at Columbia, delivered the Oliver Wendell Holmes Lecture. In his address, entitled "Toward Neutral Principles of Constitutional Law," Wechsler argued the benefits of the legal process's "transcending the immediate result that is achieved." He asked the audience to consider whether *Brown v. Board of Education* (1954), the landmark Supreme Court ruling that struck down separate-but-equal treatment in public education for black students, reflected such a process. "For me, assuming equal facilities, the question posed by state-enforced segregation is not one of discrimination at all," Wechsler said. "Its human and constitutional dimensions lie entirely elsewhere, in the denial by the state of freedom to associate, a denial that impinges the same way on any groups or races that may be involved."[8]

Scalia told biographer Joan Biskupic that he didn't attend the Wechsler lecture, but she found it "difficult not to believe" that the speech had influenced the justice. In support of this she cited an interview with Frank Michelman, co-editor of the notes section of the *Harvard Law Review* alongside Scalia and a professor at Harvard Law since 1963. Michelman "speculated" in the interview with Biskupic that the Wechsler lecture made "a lasting impression" on Scalia. Following in Biskupic's footsteps, biographer Bruce Allen Murphy characterized Scalia's denial of attendance of the Wechsler lecture as "a claim that many questioned."[9]

The prominence of Michelman in the Scalia literature, and the omission, until now, of the context necessary to assess his perspective and motives, betrays the agenda of the justice's previous chroniclers. Most early newspaper and magazine profiles of Scalia, and both previous biographies, drew heavily on the insights of the tall, mustachioed Harvard Law professor. But none, for example, mentioned *Brennan and Democracy* (1999), Michelman's admiring portrait of William J. Brennan, the liberal justice whose jurisprudence, rooted in the theory of a "living Constitution," was polar opposite to Scalia's.

In addition to "speculating" about Scalia and the Wechsler lecture, Michelman painted for one early writer a portrait of his old classmate as a boor who "delighted in chiding Stevenson liberals." In the student he knew then, Michelman remarked elsewhere, he saw nothing of the later jurist "whose opinions would grab attention, in part, for their occasional bouts of vituperation." Even a lighthearted culinary anecdote could be twisted, like floured dough, into censure. Michelman regularly regaled Scalia's profilers with his tale of working late on law review one night and watching Scalia savor some unfamiliar-looking pastries.

Scalia expressed incredulity that Michelman didn't know what a cannoli was. "Michelman did not remember getting a share," wrote Biskupic. "No," she quoted him as saying, "I think I had to go get my own." The implication was that this quotidian detail presaged some similarly uncharitable strain in Justice Scalia's jurisprudence.[10]

Michelman contested the claim that the Harvard Law faculty in the 1950s emphasized judicial restraint, neutral principles, and other conservative philosophies. "The lessons on legal interpretation and statutory interpretation and constitutional interpretation that most of us would have absorbed," Michelman told me, "came largely through what was known as the *legal process* school of thought. Legal process was a theory of collaboration across the legislative and judicial branches of government."

> Instead of taking a Congress or state legislature literally at its word when it might have cast a sentence in some more unfortunate terms that couldn't really be thought to represent the will or the intention of the legislature, it was the courts' job to provide a certain kind of assistance at that point and—I suppose within some outer limits of semantic permissibility—read the words to make good sense, to fit some attribution of statutory purpose.... It would have been lodged into the consciousness of just about everybody studying law there at that time, and that would certainly

have included Nino. And it's possible, of course, that that produced some kind of a reaction in him.[11]

The outer limits of semantic possibility! The phrase would have horrified Scalia. The idea that judges should *assist* the legislative branch, applying some *theory of collaboration* to statutory interpretation and the separation of powers—all this was heresy to Scalia, even then.

Michelman seemed unaware that his recollections of Scalia, so frequently sought out, might be colored by his philosophical opposition to the justice's views, or by resentment that the loathed originalist, the anti-Brennan, had ascended to the Court. When first contacted in 2017, Michelman was skeptical that our interview could even produce any fresh memories beyond those he had already shared with previous writers. But the slightest probing of the cannoli story unlocked one more memory, previously unreported and shocking, revealing a deep-seated antagonism that should recast our view of Michelman as a recurring source in the Scalia literature.

After he reprised his tale of watching Scalia wolf down the cannoli, I asked Michelman about Scalia's physical condition at the time. I had in mind the weight gain evident in successive yearbook photographs beginning with the ones from Xavier, when Scalia was trim and handsome, a picture-perfect soldier, through Georgetown and Harvard. "I didn't think of him as fat. He wasn't," Michelman answered. "'Husky' is what I suppose the term of art would have been." Still, Michelman couldn't help but chuckle as he recalled the nicknames coined by a law review wag: Lanky Frankie and Fat Tony.

Was Scalia aware of the nickname at the time?

Oh, yes, Michelman told me. Soon he was gleefully recalling the time, two decades after their Harvard days, when he and Scalia ran into each other at the annual convention of the Association of American

Law Schools. Fresh off his senior-level service in the Justice Department, Scalia had returned to academia and was now teaching at the University of Chicago Law School. He had arrived at the convention first and was chatting amiably with colleagues in the hotel lobby. "I was on the down escalator on my way to the lobby floor," Michelman recalled, "and I cupped my hand around my mouth and yelled down, because I saw Scalia there with a couple of other people, and I just yelled down"—

Here Professor Michelman, for the only time in our hour-long interview, adopted an exaggerated Italian accent—

"'HEY-uh, FAT-uh, TOE-nee!'"

Scalia "kind of jumped," Michelman recalled with a chortle. When Michelman stepped off the escalator, Scalia, "kind of shame-facedly, a little sheepishly," told his old classmate: "Gee, I wish you wouldn't call me that."

> **ROSEN:** Did you feel badly?
> **MICHELMAN:** No. I mean, I complied.... I thought I was just recalling, you know, in a lighthearted way, our student days. But he for some reason had begun to feel that it was a little bit against his dignity.... I didn't feel as though I had stepped across any line of civility that I should feel sorry about.

Michelman refused to recognize his catcalling of *Fat Tony* for what it was: a schoolyard taunt among grown-ups, offensive and inappropriate. He also dismissed the possibility that Scalia, at any time, could have regarded *Fat Tony* as an ethnic slur. "I don't think that thought would ever have crossed his mind," Michelman told me. "It certainly never crossed mine."

HEY-uh, FAT-uh, TOE-nee!

Even Scalia's polite request that the name be retired was "shame-faced" in Michelman's telling, a reflection of Scalia's hubris and self-regard. "I think his admonition to me," Michelman said, "was about his sense of being...on the track to some level of office or distinction, and that [the nickname] would not be helpful."[12]

*   *   *

Another editor on the *Harvard Law Review*, more kindly disposed, was a New Yorker named Robert Joost. Though Nino was Catholic and Joost Jewish, they both knew how it felt to stroll the campus of a place like Harvard in the late 1950s as an outsider. Joost's mother, Scalia recalled at Bob's funeral a half-century later, "scraped and saved" for her son, worked inside darkened offices as an after-hours cleaning lady, to give him the best possible education. Scalia also admired Joost's "fine mind." Bob, however, suffered from what is known today as bipolar disorder, as Scalia would note in his eulogy of his friend. Joost would take another eight years to graduate from Harvard Law (*magna cum laude*).

Before taking leave to grapple with chronic illness, Joost performed one last favor for Nino. It was to change Scalia's life forever, make possible his rise to the Court. Joost set Scalia up on a blind date with a petite brunette from Braintree, Massachusetts, an English major at Radcliffe named Maureen Fitzgerald McCarthy.[13]

From the start, there was a *lightning-strikes* quality to Nino and Maureen's relationship, recognizable to devout Catholics as the work of divine providence. "That was a close call," the justice remembered. "I almost didn't meet Maureen, or didn't meet her soon enough, and that would have been a great tragedy." He recalled they were introduced "by mutual friends" in December 1959. Scalia's idea of a good blind date, evidently, was to take Maureen to a law review dinner. "I recall my mom communicating to me that when they started dating, he was sort of a known figure," said Gene Scalia. "He was an impressive young guy at Harvard Law School.... I think that was part of the perception of him."

Still, Maureen thought Nino was going to be unbearably dull—*a law review dinner?*—so she contrived an excuse to bail on him early in the evening. By the appointed hour, however, Maureen found herself swayed by Nino's charm and brilliance, his quickness of mind, the animation and vigor he exuded. "I found him so interesting," she told me. "It's too bad you have to go home soon," Nino said, late in the evening. Here the Radcliffe girl contrived *another* ploy. "Mom had told Dad that her dorm had a 1:00 a.m. curfew," Meg Scalia Bryce recalled. "This was true except for the seniors, including Mom, who had 'senior privilege' and could be out until 5:00 a.m. When she realized that she was enjoying herself and wouldn't want to go back by 1:00 a.m., she told my dad that she would call the dorm and ask permission to stay out later. She pretended to make a phone call, then came back and told him that she had extended her curfew."

Or, as Maureen put it to me: "I faked that."[14]

Then Nino...*disappeared.* Maureen thought they had had such a great time; why hadn't he called her again?

"I liked her a lot but I [was] just immersed in law review stuff," the justice recalled. "I didn't ask her out again until I think it was late January or something like that."

"I didn't hear from him again until February," Maureen told me. "But it was exam time."

Scalia's Harvard pals took notice of Maureen. Law review co-editor Nathan Lewin, who was to remain a lifelong friend of the justice, saw Maureen as "this beautiful Catholic girl."

Dick Coleman thought: "What an incredible woman!"[15]

*   *   *

Maureen's parents were also remarkable people, as emblematic of the American Dream, in their way, as the Scalias. Her father, John McCarthy, son of an Irish immigrant, became a physician. Maureen's mother, Mary Fitzgerald, began working, to help support her family, after high school. Braintree was no freer of prejudice than Queens. At a time when signs read *IRISH NEED NOT APPLY*, some neighborhood parents forbade their children from playing with Maureen because she was Catholic. Dr. and Mrs. McCarthy put Maureen and older brother Forrest through college.

Petite but fiercely independent, intellectually brilliant, and impeccably mannered, Maureen inherited her steeliness from her mother, Mary. Antonin Scalia found a way to get along with his mother-in-law despite the fact that Mary, as grandson Gene Scalia recalled, had "a very, very sharp tongue. My dad used to joke about how important it was just to get a whiskey sour in front of her ASAP. Whenever he got home for the evening, that was his job: to get that in front of her and make her happy. I mean, she was a formidable person. She was tough."

When she saw Maureen getting serious with Nino, Mary muttered to her daughter about the *nice Irish boy named O'Brien down the street....* The time Gene stayed home one New Year's Eve, waiting for the ball to drop on TV, Mary bellowed at him from the stairs: *For God's sake, Gene, get the bourbon!* She, too, in the end, succumbed to Nino's charm: Mary would slap on lipstick whenever she learned Nino was due home imminently.[16]

Dr. John McCarthy died suddenly from heart failure during Maureen's third year at Radcliffe. She was devastated. But Mary insisted Maureen finish her education. Maureen drew strength from her Catholicism and the Irish gift for laughter. With her father gone, Maureen learned intimately, painfully, the fragility of life: *the need always to persevere, to conserve, preserve, stretch, adapt, make do, get the job done with whatever is at hand, no time or words to waste.* "There is very little beating about the bush" with the Irish, Justice Scalia said. "You always know where you stand.... Maureen has this endearing quality to a preeminent degree."

Faith bound them. "We were both devout Catholics," Scalia told Biskupic. "That was perhaps the most important thing that we had in common." Their politics, still embryonic, also aligned. At Radcliffe Maureen co-founded the Young Democrats but recoiled at the welfare state. "This was not how I was raised," she told Biskupic. "It was that you work hard and make your way." Intimates saw Maureen as more conservative than her husband. "There was never a time that I thought that Maureen Scalia was in the shadow of Nino," said Brian Lamb, who knew the Scalias for forty-five years. "In some respects, and I've said this many times to our friends, she was stronger politically in her views than he was."[17]

"She's very special," said Father Malcolm Kennedy, the priest of Opus Dei who described himself to me as Justice Scalia's "spiritual counsel" for many years. "She's about the only person who could really stand up to him, almost intellectually, within the family circle.... I always thought it was a very interesting dynamic there, between Maureen and Nino."

> **ROSEN:** How would you describe that dynamic?
> **FATHER KENNEDY:** Well, it was good-humored. And Nino, of course, was a commanding presence and a commanding intellect. But as I said, Maureen would have no scruples at all about challenging him.... It was a fun relationship.

In 1989, Justice Scalia aroused Maureen's displeasure by concurring in a Supreme Court opinion, written by Justice Brennan, that upheld a

First Amendment right to burn the American flag. Scalia considered himself a "law and order guy," eager to see "sandal-wearing, bearded weirdos who go around burning flags" thrown in jail; but his originalist approach to Constitutional interpretation, which recognized not merely freedom of speech but "*the* freedom of speech," sanctioned no abridgment of it. Maureen wasn't persuaded. The next morning, when Nino arrived for breakfast, he found their house festooned with Old Glory, Maureen humming "You're a Grand Old Flag." "She was tweaking him," Father Scalia told me, telling Nino, in effect: "The more important thing in your life is actually not the Court; it is marriage and family."[18]

"I think Dad would have the reputation for having more of a temper, but that's not quite fair to my mom," Meg Scalia Bryce chuckled. "She does have a temper. She can hold a good Irish grudge, but Mom is probably more even tempered, not prone to outbursts."

"We joke within the family," said Gene, "that my mother has got a much longer memory than my dad. You could get in trouble with my dad and it'd all be over the next day. With my mom, it could be a year later, you know?"[19]

*   *   *

"Nothing I learned in my law courses at Harvard Law School," the justice would tell law students, "qualifies me to decide whether there ought to be, and hence is, a fundamental right to abortion or to assisted suicide."

Scalia took all the "bread and butter" courses—*common law, criminal and civil procedure, contracts, torts, administrative law*—but even Harvard left "gaps" that he would "feel deeply...in my education as a lawyer." A clerk from Scalia's final Court term remembered him, during their interview, scanning the applicant's transcript, *summa cum laude* Northwestern, and looking up to ask, "Where's bankruptcy?"[20]

Nino was not valedictorian; but *magna cum laude*, top-five at Harvard Law, was still remarkable. "I cannot say that I look back with misty-eyed mellow reflection upon my years at Harvard," Scalia said. "They were years of really terribly hard work and I don't think I have ever studied harder, especially during the first year.... Second and third year.... I spent a much smaller proportion of time studying courses than I did on work for the law review. To some extent my grades reflected that."

Nino loved law review. In his first year, he authored a case note; in his second, he collaborated on a survey of conspiracy laws. "I had never worked as closely with other bright lawyers," he recalled. "I remember being overawed at the raw brainpower." What the geniuses around him lacked was literary skill. "I could write rings around many people who were much smarter than me," he thought.

Scalia's long hours at Gannett House, the law review offices, once exposed him to the incarnation of evil. On a Saturday afternoon in April 1959, a few hours before the review's annual banquet, an alumnus, slender and patrician, entered the building and started up the staircase, peering at framed photographs of other alumni as he went. The students didn't recognize him.

"My name is Hiss," he said at last, "and I used to be an editor here, and I thought I would come in and have a look around." It was Alger Hiss, convicted spy for the Soviet Union, released from prison: a spectral figure desperate to reconnect with a time when his name was synonymous with Eastern Establishment achievement, not espionage and perjury.[21]

*   *   *

In spring 1960 Nino brought Maureen to Trenton to meet his parents. "I must be here for a reason!" she thought. Nino knew lightning when he saw it. Ninety days after they met, they drove to New Hope, Pennsylvania. Nino had accepted a fellowship in Europe, departure imminent; so, in a restaurant—*not Italian!*—he popped the question. No, Maureen told me, he did not get down on one knee; she accepted, anyway. Her classmates gossiped: "Sure, she said yes—he's going to Europe!" "She's a Catholic—she *has* to stay with him!" Maureen paid the gossipers no mind.[22]

Tom Campion recalled an occasion during the Scalias' engagement, in mid-1960, when Nino called to ask a favor: Would Campion pick Maureen up at Sam and Catherine's, where she was staying while Nino was out of town, and take her out for the evening? Campion, then in the army, took Maureen to the officers' club at Fort Dix, where he was stationed, then back to the Scalias' home. Asked what she was like, Campion recalled, "Aside from the good looks...she was just a joy to be with." Scalia's parents adored her: "They knew their boy had chosen the right woman."[23]

On September 10, 1960, Maureen and Nino were married at St. Pius X Church in South Yarmouth. The Reverend Gerard F. Yates, S.J., of Georgetown University, officiated. Maureen's brother gave her in marriage; Scalia's friend William J. Joyce was best man. The event brought the groom his first headline—atop a photograph of Maureen, hauntingly lovely in her wedding gown, Mona Lisa smile across her lips—in the *Boston Sunday Globe*: MR. SCALIA, BRIDE ON EUROPEAN TRIP.[24]

"We wanted the same things in life," Maureen said. "This is a lot of where Catholicism comes into play," said Father Paul Scalia. "These are two people who have benefited from being raised in the Church [with] a very outward look upon things.... They meet at Harvard and Radcliffe, you know? They're not meeting at Mount St. Mary's and St. Joseph's, or Fordham Law and some Catholic women's college. And so they're rooted in the Catholic faith but then they also...engage in the world."

Their engagement came amid great change in the Church. The Second Vatican Council, which was announced by Pope John XXIII in 1959 and took place from 1962–1965, enacted reforms the Scalias abhorred. A friend said: "I can recall him being perturbed by the liberalizations in the Catholic Church."[25]

*   *   *

Among Harvard Law graduates, Scalia was unusual for not pursuing an academic position, judicial clerkship, government job, or partner track at an elite firm. Instead he secured a Sheldon Fellowship, which amounted to an all-expenses-paid European honeymoon. "The main reason she married me," Scalia later joked. "Under this traveling fellowship, Harvard gives you money to travel with virtually no strings attached, with one exception: You cannot enroll for a degree in any university, which, after seven years of college and law school, was the farthest thing from my mind!"

For the first time in his life, Nino savored a period where intense academic rigor was *not* demanded of him: the fellowship where you can't do anything, he quipped. "They just give you the money and say travel…. You do not have to devise some project that requires you to be in Florence, Italy; if you want to go to Florence, Italy, you go to Florence." The only requirements were that fellows travel every ninety days and forgo academic enrollment. "You had to write one letter to the dean of the law school saying: 'Having a wonderful time, wish you were here!'"[26]

First the couple enjoyed a brief honeymoon on Cape Cod. Then, through May 1961, Nino and Maureen traveled the Continent. Their longest residency was nearly three months in Frankfurt, where Scalia considered studying German law. The newlyweds pierced the Iron Curtain: East Germany, Poland (including Auschwitz), Czechoslovakia,

Yugoslavia. "It was the depth of the Cold War," Scalia said; in Venice, they learned of the failed invasion of Cuba at the Bay of Pigs. "I remember feeling so ashamed," Scalia said, "that our foreign policy had become such a cropper." Visiting Soviet bloc countries only deepened their antipathy to communism.

> In Warsaw we spoke to a group of students from the university.... We were treated almost like visiting royalty. It was absolutely incredible. They were so hungry for contacts with Westerners. I remember Maureen had lost one of the buttons on her coat. She had a blue cloth coat with a sort of leather button on it, and it was dangling; it was close to coming off when we arrived. And when we left, someone had taken the trouble to sew it on for her. Just one of the little incidents that I remember...their courtesy towards us.[27]

On their way back to the States, the newlyweds attended a London performance of *A Man for All Seasons*, Robert Bolt's adaptation of the life of Sir Thomas More. It was a landmark event for the Scalias. More was the sixteenth-century English chancellor and conscientious Catholic who was executed by King Henry VIII for refusing to certify the annulment of the king's marriage to Catherine of Aragon. Awaiting the executioner's axe, More proclaimed himself "the king's servant, but God's first."

The tale of unshakable Catholic faith and fidelity to the rule of law deeply touched the Scalias; after her husband's death, Maureen recalled that the play "grew in significance to us over the years." Scalia regularly quoted it, closing out law courses with a reading of his favorite passage. In it, More declares, "I know what's legal, not what's right. And I'll stick to what's legal." When More's son-in-law Roper, "a fool" in

More's eyes, counters that he would gladly trample every law in England to apprehend the Devil, More replies, "And when the last law was down, and the Devil turned round on you—where would you hide, Roper, the laws all being flat?"

Scalia's later jurisprudence—his preference for the immutability of "what's legal" over society's ever-shifting views on "what's right," his elevation of legal process over moral outcome, even when the Devil went free—embodied the core concepts of *A Man for All Seasons*.

Asked once which opera his life most resembled, the justice, a famous opera lover, demurred; most, he said, told "silly stories." The one character in literature Scalia wished to be like was More. "He was a Catholic, as I am," he said, "and that's what he died for. But the play wasn't so much about a Catholic as it was about a lawyer. The man loved the law and saw the importance of the law, even to defend ideas that he didn't agree with."[28]

*   *   *

Returned from abroad, Nino had a job lined up. He had been sitting in Gannett House one night when a man almost a decade older had wandered in. With his dark hair, glasses, and aura of Midwestern rectitude, Jim Lynn looked like a Rotary club president or trusted physician. Harvard Law '51, Lynn was recruiting for his Cleveland law firm, Jones, Day, Cockley & Reavis. Anyone toiling at that hour, he reckoned, was a top-tier student.

Cleveland? Scalia wasn't thinking along those lines.... But Lynn persuaded the young man to join him for breakfast in Harvard Square. There Scalia agreed to meet the partners at Lynn's home in Shaker Heights, an affluent Cleveland suburb, for dinner. With seventy lawyers,

Jones Day was the biggest firm in Cleveland, and among the nation's most prestigious.

At Lynn's house, Scalia found himself leaning against the fireplace, cocktail in hand, surrounded by *eight* Jones Day lawyers. All were senior honchos with decades of litigation experience, hectoring him over a law review note he had published on Sunday blue laws. *No problem!* At Harvard, Scalia had debated Nathan Lewin, a friend and co-editor, on whether it should be legal in blue-law states, where commercial sales are prohibited on Sundays, for a merchant observing a Saturday Sabbath, such as Orthodox Jews, to avoid competitive disadvantage by remaining open on Sundays. No, Scalia had argued. "He won that debate," Lewin recalled—and the following year, in *McGowan v. Maryland*, the Supreme Court ruled that blue laws do not violate the First Amendment's free exercise clause.

"We spent about two and a half hours attacking him," recalled partner Richard Pogue. The older lawyers taunted him, asking how he ever made law review. But the aces, outmatched, gave up at 3:00 a.m. "Nino loved it," Pogue said. "The intellectual combat—he just *thrived* on it." Pogue thought it the best recruiting session he ever saw. Lynn—the first practicing lawyer to recognize Scalia's potential—beamed as his recruit gave no quarter. "He already had that habit," Lynn recalled, "of getting intensely serious with those heavy black eyebrows of his scrunching up and his jaw setting so that he spoke without moving his jaw much."

The firm offered a starting associate's salary, $20,000 (around $202,000 today); Nino accepted. As Lynn later boasted to the FBI, he had "spirited [Nino] away from a Philadelphia firm which had offered him a position." In Scalia's mind, the East Coast firms were "sweat shops"; Jones Day, while top-tier, would respect his nights and weekends. In addition to informing the partners of his upcoming Sheldon

Fellowship, he cautioned them that what he really wanted to do was *teach*. "I told the people at Jones Day when I started," he recalled, "that I probably had that ambition."[29]

In fact the Scalias spent the next six years in Cleveland, "longer than I should have," the justice later conceded, simply because "I enjoyed practicing so much." After devouring Maureen's breakfast, Nino drove downtown every day to the Huntington Bank Building. He greeted fellow associates by their given names, partners by surnames. He gravitated to the Real Estate Group, led by Ray Durn. It was grunt work, typical for a first-year associate—no lofty neutral-principles talk—but Scalia's brilliance shone. "He was an intellectual, structural genius," Durn recalled.

Whatever Nino was assigned, he plunged in, inhaling the case history, knocking out the pleadings, motions, and other lawyerly work products. Scalia was admitted to the Supreme Court of Ohio in May 1962, to the U.S. District Court for the Northern District of Ohio the following year. He described this time as "an intensive education in pre-trial practice."

> I avoided specialization and handled a wide variety of matters, including litigation, anti-trust, real estate, tax, labor law, commercial law, private international law, wills, and contracts.... I prepared our clients' answers and objections to complaints, requests for admissions, and interrogatories, and prepared interrogatories, requests for admissions, motions of various sorts and briefs.... I assisted in preparing our clients' witnesses for deposition and in preparing for deposition of the plaintiffs.[30]

"He was one of the last of the real generalists," recalled partner Herbert Hansell. "He did damn near everything and he did it well."

It was untrue, as one early biographical account claimed, that Scalia "never appeared in court during his six years with the firm"; he appeared in a jury trial in federal court, several municipal actions, a pretrial conference in common pleas court, and oral argument before the Ohio Court of Appeals.

> One of the advantages of Cleveland was that the overhead was so much lower than in some of the other great legal cities, like New York, that a first-rate firm like Jones, Day could have relatively small clients. Its rates could be low enough that a very small corporation could be a client. So after two years at the place, I had my own little corporation that was my client. Any problem they had, they would call me up and it was a really wonderful feeling. I liked it.[31]

Scalia also worked with big clients: *Chrysler...Firestone...Ohio Bell...Sears, Roebuck*. The last sued its local landlord, the Cleveland Trust, after a 1960 accident in which the ceiling in a Sears store collapsed, injuring customers, damaging infrastructure and inventory, and depressing sales. "Investigation by counsel," Scalia wrote, "disclosed that the diamond-mesh lath which held the plaster (and which fell together with it) had been attached to the wooden joists with a nail significantly shorter and thinner than the metal lath trade associations...would have permitted." The jury awarded Sears $29,119.09 in damages (about $295,000 today).

Cleveland Trust appealed, arguing that Ohio's statute of limitations precluded Sears's action because more than fifteen years had passed since the construction of the ceiling, in 1935. In arguments before the Sixth Circuit Court of Appeals, Sears claimed the landlord had "constructively redelivered" the building and the ceiling at each lease renewal, the last well within fifteen years of the accident. The appellate court sided with Sears, which then negotiated a settlement Scalia termed "favorable." "Development of the legal theories underlying the case—in both trial and appellate briefs—was largely my work," Scalia said. The partners took notice.[32]

Catholicism "dominated...his thinking," but Scalia's political conservatism was also now apparent. A lawyer who interviewed with Scalia in 1963—nearly a year before Arizona Senator Barry Goldwater won the Republican nomination—recalled Scalia was already "a hard-core Goldwater person." A colleague remembered him as "one of the first Bill Buckley–type conservatives...a big *National Review* fan."[33]

In his writing Scalia seldom mentioned William F. Buckley, Jr., the urbane conservative controversialist who founded *National Review*, the leading journal of conservative opinion, to which nineteen-year-old Nino became a lifelong subscriber. Stylistically, there were differences: The patrician Buckley struck a High Oxford debating pose, marked by grandiloquent circumlocution. The kid from Queens favored a direct approach. But there were similarities, too: Both were native New Yorkers; sons of stern, principled fathers; and devout Catholics, dismayed by Vatican II, partial to Latin Mass. Both *loved* classical music and English-language arcana; both were competitive debaters and experienced TV performers with a gift for showmanship, including the deft comic touch.

Indeed, there is evidence, overlooked by previous biographers, that Buckley's rhetorical genius and permeation of the culture had struck a chord in Scalia: provided a model for how conservatives could win hearts and minds with wit and élan. During a high school commencement address in 1994, the justice referred obliquely to a "smart-aleck political commentator [who] once remarked that he would sooner be governed by the first fifty names in the Boston telephone book than by the faculty of Harvard." It was a quip Buckley had used, with variations, starting in 1961.

It was also a line Justice Scalia had recently borrowed for one of his opinions. In *Cruzan v. Missouri Department of Health* (1990), the Court upheld state officials who had blocked a woman's family from terminating her life support after a car accident left the woman in a vegetative state. Scalia agreed with the ruling but believed the majority opinion, by Chief Justice Rehnquist, should have gone farther and affirmed that federal courts had "no business" in such matters. "The point at which life becomes 'worthless,' and the point at which the means necessary to preserve it become 'extraordinary' or 'inappropriate,'" Scalia wrote in concurrence, "are neither set forth in the Constitution nor known to the nine justices of this Court any better than they are known to nine people picked at random from the Kansas City telephone directory."[34]

*   *   *

The Scalia children came swiftly: First was Ann, born September 1961. Scalia recalled that when the couple returned from Europe, Maureen was in her seventh month of pregnancy. Ann's joyous arrival came in a hospital in Hyannis, near Cape Cod, where Maureen's mother was living. Next was Eugene, in 1963; John in 1965; Catherine in 1966. Maureen joked that she and Nino were "overachievers." Nino said they were "old-fashioned Catholics... playing what used to be known as 'Vatican roulette.'"[35]

The Scalias enjoyed the close-knit community of Jones Day, where the lawyers and their wives socialized year-round. Firm members composed and staged musical revues—Scalia performed in "My Fair Laddy"—and held Christmas parties at partners' houses. Dick Pogue remembered that he, Scalia, and Jim Lynn belted out "Fugue for Tinhorns," the racetrack gambling number from *Guys and Dolls*. "Nino was always prominent at those events," his fellow associate

William Reale recalled. Partner James Courtney remembered Scalia standing in the well of a basement window outside Courtney's house, face rising just high enough to peer into the living room and mug for laughs. "I wouldn't say he's terribly good," Jim Lynn said of Scalia's piano playing. "But he likes to hammer."[36]

In March 1966, Scalia turned thirty. He still wanted to teach, an inheritance from his parents. Salvatore Eugene Scalia had warned his son: if you ever go into teaching, make it graduate-level, because most undergraduates, Sam had learned the hard way, were uninterested. "He was quite exasperated to have to teach to a class that didn't really care," Justice Scalia recalled. "They didn't have intellectual curiosity.... So he would teach to the few students there that really were interested. And I remember him saying to me he wouldn't want me to be an undergraduate professor."[37]

By all accounts Scalia was on the partner track at Jones Day; another year and he'd be *in*. But he was growing restless, and one assignment "drove him out of the firm." When a client received a demand for thousands of documents, the firm dispatched Scalia to a warehouse, three hours south of Cleveland, to review the client's archive. Valedictorian at Georgetown, *magna cum laude* from Harvard, and here he was in Lancaster, Ohio, separated from his family, entombed in legal storage, rummaging through the yellowing documents of some Midwest utility...

"It was really drudge work," Dick Pogue recalled. "And I think after that he decided, 'If this is the kind of work lawyers do, I'm going to seek other employment.'" A half-century later Pogue still remembered the shocking moment when Scalia broke the news that he was leaving. Pogue tried to talk him out of it.

It was no use. "I enjoyed practicing so much that I just sort of forgot that I was going to go into teaching eventually," Scalia recalled, "and hung around probably longer than I should have."

"He just had decided that the practice of law was not sufficiently challenging to him," said Pogue. "He wanted to get into academia where he could deal with conceptual ideas."

Scalia also took a big hit financially. Before too long he and Maureen would welcome their fifth child, Mary Clare. He understood the trade-offs. "Teaching permits you time," he said, "to live on a more human scale." But the only law schools that showed interest in hiring Nino were Cornell and the University of Virginia. He decided on Ithaca— Cornell would at least keep him in the Ivy League—but changed his mind abruptly, at the last minute. Maureen had already purchased heavy winter clothing for the kids; now they were headed to Charlottesville.

"She's never forgiven me for this," the justice would say.[38]

But the move back East reflected another consideration: a mission, a divine calling.

*   *   *

When the fire to join the Supreme Court first began burning within Antonin Scalia has remained a mystery—until now.

Family, friends, colleagues, and clerks have always been leery of ascribing the ambition to him too early, lest credence be given to the caricature of Scalia as a justice whose presence on the Court owed more to careerist politicking than to genius and industry. Scalia himself contributed to the confusion. Asked in 2008 by his friend, C-SPAN's Brian Lamb, if there had ever been "a time that you said to yourself, that you could admit saying to yourself, 'I would like to be on the Supreme Court,'" Scalia replied, "Oh, I guess only at the point where I was reputed to be on the, quote, 'short list.'"

Biographer Joan Biskupic argued that it was during Scalia's service in the Justice Department during the post-Watergate era that the future justice realized that "timing…was everything" and began "learning to play the long game." Bruce Allen Murphy, even more critical than Biskupic, cited the same era as the period when Scalia "looked to augment his resume to be in a prime position for a better job when the Republicans returned to the White House."[39]

Standing alongside President Reagan at the White House on June 17, 1986, when his nomination to the Court was announced, Scalia acknowledged that "for somebody who spent his whole professional life in the law," the event represented "the culmination of a dream, of course."[40]

So when did Scalia start dreaming of a life on the Court?

The answer comes from an unimpeachable witness, one of a trio of known survivors from Scalia's class at Xavier High School: Father Robert Anthony Connor, the Catholic priest whose friendship with Scalia, despite a quarter-century-long dormancy, stretched from boyhood to old age.

After Scalia died, in February 2016, Father Connor published a short eulogy, four paragraphs, in *National Review*. In retrospect, the essay was more remarkable for what it omitted than for what it disclosed. The clergyman related how, at twenty-three, he had abandoned medical school and made plans to travel to Rome to study with Opus Dei. This decision devastated Connor's parents, who thought their son was forsaking his future. In desperation, Mrs. Connor telephoned two men she knew her son respected, in the hope they might persuade him to reverse course.

> At my mother's bidding, Scalia and Father John J. Morrison appeared at my house in Jamaica, Queens, in June 1959. The priest tried to give me a sense of timing and proportion, which I thanked him for. Nino asked what this was all about. I explained Opus Dei…. He took in everything I said and

got it: "Sounds good to me." I don't know what he said to
my mother on the way out, but it was decisive. He had the
stature and authority, even then, to calm nerves.[41]

That was all Father Connor revealed in *National Review* about this
pivotal conversation with his friend Nino; but there was more to it.
Reached in 2020, Connor—by then eighty-five and still sharp of locution and memory, still preaching and blogging for Opus Dei—told me
he had never been interviewed about his long relationship with Scalia.
At the outset of our session, the chaplain casually told me that the
conversation with Scalia that he was about to relate for the first time,
omitted from *National Review*, was "an interesting point you'd probably want to use."

Father Connor's memory was vivid, precise. "I recall very well,"
he said. The revelatory exchange with Scalia, their shared epiphany,
occurred in the upstairs bedroom of Robert's older brother, Jim, in the
Connor home at 18206 Dalny Road in Jamaica, Queens, on the occasion when Connor's mother had invited Scalia there to talk to her son
about leaving medical school. Scalia had just completed his second
year at Harvard Law and had accepted a summer position with Foley
and Lardner in Milwaukee. When Mrs. Connor summoned him,
however, Scalia came. Connor had not seen Scalia for a few years and
was astonished to be confronted by him on the second floor of the
Connors' house.

> **FATHER CONNOR:** Scalia comes up and knocks at my
> door. He comes in and he says, "What are you doing?"....
> So I explained [Opus Dei] to him and he said to me, "Well,
> that sounds pretty good to me." ...I said, "What are *you*
> going to do?" and he says, "Oh, I'm going to the Supreme
> Court." And I said, "Well, how are you going to do that?"

And he said "I'm...going to get a position in Cleveland with this law firm that's well connected in Washington.... I will be sent to Washington, and then I will rise." That was it.

ROSEN: .... What was your response to hearing that?

FATHER CONNOR: I think I was—I was, "Okay, that makes sense, that he will be sent to Washington, and then he'll rise."

ROSEN: So that struck you as plausible, what he said—it wasn't comical or fantastical?

FATHER CONNOR: No, no, no, no, no, it's plausible. I mean, Nino was driven.... Scalia had a sense of destiny.

ROSEN: ...Do you think he regarded it as a divine calling?

FATHER CONNOR: I bet...I mean it's sort of a convergence of two transcendental moments.... He came out to ask the question, "What are you doing?" And I said, "I'm going to God," and he says, "I'm going to the Supreme Court."

As the years flew by, and the two fell out of touch, Connor often thought of his friend's prophesy. *Where is Scalia?* the priest wondered. *Where is the rising?* "I was wondering when Scalia was going to appear," he said. Finally, in 1982, he heard the news: President Reagan had nominated Scalia to the Court of Appeals. Stunned but not surprised, the chaplain wrote his old Xavier classmate the congratulatory note that revived their friendship for the remainder of Scalia's life.

You finally appeared! Connor thought.[42]

* * *

In the fall of 1967, however, Jones Day provided no path to the Supreme Court. So Nino, innately drawn to teaching, chose the route of academia. Having learned the ropes as a practicing lawyer, he would now begin imparting his knowledge to students only slightly younger than himself. At his Jones Day going-away party, Scalia broke up the crowd when he declared, "I'll be glad to get away from such a liberal place."[43]

Three weeks before he strode into Clark Hall at the University of Virginia Law School, ready to teach his first class, Professor Scalia sat quietly in his office, off the law library, making final changes to his courses. The phone rang. It was Brian Donato, a student of Scalia's in the forthcoming semester. Freshly discharged from the navy, married with two children, Donato had arranged, through naval offices, for a moving company to haul his family's furniture and effects across the country. Tragically, the moving van had crashed, killing the driver and scattering the Donatos' belongings. The shaken veteran spent hours on the phone seeking reimbursement but got short shrift from the navy, the movers, and the insurers.

Out of options, Donato scanned the list of his first-year professors at UVA and saw only one promising name: a *paisan*. Scalia listened and "couldn't have been nicer," Donato thought. Within a week—*before classes started*—Scalia called back. "I think you're going to like the outcome," he said. The Donatos received $2,000 (about $18,000 today). Stunned, Brian approached Scalia at Clark Hall to ask what his fee would be. "Dinner at your house," Scalia said, arms folded, "and I'm bringing my wife!"

The couples hit it off. Donato was another outer-borough guy: from the Bronx. The evening ended at 2:00 a.m. But if Donato imagined that shared heritage and fast friendship would bring gentle treatment in Scalia's contracts class, he was swiftly disabused. Donato's first assignment was returned with the lowest grade and Scalia's scribble: "You write like a television comedian. Your logic is A) apples, B) oranges, C) Aristotle."

Dejected, Donato returned to Clark Hall. "I just don't think I'm going to be cut out to be a lawyer," he said. "Nonsense!" Scalia barked, arms folded. "You can do this work! Besides—maybe you'll be one of those guys who gets the clients." "So I hung in there," Donato laughed a half-century later, by then a retired judge. He took a second class with Scalia, in 1969–70, on federal courts. Donato became a frequent fishing companion of the professor, godfather to one of his children—and still received a 2.5 GPA in Scalia's classes.[44]

The house Maureen had wanted, in Charlottesville's West Leigh section, was out of reach financially; but the owner, a kindly law professor named Emerson Spies, recently widowed, "quoted us a price clearly below what he could have gotten." They finalized the deal with a handshake. "Emerson as a real estate lawyer should have known better," Scalia recalled, "and I, too, I suppose, since I was coming to Charlottesville to teach contracts." Before the Scalias left Cleveland, a violent rainstorm hurled a tree limb through the front window of the Spies house. Emerson arranged its repair. "The handshake," Scalia said at Spies's funeral, "took care of it."[45]

Georgetown Today, the alumni magazine that profiled Scalia in 1975, reported teaching was his "first love." Yet the justice's previous biographers have treated his academic positions as desultory *interregna* between more colorful stints in government and on the bench. Murphy spent all of two paragraphs on Scalia's four-year tenure in Charlottesville, mainly on his law review publications; Biskupic devoted a single sentence to his years at UVA. Beyond his employment of the Socratic method—the answering of a question with a question, a staple of law school pedagogy—Biskupic recorded nothing of Scalia's teaching style, impact on students, or intellectual development.

In truth, there can be no reckoning with Scalia's jurisprudence or conduct on the Court without an understanding of his academic career. "He enjoyed being in the classroom…a manifestation of the showman in him and also his love of explaining ideas," Gene Scalia told me. "His time as a professor brought out certain traits that stayed with him throughout

his life.... What some people perceived as the contentiousness or the dis-
agreeableness that he supposedly showed at times as a justice, if you look
back to when he was a professor, he just loved a good argument."

> Sometimes we'd be sitting watching a football game on a
> Sunday afternoon and he'd wander in, pull up a chair, and
> say, "Who's playing?" and we'd tell him. And then he'd say,
> "Who are you rooting for?" He would start rooting for the
> other team—and damn if they wouldn't start winning!...He'd
> be cheering for them like he *loved* them, like he was a lifelong
> fan. And he wouldn't even know their quarterback's name,
> but he would figure it out, and then he'd start cheering that
> guy like he'd known him all his life. He just liked to debate.[46]

Interviews with Scalia's UVA law students revealed a dynamic and
exceptional teacher, even as a rookie: an educator brimming with
energy, confidence, humor, command of subject, respect for his audience, and openness to spirited engagement. "He was the best teacher I
ever had," said Arthur Schwab, a student in Scalia's 1969–70 contracts
class. "He was bigger than life.... I've never had a teacher who was that
exciting or challenging.... It was an intellectual experience that I had
never had before.... He'd pick somebody and he'd work on you for a
while during the class—you felt like you were bouncing, intellectually,
off the walls. I mean it was almost a physical experience dealing with
him, his presence."

This physicality was integral to Scalia's style. "He was continually
moving," Schwab said. To illustrate contracts law, demonstrating how
agreements are tendered, accepted, and rescinded Scalia rushed between
opposite ends of the lecture stage, trading off roles as the different parties. "Offer withdrawn!" he would yell. Again, as at Harvard, Scalia
was struck by the students' inadequacy in composition. "What these

students lacked was not the skill of legal writing," he said, "but the skill of writing at all."[47]

Laggards were treated "without mercy," students recalled. "He expected you to be prepared; and if you weren't, he kept prodding you," Schwab said. "He wasn't doing it to be mean or to embarrass; he was doing it to force you to work hard."

Later a federal judge, Schwab earned two of Professor Scalia's highest compliments. One was a summer internship at Jones Day; the other was Scalia's statement: "You're the only student in the class who can write a simple declarative sentence."

"I came out of that semester," Schwab recalled, "just so much more confident than the young guy that showed up."[48]

"He inculcated in me the sense that I could *do it*," said Donato. He recalled his mentor as even-keeled: no up days or down days, only Nino days. He was *excited* to be lecturing and supremely confident in his views. "I knew the man for forty-seven years and during that entire time we never had an argument that I won."

"He treated all of us with incredible love and respect," recalled Ralph Feil, another student in the 1967–68 contracts class. "He gave us all kinds of individual attention.... He felt that it wasn't his job to just *tell us* about it; it was his job to *interact* with us.... He loved the interaction, he loved the communication."

"He certainly was an active Socratic teacher," said Bob Dormer, another student from the 1967–68 year, who remembered the animated and friendly professor introducing hypotheticals in Italian: *un spaccato di vita*, a slice of life. The students were frequently welcomed into the Scalias' house for barbecues—until the food ran out. "Maureen, I need the rolls!" Nino would bark out; Maureen would roll her eyes. "Be juicy!" he commanded the burgers, waving his arms at the grill. Scalia attended the students' Halloween party, *sans* costume but gamely bobbing for apples in coat and tie.

Scalia's playfulness could not keep the shocking events of the sixties from intruding on his classroom. Charlottesville, by contemporaneous standards, was a conservative campus—but even there the era's upheavals were inescapable. The final exam for Scalia's inaugural class was held June 6, 1968: the morning after the assassination of Senator Robert F. Kennedy in Los Angeles. Dormer remembered Scalia addressing the students: "He commented on what a horrible event it was, and he understood that this wasn't the best time to take an exam, but that we should try and concentrate and do the best we could."[49]

*　　*　　*

None of the students recalled Scalia's expressing an opinion about the Vietnam War. As a father in his thirties, he was ineligible for the draft; as valedictorian of a military academy, he held the armed forces in high esteem. He was dismayed by countercultural contempt for the soldier and displeased when Xavier, in 1971, made regimental service optional.

In the wake of President Nixon's incursion into Cambodia and the killings at Kent State University in May of 1970, rage swept across American campuses and spread, inevitably, to Charlottesville. Encouraged by visits from Yippie revolutionary Jerry Rubin, and William Kunstler, the well-known radical attorney—a term Scalia surely found oxymoronic—antiwar activists worked to shut down the UVA Grounds. A series of marches and protests saw some law students serving as marshals, hoping to prevent violence, and others joining the demonstrators. A squadron of two hundred baton-wielding police dispersed the crowds; sixty-eight people were arrested. Citing "the alienation of American youth," UVA President Edgar Shannon urged Nixon to end the war "promptly." Local media assailed Shannon's "appeasement."

Scalia participated in a counter-protest. When word circulated that the student council, "staffed by radicals," intended to steer funds to the Students for a Democratic Society (SDS)—a leading antiwar group whose former officers would soon form the Weather Underground, a domestic terrorist cell—student conservatives sought a court injunction blocking the funding. The American Civil Liberties Union argued the council had every right to fund the SDS, but the conservative students prevailed, an outcome the antiwar litigants may have precipitated by shouting "Kill the pigs!" in court. To pay counsel, the conservative students canvassed faculty; Scalia gave $20.

That the electrified politics of the sixties stayed with Scalia—haunted him—became clear in later years. As an appellate judge in 1984, he remarked on "those days of strong feelings not too long ago when young people were certain that they had THE TRUTH and were willing to brook no opposition from existing laws or existing institutions in implementing it." When he returned to Xavier, as a justice, he noted that devout Catholics "never had that contempt for the soldier that came to the fore in Vietnam-era America."

Scalia also conjured the excesses of the left as a justice in oral argument in an abortion case before the Supreme Court, a quarter-century after the UVA protests. At issue was whether governments could create protest-free "buffer zones" outside abortion clinics. Arguing the validity of such restrictions was U.S. Solicitor General Drew S. Days III of the Clinton administration. "Those were not simply informational efforts," Days said of pro-life demonstrations in Florida, where the case originated, but were instead designed to "interfere with the processes of the clinic."

"Well," Scalia said, "calling names is designed to hurt. Calling President Nixon, to speak of recent events, a murderer, as happened in demonstrations when the Vietnam War was in progress, is designed to hurt. Does that make it unlawful?"

"It does not," Days conceded.[50]

CHAPTER IV

Open Skies

MR. WHITEHEAD: I would like first of all to introduce to the subcommittee Mr. Antonin Scalia, sitting at my right, general counsel of the Office of Telecommunications Policy.
SENATOR ERVIN: We are delighted to have him with us also.

—*Senate subcommittee hearing, February 1, 1972*

At critical points Scalia benefited mightily—as he always said—from good luck. One of the greatest strokes of good fortune was his introduction, in 1970, to Tom Whitehead: Midwesterner, electrical engineer, MIT graduate, army veteran, Nixon–Ford official, genius, visionary.

It was Whitehead—slender and dark-haired, his baby face framed by Clark Kent eyeglasses—who gave Scalia his first government job. More important, it was Whitehead who placed Scalia, and his talents, at the center of the era's most significant event: the technological revolution. Together they overhauled U.S. policy in this critical field, helping to pave the way for the innovations and transformations of the digital age.

*   *   *

Born in Neodesha, Kansas, in 1938, Clay Thomas Whitehead was the only son, with three sisters, of a chemical company supervisor and a homemaker. The Whiteheads were devout Protestants untethered to a church. Tom built telescopes and ham radio antennae in his room before enrolling at MIT. As a sophomore he worked for Bell Laboratories on pulse and analog electronics.

By 1961 Whitehead had earned degrees from MIT in electrical engineering, systems engineering, and operations. At RAND he designed deep-sea intelligence protocols, applied mathematical modeling to arms control accords, and consulted on the Apollo program. He volunteered for combat duty in Vietnam but was assigned, instead, to chemical weapons research in Maryland. He returned to RAND and MIT, earning a doctorate in management, systems, and economics. With his IBM-pinstriped look, Whitehead fit in perfectly on the 1968 Nixon campaign. At thirty, he was on the White House staff, overseeing the Atomic Energy Commission, NASA, federal maritime policy—a hugely important portfolio few others could comprehend.

It didn't take long for the systems savant to observe that federal policy on telecommunications, including oversight of space satellites and other advanced technology, was a mess: a riot of non-interoperable systems across the executive branch that cost taxpayers $60 billion. Whitehead recommended the creation of a new agency to bring the behemoth under presidential control. Nixon agreed. By September 1970, the thirty-two-year-old Kansan was confirmed by the Senate as director of this powerful new entity: the White House Office of Telecommunications Policy (OTP).[1]

The first thing he needed was a good lawyer.

*   *   *

"I went to OTP with some real reservations," Whitehead recalled. He wondered if the job would engage his gifts and whether the Oval Office would support him in inter-agency struggles. He knew he needed an ace general counsel. Scalia later wrote that the job's areas of focus included "constitutional issues, large segments of contract, corporation, and antitrust law, and regulatory legislation at every governmental level."

> The general counsel ... must combine truly outstanding legal talent with the creativity and broad perspective necessary for policy formulation ... will be required to work with top officials of other agencies such as the FCC, OMB, Justice, Defense, Commerce, and State, as well as members of the Congress and the White House staff. He must have the stature to deal with those officials on a personal basis and to assert the position of this office effectively when views conflict.

Once again Jim Lynn, who had recruited Scalia to Jones Day, propelled the younger man forward, recommending Nino when the new OTP director asked if Lynn knew any good conservative lawyers. Scalia later said he accepted the job "just to see how the big monster works." He inherited one staff lawyer and hired his own deputy and secretary.[2]

As early as December 1970—before Scalia had even started—he was receiving orders from OTP deputy director George Mansur. Whitehead was also firing off memos to "Nino Scalia" in the first week of 1971, asking the incoming counsel to draft ethics guidelines. "He was a man who had great things in mind but he was also a very practical man who could pay attention to smaller things," Scalia once joked, noting that the first assignment Whitehead gave him was to fix a traffic ticket. "I had to tell him I could not do it."[3]

OTP never grew beyond sixty employees; its offices were blocks away from the White House. An early applicant was a Purdue graduate who had majored in speech and spent two years working on Capitol Hill. Shrewd and discreet, Brian Lamb seemed all right by Whitehead, who told Lamb, "I want you to talk with Nino before we go any farther." As a PR guy, Lamb felt "mildly intimidated" by his new colleagues, "elite intelligentsia...with large computers in their head." He and Nino "just clicked," Lamb told me. "It took a while only because he never liked people that didn't stand up to him. And if he could roll over you, he would."

> We had a moment one day when the lawyers were trying to tell me what to do. And it was a very important moment, and I said to them: "Look, you do the legal stuff, I'll do the PR stuff." ...That kind of leveled things out.... I like lawyers a lot because they're smart as hell. But lawyers can be arrogant as hell and look down upon the *proletariat* like me. And they want to think that if they respect you, that you'll stand up for what you believe in. And I just remember he was that way. He will respect you if you stand up to him. He did not respect the people that he could roll over.

A former UVA colleague recommended that Scalia hire, as his deputy, a young lawyer at Covington and Burling named Henry Goldberg. Trim and athletic, Goldberg sported long hair, sideburns, and gold-rimmed eyeglasses. At thirty-five, Scalia was the old man of the office. "It was a very heady time," Goldberg recalled, as the federal government was "just beginning to grapple with where do you draw the line between computers, information processing, and communications." Other agencies were baffled: *What is telecom policy, and why is it in the White House?*

"Nino was comfortable dealing with new technology," Goldberg recalled. "He *got* the new technology, what the impact of new technology was." Yet Goldberg also realized his boss was "a little bit volatile." This impression was formed at their interview, over lunch at the Roger Smith Hotel near OTP's offices. The two men got along fine—but Scalia ended the lunch angry.

"He got into a fight with the waitress," whom Goldberg remembered as incompetent but inoffensive. "He left her a dime tip. I was appalled and said, 'Gee, let me put some more money.'"

"No," Scalia erupted, "don't you *dare* put any more money!"

"Well, don't leave *any* tip, then—a dime is an insult."

"That's just what I want to do! I'm going to put a dime down! That's the tip!"

Taken aback, Goldberg christened the incident the Dime Lunch and needled Scalia about it the rest of his life. "It proved to be typical of Nino's approach.... He had a thing with fighting with people in restaurants."

"He was a force," Lamb told me, recalling Scalia fondly, if pointedly, after his death and five decades of friendship. "You either accepted him on his terms or you didn't have a relationship."[4]

*   *   *

On December 26, 1970, Maureen gave birth to the Scalias' third son, Paul. His arrival followed that of Mary Clare two years prior.

There were now six Scalia kids, the oldest nine years old, and Maureen was home alone with them all. Her husband remained in Washington, staying at the Cosmos Club and commuting to Charlottesville on week-ends, until the family relocated to Waynewood, in northern Virginia, the following July. For all the commotion the children created, Maureen's existence in these days was marked by a profound loneliness, unique to stay-at-home moms. Her sacrifice is the hidden ingredient, the dark side of the moon, of Justice Scalia's success. Everything he accomplished, Maureen made possible.

How she must have dreaded Sunday nights, seeing Nino sail out the front door, not to return for five days.... Looking after a newborn, a two-year-old, and four other kids—by herself. *How did she manage?*

"When my parents were younger and my dad was changing jobs," Meg Scalia Bryce told me,

> that was really hard on her because she's not outgoing, and so she had to keep making new friends every time they moved. And it was heartbreaking, actually, to hear her tell it because she said, "As a mother of young children, how do you make friends? I'd see a nice lady at preschool drop-off, and so I would try to get to drop-off at the same time every day just hoping to run into her again, so that I could start up a conversation, and hopefully in a few months' time she would be a friend."
>
> What's admirable about my mom is that she never com-plained...and the same with my dad.... They never made us feel like a burden on them, and there were nine of us. I mean, we *were* a burden, but they never made us feel like that because family was *it*.... So [despite] the loneliness that my mom expe-rienced, and probably, I would imagine, some stress that my dad experienced about how to provide for us, they never made us feel that burden, which I think is pretty incredible.

"Nino had led a fairly sheltered existence prior to coming to OTP," Henry Goldberg thought. Scalia's only previous professional experience in the capital had been a brief consultancy in the Office of Hearing Examiners at the U.S. Civil Service Commission. But he loved the work. "Hearing examiners were what are now called administrative law judges...the decision-makers under the Administrative Procedure Act," Scalia recalled. "That was really my first exposure to administrative law."[5]

On March 5, 1971, Scalia received his first security clearance: top secret. He fought turf battles, interfaced with Congress, and navigated the conflicting interests of satellite corporations, telephone companies, broadcast networks, the motion picture industry, trade groups, and the *nouveau riche* barons of a new medium called cable TV. He drafted Whitehead's speeches and testimony, letters to lawmakers, memoranda to the president. On occasion Scalia signed his own memos to heavyweights such as Charles Colson, Nixon's special counsel and liaison to organized labor.[6]

Having created OTP, Nixon eyed it warily. "The White House was very political," Lamb said. "They looked at us and said: 'What are you going to do for me next?'" Whitehead and Scalia worked to shield OTP from political pressures. When the West Wing demanded the cancellation of a PBS program, Whitehead turned to Scalia. "Nino said, 'Hell, write back a memo that says it's illegal.'" Apprised that the administration's demand was lawful, Scalia shot back: "Hell, they don't know that!" Whitehead sent the memo and heard nothing further. On another occasion, Scalia rebuffed a White House order barring the airing of reruns on broadcast television.[7]

*　　*　　*

Previous biographers have treated Scalia's OTP service cursorily, in just a few paragraphs. Yet a review of his official correspondence from this period—previously unpublished and the last major corpus of Scalia's writing still unexamined outside his sealed Court papers—finds the same wit, analytical rigor, and textualist fervor that later marked his opinions.

In early 1971 America's telecom industry, still in its infancy, was a tangle of monopolies. The Bell System (AT&T) controlled the terrestrial transmission systems that supported long-distance telephone service and radio and TV broadcasting. Domestic satellites were operated by COMSAT, a creation of the Communications Satellite Act of 1962 and effectively a government monopoly. The three TV networks and PBS controlled national programming. The Hollywood studios, central to the motion picture industry, resented the advent of TV; the studios *and* the networks resented the advent of cable TV, with its insidious pay-per-view model.

At the same time, technological breakthroughs were accelerating. Attuned to them, OTP officials casually threw around terms and phrases—"mobile communications," "shared computer system"—that ordinary Americans would not hear for a quarter-century. Scalia exulted when technicians linked the Federal Telecommunications System, managed by the General Services Administration, to AUTODIN, one of two Pentagon systems. "Inter-connection between FTS and AUTODIN has been achieved," he declared; that AUTOVON, the Pentagon's voice communications system, remained non-interoperable he termed "inconvenient" and "wasteful."[8]

Scalia also understood the legal ramifications of the telecom revolution. One of his early OTP papers focused on the "protection of private rights in the Computer Society." "The era of discovery in the communications field is not drawing to an end; it is barely beginning," he wrote in 1971. Scalia foresaw the Internet, predicting "not merely additional viewing channels but also such services as long-distance shopping by

TV, instantaneous home delivery of news by facsimile reproduction, and [remote] access to libraries, accounting services, and the like."

> Electronic communications have made feasible the accumu-
> lation of data banks which contain vast quantities of infor-
> mation concerning millions of our citizens.... This
> information may be used and furnished in various ways
> which profoundly affects those citizens' lives and
> careers—employment and credit references, for example.
> Should the individual have some right to learn and correct
> this? Should any restrictions be imposed upon the extent to
> which such accumulated information may be shared or made
> available to other persons? Should some privacy safeguards
> be required?

Finally, Scalia grasped the attendant economics. He noted the communications industry had grown by 525 percent since 1950, outpacing
transportation and trade. "These figures," he wrote, "merely demonstrate the economic importance of the industry. They do not suggest its
social importance, which is even greater." There was no way "the
common-carrier monopoly now held by telephone companies should
be extended to some or all of these new fields"; private firms, he wrote,
should be encouraged to "compete for this lucrative business." That,
above all, was the Whitehead-Scalia mission: to turbo-charge the U.S.
telecom industry by injecting into it the basic tenets of free-market
capitalism.[9]

OTP's first great breakthrough was its "open skies" policy. Adopted
by the FCC in 1972, the initiative broke the COMSAT monopoly with
a radically simple idea: any company that could demonstrate the requi-
site technological prowess and capital reserves could launch a domestic

communications satellite into space. Scalia rejected the notion, propounded by rival agencies, that the policy would anger foreign nations. "This is a job that can be done promptly and well by U.S. industry," he wrote in August 1971, "at low cost and with significant effect on aerospace employment." In a memorandum to the president for Whitehead's signature, the future justice faulted the State Department for exalting diplomacy over American workers. "The Europeans do not want to see a U.S. unilateral program," he noted. "Most of the technology has been developed in this country, and U.S. industry is looking to this as a test of this administration's sincerity in standing up to the Europeans on their behalf."[10]

From "open skies" came more vigorous competition in all forms of modern communications—radio and TV broadcasting, mobile telephone service, data processing—and with it the "Computer Society" Scalia had predicted. The *New York Times*, often critical of OTP, acknowledged decades later that Whitehead and Scalia had presided over "the creation of the domestic satellite system that brought cable television and lower-cost long-distance telephone service into millions of American homes."[11]

*　　*　　*

OTP was a formative experience: Scalia learned to swim in the Washington bureaucracy. Early on, Whitehead dispatched him for a summit with DOJ's antitrust division chief to convey that OTP was "not out to be their enemy." "The general counsel of the Price Commission is a law school classmate of mine," Scalia assured Whitehead on another occasion. "I anticipate no difficulty...for us to remain informed and to have whatever legitimate input you desire." After Scalia learned congressional Democrats were summoning Whitehead for testimony, the counsel predicted an "unfriendly reception" and urged staff to "prepare...for the most likely hostile questions."

When an FCC official demanded Whitehead's budget figures within twenty-four hours, Scalia reported proudly: "I put him off until Friday." He understood the value of sequencing, controlled escalation, when to involve the boss. "There may be some risk involved in fighting this matter out," he warned in a tough spot. "I do not see any way to avoid this, however, and I do think it desirable to bring the matter to a head well in advance of Tom's departure [from Washington], so that his personal intervention can be used if necessary." "Nino has convinced me," an OTP economist wrote elsewhere, "that there may be political implications."

Scalia's papers also flashed his renowned wit. When he arranged for colleagues to attend lectures at UVA, he noted on the typed schedule, "I will be present at all sessions to add a certain degree of continuity and charm."[12]

Whitehead overruled his general counsel when, on the eve of a National Association of Broadcasters convention, Scalia urged the director to propose "some major attention-getting action...so that OTP will be prominent in corridor discussions." Like Lamb and Goldberg, Whitehead understood that Nino could get...*a little hot under the collar.* "Make it not too offensive," Whitehead once instructed him. "Polite, not belligerent."

At least once, the general counsel balked at an order. When Whitehead wanted a link drawn between antitrust suits against the TV networks and OTP's advocacy of "localism" among affiliates, Scalia sent a handwritten reply,

> Tom:
> I have tried, and there is no way I can do this. The suits don't do a thing for licensee discretion or localism. Nor do

they at all reduce network power. The nets still <u>choose</u> all their shows—they just have to let others produce + own them.

Putting in sexy language such as that which you suggest may well cause the nets to suspect that (contrary to the third ¶) we propose to bust them up.

Won't you reconsider?

AS[13]

One of Scalia's triumphs at OTP was his negotiation, over several months, of the Cable Compromise of 1971: a landmark agreement on copyright protections between the Hollywood studios, the TV networks, and the cable industry. "Nino used all of his charm and some of his wiles," Goldberg recalled. "Some people doubted that Nino could mix it up at this level, but he could." The talks made Scalia a frequent lunch partner of a legendary figure of postwar Washington: Jack Valenti, the square-jawed, silver-haired president of the Motion Picture Association of America. "He tried to play the Italian card with Nino," Goldberg chuckled; Scalia remained wary. Whenever Valenti invited Scalia to the MPAA headquarters for lunch, Scalia stopped by Goldberg's desk and made him come along. *Why?* he asked. "You know these Hollywood guys. You're going to be my witness."[14]

✳   ✳   ✳

Perhaps most important, Scalia's tenure at OTP helped prepare him for the bench. The experience, a colleague observed, "reinforced [Scalia's] general attitude toward deference" to agency rule-making and stiffened "his antipathy to using legislative history to guide court review." Judge Scalia's decision in *KCST-TV, Inc. v. Federal Communications Commission* (1983) and Justice Scalia's opinions in

MCI Telecommunications Corp. v. AT&T Co. (1994) and *National Cable & Telecommunications Association v. Brand X Internet Services* (2005) all drew on his telecom expertise. *MCI*, Goldberg thought, "could have been taken from one of his OTP memoranda."[15]

Previously unpublished, Scalia's OTP memos contain numerous examples of the incisive approach to statutory interpretation that later became his hallmark. When the United Nations tried to require the United States and other countries to secure prior approval from satellite-recipient countries for all commercial content broadcast over the satellites, Scalia rejected the intrusion on American sovereignty and liberties. "It is at least highly questionable that fundamental constitutional rights may be suppressed merely to facilitate the conduct of foreign affairs," he wrote in 1972. "It is not clear that we can prohibit our citizens from broadcasting commercial messages abroad simply because foreign governments do not wish their citizens to receive them.... This is so fundamentally contrary to the principles of our democracy, and breathes a spirit of governmental paternalism so incompatible with our institutions, that it is unthinkable that we should support it."

That same day he drafted a letter to a top State Department official, signed by Whitehead, in which the OTP director reminded the diplomatic corps never to exalt diplomacy over American citizens' rights. Rather, U.S. diplomats engaging the Soviets and others at the UN were expected to "reaffirm both our domestic Constitutional principles" and "foster the free flow of information" on the world stage. "If we do not formulate the kind of policy position I have referred to," Scalia warned, "we will be abandoning nothing less than the principle of freedom of information which we have defended at great diplomatic cost in prior international negotiations."[16]

He once urged colleagues not to "extend the scope of the discussion beyond the narrow question asked" and employed his gift for metaphor:

It is thoroughly possible (indeed, quite simple) to establish an arrangement whereby the walls in a house are owned by one individual, the windows by another, the plumbing by a third, the floors by a fourth, etc. As far as I know, it has never been done. Not because it is difficult to do, but because it is not intelligent to do. It seems to me that that is the judgment which has been made with respect to the radio spectrum; it must be "owned" and managed as a whole. Perhaps that judgment is wrong—but we lawyers have very little to do with it.

The memo also contained Scalia's fullest commentary on midcentury rot: the confluence of "crime, violence, pot and the general deterioration of that thing known as the 'social fabric.'" He worried that TV, with its power "to affect the mores of the entire community," would worsen these trends because the highest license bidder, even with no "political or ideological axe to grind...may simply find it commercially *profitable* to push sex (short of the legally obscene, whatever that is) or pot or violence."[17]

When OTP faced a decision on the Fairness Doctrine, Scalia cannily adopted the perspective of the viewer at home: "I am resigned to being sold the soap. I am willing to be advised by George Wallace to *use* the soap, or by Ralph Nader not to use it, assuming that at least someone with journalistic responsibility has determined that bathing is an important issue this week. But I am not yet ready to accept a governmental determination that I must also be shown the soapbox, simply because its owner and occupier thinks I should."

His unusual speaking style—forceful, reasoned, playful—was making an impression. Forty-five years after a Manhattan conference, in 1971, an attendee remembered that Scalia "blew the room away with his intellect."

"We knew in 1971, '72," Brian Lamb told me, "that this man would end up on the Supreme Court. There was no doubt in our mind." He and Henry Goldberg used to joke about it, when Nino would leave the room: "He's on his way!"

*   *   *

"That job as general counsel at OTP was probably the most fun I've had in government," Scalia remarked during his seventh term on the Court. He found it exciting, especially for a new agency, to make policy "with friends that are in the trenches with you.... Open Skies for satellites was the beginning of satellite communications.... We proposed breaking up AT&T in the fashion [in which] it was ultimately broken up.... We had proposals for cable television.... Our job was to try to induce the FCC to go along with those proposals, and if that was unsuccessful, to support legislation.... It was a wonderful team and we had wonderful ideas that were, for the most part, adopted."[18]

Scalia left OTP in September 1972 to become chairman of the Administrative Conference of the United States (ACUS). Colleagues chipped in for a farewell party ("$3.00 for GS-13s...$2.00 for GS-12s"), held after Scalia had moved on. ("We are not going to let him get away that easily.") Seventy-five people gathered in Tom Whitehead's outer office to toast Scalia with bourbon and a gift: a humidor for his beloved cigars.[19]

Late in his tenure at OTP, Scalia had received a letter, previously unreported, from a man who would play a central role in his future. The OTP general counsel had sought the Justice Department's opinion on whether free market competition could be introduced into domestic satellite operations: the "open skies" policy that unleashed the telecom revolution.

Scalia wrote the assistant attorney general for the Office of Legal Counsel asking "whether any entity other than the Communications

Satellite Corporation (COMSAT) can lawfully own and operate a new communications satellite system designed to improve air traffic control." While the question was narrowly tailored to the aviation industry, Scalia knew DOJ's opinion would apply to other satellite-dependent technologies. Potential obstacles, he noted, included the Satellite Act of 1962 and certain agreements the United States had signed as part of the International Telecommunications Satellite Consortium (INTELSAT).

Two weeks later, a courier delivered the nine-page reply:

> Dear Mr. Scalia:
>
> This is in response to your October 1, 1971 request for our views as to whether any entity other than the Communications Satellite Corporation (Comsat) can lawfully own and operate a new communications satellite system designed to improve international air traffic control. An administration policy apparently calls for the new system to be developed and owned by the private sector.... The new system may serve other purposes such as...to permit passengers on aircraft and in ships to place and receive telephone calls....
>
> No express provision [of the 1962 act] vests Comsat with the authority to own and control these new systems. Indeed, the Act and its legislative history infer that the creation of another entity is not precluded by the Act.
>
> Since we have not been informed of the legal arguments upon which it is asserted that Comsat has been given a monopoly to operate all new satellite communications systems, including the proposed one, we are hesitant to conclude that position is wholly tenable. In the limited time available we have developed significant arguments against the position....

We would caution that this dispute will likely arise at a later time when the Federal Communications Commission will be required to make a separate legal inquiry in connection with any licensing proceedings for the new system. By that time Comsat and any other interested organization presumably will have developed complete legal arguments in support of a contrary conclusion.

Sincerely,

William H. Rehnquist

Assistant Attorney General

Office of Legal Counsel

In their first encounter—*and for the only time*—it was Scalia assigning Rehnquist an opinion to write, and the product was classic Rehnquist: prim and dry-witted, instinctively conservative, methodologically muddled.

At the outset, the assistant attorney general delivered a light rapping of Scalia's knuckles, noting dryly that the White House was "apparently" seeking DOJ's opinion only *after* policy had been set. Rehnquist also *kvetched* about the "limited time" his office had had—*only two weeks!*—to study the matter. However, on the outcome, approving the "open skies" policy, Rehnquist did not disappoint; indeed, he neatly recast the question from whether the relevant statutes *forbade* such competition to whether they contained any explicit *approval* of monopoly.

Rehnquist first cited the statute's "express provision," a fine textualist beginning, but Scalia likely cringed at the assistant attorney general's invocation, immediately thereafter, of legislative history; nor would Scalia have overlooked the misuse of "infer" or the capitalization of "INTELSAT" but not of "Comsat." Since Rehnquist took the wrong path (legislative history) to the right destination ("open skies"), Scalia likely would have concurred in, but not fully signed, this first Rehnquist opinion he had the pleasure of reading.

Six days later, President Nixon nominated Rehnquist to the Supreme Court.[20]

CHAPTER V

Mr. Chairman

CONGRESSMAN COHEN: *Justice Scalia, you are former chair [of the Administrative Conference] and you have now got another successor.... Would you be kind enough to offer him some suggestions or recommendations on how we should proceed?*
JUSTICE SCALIA: *Do good and avoid evil.*
[Laughter]

—*House hearing, May 20, 2010*

At thirty-six, Nino exuded vigor: he played tennis and squash, jogged, swam, fished, hunted. But he smoked—pipes, cigars, cigarettes—and remained husky. A friend recalled he was "always a little chubby." His hair, swept back over his forehead and bushy eyebrows, had begun thinning. He and his large family attended Mass regularly. Peers regarded him as brilliant and fun, destined for bigger things.

Scalia also demonstrated a knack for ensnaring himself in oddball situations. Henry Goldberg, witness to the Dime Lunch, recalled the Yom Kippur when Scalia, "very curious about the fasting," opined that Jews knew how to fast *properly*. "The Catholics have gotten so soft," he said. "You skip breakfast and that's a fast? *No.* Yom Kippur fasting, you're at the hungriest, you go from dinner to dinner, it's—"

"Instead of all this bullshit," Goldberg cut in, "why don't you *join* in the fast?"

"I'm going to do it!" Scalia shot back.

"Fine," Goldberg said. Dinner on the evening before Yom Kippur would be Scalia's last meal before the fasting began.

"Water?" Scalia asked.

"No," Goldberg said. "No water. Nothing."

"Oh, that's great. That's the real way to do it!"

Scalia was instructed to arrive at the Goldberg home before sundown on Yom Kippur; they would then walk to a nearby synagogue for services before breaking the fast over dinner.

"You're on," Scalia said.

At the appointed hour he arrived at the Goldbergs' in a shocking state, barely able to stand: "a wreck...a dishrag," Goldberg recalled. He asked what the problem was. Scalia had forgotten about a tennis match he had scheduled for the day of Yom Kippur. He felt obligated to play the match *and* meet Goldberg's rabbinical challenge—no water, nothing—so Scalia had sweated for two hours without drinking anything. Now he was weak from dehydration. Goldberg wasn't sure Nino would make it to synagogue.

"Let me give you something now and get you out of your pain."

"No," Scalia insisted. "I'm going to the service."

In his "weakened condition," the future justice donned his *yarmulke* and slumped into a pew in Arlington-Fairfax Jewish Congregation.[1]

*   *   *

Established as an independent agency by statute in 1964, the Administrative Conference of the United States (ACUS) was created to study and recommend improvements in the "efficiency, adequacy, and fairness" of federal regulations; ironically, standing up the agency took *four years*. In 1968, while teaching at UVA, Scalia had served as a consultant to ACUS, in its first year of operation; as recently as February 1971, freshly started at OTP, Scalia completed an eleven-day assignment for ACUS.

Chairing this body, a kind of think tank for the regulatory state, was a dream job for Scalia at this stage: stable hours, a higher salary, a chance to sink his teeth into administrative law, which he "grew to love." The opportunity came from ACUS's departing chairman, Roger Cramton. Six years older than Scalia, Cramton was a former University of Michigan Law professor, trim and well-dressed, dark hair and sideburns, black glasses and bow tie. He had called Scalia to suggest the chairmanship of ACUS because President Nixon had just handed Cramton a coveted prize: the nomination to succeed Bill Rehnquist as assistant attorney general for DOJ's Office of Legal Counsel.[2]

Despite the written exchange with Rehnquist six days before his nomination to the Court, and the equally extraordinary interaction with Rehnquist's successor, Cramton, a few days afterward, Justice Scalia always denied seeing himself as part of a providential chain of events. This denial was unmistakable when he was interviewed, in chambers, by Judith Richards Hope.

> JUSTICE SCALIA: [Cramton] was moving on to the Justice Department to be head of the Office of Legal Counsel, to replace Bill Rehnquist, who had just gone on to the Supreme Court from that position.
> HOPE: So you saw a route?
> JUSTICE SCALIA: I had no idea.
> HOPE: You saw a pattern.

JUSTICE SCALIA: I had no idea it was to be a route, but I was nominated to replace Roger.[3]

Hope, a longtime friend of Scalia's, pressed him deftly, posing a question, then a statement, to point out that if the justice could plausibly claim not to have discerned, in the Rehnquist-Cramton-Scalia shuffle, a *route* for himself to the Court, he could not plausibly deny having observed, as every ambitious lawyer in America had, the *pattern* along which that route had been established. We can sense the justice's irritation at this audacious cross-examination: he briskly dismissed Hope's follow-up and returned them to the bare facts: "I was nominated to replace Roger." That Scalia had previously pondered the pattern Hope asked him about is evident from the fact that he didn't need to ask her, "A route to *what*?"

In truth, Antonin Scalia, best of the best, had been devising his route to the top, nurturing his vision of the American Dream, since at least the age of twenty-two in Queens in 1959, when he prophesied to Robert Connor, a future priest of Opus Dei: *"I'm going to the Supreme Court.... I will be sent to Washington, and then I will rise."*

This was not overweening ambition or crass careerism. Raised by devout and exacting parents, prodigiously gifted by God, disciplined and determined, Scalia simply understood accurately, and early in life, who he was, what the Court was, and why he belonged there. He chased that dream and never stopped, as circumstances and propriety permitted, until he achieved it. He also benefited, to be sure, from the phenomenon that was Ronald Reagan; it was Reagan's election to the presidency that made Judge Scalia, and then Justice Scalia, possible.

A seat on the Supreme Court is neither accidental nor guaranteed. Each justice arrives because he or she wanted to be there, made smart life and career decisions at key junctures to remain in contention, and caught more than a few breaks. Scalia certainly recognized divine destiny in others. Less than a year after his oral history interview, the justice eulogized Mary Lawton, a lawyer and former colleague he revered, in similar terms: "She had a confidence, an assurance, an inner balance that comes from self-knowledge, from a grasp of her proper place in the whole scheme of things. Mary Lawton never gave the impression of being accidentally where she was; she was there because she was supposed to be there, and she seemed to know it."[4]

When Scalia told Judith Richards Hope "I had no idea it was to be a route," he may have been projecting modesty, seeking to discourage further inquiry, or seeking rhetorical refuge in literalism: No one, after all, can predict life's route with certainty. In textualist terms, Scalia had said he "had no idea it *was* to be," not that he "had no idea it *could* be."

Of course he had an idea.

Of course he had seen a route.

As Father Connor said: *Nino was driven.*

*　　*　　*

President Nixon's selection of Scalia to chair ACUS made national news. The FBI opened its first background investigation into the nominee. No derogatory information was uncovered, because none existed.[5]

With fewer than a dozen attorneys and an annual budget of $750,000 ($5.2 million today), ACUS mostly relied on outside lawyers as consultants. The conference convened quarterly for a day or two, and was divided—"like Gaul," Scalia quipped—into three components: chairman and staff; a council similar to a board of directors; and an assembly that voted on recommendations. Sixty percent of members, Scalia said, were "policy-level agency people."

Scalia served as the CEO and spokesman before the White House, Congress, the agencies, the public; yet all that he was child's play. "The hardest job of the chairman," he said, "is to figure out what to study. What is it that really needs doing?" Attorneys who worked with Scalia in this period later told the FBI they found the chairman "a temperate man," an "excellent administrator," "highly regarded...for his abilities and leadership."

Many recommendations from Scalia's tenure were adopted by agencies; others—the right to counsel in parole hearings, for example—were embedded in legislation. DOJ adopted "nearly *verbatim*," Scalia noted with pride, the conference's proposed changes to the Freedom of Information Act. The Civil Service Commission adopted Scalia's guidelines for lawsuits against federal employees. And he developed a new system under which administrative law judges were made to account for backlogged dockets—delays averaging two to three years, Scalia found.

One of the things he "worried about," Scalia said, was ACUS's becoming *politicized*. Interest groups, industry, the federal behemoth itself, all sought, almost as a biological instinct, to skew the agency's recommendations in their favor. Years after Scalia's tenure, Congressman Peter King, Republican from the state of New York, proposed legislation requiring congressional approval before agencies could adopt ACUS recommendations. "Please don't do it, Congressman," Scalia warned, shaking his head, in House testimony. "It would be the kiss of death for the Congress to have it review the substance of agency rule-making."

Scalia took the no-politics rule seriously. A female conference member later testified he ran ACUS "with intellectual precision, unfailing humor, and relentless fairness...helping build a consensus even when it did not reflect his own judgment."

In May 1974, Scalia commissioned a review of the practices and procedures of the most feared and loathed government agency of all: the Internal Revenue Service. The first such study in two decades, the project cost over $100,000 ($609,000 today). Its goal, Chairman Scalia told the *New York Times*, was "to provide needed public assurance" that perennial problems at IRS—experienced by practically every taxpayer in America—"are being looked into by a responsible government agency."

Chairing ACUS allowed Nino to rub elbows with power players from across the executive branch, Congress, and the courts. "It gave him an opportunity to show his brilliance in the legal world, in the regulatory world, without being attached to somebody else," said Brian Lamb, Scalia's former OTP colleague. "He was clearly making a mark in the town."[6]

*   *   *

Scalia's previous biographers have cast his rise to the Court not as the product of a lifetime of integrity and work powered by Nino's genius, Maureen's sacrifice, and their shared Catholicism, but rather as a triumph of cynical, careerist cunning. From his critics' perspective, Scalia's chairmanship of the Administrative Conference—his immersion in the arcana of administrative law and procedure, his deep study of agency reforms—was just another hustle.

American Original by Joan Biskupic references Scalia's tenure at the conference twice in 434 pages, 6 sentences in all, and then only to serve the author's antagonism to her subject. In her jaundiced telling, the careerist narrative, ACUS simply highlights the frequency with which Scalia, as he "yearned" for more "visibility," switched jobs between 1962 and 1974. Also of interest to Biskupic is Scalia's opposition during the ACUS period, more deeply considered than she explores, to proposed expansions of the Freedom of Information Act; this she cites as evidence that Scalia, long before he became a judge, nurtured hostility to the press.

In *Scalia: A Court of One*, Bruce Allen Murphy scoffs that "even better" for Scalia than his aptitude for the chairmanship was the fact that it "involved discussions with... officials who could become instrumental in his next career move."[7]

"This man had ambition," agreed Ken Robinson, a staff lawyer under Scalia at OTP. "He came to Washington. He then managed to go from [OTP], which was a regular civil service–type job, to becoming a presidential appointee [at ACUS].... Then he went over and became an assistant attorney general.... Then he went on and became a judge.... As you know, most of these jobs, you campaign for the office; not a whole lot of jobs are dispensed just solely upon your great merit."[8]

These views of Scalia's rise to greatness are warped by ideological animus, jealousy, and ignorance. While Scalia played the game of official Washington well, he did not "campaign for" the jobs he held; to the contrary, all three of his executive branch positions—at OTP, ACUS, and DOJ—came because others put his name forward without his knowledge. Nor did Scalia take these jobs, or succeed in them, because they offered networking opportunities. Such claims denigrate Scalia's unique gifts, his multifaceted genius for research, composition, persuasion, and friendship. They also ignore his love for administrative law, a hallmark of his jurisprudence.

Eugene Scalia told me the chairmanship was important to his father's rise because through it, Scalia "learned a lot about the administrative state" and "interacted with a lot of people who cared about administrative law and running the government, *who didn't necessarily share anything else in common with him*" [emphasis added].[9]

If the careerist narrative were true, Scalia in these years—the shaggy, anything-goes 1970s—never would have been so pugnacious, nor broadcast his conservatism so openly. In March 1973, when *Jonathan Livingston Seagull* was the country's bestselling book and "Love Train" by the O'Jays was #1 on Billboard, the conservative chairman appeared on an academic panel where, as usual in that era, he was outnumbered. Convened by Fairleigh Dickinson University, the symposium examined whether attacks on the news media by senior Nixon administration officials imperiled the First Amendment.

"Antonin Scalia," the *Times* reported, "was the only panel member who saw no threat to First Amendment freedom in the criticism of the press.... But, Mr. Scalia argued, the First Amendment has always been in danger and requires constant vigilance."[10]

Book Two

STATE OF SIEGE

Chapter VI

Main Justice

Watergate had just come and was not by any means yet
gone. There a party line had been laid down, and it was
only a matter of months before the people on the other
side seized on the contradictions, charted them, comput-
erized them, gloated over them: And then, almost every
day in the right-hand column of the morning paper,
someone else was indicted. At the opposite end of the
paper, the headline reported the conviction of the poor
wretch indicted six months earlier.

—William F. Buckley, Jr., 1976

Nowhere in the U.S. government was the Watergate scandal felt more acutely than at the Justice Department, the nerve center of federal law enforcement where Nixon-era officials had helped cover up the origins of the scandal, and committed more crimes in other scandals. The tidal wave of disclosure rolled back over time, too, with revelations of abuses of power dating back to when Robert Kennedy was attorney general. With each bombshell headline and each wave of resignations and indictments, public esteem for DOJ's integrity, its commitment to the rule of law, eroded.

And no single event of the scandal hit DOJ harder than the "Saturday Night Massacre" of October 1973. When President Nixon wanted to fire Watergate special prosecutor Archibald Cox rather than surrender the secret tapes Cox was demanding, Attorney General Elliot Richardson and his deputy, William Ruckelshaus, both resigned rather than carry out the order. The unpleasant task of executing Nixon's order, perfectly legal but politically suicidal, fell to the number-three official at Justice, the U.S. solicitor general. At that electric moment, the solicitor general was a portly ginger with frizzy hair, thick black eye-glasses, and a curious mustache and beard that made him look like the king in a deck of playing cards: Robert Heron Bork, a former Yale Law professor, brilliant and complex, kindly but not egoless.

This cameo at the center of the Watergate maelstrom marked Bork's first, but not last, turn as a household name. His action embodied the highest ideals of public service, both because the president, under the law, had every right to fire Cox, for any reason or no reason at all, and because carrying out the order, after the resignations of DOJ's top two officials, spared the department further upheaval and demoralization.[1]

Reconstructing Justice, restoring its reputation for integrity, became *the* critical mission for the government lawyers of the Nixon–Ford era: it was essential to democratic government and, more broadly, to the stability of a nuclear superpower embroiled in Cold War conflicts across the globe. Shouldering this solemn responsibility was a cadre of con-scientious Republicans, Bork and Scalia among them, whose loyalties lay with the republic, not the lost cause of Richard Nixon.

*   *   *

Their unofficial leader was Laurence H. Silberman. A native of York, Pennsylvania, Larry had served in the army between his graduation from

Dartmouth and his enrollment in 1958, a year behind Scalia, at Harvard Law. In the Nixon administration, Silberman had served as under-secretary of labor and had returned to private practice by early 1974, when, following the Massacre, he was asked to succeed Ruckelshaus as deputy attorney general.

From the fourth floor of the great grey fortress on Pennsylvania Avenue insiders call "Main Justice," Silberman, like most deputies, actually ran the day-to-day operations of the department. With Bill Saxbe, a former senator and enthusiastic golfer, installed as attorney general, Silberman's influence over DOJ was nearly total. "Nobody ever saw Saxbe," one official told me. "If you had anything important to do, you dealt with Silberman."

Tall, jowly, and pugnacious, Silberman, thirty-eight, combed his unkempt sandy hair over a large forehead. Owlish glasses and a down-turned mouth projected displeasure but concealed an impish wit. Saxbe called him "meaner than a junkyard dog, honest as can be."

Every day the leadership at DOJ grappled with the prosecutions and proceedings emanating from Watergate and subsidiary scandals; with the publication, every morning, of classified intelligence in newspapers; with the stampede on Capitol Hill to rein in the powers of the presidency and the intelligence community; and with an unending series of hearings, lawsuits, subpoenas, and contempt citations targeting executive branch officials past and present. They also faced the press of the ordinary day-to-day business at Main Justice: antitrust, school desegregation, organized crime, espionage, interstate commerce, sky-jackings, narcotics trafficking, and all the other urgent issues America confronted in the 1970s. "It was," Silberman said, "like walking through a minefield blindfolded."

"He was an important figure," Eugene Scalia said of Silberman. "He hadn't been around Washington really much longer than my dad but was probably a more savvy and experienced bureaucrat, more thoughtful about the practicalities of government.... My father undoubtedly learned from him."[2]

The country was more fortunate than most Americans knew to have Larry Silberman where he was at that moment: he was smart, tough, and incorruptible. But the tasks before him were daunting.

The first thing he needed was a good lawyer.

*   *   *

"It was absolutely imperative to have a first-class legal mind," Silberman said, "and a man of courage."

The title for the job he needed to fill was so unwieldy—Assistant Attorney General for the Office of Legal Counsel (AAG/OLC)—that insiders were constantly devising pithier ones to conjure its clout:

Legal adviser to the attorney general!

General counsel to Justice!

The government lawyers' lawyer!

The president's legal adviser!

Only one stuck: *The president's lawyer's lawyer.*

OLC was responsible for determining what legal authority the federal government could cite to justify policies reaching into every corner of American life. Silberman told me OLC was "the single most important assistant attorney general spot" because the office provided binding opinions on the lawfulness of executive branch initiatives. Policy proposals, draft legislation, court filings, covert operations—OLC reviewed them all.[3]

With the Nixon presidency mortally wounded, Nino was preparing Maureen for a return to Charlottesville. His entire Washington adventure, four years running, had unfolded on a leave of absence from UVA; the dean, like Maureen, was losing patience. "At the University of

Virginia," the FBI reported in June 1974, "they have given him an ultimatum to return to the university or lose his tenure." Scalia even began moving his belongings back to the Charlottesville house, which he and Maureen had rented out to a rogue tenant ("Attila the Hun," Scalia snapped, "utterly destroyed it").[4]

Watergate dismayed Scalia. He saw in it the personal tragedy of Nixon but also the accelerating spiral of Western spiritual decline, in an age already debased by Vatican II, the counterculture, Radical Chic. "It was a sad time...very depressing," Scalia recalled. "Every day, the *Washington Post* would come out with something new.... Originally, you thought, *It couldn't be,* but it obviously was. As a young man, you're dazzled by the power of the White House and all that. But power tends to corrupt."[5]

In the summer of 1974, top-tier conservative legal talent was not so easy to find in Washington. Scalia's name was suggested to Silberman by a young lawyer who worked for him: Jonathan Rose, son of a prominent Republican attorney, had followed Scalia at Harvard Law and Jones Day. Silberman and Scalia clicked immediately at their interview. They would remain the closest friends, mutual *consiglieres,* the rest of Scalia's life. "I have never reacted as positively in interviewing anybody," Silberman said. "We were kindred souls." Scalia accepted on the spot.

He told Maureen to hold off on Charlottesville. The opportunity meant a salary cut of "several thousand dollars"—but Nino would now serve at the highest levels of government, in the job Bill Rehnquist had held when he was nominated to the Supreme Court.[6]

*   *   *

The Scalia family was still growing.

Matthew—Maureen and Nino's seventh child—arrived in May 1973.

A newborn, a two-and-a-half-year-old, four boys, three girls, the eldest only eleven...Nino consumed by work...flying around the country...How on earth did Maureen hold it all together?

If there was a group least disposed to see Nino as destined for bigger things, it was his children. They knew their father simply as Dad, a lawyer and professor who sometimes worked for the government. "As far as I was concerned," one of his daughters quipped, "Dad was a Justice Department lawyer or a law professor who couldn't seem to hold down a job."

When one of the kids took a class trip to Capitol Hill, the students were stunned to see Mr. Scalia testifying before Congress. His government ID card, to a child's eye, resembled an FBI badge; that was kind of cool. But growing up in northern Virginia, the Scalia kids knew the children of the *very* powerful: cabinet officers, senators, diplomats, people way more famous and important than Dad. "He was our father," Gene told me, "not somebody that we regarded as this awesome public figure or somebody who was on the big trajectory."

Chiefly, Dad was notable for the amusing things he said and did: his singing and carrying on, crazy driving, the improbable predicaments. "I cherish my mental snapshots of Dad on all fours, chasing us through the house as the Tickle Monster," Catherine Scalia Courtney remembered at her father's memorial. "A dollop of shaving cream on my nose when I went up to say goodbye before school. Belting out 'My Uncle Roasted a Kangaroo' or 'Mr. Froggy Went-a-Courting' at the piano."

At bedtime the originalist rejected Disney versions of *Rapunzel* or *Snow White*; instead, he would drag out an old boxed cloth edition of the Brothers Grimm with illustrations the children found disturbing. "Nino was wonderful with the kids," said a friend whose children socialized with the Scalias. "It was like he was *made* to be The Dad." "Anytime he wasn't at work," said another friend, "he was home with his children."

Marking his father's twenty-fifth anniversary on the Court, in 2011, Gene told assembled guests the Scalia kids were often asked how they felt about growing up with Antonin Scalia. "Unimpressed," Gene answered, "and in fact, a little embarrassed." One of Gene's earliest memories, from around 1968, was of Nino and the kids trudging out to the front of the Spies property in Charlottesville, Dad placing his toolbox atop a railing with a warning: "Nobody knock this box over or your name is mud!"

"We'd never heard the expression," Gene said. "We thought that was funny. And of course *he* knocked the box over. And so we were just in stitches, pointing at him, laughing at him. He's taking it in pretty good nature. And those are the kinds of memories of my dad that I cherish."[7]

In June 1974, Deputy Attorney General Silberman asked the FBI to conduct a full background investigation into Scalia. This vetting proved far more extensive than the bureau's 1972 inquiry. Individuals from every phase of Scalia's life were contacted, including one whose association dated back to 1949, when Scalia was thirteen. Declassified after five decades, these FBI records, previously unpublished, reveal as few other documents the awe-inspiring standards of excellence—*perfection*—that Scalia maintained. "[Redacted] knows of no one of higher character, associates, morals, or loyalty," read one FBI report. "[Redacted] has the highest respect for the applicant's character, associates, morals and loyalty," read another. "He knows of no one he would rather recommend for a position of trust and responsibility with the U.S. government."

"Not only is the applicant a very brilliant individual," noted a Georgetown classmate, "he is a man of sound character." Another Georgetown alumnus described Scalia's character as "of the highest caliber...one of the most honest and sincere individuals he has ever known." "Scalia has the correct temperament for a position of trust and confidence," said still another interviewee, "and would be a credit to the U.S. government." The UVA professors who were contacted told the bureau they "consider SCALIA to be [a] person of highest integrity, thoroughly conscientious, reliable." Typical was this entry: "[Redacted] advised he has known the applicant for twenty-five years. He described him as extremely honest...flawless character...legally talented, very highly thought of, has a sense of political realism, is administratively effective, fights for what he believes in, is very sober minded and businesslike."[8]

Also contacted were the Watergate special prosecutors, whose five task forces made use, in *la nouvelle vogue*, of computerized "data banks." On June 27 Silberman was apprised that a computerized search had produced "no adverse information," because, once again, none existed. On July 11 the FBI declared Scalia "highly regarded.... All knowledgeable sources contacted feel he is an outstanding attorney."[9]

On July 30, President Nixon sent Scalia's nomination to the Senate. Within a week, however, before the Judiciary Committee could take it up, the White House released the transcript of the Watergate "smoking gun" tape. On it, the president could be heard, six days after the arrests that had touched off the scandal, acquiescing in his counsel's plan to quash the nascent FBI investigation by falsely invoking the need to protect CIA operations abroad. The new evidence appeared to confirm Nixon's culpability early on. A grim-faced delegation of Republican congressional leaders, led by Senator Barry Goldwater, visited the White House to tell Nixon he would not survive an impeachment trial. In a televised address on the night of August 8, the president resigned, effective the next day.

Now the country was to have its first and only chief executive who had been elected to neither the presidency nor the vice presidency: Gerald R. Ford. The previous fall, Vice President Spiro Agnew, re-elected with Nixon in a landslide, had become embroiled in a Maryland bribery scandal unrelated to Watergate and had cut a deal with federal prosecutors to avoid prison time. The vice president resigned his office after appearing in a Baltimore courtroom and pleading *nolo contendere* to felony tax evasion charges, a spectacle unlike any in American history. To succeed Agnew, Nixon had selected Ford, then House minority leader. Genial and restrained, Ford was confirmed by the House and Senate and took his oath in December 1973; eight months later, he was sworn in as president.

Amid these seismic upheavals, Nino languished in limbo. He and Maureen didn't know whether the new president would preserve his nomination—or rescind it. Facing bigger problems, Ford allowed Silberman, the deputy attorney general, to have his choice. Here again, however, Nino was to prove unique. The peculiar circumstances of his nomination—submitted by a president freshly resigned—meant the Ford administration could not use the typical language on Scalia's commission, which would normally carry the president's affirmation that he has "nominated" and "do[es] hereby appoint" the nominee. Ford had *not* nominated Scalia; so the text was re-written for the occasion. "My commission as assistant attorney general," Scalia would later boast, "is something of a collector's item."

In a letter to the outgoing ACUS chairman, previously unpublished, President Ford accepted Scalia's resignation "with deep regret," adding, in winking tone: "You will be missed at the Conference, but my reluctance at seeing you leave that position is more than compensated by the knowledge that you are continuing to serve our Nation and this Administration as you assume your new duties as Assistant Attorney General."[10]

* * *

"The executive branch was under siege," Scalia recalled of his time at Main Justice: the post-Watergate era. Daily bombardment with leaks, investigations, subpoenas, headlines, and scandals, he said, demanded "constant exertion.... I attended a daily morning meeting in the Situation Room of the White House at which Bill Colby, the director of Central Intelligence, Jack Marsh, Secretary of the Army, Mitchell Rogovin, [an] outside counsel hired by the CIA, and a number of other high-level officials, who decided which of the nation's most highly-guarded secrets would be turned over that day to Congress, with scant assurance in those days that they would not appear in the *Washington Post* the next morning."[11]

The "siege" experience fueled a lifelong preoccupation with separation of powers. Scalia and other young Ford aides, such as chief of staff Don Rumsfeld and his *protégé* Dick Cheney, saw the executive under assault from Congress in the aftermath of Watergate. Destined for more significant roles in the Reagan era and beyond, these rising conservatives made no excuses for Watergate but recoiled at the measures enacted by the Democrat-controlled legislature—the War Powers Act, the Impoundment Control Act, the legislative veto—that upended the separation of powers. They also felt loyal to Ford, a good and honest man, innocent traveler in the labyrinths of Watergate.

Decades later, from their respective perches, Vice President Cheney and Justice Scalia moved to restore balance between the branches where possible—a life's mission—including in a famous Supreme Court case that bound them together forever. As late as 2011, in an address to lawmakers, Justice Scalia decried "the extravagant assertions of congressional power that have come before me during my years on the bench."[12]

*   *   *

Assuming his duties as AAG/OLC—taking his place after Rehnquist and Cramton—Scalia understood the power and responsibility he now wielded as *the president's lawyer's lawyer.* "It's too tendentious to call [OLC] the conscience of the Justice Department, but it has to call things straight," he said. "The job is a lawyer's job. The job is to say, 'This is what the law is, take it or leave it, like it or not.'... It was a long road back, getting the personnel of the Justice Department to be proud of themselves again. I think Ed Levi [Saxbe's successor as attorney general] was just the man to achieve that, and I think he did achieve it...I was proud to be a member of the Ford administration."

Scalia called things straight. An OLC colleague later told the FBI he was "totally objective in his formulation of opinions and interpretation of the law...allowed no politics to become involved in decisions on matters of law." In turn, Scalia "enjoyed the complete confidence" of his superiors.[13]

Awaiting Scalia's arrival at Main Justice was a lifer, a fixture at OLC since 1960, when Scalia was still at Harvard Law. Petite, brunette, and indomitable, Mary Lawton, only a year older than Scalia, had joined OLC fresh out of Georgetown Law Center. There was no one in government, or the law, whom Scalia revered more. At DOJ, "a person or persons who shall remain unnamed" urged him to fire Lawton as ideologically suspect.

"I look back on this," the justice recalled at Mary's funeral, "with such amusement.... If there was ever a public servant for all administrations— a lawyer devoted to doing her job skillfully, honestly, impartially, without fear and without favor—it was Mary Lawton. That is why she rose to become, at a very young age, the highest-ranking woman in the career civil service, and one of the most honored and respected civil servants of any shape or sex.... I never knew her to do a shoddy piece of work, to run from a fight, to shade the truth. She was a lawyer's lawyer, a counselor's counselor, an adviser's adviser."

They shared something else: swiftness to anger. In remembering this about Mary at her funeral, Scalia could well have described himself: "She could rise to wonderful degrees of anger...always an exuberant, hearty, cheerful anger. It was more fun to be in the company of an angry Mary than to be in the company of a satisfied and contented someone else."[14]

*   *   *

Scalia's first audience with a president of the United States came on August 13, 1974, when he attended a private talk by Ford on the administration's fourth day in office. The air was still thick with Watergate. Indeed, Scalia's first assignment at Main Justice plunged him into the heart of Watergate darkness: the Nixon tapes.[15]

From February 1971 to July 1973, using microphones hidden in the Oval Office, his telephones, and other locations, the thirty-seventh president had secretly amassed *3,700 hours* of secret reel-to-reel audio recordings. They captured evidence that, when exposed, implicated him in the crimes of Watergate. Now that Nixon had resigned, the question consuming the federal government, the Congress, the courts, the Watergate prosecutors, the defendants and their lawyers, the media, and the nation-at-large was: *What happens to the Nixon tapes?* They were the hottest property in America.[16]

From his brooding exile in San Clemente, the ex-president was asserting ownership. Previous presidents had simply taken their White House papers with them when they left office, and they were generally allowed, with a wave of the hand or a deed well drafted, to destroy, sell, give away, or set restrictions on access to the documents as they pleased. Federal investigators soon discovered that every president since Franklin Roosevelt had secretly recorded his conversations, in person and over the telephone—though only Nixon had installed a voice-activated system that recorded *everything*.

No one had yet donned the era's clunky headphones and trekked through all 3,700 hours of recordings, much of it inaudible, to determine whether they contained classified information, as seemed likely; additional criminal evidence, as also seemed likely; libelous statements; purely personal material; and so on. Moreover, the tapes had been subpoenaed by congressional committees and in the criminal trials of Nixon's former aides. The public's claim was compelling: the tapes and devices used, after all, had been purchased and maintained by employees of the Technical Security Division of the U.S. Secret Service, which had operated the system.[17]

Ford needed the question resolved swiftly. On the president's fifth day in office, his new White House counsel, Phil Buchen, was apprised: "Approximately 900 reels are retained on the ground floor of the Old Executive Office Building in a converted closet across from the cafeteria—sealed and secure. The room is so small that it does not have a room number." Within a week, White House aides would discover *more* tapes and designate the locked closet "Zone 128"—sometimes "Safe-Zone 128." To the new president and his aides, the tapes' presence on the White House grounds was toxic. Yet they also recognized their custodianship of the unique collection, which made the Nixon administration the best-documented regime in history.

In that first week, that meant halting attempts to spirit the tapes to Nixon's custody in San Clemente. Ford's men received word that a young White House aide entrusted with the keys to Safe-Zone 128 "was at this time packing up tapes in closet on ground floor of EOB for shipment to RMN in San Clemente."

"I told [them] to stop the truck that pulled up to the White House to take all of Nixon's papers the day after he resigned," Silberman told me, "until the Justice Department could give a legal opinion on the question."[18]

The day the Senate confirmed Scalia's nomination, Ford's staff put the finishing touches on a letter from the president to the attorney general, formally requesting OLC's legal opinion on the disposition of the tapes.[19] A draft, dated August 22 and previously unpublished, tasked Scalia with answering two questions:

1. What interests and rights does former President Nixon have in and to the papers and materials mentioned?
2. What responsibilities, if any, do persons on my staff with actual control of the papers and materials...have to the extent if any or all of such papers and materials are or become subject to subpoenas, court orders, or requests by parties to court actions, by members of the Congress, or by others for inspection, discovery, or disclosure?

Later that day, over Ford's signature, the final version—shorter, simpler—was hand-delivered to Main Justice: "I would like your advice concerning ownership of these materials and the obligations of government with respect to subpoenas or court orders issued against this government or its officials pertaining to them."[20]

Hired at OLC two days before Scalia's arrival was a young staff attorney, fresh-faced with mod sandy hair and sideburns, named William Funk. A graduate of Harvard and Columbia Law, Funk had served in army intelligence and retained his security clearances. Immediately, Scalia recruited Funk to work on the Nixon tapes case, divvying up areas of law and history for each to tackle. Unlike Scalia, Funk loathed Nixon; in his office, the young lawyer hung the president's portrait upside-down.[21]

Pressed by Silberman to turn the work product around "quickly," Scalia and Funk had inherited several opinions—all reaching the same conclusion. On August 13, as Scalia testified at his confirmation hearing, Ford counsel Benton Becker had privately advised colleagues: "Records of the Nixon administration are the property of Richard M. Nixon. He is the legal owner of all records from his administration, including, but not limited to, tapes." A presidential spokesman, citing an opinion provided by J. Fred Buzhardt, Nixon's final White House counsel, *publicly* declared the tapes Nixon's property.[22]

Scalia and Funk examined precedent dating back to George Washington; a 1935 statement by the archivist of the United States; the texts of the Federal Records Act of 1950 and the Presidential Libraries Act of 1955; and a 1974 report by the Joint Committee on Internal Revenue Taxation, which concluded "the historical precedents, taken together with the provisions set forth in the Presidential Libraries Act, suggest that the papers of President Nixon are considered his personal property rather than public property."[23]

Passages from each of these texts appeared in Scalia's final opinion, delivered to Saxbe on September 6. Working separately, Scalia and Funk arrived at the same conclusion: Nixon owned his presidential papers and tapes. "I remember how upset I was with the answer," Funk told me.

"To conclude that such materials are not the property of former President Nixon," Scalia wrote, "would be to reverse what has apparently been the almost unvaried understanding of all three branches of the Government since the beginning of the Republic, and to call into question the practices of our Presidents since the earliest times."

An early draft, previously unpublished, reveals his compositional method—and some Scalia-esque touches that did not survive. "It is true," he wrote in the draft, "that section 507 of the Federal Records Act of 1950... seemed to distinguish between official and personal papers of a President." But Scalia cited a legal opinion to the contrary issued in 1951 by OLC's predecessor agency, then displayed his keen textualist eye. He noted that 44 USC 2107(1), the section of the

Presidential Libraries Act that effectively replaced section 507 of the Federal Records Act, nowhere used the word "personal." The draft continued: "The 1955 Presidential Libraries Act, which serves as the permanent basis of the Presidential Library system, *clearly rejects the distinction and must reasonably be regarded to proceed on the premise that* a President has title to *all* the documents and historic materials—whether personal or official—which accumulate in the White House during his incumbency" [emphasis added].

In the final opinion, the concession that "it is true" that the Federal Records Act "seemed to distinguish" between different categories of presidential papers was stricken. And the final version of the passage above reads shorter, simpler: "The 1955 Presidential Libraries Act, which serves as the permanent basis of the Presidential Library system, *constitutes clear legislative acknowledgment that* a President has title to *all* the documents and historical materials—whether personal or official—which accumulate in the White House during his incumbency" [emphasis added].

On September 6, Saxbe lifted Scalia's opinion wholesale, dropped it into a letter to the president, signed it, and had it couriered to the White House.

The episode showed Scalia for what he was: principled and fearless. "It was a baptism under fire," said Jim Wilderotter, a DOJ attorney who worked closely with Scalia then. "It was not a popular decision, and Nino knew that.... We knew Congress was going to go ballistic."[24]

*   *   *

Two days later, the White House released "Saxbe's opinion" along with Proclamation 4311: President Ford's announcement that he had granted his predecessor a "full, free, and absolute pardon" covering "all offenses against the United States which he, Richard Nixon, has committed or may have committed" during his presidency.

With the pardon already triggering a furor, DOJ's finding that Nixon *owned* all his papers and tapes—and the attendant disclosure that the ex-president, armed with the DOJ opinion, had secretly contracted with General Services Administration administrator Arthur Sampson for the immediate return of the materials to the ex-president's custody, with Nixon free to destroy them in 1979—proved too much for Congress.

"Byrd Eyes Ownership of Tapes," a headline read, reporting the determination of the Senate majority whip to pass a law overturning Scalia's decision. One enterprising reporter, the *Los Angeles Times'* Ron Ostrow, tracked Scalia down to ask him about the Nixon-Sampson agreement. "I don't know anything about it," Scalia said; his work had been free of White House pressure.[25]

Senator Gaylord Nelson, Democrat from Wisconsin, introduced the Presidential Recordings and Materials Preservation Act (PRMPA). In final form, the bill conferred "complete possession and control" of the Nixon administration's 42 million papers and tapes on the administrator of General Services, who in turn would make the materials available for hearings and trials and, ultimately, public access. Senate passage came before Scalia's opinion was a month old. Exhausted by Nixon's problems, Ford signed the measure on December 19.

In 1977 the Supreme Court ruled 8–1, Rehnquist dissenting, against the ex-president's challenge to the constitutionality of the law. However, a panel of the Court of Appeals for the District of Columbia Circuit later ruled unanimously that Nixon was entitled to compensation for the government's seizure of the papers and tapes, a finding that upheld Scalia's original determination on the former president's ownership claim. In June 2000, six years after Nixon's death, the government agreed to pay his estate $18 million.[26]

*   *   *

Scalia's second task at DOJ was less weighty.

Ford's "energy czar," William E. Simon, had stripped sub-Cabinet officials of their government cars and drivers. Left "strapped" by years of government service, Silberman couldn't afford a car and considered quitting. Nino arranged for the deputy attorney general's driver to receive a police radio and gun permit; now the car was a law enforcement vehicle. "I immediately began to think of him as a Supreme Court nominee," Silberman joked at Scalia's memorial service. "I could see he would be sound on the Second Amendment."[27]

In the existing biographical literature, Scalia's tenure at OLC, starting with the Nixon tapes case, has been depicted chiefly along the careerist narrative. Upon taking office, this narrative holds, AAG Scalia tailored his opinions to please the neo-conservatives surrounding the president, Rumsfeld and Cheney, strong advocates of executive power whom Scalia considered integral to his own advancement. Cravenly currying their favor, Scalia always took the most expansive view of executive powers, sacrificing his intellectual integrity to base ambition.

In *Scalia: A Court of One*, for example, Bruce Allen Murphy writes that Scalia took the AAG/OLC job because he was "eager to get back into the political fray in the hopes that it would propel his career even higher." And in Murphy's depiction, Scalia commenced work on the Nixon tapes case with only his own fortunes in mind: "While Scalia had a duty to the new president, and a professional obligation to give his best judgment, he knew that his answer would determine how Republican political operatives who could help or hurt his career would view him.... He would earn his stripes as the legal lieutenant of chief of staff Rumsfeld and deputy chief Cheney."

The conclusion of Scalia's debut opinion—that Nixon owned the materials—Murphy casts as the product of cynical calculation: "The episode served as Scalia's executive branch calling card with the new Ford administration and the Nixon conservatives who were trying to protect themselves." The "calling card" metaphor is meant to demean Scalia, to depict him as a desperate salesman, a huckster spreading his cards around town, flashing his openness for business.

Joan Biskupic, in *American Original*, fails to recognize that Scalia's opinion in the tapes case had taken into account two centuries of presidential practice and federal statutes; instead, she sees only "the institutional mind-set of the executive branch" and Scalia's all-consuming ambition. "[The opinion] did not acknowledge the Constitutional crisis of the moment, at the heart of which were the records and tapes that were evidence of a cover-up.... He was learning to play the long game."[28]

In fact, far from thinking the decision in the Nixon tapes case would please his colleagues, Scalia privately worried just the opposite: that the men of power in the Ford administration would *resent* OLC's finding for Nixon. "It was a fairly unpopular call at the time," Scalia recalled in his 1992 oral history interview. "Frankly, I'm not sure that it was even a very welcome call to the Justice Department. I think they would have preferred to say the opposite because there was legislation [being drafted for] taking over all of these documents....

> The call I gave was, no, they belonged to President Nixon because it had simply been the tradition of presidents, ever since George Washington, that all of the papers of the president belonged to the president. They used to clear out the White House after their administration was over. George Washington took home—as I recall, they even had to go back to Mount Vernon to get a treaty that he had taken with

him. It was the only copy; they didn't know what the treaty said.... That was really the one opinion that I wrote when I was at OLC that I thought would stand a good chance of being reversed because, although I called it that way, it seemed to me such an unpopular political position.

Scalia's suspicion that his opinion displeased senior DOJ officials proved accurate. "Nixon Control of Tapes Assailed by Some Justice Dept. Experts," the *Los Angeles Times* reported. The article cited "objections inside the Justice Department" from "experts on property law" who "denounced as a sham the Ford administration's agreement giving former President Nixon control of his White House tapes and documents." Ruling for Richard Nixon was no ticket to advancement that September.

Particularly baffling is Biskupic's assertion that Scalia's opinion "did not acknowledge" the evidentiary value of the tapes for Watergate investigators and prosecutors. Biskupic fails to cite, or even mention, the final passage in Scalia's opinion, where he addresses directly the responsibilities incumbent on the personnel of the Ford administration when they faced subpoenas, court orders, and other duly authorized demands for access to the tapes. "Items within the subject materials properly subpoenaed from the Government or its officials must be produced," Scalia had held, adding that "none of the materials can be moved or otherwise disposed of contrary to the provisions of any duly issued court order against the Government or its officials pertaining to them." In other words, Scalia had ruled that the papers and tapes belonged to Nixon, but that subpoenas and court orders for access to the materials had to be obeyed.

As even Murphy acknowledges, "there was something in this opinion for Nixon's opponents." All the more puzzling, then, that

Murphy should cast the opinion as Scalia's calling card with "Nixon conservatives.... trying to protect themselves." His opinion had provided them no protection.[29]

CHAPTER VII

Blood Lust

It was just one investigation after another.
—*Antonin Scalia, 1992*

With his dark Brylcreemed hair swept straight off his mile-wide forehead, dark eyes set far apart, Jim Wilderotter had that G-Man look: He could have passed for Robert Vaughan, *The Man from U.N.C.L.E.* A New Jersey native, Wilderotter had graduated from Georgetown and the University of Illinois Law School and was already serving under Silberman as associate attorney general when Scalia arrived at Main Justice. Soon Wilderotter was promoted to associate White House counsel, tasked with coordinating the Ford administration's response to the congressional investigations of the intelligence community that were sprouting up across post-Watergate Washington.

Now retired, poring over sepia-toned photographs of himself and Scalia posing with Attorney General Saxbe and other honchos of the Ford era, Wilderotter bluntly rejected the careerist narrative: "That's just bullshit, and it goes contrary to everything that the guy did in his life and every opinion he ever wrote."

In the Watergate tapes case, Wilderotter recalled, Scalia ruled for Nixon's ownership "knowing full well that it was not the popular answer. I mean, he wasn't afraid of anybody.... He knew his opinion would piss the Congress off...that Congress would go ballistic and overrule him.... Nino knew it was coming.... The congressional investigative committees, which were basically *all* of them, had developed a blood lust that survived Nixon and was focused on the intelligence community.... All this happened on Ford's watch...Congress was still high on the blood lust."[1]

Yet to Scalia's biographers, his dual role in the post-Watergate clashes between the executive and Congress—drafting legal opinions behind the scenes, and testifying before Congress in public—offered only more evidence of Scalia's cynical jockeying for higher office while displaying his innate authoritarianism.

The careerist-authoritarian narrative that has dominated the biographical literature presents a muddled view of the man's motives: Were his opinions mere ploys, careerist moves in "the long game"—or were they genuine manifestations of an "authoritarian bent, rooted in a rule-oriented father and Catholic upbringing" (Biskupic)? Was Scalia's defense of executive power simply the means by which he sought to "earn his stripes" with Rumsfeld and Cheney—or did he invariably "stonewall and deny" the American people, and their representatives, because "Scalia believed that power could only be maintained by secrecy" (Murphy)?[2]

In their contempt for the conservatives who fought for a strong executive after Watergate, Scalia's biographers had only to follow the lead of contemporary news coverage. Every proposal that expanded the obligations of the federal government to release the records of the executive branch, no matter how voluminous or highly classified, was depicted as wise and urgent, a bulwark against what Arthur Schlesinger,

Jr., the former Kennedy adviser, called "the imperial presidency." With such proposals, members of Congress routinely vaulted themselves onto the nightly news in the guise of Champion of Openness, Slayer of Official Secrecy.[3]

The actual details of these measures, the provisions Scalia cited in his opinions opposing them, go unmentioned in the previous biographies. Neither Biskupic nor Murphy informs his reader of how sweeping the demands for "information" were, often impossible to satisfy under the time frames provided. It wasn't good government; it was *blood lust*.

Scalia's performance at OLC—the opinions he crafted, his schooling of dim-witted lawmakers on Capitol Hill—reflected neither careerism nor contempt for the American people. Rather, Scalia was applying deeply researched scholarship on the Constitution and federal case law, grounded not in some "authoritarian bent" but in devout Catholicism and reverence for separation of powers. As "the president's lawyer's lawyer" at the dawn of an accidental presidency, it fell to Scalia to defend traditional executive authority precisely when Congress, the courts, and the news media made it least fashionable.

In fact, Scalia was a profile in courage in the Ford era: one of the good guys, working around the clock and under siege, with reckless and greedy ideas flying in every direction, to preserve the powers of the presidency for the long term. He and the other men of conscience in the Republican ranks of the mid-1970s understood that Watergate and its subsidiary scandals would fade, but that the country would always need a strong executive.

*   *   *

I spoke to Nino!
Nino concurs!
Let's ask Nino!

White House aides, agency chiefs, chain smokers at Main Justice, sub-Cabinet counsel, chiefs of staff, special assistants, the men of power in the Ford administration—and some pioneer women, such as Carla A. Hills, assistant attorney general for the civil division—uttered or typed some variation of these exclamations every day from 1975 to 1977. Across the executive branch, invocations of the sacred Scalia name conveyed the imprimatur of legal sanctity.

Scalia's looked at it?

What did Nino say?

Told that Scalia had weighed in, the listener immediately felt a rush of comfort, swathed in certitude that the matter had been studied by the best of the best: When Nino gave his blessing, the recipient occupied holy ground. To Scalia's desk, accordingly, flowed an endless stream of requests for counsel on subjects weighty and arcane, urgent and desultory.

Does the Social Security Act need to be revised after the Supreme Court's decision in Weinberger v. Weisenfeld?

May the First Lady present the French prime minister with a gift donated to the White House by a French ambassador?

Should the president use an executive order to establish a council on physical fitness and sports?

Can U.S. flag tankers be exempted from oil-import fees?

Does the Endangered Species Act prevent the General Services Administration from selling millions of barrels of sperm whale oil?

If New York City defaults on $453 million in bank notes, how should its debt be restructured?

Should the FBI conduct background investigations into possible vice-presidential nominees?

On this last matter, a by-product of the McGovern-Eagleton debacle of 1972, Scalia's legal review found there was no "presidential constitutional or statutory function which would clearly support" the opening of such FBI investigations. "Neither the president nor the Congress," Scalia advised a colleague at Main Justice in June 1976, "has any responsibility or power under the Constitution to screen candidates for public office."

This opinion, previously unpublished, is notable for two reasons. First, in finding that the president and FBI *lacked* authority to investigate possible vice-presidential candidates, Scalia eschewed an expansionist view of executive power, defying the caricature of the careerist narrative.

Second, the recipient of Scalia's opinion was another ambitious young Italian American from the outer-boroughs of New York City: thirty-two-year-old associate deputy attorney general Rudolph W. Giuliani.[4]

*   *   *

After Congress passed legislation seizing the Nixon tapes, the next clash between the branches focused on proposals to expand the reach of the Freedom of Information Act (FOIA). Enacted in 1966 and used ever since by reporters and historians, activist groups and inquisitive Americans of all stripes, FOIA enables citizens to request documents from the executive branch. Congress and the courts are exempt, a key factor in the enthusiasm those branches subsequently demonstrated for FOIA.

If an agency withholds requested information, the FOIA requester can sue in federal court, where the agency has to justify its "secrecy." The growth in FOIA cases contributed to the litigation explosion of the era, forcing federal agencies to hire batteries of attorneys, researchers, and Xerox-proficient secretaries who worked on nothing else.

In 1973, a divided Supreme Court ruled in *Environmental Protection Agency v. Mink* that when federal judges presiding over

FOIA cases reviewed *in camera* the materials withheld by an agency, the court's review was limited to determining whether the material was classified, not whether classification was warranted. The ruling in *Mink* came down on January 22, 1973—the same day as *Roe v. Wade*—but did not go unnoticed. Congressman William Moorhead of Pennsylvania and other Democrats co-sponsored an amendment to the FOIA law designed to circumvent *Mink*: it required FOIA judges to determine whether documents' classifications were warranted, and if not, to order their immediate release. That judges were unqualified to make national security determinations was of little interest to the Champions of Openness and Slayers of Official Secrecy basking in favorable media coverage.

A similar bill from Senator Kennedy passed the Senate, leading to a conference bill that set tight deadlines: ten days for an agency to respond to FOIA requests; twenty days for appeals; thirty days in litigation. If the requester prevailed, the government paid litigation costs. The conference bill also empowered the Civil Service Commission (CSC) to determine whether an agency employee had wrongly withheld materials, and, if so, what disciplinary action should be taken against him.[5]

No agency chief or general counsel supported these amendments. Their objections, developed in consultation with Scalia and presented in previously unpublished memos and letters to the White House, captured in detail the problems with these proposals. Particularly troublesome was the CSC disciplinary provision. "In the Treasury Department," wrote counsel Richard Albrecht, "it is questionable whether the Civil Service Commission has jurisdiction over [appointees] and whether the agency can take disciplinary action against them." Pentagon counsel Martin Hoffmann wrote, "Members of the armed forces are entitled to carefully proscribed procedures for the impositions of administrative sanctions, and these are not compatible with the sanction provision of the enrolled bill." The Pentagon also worried about a drain on resources if DOD officers were constantly explaining classification decisions to judges.

"Classification should remain the responsibility of the Executive Branch," agreed State Department counsel George Aldrich. "It would be unsound and of doubtful constitutionality to authorize the courts to determine whether the disclosure of foreign relations information would adversely affect the national security." The Veterans Administration opposed the bill, as did the Department of Health, Education, and Welfare; Commerce; the General Services Administration; and the FBI. Even the Civil Service Commission, favored in the amendments with the new disciplinary powers, rejected them.[6]

The ultimate prey of the blood lust, of course, was the Central Intelligence Agency. Already enduring a feverish season, its secrets spilling into public view every day, Langley needed no prodding to oppose expansion of FOIA. The notion of judges' reviewing CIA's classification process was unthinkable. "I do not believe that I can effectively and securely conduct intelligence activities if a court after a *de novo* review can substitute its judgment for mine as to what information requires protection," the CIA director wrote. Naturally, Scalia agreed. He wouldn't even use the term "FOIA"; in correspondence he referred to "FIA."[7]

He knew the terrain well. As ACUS chairman, Scalia had testified against the amendments in 1973, correctly predicting they would create "an inexhaustible source of litigation" and violate separation of powers. "To commit to the judicial branch in all cases the original determination of what disclosure would be harmful to foreign policy or national defense," Scalia told lawmakers, "seems clearly improper.... I wouldn't want to make such judgments as an individual judge.... I would have to pore through all of the documents and even after I have done so, I wouldn't know whether they endanger national defense without learning a lot of other information. I presume I would have to call witnesses and whatnot. The Pentagon Papers trial demonstrates rather vividly the extreme difficulty of determining whether particular information harms the national defense."[8]

* * *

On September 25, 1974, Scalia accompanied Saxbe to a meeting with CIA director Bill Colby and general counsel John S. Warner. A month on the job, Scalia had to have felt intimidated. He was about to tango with a master.

Thin, balding, and bespectacled, William Egan Colby, a graduate of Princeton and Columbia Law, looked, in his icy greyness, like an Ivy League president. "Asked a question he did not care to answer," a reporter noted, the CIA director "would tilt back his head so light reflected off the lenses of his glasses, turning his eyes into blank white disks." An Office of Strategic Services hero in World War II, Colby later ran CIA operations in Saigon, overseeing the infamous Phoenix Program, which killed more than 20,000 Vietcong. Taking the reins at CIA during Watergate, Colby presided over the first leaks of the "Family Jewels," a seventy-page compendium of past agency misdeeds. Running CIA in the era of blood lust was an unenviable duty.[9]

Older, rumpled, Warner was also no pushover; his recent triumphs included telling the Watergate prosecutors, when they demanded access to the files of one of the arrested burglars, to stuff it. On the topic at hand, revealed here for the first time, CIA and Main Justice had serious differences. It promised to be a rocky session.[10]

Though Colby pushed back—*hard*—on the new AAG's determinations on the legal limits of CIA surveillance powers, Scalia's previous biographers have focused on a part of the meeting where Colby and Scalia were largely in agreement.

A half-century later, the official record of the Saxbe-Colby-Scalia-Warner meeting, a two-page memo by Warner, remains heavily redacted. In the declassified passages, first published in 2004, Warner credits Scalia with introducing the subject of the FOIA amendments—but only after the group had broached another, more sensitive matter, still redacted.

Scalia's previous biographers dwelt on the FOIA passages because they wished to portray the future justice, in his resistance to the proposed amendments to the law, as the ringleader of a proto-neocon conspiracy, stoking opposition to transparency in the executive branch where it hadn't existed—another entry in the careerist-authoritarian narrative. Biskupic wrote: "Scalia was in a position to help convince the president that the Freedom of Information Act amendments would thwart administration efforts related to law enforcement, the military, and foreign affairs. He was part of *a small group* of Ford officials opposed to the act's amendments—among them Dick Cheney, then deputy chief of staff to Ford. Scalia sought out officials in other agencies who objected to the amendments and urged them to voice their views" [emphasis added].

Murphy likewise fingers Scalia as the one who "began to rally the opposition.... Inside the White House, aides were telling the president that vetoing the pending legislation was sure to cause a political firestorm."

Small group? Rally the opposition? No one in the executive branch supported the amendments! "DOD will join in requesting a veto if Justice takes the lead," a CIA staff lawyer assured Warner two days *before* the session with Scalia. Moreover, Scalia's 1973 testimony shows that his views long predated his exposure to Cheney.[11]

*   *   *

Ironically, newly declassified documents show that Scalia's raising the topic of FOIA at the September 25 meeting reflected not some conspiratorial cunning on his part, but rather his last traces of bureaucratic novitiacy.

"Mr. Scalia brought up a new subject," began the fourth and final paragraph of the Warner memo, following two redacted paragraphs. "I informed him," Warner said,

> that OMB had polled us the day before by telephone, and I had indicated the Agency took a very strong position that this bill, if approved by Congress, should be vetoed. Mr. Scalia stated that, if we wanted to have any impact, we should move quickly to make our views known directly to the President. He indicated that neither State nor Defense would be recommending veto. Later in the day Mr. Scalia telephoned urging us to contact the White House, specifically [staff lawyer] Geoff C. Shepard.... I contacted Mr. Shepard and stated our position. He indicated that, in their papers to go forward to the President, they had anticipated this would be our position, but appreciated our call...."[12]

Scalia was a bit...*out of the loop.* His claim that "neither State nor Defense would be recommending veto" was inaccurate. And far from waiting for Scalia to "rally" the agency to opposition, newly declassified documents reveal that *three months before* the Saxbe-Colby meeting, in June 1974, CIA officials gave a friendly congressman "a run-down of the Agency's problems with H.R. 12471," which the lawmaker incorporated into floor remarks. *Two days* before the Saxbe-Colby session, a CIA staff lawyer asked Warner how best "to advise OMB that we request a veto."[13]

Scalia was late to the game.

Even his attempts at follow-through found him at sea. Scalia urged Colby to write to the president, and Colby did so the next day; but Warner had already told Scalia that OMB, a White House office, had polled CIA the day before. The one action Warner acknowledged having taken at Scalia's suggestion, telephoning Geoff Shepard, evoked the response that the White House had "anticipated" his sentiments.

Scalia was preaching to the converted!

* * *

That Scalia summoned the nerve to bring up the FOIA amendments at all—imposing his will on the agenda near the end of a sit-down with the legendary CIA director and his bulldog general counsel—appears all the more remarkable now that the passage of time, and the declassification process, have provided, at last, what previous biographers lacked: a window onto the main item on the agenda that morning. That was no walk in the park for Scalia, either.

While he was still wrestling with the Nixon tapes case, Scalia was simultaneously put to work, the new documents reveal, on an even more sensitive matter. Saxbe and Silberman had observed with growing alarm a series of court filings and rulings that aimed explicitly to constrain presidential power in cases involving foreign intelligence, traditionally an area of great executive latitude. These rulings had left unclear whether the CIA possessed authority to break into offices or homes overseas—or, in limited cases, on U.S. soil—to install wiretaps and other surveillance devices in the investigation of foreign intelligence cases. Saxbe asked Scalia for a formal opinion.

Two weeks after he finished the Nixon opinion, Scalia delivered a new one: a seventeen-page memorandum to the attorney general dated September 17, 1974, classified SECRET, unpublished until now. Its title was: "Use of Warrantless Trespassory Microphones in Foreign Intelligence Matters." The AAG began by noting that surreptitious entries and microphone installations dated back to the 1930s, with official approval first provided in 1940. DOJ had never put trespassory surveillance in foreign cases to a court test; the Supreme Court had never ruled on the practice. Eleven of the last twelve attorneys general, with only a brief interregnum in the 1950s, had regularly approved trespassory installations in foreign intelligence cases; this "apparently uniform practice," Scalia wrote, "must be considered to have been based upon a belief of legality.... The sober and careful judgment of many former attorneys general is certainly entitled to great weight."

Had Congress ever blessed these techniques? Scalia invoked a 1968 statute which provided that its contents should not be construed to "limit the constitutional power of the president to take such measures as he deems necessary to protect the nation against actual or potential attack or other hostile acts of a foreign power, to obtain foreign intelligence information deemed essential to the security of the United States." But Scalia took this line of reasoning only so far. He cited the "recent origin" of surveillance technology and concluded its use "has not been so visible as to warrant the inference of congressional acquiescence."

It all came down to a simple question: Warrant or no warrant? "Greater danger is to be feared from foreign attack than from domestic subversion," Scalia wrote, citing also the "special power and authority of the president in the field of foreign affairs"; these factors ensured that such installations had received "special Fourth Amendment treatment":

Neither extraordinary need nor the president's unusual powers in this field enable disregard for the Constitution, but they can help determine the meaning that should be given to a vague and flexible constitutional requirement.... Just as other circumstances and conditions can justify search and seizure without a warrant despite the language of the Fourth Amendment, so also the special needs of foreign intelligence and the grant to the president of special power and authority in this field may reasonably be thought to eliminate the warrant requirement—though not the requirement of reasonableness—in a foreign intelligence investigation.

There *are* limits, Scalia found, even on operations outside the United States. He cited the Vienna Convention on Diplomatic Relations, ratified by the United States, to conclude: "Treaty obligations prevent any trespassory activity—with or without warrant—directed against foreign embassies or consulates, or the residences of accredited diplomats." Again defying the careerist caricature, he found that international accords outweighed executive power in such cases.

Like a good lawyer, though, he found a workaround—or at least limited authority for covert actions at foreign embassies and diplomatic residences. "There may be some margin for retaliation," Scalia argued, "or application of what may be called 'the rules of the game.'" This he found in Article 47 of the convention, which allowed a host nation to apply its provisions "restrictively" if another host state nation did so. *If they've done it to us, we can do it to them.*

In conclusion, Scalia told Saxbe that the fallout from recent excesses in intelligence cases, such as the Ellsberg break-in, "urges continuation of the requirement for your personal, case-by-case approval of all warrantless surveillance." In evaluating requests, Scalia advised the attorney general to "satisfy yourself" as to the need for the information sought, a direct connection between targets and activities, the use of "minimum physical intrusion"; and enlistment of "legitimate law enforcement or U.S. intelligence personnel...through normal channels."

Scalia's September 17 opinion was an early *tour de force*. Where the attorney general had taken the tapes opinion and incorporated it into his own letter to the president, this time Saxbe preserved Scalia's opinion as a stand-alone document and attached it to his September 18 letter to Ford.[14]

＊   ＊   ＊

The Saxbe-Colby summit occurred a week later, with Scalia's September 17 memo "the principal topic," according to the heavily redacted Warner memo. Colby, wintry cardinal, blessed Scalia's product at the outset—or at least feigned as much, saying he "agreed with the general thrust." The director had a problem, however—*a concern*, as he called it. In fact, he had a few. One was Scalia's suggestion that the attorney general should only approve such surveillance installations when he was satisfied the information was needed "to protect the security of the United States against foreign powers." Colby told the DOJ officials that he hoped this requirement "would be interpreted in a broad fashion since in many respects CIA procuring of intelligence would not strictly involve the security of the U.S. in the sense of national defense."

Here sleepy Bill Saxbe, aging lion of Ohio, absentee attorney general—observed by Warner at one point to grow "rather vague" in recollection—rose to the occasion. Drawing on his old political skills, the AG intervened, deftly, to defend the work of his subordinate Scalia: "Mr. Saxbe stated that he fully understood and the intent was that this would be looked at in a broad sense." When evaluating requests for warrantless installations in foreign cases, Saxbe intended to lean forward.

Next the CIA director challenged Scalia's interpretation of the Vienna Convention. This is what was so heavily redacted in the Warner memo: the officials' discussion of the targeting of foreign diplomats by U.S. intelligence.

The CIA director had one more concern. "We have been having some problems" with DOJ, he said, on "intelligence sources and methods" legislation then pending before the Senate, on which CIA had received "different views" from the department. "The Agency regarded this as a most important matter," Colby intoned. The attorney general got the message. "Mr. Saxbe asked Mr. Scalia to look into this," Warner recalled. It was Wednesday morning; by Monday, Saxbe said, CIA could contact the AAG—not Scalia, but Vincent Rakestraw at Legislative Affairs—for an update.

At last, Colby had no more complaints.

From the outset the meeting was rough theater for Scalia. In front of Scalia's boss, the attorney general, no less a figure than William Egan Colby—legend of postwar intelligence—had attacked Scalia's work product and intimated that he had presided over an incoherent response to pending legislation. And on that issue, another AAG was made CIA's point of contact. To Saxbe's credit, the attorney general had backed Scalia up. But legends can be devious.

＊　　　＊　　　＊

Unconvinced by Saxbe's assurances, Colby took his case directly to the president. The CIA director wrote Ford a *second* letter on September 26, separate from the FOIA letter, effectively overruling the language of Scalia's September 17 memo. This letter, stamped SECRET but now declassified, and also previously unpublished, was Colby's attempt at end-running Scalia.

It began by endorsing Saxbe's call for the president to approve the foreign-intelligence surveillance powers outlined in the Scalia memo. But Colby conveyed his "serious concern" with Scalia's proposed work-around for the Vienna Convention: *if they've done it us, we can do it to them.* Colby wanted *blanket* authority, whether a foreign intelligence agency had acted against the United States or not. "There could well be situations," he wrote, "where this government would not be aware of such practices. Furthermore, I am persuaded that there will be occasions in the future where circumstances warrant such surveillance by the United States in any case."

Colby also advanced a legal argument Scalia had eschewed: that "the inherent power of a sovereign overrides the provisions of a treaty." The CIA, he lectured the president, "was created by the Congress with full recognition that it was to conduct espionage on behalf of the United States Government.... [T]he constitutional power of the President, bolstered by congressional recognition, overrides these particular provisions of the [Vienna] Convention."

The CIA director assured Ford that CIA and Main Justice had come to an agreement that Langley would conduct no electronic surveillance *within* the United States "without [the attorney general's] prior personal approval." The same held true, Colby wrote, for surveillance of Americans abroad.

But what if Saxbe withheld his approval? Here, in his final two paragraphs, Colby went for broke. He told the president that CIA should enjoy final authority, even if the attorney general disapproved, and *ahead* of presidential notification, and even for operations on *domestic* soil: "If at some time in the future the Attorney General does not approve a requested trespassory electronic surveillance in the United States for foreign intelligence purposes solely because the agency cannot establish that the foreign country concerned engages in similar practices against the United States, I propose that the agency proceed to conduct such an operation. However, I further propose that I immediately report such action to you for your personal review."

Even more audacious, Colby made clear in closing that he wasn't seeking Ford's *approval* for the new policy; rather, the director presumed the president's acquiescence, and if Ford didn't like it, he had to *opt out*: "Unless you see objection to this procedure, I will follow it with respect to our foreign intelligence operations of this type."

The audacity rankled White House counsel Phil Buchen, who wrote to National Security Advisor Brent Scowcroft: "In view of the apparent Congressional opposition to continuing foreign intelligence wiretaps...I suggest we defer consideration of the Attorney General's opinion and the CIA recommendation." On October 10, 1974, Ford met with Saxbe and, according to Buchen's previously unpublished memo to General Scowcroft, they "agreed last two paragraphs of Colby letter...should not be implemented...until NSC meets (with AG present) to review whole policy for consideration by the President."[15]

The end-run had failed! Sleepy Saxbe had stood up for Scalia again.

In his tango with the master, Scalia had made a few missteps but held his own. He had succeeded in getting CIA to convey anew to the White House, albeit unnecessarily, the agency's opposition to the FOIA amendments; and he had prevailed on the main issue when Saxbe and Buchen short-circuited Director Colby's attempted end-run around Scalia.

*   *   *

A week after the showdown with CIA, Scalia drafted a veto message for Ford's signature for the Moorhead-Kennedy bill. "I think it makes a strong case," Scalia told a colleague, "readily understandable by the public." That Scalia *still* didn't grasp the depth of opposition to FOIA across the executive branch was clear from his October 3 memo to Geoff Shepard of the White House, to which Scalia attached the draft veto message: "I hope serious consideration will be given to what a veto message might look like before a veto is ruled out as entirely impracticable."

Ruled out? The declassified record makes it clear that opposition to the FOIA amendments was instant and widespread, with the momentum building *towards* veto, not against it, as Scalia feared. Composed in first person for the president's review and previously unpublished, Scalia's draft message zeroes in on a provision of the amendments that had escaped the notice of the White House and the agencies. "As the legislation now stands," Scalia wrote, "a determination by the Secretary of Defense that disclosure of a document would endanger our national security must be overturned by a district judge if, even though it is reasonable, the judge thinks the plaintiff's position just as reasonable. And if the district judge's decision of equal reasonableness is based upon a determination of fact, it cannot even be undone by a higher court unless 'clearly erroneous.'"

"Such a provision not only violates constitutional norms, it offends common sense," Scalia wrote.

> Confidentiality can simply not be maintained if many millions of pages of FBI and other investigatory law enforcement files become subject to compulsory disclosure at the behest of any person, except as the government may be able to prove to a court—separately for each paragraph of each document—that disclosure "would" cause a type of harm specified in the amendment. Our law enforcement agencies do not have, and assuredly will not be able to obtain, the large number of trained and knowledgeable personnel that would be needed

to make such a line-by-line examination with respect to information requests that sometimes involve hundreds of thousands of documents.... An agency like the Immigration and Naturalization Service...receives almost 100,000 requests a year for information contained in 12,000,000 files kept at sixty-seven locations.

On October 17, 1974, Ford vetoed the bill. The White House statement leaned heavily on Scalia's draft. Phil Buchen lacked Scalia's theatricality, however. Where the AAG had written that the equal-reasonableness provision "not only violates constitutional norms, it offends common sense," the final version of Ford's veto message, prepared by Buchen, said only that the provision "would violate constitutional principles."[16]

Thirty-three days later, the ninety-third Congress, filled with blood lust, overrode Ford's veto. "It is unlikely that Scalia had even tried to count the votes," snaps Biskupic. "He would prove time and again that he did not grasp—or care to grasp or bow to—the ways of Capitol Hill."[17]

Biskupic's indictment is curious, for it is premised on the mistaken assumption that the assistant attorney general, rather than advising the executive and attorney general at whose pleasure he serves, should "bow to the ways of" the legislature. Moreover, in faulting Scalia for never having tried to "count the votes" on the House and Senate floors, Biskupic suggests the Office of Legal Counsel should have elevated politics over the law.

* * *

Now Scalia was a regular attendee of the morning meetings in the White House Situation Room—seated across from Colby and Warner. "Every morning we would decide how many of the executive's most confidential documents about covert operations and all other matters would be turned over" to select congressional committees, Scalia recalled.

Dominating the headlines across 1975–76 were two select congressional committees, known colloquially as the Church and Pike Committees, after their respective chairs, Senator Frank Church of Idaho and Congressman Otis Pike of New York. "One of the consequences of these investigations," Justice Scalia recalled at a national security conference in Ottawa, Canada, in 2007, "was an agreement by the CIA that all covert actions would be cleared through the Justice Department. So believe it or not, for a brief period of time, all covert actions had to be approved by me. Needless to say I did not feel that this was an area in which I possessed a whole lot of expertise. Nor did I feel that the Department of Justice had a security apparatus necessary to protect against a penetration by foreign operatives. We had enough security procedures to frustrate *La Cosa Nostra* but not the KGB."[18]

Most of Scalia's work on covert operations remains classified—but enough has emerged to confirm he was consulted on the nation's most sensitive diplomatic, military, and intelligence matters.[19] He made, for example, a small but significant cameo in the dramatic events of April 30, 1975: the fall of Saigon. "On the afternoon of that day, I received a request for an opinion from the White House," Scalia said in a previously unpublished account, "the answer to be delivered no later than, as I recall, 8:00 p.m.

> The White House wanted to know whether the War Powers Act—which prevented the introduction of American military personnel into combat situations without the express consent of Congress—whether that act prevented the dispatch of helicopters to evacuate American personnel, and friendly Vietnamese, from the roof of the United States Embassy. I

gave an opinion saying no, but I vividly remember thinking, "My God, if I say yes, would the operation be called off on advice of the counsel? What has the world come to?"

To intimates Scalia confided his astonishment that the kid from Queens stood astride the American intelligence apparatus, a position he had never envisioned or sought. He had come a long way from the collapsed ceilings of his Jones Day days: now his counsel was sought on assassinations and embassy evacuations. Bill Funk once accompanied Scalia to the State Department for a classified briefing about one of CIA's overseas collaborators. It was, Funk said, "the kind of information you don't want to have. But he always wanted sort of a witness.... I do remember, when we got the name of this foreign asset, when we were riding back from the State Department, he said, 'Why should I be getting this stuff? This is crazy.'"[20]

*   *   *

From his "war stories" in the Intelligence Reformation, Scalia took away two lessons. The first was structural. "The problem before the regularization of national security and intelligence activities was simply that there were no rules," Justice Scalia said. "When I first encountered this area, in the 1970s, the nature of those activities was virtually unknown.... President Ford's 1976 executive order [No. 11905], continuing through the enactment of FISA [in 1978] and its revision in 1994, enactment of the Patriot Act in 2001, and successive revisions on the governing presidential executive order, the who and the why, the *dos* and the *don'ts,* of our national security and intelligence activities are out on the table."

The second lesson was a warning against "over-lawyering" the subject. "The army that hits the beaches when they've got their legal advisors," Scalia said, "is asking for trouble."[21]

CHAPTER VIII

Wonderfully Intimate

Good friends deserve constant attention.

—*Antonin Scalia, 2001*

On February 2, 1975, Bill Saxbe resigned as attorney general to serve as U.S. ambassador to India. His successor at Main Justice would exert a profound influence on the direction of Scalia's life and career.

At sixty-three, Edward Hirsch Levi, bald and bow tied, was one of the most respected minds in the law. The former dean of the University of Chicago Law School, now the university's president, had attended child-prodigy courses there at age five. Unlike recent attorneys general close to the presidents they served—Bobby Kennedy, John Mitchell—Levi had never met Gerald Ford before he was summoned to the Oval Office to be offered the job in December 1974. "I needed this like a hole in the head," he said, but "when the president urges you very strongly, he's in a very persuasive position." The Senate approved Levi unanimously.[1]

Silberman was also moving on. Ford asked him to stay as Levi's number-two, but the deputy knew his broad sway at DOJ was over. He accepted an appointment as ambassador to Yugoslavia. At Main Justice, the besieged fortress, he and Scalia had forged a lifelong bond. "Whenever one of us was offered something," Silberman told me, "we always called each other to talk it over." When Scalia, in years to come, needed a lawyer of his own, he turned to his former boss.

While the new attorney general was reserved and bookish, qualities that Scalia, a scholar himself, appreciated, the former dean could also be *ruthless*. "Edward Levi had a sharp tongue," Scalia recalled, "deployed to devastating effect upon the self-important and the self-assured." Bob Bork, a former Marine, considered Levi "the intellectual version of a Marine boot camp drill instructor." At Levi's memorial, Scalia recalled fondly, "He never did lose a certain air of scholarly detachment.... One evening, for some reason, I had occasion to drive him home (usually, of course, he had a driver). I knew the general neighborhood in which he lived, but not the precise street and house. As we neared our destination, I asked him to give me directions. He said he didn't have the slightest idea; the driver just let him off every night, and he went in."

Within the absent-minded professor, Scalia glimpsed steel. The justice recalled that "Levi courageously continued to authorize physical entries for foreign intelligence and national security purposes when he believed they were justified—but thanks to the [rulings] of the D.C. Circuit, he did so at great personal risk." In *U.S. v. Ehrlichman* (1976), for example, the Court of Appeals upheld the criminal convictions of former Nixon White House aide John Ehrlichman that stemmed from his authorization, in 1971, of the infamous burglary at the office of Daniel Ellsberg's psychiatrist. The CIA-trained burglars employed by the White House for the job, known colloquially as "the Plumbers," had sought evidence that Ellsberg, in addition to leaking the Pentagon Papers to the *New York Times*, might also have delivered the classified documents to foreign adversaries. The D.C. Circuit held that the government enjoyed no exemption from warrant requirements simply because the case involved foreign intelligence.

Levi's chief contribution was restoring integrity to Main Justice and particularly to its use of surveillance: the galvanizing issue of the post-Watergate era. In later years, Justice Scalia saw some of that probity lacking. "I would be willing to wager," he said in 2007, "that Edward Levi was more demanding in his requirements for black bag jobs than is the FISA [Court]."[2]

*　　*　　*

Along with Silberman and Levi, Scalia befriended a third DOJ official during this period: Solicitor General Robert Bork.

In the mid-1970s and early '80s, Bork was *the* rising star among conservative lawyers, a perennial subject of Supreme Court buzz: *the next Rehnquist*. It wasn't his looks: portly and bespectacled, Kent cigarette drooping from a corner of his mouth, Bork was, as a reporter wrote, "a bear of a man with a scraggly red beard...untamed frizz on a balding pate...[and] an outsize love for food and drink." Dispatched by the Marine Corps to China at the end of World War II, Bork returned home to graduate, like Levi, from the University of Chicago and its law school: preeminent bastion, in elite academia, of conservatism.

Initially a New Deal liberal, Bork evolved into a libertarian free-market champion. In 1962, after eight years practicing law, one in New York, seven at Kirkland and Ellis in Chicago—both he and Scalia cut their teeth at Midwestern firms—Bork moved his wife and three children to New Haven to teach antitrust law at Yale. In the professor's supple mind, the law sometimes became an abstraction; this tendency could make the professor, renowned privately for geniality, kindness, and wit, appear coldly indifferent to real-world consequences. An early example was a 1963 essay for *The New Republic,* "Civil Rights—A Challenge," in which Bork warned that "justifiable abhorrence of racial discrimination" might produce legislation "by which the morals of the majority are self-righteously imposed upon a minority," a development "subversive of free institutions."

By the late 1960s Bork was appalled, like Scalia, at the excesses of the campus left and the activism of the Warren Court. In a 1971 speech published in the *Indiana Law Journal,* Bork, forty-four, cast the thunderbolt that elevated him to god-like status on the right. Entitled "Neutral Principles and Some First Amendment Problems," the essay expanded on Herbert Wechsler's decade-old maxim that the Court must apply "neutral principles" without regard for outcomes. "If judges are to avoid imposing their own values upon the rest of us," Bork argued, "they must be neutral as well in the *definition* and *derivation* of principles" [emphases in the original].

This attack on the Warren Court electrified the nascent conservative legal movement: "A Court that makes rather than implements value choices cannot be squared with the presuppositions of a democratic society. The man who understands the issues and nevertheless insists upon the rightness of the Warren Court's performance ought also, if he is candid, to admit that he is prepared to sacrifice democratic process to his own moral views. He claims for the Supreme Court an institutionalized role as perpetrator of limited *coups d'etat.*"[3]

Scalia saw in Bork "a rare combination of integrity and intellectual brilliance," as well as bravery. "He was the intellectual point-man for the movement to curb the pretensions of the Warren Court and return the meaning of the Constitution to what it said," Scalia recalled. "All discussions of 'original intent' relied heavily upon his fertile and often combative scholarship. He became more than a leader of change; he became, for the opposition, the very *symbol* of change."[4]

By March 1973, Bork had risen to solicitor general, DOJ's number-three position. The solicitor general manages the department's litigation before the Supreme Court and frequently appears before the justices to present oral argument. The office worked closely with OLC. But it was the Nixon-era scandals that catapulted Bork to nationwide fame. He played a critical backstage role in nudging Spiro Agnew to resign; and it was Bork, ten days later, who carried out Nixon's order to fire Archibald Cox in the "Saturday Night Massacre." Largely forgotten was Bork's preservation of the special prosecutor's staff; his order that they continue their work; and his appointment of Cox's successor, Leon Jaworski, who steered the investigation through Nixon's resignation and his aides' convictions. Bork's integrity and coolness under fire helped the country navigate the catastrophe of Watergate—yet liberals denounced him. "I never knew Bob to be a man who deeply admired Richard Nixon," Scalia said, "but he became The Man Who Fired Archibald Cox."

"My parents were very close to Judge Bork and his first wife, Claire, who died of cancer before Bork became a judge," Gene Scalia told me. "They were a really tight foursome.... The Bork kids were a little bit older than the Scalia kids but the families would do things together.... Bork was ten years older than my dad and had held a more senior position, was better known; but they were very good friends.... My dad told me once, after a party everybody had left: 'That's why you should work hard in school—so you can succeed and have friends like Robert Bork.'"[5]

In time, however, fate and circumstance, the swaying tides and sharp turns of adult lives lived in full, would place a strain, unspoken but unmistakable, on Nino's cherished friendship with Bob Bork.

✻ ✻ ✻

Working with Levi was "one of my life's great privileges," Justice Scalia said, but he also remembered the AG for "one of the more embarrassing incidents in my Washington career." This occurred when the Scalias hosted Claire and Bob Bork and Kate and Ed Levi for dinner.

Bells rung and greetings exchanged, Nino, in festive mode, took the guests' cocktail orders, then strolled jauntily to the liquor cabinet, which sat on the living room floor. *The key was missing—and the cabinet was locked.* "The obvious culprit was our toddler, who had evidently taken the key and dropped it who knows where," Scalia recalled. "I will never forget the image of the attorney general, the solicitor general, and I—and I think Kate joined us—crawling around on our hands and knees on the living room Oriental rug, feeling for the missing key."

Michael Uhlmann, AAG for the Office of Legislative Affairs from 1975 to 1977, also worked closely with Scalia, sometimes testifying alongside him at hearings. "In the course of defending the executive against the tirades and heresies of Congress," Uhlmann recalled, "we all became wonderfully intimate friends." He and Nino used to knock back Scotch and jot ideas on legal pads. When Uhlmann brought his parents to Main Justice, the group boarded the private elevator that connected to Bork's third-floor office. Unexpectedly, the elevator descended to the garage, where Bork got on, late for visitors awaiting him. Twenty feet up the elevator stopped; for an *hour* the SG remained trapped with the Uhlmanns. "Nino's contribution was to shout down the elevator shaft, 'Suppose we lower the Bible down!'"[6]

"All the time!" Silberman told me, when asked if Bork and Scalia disagreed much. In his final public speech, in January 2016, Justice Scalia remembered tweaking Bork whenever the solicitor general's staff, in court pleadings, cited *Church of the Holy Trinity v. United States* (1892). That was the landmark Supreme Court decision in which the justices, ruling in favor of a New York church that had retained a British rector in plain violation of an existing statute, held that judges must sometimes look beyond "the letter of the statute" to divine "the intention of its makers." "Whenever the solicitor general's office wanted us to ignore the text of the statute, it would cite *Church of the Holy Trinity*," Scalia said. "I used to ask the assistant SG arguing the case, 'Is this the *Holy Trinity* team today, or do you want us to follow the law?"[7]

Silberman recalled one row between the two men so intense that its resolution required inspired improvisation. "I ought to discuss this with the attorney general," Silberman said, leaving Bork and Scalia fuming as he rode the private elevator one floor up. What Larry knew, and his subordinates did not, was that the AG was out of town; the deputy contentedly burned a Marlboro while the combatants, a floor below, cooled off. Rejoining them, Silberman theatrically invoked the will of the attorney general before delivering an edict he had dreamt up on the elevator ride down; Bork and Scalia stalked off. "Nino was mad as hell that I pulled that," Silberman told me with undisguised delight, "when he found out."[8]

✳   ✳   ✳

The toddler who was "the obvious culprit" in the subversion of the Scalias' liquor cabinet was Matthew. In their mass production of kids, Maureen and Nino were finally slowing down. Twenty-two months had separated the births of their first two children, and the next three all arrived within eighteen months of each other; thereafter, the gaps grew longer, with the next three arriving at intervals of two, two and a half, and two and three-quarters years. The greatest distance separated their eighth child, Christopher, born December 1975—the boys' decisive fifth vote—and Margaret Jane ("Meg"), the fourth girl, forever known as The Youngest, born in Palo Alto in October 1980, nearly five years later.

"He always said he was going to have a baseball team," remarked Scalia's Aunt Lenora. In all, the births, which commenced when Maureen was twenty-one, spanned nineteen years; nearly *seven years* of her life were given over to pregnancy, most of it with multiple children to look after.[9]

Whenever anyone asked him about the rigors of raising such a large family, Scalia denied a significant role. This emerged as a recurring refrain in the literature on him, with Scalia's ambivalence about the situation—a hint of remorse—an element from the beginning. While it was less common for husbands to attend childbirths in those years, Scalia witnessed only one of his children's births: the last, after a doctor "practically locked him in the delivery room." For the other eight, he recalled driving Maureen to the hospital "a couple of the times." "Scalia enjoys a large family," *Georgetown Today* reported in 1975, "but regrets that his work week allows him less time than he would like with the children."

At a Federalist Society gala in 2006, Justice Scalia, then in his twenty-first term on the Court, brought Maureen to the podium. Never a seeker of the spotlight, Mrs. Scalia smiled shyly and examined the floor as the justice described her as "the best decision I ever made, the mother of the nine children you see, and the woman responsible for raising them with very little assistance from me.... And there's not a dullard in the bunch!"

In 2008, when Scalia granted his first broadcast television interview, to CBS News' *60 Minutes*—a series of sit-downs with Lesley Stahl recorded at the Court, the Scalias' home, Nino's childhood home, and P.S. 13 in Queens—the justice signaled that with his children grown and raising kids of their own, he no longer harbored "regrets" over how little time he had been able to devote to his sons' and daughters' day-to-day lives.

> **STAHL:** The justice told us that he didn't go to the soccer games and the piano recitals and things. You know, there are people—
> **JUSTICE SCALIA:** You know, my parents never did it for me and I didn't take it personally. [affects mock-crying face]

"Oh, Daddy, come to my softball game!" I—I mean, it's my softball game; he has his work; I got my softball game. Of course, [gestures toward Maureen] she was very loyal; she went to all the games.

MAUREEN SCALIA: Most. I would get five minutes at each on a Saturday. [laughs]

"Mr. Justice," he was once told by another interviewer, "we know you love children—"

"Where did you get that?" he interjected.

"You have nine of them."

"No," he said. "It means I love my wife."[10]

*   *   *

This self-portrait—the father of nine minimally involved in the rearing of the brood, regret an early theme—raises important questions about Scalia's life: how he lived it, how he understood it. Was Nino exaggerating, in a chivalrous feint toward Maureen, or was he really just home for dinner, as he maintained, while she did everything? On this important point—personal, not legal, but defining—how literally should the textualist be interpreted?

"He was not in any way an absentee father," Gene Scalia told me. "At times, he was traveling; he certainly was very busy":

> You're writing a book about my dad and not my mom. But I remember I was in high school [when] she talked about the demands on her time of having all these children. She said, kind of thankfully, that she found that she'd always been able to give each of her children the time they needed when they really needed it.... What she did is amazing.... I could name

you a lot of Supreme Court justices, but I'm not sure I could name you as many mothers who pulled off all my mom did.... She did, in fact, raise nine children while also managing the household budget and often the house itself.

"As he used to say," remarked Catherine Scalia Courtney, "he did the Constitution, and she did everything else. The day-to-day running of the business that was a large family fell to Mom.... During those nomadic years, between Jones Day in Cleveland and Dad's appointment to the appeals court in Washington, we moved eight times":

Packing up a huge household for each of those moves, making sacrifices to stretch a public service salary to feed and clothe a large family, fighting to raise us in the Catholic faith in an increasingly secular world—she supported him and stood by him so he could focus on what they both saw as his vocation.... Anyone who knows Mom knows that she is as smart as, dare I say smarter than, Dad.... If it was help with math homework, you wouldn't go to him.... He always ended up doing what she told him to. This was their *shtick*.

Father Paul Scalia thought it "too stark" to say his dad hadn't done much: "It's not like he came home and he was a nonentity. He was certainly present." Maureen was *more present*. From boyhood, the future priest recalled the Scalia homes' always having a study: Dad's place of isolation and labor, where disruption was tolerated only infrequently. "You'd knock on the door and interrupt and go and talk to him about something, but you knew he was working.... Mom is the one who's on top of things...for school, for our sports. She knows our friends and things like that."

"I cannot claim that I had, personally, a great hand in the raising of the children," Justice Scalia said in his 1992 oral history, his most expansive comment on the subject.

> Most of the decisions concerning the children have been made by Maureen. I must say I have not been the—what should I say?—hands-on kind of a father that some, perhaps, are.... In all the jobs I've had, whether it was in the federal government, or teaching, or in [private] practice, I've always been home for dinner, family dinner, every night; so the kids always know that their father is there if they need anything. And if they want to talk to me about anything, I'm there. But basically Maureen has shaped their lives much more than I have: looked out to see that they took the right courses at school, that their teachers were good ones, and that they were getting the kind of attention they should.

Money was a constant concern for Maureen; her husband's soaring professional trajectory was noteworthy for how financially unrewarding it had proved. "[Scalia] has shown a remarkable disregard for making a lot of money," the *Los Angeles Times* reported in 1986. "He's never been one who cared a fig about making money," agreed a colleague. Or as Maureen put it, "This was a man who had seemed to spend so much of his career looking for a job that would pay less than the one he had at the time."[11]

Scalia's work at Main Justice was starting to mean more absences from home. During one clash with Congress, Scalia and Funk reviewed classified documents in the Situation Room into the wee hours and grabbed a few hours' sleep on White House couches. And foreign travel became more frequent. In January 1975, when the Scalias' seven children ranged in age from twenty-two months to thirteen years, Nino spent four days in Mexico City at an American Bar Association gathering. That summer, when Maureen was four months pregnant with Christopher, Nino jetted off to Montreal and Quebec for six days—more ABA. The following year brought a ten-day jaunt to Italy; three days in London; and two trips to West Germany, in January and July, totaling two weeks away from home.[12]

For Maureen Scalia—*strong and brilliant, resourceful and tireless, living, loving saint*—these were the hardest days.

*   *   *

This period also witnessed the birth of a lifelong obsession: Scalia's reverence for *The Federalist* papers. This is the collective title given to eighty-five articles in various periodicals across 1787–1788, secretly written by Alexander Hamilton, James Madison, and John Jay and published under the pseudonym "Publius." They made the case for ratification of the Constitution.

Whenever Justice Scalia lectured to law students, which was all the time, he asked: How many of you have the read *The Federalist* papers? "I have never seen more than about 5 percent of the students raise their hands," he lamented, "students at the nation's elite law schools." Law professor John Baker, who taught separation of powers with Scalia for three decades, asked him: When did *you* start reading *The Federalist* papers?" "In the Office of Legal Counsel," he said. "I had to learn it then."

Yet if Scalia was already gripped by originalism and textualism, he wasn't impressing it on his subordinates. "At that point, Scalia had no track record for what he eventually became famous for," Funk told me.

ROSEN: In whatever occasions you would have had to discuss approaches to statutory interpretation with him—and

I gather there would have been such occasions—he was not a champion of originalism or textualism at that point.

FUNK: That's correct.... If he was, he kept it pretty well hidden.... It wasn't something that he suggested as an approach.... Usually, the questions at OLC...[we] were looking at essentially the language of the statute and the context of the statute and the legislative history: all those sort of traditional tools of statutory construction.[13]

Mike Uhlmann wondered if he had lit the spark. At their first meeting, over lunch in 1970, Uhlmann arrived late, saying, "I'm sorry, I was making legislative history." He shared tales from the Senate Judiciary Committee, where aides were known to "clean up" their bosses' floor remarks for the *Congressional Record*; some, he said, took "rather greater liberties with the text." He explained how Ted Kennedy and other leading Democrats exploited legislative history: For the most controversial provisions of a proposed law, passages that could never prevail in floor votes, the lawmakers sprinkled the committee process with statements of "intent," confident that liberal judges, on their inevitable strolls through the garden of legislative history, would later find these seeds. "I cannot and will not say that this was the beginning of that thought process, which resulted in Scalia's revolution—I think fairly it can be called that—on the misuse of legislative history," Uhlmann said after the justice's death. But Scalia was definitely "intrigued" that afternoon: "I don't think he really knew how mischievous that business could be.... Obviously, he had thought about it before, but this, I think, got him going."[14]

In May 1973, in his first appearance as a witness before Congress, Scalia expressed doubt that a measure proposed by House Democrats would achieve its aims "unless you puff it up with good legislative history." The comment was unusually ambiguous for Scalia, simultaneously conceding the practice's validity ("good legislative history") while assailing its fraudulence ("puff it up").

Main Justice had only deepened his skepticism. He still referenced legislative history in some of his opinions, but his impatience was growing. "When I was head of the Office of Legal Counsel," he would recall, "60 percent of the time of the lawyers on my staff was expended finding, and poring over, the incunabula of legislative history. What a waste."[15]

CHAPTER IX

Il Matador

> *CONGRESSMAN GIAIMO: When did you become*
> *involved in this controversy and this struggle?*
> *SCALIA: I have been on the outside of it—*
> *GIAIMO: I am not interested in how long you were on*
> *the outside, I want to know when you got on the inside*
> *of it.*
> *SCALIA: It depends on what you mean by on the inside.*
> *GIAIMO: That depends on what you mean by on the*
> *outside.*
> *SCALIA: I guess it does. I guess we agree then.*
>
> —*House Select Committee on Intelligence, November 20, 1975*

In February 1976, some officials in the Ford administration wanted to make Scalia chairman of the Federal Trade Commission. The White House and DOJ moved swiftly to quash the idea. "I want to point out how valuable it is for you and the White House staff to have Scalia remain in his present position," Phil Buchen, the White House counsel, wrote to President Ford. "I know that Ed Levi considers him among his most valued assistants, and it would be a severe loss to the attorney general as well as to the Department of Justice if Scalia were to be asked to leave his present position. Scalia is a remarkably bright and resourceful attorney and a prodigious worker. I can think of no one else over at Justice who could adequately take his place.... Even a competent newcomer would require time to begin to match Scalia's performance."

His tone almost desperate, Buchen listed the areas in which Scalia had proved invaluable: executive privilege, intelligence oversight, federal election law. "Scalia directs all the legal research and provides the advice needed," Buchen summed up, "to deal with the major issues that affect the presidency and operations of the Executive Branch." Ford was swayed; Scalia stayed put.[1]

It was also in this period that Scalia, for the first time, drew consideration for the Supreme Court. In November 1975, following the retirement of Justice William O. Douglas, the president asked Levi to compile a slate of prospective successors. In Levi's alphabetized listing of eighteen judges, law professors, and lawmakers, biographical sketches attached, Scalia came eleventh; Bob Bork was third. Levi pared the list down to ten, with Scalia among those eliminated. The three finalists were Bork; Dallin Oaks, president of Brigham Young University; and Judge John Paul Stevens of the Seventh Circuit. Ford chose Stevens. There is no indication in the record that Scalia knew of his ascension to the list, but it seems likely he would have learned of it somehow.[2]

Mere inclusion heralded Scalia's arrival as a major figure in American law. And a date with the Court was not far off.

*   *   *

With Congress under Democratic control, every Ford administration official summoned to testify at congressional hearings knew to expect rough sledding. Scalia not only held his own in these confrontations; he *ran rings* around the lawmakers. His performance in congressional hearings, alternately trenchant and humorous, revealed Scalia as a brilliant practitioner of oral argument. Fifteen years of teaching and legal experience had sharpened the debating skills he brought from Xavier and Georgetown. A natural performer, veteran of radio and television in his teenage years, Scalia grew into the role of *Il Matador*, knowing when to sidestep the onrushing bull, when to spear him, how to please the audience.[3]

The mismatch between *Il Matador* and his questioners on Capitol Hill was on display in Scalia's earliest congressional testimony, in May 1973, at a House Governmental Operations hearing. Most lawmakers had never conjugated Latin or carried championship debate teams. When the ACUS chairman argued presidents must have candid advice, that executive branch officials must be free to "open up and brainstorm" without fear their counsel will be disclosed to Congress, Scalia drew challenge from Republican Pete McCloskey of California.

McCloskey asked if an executive branch official would be "inhibited" in giving advice to his bosses if he knew the advice would be made public.

"I can't really believe," Scalia answered, "that you are asserting that a man speaks on the record with the same freeness that he speaks in private."

The spear: *Il lancia!*

When Scalia noted that the government's withholding of information can sometimes protect innocent citizens, as in grand jury proceedings, McCloskey said, "That method worked fine until grand juries began to be abused by a law enforcement agency that used them for their purposes."

"I am not urging that this provision be abused," Scalia returned. *Il lancia!*

When the congressman, indefatigable in errancy, sought to discredit Scalia by association, invoking the name of Richard Kleindienst, the attorney general who had resigned the previous month in Watergate, Scalia employed humor: *il mantello rosso*, the red cape. "I have taken no position on the matter," he deadpanned, "and I hope not to."

"I value very much your wisdom, experience, and sincerity," McCloskey finally concluded, exhausted, his snorting rushes of no use against the superior intelligence and ringmanship of *Il Matador*.

But before he yielded, the congressman had one small request: he asked if Scalia could provide written examples of instances when executive branch officials would have withheld their advice if they knew their counsel would be made public.

"That request, I think, is clear, isn't it?"

"That is such a reasonable request," Scalia replied, "I don't see how I could refuse it."

It was, of course, a preposterous request: *Compile a list of past events that wouldn't have occurred if some past condition had been altered*. There is no evidence Scalia followed up.[4]

*　　*　　*

In April 1975, as assistant attorney general, Scalia testified before another House subcommittee, this time opposing legislation creating a "shield" for newsmen. The proposal would have allowed journalists to withhold evidence subpoenaed by grand juries. As with FOIA, the measure was more sweeping than was widely reported: *anyone* who gathered information with an eye toward "publishing" it could assert the privilege.

Scalia drew from the era's headlines. Suppose a news crew filmed an attempted assassination, he told the lawmakers; under the proposed shield law, the government could not obtain the footage even "to prevent the indictment of individuals...wrongfully accused." The assistant attorney general also invoked Patty Hearst, the nineteen-year-old heiress kidnapped by the radical Symbionese Liberation Army (SLA). Under psychological duress, the Berkeley student had joined her captors; bank surveillance had captured her toting a rifle during an SLA robbery. If the shield law were enacted, Scalia warned, police could not access the raw footage, making a "mockery" of the law enforcement process. "The public would in effect be told: Establishing the conditions which make such a [television] program possible is more important than the relatively inconsequential interest of capturing individuals who may have violated our laws and who may injure our citizens again in the future. The freedom of the press is important, but it must be protected in a way that does not bring the law enforcement process into contempt."

Democrat Robert Kastenmeier of Wisconsin objected: "If [newsmen] were not able to proceed in confidence in some cases, the public and law enforcement would not have other information and evidence available upon which people, in fact, could be brought to justice."

Scalia asserted that DOJ guidelines for serving subpoenas on news organizations, issued by John Mitchell in 1970 and since revised, were "reasonable, responsible, and effective in preventing abuse." The relatively few instances when newsmen withheld information even under subpoena, Scalia argued, showed such disputes were soluble through "wise exercise of administrative discretion" and did not require new legislation.

A Republican on the panel expressed incredulity at Scalia's faith in the executive. "Surely like all of us . . . you have read of abuse," Republican Tom Railsback of Illinois said. He referenced the "common practice" of prosecutors' seizing news footage of riots. "Many times that resulted in nothing being learned at all."

> **RAILSBACK:** But it put . . . the people who had covered that
> riot in the position of having to produce films that were never

shown, that were outtakes, at some expense to that company. You are certainly aware of those charges.

SCALIA: I think I am aware of some of those; but I must say that those are not the situations that arouse the most sympathy in me.

A comic moment from *Il Matador*!

Now Railsback asked, "Do you think that an investigative reporter on occasion has served a useful purpose in disclosing evidence of corruption or mismanagement, and in some cases, crimes?"

Now, *il mantello rosso*: "There is no question, sir. That is what makes the problem a difficult one."

Railsback persisted, arguing that the DOJ guidelines, Scalia's model for how to resolve disputes between police and reporters, did not apply to the states. Scalia conceded the states had no guidelines, a feint by *Il Matador*, before noting "they do have legislatures; and if the abuse exists, I see no reason why the federal government has to take it upon itself to severely restrict a fundamental power of state government, the power to obtain information."

Il lancia!

Democrat George Danielson of California decided he was going to rough up *Il Matador*. "That was not my question," he snapped at Scalia. "Let me know when you are done because I want to ask you my question."

"I thought I understood your question," Scalia replied.

"No, you did not," the congressman said. Danielson asked whether federal judges could quash subpoenas; yes, Scalia answered. "I had a little trouble getting it out of you," Danielson said, "but that is on your side."

"I certainly did not intend to hinder you in your effort."

"Sir, you are much too defensive," Danielson concluded. "I am simply trying to get the facts out."

Father Robert Drinan, a Jesuit priest and liberal Democratic congressman from Massachusetts, wondered if Scalia thought the husband-and-wife privilege afforded any shield. "I am not a great fan of the husband-and-wife evidentiary privilege," Scalia said. "About every prominent scholar in the field of evidence...abhors all categorical privileges."

> **FATHER DRINAN:** How about attorney-client—you take that on, too, huh?
> **SCALIA:** On an absolute basis, I think there is abhorrence for that.
> **FATHER DRINAN:** Your first norm seems to be whatever is good for law enforcement is good for the country.

Had Father Drinan stopped there, he might have impaled *Il Matador*—or at least enjoyed the last word. But the congressman then accused Scalia of pressing a "distortion" of the shield bill, adding "confidentiality is essential to that bill." In fact, Scalia understood the Democrats' legislation better than Father Drinan did. "No, sir, it is not," Scalia said. "It is only essential at the trial stage. There is no way [under the proposed legislation] to get any information, confidential or non-confidential, before the trial stage."

Il lancia!

Wounded and frustrated, his snorting rushes coming to nothing, Father Drinan, like Danielson before him, lashed out.

> **FATHER DRINAN:** You just want us to go on nagging you every once in a while so that somewhere you people will be

honest. That is what you are telling me—no more regulations; the attorney general's list is perfect; no more federal law; just keep nagging us.

SCALIA: I am not encouraging that, Mr. Drinan. I am just observing that it is going to happen, and I think that it is good that it should happen.

Democrat Edward Pattison of New York asked if Scalia thought confessions to a priest warranted exemption from subpoena power. In the devout Catholic witness, this, at last, touched a nerve. Scalia conceded the use of state power to pierce "the confidential seal of confession...would be a deep incursion into the practice of freedom of religion."

The hearing ended with the assistant attorney general's agreeing to provide the subcommittee with records of subpoenas served on reporters. The newsmen's shield bill died in committee.[5]

*   *   *

Two months after the hearing, Scalia participated in an American Enterprise Institute symposium at the National Press Club on the same subject, broadcast on PBS. Also on stage were Floyd Abrams, who represented the *New York Times* in the Pentagon Papers litigation; scholar Edward Epstein; and the *Los Angeles Times*' Jack Nelson, a Pulitzer Prize–winning reporter.

AEI's videotape marks the earliest known recording of Scalia. He was heavyset and vibrant, a charming combination of Ivy League intellect and Queens street sense. Host Peter Hackes struggled to pronounce his name "SKEH-lee-uh...Scah-LEE-uh...SKULL-ee-yuh." A soft-spoken Alabaman, Nelson pressed for the reporters' shield in a Southern drawl. "If the Nixon administration, for example, had been able to subpoena Woodward and Bernstein...and learned confidential sources," Nelson argued, "you would have never had Watergate uncovered."

"Well," Scalia quipped, "Mr. Nelson's view is the most rational, next to what I think is the correct one, and that is that there should not be a newsman's privilege." The audience, and Nelson, broke into laughter.

> SCALIA: If you have [a shield] that's unqualified, you just can't live with it. And if you have one that's qualified, it just doesn't work.... It really doesn't help the discussion to put the whole thing in the context of the Nixon administration's subpoenaing of newsmen. It normally isn't the Nixon administration; it's normally a court in a criminal case. And as often as not, they are subpoenaing the newsman not on behalf of the government but on behalf of the defendant.
> NELSON:...The subpoenaing of reporters did not begin, though, by the Justice Department until the Nixon administration.
> SCALIA: I doubt very much whether that's true.[6]

Stymied, Nelson cited Scalia's congressional testimony invoking the Patty Hearst case. The reporter claimed that the hypothetical Scalia had conjured—a TV interview with the heiress, withheld from investigating authorities—could somehow aid law enforcement. "You would know a hell of a lot more about Patty Hearst...than you did before," Nelson said. Scalia's response provoked his first clash with Abrams, the era's preeminent First Amendment lawyer, and a flash of the Scalia wit.

> SCALIA: I don't know where Patty Hearst is on the FBI's most-wanted list, but let's assume she's number one. And

there she is, big as life on the screen, in living color.... I just don't think a society can take its law enforcement efforts seriously if it can allow something like that to occur.

ABRAMS: We've done that in twenty-four states where we have privilege laws.... In New York, for example, if that interview did occur with Patty Hearst, the New York state authorities could not require a newsman to disclose the source of that.... The country hasn't exactly collapsed.

SCALIA: I think if Patty Hearst would offer it [snaps fingers], there's somebody who would snap it up like that.... That would just have an enormously corrosive effect upon not just law enforcement but the entire society's respect for law.

NELSON: [jabbing pen in Scalia's face] Wouldn't the FBI and the Justice Department know a lot more about Patty Hearst if they saw her interviewed on television than they know right now? I mean—

SCALIA: [laughing] No, not necessarily. I guess they'd have a current photograph of her; that might be helpful. [laughter]

NELSON: It might be.

EPSTEIN: But she might be disguised.

SCALIA: You're seriously asserting that this would be a help to law enforcement efforts?

NELSON: Well, I don't know, but I'm not saying—it wouldn't be a hindrance.

ABRAMS: I would seriously assert that it's a help to the public to be able to watch an interview with Patty Hearst rather than not. And the effect of what you're saying is that, in the future, at least, you couldn't.

SCALIA: What if it was Jack the Ripper? Would that make any difference? I mean, here is Jack the Ripper in living color, you know. [wiggling fingers, audience laughing] "Hi, out there, you know. I'm interviewed on television. I know the police can't get this film and they can't find out where I'm being interviewed, because the laws we live under say it's more important to watch me than it is to catch me." [laughter and applause][7]

In the age of blood lust, the Ford administration wound up on the receiving end of subpoenas from committee chairmen: the Champions of Openness, Slayers of Official Secrecy. Congressman Pike and Senator Church exposed a vast array of covert operations from the 1950s onward, including violations of CIA's charter. They were also unabashed publicity hounds. This occasioned Justice Scalia's recollections of Situation Room sessions where "the nation's most highly-guarded secrets would be turned over that day to Congress, with scant assurance...they would not appear in the *Washington Post* the next morning."[8]

The blood lust even targeted Scalia, with lawmakers threatening to hold him in contempt of Congress. At issue were documents filed with the Department of the Interior by U.S. oil exporters, under a statute that guaranteed the papers' confidentiality. The exporters had to report to Interior whether Arab nations, during their oil embargo against the United States, had pressured the firms to disclose sales to Israel. The Ford administration withheld the papers. "The congressional committee did not take this well," Justice Scalia recalled.

They demanded that Interior turn over those documents. They also sent investigators around to my office who interviewed my lawyers—just burst in upon them without ever asking my permission, without ever coming to see me—and sought to interrogate them about how [OLC's] opinion had been prepared. I of course told them not to talk to the investigators.... Because of my refusal, I was scheduled to be

considered for contempt of Congress.... The problem was
solved in the way these problems are usually solved: [Interior
Secretary] Rogers Morton...turned over the [documents],
despite our advice.[9]

On November 19, 1975, Ford's men summoned the assistant
attorney general to the Situation Room on short notice. "The White
House called up Scalia and said, 'We have a problem; can you come
over and help us?'" William Funk told me. "We spent from the afternoon all the way through to the next morning at the White House,
trying to assess the situation, what exactly it was [the Pike Committee]
wanted, what exactly was the response to it, what might, in fact, be
given to them."[10]

Following their all-nighter, Scalia and Funk appeared before the
committee at 10:00 a.m. Minutes earlier, Scalia had completed a
twenty-three-page opening statement, still "in rough form," he cautioned lawmakers. Time had not allowed for photocopying. Ten sentences in, Pike cut him off.

> **PIKE:** Mr. Scalia, do you want to read your whole statement
> without interruption? Since we don't have a copy of your
> statement, it is going to be very difficult for me to remember
> everything you say until you have finished.
> **SCALIA:** Sir, I don't mind, but I think you may be troubled
> about some concerns which will be handled later.

Pike's opening concession—that he lacked the acuity to follow the
witness's opening statement without reading along—set the tone.

Whenever Scalia resumed, Pike interrupted. He asked for copies a
second time. "I do not have a prepared statement in a form that could
be copied, sir," Scalia explained again. "This meeting was set up rather

quickly, as you know, and I will be happy to have it typed in more presentable form and distribute it to the committee afterward."

"I thought you were reading," Pike said. The chairman simply could not comprehend that Scalia's statement was suitable for reading into the record but not for formal submission.

Scalia resumed. Sixty seconds later, Pike cut him off again.

*   *   *

What had brought Scalia before the Pike Committee—his first turn in the national spotlight, at the epicenter of post-Watergate Washington—was the panel's aggressive action a few weeks earlier.

On November 7, a Friday, the committee had dispatched seven subpoenas against executive branch personnel. All demanded production of vast reams of classified documents within *two working days*. Two recipients, including CIA Director Colby, were named; five subpoenas were addressed to "the Assistant to the President for National Security Affairs, or any subordinate officer, official or employee with custody or control of the items described in the attached schedule." One subpoena targeted the "40 Committee," the elite National Security Council group that approved covert operations.

Chaired at the time by Henry Kissinger, the 40 Committee dated back, under different names, to the Eisenhower era. Pike demanded the Ford administration produce "all 40 Committee and predecessor committee records of decisions taken since January 20, 1965." *Ten years of interagency decision-making on covert operations, to be located, reviewed, redacted, copied, and sent to Capitol Hill—over a weekend!*

To their impossible demands and compliance windows, the subpoenas added other self-defeating problems. One misidentified its target agency, mistaking a joint U.S.-Soviet council, an international body, for a unit of the executive branch. The other defective subpoenas, intended for Kissinger, were the five addressed to the assistant to the president for national security affairs. For more than two years, starting in September 1973, Kissinger, in unprecedented fashion, had held the dual roles of White House national security advisor (formal title: assistant to the president for national security affairs) and secretary of state. On November 3, 1975, four days before the committee's subpoenas arrived, Ford had removed Kissinger as national security advisor and left him at the helm of State. As a technical matter, then—and well-drafted subpoenas are technical instruments—the five subpoenas had been addressed not to an individual but to a vacant position, and thus were unenforceable.[11]

Adopting a far more conciliatory approach than subsequent presidents would exhibit, Ford and his aides scrambled to comply with five of the subpoenas; still, the press decried the administration's secretiveness. In fact, Assistant Attorney General Scalia—bleary-eyed in the Situation Room with Funk, struggling to reconcile the sweeping demands and impossible timetables—invoked executive privilege sparingly. He withheld State Department recommendations to the 40 Committee and insisted that, rather than ship forty thousand pages of classified documents to Capitol Hill, the materials had to be reviewed by the lawmakers and their staffs in a secure facility, later the standard practice.

Pike saw a better headline. Acting on a motion from Democrat Ronald V. Dellums of California, an African-American firebrand and far-left liberal, the committee voted, largely along party lines, to recommend that Congress hold Kissinger in contempt. Pike moved forward with the contempt vote despite backstage "pressure...from many sources, including the speaker and key congressional leaders." It was a cheap publicity stunt, a first in American history that placed the secretary of state at risk of a three-year prison term and $3,000 in fines.

Scalia was dispatched to the Pike Committee to argue for the contempt citation to be withdrawn.[12]

*   *   *

Scalia's opening statement summarized the subpoenas' terms, as best the sloppy draftsmanship allowed, and outlined the administration's compliance. Pike remained *apoplectic* that the witness wanted to *read* his statement into the record. "I normally don't mind being interrupted in the course of a presentation," Scalia finally said, "but I think it will be easier if you let me proceed."

"I don't know how long your prepared statement is but we can't remember everything you will have said," Pike complained again; *taking notes* never occurred to the chairman. "You ask us to sit here while you read twenty-three pages of a statement, which would be called, I believe, in any court, a self-serving document," he complained. "There are going to have to be interruptions."

Scalia argued that just because a National Security Council secretary had accepted service of the five defective subpoenas, intended for Kissinger but addressed to a vacant office, did not mean the administration, or Kissinger, was obligated to comply with them. Enraged at Scalia for exposing the committee's slipshod work, Pike snorted that *Il Matador* was out of bounds.

> **PIKE:** I frankly am not going to spend the morning arguing the legal case, which is not proper argument here.
> **SCALIA:** I thought that is what the committee had before it in deciding whether somebody [was in contempt]—
> **PIKE:** What the committee has before it at the moment, as I judge it, is you saying we served the wrong guy and...we

should have addressed our contempt citation to some
secretary.

SCALIA: You didn't serve the wrong guy, Mr. Chairman.
You brought your citation of contempt against a person who
had not been served.... Secretary Kissinger did not believe,
or have any reason to believe, that he had responsibility for
compliance with those subpoenas.... He would have known
nothing about it.

Far from hiding behind official secrecy, Scalia apologized for not
turning over more documents. He had spent the intervening weeks interviewing staff and determined that while the administration "did not
display that degree of cooperativeness...which has been our objective,"
no "contumacious" intent was involved, nor any of "the kind of malicious-
ness that should appear before you take this drastic step." Where the
witness displayed the crisp reasoning of a Jesuit-trained logician, a top-tier
attorney, the panel's members struggled to comprehend basic facts.

PIKE: We subpoenaed the minutes.
SCALIA: No, you didn't.
PIKE: I think we did.
SCALIA: No, sir. Just certain portions.... We cannot pos-
sibly deal with the committee if the understandings keep
changing.
PIKE: ... I understand—or at least I *think* I understand—
what you are saying.

Dellums, sponsor of the contempt charge, confessed, "I have great
difficulty following this."

"You have been making a lot of statements here," complained
Democrat Robert Giaimo of Connecticut, "to which I am trying to pay
close attention."

"I was not trying to be cute," Scalia replied.

At one point—*blood lust!*—the lawmakers all but accused Scalia of *lying* when he testified he had not attended a particular White House strategy session. *Finally, a lawmaker rose to his defense!* It wasn't one of the Republicans...somnambulant creatures accustomed to minority status. Instead, it was Democrat Philip Hayes of Indiana, who chastised his fellow Democrats for their treatment of Scalia. "I really don't think it is proper to engage this gentleman in this kind of discourse," he said, probing "what is inside his head or where he has been traveling."

When the Democrats argued that a sitting president could not assert executive privilege over his predecessors' materials, Scalia snapped that their argument "does not make much sense. Why does a fact which is a sensitive military or foreign affairs secret on January 19 suddenly become non-secret on January 20?" The witness kept vague how far in time the privilege extended. "I am not asserting that executive privilege can be asserted all the way back," Scalia said. "It is, rather, you who are asserting it cannot be exercised even one president back."

Il Matador inflamed his attackers. Now the Democrats bristled at Scalia's requirement that the subpoenaed materials be examined at a secure facility. "To provide such information, identified by country and names of individuals regarding all covert operations over a ten-year period—to be held in one place and to be distributed freely within and among the committee and its staff—would provide a security threat of unacceptable dimensions," Scalia countered. No, the Democrats responded: Subpoenas meant *turn over* records, not *make them available.*

DELLUMS: We are asserting a right and you are asserting some reasons why you cannot comply.
SCALIA: I am saying we both have interests involved here, and I hope we can work it out so they can be accomplished. If you have access to the information you want, that is what

you are most interested in. If we don't let these documents
float about the place, that is something that we are very much
interested in....
DELLUMS: For you to sit here and assert a theory of "security risk" is a challenge to the integrity of this committee....
I do not believe you have the right to challenge the integrity
of this committee. To assume the documents are "floating
around" someplace is absurd.... We have not been about the
business of leaking any materials.

Dellums's statement that the witness had no right to challenge the
committee's integrity, as Stalinist a sentiment ever heard on Capitol
Hill, Scalia allowed to pass; he saw value in retreat.

DELLUMS: How can you say these documents would be
"floating around" someplace?
SCALIA: I withdraw "floating around." I should not have
put it that way.

A setback for *Il Matador*—but not for long. "My point stands," he
told Dellums, "that we want the minimum possible circulation of this
material, even in very secure places."

"I think there have been egregious leaks of information," declared
Republican Robert McClory of Illinois, "and they have been
damaging."

With Democrat Les Aspin of Wisconsin, a future defense secretary,
Scalia's patience wore thin.

ASPIN: When you talk about all of those pieces of paper in
one stack—regarding all of the covert operations—would

that be available to read over in the executive department?
If one member of the committee were to take an afternoon
and go over there, is that what you are offering?
SCALIA: I don't know the physics of it, Congressman.

Now Dellums jumped back in.

DELLUMS: You think that maybe somebody might steal the
documents if they are over here. There is no other rhyme nor
reason for it.
SCALIA: I think it demonstrates that we don't mistrust you
at all; it is just your safes. We would rather have [the mate-
rials] where we can look after them....
PIKE: This has just degenerated.

Closing the hearing, Pike congratulated the witness sarcastically.
"You can go back to those who sent you and say you did indeed accomplish your purpose," the chairman snapped. "You stopped the committee for one more day."

"It is a serious matter you are considering," Scalia shot back. "And
I think it is worth a couple of hours before you cite a secretary of state
for contempt for the first time in the history of the country."

Congressman Hayes, Scalia's Democratic defender, rose to his
defense once more: "You have done an excellent job of presenting a
good deal of new and fresh information."

Dellums, the only member to stagger *Il Matador*, sought a final
moment of glory. The committee had taken testimony, he said, establishing that some of the covert projects "at best are dubious and are at
worst outright illegal, a sham and a tragedy."

"Stupidity," Scalia replied, "is still not unlawful."[13]

*   *   *

The mismatch was equally glaring in the Senate. Scalia's most memorable appearance before the upper chamber included a series of pointed exchanges with Democrat Edmund Muskie, Lincolnesque Mainer, the 1968 vice presidential nominee and failed presidential aspirant of 1972. The Intelligence Reformation offered Muskie a face-lift: Champion of Openness, Slayer of Official Secrecy.

In October 1975, Muskie's subcommittee considered legislation to restrict further the administration's ability to withhold documents from congressional committees. *Il Matador* opened with *il mantello rosso*. "I realize that anyone saying a few kind words about executive privilege after the events of the last few years is in a position somewhat akin to the man preaching the virtues of water after the Johnstown flood, or the utility of fire after the burning of Chicago. But fire and water are, for all that, essential elements of human existence."

Incensed by the attempt at humor, Muskie rushed forward, accusing Scalia of trying to "reduce the issues to absurdities." Any principled defense of executive power, of the need for the president to respond selectively to congressional demands, especially in national security matters, was seen, in the eyes of Muskie and the reporters present, as absurd…shocking…*rude.*

Unlike Pike, the chairman allowed Scalia to finish his opener—but not without first declaring offense at it. "I will listen to the rest of your statement," Muskie allowed, "but I have listened for ten pages here to the logic that is the most incredible exposition…that I have been exposed to in all of the time I have been in the Senate."

Muskie's confession that he resented listening to testimony longer than ten pages went unreported by the press.

"Before I know it," he thundered, all revved up for the cameras, "you are going to be challenging my right as an individual senator to bring up [a] question!"

Unfazed, Scalia declared the legislation "inappropriate": "Ultimately, the president has a personal constitutional responsibility to make his own judgment as to what information within the control of the executive branch must be protected.... I hope that whatever action your committee takes with respect to the present legislative proposals, you will not seek to eliminate a vital element of our system merely because it may sometimes have been abused."

The entire concept of congressional oversight, the "astounded" chairman harrumphed, was "challenged by your logic." United Press International reported: "The Justice Department, its views evidently unchanged from the Watergate days of the Nixon administration, insisted yesterday the president may keep anything he wishes secret from Congress. Assistant Attorney General Antonin Scalia argued before a Senate intergovernmental subcommittee that the president has a right 'and indeed duty' under the doctrine of executive privilege to protect information he deems sensitive."

The article ran across the country, beneath headlines such as "Justice Department Backs Top Secrets" (*Valley Morning Star*, Harlingen, Texas); "Vast Privilege Is Claimed" (*Indianapolis Star*); and "President Rules What Is Secret" (*Daily Record*, York, Pennsylvania).[14]

*   *   *

These encounters never rattled or enraged Scalia; they *disappointed* him. Since his teenage years, Nino had *loved* robust debate. "Competitions of the mind came naturally to him," a clerk observed, likening the justice to "the chess master who comes to the park on a Saturday morning and is disappointed to see just ten other chess players willing to take him on." But robust debate was not the hallmark of the Democrats' post-Watergate congressional hearings: arid theaters of antagonism and mediocrity, relentlessly partisan, often confused, what

Scalia had in mind when, in 1978, he described the House as a "quint-essentially human" institution.[15]

Fortunately, high office also afforded his first appearance in the Washington institution worthiest of his gifts. On January 19, 1976, Scalia made his first and only appearance *before* the Supreme Court. A custom at Main Justice held that the solicitor general—Bob Bork, in this case—afforded each assistant attorney general an opportunity to present oral argument before the Court. "Most did not," recalled Frank Easterbrook, then an assistant to Bork, later a judge on the Seventh Circuit, "but Nino Scalia wanted to argue. Bob gave him a choice of cases—no surprise, since the two were close friends and Bob had great respect for Nino. Nino picked *Dunhill* because the subject interested him."

Alfred Dunhill of London, Inc. v. Republic of Cuba had originated as a financial dispute between a leading cigar manufacturer and American-based importers, brought about by the Castro regime's nationalization campaign of 1960. The U.S. government was not a party to the case; but the Ford administration filed an *amicus*, or "friend of the court," brief. Scalia was there to argue it.[16]

Presiding on that chilly morning was Chief Justice Warren Burger. Serving his seventh term on the Court, Burger was the very picture of a chief justice: tall and hefty in the robes, white hair, stately baritone. While he looked the part, the Nixon appointee had proved a disappointment to conservatives, who saw him more focused on reforming the Court's creaking administrative structure than on overturning the sweeping liberal jurisprudence of his predecessor, Earl Warren.

Burger knew how to move things along, though, and he opened *Dunhill* briskly, like a board chairman, calling company attorney Victor Friedman to the lectern. Friedman got one minute into his presentation before Justice Rehnquist—vaulted there from the very job Scalia now held—interrupted with a question. Twenty-five minutes later, it was Scalia's turn.

Spinning silently in a corner was the Court's taping system, a presence at such proceedings since 1955. The timber of Scalia's voice, at thirty-nine, was reedy, high-pitched, his Jersey-Queens roots discernible only occasionally—*vie-tality for "vitality," buh-low for "below"*—in a professorial presentation that also had its rough spots.[17]

As Scalia approached the lectern, the only audible sound was some muffled coughing. No one introduced the assistant attorney general; he seemed uncertain when to start until an unknown voice, off the bench, said softly, "Go ahead." "Mr. Chief Justice and May It Please the Court": Thus began Antonin Scalia's Supreme Court career. Dressed in the formal English "morning clothes" required of attorneys before the Court in those days—long-tailed coat, tie, and striped trousers—Scalia announced that he was there to argue an issue not centrally before the Court; his concern, instead, was a lower court ruling in the case which, if mutely accepted by the justices, threatened to "destroy" a long-held position of the United States.

At issue was the doctrine of sovereign immunity: the circumstances under which a sovereign state can be sued. The administration wanted the courts to bless a "restrictive" form of the doctrine, which would allow lawsuits only to contest "official" actions, not "commercial" ones such as the Cuban government's repudiation of its obligation to pay its debt to Dunhill.

The newcomer's first display of hesitancy came around ninety seconds in, when, momentarily at sea, Scalia emitted a word—*a sound*—detested by champion debaters: "Uh." A minute later, however, came the first Scalian turn of phrase, the first flash of the liveliness that would later define his oral argument from the bench: "It would surely reduce the law to ineffectiveness, and perhaps expose it to ridicule,"—*ridicule! the worst fate on the streets of Queens!*—"if [Cuba], having being denied the claim of sovereign immunity, were able to achieve precisely the same result by simply appearing [in court] and repudiating the obligation."

Attacking the Cuban government's brief, Scalia summoned his Xavier theatre days. "Respondents' brief seeks to *calm* our fears on this point," he said—openly sarcastic, he lingered over "calm," gave it a downward lilt, like the soothing doctor in an aspirin commercial—"by assuring us that repudiation of a commercial obligation will be unlikely.... The trouble with all of these hopeful assurances is that they are destroyed by the experience of this very case. There could not have been a more naked repudiation.... There is no high political background here. It is simply a question of a lot of money; and until it was clear that it involved a lot of money, Cuba did not care about the point."

Even by the standards of the era, when oral argument was less interruptive, the justices appeared...sleepily uninterested. Scalia spoke for nearly *eight minutes* without interruption. The assistant attorney general didn't understand the reason for this Great Silence, and he didn't like it: reprising the written brief in oral argument, Scalia always maintained, was no use, no fun.[18] Weren't they all there, in the elite ring, the Marble Temple, to explore, in lively oral argument, the issues raised by the brief?

Given the Court's slow march toward diversity, it was remarkable, in retrospect, that the justice who first interrupted Scalia—the first to address him at Court—was Thurgood Marshall. The moment pulsed with significance: the first African-American justice welcoming the first Italian-American justice, ten years ahead of his arrival as a peer.

Unfortunately for Scalia, things went south from there.

*   *   *

Marshall interrupted just as Scalia was arguing that sovereign immunity came with a "territorial condition," meaning the act of state must have been performed within the government's own territory to warrant coverage under the doctrine. Here the AAG made his first reference, obliquely, to the textualist enterprise. "One may interpret that territorial condition literally, I suppose," Scalia said. Later on, he noted that the government's *amicus* brief discouraged such literalism. Marshall saw an opening. If the "territorial condition" required that the act of state be committed within its territory to qualify for protection under sovereign immunity, couldn't Cuba claim that its rejection of payments to Dunhill had been approved by authorities physically located in Havana?

But Marshall—his voice raspy, his speech less formal than that of the other justices, unburdened by academic affect—didn't frame it that way.

"Mr. Scalia"—he pronounced it right—"is that statement of the lawyers contradicted anyplace up until now?"

For Scalia, time and space stopped. Marshall's question was impenetrably vague: Did he mean "of the lawyers" (plural) or "of the lawyer's" (singular)? Which statement? Contradicted how? By whom? Where?

It was the only way to shut Scalia down: sheer incomprehensibility.

He stood there mute, frozen. Probably twenty years had elapsed, Xavier days, since he had last staggered so badly in debate.

Five seconds of silence passed.

At last, from the lips of the kid from Queens, struggling for direction, came...*nothing*...just an audible *croak* from the back of his throat.... Instantly, Scalia recognized the unacceptability of this—*croaking in the Court!*—and opted for the minimal upgrade of "Ahhhm—"

When "Ahhhm" came to an end, another two full seconds passed.

The Court was quiet as a church! Scalia was reeling!

A rookie in the elite ring, *Il Matador* lacked the self-assurance to force Justice Marshall to clarify his question with a return question: the Socratic method Scalia had mastered at UVA. So he took a shot in the dark, switching the issue from contradiction to *authorization*. "No, sir, I don't believe there was any—any contrary evidence adduced that the—that the lawyer was *not* authorized," he said, before declaring the subject irrelevant:

"I do not think that... whether the statement of the lawyer was in fact authorized is really present in this petition."

"The statement made—authorized—is made in Cuba?"

Scalia was flummoxed again.

Three seconds of silence passed.

Finally, he stammered: "There's—I, I—I don't know, sir. I—I don't believe there's anything, uh, in the record which shows where—"

> MARSHALL: Okay, you say it's here, but the statement was that something was done in *Cuba*.
> SCALIA: Well, certainly something was done in Cuba, but I would not consider a government—
> MARSHALL: [sing-song tone] But if the government had any contrary evidence of any kind, I would assume they would have shown.

Now Scalia posed a question; it was time to nail down the subject.

> SCALIA: Contrary evidence to what effect, sir?
> MARSHALL: The fact that he wasn't talking about the truth.
> SCALIA: Yes, I think that is correct.

Scalia's admissions of uncertainty ("I don't know, sir.... I think that is correct") made a muddled start to his exchange with Marshall. Belatedly, Scalia moved to reclaim control.

MARSHALL: And the fact that the government hasn't produced it after all these years leads me to what conclusion?

SCALIA: I think [to] the conclusion that the statement of the lawyer was authorized. And—and again, I am not contesting that. But the point is...the authorization to the lawyer, even if it was given in Cuba, does not constitute a public act any more than the authorization by the president to one of his delegates in the United States to do a particular act constitutes the act itself.

Marshall was exasperated. "Let me ask you one more question: Do you want *Sabbatino* overruled or not?"

The justice was referring to *Banco Nacional de Cuba v. Sabbatino*, a 1964 opinion in which the Court had overturned two lower rulings finding that Cuba had violated international law when it forced a sugar distributor, through confiscation, to contract with a state-run bank. In an 8–1 opinion by Justice Harlan, the Court declined in *Sabbatino* to decide the validity of a decree by a foreign government that had no treaty with the United States.[19]

Again, Scalia was stopped cold.

Three more seconds of silence passed.

"Yes, sir, that—" He paused again. "Well—I—I think as, as described in the government's brief, we think that the issue of *Sabbatino* is not involved.... If however, the Court should disagree...and if the Court should find that when *Sabbatino* spoke of an act of state, it meant an act of state...could even consist of a simple repudiation of a contractual obligation, then I would assert that *Sabbatino* should be reexamined."

The remainder of Scalia's time was less fraught—but still arduous. Justice Powell, genteel Southerner, interrupted to ask, "Mr. Scall-yuh, does any country that you know of concede or admit today that it applies the Act of State Doctrine to commercial transactions?"

Three more seconds of silence passed, again.

"The, uh—the—it is—it is said that the Act of State Doctrine is applied by a number of other countries," Scalia stammered, "but their application is a good deal less clear than our own...a good deal less rational."

A further exchange with Powell, who seemed satisfied—and then it was over. Dunhill had conceded fifteen minutes for Scalia to argue the government's *amicus* brief; he had consumed eighteen.

"I see that my time has expired, thank you."

In the elite ring, *Il Matador* had been bloodied.

Book Three

THE CHICAGO FIRE

CHAPTER X

Growing Oaks

*A whole lot of what I am intellectually is attributable to
this place.*

—Antonin Scalia at the University of Chicago Law School,
February 2012

The Court sided with Dunhill.

Il Matador, though bruised and bloodied, had prevailed.

Victory in the elite ring marked a milestone moment in Scalia's life, one his parents lived to see. It was not lost on him that the opportunity had come courtesy of a colleague and friend: Bob Bork.[1]

The experience with Justice Marshall had also provided a valuable reminder: despite his long dominance in debate, from Xavier to Congress, Nino, like any other accomplished practitioner, still had room to improve. He learned anew to be prepared for anything, to meet imprecision, or even inscrutability, from an interlocutor with disciplined directionality, harnessed always to the central business of *persuasion*. Hearings led by batty committee chairmen lasted for two hours; in oral arguments at the Court, rapid-fire engagements with top legal minds, success was measured in seconds. Surely Scalia—*be ye perfect*—knew his debut had been rocky.

But he never betrayed it. Scalia's only public comment on his experience in *Dunhill* came, unprompted, in an interview with his co-author Bryan Garner in 2014, thirty-eight years after the fact. Of his struggles under Marshall's questioning, Scalia said nothing; instead, he expressed disappointment that the justices had waited eight minutes to engage him: "It was awful. I looked from face to face. I'm just saying what I've already said [in the brief]. I'm like, 'Come on, you guys, give me a hand here. How can I help you? What are you concerned about?'"

Still, in *Making Your Case: The Art of Persuading Judges* (2008), co-authored with Garner, the justice may have had *Dunhill* in mind when he urged intensive preparation before oral argument; after all, a question from the Court about the record in *Dunhill* had reduced Scalia to the lamest reply: *I don't know.* "Knowing your case means, first and foremost, knowing the record," Scalia and Garner wrote. "You never know until it is too late what damage a gap in your knowledge of the record can do."[2]

Descending the Court's fifty-three marble steps that morning, Scalia knew he needed to be *better*. But he also knew that when he returned to the Court—*I will rise*—he would be a rookie no more.

＊　　　＊　　　＊

A milestone moment for the future justice, *Dunhill v. Cuba* has been largely, and curiously, ignored by his previous biographers.

Bruce Allen Murphy's *Scalia: A Court of One* (2014) simply does not mention *Dunhill*, as if it never happened.

In *American Original* (2009), Joan Biskupic breezes past the event: a single paragraph, 104 words, with no reference to the recording and no quotation from the arguments. In this drive-by treatment, the only quoted remark is a pencil notation made by Justice Blackmun, unsealed in 1999, describing Scalia as "plump." Biskupic tells her readers she asked about *Dunhill*, and the justice "remembered little about the argu-ments or the case." Familiarity with the record on the part of his inter-viewer might have helped.[3]

What explains these omissions? After all, hostile biographers might have exulted in Scalia's rough performance in *Dunhill*, his silences and stammering before the legendary Thurgood Marshall. But Biskupic and Murphy may have made a different calculation: that dwelling on, or even mentioning, Scalia's debut at the Court—two months shy of his fortieth birthday, a decade before his investiture—was best avoided, lest they acknowledge the aura of inevitability that attended Scalia's rise, some-thing his biographers apparently found absurd...shocking...*rude*.[4]

*   *   *

On November 2, 1976, President Ford lost his bid for election in his own right to Democratic nominee Jimmy Carter.

"The people threw us out," Nino liked to say.[5]

Over the preceding year, as he advised the president and attorney general on issues ranging from covert operations to the insolvency of New York City, Scalia had had ample time to ponder his next move if Ford lost. He could practice law again, which would mean more money and stress; or teach law again, which he loved. In Nino's mind, aca-demia would allow him to write provocatively on legal issues, as Bork had done. This in turn would position him nicely for a federal judgeship in the event the Republicans reclaimed the White House in 1980—and without all the conflict-of-interest baggage that came with charging clients $1,000 an hour.

Scalia and his most ardent defenders—his family and former clerks—have always bristled at suggestions that he was, in his rise to greatness, so calculating and strategic. The fact is that for someone in his position *not* to have thought in such terms, *not* to have surveyed

cannily the prospects before him—he had just made the Ford administration's short list of potential Supreme Court nominees and argued
before the Court—would have required a flight from reality, or dullness
of perception, unknown in the man. Grateful inheritors of the Scalia
legacy should acknowledge not only that he *did* think this way, of neces-
sity, but that he was *right* to have done so; that the United States, and
those closest to him, were *better off* that he did so. Any honest account
of Scalia's life will record as much, with undiluted admiration for his
genius, hard work, religious devotion, and liveliness of mind and spirit.

However, Nino also had a wife and eight kids—the eldest fifteen
and college-bound—to consider; his ambitions could not override
all that.

The next step on his path emerged from his deep bond with
Ed Levi.

> It was largely through his urging that I interviewed at the
> law school at the University of Chicago.... I spent a half a
> year, after leaving OLC, here in Washington so that my
> children could finish their school year. And during that half
> a year, I taught at Georgetown and I was a scholar in resi-
> dence at the American Enterprise Institute, where I made
> friends with some other interesting people that have been my
> friends since, such as Irving Kristol...Jeane Kirkpatrick;
> Walter Berns. And then the next summer [1977] I went to
> Chicago and began resuming my career as an academic.[6]

Levi later said exposure to Scalia's mind left him in "awe." On
January 6, the Associated Press reported Levi "probably" would return
to Chicago, adding, "Robert Bork, once a student of Levi, and Antonin
Scalia...also may go." In fact, Bork returned to Yale.[7]

Another factor made the move attractive for Maureen and Nino. Chicago paid *full tuition costs* for enrolled children of faculty members; if enrolled at another college or university, the school matched tuition costs up to Chicago's. "Scalia, a devout Catholic," *Newsweek* reported in 1986, "accumulated so little wealth from teaching and government work that when he left Washington, friends say he chose the University of Chicago at least in part because it would pay tuition for his children." "He chose Chicago, according to University of Virginia professor A. E. Dick Howard and other colleagues," reported *American Lawyer*, "in part because the school paid tuition for faculty children—and Scalia had a houseful of them." No Chicago professor had ever planned such ambitious exploitation of the policy. "There was a joke," Gene Scalia recalled, "that my father was the highest-paid man in academia."[8]

In early 1977, Scalia visited the Chicago campus for a job interview arranged by David Currie, a former Harvard classmate teaching there. "He cut a large figure," recalled Richard Epstein, another Chicago professor present for the interview. Swiftly the talk turned to a subject Nino knew well. "For Scalia, there was no middle ground.... He was a passionate and articulate defender of executive privilege, [noting] that this was an issue that was not defined by party, but by role. Repeatedly, he stressed that every president of both parties had taken this view, which he thought that the constitutional system of separation of powers required." Besides Scalia's qualifications and friendship with Levi, the professors believed he had "given the impression that he planned to make his career in academia," and voted to hire him.[9]

On January 14, 1977, Scalia signed his resignation letter to the president, effective at noon on the twentieth. "I am grateful for your affording me the opportunity to serve the United States," Scalia wrote.

As you leave office, the country is more united and tranquil
than it has been for many years, largely because of the personal qualities which you brought to the Presidency. May I
add my own thanks to those of the nation for your steady
and trustworthy leadership in difficult times.

> Respectfully,
> Antonin Scalia

In a letter addressed "Dear Nino" and signed "Jerry Ford," dated
January 18 and previously unpublished, the president accepted. Ford
made clear he knew the central role *the president's lawyer's lawyer* had
played: "I know that yours has been a difficult and challenging assignment, and you have served the Department and this Administration
with great distinction."[10]

✳   ✳   ✳

The American Enterprise Institute (AEI) was founded in New York
City in 1938 as the American Enterprise Association. Its mission was
to advocate for "greater public knowledge and understanding of the
social and economic advantages...of the system of free, competitive
enterprise." Founder Lewis Brown and the trustees were all titans of
finance and industry (derided by Biskupic with a swipe at "the corporate
bent of the AEI crowd"). The group published papers widely read on
Capitol Hill. Under the leadership of William J. Baroody, AEI took its
current name and became a full-fledged research institute. By the time
Baroody stepped down, in 1978, AEI staff had grown from 5 to 125
and its annual budget from $80,000 to $8 million. Bringing Scalia
aboard was a final masterstroke of his tenure.[11]

DOJ had exposed Scalia to "all aspects of federal constitutional
and statutory law," as he put it. This versatility, and his liveliness, made

him a clutch utility player for AEI, suitable for any symposium or anthology.

Let's put Nino on the panel!

Nino can write something for us!

With its emphasis on free enterprise, AEI found particular value in Scalia's passion for administrative law. His gift for treating complex issues in layman's terms enabled the institute to educate policymakers and the public on the work of federal regulatory agencies, codes of conduct that Scalia had crafted and enforced as OTP counsel and evaluated and reformed as ACUS chairman. By now, he had strong opinions on the limits of agency power over private enterprise; the role of congressional oversight; and the deference judges should accord agency decisions. The growth of the regulatory behemoth was of paramount concern to conservative intellectuals in the 1970s, and Scalia, with his broad experience in administrative law, possessed unrivaled expertise.

When he arrived, AEI was launching a bi-monthly publication on the subject. In its inaugural issue, *Regulation* vowed "a response to the extraordinary growth in the scope and detail of government regulation.... The longer-range purpose is to foster an analytical approach to regulation.... The editors of this journal recognize that, in a complex industrial society, a substantial measure of regulation may be necessary. We are committed, nonetheless, to the ideal that this regulation should be sensible, cost-effective, and as unburdensome as the nature of its objectives will allow." *Regulation* soon became known, like Scalia, as "scholarly but sprightly." He and co-editor Murray Weidenbaum, a former Treasury official, contributed unsigned pieces to the "Perspectives" column.

These were heady days for AEI. In the Republican primaries of 1976, Ronald Reagan had mounted a formidable challenge to President Ford, hoisting the banner of the right for the first time since the

Goldwater debacle. AEI emerged as *the* place to be in Washington for the right-wing intelligentsia, the GOP government-in-waiting.

Also installed at AEI, Silberman remembered fondly the brown-bag lunches he and Scalia enjoyed with Kristol and Kirkpatrick, Paul McCracken, Herb Stein, Jude Wanniski, Ralph Winter.... As usual, Bork, affiliated with AEI since 1964, was a step ahead of Nino. The organization's promotional literature showed Bork in his DOJ office, grinning with phone to ear, feet propped on desk; Scalia appeared stern-faced, pipe in mouth.[12]

*   *   *

The Scalias moved to Chicago, Gene remembered, on August 16, 1977: the day Elvis died. Maureen and Nino had purchased a former fraternity house on Woodlawn Avenue, three blocks from campus, in Hyde Park. Scalia's parents, Sam and Catherine, visited; the old man gave Christopher a water gun.[13]

The University of Chicago Law School was a Midwestern bastion of academic conservatism. Scalia called it "one of two or three of the most formidable intellectual institutions in the world." In the 1930s the faculty had advanced free-market principles, spawning the "Chicago school of economics"; at the same time the law school pioneered the application of economic theory to legal analysis, a *law-and-economics* approach that proved equally influential.

Nino taught contracts to first-year law students; to second- and third-years he taught administrative and constitutional law. "He loved teaching law, perhaps because he loved ideas and understood their power," recalled Bradford Clark, who clerked for Justice Scalia in 1989–90 and later taught at Harvard, among other top law schools. "He once told me that law professors have their greatest impact through teaching rather than scholarship."[14]

As he did everywhere else, Scalia made friendships in Chicago that lasted the rest of his life. One was with thirty-year-old Professor Geoffrey Stone, a former clerk to Justice Brennan. Their daughters attended school together. Both taught con law. And both *loved* to argue. "We agreed about almost nothing, and we argued constantly," Stone recalled. "But our arguments, though intense, were always respectful." Stone recalled Scalia's joining the professors' monthly poker game. "He'd always wear a beat-up old fishing hat—as if it were a symbol of his night out with the boys. He wanted to have us play games that were off the beaten path. One was a version of poker where each player would hold a card on their forehead, where other players could see their card but the holder was blind. He got a kick out of things like that and was a fun person."[15]

Like the students in Charlottesville, students at Chicago found Nino and Maureen open and kind. "His wit in the classroom set him apart," recalled Thomas Dulcich, later a fellow of the American Council of Trial Lawyers. "When you were with Antonin Scalia, he took an interest in you. It wasn't him *up there* and you *down there*. He was a warm human being who appreciated those people around him." Lee Liberman, a Yale graduate and fellow New Yorker, took con law and administrative law with Scalia at Chicago. The classes were "formative intellectual experiences.... I really think about the structure of government in a way I learned from him. He had this Joe Six-Pack character.... When legal doctrine was just getting too disconnected from reality, he would ask: 'What would Joe Six-Pack think about this?'"[16]

The FBI later reported that Scalia was "consistently rated highly as a professor by the [Chicago] student body on their faculty evaluation sheets." But the Chicago years, by all accounts, did not reprise the sunny academic life the Scalias had enjoyed a decade earlier at UVA. A faculty member observed that Nino was "never part of the law school's inner circle." A colleague said Scalia disliked playing "second fiddle" to the law school's dominant intellectual figure, Professor Richard Posner, whose name was synonymous with *law-and-economics*. Scalia wrote and argued brilliantly, appeared frequently on television, but had not done Big Think: He was responsible for no theorems, no books, no Posnerian school of thought.

"Nino wasn't happy at Chicago," a friend said, "chiefly because Maureen wasn't happy." Raising eight children as devout Catholics in northern Virginia in 1976, with your husband often gone, was challenging enough; the setting of Chicago—vastly larger, more dangerous—made things harder on Maureen. She felt unwelcome on campus. "When they were at the University of Chicago," Silberman told me, "she, and thereby Nino, felt quite uncomfortable because most of the women, either on the faculty or married to the faculty, had careers and looked down upon Maureen as 'just' a home mother."[17]

Even finding a church proved difficult. "Our Sundays in Chicago were especially adventurous," recalled Mary Clare Scalia Murray. "Rather than walking ten minutes to the neighborhood church, Dad drove us thirty minutes to a city church led by Italian priests whose accents were so thick I never knew when they were speaking English or Latin."

At UVA the students offered only glowing reviews of Scalia's teaching style; at Chicago, students cited his frequent trips to Washington and complained he "wasn't always as well prepared for class as they would have liked." And he reportedly "scared the wits out of some of his students." Mary E. Becker, one of 165 students in Scalia's first-year contracts class, recalled he was "unrelenting on preparation. You had to work hard to keep from being humiliated. He would call on you whether you were ready or not. It was frightening."[18]

Another former student, who took the contracts class in 1977–78 and requested anonymity to speak freely, told me Scalia was "widely hated as one of the worst professors at the law school. He was kind of an asshole. Most professors, if they ask a hypothetical and the student doesn't know the answer, they move on. He would push and push, really embarrass the student." On one occasion, when four consecutive students confessed to unpreparedness, Scalia abruptly left the classroom.

The students of those years, the era of *Animal House* and *Caddyshack*, sometimes exhibited an irreverence Scalia abhorred. His contracts law students once turned his teaching tools against him—for satire. To enliven the dry subject Professor Scalia liked to present the cases as disputes over Albemarle Pippins: a strain of apple Thomas Jefferson had cultivated at Monticello. Now came a banging at the classroom door. In strolled a second-year female student in a farmer's daughter get-up: red-check shirt, overalls, hayseed in mouth.

"Antonin Scalia?" she said. "We got yer shipment for ya! C'mon, boys, bring 'em in!"

On cue, a stream of male students, costumed as farmers, burst in, pushing carts filled with apples.

"These here," the farmer's daughter bellowed, "are yer Alba-marle Pippins!"

Laughter! Commotion! Bedlam!

An organizer of the prank—a woman who confessed to having previously found Scalia "an energetic teacher" who "brought a sense of lightness and humor to the classroom" and "seemed intent on making contracts fun"—recalled his reaction. "For a few minutes, we enjoyed the pleasant delirium of group participation in a shared joke."

Then Scalia stopped…smiling. He didn't merely stop—his entire demeanor changed. Perhaps he suddenly felt we were laughing *at* him, not *with* him. That perception couldn't have been further from the truth, but it might explain the transformation that took place. One moment, Scalia was the jovial teacher, absolutely certain of his abilities and completely secure in the admiration of his students. In an instant, his entire affect changed. "That's enough," he said angrily, dismissing the farmer actors. Our laughter died down in a hurry as we returned to the case at hand.

Scalia likely saw the incident as his father, that educator of highest standards, would have: as a violation, a defilement, of the classroom. After this, the woman said, there was "no more cheerful repartee"; he "never recovered his prior avuncular manner, preferring instead to grill students harshly." The next term, with a fresh crop of students, she observed how he "regained his equilibrium and once again displayed a spirited and brilliant teaching style."[19]

*   *   *

"When you ask Nino for a spark of creativity, what you get," said Anne Brunsdale, "is the Chicago Fire. There is no halfway with him."

No one worked more closely with Scalia at *Regulation*. She never received the editor's title, but Brunsdale ran the magazine while Scalia and Weidenbaum, pursuing their academic and professional careers, trekked to Washington and worked from afar. "She was certainly very integral to *Regulation* being the big success that it was," a colleague remembered.

A Minnesota native, Brunsdale earned degrees in political science and Far East studies from the University of Minnesota; three years later, in 1949, came a second master's, in comparative government, from Yale. Divorced from Yale professor Willmoore Kendall, early mentor to Bill Buckley and *National Review*, Anne, like Buckley, served briefly in CIA. She joined AEI in 1967 and was soon overseeing publications. In 1985, President Reagan nominated her to the International Trade

Commission, which she chaired from 1989 to 1990. She was "a woman who speaks strong truths gently."[20]

It was Anne who recruited Scalia to *Regulation*: "I thought Nino.... might provide that extra spark.... His commitment to his ideas and his ventures is always total and his contributions are consistently large.:... His submissions to the magazine reflected his personality: a little bit of self-deprecating humor combined with keen insights, devotion to principle, and a free and lucid writing style. And all of us at the magazine vividly recall his editing.... We were truly amazed that someone so busy and eminent could care so deeply about words, about making words flow, and about finding the particular phrase that summed everything up."[21]

Scalia's debut essay for *Regulation* was entitled "The Judicialization of Standardless Rulemaking: Two Wrongs Make a Right." "The subject of the present article is administrative procedure," he announced. "By nature, it is an arcane, bloodless, and thus unattractive subject of study—for regulators no less than the readers of *Regulation*."

Brunsdale hadn't read many openings like that!

"Nino could get away with that sort of thing," she said, "because he lied: in his hands, the subject was not arcane, bloodless, or unattractive; he made it relevant, robust, and interesting."

The article inveighed against federal judges who engaged in "vaguely moralistic tinkering" with agency rulemaking. Early on Scalia invoked legislative history, quoting at length, and respectfully, from House and Senate committee reports.[22]

By the time of his second *Regulation* article, however, in the March–April 1978 issue, Scalia had turned decisively against the practice. In "Guadalajara! A Case Study in Regulation by Munificence," Scalia examined the constitutionality of quotas for foreign immigrants imposed on the admissions boards of U.S. medical schools. He wrote sarcastically of what "the legislative history solemnly announced," adding that a particular interpretation of a law "is not inconsistent with the legislative history of the provision, because almost nothing is." He appended *three pages* of muddled House debate, saying they read "as though written by Lewis Carroll for Abbott and Costello."

Scalia's writings for *Regulation* revealed a love higher, even, than his passion for administrative law: separation of powers. Challenging the "Guadalajara provision" of the Health Professions Educational Assistance Act of 1976, fourteen medical schools—Yale, Johns Hopkins, the University of Chicago, and Stanford among them—had rejected federal funds rather than meet mandated quotas for foreign-born admissions. To Scalia, the case embodied "the phenomenon of expanding federal regulation...characterized by broad discretionary authority in an executive agency":

> Whatever one might think of broad delegation as a general matter, delegation with what might be termed acknowledged absence of congressional agreement is a deplorable distortion of democratic processes. With the ordinary broad delegation, there is at least a genuinely assumed social consensus which it is the task of the agency to translate into specific detail. Delegation in acknowledged absence of agreement, on the other hand, intentionally confers upon the agencies or the courts that function of reconciling or subordinating conflicting private interests which is preeminently the task of the political branch.[23]

It wasn't long before *Il Matador* returned to the ring. In February 1977, Scalia testified before the House Government Operations Committee, opposing one of the first initiatives of the Carter White House: an executive branch reorganization plan that subjected presidential action to potential nullification under a "one house veto" provision.

Scalia cited the fact that Carter had already presided over a significant pay raise for federal employees—and members of Congress—without a vote by either chamber, derided by Scalia as "legislation by inattention."

The reorganization plan was unconstitutional, he said, "because its obvious purpose is to enable a change in the law without a vote by both houses of Congress.... It will indeed be disappointing if the first two major legislative steps taken by this new post-Watergate Congress turn out to be the 'look-ma-no-hands' pay raise followed quickly by the establishment of provision for 'blindman's-bluff' reorganization."[24]

The following year, Scalia argued before a Senate subcommittee that parents of parochial school students should be eligible for federal tuition tax credits. "I will not take much of your time," he told lawmakers, "partly because you have wisely not agreed to give me much of it." He framed the issue in terms of religious freedom, suggesting that the current prohibition on the tax credit was an outcome worthy of Soviet communism: "Is it conceivable that in this country—as opposed, let us say, to Hungary—it is not only proper but necessary to single out for special discrimination those parents who choose to follow the long American tradition of religious schooling?"

His argument included a bold attack on the "utter confusion" of the Supreme Court in "the church-state area." Citing a series of rulings spanning thirty years, he showed how the Court had sent sharply mixed messages about how it interpreted the First Amendment's Establishment Clause: "Congress shall make no law respecting an establishment of religion." Scalia couldn't tell whether the Court intended to enjoin the government from favoring one religion over another, or from providing any government benefits to any religious group. "The Supreme Court has, for example...approved state provision of textbooks for use in sectarian schools...but has disapproved provision of other instructional materials and equipment.... It has sustained state exemption of churches and places of worship from property taxes...but has, in certain other circumstances, stricken down state income tax remission for tuition payment to sectarian schools."

Foreshadowing his later jurisprudence, Scalia in his testimony took special aim at *Lemon v. Kurtzman* (1971). Authored by Chief Justice Burger—and joined by his fellow Nixon appointee, Justice Blackmun—*Lemon* struck down two state laws that had provided government funding to parochial schools, including for teacher salaries, finding the measures violated the Establishment Clause. For future statutes to survive judicial review, *Lemon* established a three-pronged test. The law must have a secular purpose; its principal or primary effect must neither promote nor inhibit religion; and it must not foster "excessive government entanglement" with religion. "These tests," Scalia testified, were "less tools of analysis than convenient bases for rationalizing results reached in some other fashion—convenient because they may be applied strictly or liberally, rigidly adhered to or virtually ignored, in order to support the outcome."

Democrat Daniel Patrick Moynihan of New York, liberal polymath and former U.N. ambassador, a co-sponsor of the legislation providing the tax credits, agreed—but still drew the witness's rebuke.

> **MOYNIHAN:** Yesterday, Professor Scalia, we heard testimony in which was solemnly proposed to us a kind of doctrine of constitutional fatalism. We were advised that having taken an oath to support the Constitution of the United States, we dare not propose any legislation which the Supreme Court may hold unconstitutional.... Professor Scalia has almost suggested that you won't find your answers in law....
>
> **SCALIA:** Let me make it clear what I have said and what I haven't said.

Moynihan backed off:

MOYNIHAN: Don't let me tell you what you have said.
SCALIA: I am not saying the Congress should never look to an established body of Supreme Court opinions which sets forth a consistent constitutional philosophy and a clear line of precedent. What I am suggesting is that the confused series of cases dealing with church-state is an embarrassment. It makes no sense. The principles enunciated are not indeed followed by the decisions.... The thing is evolving and changing as we go along.[25]

Scalia's legal philosophy—*originalism, as practiced through textualism*—was taking shape. The meaning of a law, and accordingly its interpretation by judges, should not *evolve and change* over time; rather, the interpretation should adhere to what the law meant, *what it was widely understood to mean*, at the time it was enacted. And this was best discerned from the law's text, not its legislative history. What Congress voted on, what the president signed, were laws with specific texts—not floor speeches or committee reports. The text *was* the intent.

*　　*　　*

When Walter Olson arrived at AEI headquarters in Dupont Circle for an interview with Scalia, hoping to land the job of associate editor of *Regulation*, the twenty-six-year-old Yalie, bespectacled and slight of build, stood even chances. He had Anne Brunsdale's recommendation; but she feared he was too timid for Scalia. "He sized me up as pretty wimpy," Olson recalled.

Scalia wanted someone unafraid of challenging the contributors: lawyers and economics professors, regarded by *Regulation* staff as "some of the most arrogant people in the world." Olson launched into a critique of Scalia's most recent article. This Scalia "loved, loved, loved," electing to "drop the job interview in order to argue about ideas" for the rest of their session. "I battled for my barely-out-of-college libertarian views, which he countered in a pleasant enough fashion but clearly saw as naïve." When Olson left, Scalia said: "You win, Anne. As usual, you're right."

Until Bryan Garner co-authored two books with Scalia, in 2008 and 2011, Brunsdale and Olson were the editors who worked most intimately with Scalia as a writer. They read his drafts, incorporated his edits, talked craft at length. "It was an immense privilege," Olson said, "to have our relationship be one about words and language.... He loved nothing better than to stop what everyone was doing in order to make sure that we all worked through a style point...the rhythm of a sentence, obscure usage of an idiom.... He loved the fact that Anne and I were just as drawn to those issues as he was.... He wouldn't just write in his preferred correction on the thing; he would bring it up so that we could talk about it because he so enjoyed talking about style points."

Always, Scalia was theatrical. "He was so expressive," Olson recalled, "the way he would hold himself and turn and cock his head.... You always wanted to be watching him because that was part of the story of his communication.... He had a wonderfully expressive face, wonderfully expressive gestures and manners.... It was as if he was onstage."

Central to Scalia's persona in those years was his smoking. "That pipe was such a prop!" Olson chortled. "He had all these gestures that he would do with the pipe.... After he'd made a point, he'd take a puff in order to signify that he was pleased with how he had phrased that. I mean, he used that pipe just as it might be used on a stage."[26]

*   *   *

Nino's energy was unlimited: grading papers, knocking out an article for *Regulation*, testifying before Congress, enlivening a TV debate, chairing a section of the American Bar Association, mentoring a student, catching a flight.... In all these endeavors, Scalia maintained the highest caliber of intellectual and personal conduct, flashing his trademark wit and conveying, to ally and foe alike, that he never took himself too seriously. Only Maureen—keeper of their lives, children, house—exhibited deeper reserves of energy.

Twice Scalia appeared on a TV show called *The Advocates*. Recorded before a live studio audience, the PBS production featured two opposing policy advocates who, under the direction of a well-known moderator, examined expert witnesses. "Mr. Scalia, the floor is yours," announced Marilyn Berger, previously of NBC News, the moderator for Scalia's debut, in May 1978. The subject, again, was tuition tax credits.

"Thank you," Scalia said as he rose, his face a courtly grimace. He wore a dark three-piece suit, red-and-blue striped tie, and ill-fitting Oxford-blue button-down. He presented earnestly, glancing at index cards, sweating under the studio lights, the Jersey-Queens accent escaping only intermittently. Scalia called as witnesses Republican Senator S. I. Hayakawa of California, the former university president who had famously confronted radical students in the 1960s; and Walter Williams, an African-American economist from Temple University.

As direct examiner, a role he would never reprise after his turns on *The Advocates*, Scalia brought his theatricality to bear: rising from his table, Perry Mason style, strolling around it, looking down, cupping his chin, resting on one leg at table's edge, hands clasped. He employed leading questions ("Senator, why is it that you believe that there is a need for some assistance, particularly at the college level?") and more circumlocutory approaches, including feigned adoption of the opposition argument for the purpose of dispelling it ("Wouldn't the proposal, Mr. Williams, further the segregation of our schools?"). Scalia was unafraid to grapple with race.

> **SCALIA:** Mr. Williams, if you were to select, out of all the available devices, some device that would assure as much as possible racial and socioeconomic homogeneity in a school, could you think of anything any better than a mandatory neighborhood school?
> **WILLIAMS:** I couldn't think of anything better.... If one looks at SAT scores and the performance, particularly, of minority children, one would think that either blacks are genetically inferior or that the Ku Klux Klan was the superintendent of schools. [laughter, applause]

Challenge came from Albert Shanker, the shaggy-haired math teacher whose combative leadership of the American Federation of Teachers had made him an unlikely celebrity. While he spoke, Scalia paced like a tiger.

> **SHANKER:** We have the most powerful nation in the world, one of the richest, a nation that's enjoyed liberty and freedom longer than any other in the history of mankind. And I think we owe a lot of that to our public schools.... This proposal could completely destroy that public school system.
> **SCALIA:**...It's the same argument that used to be made in the early days of this Republic...by those people who favored an established church. They used to say, "Look, we don't require you to belong to the Church of England; we have

freedom of religion in this state. But we have a state church
here. You're welcome to come to it for free; if you don't want
it, go to another one, but [slaps his own chest] don't expect
us to pay for the other one." Why is it different for the
schools?

SHANKER: Well, you're turning the whole argument on its
head.... In one case, the taxpayers in the country would be
establishing a church. And in the other case—

SCALIA: They would be establishing a school!

SHANKER: Yes, we are establishing a public institution to
serve the purposes that the people and their elected representatives decide on. Not to teach in a foreign language, to teach
in ours.

Left unexamined was Shanker's likening of faith to a *foreign* pursuit, conducted in some language other than *ours*.[27]

*   *   *

The most important AEI debate in which Scalia participated was
videotaped in Washington in December 1978. For "An Imperial
Judiciary: Fact or Myth?" Scalia found himself seated at the far end of
a crowded news anchor desk, a crude AEI sign dangling overhead. He
sported a pale grey three-piece suit with patterned blue shirt and red
paisley tie; it was as if someone, likely Maureen, had told him that if
he was going to be on TV all the time, he needed to jazz up his ward-
robe. At Scalia's elbow, like in old times, sat Larry Silberman; at the
center was moderator John Charles Daly, a former ABC News executive
(and son-in-law of Earl Warren); and then the panel's liberals: Ira
Glasser, executive director of the American Civil Liberties Union
(ACLU) and Professor Abram Chayes of Harvard Law.

Silberman delivered the opening argument: an imperial judiciary indeed existed, with judges "seeking successfully power at the expense of the other two branches and, to an extent, at the expense of society as a whole."

Arguing in opposition was Glasser. Thin and bald, long brown hair drooping over his collar, long nose separating his droopy brown eyeglasses from his droopy brown mustache, Glasser resembled Mr. Potato Head and spoke with a New Yawk accent: the embodiment of the egg-headed liberal, brilliant and articulate, seen all the time on PBS in the 1970s. He made, for Scalia, a formidable opponent.

Without judges' imposing mandates and timetables on administrative entities, Glasser argued, all kinds of corrupt institutions—prisons, mental hospitals, foster homes—would claim more innocent victims. Scalia's counter-argument brought his first public comments on abortion.

> GLASSER: What you are confronted with is a right without a remedy, and the court is then involved, and the lawyers on both sides are involved, in a kind of ongoing external administration of those agencies. Now, I can see that that's a real problem. But to simply say that the courts shouldn't be involved in that is to cede all of that to the legislatures, and to simply assume...that there *will* be rights, there *won't* be remedies. And therefore, I think, in the end, there won't be rights.
>
> SCALIA: Well, what the argument is about in most of these cases—*most* of these cases—is not whether there's a right or not, but whether in fact the right has been adequately observed.... You can speak very facilely of rights. *Where are there rights and where are there not?* That is another judgment that the courts have been increasingly willing to arrogate to themselves. In the abortion situation, for example,

whether, indeed, the right that exists is the right of the woman who wants an abortion to have one, or the right of the unborn child not to be aborted—who knows? In the past that was considered to be a societal decision which would be made through the democratic process. But now the courts have shown themselves willing to make that decision for us. That's, I think, the major objection that most people have with the direction in which the courts are now going, and the major reason why many people believe it is indeed an imperial judiciary.

In his assault on judicial overreach Scalia was establishing himself as a leading critic of the Warren and Burger Courts, a near-peer of Bob Bork. "I think they have gone too far," he told the AEI audience. "They have found rights where society never believed they existed."

"Let's not forget to blame the Executive Branch," Scalia added—a far cry from the caricature of him as abjectly devoted to the executive. "What the executive has been doing for many years is going up to the Hill and seeking broad statutes, because they were under the impression that 'The more vague the statute, the more discretion I have.' What they have found in recent years, however, is the courts are suddenly beginning to pretend that these absolutely meaningless phrases *have* meaning! And so instead of arrogating discretion to the executive, they find, to their horror, that the discretion is sucked right over into the courts!"

His sharpest thrusts were reserved for the Supreme Court. In retrospect, his remarks previewed how he would behave as *Justice* Scalia: his approach to constitutional and statutory construction, the limitations he intended, unlike the current justices, to observe.

"I draw the line at the point where the Court plucks out of the air a principle of action that is not now considered necessary by a majority of the people in the country, nor was ever considered necessary," he

said. "An example would be the Court's decision on capital punishment." This was a reference to *Furman v. Georgia* (1972), which had
held the death penalty unconstitutional. "There is simply no historical
justification for that, nor could the Court claim to be expressing a
consensus of modern society.... The same could be said about the abortion decision." This, of course, referred to *Roe v. Wade* (1973), which
had legalized abortion.

"It is very hard to tell you where the line between a proper and an
improper decision should be drawn. It would fall short of making fundamental, social determinations that ought to be made through the
democratic process, but that the society has not yet made."

Again, Glasser carried the opposition. He could not accept Scalia's
prescription that society should decide life-and-death issues in legislatures, without judicial intervention; the ACLU executive conjured the
specter of majoritarian tyranny. He returned the panel to race.

> **GLASSER:** I think the problem with continuing to refer to
> what the consensus of society is, Nino, is that the Court is
> charged with making decisions precisely on behalf of minori-
> ties and against the consensus.... If you had left it to the
> consensus in 1954, the Court would have been disabled from
> ruling in the school desegregation case [*Brown v. Board of
> Education* (1954)].
> **SCALIA:**...I do not believe that is true. Most of the country
> did *not* consider separate black schools proper in 1954. In
> any event, the results of that decision have been very good.

When Silberman cited forced busing as another example of judicial
imperium, Glasser resorted to semantics—and Scalia was ready to
pounce. The students, Glasser said, "do not object to being on a bus;
they object to where the bus is going."

Scalia cut him off, hands raised in mock captivity. "We could say the same thing about a person who is kidnapped.... 'I don't mind being in the car, I just care about where the car is going!'"

Riotous laughter, followed by applause.

"You can say that," Glasser replied. "I can't say that."[28]

*   *   *

For all Nino's frenetic activity—his winning performances on lecture and debate stages, the frequency and brilliance of his published works, the notice he was drawing from colleagues, editors, TV and radio producers—Chicago remained, on balance, an unhappy place for Maureen. That this was so is clear from Nino's repeated efforts to leave.

When Justice Scalia lectured at Washington and Lee University Law School in 2005, he told the audience he had interviewed for the deanship there while he was still teaching at Chicago; indeed, he had spent two days visiting the Washington and Lee campus, in Lexington, Virginia, in November 1981, and had returned with Maureen for another two days the following February. "I don't know how it would have turned out," he joked.

Nino wasn't so desperate to leave that he would accept *any* position at *any* other school. According to one account, between 1972 and 1982, including their time in Chicago, Scalia turned down deanship offers from five law schools—UVA and Georgetown, two of his former academic homes, among them—as well as an executive position at the University of Montana.[29]

In another of Scalia's attempts at bolting Chicago, previously unreported, he sought a return to lucrative private practice—with assistance from his *consigliere*. "I've never told this to anyone else," Judge Silberman said to me in chambers at the D.C. Circuit in Washington in 2017. He disclosed that Scalia had telephoned him in

1979 to ask if Nino could join Morrison & Foerster, the San Francisco–based law firm where Silberman, a senior partner, represented the nation's eighth-largest bank and other powerful clients. Larry was eager to bring his best friend aboard. As a former deputy attorney general, his stature at Morrison unrivaled, he thought the task would be easy; instead, he found himself "rather frustrated" when the firm rejected Scalia. The partners recognized him as "a first-class intellectual," but asked Silberman, "What clients would he be able to bring?"[30]

A third attempt succeeded, at least temporarily. In mid-1980, Scalia accepted a visiting professorship at Stanford Law School. "They moved the family from Chicago to Palo Alto for just a year," Gene Scalia recalled. "Pretty big hassle, but [Mom] enjoyed that year."

So did Scalia, according to Gene, who recounted the occasion when, not long after this, he had asked his dad where he should attend law school. "Stanford," the elder Scalia said. "The sun is shining year 'round. I biked to and from the law school every day. I lost thirty, forty pounds—best shape of my life. The kids are out there throwing the frisbee, just hanging out, loving life. It's just a beautiful place to be."

Then he wavered. "Chicago, there is just this intensity about it.... The environment is crackling with ideas. People are constantly talking, debating, just loving their studies, their scholarship."

"It sounds like I should go to Chicago."

"No, I'd go to Stanford."

Gene chose Chicago.[31]

The exchange reflected the happiness the Scalias found in northern California. Maureen, grateful to have escaped Chicago, was pregnant with the Scalias' ninth child; their Palo Alto rental home had a swimming pool.

From one of Scalia's former students at Stanford, however, a different account emerged, echoing the whispers in Chicago: of Nino as an outsider, a winning personality nonetheless marginalized. "Professor

Scalia cut an odd figure at Stanford," wrote John Schapiro, a finance lawyer, after the justice's death. "In an atmosphere of perpetual sunshine and informality, he wore a dark suit, white shirt, and tie every day, and walked slightly hunched forward, with his head down, as though a stiff wind off of Lake Michigan and a bit of a snow squall accompanied him wherever he went."

Schapiro's account, the only detailed portrait of Scalia at Stanford ever published, is worth quoting at length:

> Today, it is universally accepted that he was a brilliant scholar, but the elite law school faculties of the late '70s did not see him that way. To left-wing faculty—a majority at most law schools, although not Chicago and not really Stanford—he was simply anathema, a right-wing hatchet man....
>
> He was out of step with conservative legal scholars as well. The most exciting group of right-wing scholars then was engaged with bringing the rigor of economic analysis back into law.... Their crusade had nothing to do with originalism or social conservatism.... Scalia did not fit well with either group of conservatives.... What the rest of them all had in common was that you had to be as smart as they were to do what they did. It was a game only the elite could play. That wasn't Scalia's approach at all. His focus on original intent and clear statutory language was easily comprehensible by anyone, which made his academic work seem lowbrow to his peers....
>
> Finally, he was deeply religious, and Catholic, in a movement where neither was common at the time.
>
> Without warm relations with fellow faculty, Scalia came most alive with students. He just loved talking, and arguing, about law. He loved to bait left-leaning students into

challenging him, and then to show them how their own principles should lead them to conservative results. His conservatism was thoroughly democratic and blue-collar. He did not waste breath defending wealthy businesses or the Establishment. He, like the liberal students, sought social justice for all, but he believed that was most easily achieved through conservative values, clear rules, and limited government discretion.

He was exactly as everyone now knows him to have been: funny and sharp, funny and a little mean.... The door to his office was always open, and he was always in it, and he was always ready to argue about law.

Scalia might not have disputed this account. He spoke of "the Christian as cretin," the sense of *apartness* felt acutely by devout Catholics; and he told Biskupic that conservative professors back then were invariably made to feel "isolated, lonely...like a weirdo."[32]

*   *   *

In Palo Alto, Scalia took a phone call from a first-year law student back in Chicago, a native New Yorker named Lee Liberman.[33] She and another student, David McIntosh, a friend from undergraduate days at Yale, were forming a group of conservative law students on the Chicago campus. Another Yale friend, Steven Calabresi, now at Yale Law, was doing the same in New Haven. At Harvard, their ally was Spencer Abraham, founder of the conservative *Journal of Law and Public Policy* (later secretary of energy in the Bush-Cheney administration and U.S. senator from Michigan). The group's modest aim was to establish a few more campus chapters. For their name they chose The Federalist

Society, patterned after *The Federalist* papers; for their logo, a silhouette of James Madison.

Liberman asked Scalia if he would serve as faculty adviser for the Chicago chapter.

> **ROSEN:** Why did you choose him?
> **LIBERMAN:** We actually had a lot of choices at Chicago.... But he seemed to have a good combination of being involved in sort of the world of ideas, but also some sense of how those ideas play out in practice in the real world, and therefore somebody who would be particularly good for this purpose.

Scalia accepted. Immediately—*ask for a spark, get the Chicago fire*—he was making suggestions, placing calls. "He was delighted that there were people interested in some competing ideas to the pervasive liberal orthodoxy," Liberman told me.

Scalia's early contributions were profound. He connected the Yale and Chicago chapters with his new friends in Palo Alto, helped the Society secure office space, and steered its leaders to a $20,000 grant (about $63,000 today) from a foundation run by Ford-era colleagues and AEI. As the group planned its first symposium, at Yale in April 1982, Scalia agreed to speak and lined up other speakers. The Scalias even hosted out-of-town FedSoc members. A historian of the movement identified Scalia as "the most important elite sponsor of the Society in its early years." "His involvement at the beginning was quite significant," Liberman said, "and his staying involved was also significant."

It wasn't just Scalia's energy and organizational muscle that helped propel the Society; it was his ideas. Leonard Leo, who joined the Federalist Society in 1991 and helped build it into the powerhouse it is today, recalled that originalism and "the structural Constitution"—separation of powers, federalism—were emerging as the chief preoccupations of the burgeoning conservative legal movement. "He was leading those charges," Leo told me.[34]

Another important early supporter was the founding faculty advisor at Yale: Robert Bork. Calabresi—who later clerked for Bork and Scalia on the Court of Appeals—said Bork "did more than anyone else...to help create, nourish, and legitimize the Federalist Society." At its first event, in New Haven, attended by 200 students from across the country, Scalia had a slot on the speakers' roster—but the keynoter was Bork.

Judge Bork's speech made headlines: a blistering attack on the intellectual incoherence, and susceptibility to public criticism, of the Supreme Court. "The Court responds to the press and law school faculties," Bork said, in remarks the Associated Press described as "unusual" for a federal judge. "The personnel of the media are heavily left-liberal.... Law school faculties tend to have the same politics.... When the Court nationalizes morality, it strikes at federalism in a central way."[35]

The response was overwhelming. Students at unaffiliated schools deluged the "FedSoc" founders with inquiries about new chapters. The group's membership ranks, geographic footprint, annual budget, and professional influence swelled over the next decade and "never stopped growing," as Bruce Allen Murphy acknowledged. Within a year of the inaugural event, the group boasted 17 chapters; by 2000, it had 25,000 members, with chapters for practicing lawyers in 60 cities and student chapters on 140 campuses. The founders took top-level jobs in the Reagan-era Justice Department and as clerks to federal judges.

Today the Federalist Society is undeniably the nation's premier institution for conservatives in the law, with 70,000 members, chapters at every accredited law school in America (and in numerous foreign countries), four alumni on the Court, and thousands more seated on state and federal courts. Tax filings for 2019 showed revenues exceeding

$23 million. Many federal judges appointed by George H. W. Bush and George W. Bush were members or approved by the Society. That influence extended beyond Scalia's death: President Trump appointed more than 200 federal judges, a record, consisting almost entirely of Federalist Society members and alumni.

"We thought we were just planting a wildflower among the weeds of academic liberalism," Justice Scalia said on the group's twenty-fifth anniversary. "It turned out to be an oak."[36]

CHAPTER XI

Bitterly Disappointed

The waiting is the hardest part.
—*Tom Petty, 1981*

Nino put out his cigarette and clambered aboard the small stage with the anchor desk. AEI's new backdrop was a pale-blue screen, lending the proceedings a futuristic vibe. The debate, convened in May 1979, again moderated by John Charles Daly, was entitled "A Constitutional Convention: How Well Would It Work?" Besides Nino, the eminent thinkers on-set included Walter Berns, an AEI scholar who had taught at Yale; Gerald Gunther, a Stanford Law professor who had clerked for Chief Justice Warren; and Paul Bator of Harvard Law. Nino was heavier and had returned to conservative attire: a gray three-piece suit, Oxford blue shirt, and red, white, and, blue–striped tie.

The idea of a constitutional convention was in the air. Thirty states had petitioned for an amendment requiring the federal government to maintain a balanced budget. Turning to Scalia, Daly quoted from Richard Rovere, who had argued in the *New Yorker* that a constitutional convention unlimited in scope could produce radical outcomes:

abolition of the Bill of Rights, elimination of the Supreme Court, reinstitution of slavery.

Throughout the apocalyptic litany, Scalia signaled his impatience with an arched back, raised eyebrows, folded hands, and a slight smile. Daly asked what would come from a convention unlimited in scope.

"I suppose it might pass a bill of attainder to hang Richard Rovere," Scalia snapped, "just as it's possible that the Congress tomorrow might pass a law abolishing Social Security as of the next day, or eliminating Christmas." There was, Scalia conceded, "an iota of truth to Richard Rovere's absurdities": the infinitesimal risk of the convention's being hijacked. The alternative, Scalia argued, was the *status quo*, which "provides no means of obtaining a constitutional amendment except through the kindness of the Congress, which...likes the power...[and] does not want to have amending power anywhere else."

In June 1978 California voters had approved Proposition 13, amending the state constitution to require a balanced state budget. Scalia heard "a great cheer about the country.... It was a sort of amazement that, by golly, the people—when they really want something badly enough—can really get it.... Now what we need is some means at the federal level like Proposition 13. The Constitution has provided it. I suggest that if the only way to clarify the law, if the only way to remove us from utter bondage to the Congress, is to take what I think to be a minimal risk on this limited convention, then let's take it."

Berns argued the Supreme Court should exercise judicial review over the convention's amendments. "Put me down for objecting to the Court getting into it," Scalia cut in. He combined his old Xavier theatricality with a vision of America's future that bordered on fatalistic. "Somehow the federal legislature has gotten out of our control and there is nothing we can do about it," he said. "One can say the same thing about the federal judiciary.... I'm not sure how much longer we have. I am not sure how long a people can accommodate itself to directives from a legislature that it feels is no longer responsive, and to directives from a life-tenured judiciary that was never meant to be responsive, without ultimately losing its sense of control of its own destiny."

The Supreme Court was soon to issue a landmark affirmative action ruling. Sarcastically, Scalia clasped his hands and looked up to the heavens. "We are all sitting, breathless, waiting for the Supreme Court to tell us what our fundamental beliefs are with respect to this particular issue.... We have no recourse. There's not a whit of a chance that the Congress will overturn any decision that the Supreme Court comes down with.... Unless this alternative method of amending the Constitution is adopted, we will continue [taps desk] to live under that kind of—what I consider an inanely nondemocratic system."

This was Scalia's fullest exploration of the *malaise* of the Carter years. "There is a widespread, deep feeling of powerlessness in the country," he said.

> The people do not feel that their wishes are observed. They're heard but they're not observed, particularly at the federal level.... The basic problem is simply that the Congress has become professionalized. It has an interest, much higher than ever existed before, in remaining in office. It has a bureaucracy that is serving it. It is much more subject to the power of individualized pressure groups as opposed to the unorganized feelings of the majority of the citizens. All of these reasons have created this feeling—which is real and which I think has a proper basis—of powerlessness.[1]

To watch Scalia's old televised debates, five decades removed, is to behold—*immediately, unmistakably*—a figure fundamentally different from his co-panelists on the clunky-*futura* anchor desk. He is quicker, livelier, readier for primetime, at once more casual and more intense, his range of gesture and expression wider, a more seasoned performer, more committed to the competitiveness of debate, to showmanship.

"He disdained the hedges, doubts, and qualifications that are the common fare of academic debates," a Chicago colleague observed. The other panelists were... ordinary academics. To them these occasions were... educational *fora*... restrained affairs with room, maybe, for a professorial quip or two. The kid from Queens was there to *win*: he argued ferociously, raising and lowering his voice, eyes wide here, brow furrowed there, pointing, waving, joshing, taunting, outsmarting, outpointing.

Audiences loved it. They appreciated Nino's abandonment of academic affect, his ingenious on-the-fly reduction of complex issues to layman's language, his biting humor. When the attendees laughed or applauded, invariably it was for Scalia.[2]

*　　*　　*

In Ronald Reagan's march to the 1980 Republican nomination, Larry Silberman played a major backstage role. The former deputy attorney general and ambassador co-chaired Reagan's foreign policy and judicial-selection committees, gave him briefings, and even made a secret trip to Central America, at Reagan's behest, to assess Nicaragua's Sandinistas.

Silberman also formed a group called Law Professors and Lawyers for Reagan. "Every law professor on that list subsequently became a judge," he later boasted. On it were Bork and Scalia.[3]

"Scalia came into my office to announce that it was time for conservatives like us to get off the sidelines and stand four-square behind Ronald Reagan," recalled Chicago colleague Richard Epstein. It was clear, Epstein wrote, that Scalia saw academia "only as a way station...to a political appointment or judicial nomination."[4]

Three weeks after the birth of the Scalias' ninth child, Margaret Jane, and a week ahead of the election, Nino's name appeared in a full-page advertisement in newspapers across the country. Forty-four "leading members of the Bar," also including Bork, Buchen, and Silberman, but not Epstein, affirmed, "Ronald Reagan Will Take Partisan Politics Out of Judicial Selection."

On November 4, Reagan trounced Carter in a historic landslide.

For the American right, it was a singularly exciting time. Chastened after the Goldwater debacle of 1964, its torch kept lit through the dark years of Vietnam, *détente*, and Watergate by the likes of Reagan, Buckley, Kirkpatrick, Milton Friedman, and Thomas Sowell, *movement conservatism* had triumphed at last. At AEI hopes ran high that the new president would lead a counter-revolution of judicial restraint and free market principles, taming the regulatory leviathan, runaway Congress, and imperial judiciary.

Scalia knew it wasn't that simple. "Even if the philosophical makeup changes relatively soon," he wrote shortly after the election, "there will still be a large amount of agency business from the last administration—pending rulemakings and prosecutory actions—that is already in the pipeline and cannot realistically be turned off. There is, moreover, an absolute limit to the degree of restraint that can be imposed upon a mission-oriented career bureaucracy without utterly destroying morale and effectiveness."[5]

Six days after the election, the Reagan transition team announced the findings of its regulation task force. Murray Weidenbaum, Scalia's co-editor at *Regulation*, was chair; members included Bork and Scalia. The group recommended a year-long moratorium on new regulations and reorientation of rulemaking to accord greater weight to net economic impact: *law-and-economics*. The following month AEI and *Regulation*—now in the live-event space—sponsored a panel on the subject. Identified as a Stanford Law professor, Scalia counseled his conservative colleagues to look beyond staffing. "Replacing their bureaucracy with ours does not solve the underlying difficulty," he warned. "The point is that no bureaucracy should be making basic social judgments."[6]

*   *   *

"In the past four years," Scalia wrote in December 1980, "the Federal Trade Commission (FTC) has vied with the Occupational Safety and Health Administration (OSHA) for the title of Most Unpopular Agency."

To engage the lay reader on a topic as dry as administrative law, Scalia invoked school-age popularity contests, a doleful memory worthy of Charles Schulz, and employed Ironic Capitalization, a stylistic innovation of the New Journalism. Such deft literary touches reflected Scalia's openness, in oral and written argument, language and logic, to forms of expression, whole modes of persuasion, never before employed by legal scholars. "Fancy that!" he exclaimed in a law review article.

Scalia's insistence on popular understanding was his hallmark. In the Ford White House he had insisted drafts be "readily understandable by the public." Agency rules, he said, should be comprehensible to "a person of average intelligence and experience." His editorials for *Regulation*, a reader found, were "marked not only by a coherence that made their subject matter accessible to any layman but also by a sharp sense of humor that was all the more welcome for being completely unexpected." The FBI reported that he had the "ability that all attorneys strive to achieve...[to] present complex problems in a simple sort of way." A colleague said, "He has the ability to write about the law and make it accessible to individuals not in the legal field."

This egalitarianism was on display in Scalia's earliest writing, for which he invariably chose jolting or amusing titles. A 1971 article in *Virginia Law Review* was entitled "Appellate Justice: A Crisis in Virginia?" Another early title was: "Asymmetry Is an Unbalanced View." His 1972 speech to the Federal Communications Bar Association invoked the nursery rhyme "Don't Go Near the Water." "For those of you who did not have the same childhood as I," Scalia quipped, "the rhyme goes as follows:

> Mother may I go out to swim?
> Yes, my darling daughter.
> Hang your clothes on the hickory limb,
> But don't go near the water.

"Little did I suspect when I first heard those lines that they were an allegory of Melvillian proportions," Scalia continued, "intended to describe the mandate of the Congress to the Federal Communications Commission under the Communications Act of 1934."[7]

Nursery rhymes!

Melvillian proportions!

The Bar had never seen anything like it.

*　　*　　*

Scalia's wit imbued his legal writing and speeches with a dose of Everyman realism, reminders of shared humanity. This consideration distinguished him from other scholars, endeared him to audiences.

"Guadalajara! A Case Study in Regulation by Munificence" was followed by "The Legislative Veto: A False Remedy for System

Overload." His ABA "Chairman's Message" was titled, "Support Your Local Professor of Administrative Law." "The Freedom of Information Act Has No Clothes," blared the cover of *Regulation*. FOIA, he wrote, was "the Taj Mahal of the Doctrine of Unanticipated Consequences, the Sistine Chapel of Cost-Benefit Analysis Ignored."

Moderating a panel in 1980, Scalia introduced Morton Halperin, the former National Security Council official, by joking that Halperin was proud he never received a law degree; then Scalia introduced his pal Mike Uhlmann: "Unlike Mr. Halperin, he made the mistake of going to law school." A month later, at a Notre Dame conference, Scalia titled a paper about tuition tax credits: "On Making It Look Easy by Doing It Wrong: A Critical View of the Justice Department." In mock-Biblical language, he assailed the incoherence of the Court's recent rulings on church and state.

> Thou mayest provide bus transportation to and from school for parochial school students; but thou shalt not provide bus transportation to and from field trips.... Thou mayest exempt from real estate taxes premises devoted exclusively to worship of the Almighty; but thou shalt not... permit parents an income tax remission for tuition.... I envision these commandments not as engraved upon tablets of stone but as scribbled on one of those funny pads that children use, with a plastic sheet on top that can be pulled up to erase everything and start anew.[8]

Two of Scalia's law review works endured. "Vermont Yankee: The APA, the D.C. Circuit, and the Supreme Court" (1978) addressed the Court's recent decision in *Vermont Yankee Nuclear Power Corporation v. Natural Resources Defense Council, Inc.* Authored by Justice Rehnquist, the 7–0 ruling rebuked the D.C. Circuit, one rung below the Supreme Court, for having "improperly intruded into the agency's decision-making process."

Back in 1971, in full compliance with Administrative Procedure Act, the Atomic Energy Commission (AEC) had granted a private company, Vermont Yankee, a license to operate a nuclear power plant. Stacked with liberal activist judges in the 1960s and '70s, the D.C. Circuit, responding to litigation brought by environmental groups, had ordered AEC to apply to Vermont Yankee's license application—*retroactively*—environmental-impact standards *not yet enacted* when the agency had issued the license. The appellate court, Rehnquist thundered, had "seriously misread or misapplied [relevant] statutory and decisional law cautioning reviewing courts against engrafting their own notions of proper procedures upon agencies entrusted with substantive functions by Congress."

In the age of the imperial judiciary, Scalia was astonished but happy to see Rehnquist, however belatedly, leading the Court in "abjuring judicial responsibility for the development of federal administrative procedure." Still, one ruling was not enough to prove the Court's commitment. "Whether the abjuration is real...and whether realistically it can be followed," Scalia wrote, "are issues of major importance in administrative law."

> The case brings into question the ability of the Supreme Court to establish coherent principles of law in an area which has been largely the province of the D.C. Circuit. More precisely, it brings into question the willingness of the D.C. Circuit to be guided by the Supreme Court. Finally, the case suggests both the need for a major revision of the Administrative Procedure Act and the impossibility of any successful revision so long as current assumptions about the purposes of such legislation are retained. That is to say, it

suggests the indissoluble link between procedure and power, which must determine where and how procedures are made.[9]

Scalia's other law review triumph was bannered, uniquely, as "COMMENTARY" in *Washington University Law Quarterly*. The title was also unique: "The Disease as Cure: 'In Order to Get Beyond Racism, We Must First Take Account of Race'" (1979). The use of a *quotation* as the subtitle reflected the author's stylistic irreverence and, too, his disdain for the quote, taken from a recent affirmative action opinion by liberal Justice Harry Blackmun. It was an *in-your-face* move by the kid from Queens.

"Every panel needs an anti-hero and I fill that role on this one," Scalia began; once again, he displayed no fear of tackling race on the national stage. "I have grave doubts about the wisdom of where we are going in affirmative action, and in equal protection generally. I frankly find this area an embarrassment to teach."

Challenging the morality of affirmative action back then required immense courage. It risked the censure of *l'académie* and the ineradicable label, in mass media, of *racist*. But Scalia—devout Catholic, loving husband and father, top-ranked scholar, Latin speaker, indefatigable worker, eminent lawyer, well-regarded neighbor, holder of high office, practitioner of the most principled standards of human conduct, kid from Queens, embodiment of the American Dream—feared the condemnation of no man. He simply reckoned, from a moral and legal foundation that included the immigrant perspective, that affirmative action—*the state-sanctioned use of racial quotas in admissions, hiring, and contracting*—was reverse racism: a violation of law, by the imperial judiciary, in the name of law.

"Here, as in some other fields of constitutional law," he wrote, "it is increasingly difficult to pretend to one's students that the decisions of the Supreme Court are tied together by threads of logic and analysis—as opposed to what seems to be the fact that the decisions of each of the justices on the Court are tied together by threads of social preference and predisposition. Frankly, I don't have it in me to play the game of distinguishing and reconciling the cases in this utterly confused field."

Central to the confusion was the Court's byzantine ruling in *Regents of the University of California v. Bakke* (1978). Twice in two years, Allan Bakke, a white man from California, had applied to, and been rejected from, the UC Medical School at Davis. He sued after learning that the school devoted 16 percent of its slots to minorities, and that his grades and test scores had exceeded those of all minority students admitted in the two-year span. Claiming discrimination on the basis of his race, Bakke argued the university had violated the Equal Protection Clause of the Fourteenth Amendment and the 1964 Civil Rights Act.

The Burger Court fractured badly: four justices upheld the constitutionality of racial quotas in higher-education admissions; four found the practice unlawful; and one, Justice Powell, in a lone opinion, selected from the buffet before him. Powell held that governmental racial distinctions of any sort are "inherently suspect" and should only be employed after "the most exacting judicial examination" identifies a "compelling" state interest in them. "We later learn," Scalia said, "that the 'compelling' interest at issue in *Bakke* is the enormously important goal of assuring that in medical school...we will expose these impressionable youngsters to a great diversity of people." *Impressionable youngsters—the sarcasm!*

Diversity, in *Bakke*, meant racial quotas. "I suspect that Justice Powell's delightful compromise was drafted precisely to achieve these results," Scalia scoffed, "just as, it has been charged, the Harvard College diversity admissions program, which Mr. Justice Powell's opinion so generously praises, was designed to reduce as inconspicuously as possible the disproportionate number of New York Jewish students that a merit admissions system had produced."

Tough stuff! No one made the moral case against affirmative action in that time more forcefully or fearlessly. But Scalia was only warming up. He had special words for Justice Byron White and John Minor Wisdom, a Fifth Circuit judge who had issued landmark desegregation decisions in the 1960s and was now ruling in favor of affirmative action. In rebuttal, Scalia invoked his own family's story—the immigrant experience, the American Dream—to expose the fallacies of the affirmative-action mindset, exemplified, he wrote, "when John Minor Wisdom talks of the evils that 'we' whites have done to blacks and that 'we' must now make restoration for."

> My father came to this country when he was a teenager. Not only had he never profited from the sweat of any black man's brow, I don't think he had ever seen a black man. There are, of course, many white ethnic groups that came to this country in great numbers relatively late in its history— Italians, Jews, Irish, Poles—who not only took no part in, and derived no profit from, the major historic suppression of the currently acknowledged minority groups, but were, in fact, themselves the object of discrimination.... If I can recall in my lifetime the obnoxious "White Trade Only" signs in shops in Washington, D.C., others can recall "Irish Need Not Apply" signs in Boston, three or four decades earlier.... Some or all of these groups have been the benefi- ciaries of discrimination against blacks, or have themselves practiced discrimination. But to compare their racial debt—I must use that term, since the concept of "restorative justice" implies it; there is no creditor without a debtor—with that of those who plied the slave trade, and who maintained a

The Scalias in Italy, circa 1909. The boy at bottom right is Salvatore Eugene Scalia, the justice's father; at lower left is Salvatore's sister Carmela; Justice Scalia's grandparents Maria and Antonino, top row, center. *Courtesy of the Scalia family*

The justice's parents: Salvatore Eugene Scalia, also known as Sam, and Catherine Panaro Scalia. Sam had emigrated from Sommatino, Sicily; Catherine was born in Manhattan to Italian immigrants. They were married in August 1929. *Courtesy of the Scalia family*

Antonin Scalia, also known as Nino, photographed in 1937. He was born at Mercer Hospital in Trenton, New Jersey, on March 11, 1936. *Courtesy of the Scalia family*

Antonin Scalia with his Boy Scout troop, second row, sixth from left. *Courtesy of the Scalia family*

Sixth grade class photo, P.S. 13, Queens, New York, 1947, Scalia in the second row of desks, third from left. *Courtesy of the Scalia family*

Elementary school graduation photo, June 1949, Scalia third row from bottom, second from left, and in insert. *Courtesy of the Scalia family*

Leading the Xavier High School Regimental Band, 1953. Scalia played French horn only passably but became the band's commanding officer, unprecedentedly, as a lieutenant colonel. Robert Connor is in the second row, second from right. *Courtesy of Xavier High School*

Playing Macbeth at Xavier, 1953, opposite John Gallagher's Lady Macbeth. "Probably the most significant thing I've done," the justice said decades later. "You know how many lines there are in Macbeth?" *Courtesy of Xavier High School*

Second from right on the Xavier debate team, 1957, beside Jesuit Father Richard Hoar. *Courtesy of the Scalia family*

As Xavier's valedictorian, Scalia earned a 97.5 average and medals for general excellence, English, Latin, Greek, modern languages, religion, debating, and dramatics, a silver key for speech, and a gold medal for the Glee Club. *Courtesy of Xavier High School*

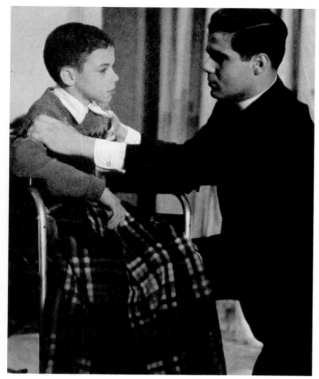

Scalia plays a priest, opposite actor Paul Fuqua, at Georgetown University, 1957. Scalia contemplated entering the priesthood but ultimately decided, "He wasn't calling me." *Courtesy of the Scalia family*

Harvard Law Review, 1960. Scalia is second row, third from left. Next to him, fourth from left, is Philip Heymann, a future Watergate prosecutor and deputy attorney general. In the same row, at far right, is Frank Michelman. *Courtesy of Harvard Law School (photograph by Murray Tarr Studios)*

On September 10, 1960, at Saint Pius X Church in South Yarmouth, Massachusetts, Scalia married Maureen Fitzgerald McCarthy, a Radcliffe student from Braintree. "Anyone who knows Mom," their daughter Catherine once said, "knows that she is as smart as, dare I say smarter than, Dad." *Courtesy of the Scalia family*

Left to right: bridesmaids Jane Waldman and Jane Otte, newlyweds Nino and Maureen, best man William Joyce, bridesmaid Janet Martin. *Courtesy of the Scalia family*

September 1962, when Nino was in private practice with Jones Day in Cleveland. A year earlier, the couple had celebrated the birth of their daughter Ann, the first of nine children. *Courtesy of the Scalia family*

Professor Scalia taught at the University of Virginia School of Law from 1967 to 1971. "Best teacher I ever had," a student recalled. "Bigger than life.... I've never had a teacher who was that exciting or challenging." *Courtesy of the Scalia family*

Clay T. Whitehead, known as "Tom," director of the White House Office of Telecommunications Policy in the Nixon administration, hired Scalia as general counsel. *Courtesy of Margaret Whitehead*

"We knew in 1971," said OTP colleague Brian Lamb, "that this man would end up on the Supreme Court." *Courtesy of the Scalia family*

Justice Department leadership, 1974. Attorney General Saxbe sits at center, Scalia standing behind him. Laurence Silberman is seated second from left, Robert Bork at far right. Carla Hills stands third from left, Jim Wilderotter, fifth. *National Archives and Records Administration*

Assistant Attorney General Scalia, at far right, participates in a meeting with President Ford and his advisors on school desegregation in the White House Cabinet Room, June 2, 1976. *Courtesy of the Gerald R. Ford Presidential Library and Museum*

Starting with teen programs in the 1950s, Scalia appeared frequently on television, including in this American Enterprise Institute debate, July 29, 1975. *Courtesy of the American Enterprise Institute*

Debating the imperial judiciary at another American Enterprise Institute event, December 12, 1978. *Courtesy of the American Enterprise Institute*

In a May 1978 episode of the PBS program *The Advocates*, Scalia conducts direct examination of Republican Senator S. I. Hayakawa of California on tuition tax credits. *Courtesy of GBH Archives*

Seated alongside James C. Miller III on another American Enterprise Institute panel, 1980. Alternating between cigarettes, cigars, and pipes, Scalia never completely gave up tobacco. *Courtesy of the American Enterprise Institute*

Scalia taught at the University of Chicago Law School from 1977 to 1982. *Courtesy of the University of Chicago Law School*

Cathedral of St. Matthew the Apostle, Washington, D.C., October 30, 1982. From left, Judge Scalia, Judge Abner Mikva, George Will, Donna Pohl, newlyweds Mary Ellen Bork and Judge Robert Bork, Howard Crane, Keith Jones, Stuart Smith. *Courtesy of Mary Ellen Bork*

The United States Court of Appeals for the District of Columbia Circuit, circa 1984. Bottom row, from left: Malcolm Wilkey, J. Skelly Wright, Chief Judge Spottswood Robinson, Edward Tamm, and Patricia Wald. Top row, from left: Scalia, Ruth Bader Ginsburg, Abner Mikva, Harry Edwards, Robert Bork, and Kenneth Starr. *U.S. Court of Appeals for the D.C. Circuit*

With William Rehnquist at a session of the Administrative Conference of the United States, June 1986. The careers and fates of the two jurists, friends and poker buddies, entwined at key junctures. But Scalia never forgot that Rehnquist told him, prior to their service on the Court together, "Nino, don't worry so much about the reasoning, just get the right result." *Courtesy of the Harvard Law School Library*

At the White House on June 17, 1986, President Reagan announces the retirement of Chief Justice Warren Burger, at far right, and the nominations of Associate Justice William Rehnquist to succeed Burger and of Scalia to succeed Rehnquist. *Courtesy of the Ronald Reagan Presidential Library and Museum*

The Supreme Court nominee returns to the Oval Office, July 7, 1986, because no suitable photographs had been taken when President Reagan offered Scalia the nomination in the same setting on June 16. *Courtesy of the Ronald Reagan Presidential Library and Museum*

At his confirmation hearing before the Senate Judiciary Committee, August 5, 1986, Scalia listens to Democratic Senator Patrick Leahy of Vermont (back to camera). Fred McClure and John Bolton can be seen over Maureen Scalia's left shoulder. A tired Meg Scalia, age five, sits with her mother. *C-SPAN*

In a private gathering in the White House Blue Room prior to the swearing-in ceremony, September 26, 1986, President Reagan congratulates Maureen Scalia. Also pictured, left to right: Elvera Burger (partially obscured), First Lady Nancy Reagan, Chief Justice–designate Rehnquist, Nan Rehnquist (in profile), and Justice-designate Scalia (obscured). *Courtesy of the Ronald Reagan Presidential Library and Museum*

In the White House East Room on September 26, 1986, Chief Justice Burger swears in Justice-designate Scalia. *Courtesy of the Ronald Reagan Presidential Library and Museum*

In chambers before the investiture ceremony at the Supreme Court, September 26, 1986. Front row, from left: Margaret, Justice-designate Scalia, Christopher, Mary. Back, from left: Maureen, Ann, Catherine, Matthew, Eugene, Paul, and John. *Bob Daugherty/Associated Press*

The Rehnquist Court, November 12, 1986. Bottom, from left: Justice Thurgood Marshall, Justice William Brennan, Chief Justice William Rehnquist, Justice Byron White, Justice Harry Blackmun. Top, from left: Justice Sandra Day O'Connor, Justice Lewis Powell, Justice John Paul Stevens, Justice Scalia. *Collection of the Supreme Court of the United States*

formal caste system for many years thereafter, is to confuse a mountain with a molehill. Yet curiously enough, we find that in the system of restorative justice established by the Wisdoms and the Powells and the Whites, it is precisely *these* groups that do most of the restoring. It is they who, to a disproportionate degree, are the competitors with the urban blacks and Hispanics for jobs, housing, education—all those things that enable one to scramble to the top of the social heap where one can speak eloquently (and quite safely) of restorative justice.

No creditor without a debtor: Scalia offered the unwelcome reminder that affirmative action schemes always had innocent victims, like Allan Bakke, built into them. As a final demonstration of the "pretense or self-delusion…in all that pertains to affirmative action," Scalia presented a Swiftian "modest proposal" for enforcement of the Court's vision: an accounting scheme for the transactions of the "restorative" process.

Employing sports-betting lingo—*kid from Queens!*—Scalia proposed the Restorative Justice Handicapping System. His explanation of "RJHS" contained some of Scalia's greatest writing: political satire worthy of Orwell or Vonnegut, by turns dark and hilarious, unheard of in academia. "I only have applied [RJHS] thus far to restorative justice for the Negro, since obviously he has been the victim of the most widespread and systematic exploitation in this country," Scalia noted, assuring "a similar system could be devised for other creditor-races, creditor-sexes or minority groups."

Under my system each individual in society would be assigned at birth Restorative Justice Handicapping Points, determined on the basis of his or her ancestry. Obviously,

the highest number of points must go to what we may loosely
call the Aryans—the Powells, the Whites, the Stewarts, the
Burgers, and, in fact (curiously enough), the entire composition of the present Supreme Court, with the exception of
Justice Marshall.

This grouping of North European races obviously played
the greatest role in the suppression of the American black.
But unfortunately, what was good enough for Nazi Germany
is not good enough for our purposes. We must further divide
the Aryans into subgroups.... The Irish (having arrived later)
probably owe less of a racial debt than the Germans, who in
turn surely owe less of a racial debt than the English.

It will, to be sure, be difficult drawing precise lines and
establishing the correct number of handicapping points, but
having reviewed the Supreme Court's jurisprudence on abortion, I am convinced that our justices would not shrink from
the task....

One must in addition account for the dilution of blood-
lines by establishing, for example, a half-Italian, half-Irish
handicapping score. There are those who will scoff at this as
a refinement impossible of achievement, but I am confident
it can be done, and can even be extended to take account of
dilution of blood in creditor-races as well.

Indeed, I am informed (though I have not had the stomach
to check) that a system to achieve the latter objective is already
in place in federal agencies—specifying, for example, how
much dilution of blood deprives one of his racial-creditor
status as a "Hispanic" under affirmative action programs.

Moreover, it should not be forgotten that we have a rich
body of statutory and case law from the Old South to which
we can turn for guidance in this exacting task.

The sarcasm! The fearlessness!

Equating affirmative action, sacrosanct bequeathal of enlightened postwar liberalism, with Jim Crow and Nazism! Depicting Lewis Powell and John Minor Wisdom poring over the law books of the Old South. Scathing, devilish, unprecedented in law review! Blackmun's memorable turn of phrase—"In order to get beyond racism, we must first take account of race"—poisoned the well of legal discourse, Scalia argued. Now he dropped the Swiftian pose.

> I trust you find it thoroughly offensive, as I do. It, and the racist concept of restorative justice of which it is merely the concrete expression, is fundamentally contrary to the principles that govern, and should govern, our society. *I owe no man anything, nor he me, because of the blood that flows in our veins.* To go down that road (or I should say to return down that road), even behind a banner as gleaming as restorative justice, is to make a frightening mistake. This is not to say that I have no obligation to my fellow citizens who are black. I assuredly do—not because of their race or because of any special debt that my bloodline owes to theirs, but because they have (many of them) special needs, and they are (all of them) my countrymen and (as I believe) my brothers. This means that I am entirely in favor of according the poor inner-city child, who happens to be black, advantages and preferences not given to my own children because they don't need them. But I am not willing to prefer the son of a prosperous and well-educated black doctor or lawyer—solely because of his race—to the son of a recent refugee from Eastern Europe who is working as a manual laborer to get his family ahead. The affirmative action system now in place

will produce the latter result because it is based upon concepts of racial indebtedness and racial entitlement rather
than individual worth and individual need; that is to say,
because it is racist. [emphasis added][10]

"Disease As Cure" was one of the bravest, toughest, most brilliantly
argued statements on race and law in the twentieth century. Scalia's
free-wheeling literary style never caught on in law review; but he had
made his mark. "He encouraged us to do the kind of scholarship that
might *actually* help lawyers and judges in their work," said Brad Clark,
a former clerk. "Law has meaning only in context.... In his view, law
professors could provide a valuable service to the Court and to the
profession by recovering lost context and meaning."[11]

*   *   *

On January 20, 1981, Chief Justice Burger swore in Ronald Reagan
as the fortieth president of the United States. In the preceding weeks,
Scalia had let it be known, through Silberman and others, that he
wanted to serve as solicitor general: the last post Bob Bork had held in
government. As a former AAG who had argued before the Court, Scalia
was a natural candidate.

The transition team flew Nino in from Palo Alto for an interview
with the new attorney general. William French Smith, a partner at
Gibson Dunn's Los Angeles office, had known Reagan since the
mid-1960s and had been his personal attorney. "Courteous demeanor,
conservative clothes, and gray hair made him look the very model of a
lawyer," the *New York Times* observed. Descended from an old New
England family, Smith had graduated from Harvard Law and served
as a naval officer in World War II. His bearing, unlike that of the kid
from Queens, was quintessentially patrician: "cool in difficult

circumstances," a reporter remarked, "intensely private, almost passionless." Scalia thought the interview went well.

But the process dragged.

The administration was looking at two other candidates: Judge Dallin Oaks of the Utah Supreme Court; and Rex Lee, a former AAG for the Civil Division, now dean at Brigham Young Law School. For the first time, Scalia benefited from his ethnic heritage: a letter-writing campaign on his behalf, mounted by Italian-American Republicans and advocacy groups, had quietly commenced in December 1980.[12]

"I almost could have flipped a coin. It was that close," Smith said. He chose Lee (father of future U.S. Senator Mike Lee). Smith telephoned Scalia in Palo Alto to deliver the blow. "I was bitterly disappointed," the justice told Biskupic in 2007. "I never forgot it." Maureen wept.[13]

Silberman knew the real problem. Larry's stature in Washington and his work on the Reagan campaign had made him an insider; on his recommendation, Smith hired Ed Schmults, a former counsel to President Ford, as deputy attorney general. Silberman had put in a good word for Nino for the solicitor general job. But after the new attorney general interviewed Scalia, Smith confided: *Larry, I don't like Nino.* "This was the only person I ever knew who didn't like Nino," Silberman told me.[14]

For Scalia, the episode plunged him back to the hurt feelings of 1953, his last bitter disappointment, when Princeton rejected him. At that interview, Scalia later recalled, he could feel his interviewer's Anglo-Saxon elitism, could sense the conviction that the Italian kid from Queens was *not the Princeton kind*, code for *not WASPy enough*. And now here was William French Smith, white-haired eminence of the bar, scion of Old New England, WASP among WASPs, judging Nino *not the solicitor general kind*. Given the role of the solicitor general, arguing before the Marble Temple, it was as if Smith had pronounced Scalia *not the Supreme Court kind*. "Nino," another colleague recalled, "got angry about that."[15]

*   *   *

Scalia never thought of himself as a victim of discrimination. Outside of a few comments in childhood and the Princeton interview, he pointed, in his many interviews, to no other instances of it. Yet Scalia's career in Washington and Chicago saw numerous occasions when his Italian heritage was invoked or insulted, often to his face or with his knowledge. Sometimes it was in good humor, often not; either way, it was a more frequent occurrence in Scalia's life than he cared to acknowledge.

In 1973, when Scalia served as chairman of the Administrative Conference, his first public-facing job in government, Robert S. Boyd, the Pulitzer Prize–winning Washington bureau chief for the Knight newspaper chain, took readers on a weekday tour of the capital. The aim was to show that, Watergate aside, the gears of government ground on. At a downtown news conference, Boyd wrote in his syndicated column, a "swarthy, crew-cut lawyer named Antonin Scalia announced a plan to organize a nationwide system of small, neighborhood courts." Another paragraph detailed the proposal without reporting Scalia's title: just surname and *swarthy*.

In 1974, Attorney General Saxbe held a picnic for DOJ officials and their families. Scalia brought a box of bocce balls. Looking on quizzically was Herb Petersen, assistant attorney general for the Criminal Division. Scalia saw Petersen's perplexed expression and decided to needle him a bit.

"You do know what bocce balls are, don't you, Herb?"

"Nino," Petersen replied, "as head of the Criminal Division, we handle a lot of organized crime cases. And any time we see grown men playing bocce, we send for an FBI camera team and microphone team." For his gentle ribbing of his colleague, Scalia got zapped, right between the eyes, with the suggestion that all Italians belong to *La Cosa Nostra*.

In 1975, David Broder, syndicated *Washington Post* columnist and also a Pulitzer winner, reported on a Senate subcommittee considering proposed constitutional amendments. The column identified Scalia as assistant attorney general and quoted him—but added parenthetically that he "must have transferred from the music department with a name like that."

In 1976, when Scalia argued *Dunhill v. Cuba* before the Supreme Court, Justice Harry Blackmun, sixty-seven-year-old native of rural Illinois, author of *Roe* and *Bakke*, gazed upon the formally attired attorney before him, representing the federal government, and scribbled: "plump, dark."

Shortly after that, most egregious of all, came the time when Frank Michelman, Scalia's old co-editor at *Harvard Law Review*, catcalled the former assistant attorney general, now an AEI scholar and professor at the University of Chicago Law School, from a descending escalator during a crowded legal conference: "HEY-uh, FAT-uh TOE-nee!"

These are just the recorded instances, unreported by previous biographers. Scalia's opposition to identity-group politics and its statutory spawn only reinforced his disinclination, innate and unyielding, ever to depict himself as a victim. To be sure, prejudice played less of a role in Scalia's life than it did for many sons of Italy; but it was there the whole time, in recurring episodes Nino chose, early on and wisely, to ignore.[16]

*   *   *

In Palo Alto, Scalia kept speaking, publishing, writing, lecturing, mentoring—but the waiting, the limbo, the purgatory, the not knowing, was difficult for such an energetic, ambitious man. In early February he published additional thoughts on regulatory reform for the new administration to consider. They included an admonition against the idea, popular among conservatives, of subjecting all new agency rules to strict cost-benefit analysis. The danger, Scalia explained, was that the same analyses would also apply to rules the Reagan administration wanted to *undo*: "The elimination of regulation will be subjected to a burden of proof that the original adoption of regulation never confronted." Disputes over the cost-benefit threshold would shift to the courts, Scalia added, where the imperial judiciary would invariably allow existing regulations to stand. The administration disregarded Scalia's advice. On February 17, President Reagan issued Executive Order 12291, imposing a strict cost-benefit analysis standard on all new federal regulations.[17]

For that reason, it was probably a mistake for AEI to ask Nino to moderate its panel event on Executive Order 12291. Scalia's guests that April morning were Weidenbaum, now chairman of the White House Council of Economic Advisers; and James C. Miller III, executive director of the regulatory task force chaired by Vice President Bush. Anne Brunsdale chimed in here and there, but true to form, mostly ceded the stage to Nino.

It wasn't just that the administration had chosen to pursue regulatory reform with the instrument Scalia considered least effective; something else gnawed at him. In the Reagan revolution, Weidenbaum and Miller had received the call to battle, the *summons*; Scalia had not. He was still sitting on the sidelines, hosting panels.

Where the ostensible subject that day was the Reagan administration's progress on regulatory reform, and Scalia, a comrade in the great campaign, was expected to support the panelists in presenting a positive picture of that progress, they instead found their host doing the opposite: putting them through the wringer, posing the hardest questions, dourly pronouncing their enterprise doomed to failure.

Scalia's performance went beyond intellectually rigorous let-the-chips-fall explication; his relentlessness in the torment of the panelists betrayed bitter disappointment that they had received the summons and he had not, and that his advice on regulatory reform had been discounted.

An amiable-looking *mensch* from the Bronx, his brown comb-over in mad flight from the side of his head, Weidenbaum was President Reagan's chief economist. His hostility to over-regulation was legendary. "Don't just stand there," he told aides, "*undo* something." Jim Miller, raised in Conyers, Georgia, was husky and keen-eyed, a ring of blond hair orbiting his Mr. Clean dome. He had earned his Ph.D. in economics at UVA when Scalia taught there and later served as White House budget director.

Scalia opened by reading the president's statement. "I came to Washington to reorganize a federal government which had grown more preoccupied with its own bureaucratic needs than with those of the people," it said. "This executive order...requires every agency to undertake a systematic sunset review of existing regulations...to eliminate those which are unnecessary...to reduce the burden to the minimum."

"That's not bad," Weidenbaum said. *Scalia had sprung a trap:* the statement was from President Carter.

"This whole thing has a certain air of *déjà vu* about it," Scalia said. "What is it about President Reagan's order that makes it a significant improvement over Carter's system?"

"The man who signed it," Weidenbaum shot back.

"One wonders whether the executive order was really necessary or desirable," Scalia continued. "I've done a rough chart of how long it will take to get out a rule under the new procedure."

Adding up all the delays he saw in the process—some familiar, such as public comment periods, others unique to the Reagan-Bush program—Scalia reckoned it would take agencies at least seven months to enact a rule, "ninety days longer than under the [Carter] system."

"At the maximum," Miller interjected.

"In my experience with agency processes," Scalia said, "maximums tend to become the norm."

Next Scalia took aim at the cost-benefit standard. "How do you propose to value human life?"

"Very carefully," Weidenbaum replied.

Scalia asked how far along the effort to develop regulatory budgets was.

"Not very far," Miller conceded.

Scalia wanted to know whether the administration conceded that it lacked the legal authority to extend its order to the independent agencies.

"No," Miller snapped, "it does not so concede."

"When you gentlemen were out of government," Scalia said, "you generally agreed that there are too many vague and standardless statutes on the books. Now that you're in power, do you feel any differently?"

What the hell kind of panel was this?

Here were the two top economic advisers to the new conservative president, visiting AEI to tout the administration's bold agenda for taming the behemoth, and Nino Scalia, their erstwhile ally, was taking them apart!

"Frankly," Scalia chided Miller at one point, "I'd expected a more encouraging answer."

The panelists would have fared better at Brookings!

Finally, Scalia asked how many employees the task force had. With detailees from OMB, Commerce, and other offices, Miller counted ninety.

Scalia dismissed the entire enterprise: "To me, it is almost unthinkable that with a staff of that size you'll be able to do a thoroughgoing review of proposed regulations, not to mention the more long-range tasks of reviewing existing regulations, considering what statutes should be amended, developing a regulatory budget, and maybe working up a system for follow-up monitoring. I cannot imagine how just ninety men and women, strong and true, can do all of that."

"If you're the toughest kid on the block," Miller replied, "most kids won't pick a fight with you."

But Scalia had done just that—and left his comrades bloodied.

Four months later Scalia swung his axe again. The White House was taking the easy way out; the only way to tame the behemoth was legislation defining the agencies' powers and limits. "The jubilation of regulatory reformers at having finally brought rulemaking under control should be somewhat restrained," he wrote in *Regulation*. "The assumption that control of rulemaking constitutes control of law-making is simply not correct."

As late as February 1982, the summons *still* not having arrived, Scalia dismissed the administration's cost-benefit standards as "a mirage" and blasted the "deregulatory lethargy of the independent agencies in this administration." Privately, he worried regulatory reform was "losing momentum," risked "ending up as a kind of Henry George Society, meeting once a year to dream about what might have been."

Strong medicine for one's friends—and hardly the moves of a man animated solely by careerism. "He was prepared to express a [contrary] view...at a time when he had nothing to gain," recalled Larry Simms, a former colleague. "A lot of people would have kept their mouths shut."[18]

*　　*　　*

In June 1981, as the Scalias' West Coast retreat neared its end, Supreme Court Justice Potter Stewart, an Eisenhower appointee who had just completed his twenty-third term, announced his retirement, effective July 3. It was the Court's first vacancy since 1975. Newspapers nationwide mentioned Scalia's name, invariably after Bork's, as one of the candidates President Reagan was said to be considering for the seat. Ultimately, making good on his campaign promise to appoint the first female justice, Reagan selected Sandra Day O'Connor, a fifty-one-year-old judge on the Arizona State Court of Appeals, previously the majority leader of the state Senate.[19]

The following month, Scalia awakened to the *New York Times* headline: "Bork Held to Be Choice for Court." The article quoted senior Reagan aides—*an authorized leak*—as saying the president intended to nominate Bork to the D.C. Circuit: the appointment Scalia coveted. Reagan hoped to place the country's foremost conservative scholar on the appellate court "generally considered one of the most liberal in the nation."[20]

Three times in seven months Scalia had been passed over.

For Nino and Maureen, there was little to do but wave goodbye to the California sunshine and settle in for another brutal winter in Chicago. Nino had a living to earn. Somehow he found time for a lucrative side practice in consultancy and appellate litigation, with government and corporate clients.

In late 1978, the Federal Trade Commission retained the professor's services in a monopoly case the agency had brought against the country's leading cereal manufacturers: Kellogg, General Mills, General Foods. Six years into the litigation, approaching the end of the hearing phase, the administrative law judge presiding in the matter had abruptly retired, only for FTC to rehire him, at a higher salary, as a consultant. The Titans of Breakfast cried foul, demanding the judge's disqualification and a retrial. "It was fairly clear," Scalia admitted, "that disqualification was necessary." FTC wanted to install a new judge with no retrial and incorporated Scalia's "written and oral advice" into its arguments. In the end, FTC appointed a new judge and authorized him to determine which evidence, if any, warranted rehearing.[21]

That same year, Scalia worked *against* the federal government in a different case—which his deep-pocketed client, ignoring the professor's advice, lost. Dresser Industries, a Dallas-based energy firm, had decided in 1975 to participate in a "voluntary disclosure program" offered by the Securities and Exchange Commission to companies that had paid bribes to foreign nationals. The company cited assurances from SEC staff that evidence amassed in Dresser's internal inquiry would not be seized by the feds; while the firm was investigating its far-flung operations, concerned about the safety of employees abroad, the Justice Department established a task force, staffed with SEC lawyers, to prosecute cases arising out of the program. Soon, Dresser faced subpoenas from both a grand jury *and* the SEC; a move to quash the subpoenas, citing SEC's early assurances of confidentiality, was rebuffed by the district court.

For Dresser's appeal to the D.C. Circuit, the company's powerhouse law firm, Baker & McKenzie, brought in a hired gun: Nino Scalia. Serving "of counsel," working behind the scenes, the professor developed novel legal arguments, including the contention that SEC's cooperation with DOJ infringed on grand jury authority and violated grand jury secrecy rules. A three-judge panel of the D.C. Circuit court, unaware of Scalia's participation, ruled in a way that, as he put it, "gave Dresser much of what it sought." While the SEC subpoena was not thrown out, the agency was forbidden from sharing the "fruits" of its civil discovery with DOJ.

Both Dresser and SEC found this result unsatisfactory, however, and moved for a rehearing *en banc*: with the full roster of judges on the D.C. Circuit participating. Scalia appears to have counseled against such a move—and to have been overruled by Dresser, the law firm, or both. Sure enough, in 1980, the full appellate court vacated the decision of the three-judge panel and found the cooperation between SEC and DOJ entirely proper. Scalia helped draft a petition to the Supreme Court, urging a stay of the D.C. Circuit order; the Court granted the stay. He then helped draft a petition of *certiorari*, asking the Supreme Court to hear Dresser's appeal; this the justices rejected.[22]

The most significant case Scalia worked on was *Immigration and Naturalization Service v. Chadha*. In 1966, Jagdish Rai Chadha, a Kenyan native of Indian ancestry, moved to Ohio for university studies. After his student visa expired in 1972, the Immigration and Naturalization Service (INS) allowed Chadha, then completing his master's in political science, to remain in the United States, accepting his claim that racial violence in Kenya posed an "extreme hardship."

Under a provision in the Immigration and Nationality Act of 1952, however, either chamber in Congress could veto such a decision by passing a mere resolution. In 1975, Democratic Congressman Joshua Eilberg of Pennsylvania, chair of an immigration subcommittee, asserted that Chadha and five other named "aliens" had failed to show "extreme hardship" and introduced a resolution vetoing the halt in their deportation proceedings. It passed the House without debate or vote.

Chadha and INS jointly petitioned the Ninth Circuit. Lawyers for the House and Senate filed *amicus* briefs. The appellate court sided with Chadha, finding the legislative veto violated the separation of powers. The INS again halted Chadha's deportation. The Supreme Court heard oral arguments in *Chada* twice in 1982. That the justices granted *certiorari* was exciting news to Scalia; for *years* he had been inveighing against the legislative veto as a "threat to democratic self-government." As an ABA section chairman, he helped draft an *amicus* brief in *Chadha*, "most (but not all) of its text...my work." Scalia argued that all legislative vetoes were unconstitutional because "they permitted legislative interference in executive functions and purported to authorize the

legislature to take acts of legislative character and effect without following the procedures mandated by the Constitution."

On June 24, 1983, in a 7–2 ruling, the Court struck down the legislative veto. The device may have served as a "convenient shortcut" for
Congress to override the executive, Chief Justice Burger wrote, but "the
action taken here by one House…was essentially legislative" and
involved "determinations of policy that Congress can implement in only
one way…bicameral passage followed by presentment to the
president."

The ruling's implications extended beyond the fate of the victorious
Kenyan on whose behalf the Chicago professor had drafted ABA's
amicus brief. The *New York Times* reported that the ruling "may profoundly alter the balance of power between the White House and
Congress."[23]

*   *   *

At last the summons came: the White House offered Scalia a seat
on the Seventh Circuit. It was an enormous opportunity: a federal
appellate court, one rung below the Marble Temple, covering Illinois,
Indiana, and Wisconsin. Most lawyers would consider it the apex of
their careers. John Paul Stevens served there before President Ford
nominated him to the Court.

Scalia didn't want it. He had his eye on the D.C. Circuit, where
administrative law dominated the docket, where presidents most frequently found Supreme Court nominees—where Bork now sat.

But who knew when the D.C. Circuit would see another vacancy?
Wouldn't it be smarter to take the Seventh Circuit now?

That Scalia sought, and would likely receive, nomination to the
appellate bench was common knowledge on the campuses where he

taught. "Nino Scalia told our law school class in 1980 at Stanford that he was leaving for the D.C. Circuit and that he would then be appointed to SCOTUS by Reagan," recalled a former student, a Scalia admirer. "He was as excited as a student about the prospect, and also let us know, I believe, to assure us he wasn't abandoning us for nothing."[24]

"He was very actively politicking for a place on the D.C. Circuit," a student of Scalia's during his final year at Chicago, also an admirer, told me. "Word around the law school," another Chicago student recalled, "was that he was about to be nominated to the D.C. Circuit." So loud was the buzz that, *in advance* of the nomination, this student cleverly arranged an interview with Scalia for a clerkship—and got one.[25]

"He always wanted to be a judge," said Richard Epstein, Scalia's Chicago colleague. "Scalia was always in politics.... He wanted to be in Washington." Nino had made up his mind. "He told me he would not take a position on the Seventh Circuit."

The instinct of Scalia, veteran poker player, was to gamble.

"Hell," he thought, "I'll wait."[26]

Chapter XII

Judge Scalia

> **BRIAN LAMB:** *Was there ever a time where you*
> *thought that you wanted to be a federal judge before*
> *you were appointed?*
> **JUDGE SCALIA:** *Oh, I can't—I can't really say I*
> *ever—I had ever set that as a goal or an ambition, no.*
> *Until—until the time when it was offered, I really hadn't*
> *thought of it.*
>
> *—April 1986*

On May 31, 1982, Judge Roger Robb, a Nixon appointee to the D.C. Circuit, assumed senior status. *Here was the vacancy Scalia had coveted—six months after Bork's ascension to the same court.* If Scalia got the nod and were confirmed, he would enjoy life tenure on the body "widely regarded as second only to the Supreme Court as the nation's most powerful court."[1]

The first eighteen months of the Reagan presidency had brought Scalia recurring disappointment: Rex Lee's getting the solicitor general job; all the major regulatory chairmanships going to others; Reagan's selection of Sandra Day O'Connor for the first Supreme Court vacancy, Bork for the first D.C. Circuit vacancy.

In this anxious year of Scalia's life and career, the waiting inevitably created apprehension about the future. Maureen had wept, after all, when Nino lost the solicitor general's job to Rex Lee. But declassified documents show they needn't have worried.

Immediately after Reagan's election, influential individuals and groups went to work on Scalia's behalf: bringing him up in conversation, writing and telephoning decision-makers, urging them to consider the Chicago law professor for executive or judicial office. The entreaties were well received. For Reagan's aides, finding the right spot for Scalia was not a matter of *if* but *when*.

His chief booster, yet again, was Silberman. He buttonholed Reagan's top advisers—the heavy hitters: James A. Baker, Bill Clark, Ed Meese, William French Smith—and urged them to give the administration's first Court appointment to Bork, Scalia, or Posner ("a Protestant, a Catholic, and a Jew," Silberman told me). *Who's Scalia?* "William French Smith knew who he was, but Baker and Clark didn't know who Scalia was."

To Scalia's sterling qualifications Silberman added an argument he thought his listeners, always politically attuned, might find appealing: After Polish Americans, the country's 30 million Italian Americans made up the largest ethnic group that trended Republican. And to that community, an Italian American on the Supreme Court would mean more than an Italian-American president, Silberman told his colleagues, "because of the Mafia stereotype."

Whereas presidential campaigns were rough-and-tumble affairs, arenas in which false charges and private deals have always been commonplace, the Supreme Court was an institution of a higher order, swathed in a near-holy shroud of mystique and prestige...*the Marble Temple*...the pinnacle to which only the worthiest ascended. In Scalia's case, this meant the son of an immigrant...a model of incorruptible genius, piety, and industry…the incarnation of the American Dream.[2]

The Italian-American push for Scalia began in December 1980 and continued across the next year. Jack Burgess, public liaison at the White House, apprised Fred Fielding, White House counsel, in August 1981, "I have been contacted by several Italian-American leaders regarding Nino Scalia, who is rumored to be a top candidate for judge on the D.C. Circuit Court of Appeals. His appointment would be enthusiastically received in the Italian-American community."

Days earlier, Fielding had heard from Bob Saloschin, Scalia's DOJ colleague in the post-Watergate era. "The period in question was one that involved many matters of great complexity and high stress, with which Nino and I had to cope," Saloschin wrote. "Nino Scalia has in pre-eminent degree those personal qualities of intellect, industry, experience, and temperament which qualify him for superior public service as a federal appellate judge."

Silver-haired and jowly, Fred Fielding was one of the Reagan era's savviest players. He had cut his teeth in Watergate—the rare figure who kept his nose clean, never came under threat of indictment, despite having served at the epicenter of the scandal as deputy White House counsel under John Dean. To the Scalia encomia that reached him, Fielding replied with a mix of agreement ("Mr. Scalia's record speaks for itself; he certainly merits serious consideration for appointment to the federal bench") and gentle let-down ("Quite frankly, at this point, another candidate [Bork] has been identified for this position. This is not to in any way denigrate Nino's qualifications, nor his capacity to be considered for another spot on that court—his qualifications make him eminently qualified to sit there").[3]

The wild card was William French Smith. The patrician attorney general had thwarted Scalia's solicitor general ambitions—"I don't like Nino"—and no one knew if he would defy the current now running strongly in favor of *some* kind of appointment for the Chicago professor.

*   *   *

On March 24, 1982, the FBI opened a background investigation into Scalia, his third in ten years, identifying him as a potential nominee for "circuit court judge/District of Columbia." On April 2, the *Washington Post* reported Robb's retirement; three days later, the FBI interviewed Scalia and he signed a waiver allowing the IRS to release his tax records.

Once again, the vast machinery of the world's pre-eminent law enforcement organization cranked into gear, no resource spared, to locate derogatory information of any kind that might possibly exist, anywhere in the world, about Antonin Scalia; and once again, the exercise proved desultory because none existed. Field offices from San Francisco to Tampa Bay dispatched FBI special agents to fan out across neighborhoods, campuses, and offices, run searches on data banks, and review every detail of every phase of Scalia's life, and once again the Information Age dragnet yielded only the highest of testimonials.

The dozens of men, and handful of women, who submitted to questioning included intimates and acquaintances from Nino's school years and private practice at Jones Day, his professorships and government positions, neighbors, politicians, civil rights activists, religious leaders—even the dozen or so judges who, if Scalia were confirmed, would welcome him onto the D.C. Circuit.

All that emerged was Scalia's brilliance, vibrancy, and integrity. He was routinely described in terms such as "one of the smartest human beings he knows"; "one of the most erudite and competent attorneys he has known"; "one of the most intelligent individuals he has ever worked with"; "one of the highest intellects he has encountered."

The interviewees praised him as "delightful and sensitive," "able to put people he meets at ease," possessor of "a marvelous and persuasive speaking manner," "friendly, witty, lively," "a very religious Catholic family man," "a tremendously hard worker," "a universal man" with "fair knowledge of the classics," "speaks Latin and French," "does not drink to excess," "plays doubles tennis," "a person of multi-talents" that included "singing and playing the piano," "charming, friendly, affable," "very dynamic," "quick witted with a warm sense of humor," "even-tempered and totally in control of all aspects of his life," "honest and church-going," blessed with a "good sense of humor...family oriented."

Most important for the bench, the bureau concluded that Scalia was "of unimpeachable character." The interviews had uncovered only "the highest regard for his professional capacity and his personal integrity," "a model family man...his reputation...above reproach," his "impartiality, objectiveness, professional ethics and competency... above reproach."

Asked whether Scalia would make a good judge, the interviewees agreed they "could not offer a better qualified person for the position of U.S. circuit court judge"; "the government could not have a better candidate for a position as a judge"; "there is no one more qualified than Scalia to [be] a federal judge."

The FBI interviews tell us more about Scalia than any other document, including his signed opinions, for they afford an unrivaled window onto his *character*: the single attribute, as his father instilled in him, that unlike brains or muscles was never to be put up for sale. Would that every life repaid such close scrutiny with such superlative results.

In this season of Ninomania only one interviewee, a Washington lawyer whose name remains redacted, offered critical comment. "The only fault [Scalia] has is that he becomes arrogant at times," this individual said; still, the interviewee described Scalia as an "excellent attorney" and said he "knew of nothing adverse regarding [his] character, associates, reputation, or loyalty." The interviewee "never had any problems with" Scalia and "did not believe his arrogance would affect his judgment."

The 1982 investigation also proved prescient in jurisprudential terms. "Scalia's views on civil rights totally lack prejudice," declared a Washington lawyer. A Stanford colleague described him as "even-tempered and free of any prejudice towards...any class of citizens." A third attorney discerned in the future justice a "moral dedication to civil rights." Also on display were his open-mindedness and civility. "He and Scalia have not always agreed," the report said of a Jones Day colleague, "but [Scalia] has demonstrated he will listen to those arguments contrary to his opinion and then completely consider and value those other opinions." A D.C. Circuit judge remarked that Scalia "has the talent of disagreeing without being disagreeable." This same judge added that Scalia "could stand to lose perhaps five to ten pounds"—and that he had already written to Scalia to welcome him to the D.C. Circuit.[4]

*   *   *

William French Smith remained a problem. When Robert Bork, vaunted figure, approached Smith to endorse Scalia for the solicitor generalship, Smith had erupted: "No way! This son-of-a—"

"Nino pissed him off," said Ray Randolph with a chuckle.

Judge Randolph served on the D.C. Circuit from 1990 to 2008. A dean *emeritus* of the Washington legal fraternity, he recalled wistfully the titans of an earlier generation in a recent interview. Randolph, too, had cut his teeth in Watergate: he was deputy solicitor general under Bork. The two remained close ever after. Randolph also got to know Scalia: they went fly-fishing in Alaska, hunted quail and pheasant, talked *Roe* in the wild. Chortling again, Randolph recalled how he and Nino used to get "plastered" at annual gatherings of the Grand Cru Club in Washington, Nino telling the same lame joke twenty years in a row. "He was terrible!" Randolph said of Scalia as an outdoorsman. "But he was a trooper."

In a previously unreported account, Randolph said the impasse with the attorney general was resolved by Nino's friend and colleague.

> **RANDOLPH:** Bob Bork got a hold of Nino and [got him to] apologize to William French Smith, as a result of which Nino got on the D.C. Circuit.
> **ROSEN:** Bork smoothed it over; is that what you're telling me?
> **RANDOLPH:** Exactly. Bob told me this many times—and Nino confirmed it.[5]

Randolph recalled that Scalia had responded to some overture from the attorney general, perhaps the Seventh Circuit offer, in a way Smith had found off-putting. Smith's relinquishment of the grudge was certified with his signature—*stately, flowing, all three WASP patrician names*—on a memo to Reagan, dated July 6, forwarding the nomination papers. "[Scalia] bears an excellent reputation as to character and integrity, has judicial temperament and is, I believe, worthy of appointment as a United States Circuit Judge," Smith wrote. "I recommend the nomination."

Three days later, the White House counsel's office advised the president that the other heavy hitters—Baker, Meese, and Ed Rollins—

agreed on nominating Scalia. Fred Fielding urged the president to sign the form and telephone Scalia. Reagan agreed and signed the papers. A few days later, he received a synopsis of Scalia's career and home and office numbers.

On July 13, 1982, Nino Scalia, the kid from Queens, answered his telephone in Chicago and heard a White House operator announce the president. With his cheerful Irish *brio*, Reagan offered the professor the nomination; Scalia accepted. A terse White House press release went out the next day. No newspaper reported the event.[6]

*　　*　　*

For Scalia himself, it was a pinnacle moment, a dream come true: *the American Dream*. The nominee's immigrant and first-generation parents, the hard-working devout Catholics whose sacrifices had made the moment possible, had lived to see it. Not that Nino expected any display of emotion from his father. Sam and Catherine had moved back to Trenton. Even in retirement, even after Nino became *Judge Scalia*, the old man would rebuke his son for reading *Peanuts* and mark up his opinions in red.... But deep down, Sam took pride in Antonin's achievements. "He was gifted," the old man said in the one interview he ever gave, unmentioned in previous biographies. "He was good at anything he did.... He picked up the guitar in nothing at all. The minute I put him on a bicycle, he took off—*whoosh!*"[7]

For Maureen and the children, Nino's ascension to the bench never eclipsed his status as husband and father. But now even his family, all ten of them, were obliged to recognize something about Dad that professional colleagues had long known: that he was a larger-than-life figure, that the still-unfolding narrative of his career traced an ascendant arc, that his work held important meaning for American law and society, and that he was destined for greatness.

The family understood as never before how Nino's talents and energies, his endemic absences—"he worked many long hours, into the night and weekends," a Justice Department colleague had told the FBI—had all been directed not at the attainment of higher office but to the higher callings of God, law, and nation, causes larger than himself. Nor was Scalia's embodiment of the American Dream, the power of his family story, lost on Maureen and the kids. Even to those most familiar with his human flaws, Nino now had a new aura: *judge*.

Much work lay ahead. But it was a moment—after so many family sacrifices and the agony of waiting—for rejoicing. In the Scalia home, where nine children ranged from twenty-one months to twenty-one years, it also meant a familiar ritual: *moving*, this time back to Washington, the eighth time the Scalias had been uprooted since 1962, and the last.[8]

The D.C. Circuit was the perfect fit. "He was very interested in the docket of the D.C. Circuit," Gene Scalia told me. "He had been writing about the D.C. Circuit while a professor, and now had an opportunity to address as a judge some of the things that had really been on his mind—and to some extent had been disturbing him—while he was a professor."[9]

Word of the nomination spread swiftly. At the Cleveland offices of Jones Day, the first institution to recognize Scalia's genius, the partners were seen "celebrating." Less thrilled was Anne Brunsdale: "I was, as they say, conflicted. I didn't want to lose him...not to the Court of Appeals."[10]

Father Connor, Scalia's pal from Xavier and beyond, sat down in an Opus Dei center in New Jersey to write the congratulatory note that would revive their friendship after two decades of dormancy. The epiphany Robert Connor had shared with Nino Scalia—that intense moment in the Connor family home in Queens in the summer of 1959, when Bob declared his commitment to Opus Dei and Nino declared "I will rise" to the Supreme Court—had never been forgotten by Father Connor.

For twenty years the priest had looked for some sign of Scalia's rising: "I was wondering when Scalia was going to appear." Now it had come. Father Connor minded his tone. "I didn't say that, of course, but [I thought] *you finally appeared!*"[11]

*   *   *

Maureen was right again: Nino's new job paid less than his last one. Between his Chicago professorship, AEI residency, and consulting and speaking fees, financial records showed, Scalia earned $100,350 in 1982; as a federal judge his annual salary would be $74,300. While he could continue giving speeches, his lucrative consulting work—which had netted $50,000 from AT&T, Sidley & Austin, and others—was gone.

Some who knew him expressed concern. David McIntosh, the former Scalia student and co-founder of the Federalist Society at Chicago, remembered being "excited for him" but asking him how he was going to raise nine kids on a judge's salary. Scalia, half-smiling, said, "I'll just buy a cheaper brand of beer."[12]

In some precincts the move was seen as...*a step down.* Scalia's daughter Catherine was studying in Germany at the time. Asked her father's profession, she said, "He's a professor." *Wow!* came the reply from the foreign students, who thought a professorship a big deal. For good measure, Catherine added: "Not only that—he's going to be a judge!"

The students' faces sagged.

The position didn't carry the same prestige in Europe. There judges were merely civil servants. The sentiment aligned with Scalia's own view of a judiciary whose powers were properly circumscribed.[13]

*   *   *

Confirmation was never in doubt. Republicans controlled the Senate and Scalia was "an obvious choice" who "came up on every list" of nominees. Yet the ABA committee that evaluated nominees only rated Scalia "qualified": the lowest passing grade. *What the hell?* Scalia had chaired an ABA section, moderated ABA panels, published in ABA journals. The rankings of "well qualified" and "exceptionally well qualified" were reportedly withheld because they required "substantial courtroom experience." "Slanderous nonsense," fumed a White House lawyer.[14]

On August 4, Senator Strom Thurmond of South Carolina, the eighty-four-year-old Judiciary Committee chairman, cracked the gavel to open Scalia's confirmation hearing. Three other nominees—Michael Mihm, Bruce Selya, and Harry Wellford—shared the witness table with him that day. Republican senators on the panel included Bob Dole of Kansas; Arlen Specter of Pennsylvania; Orrin Hatch of Utah; Jeremiah Denton of Alabama; and Charles Grassley of Iowa. The Democrats included Robert Byrd of West Virginia; Ted Kennedy of Massachusetts; Pat Leahy of Vermont; and the committee's ranking member, a third-term Delawarean, garrulous and ambitious, named Joseph R. Biden, Jr.[15]

"He has nine children he will be bringing down to Washington, D.C.," joked Senator Charles Percy, Republican of Illinois, Scalia's sponsor. "We are depleting our population in Chicago with that exodus."

"Do you solemnly swear that the testimony you shall give in this hearing shall be the truth, the whole truth, and nothing but the truth, so help you God?"

"I do," Scalia said.

The chairman quoted Scalia's recent *Regulation* article, "The Freedom of Information Act Has No Clothes." What did Scalia regard as the "major problems" with FOIA?

"Let me make clear at the outset, Mr. Chairman," Scalia replied, "that that article came from the days which, if I am confirmed, would be bygone days—days in which as a private citizen I could comment on the wisdom of laws which the Congress had enacted. Needless to say, my views on the wisdom [of a law] would have nothing to do with my interpretation of it were I sitting as a judge."

After some brief back and forth on FOIA, the chairman asked what criteria Scalia would use to recuse himself from cases on account of conflicts of interest. The witness said he would

> consult...the canons of judicial ethics. As far as my own personal soul search is concerned, I would disqualify myself in any case in which I believed my connection with one of the litigants or any other circumstances would cause my judgment to be distorted in favor or against one of the parties. I would furthermore disqualify myself if a situation arose in which, even though my judgment would not be distorted, a reasonable person would believe that my judgment would be distorted. That does not mean anybody in the world, but a reasonable person.

Thurmond had a final question. "What is your understanding of the term 'American federalism,' and to what extent, in your view, is the Tenth Amendment to the Constitution an affirmative grant of authority to the states?"

"What I understand by American federalism," Scalia answered,

> is our system of dual sovereignty, so to speak, whereby the federal government has jurisdiction over certain matters and the states have jurisdiction over certain matters. As to whether the Tenth Amendment is a grant of any authority

to the states, the states did not need a grant of authority. The Supreme Court has said in some cases that the Tenth Amendment is redundant, and I think that is accurate.... It is clear under the original Constitution that the federal government is a government of specified powers, and that unless those powers have been affirmatively granted to the federal government, they automatically remain with the states.

No other senator requested recognition or objected to the placement of Scalia's biography in the record. Thurmond excused the witness with a courtly farewell: "I hope you have a nice service on the bench." The Senate approved Scalia's nomination the next day.

On August 17, 1982, the kid from Queens received his commission and took his oath as judge on the United States Court of Appeals for the District of Columbia Circuit: "I, Antonin Scalia, do solemnly swear that I will administer justice without respect to persons, and do equal right to the poor and to the rich, and that I will faithfully and impartially discharge and perform all the duties incumbent upon me as a circuit court judge under the Constitution and laws of the United States. So help me God."[16]

Book Four

OUR COMMON ENTERPRISE

CHAPTER XIII

Particularly Dangerous

The main business of the lawyer is to take the imagination, the mystery, the romance, the ambiguity, out of everything that he touches. It is not for nothing that the expression is "sober as a judge," rather than "exciting as a judge" or "inspiring as a judge."

—Antonin Scalia, 2005

When Scalia donned his robes at the start of the Fall 1982 term, "his forcefulness and political savvy took some of his colleagues by surprise," *American Lawyer* reported. "They assumed Scalia would defer—at least initially—to Bork. Scalia did nothing of the kind.... One of the first things the other judges noticed was that the newcomer was nosing into their opinions. Unlike most members of the court, Scalia pores over other judges' drafts, covering them with detailed and often critical marginal comments, even if he isn't on the panel deciding a case. Several of the judges say they like the attention; none admitted to disliking it, although some clerks say they find it excessive."

"When I first joined the D.C. Circuit," Scalia recalled, "I tended to treat the proposed opinions authored by my colleagues as I had been accustomed to treating the proposed law review articles circulated by my academic colleagues.... I would not just suggest a correction of what seemed to me mistakes or misstatements; I would also offer what seemed to me helpful suggestions for improvement."

The chief judge was annoyed. Edward Allen Tamm, an LBJ appointee, invited the newcomer into chambers on a pretext. "When our conversation was over," Scalia said, "he stood up from his desk, walked over to his judicial commission hanging on the wall, peered at it thoughtfully and said, 'You know, Nino, I've read this commission over and over again, and nowhere does it say I have authority to edit other judges' opinions.'" Scalia took the hint, thereafter restricting his commentary on Tamm's opinions, as he quipped, to when Tamm "seemed to be overruling *Marbury v. Madison*."[1]

*   *   *

Bork, for his part, was finding it...*hard to keep up.* "When I first came to the court, [the case load] seemed very heavy," he acknowledged; the clerks whispered he was "falling behind." In his first two years on the bench, Bork authored thirty majority opinions, "somewhat fewer than might be expected," as a conservative court-watcher remarked at the time.[2]

Cases before the D.C. Circuit were heard and adjudicated by three-judge panels; in some instances, federal district judges, drafted from one rung below the appellate ranks, or retired appellate judges, enjoying "senior status," were enlisted to fill out a panel. If the losing party in a panel decision requested it and a majority of the judges approved, a case could be re-argued *en banc*, meaning before the full circuit court. The full court would then issue a ruling either upholding or overturning the original panel decision. If the Supreme Court declined to hear an appeal of a decision rejecting *en banc* proceedings, then the panel decision stood as the law of the land. Scalia disliked the rehearings: "When we sit *en banc* it is a much more ponderous group to bring to a consensus than is a panel of three."[3]

The cloistered appellate process—a dozen-plus judges working in groups of three—fostered collegiality, even intimacy. Judges and their clerks casually dropped by each other's chambers to argue and banter. Judge Abner Mikva, a Carter appointee, recalled Scalia as having "a good sense of humor, lots of human qualities, an uproarious laugh...the kind of person you can pop in on and say, 'What do you think about this?' He'll drop what he's doing and start to *kibbitz* with you."

Bork's experience was far different. "You don't drop in on a judge.... It was regarded as an imposition," he recalled. "You sit all day in chambers by yourself working on these things and then you go home and talk to the dog at night. It's a very isolated lifestyle."[4]

Until Bork arrived, the Court's junior judge was a diminutive, owlish New Yorker, a witty and fearless liberal named Ruth Bader Ginsburg. Appointed by President Carter in 1980, "R.B.G.," as she signed her notes and memoranda, welcomed the newcomer with a party in her Watergate apartment. Scalia "made himself the centerpiece" of the evening, one of the judge's wives recalled. "He was very jovial, thinking himself very clever and full of himself. But nothing that was obnoxious. It was quite pleasant."[5]

Where the other judges favored IBM-blue typeface on their stationery, suitable for Postal Service forms, Scalia opted for severe, black Gothic lettering, the kind used in the *New York Times* logo and nineteenth-century German sheet music. He also installed in chambers a new kind of machine, useful, he reckoned, in the composition of his opinions: a word processor.

District Judge Oliver Gasch, an LBJ appointee, found the sight astonishing. "I shall always remember going up to confer with Nino Scalia,"

Gasch recalled in 1992, "and here he was in front of his computer, banging out things…and erasing lines and restoring some lines…. It was the first time I had ever seen a judge work at a computer."[6]

*   *   *

Legal scholar Ralph Rossum first met Justice Scalia in July 1987, when they co-taught a summer course at the University of Aix-Marseille Law School, in the south of France, on the American Founding. Two decades later Rossum published *Antonin Scalia's Jurisprudence: Text and Tradition* (2006), an admiring though not uncritical study of Scalia's hundreds of published opinions, widely regarded as definitive. "When he became a judge," Rossum wrote of his friend, "he knew how law is practiced, taught, and used for corporate, political, and constitutional objectives."[7]

Scalia's first signed opinion was a dissent. Joined by two other conservative judges, George MacKinnon and Bork, Scalia objected to a decision denying *en banc* review of a case—*Washington Post v. United States Department of State*—on which a three-judge panel, one that had not included Scalia, had already ruled. The subject matter was the Freedom of Information Act, Scalia's longtime preoccupation. Ron Kessler, an acclaimed *Washington Post* reporter, had used FOIA to request State Department documents listing classified expenditures. The D.C. Circuit panel had upheld a lower court order compelling the government to turn over the documents, and remanded, or returned, the case to the lower court for additional action.

In Scalia's eyes, this was a teachable moment for his new colleagues on two fronts: executive power and statutory construction. "We believe this case should be reheard *en banc*," Scalia wrote for the minority on December 28, 1982, "not merely because the effect of the panel decision is to overturn a congressionally approved tradition and practice of confidentiality in foreign affairs matters that is almost two centuries old.... Rather, the source of our concern is that in arriving at that surprising result the panel decision embraced a process of statutory interpretation that makes nonsense of legislation enacted *after* the 1976 Amendments."

Scalia opposed the grafting of new meanings onto existing laws. But in liberal law circles in the early '80s, the newest trend in jurisprudence was something even worse than that, called *prospective pre-emption*. This was the idea, preposterous on its face, that a judge could find that a law "prospectively pre-empted" a subsequent law that explicitly contravened the earlier one. "The opinion of the panel barely mentions the 1980 statute," Scalia marveled in *Post v. State*. "The theory of 'prospective pre-emption' which the panel decision represents is sure to confuse the application of future laws.... We hardly think that the language of the 1976 statute and its legislative history provide such a clear answer...that the later legislation cannot be accommodated, as traditional canons of interpretation would demand. That is the course we would follow, making it unnecessary to remand the case in the hope that the district court might devise some way to undo the harm produced."[8]

The dig at the majority's order to remand served notice that Scalia intended to bring to the bench the same modes of argument, incisive and rigorous, comic and scathing, that he had honed while teaching at Chicago, when the opinions of the D.C. Circuit frequently attracted his pen. We can only imagine the quizzical look elicited when a Chicago professor told Scalia, shortly before he ascended to the bench: "It's really regrettable that you won't find in your new work as a federal judge the same range of spirited expression that would be available to you if you were a faculty member."[9]

＊   ＊   ＊

Asked if anything surprised him when he first donned the robes, Scalia said: "I've been surprised at how little I've been surprised."

Before issuing his first signed opinion, Judge Scalia gave his first speech as a judge: at Lehigh University in northeast Pennsylvania. Advertised in the local paper, delivered to a packed house at the Sinclair Laboratory Auditorium on the evening of September 13, 1982, the lecture was entitled: "Regulatory Reform—Realities and Illusions." "Regulatory reform is one of the most significant developments in U.S. government theory since the New Deal," he declared.[10]

Scalia's next mark, again in dissent, came in a freedom of speech case where the other appellate judges threw *their* first jabs at the newcomer—but in which supreme validation ultimately belonged to him. In *Community for Creative Non-Violence v. Watt*, activists against homelessness appealed their loss in the lower court, which had found the National Park Service had acted lawfully when it issued a demonstration permit that allowed the protesters to erect encampments on NPS grounds but forbade sleeping in them. The activists' professed means of protest, on the National Mall and in Lafayette Park, *was* sleeping. Such conduct, the Park Service said, violated anti-camping measures; the protesters asserted sleep as a form of speech protected by the First Amendment.

At oral argument in December 1982, Scalia signaled his incredulity. "Can any conduct be symbolic speech?" he asked attorney Arlene Kanter of the Institute for Public Representation, arguing on behalf of the protestors.

"Is it symbolic speech," he pressed, "if a person who objects to a law about spitting on public streets decides to spit publicly to show his disdain?"

Kanter conceded the point: "Conduct that is merely performing an act that is counter to the law is not really symbolic."

After a "divergence of views at conference," the D.C. Circuit sided with the protestors. "There can be no doubt," Judge Mikva wrote for the majority on March 9, "that the sleeping proposed by CCNV is carefully designed to, and in fact will, express the demonstrators' message that homeless persons have nowhere else to go." To the majority, virtually *nothing* could be ruled out as constitutionally protected speech.

Scalia, Bork, MacKinnon, and Tamm concurred in the main dissent, penned by Judge Malcolm Wilkey, a Nixon appointee. Even if sleeping were *fully* protected by the First Amendment, Judge Wilkey reasoned, the camping ban was lawfully enacted under regulatory authority; and by the definition of camping provided, "what appellants propose is clearly camping." But Scalia also filed a separate dissent, again joined by MacKinnon and Bork, because he wanted "flatly to deny that sleeping is or can ever be speech for First Amendment purposes." He found it "difficult to conceive of any activity inherently less expressive than the act (if it may be called that) of sleep." The entire debate, he lamented, offered "a commentary upon how far judicial and scholarly discussion of this basic constitutional guarantee has strayed from common and common-sense understanding." With his dissent in *Watt*, Scalia planted an obelisk for textualism:

> I start from the premise that when the Constitution said "speech" it meant speech and not all forms of expression. Otherwise, it would have been unnecessary to address "freedom of the press" separately—or, for that matter, "freedom of assembly," which was obviously directed at facilitating expression. The effect of the speech and press

guarantees is to provide special protection against all laws that impinge upon spoken or written communication.... To extend *equivalent* protection against laws that affect actions which happen to be conducted for the purpose of "making a point" is to stretch the Constitution not only beyond its meaning but beyond reason, and beyond the capacity of any legal system to accommodate.

To make the First Amendment "ridiculous and obnoxious," he warned, is to "endanger the great right of free speech...more than the Park Service regulation in question menaces free speech by proscribing sleep."

Ridiculous? Obnoxious? The majority responded in kind. Judge Mikva dismissed "the arbitrary, less-than-fully baked flavor of Judge Scalia's theory," mocked his "narrow reading of...the Bill of Rights," questioned his understanding of the "First Amendment's values," and sniffed that "his attempt at tight, tidy analysis does not yield sensible results."

Scalia had the last laugh. In a 7–2 ruling, the Supreme Court overruled the D.C. Circuit—*sided with Scalia*—and held the Park Service could lawfully restrict camping to designated areas.[11]

Not bad for a kid from Queens.

*   *   *

In March 1983 a panel led by former Chief Judge J. Skelly Wright, a Kennedy appointee, heard oral arguments in *Chaney v. Heckler*. Eight prison inmates in Texas and Oklahoma, all sentenced to death, had sued to halt the use of barbiturates and paralytics in capital punishment. They claimed the Food and Drug Administration (FDA) had not discharged its regulatory duty, under the Food, Drug, and Cosmetic Act of 1976, to assure that all "new drugs" are "safe and effective." By allowing the use of the drugs on Death Row, the prisoners argued, FDA had "arbitrarily and capriciously refused to prevent the use of drugs not proven 'safe and effective' as a means of human execution."

You couldn't make this stuff up.

The FDA commissioner argued that his agency enjoyed no authority over state-sanctioned lethal injection, and that even if it did, FDA would exercise its "enforcement discretion," well established in administrative law, to allow the practice. Only when the agency perceived a "serious danger to the public health" would it take action, and the commissioner saw no such hazard in lawful state executions. The lower court dismissed on summary motion, without a trial, because "decisions of executive departments and agencies to refrain from instituting investigations and enforcement proceedings are essentially unreviewable by the courts."

The D.C. Circuit, eager to limit capital punishment, overturned. "Such drugs pose a substantial threat of torturous pain to persons being executed," Judge Wright wrote. "Even a slight error in dosage or administration can leave a prisoner conscious but paralyzed.... Decency demands that the life be taken without cruelty. The Eighth Amendment embodies society's requirement that the means of punishment not be barbarous or torturous."

Issued in October, Wright's opinion ordered FDA to "fulfill its statutory function" and investigate whether the prescribed drugs were "safe and effective" for *capital punishment*.

Again, Scalia could not hide his incredulity. "There is ultimately no special factor to support the extraordinary assertion of authority to control the agency's enforcement discretion," he wrote.

> The public health interest at issue is not widespread death or permanent disability, but (at most) a risk of temporary pain

to a relatively small number of individuals.... Moreover, it is not a matter of pain versus no pain, but rather pain of one sort substituted for pain of another.... In these circumstances, it is hardly clear error [by FDA] to determine that lethal injection statutes do not pose a 'serious danger to the public health,' justifying the diversion of FDA enforcement resources from other projects. Indeed, it seems to me the conclusion that they do pose a serious danger is fanciful.

Where Scalia blasted the majority for conveying "disdain for the plain meaning of statutory language," the majority sneered that Scalia's invocations of precedent carried an "anachronistic ring." He shot back: "If the clear statements of this court...become downright anachronisms in nine years, we should perhaps stop publishing our opinions. Fancy, however, that the sound which the majority heard was not an anachronistic ring at all, but the stifled cry of smothered *stare decisis*, or perhaps the far-off shattering of well established barriers separating the proper business of the executive and judicial branches."

For the core absurdity of Judge Wright's opinion—its equation of condemned prisoners, minutes away from state-sanctioned death, with the legions of Americans purchasing aspirin, lipstick, and other FDA-regulated products, an argument *American Lawyer* termed "far-fetched"—Scalia reserved his sharpest thrust:

The condemned prisoner executed by injection is no more the "consumer" of the drug than is the prisoner executed by firing squad a consumer of the bullets.... If speculations as to motivation are to be indulged in, I would suggest that the agency was properly refusing to permit its powers and the laws it is charged with enforcing from being wrongfully enlisted in a cause that has less to do with assuring safe and

effective drugs than with preventing the states' constitutionally permissible imposition of capital punishment. This court
should have done the same. It is our embroilment, rather
than the FDA's abstention, that is remarkable.

In January 1984 the D.C. Circuit denied *en banc* review.

Once again the case went to the Supreme Court, and once again
the Court overturned—*siding with Scalia*—citing the statutory interpretation and separation of powers arguments he had marshaled.[12]

*   *   *

Stout and broad-faced, J. Skelly Wright sported thinning brown hair
atop a balding pate, bushy brown eyebrows, giant apple-cheeks, and a
prominent chin. A native of New Orleans and a World War II veteran,
Wright had served on the D.C. Circuit since 1962. For the three years that
preceded Scalia's arrival, 1978–81, Wright was chief judge. Scalia looked
up to the older man. As a district judge, Wright braved a cross-burning
on his lawn, among other threats, to issue landmark desegregation orders
that transformed the schools and mass transit of his native New Orleans.

At the appellate level, under the long tutelage of Chief Judge David
Bazelon, Skelly Wright developed into "one of the most liberal judges
in the nation's court system." He was the lone dissenter when a panel
temporarily blocked the *Washington Post* from publishing the Pentagon
Papers. And he advocated for judicial activism, holding in a 1971 ruling
that among a judge's functions was "to see that important purposes,
heralded in the halls of Congress, are not lost or misdirected in the vast
hallways of the federal bureaucracy."[13]

But now something was wrong.

Among the judges and clerks, it was an open secret that Wright was
lapsing into dementia. "He was literally getting lost," a Scalia clerk

recalled. "He would wander out of his office and he couldn't find his way back." Wright's clerks had taken over. For oral arguments, they typed up note cards from which the former chief dispassionately read questions to the lawyers before him. One time Wright got his note cards mixed up and began posing questions utterly unrelated to the case at hand; the lawyers before the bench exchanged nervous glances until Judge Patricia Wald, a Carter appointee, gingerly alerted Wright to the problem. He snapped at her. "It was really, really embarrassing for Judge Wright," recalled the Scalia clerk.

> I remember walking back to chambers with Judge Scalia, or talking to him in chambers afterwards, and he was really angry.... [Wright] was a courageous judge. I mean, he obviously was in totally different parts of the ideological spectrum than Judge Scalia was, but Judge Scalia really admired him. And he thought it was very disappointing to see that—basically, in order not to tip the court to the conservatives, which was going to happen eventually, anyway—that the liberal judges would let Judge Wright embarrass himself that way in court.[14]

Clerks were a new feature of Scalia's life. His approach to them was unusual. Generally he spared clerks from preparing "bench memos": ten-page summaries of the cases judges can review in advance of critical junctures, such as oral arguments, or conference, where the judges met privately, discussed how they planned to vote on selected cases, and authorship of majority opinions and dissents was assigned. Most judges and justices depended on bench memos; but Scalia devoured the briefs filed in each case himself—even the *amicus* briefs!—and had no need for summaries.

He allowed clerks to compose draft opinions but frequently revised them so heavily that the final product bore little resemblance; in cases that animated him, he dispensed with drafts and composed the opinions himself. "Scalia cared deeply and profoundly," a D.C. Circuit clerk recalled, "about getting it right. Law clerks learned early on about 'the cart,' on which we had to put every source that we cited in a draft so that he could read the sources for himself to make sure that we characterized them correctly. The fact that he would usually delete whatever drafts we had given him and start over from scratch made that practice seem a tad puzzling at times, but he maintained that the drafts helped him. And it was certainly better for us to believe that than to believe the alternative."

What Judge Scalia loved above all was engaging his clerks in *impromptu* oral argument. The former professor still relished the Socratic method, devil's advocacy, thrashing out issues with young lawyers whose brilliance and work ethic augured impressive careers of their own: teachers and deans, top-tier counsel, judges, Cabinet members, a presidential candidate, even a Supreme Court justice. After a few terms, Scalia started hiring, among his trio of clerks for each term, a "counter-clerk": an avowed liberal who could challenge the judge's entrenched views, in the ceaseless *kibitzing* and case dissection, with skill and respect.

Once again the Scalias were warm and welcoming, opening their doors to what Nino called *the clerkorati*. He led clerks on jogs around the Mall; brought them to Mass; hosted them at A.V. Ristorante, his favorite restaurant, where consumption of red wine and anchovies became a clerk's duty. "It was a wonderful, wonderful opportunity. My career has been all downhill since," said Patrick Schiltz, who clerked for Scalia twice—in his final term on the D.C. Circuit and his first on the Supreme Court—and became a federal judge in his own right.

Michael Brody, who clerked for Scalia in the 1983–84 term, recalled his meticulousness on the bench and his warmth off of it: "Scalia was a very careful judge. I learned a lot from him. He made sure his opinions were correct before they went out of chambers."

On Christmas Eve the clerks went caroling outside the judges' homes. "Most of the judges greeted us warmly, smiled, and sent us on our way," Brody recalled. "Scalia invited us in.... He played the piano and sang a duet with one of the clerks. His wife served us punch and cookies."[15]

✻   ✻   ✻

Scalia's status had changed—but his personality hadn't.

One night in this period, he and Maureen met up at Galileo's, a fashionable restaurant in Northwest Washington, with Tom and Margaret Whitehead, Henry Goldberg and his wife Kim Hetherington, and Brian Lamb and his date: a reunion of the old crowd from the White House Office of Telecommunications Policy.

The group had just gotten seated and was looking over menus. "Nino had his pipe," Lamb recalled. "And down at the bottom of the menu, it said NO PIPE SMOKING, big letters. And the *maître d'* came over to the table and said, 'I'm sorry, sir, but there is no pipe smoking allowed here. You'll notice it's on your menu.'"

> **LAMB:** Nino threw the menu down on the table, got up, and walked out of the restaurant, leaving his wife. We all looked at her immediately and started laughing because he was just throwing a fit. And we said to her, "Do you want to go?" and she said, "No, no." Because we had agreed that we were going to go down the street a block and have an after-dinner drink at a hotel. And [Maureen] said, "No, he'll be at the

hotel when we get there." And when we walked into the hotel, there he was, sitting right there waiting on us.

ROSEN: What do you take from that story?

LAMB: He was stubborn, and he always knew that he was right.... I mean, that's just the way he was. I don't mean this to be critical of him, and it's not my job to do that. It's just that he was a *happening*, and when you were around him, you either took him the way he was or [not].... He didn't care, when it came to his positions in life, whether you liked him or not; he was sure that he was right.

"He had a thing with fighting with people in restaurants, going back to the beginning," said Goldberg, who also recalled the Galileo eruption. "[Maureen] was like, 'Hey, just let him be. He'll get over it. He'll calm down. Don't go out of your way. We're not going to leave the restaurant. Just relax.'"

Goldberg added a critical element to the story—if not a saving grace, at least a mitigating detail. At the time the *maître d'* cracked down on Nino, other diners were *smoking cigarettes*. "Nino pointed out to the *maître d'*: 'What do you mean, no smoking? There are people at the table over there smoking cigarettes!' And the guy said, 'Yeah, but cigarettes are okay; no pipes or cigars.' Nino found that to be denial of equal protection...and the unfairness of that...set him off. So a ban on smoking uniformly applied probably would have been okay, but not a policy that was discriminatory."

Scalia knew he could be a handful—and so did Maureen.

"He was very conscious of the swath that he cut, his own ebullience, and how that could be difficult for people," Goldberg told me. "Maureen was a saint because she put up with that. But she also had a very clear-eyed view of Nino and would not put up with his bullshit."[16]

*   *   *

Scalia's first unanimous opinion returned him to his post-Watergate roots: the continued controversy over executive surveillance powers.

In *United Presbyterian Church v. Reagan,* activist clergy and their political allies, including Congressman Ron Dellums, challenged the legality of Executive Order 12333. Signed by President Reagan in December 1981, the order was, as Judge Scalia noted, "the most recent in a series of executive orders, dating back to the Ford administration"— a subtle nod to Scalia's own prior work—aimed at clarifying the powers of the intelligence community.

The plaintiffs alleged that Reagan's executive order condoned illegal surveillance, producing a "chilling effect" that inhibited them from free participation in First Amendment–protected activities. The district court had dismissed the suit, and barred discovery, on the grounds that the plaintiffs lacked *standing*: the legal principle that only individuals and groups with legitimate disputes, rooted in real or threatened injuries, not theoretical assertions of harm, can pursue legal action in the courts.

Writing for a panel that also included Bork, Scalia upheld the lower court finding that the church and other activists lacked standing. "To give these plaintiffs standing on the basis of threatened injury would be to acknowledge, for example, that all churches would have standing to challenge a statute which provides that search warrants may be sought for church property if there is reason to believe that felons have taken refuge there. That is not the law."[17]

Scalia linked standing to separation of powers, staking out new ground. For courts to accord standing to unworthy litigants imposed judges' wills over the political processes performed by other branches. A narrow view of standing comported with Scalia's belief in the "properly limited role of the courts in a democratic society."

In *Moore v. U.S. House of Representatives*, eighteen members of Congress appealed the dismissal of their challenge to the Tax Equity and Fiscal Responsibility Act. The lawmakers argued that the 1982 law, which had originated in the Senate, contravened the Constitution's Origination Clause, which provided that all "bills for raising revenue" must originate in the House. The district court had dismissed for lack of standing.

For the D.C. Circuit, Malcolm Wilkey authored a majority opinion that upheld dismissal, calling it "a proper exercise of the court's discretion," while also finding the appellants had standing to file suit. Scalia could not go along:

> I write separately because, while agreeing that we should abstain from deciding this dispute, I view that abstention to be the result not of our discretion but of constitutional command.... We sit here neither to supervise the internal workings of the executive and legislative branches nor to umpire disputes between those branches regarding their respective powers.... To convert standing into equitable discretion, as though it makes no great difference, is to toy with the separation of powers.[18]

*   *   *

"It's very difficult to be Robert Bork," Mike Uhlmann once remarked, when asked to fill in for Bork, at the last minute, on an ABA panel. "Indeed, if the truth be told, even Bob Bork has trouble being Bob Bork."[19]

For the bearded don of the conservative legal movement, life had been a roller coaster of late. On December 8, 1980, Claire Davidson Bork, Bob's wife of twenty-eight years, his "intellectual partner," mother of their three children, one still a teenager, died after a nine-year battle with cancer. Devastated, Bork left Yale to practice law in Washington.

On December 7, 1981, President Reagan appointed Bork to the D.C. Circuit. Six months after that, while lecturing at the Ethics and Public Policy Center in Washington, the judge met an employee there, fifteen years his junior, named Mary Ellen Pohl. Vivacious and open-faced, her blonde hair sculpted short like Nancy Reagan's, Mary Ellen held three degrees, including a master's in theology from Catholic University. She had recently quit the Sacred Heart religious order, where she had been a nun since 1965. "It wasn't so much that I left the order," she told me. "It was that the order left me."

After three dates, she and Bob decided to marry. Mary Ellen felt readily accepted by Bork's children. "They knew that their father had done a great deal for their mother when she was sick for so many years; so they did not have any ill feeling towards me at all," Mary Ellen told me. "I didn't know any priests or nuns," Bork recalled. "I hadn't been to any church for years and years until I began going to Sunday Mass with my Mary Ellen." He converted to Catholicism.

When they wed at the Cathedral of St. Matthew the Apostle in Washington, on October 30, 1982, Scalia—along with Ray Randolph, Abner Mikva, George Will, and others—served as a groomsman. Photographs from the Borks' private wedding album, previously unpublished, capture the depth of the relationship between Bork and Scalia. While the groomsmen included other accomplished men, Bork and Scalia loomed as the dominant figures—the scale of their ambitions and entwined destinies elevating them above the others. While the Scalias mourned the loss of Claire, they were warm and welcoming to Mary Ellen, even hosting the couple's wedding-eve rehearsal dinner at the Cosmos Club.

Things were looking up for Bork. He was universally regarded as next in line for a Court nomination when a vacancy arose—and he was in love. "Around Mary Ellen," a reporter observed, Bork "lightens up…beams happily…there is lightness in his step." "[Nino] was one of the first people that Bob wanted me to meet," she recalled. "I think they both had tremendous respect for the gifts of each other and they both shared deep conservative values."

> And since that was part of the culture war, as well—you know, legal battles—they saw each other as kind of partners.… Bob was one of the first people to really talk about originalism, and Nino, of course, is known for originalism, too, and textualism. But Bob thought as the years went by that their views were a little different, because Nino was more tuned into analyzing the text. And Bob was all for that, but he also thought history was very, very important. And later on, he said to me he thought that maybe his position was leaning more towards giving more weight to history.[20]

Ultimately it would be their shared love, the law—silent partner in Bob and Nino's friendship all along—that drove the wedge between them.

*   *   *

On May 4, 1978, famed syndicated columnists Rowland Evans and Robert Novak raised alarms about the prospective appointment of Bertell Ollman, a Marxist, to a departmental chairmanship at the University of Maryland. The column, published in the *Washington Post* and hundreds of other outlets nationwide, anonymously quoted a political scientist at "a major eastern university whose scholarship and reputation as a liberal are well known" as saying, "Ollman has no status within the profession."

Claiming he was "widely esteemed among his colleagues," Ollman filed a $6 million defamation suit. Finding the column a straightforward expression of opinion protected under the First Amendment, the district court dismissed *Ollman v. Evans and Novak* on summary motion. The D.C. Circuit splintered; its official syllabus, from December 1984, was comically unwieldy, requiring eight paragraphs to recount how the judges voted.

Writing for the majority, Judge Kenneth Starr unveiled a four-pronged test for distinguishing between *assertions of fact* and *expressions of opinion*, with their differing claims to First Amendment protection, organized around dense concepts like *precision-indefiniteness* and *verifiability-unverifiability.*.... In the end, Starr affirmed the lower court: "The reasonable reader who peruses an Evans and Novak column on the editorial or Op-Ed page is fully aware that the statements found there are not 'hard' news."

Bork's concurrence—agreeing with the outcome but differing over legal reasoning—conceded that "the kind of commentary...Rowland Evans and Robert Novak have engaged in here is the coin in which controversialists are commonly paid." But Bork urged his colleagues not to succumb to the "temptation" to distinguish neatly between *opinions*, protected, and *assertions of fact*, unprotected.

"Judges generalize, they articulate concepts, they enunciate such things as four-factor frameworks, three-pronged tests, and two-tiered analyses in an effort, laudable by and large, to bring order to a universe of unruly happenings and to give guidance for the future to themselves and to others," Bork wrote. "But it is certain that life will bring up cases whose facts simply cannot be handled by purely verbal formulas.... When such a case appears and a court attempts nevertheless to force the old construct upon the new situation, the result is mechanical jurisprudence."

What was this?

Robert Bork, bearded Moses of originalism, godfather of conservative legal philosophy, was singing tunes that could have come from the lips of William J. Brennan or some other liberal champion of the living Constitution. The idea that the meaning of a law might require "evolution," as Bork also wrote in his opinion, that today's federal judges, confronted with "modern problems," should take an elastic view of statutory interpretation—why, it was *heresy!*

To Scalia, it was as if his newlywed friend had taken leave of his senses. Bork's argument that "old categories...applied woodenly, do not address modern problems"; the fact that he "confessed" that his approach involved "admitting into the law an element of judicial subjectivity"; these constituted betrayals of the principled, reasoned originalism Bork had pioneered and Scalia had honed. Here they were, freshly installed by a conservative president on the nation's second most powerful court, their influence on American law never greater—and Bork was going wobbly?

Scalia, Last Originalist Standing, joined in one of two existing dissents and filed one of his own aimed explicitly at Bork: "I write separately to survey in somewhat greater detail the concurrence's more scenic route.... It is difficult to see what valid concern remains that has not already been addressed by First Amendment doctrine and that therefore requires some constitutional evolving."

Scalia believed Evans and Novak *had* libeled Ollman. The columnists' use of the anonymous quotation from the liberal political scientist to illustrate Ollman's purported lack of status in the profession amounted, in Scalia's eyes, to "a classic and coolly crafted libel"—not mere expression of opinion, but a foray into factual reportage. Bork and the others, Scalia thought, had failed to understand this:

[Evans and Novak] went even further out of their way to dissociate this factual statement from their opinions: they put it

in the mouth of one whom they describe as (1) an expert on
the subject of status in the political science profession, and (2)
a political *liberal, i.e.,* one whose view of Ollman would *not*
be distorted on the basis of greatly differing political opinion.
They were saying, in effect, "This is not merely our prejudiced
view; it is the conclusion of an impartial and indeed sympathetic expert." Try as they may, however, to convey to the
world the *fact* that Ollman is poorly regarded in his profession, the concurrence insists upon calling it an opinion. It will
not do. [emphases in the original]

What really "troubles me," Scalia added, was Bork's embrace of
"judicial subjectivity" to address modern problems: "It seems to me
that the identification of 'modern problems' to be remedied is quintessentially legislative rather than judicial business...that the remedies are
to be sought through democratic change rather than through judicial
pronouncement."

Scalia was effectively telling his dear friend: Rather than encourage
judges to place new, "evolve[d]" meanings on existing laws to address
changed circumstances—*the very activity of the Imperial Judiciary that
Bork and Scalia had spent fifteen years denouncing*—the people, acting
through their legislature, should identify which circumstances required
new laws with new meanings.

Bork didn't take it well. When he received Scalia's draft dissent in
chambers, he crafted a sharp riposte to his younger friend. Most important to Bork was to dispel the notion that he had betrayed originalism;
his fortunes could brook no suggestion from Scalia, nor anyone else, that
Moses had cast aside the tablets. Such a view could undermine Bork's
jurisprudential legacy—and his chances for a Court nomination.

"Judge Scalia's dissent implies that the idea of evolving constitutional doctrine should be anathema to judges who adhere to a

philosophy of judicial restraint," Bork wrote in his final opinion. "But most doctrine is merely the judge-made superstructure that implements basic constitutional principles":

> When there is a known principle to be explicated the evolution of doctrine is inevitable.... Why is it different to refine and evolve doctrine here, so long as one is faithful to the basic meaning of the amendment, than it is to adapt the Fourth Amendment to take account of electronic surveillance, the Commerce Clause to adjust to interstate motor carriage, or the First Amendment to encompass the electronic media? ... To say that such matters must be left to the legislature is to say that changes in circumstances must be permitted to render constitutional guarantees meaningless.

Then Bork *really* let loose, arguing it was Scalia, not he, who misunderstood the role of courts in American society: "There would be little need for judges—and certainly no office for a philosophy of judging—if the boundaries of every constitutional provision were self-evident. They are not.... A judge who refuses to see new threats to an established constitutional value, and hence provides a crabbed interpretation that robs a provision of its full, fair and reasonable meaning, fails in his judicial duty."

On August 27, 1984, Judge Scalia sent his colleagues a signed memo, unpublished until now, to which he attached a new dissent designed to "respond to Judge Bork's revisions." Scalia bristled at Bork's condescending tone: "I am not in need of the concurrence's reminder that the Fourth Amendment must be applied to modern electronic surveillance, the Commerce Clause to trucks and the First Amendment to broadcasting. The application of existing principles to new phenomena—either new because they have not existed before or new because they have never been presented to a court before—is what I would call not 'evolution' but merely routine elaboration of the law."

Evans and Novak won the case, the University of Maryland rescinded its offer, and the Marxist professor taught at N.Y.U. for decades afterwards.

For Bork, however, the sting of Scalia's attack endured; it was as if a church founder had been excommunicated by one of his disciples. Five years later—after life and politics had settled with cruel finality the friendly rivalry between them—Bork revisited *Ollman*, and Scalia. This time, with his old friend on the Supreme Court, Bork fashioned an even harsher rebuke. "The fact that doctrine changes," Bork wrote in *The Tempting of America: The Political Seduction of the Law* (1989), "unsettles some who, like myself, object to courts that go beyond constitutional principle. It should not. I tried to explain this in *Ollman v. Evans*." Without naming Scalia as the author, Bork lashed out at the "one dissent" that "complained that I was creating new law.... If one cannot see where...the adjustment of doctrine to protect an existing value ends and the creation of new values begins, then one should not aspire to be a judge or, for the matter of that, a law professor."[21]

*   *   *

As cracks formed in his bond with Bork, Nino was forging a new, deeper friendship with another D.C. Circuit judge: Ruth Bader Ginsburg.

"A few comments for Judge Scalia, with admiration, as always, for his style," she wrote affectionately to Scalia, cc'ing Bork, in a memo dated August 23, 1984, previously unpublished. None of the other judges wrote the way she and Nino did. They brought out the best in each other. In their exchanges of drafts and memoranda, where the judges hammered out disagreements or failed to do so, Ginsburg flattered and needled Nino, challenged and cajoled him, recruited him and sometimes worked against him. Her August 23 memo took aim at his dissent in *Ollman*, starting with his finding of a "coolly crafted libel."

> Cooly [*sic*] crafted? Have you prejudged the *Times v. Sullivan* malice requirement? (Otherwise, yours is a beautifully crafted opening paragraph.)
>
> Is it defamatory to publish "Ginsburg is an incompetent judge, law teacher, parent, spouse"? "RHB [Robert H. Bork] was an incompetent SG [solicitor general], advocate, constitutional law thinker"? (Who defines competence, status? In soft disciplines aren't they fuzzy notions?)
>
> How much of what is said [in your dissent] would apply to the Supreme Court's decision in *Times v. Sullivan*?
>
> R.B.G.

In *New York Times v. Sullivan* (1964), the Court had held unanimously that for public figures to prevail in libel claims, plaintiffs must prove not only that the statement was false but that it was made with malice: reckless disregard for the truth. Scalia's two-page reply to Ginsburg, composed the same day as her memo and also previously unpublished, captures his recognition of a legal mind, and a linguistic sensibility, equal to his own. "As to the first" question, he wrote, "I plead guilty."

Few people ever coaxed such an admission from Antonin Scalia.

Yes, he was acknowledging, he held *Sullivan* in low regard.

"As to the second," Ginsburg's questions about "incompetence," he continued, again playfully:

> Although in some contexts these statements would assuredly be libelous (*e.g.*, "The ABA Committee on Judicial Appointments

concluded that Ginsburg was an incompetent judge"), in a proper "political controversy" context they would be statements of opinion. When Jesse Helms says, in the course of a diatribe against the Warren Court, that Earl Warren was an incompetent judge, it will be understood that his assessment of competence is largely informed by political opinion. Had Evans and Novak said that Ollman was an incompetent political scientist, I might let them off.... They went out of their way to appeal to an objective, non-political, non-opinionated, factually ascertainable standard: Ollman is regarded by his peers as a hack. The reason that statement is more persuasive is precisely because it is more libelous.

Scalia then responded to Ginsburg's invocation of *Sullivan*. That ruling, Scalia noted, "did not purport to be changing First Amendment law in response to 'modern needs.' To the contrary, it took pains to point out that it was not departing from prior law." Scalia took issue with Bork, whom he copied on the exchange: "Judge Bork's opinion, by contrast, while at some points disguising its thrust...rests upon the novel proposition that a decent amount of defamation in the context of political commentary is okay. (I will try to make this clear in a few revisions to my earlier draft.) I am not unsympathetic to that proposition, but in no way can it be thought to be anything but a major change in the law."

While Ginsburg enjoyed her friendly exchanges with Scalia, she was also writing privately to Bork to fortify him against Scalia's onslaught. "In the next few days, I must vote in this case," she wrote Bork on November 26, in a previously unpublished memo, "because I'm off to Captiva Island.... I would have been delighted to concur in your opinion.... However, the four paragraphs running from p. 7 to p. 10, answering Nino's challenge, include comment on 'known' (framed) vs.

'new' constitutional rights that close me out. I believe you can answer Nino effectively without including passages I must resist."

> The key point to be made in response to Nino is that when a case involves a constitutional principle over which judges have been given stewardship, it is our responsibility to say how that principle may be protected as the world changes. Why is it necessary, in making that point, to [mention] "thrust[ing] into the Constitution rights or values that the Framers did not place there"? All agree that the speech/press clause is in the constitution. So why can't you move (and carry me with you) directly to the discussion of adapting the unchanging value to new circumstances?
>
> Attached, a proposed revision for your consideration. If it doesn't satisfy you, please suggest an alternative composition that will enable me to join your opinion.
>
> R.B.G.

Shaken by his friend's censure, Bork incorporated Ginsburg's changes—word for word, in spots—and she joined his concurrence.[22]

*   *   *

Scalia was now the court's driving force. In *CCNV v. Watt*, the sleep-equals-speech case, Judge Wilkey explained to the other judges how Scalia had "pointed out that my proposed opinion would be stronger" if it avoided a "controversial question on which there is little Supreme Court guidance" and focused instead on administrative law. "Accepting this helpful criticism," Wilkey continued, "I suggest striking pages 7 and 8 and notes 24–36 of my original draft proposed opinion and replacing them with the attached, principally drafted by Judge

Scalia." "I concur," Bork scribbled; Judge Harry Edwards likewise agreed to "rewrite parts II. & III. of my opinion to take account of Judge Scalia's proposed modifications."[23]

A pioneering African-American law professor at Harvard and the University of Michigan, Edwards was a Carter appointee but valued Scalia's approach to the law and his colleagues: "If you get to a point in discussing a thesis when he doesn't have an answer, he's not going to hardline you just to get a result."[24]

The papers of Scalia's deceased colleagues on the D.C. Circuit, unsealed by the Library of Congress and examined here for the first time, capture the steady growth of Scalia's influence. How a case should be decided; what language to use—and to avoid—in the opinion; the rules governing appearances by attorneys; the running order of the cases at oral argument—on all this and more, the judges followed Nino's lead.

In April 1983, with Scalia having been on the bench less than a year, R.B.G. witnessed, and memorialized, the extraordinary power of persuasiveness the new judge exerted over his colleagues, even liberals such as herself and Patricia M. Wald. The case was *Ryan v. Bureau of Alcohol, Tobacco and Firearms*, examining whether certain ATF documents were "tax records" and thus could be withheld under FOIA. When the judges met at conference, Scalia cautioned them against embroiling the appellate court in disputes over subtle differences in filing forms—and overcame some resistance. Ginsburg's conference memo, prepared for the other judges in April 1983 and previously unpublished, reports:

> Judge Scalia suggested that any attempt to distinguish between forms immediately usable to determine someone's tax liability and forms that are merely preliminary steps toward that end, might set dangerous precedent. The agency

would have to categorize forms; lawyers could seize on the decision to urge the form they seek is merely preliminary or is not sufficiently connected to ascertaining tax liability. Although RBG and PMW initially inclined the other way, all agreed that this was a case of small importance and should not be used to set potentially important precedent. On further thought RBG is convinced that AS's position is right....

R.B.G.

"AS was attracted," read another Ginsburg conference memo, five days later, "to the potential this case may have for an airing of his views on 'substantial evidence' vs. 'arbitrary and capricious.' On that basis the opinion was assigned to him."[25]

Admiration for the power of Scalia's mind swept the judges' chambers. "I have reshaped *Goodrich* along the lines you suggested," Ginsburg informed Scalia in July of 1983.

"Herewith a revised memorandum," wrote Tamm the following year, "supplemented by suggestions from Judge Scalia."

"The standing issue about which Judge Scalia expressed concern is...pertinent," Mikva noted in January 1985.

"I agree that footnote 8 was unnecessarily ambiguous," Ginsburg conceded that April, "and therefore am making the change Judge Scalia recommended." A few weeks later, R.B.G. forwarded a separate draft opinion "borrowing liberally from Judge Scalia's."

That spring, Pat Wald wrote to Scalia, "As suggested, I have deleted the discussion of legislative history"; of another of his recommendations, she acknowledged: "I have fully incorporated the substance of this suggestion."

"Judge Scalia's suggested revisions are fine with me," Ginsburg wrote in July. "The changes suggested by Judge Scalia," Judge Carl

McGowan wrote, "have been incorporated.... The opinion is now on its way to the printer."

"I have altered p. 7 precisely as you suggested," Ginsburg wrote Scalia the next month, and again, to Mikva and Scalia, in October: "I concur in... Judge Scalia's suggested clarifications."[26]

His influence was not just episodic but institutional. Until his arrival, the names of the judges on a given panel were not disclosed until the day of oral argument. Scalia challenged this at conference. "Why shouldn't we let the lawyers know who the judges are, as long as we don't give them continuances?" he asked. "They have to understand they can't do any shopping if they don't like the panel."

"Well," another judge said, "if they know [who] the panel is... I guess they might settle the appeal."

"So," Scalia replied, "isn't that something we should encourage?"

"He was right," Mikva recalled. "That was Scalia's contribution to our procedures."[27]

*   *   *

"Everything about Scalia's first year-and-a-half on the bench indicates that he would be not only a conservative justice but also an influential one," legal analyst Richard Vigilante observed in early 1984. He saw Supreme Court material: "No majority opinion filed by Scalia has ever been reversed *en banc*. But of the nine cases in which Scalia had written dissents as of December 1983, four had been accepted by the Supreme Court for review.... Scalia is also one of the best writers on the federal bench, and history shows that a well-written opinion can have far more influence even than it deserves."

American Lawyer agreed: "In a short time, he has distinguished himself.... His aggressively argued, deeply conservative opinions have grabbed attention and earned him a place as a leader of the court...."

One of the things attracting attention to Scalia is how well his opinions have fared before the Supreme Court. Of the eleven cases in which he has written dissents, *cert* was requested in four and granted in three. Of the fifty-three cases in which he wrote majority opinions, *cert* was requested in four cases; all were denied. In other words, the High Court has sided with Scalia in seven of eight reviews."

Now the media, beholden to horse-race narratives, played up the Bork-Scalia rivalry. "Outshining Bork," read one headline. The former solicitor general was said to be "uninterested in the unbalanced diet of administrative law cases" before the court, while lawyers arguing before the D.C. Circuit encountered in Scalia a "phenomenally well prepared" jurist. "I'm not bored," Bork insisted, while conceding he missed his beloved antitrust cases; Scalia, meanwhile, was heralded as the "Live Wire on the D.C. Circuit." There was, at bottom, a charm gap. While interlocutors found Bork "imposing," attorneys thought Scalia "comes across as a knife-fighter, but a friendly knife-fighter."

"When he was appointed in 1981, Bork was dubbed justice-in-waiting," reported *Newsweek*. "He's still waiting and, in news media circles at least, has been momentarily eclipsed by Antonin Scalia, a former University of Chicago Law professor who could be the first Italian-American named to the High Court. At forty-nine, Scalia, who is routinely referred to as Nino by journalists who couldn't pick him out of a lineup, is nine years younger than Bork and may be even more conservative."

Long accustomed to primacy in the conservative legal world—*Moses with the tablets*—Bork exuded humility when, for the first time, reporters started asking about the junior colleague who had followed him to Main Justice, AEI, and the D.C. Circuit: all critical junctures where Bork had given Nino a hand up the ladder. "I'd be delighted if he got [a Court nomination]," Bork said. "He's too good a friend to get into competition with."

When Scalia was nominated to the Court of Appeals, the similarity between the two men and their legal philosophies was the talk of the town, with the buzz focused on the shifting ideological balance on the D.C. Circuit; now, in the feverish speculation about a Supreme Court nomination, it was the *differences* between Bork and Scalia—*their ages, personalities, suitability for promotion*—that filled the air.

Many believed that Scalia, with his wit and charm, would prove more persuasive on the Court than Bork, the dour don. "Lawyers who don't share Scalia's conservative philosophy now say they consider him particularly dangerous," reported Stephen J. Adler, "because he seems to be so widely liked and appears likely to excel at building majorities for his positions."[28]

CHAPTER XIV

Inevitable Hour

*I just sort of kept my nose to the grindstone and, I mean,
that's the secret. Just between you and me, there's a
whole lot of luck involved, okay?*

—Antonin Scalia, 2008

S calia's judicial philosophy emphasized three principles: separation of powers; the modest role of judges and courts; and the centrality of original meaning, with textualism as the metal detector to find it, in the larger enterprise of statutory interpretation.

In *Illinois Commerce Commission v. Interstate Commerce Commission* (1984), a dispute over the boundaries of federal and state regulatory authority, Scalia's solo dissent declared that the original meaning of a law "is best found in the language of the statute." It was a revolutionary notion: "Legislative compromise (which is to say most intelligent legislation) becomes impossible when there is no assurance that the statutory words in which it is contained will be honored."[1]

In *Gott v. Walters* (1985), Scalia wrote the decision in a case that examined whether the Veterans Administration had properly enacted rules for the processing of veterans' radiation-exposure claims. The lower court sided with the veterans challenging the rules, but Scalia found the VA administrator's actions were non-reviewable by the courts; the text of the statute, he noted, stated explicitly that the decisions of the administrator "on any question of law or fact under any law administered by the Veterans' Administration providing benefits for veterans and their dependents or survivors shall be final and conclusive and no other official or any court of the United States shall have power or jurisdiction to review any such decision."

Judge Wald dissented: "I simply cannot believe that [the statute] was intended to allow the VA to defy with impunity the traditional, government-wide constraints on agency action embodied in the Administrative Procedure Act's rulemaking provisions."

Writing for a majority that included Bork, Scalia argued the statute *was* the intent: "What is truly incomprehensible to [Wald], and to those courts that have improvised assorted non-statutory limitations upon the scope of [the law], is...the whole concept of a system of administrative justice, even in a field of government benefits, without general judicial supervision. That concept, however, is precisely what the veterans' benefit laws enacted, plainly rejecting the judicialization, and even the lawyerization, of this field."[2]

In *Hirschey v. Federal Energy Regulatory Commission (FERC)*, the proprietor of a hydroelectric power plant had prevailed over the regulatory behemoth in litigation and was seeking attorneys' fees. Scalia filed a concurring opinion that mounted his strongest opposition yet to the use of legislative history in statutory interpretation. "I frankly doubt that it is ever reasonable to assume that the details, as opposed to the broad outlines of purpose, set forth in a committee report come to the attention of, much less are approved by, the house which enacts the committee's bill," he wrote. "And I think it time for courts to become concerned about the fact that routine deference to the detail of committee reports, and the predictable expansion in that detail which routine deference has produced, are converting a system of judicial construction into a system of committee-staff prescription."[3]

Scalia also maintained a robust speaking schedule, with more than two dozen appearances in his first two years as a judge: lectures at Harvard, Princeton, and Yale, the Aspen Institute, Federalist Society events, a prayer breakfast, a law review banquet, a conference in Tuscany, judicial gatherings, moot court competitions, and, most improbably, an impromptu debate with Chicago frenemy Richard Epstein at the Cato Institute in Washington, followed by dueling articles and a short book, *Scalia v. Epstein*: the first book with Scalia's name in the title.

On May 20, 1984, Scalia delivered his first commencement address: at the University of Dayton Law School in Ohio. He channeled the same humor, and the disarming declarations of dullness, that had enlivened *Regulation*. "I have suffered through *many* commencement addresses," he began. "Needless to say, I do not recall the point or even the subject of any commencement address I have ever heard."

Scalia's aim was to convey to the graduates the meaning of a life in the law. "There is a profound spiritual connection between a human being and his or her work," he said. "It is less true that we are what we eat than that we are what we *do* to eat." He dismissed the common notion that by "becoming lawyers, you have probably lost your immortal soul." While lawyers were frequently scolded in Scripture, he quipped, "the proper lawyers in the New Testament are probably tax gatherers—and they fare pretty well." He listed the unappealing traits of lawyers—*preciseness, attentiveness to flaws, world-weary cynicism*—but portrayed the profession as the crosswalks of society. "We have seen so much of the world *vicariously*, through the innumerable cases we have read, covering the entire spectrum of human experience.... By and large, human fault and human perfidy are what the cases are about.... We have seen the careless, the avaricious, the criminal, the profligate, the foolhardy parade across the pages of the case reports. We have seen evil punished and virtue rewarded. But we have also seen prudent evil flourish and foolish virtue fail. We have seen partners become antagonists, brothers and sisters become contesting claimants, lovers become enemies.... Expect to find here no more a dreamer than a poet" [emphasis in the original].

The promise of lawyers was not a particular outcome to a case but the *process* that delivered outcomes: "Process is what we are all about! Lawyers really have no more interest than anyone else—and no more expertise than anyone else—in what the *substance* of our laws should be. If you want to know whether deregulation is good or bad, ask an economist. If you want to know whether indeterminate prison sentences are good or bad, ask a criminologist or penologist. What lawyers are good at, what lawyers are *for*, is implementing these decisions in a *manner*, through a *process*, that is fair and reasonable" [emphases in the original].[4]

Not everyone was a fan of the Scalia songbook—not even every conservative. Former Nixon White House speechwriter William Safire, by then a Pulitzer Prize–winning columnist for the *New York Times* and acclaimed expert on language, had quietly taken the measure of the "Live Wire," this Nino Scalia with his sharp pen and tongue, his equal aptitude for writing and speaking, the federal judge who had appeared so often, as an academic, on television. "The new justice of the Supreme Court," Safire asked readers in his "Office Pool" column of December 31, 1984, "will be (a) Paul Laxalt; (b) Robert Bork; (c) Antonin Scalia; (d) William Clark."

Four months later, Scalia's future prospects squarely in sight, the columnist took his shot. "Free Speech v. Scalia," read the *Times* headline of April 29, 1985: the highest-profile attack on Scalia to date. In a single stroke, Safire gave birth to the careerist narrative and to the caricature of Scalia as an ayatollah in judicial robes. "If you were a lawyer and wanted to become the next chief justice of the United States," the column began, "what cause would you embrace, or philosophy would you expound, to ingratiate yourself with Ronald Reagan?"

> Strict constructionism? Judicial restraint and respect for prec-
> edent? No, that old-time conservative stuff has lost its appeal
> to an administration eager to use the courts to reverse deci-
> sions made in the last generation. These days, the way to a
> president's heart is to espouse government secrecy and to
> march in the vanguard of the media-haters. Consider the
> meteoric rise to contention for the next High Court vacancy
> of Antonin Scalia, forty-nine years old, who has shown him-
> self to be the worst enemy of free speech in America today.

For the first time, Scalia endured the experience of being vilified in the press: his life, writing, and conduct cast not as genuine expressions of piety, legal training, and philosophy, but as shameless gambits to "ingratiate" and advance himself. "Three years ago, as a professor," Safire wrote, Scalia "focused White House attention on himself in an interview with *U.S. News* about the Freedom of Information Act." Had Safire, renowned for investigative zeal, done his homework, he would have known that the opposition to FOIA that Scalia had expressed in his January 1982 interview with *U.S. News & World Report* dated to the Nixon era—and that that opposition was rooted in Scalia's under-standing of the law and in his executive branch experience, not self-interest.

While conceding that Scalia's appointment to the D.C. Circuit was "not solely because of publicity," Safire claimed Scalia's opinions were crafted for that reason. Thus his dissent in *Ollman v. Evans and Novak*, finding libel by Safire's celebrity-columnist brethren, was not the result of a close examination of the relevant texts, statutory and syndicated, but rather the means by which the careerist "endeared himself to the press-bashers." Scalia's opinions constituted "the most egregious assault on freedom of speech since the silencing judgment against William Cobbett" in 1809. Having assailed his subject's character, Safire ended with a half-hearted disavowal of that intention. "Do I here impugn a jurist's motive, suggesting that he is throwing red meat to the young lions at Justice and in the White House in order to fatten his chances for advancement? On the contrary, I suspect Judge Scalia has persuaded himself that institutional privacy outweighs personal privacy.... But...when recommendations for the High Court are made to the president...the posture of being the fiercest opponent of the First Amendment does not hurt a judge's chances."

The tone was unusually personal, redolent of more than mere jealousy at a rival ascendant; this sounded like *hatred*. What spawned it?

Previously unreported—undisclosed by Safire in the column, as ethical canons warranted, or at any other point in his long journalism career, and unmentioned by previous Scalia biographers—was the fact that the judge had recently authored a unanimous decision for the D.C. Circuit rejecting an appeal filed by...Safire's brother.

In *Safir v. Dole*, published September 30, 1983—eighteen months before Safire's attack—the D.C. Circuit had ruled against Marshall Safir, proprietor of a shipping business bankrupted in 1967. After larger carriers were sanctioned for predatory pricing, Safir, a small-timer, secured a $2.5 million settlement; but a lower court had rebuffed his demand for a share of government subsidies provided to the larger carriers.

"Even a sketch of this protracted controversy can hardly be brief," Scalia wrote with undisguised annoyance. "We find that there is no reasonable likelihood that Safir will in the future be a competitor of these companies.... The relief he seeks is therefore not likely to benefit him in any legally cognizable fashion.... He thus lacks standing."

Scalia scoffed: "To continue to believe [Safir a viable competitor] would be...to ignore the accumulating evidence of the past sixteen years, in which Safir's only known participation in the shipping business has been his *pro se* prosecution of this litigation."

The next three years brought additional verdicts: in federal district court, at the Second Circuit Court of Appeals, and, once again, at the D.C. Circuit, after Scalia left, designating Safir a "vexatious litigant": a menace to the courts, representing himself in frivolous lawsuits and appeals, scheming in vain to reverse financial losses from the 1960s.

Imagine the anger that coursed through William Safire, *New York Times* columnist, Pulitzer Prize–winner, pillar of the establishment, when Nino Scalia—*rising star, enshrined on the columnist's own Supreme Court short list*—used his wickedly sharp pen to expose the fakery of Marshall Safir, bringing down on the charlatan the full force of the Court of Appeals.[5]

How might the columnist get even?

*   *   *

Just before Christmas 1985, Sam Scalia suffered a stroke at his home in Trenton and collapsed to the floor. When Catherine, already weak of heart, discovered him, she went into cardiac arrest and died on the spot. Rushed to Mercer Medical Center, Sam "lingered for a couple of weeks," conscious only intermittently; he died there on January 6, 1986, at eighty-two. He and Catherine, eighty, were buried together at St. Mary's Cemetery in Trenton. They had been married fifty-six years. On his deathbed, the old man recited from memory Thomas Gray's epic poem, "Elegy Written in a Country Churchyard" (1750).

The curfew tolls the knell of parting day,
   The lowing herd wind slowly o'er the lea,
The plowman homeward plods his weary way,
   And leaves the world to darkness and to me....
The boast of heraldry, the pomp of pow'r,
   And all that beauty, all that wealth e'er gave,
Awaits alike th' inevitable hour.
The paths of glory lead but to the grave.

In Sam's only published remarks—a newspaper interview conducted
two months before he died, unmentioned by previous Scalia biographers—
the old man's admiration for his son, the appellate judge and Supreme
Court contender, was laced with a hint of disapproval, of reproach, that
the boy hadn't worked hard enough, hadn't suffered enough, to have
earned his success. "He was gifted...good at anything he did," Sam told
the *Trenton Times*. "He played the piano when he was very young and I
wondered how he managed to do so well and practice so little."

After his parents died, Scalia found in his mother's effects a collection of letters she had received from the parents of her elementary
students, attesting to her impact on them. Asked in 1986 which family
member most influenced him, Scalia replied: "I used to think my father,
not because he took me in hand that much, but simply because he was
a constant role model of application. He was a very disciplined man,
energetic, and believed that one should not waste time, squander one's
money or one's talents.... So he doubtless had a great influence on me.

"But, really, the older I get, in looking back and talking to some
relatives...and seeing how hard it is to raise my own children, I guess
I have become more and more aware of how much influence my mother
had upon me.... She was an intelligent woman, a great school
teacher...not the intellect that my father was, yet I am not sure that she
didn't have more to do with how I turned out than my father did."[6]

*   *   *

Scalia's schedule left little time for grieving. Four days after his father's death, the judge sat for oral argument; ten days after that, he lectured at the University of Texas on "Legislative History: Judicial Abdication to Fictitious Legislative Intent." Scalia's opposition to legislative history left a question: How else should judges interpret a statute when its text is unclear, and textualism is of little help in divining original meaning?

His answer came in the First Amendment case *In re Reporters Committee for Freedom of Press,* in which Scalia, writing for the majority, rebuffed reporters' demands for access to depositions and other discovery documents while a libel lawsuit, brought by the president of Mobil Oil against the *Washington Post,* was underway. "The Supreme Court has not spoken to the existence of a First Amendment right to court records of civil proceedings," Scalia found. In the absence of clear constitutional text or precedent, he wrote, the judges should consider "historical tradition."

This was a landmark for Scalian originalism, the introduction of a second tool: "An historical tradition of at least some duration is obviously necessary, particularly to support a holding based upon the remote implications of a constitutional text.... With neither the constraint of text nor the constraint of historical practice, nothing would separate the judicial task of constitutional interpretation from the political task of enacting laws currently deemed essential."[7]

The most politically significant decision from Scalia's tenure on the appellate bench—the one that drew the most news coverage and cemented his status as the leading contender for the next Court vacancy—was, ironically, displeasing to conservatives. The ruling in *Synar v. United States,* published in February 1986, was *per curiam* ("by the court" in Latin), meaning unanimous and anonymous.

Everyone in Washington knew, however, that Scalia was the author—
"his fingerprints," Ralph Rossum wrote, were "all over it"—and the
ruling established him as one of the country's foremost jurists. Even
more unusual, *Synar* was heard by a district panel, with Scalia the only
appellate judge serving on it.

At issue was the Balanced Budget and Emergency Deficit Control
Act of 1985, also known as Gramm–Rudman–Hollings, after its spon-
sors: Republican Senators Phil Gramm of Texas and Warren Rudman
of New Hampshire and Democratic Senator Ernest Hollings of South
Carolina. The measure restricted annual federal spending to a "maximum deficit amount," to be reduced each fiscal year until the deficit
was eliminated in 1991. In the event that the behemoth exceeded its
spending limits, the law empowered the comptroller general, after
receiving recommendations from the Office of Management and Budget
and the Congressional Budget Office, to compile a final report specifying which budget items were to be cut; then the president of the
United States was required to issue a "sequestration" order implementing the cuts specified by the comptroller general.

President Reagan signed the measure that December. "Deficit
reduction is no longer simply our hope and our goal," he declared in a
signing statement, "deficit reduction is now the law." But the president
also cited "serious constitutional questions raised" by the powers
granted the CBO director and comptroller general—two agents of
Congress unaccountable to the chief executive, now invested with
executive functions that, as Reagan noted, "may only be performed by
officers in the executive branch."

On the day Reagan signed Gramm–Rudman into law, Representative
Mike Synar, an Oklahoma Democrat who opposed the measure, filed
suit against it. A week later, eleven other members of Congress joined
the litigation, as did other plaintiffs. The Senate and the speaker of the
House filed motions. DOJ exhibited a split personality: contesting the

constitutionality of the Comptroller General provisions while opposing Synar's standing to sue.

At oral argument on January 10, 1986, Scalia's questions "dominated the hearing that ran for nearly three hours," the *Baltimore Sun* reported. The judge "jousted repeatedly" with lawyers for Synar, summoning "his sharpest and most persistent questioning to test the broad constitutional challenges mounted against the law." A reporter for the Gannett News Service likewise observed that Scalia, "often mentioned as a possible next U.S. Supreme Court nominee...seemed unimpressed by the arguments against the bill." "Haven't they made the hard decision?" Scalia asked about the lawmakers who adopted Gramm–Rudman. "Congress decided that what it wants to do is balance the budget and do whatever it takes to get us from here to there."

The Associated Press portrayed the case as "the most significant separation of powers dispute in the federal courts since the Supreme Court in 1974 ordered then-president Richard Nixon to surrender his Watergate tapes." Scalia's role in that earlier controversy had been central; and since *Synar* also posed major issues of standing, the case was practically *built* for Scalia.

At oral argument, it turned out, the former professor had been playing devil's advocate. Scalia held that Synar possessed standing to sue, but that the comptroller general provisions were unlawful: "The Constitution implicitly confers upon the president power to remove civil officers whom he appoints, at least those who exercise executive powers," he wrote.

> Since the powers conferred upon the Comptroller General as part of the automatic deficit reduction process are executive powers, which cannot constitutionally be exercised by an officer removable by Congress, those powers cannot be

exercised and therefore the automatic deficit reduction process to which they are central cannot be implemented....

It may seem odd that this curtailment of such an important and hard-fought legislative program should hinge
upon the relative technicality of authority over the
Comptroller General's removal... But the balance of separated powers established by the Constitution consists precisely of a series of technical provisions that are more
important to liberty than superficially appears, and whose
observance cannot be approved or rejected by the courts
as the times seem to require.

That July, in an expedited decision reflecting the gravity of the case,
the Supreme Court sided with Scalia and held Gramm–Rudman
unconstitutional.[8]

*   *   *

On May 27, 1986, Chief Justice Burger sent word to White House
chief of staff Don Regan, steely former titan of Wall Street, that he
wanted to see the president. The request was unusual, and Burger's
advanced age—almost seventy-nine—left Regan "suspecting that
Burger had real news" to deliver: possibly a retirement announcement.
Regan scheduled an immediate audience with the president and dispatched an aide, Tom Dawson, to meet the chief at a "little-known
entrance" to the White House.

With his stately bearing, white hair, and baritone, a veteran of
presidential intrigues since the Eisenhower era, Burger still cut an imperial figure. He cannily brought along Fred Fielding, White House
counsel in the first Reagan term and universally trusted, as a witness.
In the Oval Office they were greeted warmly by the president and

Regan. After pleasantries, Burger focused on his work *outside* the Court: as chairman of the Commission on the Bicentennial of the Constitution, an advisory panel created to help commemorate the two-hundredth anniversary, then fifteen months away, of the country's founding document. The project needed Burger's attention...*fundraising difficulties were averred to*...Only at the end did the chief let it drop: In view of his age and bicentennial duties, he wished to retire at the end of the Court's current term, a month away.[9]

Burger's news was momentous—but did not catch the administration by surprise: five of the nine justices were seventy-five or older. "From early 1981, we had been looking at a whole host of people for judicial appointment," former attorney general Ed Meese told me. Only sitting judges and justices, the president reckoned, would have the track record to demonstrate adherence to his judicial philosophy. The DOJ working group carried a suitably Star Chamber title: the Special Project Committee. This degree of preparedness gave the White House a head start on the selection process and helped, as Regan said, to "minimize the possibility of premature disclosure of the chief justice's intentions" to the news media.

The earliest White House list of candidates to fill the Burger vacancy included eighteen names. Bork was first, Scalia second. Soon the list was whittled to eight: joining Bork and Scalia were Justices Rehnquist and O'Connor, plus four other appellate judges, among them Anthony Kennedy of the Ninth Circuit. By June 5 the triumvirate running the process—Regan, White House counsel Peter Wallison, and Meese—had four "leading candidates": Rehnquist and O'Connor, Bork and Scalia. Assistant Attorney General Brad Reynolds, head of the Special Project Committee, thought Rehnquist, serving his fourteenth term, would decline the chief justiceship. Rehnquist was "tired," Reynolds said, "and probably would not want the added administrative burdens."[10]

*   *   *

Alan Charles Raul was thirty-one years old and only two months on the job as associate White House counsel when Wallison tasked him with reviewing the "voluminous" files DOJ had compiled on Bork and Scalia. Wallison wanted assessments of the two men's suitability for the president's selection and their "confirmability" if nominated.

"Scalia is uniformly considered a first-rate legal scholar," Raul reported.

> Even liberal Democrats concede this. The confirmation process, consequently, should be relatively easy.... Also enhancing Scalia's confirmation prospects, I would imagine, is the fact that he is an Italian-American—he would be the first appointed to the Supreme Court.... He does not seem to have antagonized any particular groups or powerful individuals in his rise to prominence.... Scalia writes well and is accessible to the non-lawyer. Though he is called an arch-conservative, he is also an independent thinker who does not bend his principles to suit the circumstances.... In 1985, he struck down part of a deregulatory scheme adopted by FERC.... In another case, Scalia, joined by Judges Bork and Starr, decided that Washington's [transit authority] acted unconstitutionally in refusing to rent subway advertising space to someone who wanted to post an anti-Reagan photo-montage.

Scalia's track record made clear, Raul said, that he "would not be an activist...or rely on his own preferences to fill interstices in legislation...[that] he would resist stretching the terms of legislation beyond what Congress narrowly addressed.... Strong emphasis on 'separation of powers' is the hallmark of his jurisprudence."

Evaluating Bork, the scouts all conceded Moses' primacy, his progenitorship, in the conservative legal movement; but they also signaled, for the first time, that insiders harbored some doubts about Bork...dark rumblings that the Godfather, towering figure though he was, was not without certain...shortcomings...personal *and* jurisprudential...factors that conspired to make his selection, which for so long had seemed a *fait accompli*, now seem...*problematic*. Judicial restraint was "a standard conservative theme in part because Robert Bork has been espousing it for the last twenty years," the DOJ analyst acknowledged. "Our underlying model of a conservative jurist has been profoundly influenced by Bork's work."

As Raul noted, however, many conservatives had found Bork's decision in *Ollman*, with its call for an "evolution" in First Amendment jurisprudence, "disturbing." "Scalia, in dissent, rightly criticized this opinion," Raul wrote. "Perhaps it is best viewed as an isolated misstep."

But the DOJ assessment went further, finding Bork's "deeper political convictions" had grown "obscure" on the bench. "Ten years ago, he readily would have been classified as part of the libertarian wing of the Classical Liberalism, as represented by the Chicago School," the scout said. "Since then...Bork has moved in the direction of communitarianism and traditionalism. He has spoken in [ways that] would have shocked the author of *The Antitrust Paradox*"—Bork's 1978 masterpiece.

There were other problems. Some of Bork's Nixon-era filings as solicitor general, "particularly in the civil rights area...were clearly erroneous," DOJ analysts concluded. He still carried baggage from the Saturday Night Massacre, particularly, as Don Regan noted, among "the large company of doctrinaire liberals in the Congress, the press, and the Democratic Party who did not believe that the Watergate scandal should be permitted to fade away." And despite being known to friends as "a tremendously warm human being and very witty," the judge's persona somehow seemed *gloomy, prickly, lethargic*. "Conflicting views have been expressed on the warmth of his personality and the extent of his humility," one scouting report said. "He is fifty-nine years old, smokes heavily, drinks somewhat and engages in little if any exercise." Scalia, by contrast, was reported, accurately, to be "extremely vigorous and dynamic...an extroverted, hail-fellow-well-met type."

Only a few years earlier, the two judges had been seen as two of a kind, their names spoken in tandem so regularly they blended into one proper noun: *BorknScalia*. Now official Washington focused on their differences, their dissimilarities. "[Bork's] star has dimmed somewhat with the addition of other conservative legal academics to the federal bench," the DOJ analysis noted. "Scalia is nine years younger than Bork, and perhaps more conservative," Raul wrote. Where conservatives found Bork's heresy in *Ollman* "unsettling," Scalia was seen authoring "the most important opinions of any appellate court judge during the last four years, without a single mistake."

Scalia's nomination posed only two potential problems. The kid from Queens was "prone to an occasional outburst of temper"; and there was what Raul called "Safire's attack." Reagan aides wondered whether the attention the *Times* columnist had drawn to Scalia's First Amendment decisions might prompt the news media, in the hothouse atmosphere of Senate hearings, to target Scalia for destruction. "Judge Scalia's approach [in defamation cases] is anathema to the media since it would allow a greater number of libel cases to proceed," Raul noted. "Other than Safire, however, the media appear to have treated Scalia extremely well."

With the 1986 midterms approaching, the scouts considered that the Democrats might reclaim control of the Senate. With Joe Biden likely to chair the Judiciary Committee, the consensus was that Bork could fare *better*. "Senator Biden…has noted that he voted to confirm conservative [appellate] nominees such as Bork, Scalia, and Posner," the scouts noted. Bork was also seen as more likely to be confirmed by a Democratic Senate because he is 'much older and less radical than some of the alternatives'…as liberal a nominee as the Democrats believe they will get." Administration officials also thought the news media would "be kind to Bork because of his strong support for the First Amendment in…*Ollman*."[11]

These predictions, as in all scouting reports, varied in their accuracy.

*   *   *

Four years earlier, when Scalia was still at Chicago and FBI agents were fanned out across the country vetting him for the appellate bench, a former student, Lee Liberman, who had recruited Scalia as faculty advisor to the fledgling Federalist Society, approached him again. In Scalia's campus office, she asked if he would be a reference on her clerkship applications.

"Here's my list of judges I'm wondering if you could write for me to," she said.

"Oh, I'm not going to be able to write for you," Scalia replied.

"Oh, my God," Liberman thought. "What did I write in that ad law exam?"

"Don't worry, your future is assured," Scalia deadpanned. "I'm being nominated to the Court of Appeals myself.… If I'm confirmed, I'd like you to come clerk for me." Liberman did, in the 1983–84 term.

Now, as the White House raced to fill the Burger vacancy in secrecy, DOJ officials decided they needed still another evaluation of Scalia's track record, a deeper dive; after all, the existing DOJ and White House analyses, including Raul's, had totaled only a few pages. The task of preparing this more thorough review fell to the associate deputy attorney general, a fast-rising star from the Federalist Society unabashed in her bias: Lee Liberman.

Fourteen pages long, studded with citations from two dozen cases, the Liberman memo was the first sustained examination of Scalia's appellate jurisprudence. "Scalia has been the conservative judge the most to be reckoned with on the D.C. Circuit.... He has written many of the most important opinions written recently by any federal judge," she wrote. "I did not find a single opinion in which either the result reached or the ground of decision seemed problematic."

The Liberman memo contained insight absent from the other reports. "He is extremely aggressive and successful in spotting jurisdictional issues on his own when they are not briefed," she noted.

> In *Arellano v. Weinberger*, at his instigation the court ordered the Act of State defense briefed. The grounds Scalia used in dismissing the suit also had not been briefed and he also noted a possible standing issue [DOJ] had not discussed. In *Gott v. Walters*, he raised the question whether judicial review was precluded by statute when no party had briefed it.... In *Maryland People's Counsel v. FERC*, he raised a standing issue that FERC had completely missed. In *ATA v. ICC*, he raised a ripeness issue ICC had missed.... This is an important ability.... It is very helpful for the Court to be sensitive to separation of powers problems even if the executive is not. Having a justice with Scalia's instinct for discovering these issues could be vital in those circumstances.

Like the other scouts, Liberman marveled at Scalia's "very successful" record at the Court, which "has not yet reversed any of his decisions." She lauded his attention to standing as an element of separation of powers; his support for executive authority ("very strong"); his opposition to *Roe* and affirmative action; his "engaging personality" and "superb" writing style ("the kind of flair that helped Holmes, Frankfurter, Black, and Harlan exercise influence even beyond the force of reasoning"); his deference to agency discretion ("affirmance of the agency twenty-one times and reversal only eight, all of which were justified"); and his instinct for how and when to overturn precedent.

"In light of some of the Supreme Court's cases, our candidate will need a willingness to depart from previous cases, and a strategic grasp of how to go about doing so," she wrote. "Scalia has a very strong record in this area both on and off the bench."

> He suggested in *CCNV v. Watt* that the Supreme Court rethink its entire "symbolic speech" theory, while explaining how all its previous cases could be reconciled with his approach. He found a very narrow way of reading an incomprehensible Justice Stevens [decision] in *Tavoulareas v. Washington Post*. He indicated that he favored overruling *New York Times v. Sullivan* in *Ollman*. He joined Bork in mocking the privacy cases in *Dronenburg v. Zech*. Undeterred by the full court's vacation of his *Ramirez* opinion, he reinserted his theory into his opinion in *Sanchez-Espinoza*.... Before becoming a judge, Scalia also expressed strong views against giving the Supreme Court's holdings in the religion cases any significance beyond their particular facts.

The final factor was work ethic. "Scalia does more work himself on every opinion than any other judge in the circuit," Liberman wrote. "He writes from clerks' drafts, but reworks them so completely that they are unrecognizable. This approach avoids any possibility that the views of his law clerks rather than his own will determine the outcome of cases."

Here, unlike any other scout, Liberman spoke from experience. Yet even her insight was limited: Liberman's bosses at DOJ hadn't told her *why* she was evaluating Scalia. "I didn't know there was a vacancy," she told me. "I thought we were just doing it, you know?"[12]

*   *   *

On the balmy afternoon of June 9, President Reagan welcomed Regan, Wallison, and Meese to the Rose Garden. From Reagan's diary: "A meeting with Ed M. re the replacement on Supreme Ct. for Chief Justice Burger. Only 4 of us are involved in this which must remain quiet until we're ready to announce. Curiously enough each of the 4 of us came up with the same choice for Chief (Rehnquist) & the same choice of a replacement then for Rehnquist."

The attendees all remembered this meeting differently. Wallison said the session lasted forty minutes, with Rehnquist, Bork, and Scalia emerging as the "most promising" candidates for the president. "He seemed intrigued by Judge Scalia," Wallison recorded in an August 1986 memo to the file, because Scalia "was young enough to serve on the Court for an extended period of time, and [would] be the first Italian-American appointee."

Yet in oral history interviews conducted in 2000 and 2003, Wallison disclosed for the first time that Reagan initially considered nominating Scalia to the chief justiceship. Meese argued that Rehnquist should succeed Burger, with a new associate justice chosen to fill the Rehnquist seat. In addition to Rehnquist's obvious qualifications, there was some concern that, if passed over, he might retire from the Court altogether.

In the literature of the Reagan presidency, nowhere are the president's precise reasons for choosing to elevate Rehnquist explicitly set forth; his diaries are sparse on the subject. Wallison's revelation that

Reagan considered nominating Scalia to the chief justiceship opens a new dimension in our understanding of the chief executive's decision-making at this critical juncture in American history. *What might a Scalia chief justiceship, commencing in October 1986, have looked like?* No one doubted Scalia was up to the job. Perhaps the president felt that Rehnquist, the conservative "Lone Ranger" of the Court since 1972, solo dissenter in forty-seven cases, had earned the promotion; perhaps, too, the plan's elaborateness, a two-step akin to a trick play on the gridiron, appealed to the Gipper.

According to Don Regan's 1988 memoir, *For the Record,* Wallison urged the president to pair Rehnquist with Bork, on the grounds that the dour judge would draw less scrutiny alongside the more senior nominee, reviled by the left since 1971, thereby improving Bork's chances of confirmation. John Bolton, assistant attorney general for legislative affairs, agreed: "Getting Bork on *then* was the best way to do it. And if there was another nomination later, you could nominate Scalia; it would be easy." Regan vetoed the idea, recalling in his memoir that he told the others "waving two red flags before the enraged liberal bloc on the [Judiciary] committee would be too much." Meese agreed, Regan wrote.

In his own memoir, *With Reagan: The Inside Story,* Meese, long considered the closest of Reagan confidantes, made only fleeting mention of the Scalia nomination. Still sharp of mind and locution in a recent interview conducted as he approached ninety, Meese recalled vividly the precise moment Reagan settled on Scalia: "When he was making the decision, he chose Scalia for one reason and only one."

> **MEESE:** Bork was a heavy smoker, actually, and was older and in less good health. And so it was on that basis that the president chose Scalia, specifically on the probable longevity.

ROSEN:... How was considered the factor of Scalia's being the first Italian-American?

MEESE: That really was kind of an after-thought. It was kind of an extra bonus after he selected Scalia.

Wallison remembered Scalia's Italian ancestry as the *decisive* factor in the president's decision. In his oral history interviews, Wallison disclosed the pivotal exchange, omitted from his 1986 memo to the file, that he had with President Reagan at the moment of decision. "Reagan asked me whether Scalia was of Italian extraction," the former counsel told political scientist Martha Kumar. "I said, 'Yes, he's of Italian extraction.' Reagan said, 'That's the man I want to nominate, so I want to meet him.'"

"Once the president learned that Scalia would be the first person of Italian-American descent to be on the Supreme Court," Wallison continued, "that's all he wanted to hear. That was it. He wanted to be the president to appoint the first Italian-American to the Supreme Court.... He had all the usual American instincts: we don't have an Italian-American on the Court, so we ought to have one. He really felt good about doing that. It wasn't principle so much as that kind of emotional commitment."

A meeting with Rehnquist was set for two days later. Again, Regan's staff handled the logistics, sneaking the sixty-one-year-old associate justice through an underground tunnel linking the Treasury Department to the White House. Waiting in the Oval Office were the president, Regan, Meese, and Wallison. Regan made small talk, but Rehnquist was immovable. "Rehnquist," Wallison recalled, was "as shy as anyone I've ever met in public life... very awkward in these kinds of meetings. He looks at his shoes." When the president cut, gently, to the chase, informing Rehnquist that Burger intended to retire, the justice was unfazed. Reagan asked if Rehnquist would serve as chief; the latter said he'd be "honored." Told that two judges were under consideration for the new vacancy, Bork and Scalia, Rehnquist, dry and wry, said only that he held each in high regard.

When Rehnquist left, whisked back through the tunnel, the president said he wanted a meeting "as soon as possible with Judge Scalia." Regan placed the call. Scalia agreed to meet with the president on Monday, June 16.[13]

CHAPTER XV

The Culmination

BRIAN LAMB: *You can't pick up a magazine or a news-*
paper when it writes about this court in which they don't
mention you and Judge Bork—and lately, they've men-
tioned you a lot more than Judge Bork, because of the
Gramm–Rudman decision—as an obvious candidate for
the Supreme Court. What does that do? I'm sure your
friends must say something to you about that, your col-
leagues. Does it bother you?
SCALIA: *[smiles, touches nose, hesitates for five seconds]*
Well, Mr. Lamb, you must know that it is a—your name
being mentioned for a job like that is about the—you
know, that plus whatever a token on the New York sub-
way now costs will get you into the New York subway.
It's very much a matter of lightning striking.

—C-SPAN, April 1, 1986

Until the telephone rang with Don Regan on the line, Scalia had *no*
idea a Court vacancy had opened up. Of the Hitchcockian machi-
nations that revolved around him in May–June 1986, consuming the
president and his top aides—*black binders, government limousines,*
secret tunnels—the judge was blissfully unaware.

331

Speculation about Scalia's rise was growing, however. The *New York Times* described him on May 24 as "highly conservative," on June 1 as "well regarded." On June 3, the *Pittsburgh Post-Gazette* named him a "possible Supreme Court nominee." On June 12, the day Reagan met with Rehnquist, a wire service listed Bork and Scalia as "the administration's leading candidates" for a justiceship. The *American Bar Association Journal* polled fifteen experts; Scalia captured four ballots to Bork's three.[1]

Scalia admired President Reagan deeply. In November 1985, the judge had flown to UCLA Law School to lecture the Federalist Society audience on the "fiction" of legislative intent. Afterward, the guest of honor was feted at Chaya Brasserie, a trendy Franco-Japanese fusion spot in West Los Angeles. Scalia "was already a hero to us," recalled James Swanson, a co-founder of the FedSoc chapter, the student who had invited Scalia and introduced him at his lecture, "and he was so friendly, so curious about what our plans were...if we wanted to go to Washington and work in the Reagan administration."

> At dinner Judge Scalia was a wonderful guest, and he treated us to his legendary warmth, wit—and strong opinions. The judge led the conversation, which jumped from topic to topic, from originalism to pop culture, from President Reagan to communism. At that moment Judge Scalia pounded his fist on the table and he exclaimed: "There *is* a difference between East and West!" He pounded the table again. "There *is* a difference between right and wrong!" He pounded the table a third time. "There *is* a difference between good and evil!" He pounded the table a final time. "And it should be *said*, and said *often*!"

Asked what had provoked the judge's display of emotion, Swanson told me, "He just got very passionate about his views of freedom vs. communism and Reagan and the Soviets."[2]

*   *   *

Hanging up with Regan, Scalia made an instant decision: *Tell no one but Maureen*. He was still stinging from losing the solicitor general's job back in 1981. Nino understood the meaning of the call: a Court vacancy had opened up, and he was being evaluated for it, maybe being offered it. But in case his expectations proved ill-founded, he kept Monday's meeting at the White House close to the vest. "I was floating around all weekend," he recalled, "hoping it wouldn't end the way it did [in 1981]."

The following morning, June 14, a Saturday, Attorney General Meese convened a conference on economic liberties at the Justice Department. Scalia was a featured speaker. When Scalia took the podium, only he and Meese knew that Scalia would be meeting with the president in forty-eight hours. "We didn't tell him the purpose" of the meeting, an administration official later told reporters. "But he's over twenty-one and he knows that the president doesn't call you over to talk about nothing."[3]

Seated at Scalia's table that Saturday were Meese, Bork, and Richard Epstein, also a speaker. As a professor, Scalia began, "I was fond of 'teaching against the class'—that is, taking positions that the students were almost certain to disagree with.... It is neither any fun nor any use in preaching to the choir.... This endearing quality of saying the right thing at the wrong time is the secret of my popularity." For his speech, Scalia said, he had been "initially at a loss to think of a subject that would be sufficiently obnoxious.... As I was musing in my chambers over this perplexing problem, the room was filled with the sound of a voice—loud, though it was a whisper.... It said: CRITICIZE THE DOCTRINE OF ORIGINAL INTENT. The voice, I must admit, sounded a little like David Bazelon. Then again, it sounded a bit like Robert Bork."

After tweaking his friend, now that he had good reason to believe their rivalry would soon be over, Scalia drew an even sharper line between himself and his tablemates. He distinguished between *original intent*, espoused by Bork and Meese, and *original meaning*, which Scalia believed judges should employ in statutory interpretation. A more cautious man, less principled, would have chosen less provocative material for the day. Meese had the president's ear; one word from him and Monday's meeting could be scuttled altogether. But Scalia, contrary to the careerist caricature, wanted to make his argument.

"Even if you believe in original intent in the literal sense," he said, "you must end up believing in original meaning, because it is perfectly clear that the original intent was that the Constitution would be interpreted according to its original meaning." To Scalia, it all boiled down to one question: "What was the most plausible meaning of the words of the Constitution to the society that adopted it—regardless of what the Framers might secretly have intended?" He closed with a premonition: "I suppose I ought to campaign to change the label from the Doctrine of Original Intent to the Doctrine of Original Meaning. As I often tell my law clerks, terminology is destiny."[4]

During the luncheon, the conversation at the head table turned into a debate over the Commerce Clause. "Scalia took a strong line in favor of judicial restraint," Epstein recalled. "As was his wont, Bork was all over the place, thinking aloud and trying to get to the bottom of something." As the discussion intensified, an aide approached Meese and notified him that he was needed at the White House immediately. Meese left, and "Scalia's nomination to the Supreme Court was announced shortly thereafter," Epstein said. "History often turns on strange coincidences."[5]

The luncheon was the last time Bork and Scalia would see each other before fate—and Ronald Reagan—changed their lives, and friendship, forever.

*   *   *

Scalia arrived in the Oval Office at 3:28 p.m. He was greeted by the president, Regan, Wallison, and Meese. According to the official memo prepared by the White House counsel, Reagan "came right to the point," apprising the visitor of Burger's retirement and Rehnquist's appointment to succeed him. Scalia, the president said, was "the choice of all of us" to succeed Rehnquist. The judge expressed gratitude. Reagan offered the seat "right on the spot" with "very little ceremony," and a "delighted" Scalia accepted immediately, saying, as Rehnquist had, that he would be "honored." All agreed that to prevent news leaks, the dual announcement should be made the next day. Scalia left at 3:48 p.m.[6]

The kid from Queens had risen.

THE SUPREME COURT

He had made it!

All the work, the *work*, the grinding, grueling *work*, the *hours and hours and hours* of studying, conjugating, teaching, writing, lecturing, debating, publishing, editing, moving, flying, testifying, and *praying*, had led him at last, at the inevitable hour, to his God-appointed destiny: the Marble Temple, pinnacle of the law. A quarter century had passed since Nino's Dalny Road prophecy to Bob Connor: "I'm going to the Supreme Court.... I will rise."

First thing: give thanks to God. Next: tell Maureen, and thank her, too. Then: round up the children, ages five to twenty-four, and make sure they all have clean clothes for the announcement. "Tomorrow's going to be a circus," he and Maureen agreed.

When he got back to chambers, the judge called in his most trusted clerk, Patrick Schiltz, and confided the news: the Burger-Rehnquist-Scalia shift at the Court. "I mentioned how sad it was that his parents hadn't lived to see that," Schiltz told me. "That is the only time I saw him get really emotional about it. He choked up and kind of wiped away a tear and agreed that he was sad, too. But we both said they were in Heaven looking down and they must be very happy."[7]

*   *   *

Nino had risen. And the first thing he needed was a good lawyer.

Eight months earlier, in October 1985, Larry Silberman had been sworn in as the newest Reagan appointee, following Kenneth Starr, on the D.C. Circuit. Thus began an extraordinary four-decade second career for Silberman, one that exceeded, against tall odds, the historical significance of his first, when he had served as under-secretary of labor, deputy attorney general, intelligence advisor, and Iron Curtain ambassador.

In addition to writing dozens of seminal appellate decisions— including in *District of Columbia v. Heller*, which, upheld by the Supreme Court, paved the way for the legalization of handgun ownership across America—Judge Silberman co-chaired the Commission on the Intelligence Capabilities of the United States Regarding Weapons of Mass Destruction, the independent panel created by the Bush-Cheney administration to examine intelligence failures in the run-up to the Iraq War.

Interviewed in chambers a few blocks from the Capitol in May 2017, the old lion, still scrappy and acerbic at eighty-one, nattily attired in tweed sportcoat and tie, smiled at the memory of joining the D.C. Circuit. Bork and Scalia, Silberman's former subordinates at Main Justice, "never let me forget" he was now junior to them.

Silberman knew Bork well; but Larry and Nino were best friends. They could be merciless when ribbing each other. It was Scalia who "talked me into serving" on the D.C. Circuit, Silberman said. "Bork had told me I'd be bored. Scalia said: 'I think you'll love it—you're at least half of an intellectual!'" As a judge Silberman once made the mistake, in private conversation, of using the Latin term *dubitante*. "You don't even know what *dubitante* means!" Scalia snapped. How many lunch hours they passed at the A.V. Ristorante, trading ethnic jokes, knocking back what Silberman called "dago red wine." Friends impersonated Larry to poke fun at how often he placed himself at the center of major events: "So I said, 'Harry, for Chrissakes—drop the fucking bomb!'"

Larry and Nino: Together they rose through official Washington in the 1970s and '80s, an affectionate, wise-cracking Odd Couple whose friendship was never afflicted by the rivalry that colored Scalia's relationship with Bork. Silberman told me that he recognized upon *meeting* Nino, in 1974, that he was destined for the Court. This shared ambition—Silberman was short-listed three times by Republican presidents—was something the two men, mutual *consiglieres*, discussed candidly. "Whenever one of us was offered something, we always called each other to talk it over," Silberman said. "Nino was afraid that if there was a vacancy—he confided in me ruefully—the president would be inclined to fill 'the Jewish seat' and I'd get it."

In a previously unreported episode from June 1985, a year before Scalia's fateful meeting with President Reagan in the Oval Office, Attorney General Meese, confronted with the resignation of Rex Lee as solicitor general, had quietly approached Judge Scalia and asked him to resign from the D.C. Circuit to succeed Lee: the very man William French Smith had chosen over Scalia back in 1981.

"My dad was very torn," Gene Scalia told me, "because he was interested in being on the Supreme Court and he figured if he became solicitor general, that would be a useful credential and he would be in the good graces of the administration.... I do remember evenings at the counter in the kitchen, where my dad would have his whiskey sour and cheese and crackers and read the comics before sitting down for dinner. I do remember a couple discussions about whether he should take that job, and my mom and him talking it through, and his being very unsure what to do."

"Don't do it," Silberman advised. "Your chances of going to the Supreme Court are better where you are than if you become solicitor general."

Scalia was still torn.

"Do you want to go back to private practice?"

"Why are you asking me that?"

"Because Nino, when you are no longer SG, you're not going to be a judge again. You can't go back on the D.C. Circuit."

Scalia followed the wise counsel of his Jewish *consigliere*.

"I've got a job I like," Nino thought. "I could take SG and not like it, and it's a two to three-year job—and then where am I?"

Now, fresh from the Oval Office meeting with Reagan, Scalia turned to Silberman again: "I'm going to need a lawyer. Will you represent me?"

Silberman was ideal: He was a friend; he knew the ins and outs of judicial nominations; and as he put it to me, decades later: "I was free!"

At that moment, Silberman's daughter was living in the Scalias' Chicago home with other renters. She told her father she believed Scalia wanted them out. Silberman asked why. Because the judge hadn't sent the tenants a bill, she said. Larry called up Nino and asked if he wanted Silberman's daughter to move out.

"No! Why do you ask?"

"Because you never sent them a bill."

"Oh, my God!" Scalia said, dumbstruck.

The episode introduced Silberman to a recurring feature of his counsellorship to Scalia—the absent-minded professor, particularly in finance. Digging into Scalia's disclosure forms, Silberman found a

$50,000 accounts-receivable from AT&T that puzzled him. "Oh, I did some consulting work for them a few years ago," Scalia answered.

"Well, you never sent them a bill!"

Scalia asked if he should send AT&T a bill now.

"Jesus, Nino, no! You're up for the Supreme Court!"

A few weeks later Scalia came to Silberman in a state of anxiety. Senator Robert Byrd, Democrat of West Virginia, had invited Scalia to appear at a Columbus Day parade.

"Does this mean I have an ethical problem?"

"You dummy! It means you're going to be confirmed!"

ROSEN: Not too many people probably ever addressed Antonin Scalia as "you dummy."

SILBERMAN: [laughs] He was impractical. He didn't understand politics at all.

Estrangement from finance was part of "the wholly impractical life he led," Silberman said, in stark contrast with Maureen, whom Silberman described as "a brilliant woman...profoundly conservative...the dominant force."[8]

*   *   *

At the White House and Main Justice, the vast machinery required to submit and confirm *two* Court nominees cranked into gear. The announcement was set for 2:00 p.m. in the White House briefing room on Tuesday, June 17. Two hours beforehand, Don Regan summoned senior staff, including communications director Pat Buchanan and acting White House press secretary Larry Speakes, to break the imminent news to them. Buchanan, the conservative stalwart who had urged Reagan a year earlier to select Scalia over Bork, shouted, "Yes!" and pumped his fist. All were sworn to secrecy. Speakes issued a press release announcing a 2:00 p.m. event, after which "all the phones in the White House lit up," as reporters tried to learn the topic of the president's remarks. Scalia arrived, unnoticed, in a "battered" compact car while Burger, forswearing discretion, pulled up in his official black limousine emblazoned with the Court seal in gold. The secret held.[9]

At 1:57 p.m., Scalia was ushered into the Oval Office. There stood Reagan, Regan, Wallison, Meese, Burger, and Rehnquist. The men chatted amiably for two minutes. Over at the Court, Burger had arranged for his fellow justices to receive copies of the chief's official retirement letter ten minutes before the announcement. Stunned, the justices gathered around the TV in the chief's conference room to take in the news like the rest of the country. Rehnquist's absence was not unnoticed.

Now the elite group, led by the president, traversed the short, carpeted path from the Oval Office to the briefing room. A door opened, cameras clicked, lights flashed. Reagan, trailed by Burger, Rehnquist, and Scalia, clambered to the elevated dais and the presidential podium. Clad in a charcoal grey suit and red tie, Scalia, shorter and darker than the others, the only man onstage unknown to the public, stood alone to Reagan's right—screen left for Americans tuned in across the country—with Rehnquist and Burger shoulder to shoulder on Reagan's left. "There was an audible gasp when the three jurists appeared," Wallison wrote. Pleased the press was caught off guard, Reagan opened with a shake of his head and a triumphant "Heh!"[10]

Minutes earlier, at the Department of Education, Gene Scalia, then a speechwriter for Secretary Bill Bennett, one of his dad's poker buddies, marched into the office of the chief of staff, William Kristol.

"We've got to turn on the TV."

"Why?"

"Bill, trust me. This is going to be good."

The three gathered at a TV. Gene smiled.

For Antonin Scalia, the pairing with Rehnquist carried special significance. Back in October 1971, when Rehnquist had been named to the Court, he was serving as assistant attorney general for the Office of Legal Counsel and had corresponded with Scalia, on telecommunications law, less than a week earlier. When Roger Cramton succeeded Rehnquist, Scalia had succeeded Cramton; later still, Scalia succeeded them both at OLC.

Now Rehnquist's rise had again aided Scalia's: their names and faces would be linked, in history and the public imagination, forever. Scalia liked and admired Rehnquist, even when they didn't agree. They were part of a regular poker game, and in such settings Rehnquist was affable and dry-witted. He once told another justice that Warren Burger's opening remarks at Court conferences went on so long they sounded "like a Southern novel."

But as Scalia looked across the White House stage at Rehnquist—in this, their moment of shared supreme triumph—he surely remembered something Rehnquist had said to him recently, during Scalia's time on the D.C. Circuit, previously unreported: "Nino, don't worry so much about the reasoning, just get the right result." The remark haunted Scalia the rest of his life. Fond though he was of Rehnquist, that was *not* the kind of justice Scalia intended to be.[11]

*   *   *

President Reagan began by disclosing Burger's secret visit of May 27; the quiet work done to develop recommendations; and his decisions to nominate Rehnquist and, "upon Justice Rehnquist's confirmation," Scalia. "In choosing Justice Rehnquist and Judge Scalia, I have not only selected judges who are sensitive to [judicial restraint], but through their distinguished backgrounds and achievements, reflect my desire to appoint the most qualified individuals to serve in our courts.... Judge Scalia has been a judge of the United States Court of Appeals for the District of Columbia Circuit since 1982. His great personal energy, the force of his intellect, and the depth of his understanding of our constitutional jurisprudence uniquely qualify him for elevation to our highest court."

Reagan closed with praise for Burger, saying the Court under his seventeen-year tenure as chief had "remained faithful to precedent, while it sought out the principles that underlay the Framers' words." Scalia and the Federalist Society felt differently about the Burger Court, whose bequeathals to American law had included *Roe* and *Bakke*; but Reagan was being gracious. "God bless you," he said, turning to leave as the reporters shouted questions. Reagan tried to beg off, but the reporters kept clamoring. Already familiar with Rehnquist, they made Scalia their focus.

> **CHRIS WALLACE/NBC NEWS:** Are you satisfied that the judge agrees with you on the abortion issue?
> **REAGAN:** I'm not going to answer any questions. If I start answering one, I'll—
> **SAM DONALDSON/ABC NEWS:** Mr. President, what was the process which led you to Judge *Scah-lee-ah*? Did you know him before? Did people come to you and recommend him? What was the process?
> **REAGAN:** I'd previously appointed him into his present judgeship.

Amid the din, the president turned to Wallison.
"Can I go now?"
"Yes," the counsel said. "You can go."

Reagan left and Burger took the podium, jovially holding forth on his legacy, future, and health ("never felt better").

> **REPORTER:** Do you approve of the appointment of Judge Scalia?
>
> **BURGER:** Well, the Constitution doesn't give the chief justice any authority on the subject.... I've known Justice Rehnquist as a colleague for now, what, fifteen years?...And I've known Judge Scalia since the time he was an assistant attorney general. He's participated in extrajudicial activities, like being a member of the American team visiting England to study some of their methods. We are not close friends. I have a high regard for each of them, a high regard.
>
> **REPORTER:**... You know Judge Scalia better than anybody else in this room. Give us a little sense, if you would—
>
> **BURGER:** No, I wouldn't say I know Judge Scalia better than anyone else in this room.
>
> **REPORTER:** Better than anyone else on *this* side of the room. [laughter]
>
> **BURGER:** Then some of you haven't been on the job, doing your homework.

The shouting! "Can we talk to Judge Scalia?" "Can we ask Judge Scalia about his background?" The hounds were on the scent of the new guy, eager to pin him down on *Roe*. But the hounds would have to wait; Rehnquist was next up to the microphone. The justice said he was "deeply gratified" by the president's confidence and would do his best to "deserve" it. Queried on his health, Rehnquist parried cannily: all questions that might bear on his confirmation he would defer until his Senate hearing.

Now it was Scalia's turn to meet the press. With his debate-show appearances in the 1950s, and his extensive work with AEI, PBS, and other TV producers, Scalia had undoubtedly logged more time on television than all the sitting justices and their predecessors combined. Yet even for so practiced a performer as *Il Matador*, the super-charged moment—the White House setting, the live coverage, reporters shouting—was new and, judging by the look on Scalia's face, a bit unnerving.

Until it was time for him to speak, Nino cautiously clasped his hands while Rehnquist, long a made man, casually shoved his hands in his pockets and Burger, sovereign, stood with arms folded. But Scalia was ready for his close-up. His first public comment on the national stage flashed his sense of humor.

> **ANDREA MITCHELL/NBC NEWS:** Judge Scalia, can you share your thoughts with us as a new nominee—as much as you can say about your philosophy?
> **SCALIA:** Yes, on the substance of it, I think I'm with Justice Rehnquist. I—I know a good idea when I hear one. [laughter]
> **MITCHELL:** What about your personal thoughts?
> **SCALIA:** Oh, my personal thoughts are, for somebody who spent his whole professional life in the law, getting nominated to the Supreme Court is the culmination of, of a dream, of course. And I'm—I'm greatly honored that the president would have such confidence in me and hope that the Senate will do so, as well. And I'll certainly do whatever I can to live up to it.

The reporters wanted to know if Reagan's aides had asked Scalia about *Roe*. The Senate could ask that, Scalia replied, but for now he was going to respond as Rehnquist had. Then they asked if Scalia thought his nomination was going to prove controversial. "I've no idea," he snapped. "I'm not a politician."

> **DONALDSON:** Judge *Scall-ya*, would you call yourself a tough judge?
> **SCALIA:** [pauses] Uh, I—I think that's—that's in the category of questions I think—
> **MITCHELL:** Can you tell us when you were first approached by the administration? . . .
> **SCALIA:** I think if the president wants that to be known, I'm sure he'll tell you.
> **LESLEY STAHL/CBS NEWS:** . . . Judge *Scall-ya*, could you tell us where you went to school and what your background is?
> **SCALIA:** Sorry, that's—
> **SPEAKES:** We have that in the bins.
> **REPORTER:** . . . Judge *Scall-ya*, many of the judges appointed by this administration are said to have been subjected to a rigorous screening process conducted under Attorney General Meese. Were you at all—*Roe v. Wade* aside—asked any of your positions on various points of law?
> **SCALIA:** I have—I have no idea what, what the screening process was. And again, you'd have to ask the attorney general.
> **WALLACE:** No one spoke to you, sir?
> **SCALIA:** Uh—I speak to people all the time.

These early exchanges anticipated Scalia's interactions with the press for the rest of his life: questions that, in his eyes, ranged from ill-conceived to moronic, answers that alternated between bemused and bothered. An end was called to the Q&A. But the hounds had one final piece of business. They asked how to pronounce "Scalia," then "Antonin."

*   *   *

June 17, 1986, Announcement Day, marked the great dividing line in Scalia's life: the moment he became a national figure, his rising beamed coast-to-coast, an instant celebrity, symbol, and myth. The public beheld a short, stocky judge with thinning black hair and intense dark eyebrows, the son of an Italian immigrant with a sharp wit and jovial smile, at once cocky and humble, an overnight sensation: sharing the White House stage with Ronald Reagan, Warren Burger, and William Rehnquist, titans all.

CHAPTER XVI

The Nominee

*Supreme Court appointments are the premier spoils of
presidential politics. Each appointee is 20 percent of a
majority at the apex of one of the three branches of
government, the branch that has assumed custody of the
issues (race, abortion, etc.) the political branches have
been pleased to relinquish. The departure of Warren
Burger, the elevation of William Rehnquist, and the
nomination of Antonin Scalia are important episodes in
the process of lengthening the shadow today's president
will cast into tomorrow.*

—George F. Will, 1986

How Nino and Maureen celebrated his nomination, the culmination, *the incarnation*, of their dreams—Scalia's, Maureen's, the
American Dream, seamlessly entwined—is not recorded. Once again,
the pace of events afforded little time for emotion. The nominee faced
a fourth FBI background check, questionnaires and financial disclosure
forms, meetings with senators, mock hearings, and, finally, the confirmation hearings themselves, before the Senate Judiciary Committee.
There were also ramifications for Maureen and the nine Scalia children.

Their father was suddenly one of America's most famous men, his family now subject, in ways obvious and subtle, to the perils of fame.

For the next ninety days, Scalia lived in a cocoon, encircled by White House and DOJ staffers, handlers, clerks, sherpas: the human capital invested to keep nominees away from the media and on track to confirmation. With C-SPAN carrying the hearings live, and CNN capable of doing so, the mid-1980s media landscape resembled today's more closely than that of the Watergate era. Reagan's aides, and the nominees, understood themselves to be operating in a modern arena, governed by global satellite communications, 24-7 news coverage, and hostile advocacy groups. The White House reporters who peppered Scalia were a modern press corps, playing for keeps; and Senate Democrats, while in the minority, were gunning for Rehnquist. The stakes were high. *Newsweek* noted that Scalia could serve on the Court "beyond the year 2010." Speaking to the *Wall Street Journal*, a senior administration official called the nominations "the most significant move" of the Reagan presidency.[1]

*   *   *

"Judge with Tenacity and Charm," declared the *New York Times*.

"Scalia Described as Persuasive, Affable," agreed the *Los Angeles Times*.

"Scalia Seen as Major Force on the Supreme Court," noted the *Christian Science Monitor*.

"Confirmation of Justices Predicted by End of Year," reported the *Washington Post*.

Here, in Scalia's baptismal news cycle, emerged the broad outlines of the coverage he was to receive, as justice and celebrity, symbol and myth, for the rest of his life. Ignorant of Scalia's existence until Tuesday, unaware of the trails he had blazed through academia and the appellate bench—"His opinion on the Court's decision is not known," the *Chicago Tribune*, of all outlets, falsely reported about *Roe*—the press struggled to catch up. But reporters are quick studies, and after calls to sources they captured accurately the high esteem for Scalia and his conglomerate of skills.

"It is his combination of affability and acumen, of energetic fervor and astringent intellect, that makes him potentially one of the most influential of justices," reported *Time*. "Through his considerable powers of persuasion," said the *Monitor*, "Scalia may wind up altering the balance—and thus the outcome of close decisions." "Judicial foes and supporters alike describe Antonin Scalia...as an aggressive conservative who combines persuasive powers with unusual affability," the *Los Angeles Times* said.

However, the moment also gave flight, among the Washington press corps, to the careerist narrative that Safire, the opinion columnist with a grudge against Scalia, had floated the year before. That Scalia perfectly embodied the philosophy of judicial restraint championed by Reagan and Meese seemed beyond the imagination of the news media. Such powerful synchronicity could not be organic; it had to be the result of Scalia's *actively auditioning* for Reagan, flashing his card, earning his stripes.

"In his opinions," said the *Washington Post*, Scalia "appeared to go out of his way to express views consistent with those of the Reagan administration.... That practice fueled speculation in legal and political circles that he was actively campaigning for a high court nomination." "A few of Scalia's colleagues on the Court of Appeals," reported *Time*, "suspect that he wrote a number of strongly-worded dissenting and concurring opinions on the conservative side of cases simply to advertise that he was 100 percent in accord with Reagan's views."

The cheapest shots came from *Daily News* columnist Jimmy Breslin, the celebrated "Bard of Queens," who took the R train to scope out Scalia's boyhood neighborhood in Elmhurst. The people there,

Breslin wrote, were "pure Queens.... Their major asset was their obsti-
nacy." He depicted the neighborhood—and by implication, Scalia
himself—as insular, bigoted, conceited:

> Scalia, as Roman Catholic as a retreat, was forced to attend
> Boy Scout meetings at the Methodist church because
> the natural place for a Boy Scout troop in Elmhurst,
> St. Bartholomew's Roman Catholic Church on Ithaca Street,
> had an Irish pastor at the time who would not allow a Boy
> Scout troop in his place because he might wind up with
> Protestants and, God forbid, a Jew inside his halls....
> [Xavier] was fully integrated: half Irish and half Italian.
> Scalia, in a Catholic school, was in an atmosphere that
> causes students to feel superior to begin with. As the school
> was Jesuit, the atmosphere was also one of being superior
> to all other Catholics. And then since Xavier was a military
> school, its students were aggressively superior.

Editorial opinion split along ideological lines. "Although we might
not agree with Antonin Scalia on every issue," said the *Wall Street
Journal*, "he is an excellent choice. Even before he joined the [bench]
he had come to our attention as the editor of *Regulation* magazine and
as one of the crew of bright young scholars teaching at the University
of Chicago Law School. His specialty is separation of powers.... Scalia
is [also] an expert on how the post–New Deal regulatory system works,
and especially on how it fits—and doesn't fit—into this careful system
of checks and balances."

The left-leaning *Baltimore Sun*, conceding Scalia's "impeccable"
credentials, took a dimmer view: "We question his marketplace
approach to the law—is this or that constitutional right worth the price
paid to protect it? We certainly question his view that the press does

not deserve the freedom to probe and write about important individuals and institutions. He may not be, as [William Safire] called him last year, 'the worst enemy of free speech in America today,' but he's no Warren Burger, either."[2]

Reactions across Washington also split along ideological lines. "Senate Republicans Praise Choices," the *Los Angeles Times* reported. Democratic lawmakers, aghast that Reagan even *had* another opportunity to appoint a justice, labeled his choices "very frightening," with Scalia depicted as "even more of a conservative hard-liner" than Rehnquist. Senator Biden, ranking Democrat on the Judiciary committee—who had approved Scalia's nomination to the D.C. Circuit—was all over the place. On one hand, Biden conceded that Rehnquist and Scalia were "in a different league intellectually" from most nominees; on the other, he argued that while Scalia was "unquestionably qualified" to sit on the appellate court, it was "an open question whether he is qualified to sit on the Supreme Court."

With Rehnquist sure to draw heavy fire, however, and Scalia's credentials so impressive, the consensus foresaw little opposition for him. The Democrats on the D.C. Circuit endorsed him. Judge Mikva spoke of his "delightful colleague...good sense of humor, lots of human qualities, an uproarious laugh." "I think he does listen, he has an open mind, he enjoys the dialogue," Judge Wald told the *Post*. "I do have the sense he has strong feelings about particular things, but that he does come to each case willing to listen to both sides."

Other Senate Democrats on the Judiciary Committee followed suit. Pat Leahy of Vermont called Rehnquist and Scalia "very competent, highly qualified men." The *New York Times* heard "lawmakers from both parties" agreeing that Scalia's "intellectual brilliance would mute criticism from senators who disagreed with his conservative rulings." *U.S. News & World Report* predicted that both Rehnquist and Scalia were "likely to sail through Senate confirmation."[3]

To liberal lawyers and advocacy groups, however, the bipartisan spirit that greeted Scalia on the Hill was deeply disappointing. These activists would not allow his nomination to go unopposed. Alan Dershowitz, then a liberal Harvard law professor, branded Rehnquist and Scalia "two of the finest nineteenth-century minds in America." Laurence Tribe, also a liberal Harvard Law professor, took the matter more seriously, calling the nominees "distinguished and bright men," jurists "of tremendous affability," and warning, "There is no doubt that Scalia will shift the balance of the Court over the long run because he is so much more intelligent and powerful and affable than Warren Burger."

Social justice warriors, civil rights groups, women's organizations: The mobilization was underway. But they started from a disadvantage: the American Bar Association—which had withheld its highest rating during Scalia's nomination to the D.C. Circuit—now ranked him "well qualified" for the Court, following an "exhaustive investigation" by ABA's Standing Committee on the Federal Judiciary. Their unanimous opinion held Scalia "among the best available for appointment to the Supreme Court," saying he had demonstrated across his career "outstanding competence, the highest integrity, and excellent judicial temperament."

The ABA inquiry was more comprehensive than the FBI's. The dean and faculty of the University of Michigan Law School were enlisted, along with leading lawyers and law students, to review Scalia's opinions. More than 340 interviewees were questioned, including more than 200 state and federal judges, among them the justices of the Court and Scalia himself. "Most of those who know him spoke enthusiastically of his keen intellect, his careful and thoughtful analysis of legal problems, his excellent writing ability and his congeniality and sense of humor. Almost all who know him, including those who disagree with him philosophically and politically, expressed admiration for his abilities, and for his integrity and judicial temperament."[4]

"Liberals Portray Scalia as Threat but Bar Group Sees Him as Open," the *New York Times* reported. This was when the playbook was written: If a conservative Court nominee was well qualified and unburdened by any hint of questionable prior conduct, then the liberal line of attack was to declare the nominee's views *extreme*—racist, sexist, repressive. "There is room in the courts for conservatives," said Ralph Neas, executive director of the Leadership Conference on Civil Rights. "But this man is not within the parameters of acceptability. He has shown a remarkable insensitivity to victims of discrimination." Eleanor Smeal of the National Organization for Women said the judge's views were "totally out of keeping with where we are in today's society."[5]

*　　*　　*

For one interest group, the Scalia nomination triggered an explosion of pride and joy. Not since Rocco Marchegiano of Brockton, Massachusetts, captured the world heavyweight championship in 1952 had the Italian-American community rejoiced like this. Scalia's rise meant even more because his achievement, unlike Rocky Marciano's, was purer, wholly intellectual, academic: untainted by the violence of the ring and the dishonor of organized crime, which had periodically controlled professional boxing.

The 1980 Census listed 23 million Americans of Italian descent, roughly 9 percent of the population. Recent years had witnessed numerous ground-breaking appointments and achievements, including the crusading Watergate roles of Judge Sirica and House Judiciary Chairman Democrat Peter Rodino of New Jersey; the ascent, in 1978, of A. Bartlett Giamatti to the presidency of Yale; Mario Cuomo's election as governor of New York in 1982; and the selection, two years later, of Geraldine Ferraro as the Democratic vice presidential nominee.

The preceding generation had produced several films, Oscar winners and box office gold, with Italian themes, including *The Godfather* (1972) and *The Godfather: Part II* (1974), *Rocky* (1976), and *Saturday Night Fever* (1977). These landmark works celebrated the community even as they stirred ambivalence within it.

Scalia trumped all that. When he donned the robes of an associate justice, his honor would be pristine, holy, *supreme*. "Italian Americans throughout the nation are thrilled and over-joyed," Charles Porcelli, president of the Joint Civic Committee of Italian Americans, wrote President Reagan on June 19. "The long-sought dream of Italian Americans is now at long last a reality...Italian Americans everywhere are eternally grateful.... Judge Scalia is eminently qualified and has the wholehearted support of all Italian Americans as well as the many ethnic groups in the country. His selection has heightened the spirit and morale of our people.... We are convinced that Judge Scalia will perform with dignity [and] dedication and will be guided in his decisions on the basis of what is in the best interests of all Americans regardless of race, creed, or social status."

By recognizing "the tremendous academic and professional accomplishments of this unique individual," wrote Dante Sarubbi of New Jersey, "you have brought honor to all Italian-Americans." Bruno Giuffrida, head of the Supreme Lodge of the Order Sons of Italy, thanked Reagan for embracing those "who have heretofore been denied access to America's highest court." "Our deepest thanks for your courage and understanding," cheered the country's largest Italian-American service organization. "Antonin Scalia will make you proud of your choice and will help make America even greater.... You should be credited with the foresight you have in America's finally realizing that intelligence, justice, humaneness, and knowledge of our laws exist in the Italian community just as they exist in other heritages which make up America."

"The Italo-American community for many years has attempted to convince past presidents of these United States that simple justice and equity cried out for an appointment of an American of Italian descent to the Supreme Court," wrote Frank Montemuro, Jr. "Our pleas were made to Presidents Franklin Delano Roosevelt, Truman, Eisenhower, Kennedy, Johnson, Nixon, Ford, and yourself. They all listened.... Only you heard."[6]

*   *   *

White House aides moved swiftly to maximize the appointment's political value. "Italian American organizations will highlight the Scalia nomination," Mari Maseng of the Office of Public Liaison wrote the president. Maseng wanted to blast out a Reagan-Scalia photo on June 23, but no good photo of them had been taken, and Reagan was now in California. On July 7, Scalia returned to the Oval for the photo session. The official contact sheets of the White House photographer show the Gipper cracking Scalia up.

No Court nominee had ever benefited from as elaborate a publicity campaign as the one Maseng and Linas Kojelis, special assistant to the president for public liaison, orchestrated for Scalia:

1. <u>Mailings</u>: Mail press releases and transcripts of White House Press Room statements on appointment...to Italian American media and leadership. (Completed on 6/20.) ...
2. <u>Press Conference for Italian American media</u>: Invite Italian-American media representatives to White House for briefing on domestic and foreign policy issues. Includes briefing by Pat Buchanan....

3. <u>Presidential Briefing for Italian-American leaders</u>: Host White House briefing on domestic and foreign policy issues in Cabinet Room with Presidential drop-by.

There were seven points in all, including enlisting Vice President Bush and his official residence in the campaign; dinners to be held by Italian-American groups; a Capitol reception to be hosted by Congressman Rodino, a Democrat and "one of the deans of the Italian congressional delegation."[7]

*   *   *

A few hours before the big announcement at the White House, Judge Bork trudged through the mural-covered halls of his old haunt: Main Justice. His summons, on short notice, was odd. He had broken bread with Meese at DOJ just three days earlier, at Saturday's conference on economic liberties, where Nino, *the ham*, had tweaked him from the podium.

Bork, too, was over twenty-one, and knew the summons meant either that he was being nominated to the Court—or that Nino was. Who met with Bork at DOJ that morning, what was said, is nowhere recorded. At 2:00 p.m., however, Bork watched on TV along with the rest of the country.

There was Nino Scalia, Bork's dear friend, practically his protégé, onstage at the White House, shoulder to shoulder with Reagan, Burger, and Rehnquist, titans all. His rivalry with Nino was over...was this really how it ended? With Bork as the Salieri to Scalia's Mozart?

Now reporters were lighting up Bork's phone...with questions about *Nino*. The newspapers had got wind of Bork's visit to DOJ that morning. Joseph Volz of the *Daily News* reported that Bork was summoned to "get the word that he was not stepping up but that his colleague on the same appellate bench would." Ron Ostrow and Philip Hager of the *Los Angeles Times* reported that Bork had been assured of receiving the *next* vacancy. "Bork would not comment," Ostrow and Hager wrote. "Bork declined comment," Volz reported, beneath a headline reading, "Scalia Beat Bork for Post."

Salt in the wound!

The articles contrasted Scalia's "vigor" and "robust health" with Bork's pallid appearance. "Bork is fifty-nine, smokes heavily, and is overweight," the *Los Angeles Times* reported as fact.

The *New York Times'* James Reston, dean of the Washington press corps, described Bork's fate as the "one surprise" in the rise of Scalia: "While it is agreed here that he is articulate and personable, it was thought that Robert Bork...had a more brilliant career, and having been passed over once despite the recommendation of the conservative wing of the Republican Party, would this time be chosen.... Judge Scalia, a Roman Catholic who would be the first justice on the Court of Italian descent, is thought to be a more reliable conservative."

Bork had waged his lonely war on the Warren Court, birthed the modern conservative legal movement, and achieved the status of a national figure while Scalia was still at OTP negotiating cable contracts...and now Nino was more reliably conservative than the godfather, the don of originalism?

The rivalry had been on display at least since *Ollman*. "It colored their relationship personally in some subtle ways," Silberman observed, "became a little strained.... This is human nature." Gene Scalia recalled that it was his father, not anyone at DOJ, who had broken the news to Bork.

EUGENE SCALIA: I know that after my dad met with the White House and was offered the job by President Reagan, he came back to the court and visited Judge Bork in his chambers to tell him. And that was obviously a hard conversation to have.

ROSEN: Is that all we know about that conversation?

EUGENE SCALIA: It's all I know about it.

"Bork deeply resented that Nino got picked first," Silberman told me. Bork chalked it up to the *Italian thing*. Speaking to Silberman, he wondered aloud whether "ethnicity will rule again" when the next vacancy arose.[8]

*   *   *

The first demand on Scalia was the placement of calls to five Senate leaders: Majority Leader Bob Dole; Strom Thurmond, president *pro tempore* and chairman of the Judiciary Committee; Alan Simpson, majority whip and Judiciary Committee member; Minority Leader Robert Byrd; and the Committee's ranking Democrat, Joe Biden.

A June 19 staff memo, captioned SUBJECTS FOR DISCUSSION WITH JUDGE SCALIA and previously unpublished, advised the director of the White House legislative affairs office: "You should impress on him the importance of working with this office...that this office has the lead."

> Advise him that the nomination papers will be transmitted to the Senate today...so as to allow the clock to start ticking in the Judiciary committee. Chairman Thurmond intends to hold [Scalia's] confirmation hearing shortly after [the hearing for] Justice Rehnquist is completed.
>
> Advise him we will start setting up courtesy calls after the Congress returns from the July 4th recess...Senator Thurmond has pledged to speed the process up, so it is probable that

confirmation will take place before the August recess.... Justice Department, in the guise of John Bolton, will prepare briefing books on the senators, their concerns and special interests in the judicial field.

At the appropriate time, a mock hearing will be scheduled, to give Scalia a "feel" for his hearing.

Scalia's first meetings on Capitol Hill, scheduled for July 15, were with Senators Howell Heflin, Democrat of Alabama, and Alfonse D'Amato, Republican of New York and a fellow *paisan*. The next two weeks were a blur, as Scalia and his handlers rode the elevators up and down the Hart and Russell Senate Office Buildings for cordial conversations with two dozen of the chamber's major and minor figures: Dole, Kennedy, Moynihan, Leahy, Arlen Specter, Paul Simon, Orrin Hatch, Chuck Grassley, Mitch McConnell.

At Scalia's side was Fred McClure, the White House lawyer and legislative aide—young, savvy, African-American—who shepherded Scalia through the confirmation process. "He was absolutely enthusiastic about doing it," McClure said of the Senate sit-downs. "He was looking forward to it. I mean, it was like it was one of those things he had been kind of waiting on all his life...the next step to the brass ring."

Il Matador charmed and dodged with ease. No one made it easier, though, than D'Amato, another Italian American from New York, a year younger than Scalia. "I would have sworn that I was at some type of Italian reunion," McClure told me, his account previously unreported. "[D'Amato] was just busting at the seams and excited about Scalia.... They had a lot in common."

After they got through hugging and shucking and jiving with each other, we sat down. Al went over to his television and he pulled up some videotapes.... He said, "Nino, you've got to see this! You've got to see my mama, who is in my commercials this year!" And we watched Alfonse's re-election commercials for the United States Senate, where his mama talked about what a wonderful young man he was, or son he was. That was the *complete extent* of the interview.... We saw, like, three of the commercials she had shot and put together for Al.... We went outside and then [D'Amato] told the press how much he loved Nino Scalia and what a great justice he was going to be.[9]

Next came Scalia's "murder board," a kind of mock-confirmation hearing in which White House and DOJ staffers bombarded the nominee with difficult questions. "He was very confident," recalled Pat Schiltz, the circuit court clerk who assisted Scalia during the confirmation process and attended the murder boards. "Maybe Maureen would say something different, that he was spending every night at home working until midnight getting ready; but my impression was that he wasn't really sweating his confirmation hearings and that he didn't put a ton of time into preparation."

The sessions were held at the Old Executive Office Building. Word reached the group that Arlen Specter was planning to ask Scalia if he accepted as "settled law" the case of *Marbury v. Madison* (1803), the seminal ruling that established the Court as the final arbiter on the constitutionality of federal law and executive action. The decision had enshrined the concept of judicial review in American civic life; surely Scalia could endorse *Marbury*? Silberman had already advised against it: "If you answer on one case, you'll have to answer them all."

"I'm not going to admit to anything as settled law," Scalia declared to the group.

He was soon forced to recalibrate. Brad Reynolds, the assistant attorney general who had overseen the DOJ scouting effort, appeared in Scalia's chambers during this time with a question: "When you're asked about *Brown v. Board*, how are you going to answer?" *Brown, et al. v. Board of Education of Topeka, et al.* (1954) was the landmark Court ruling that held racial segregation in schools unconstitutional: the masterstroke of the Warren Court, *truly* settled law, effectively beyond criticism. "That was a really tough, hard conversation.... Reynolds was pressing him," Schiltz recalled. "Are you going to refuse to say that *Brown v. Board* was right? ... Your choices are: refuse to say whether you think it's right; say that you think it's right and then have to reconcile it with textualism; or say that you think it was wrong. That's the one time I can remember him struggling to get ready for the hearings.... It was the one thing where I saw him really have to furrow his brow and think about how he was going to answer.... *Brown v. Board* was a stand-in for when you're asked about this landmark or that landmark.... Where are you going to draw the line?"[10]

The FBI opened a new background investigation into Scalia, his fourth in fourteen years. Compared to the earlier exercises, the 1986 effort was...*half-hearted*. In part this owed to timing. Satisfied with the 1982 investigation and determined to avoid news leaks, the White House had concealed the nomination from the FBI: not until the day *after* Reagan announced Scalia's nomination to the world was the bureau tasked with vetting the judge. "The president of the United States is considering appointing this individual to the Supreme Court," the FBI director advised all field offices, comically, on June 18.

Top FBI officials also saw little need for a reprise; resources were scarce, and they had already determined, in painstaking fashion, that Scalia lived an exemplary life. The judge completed and signed Standard

Form 86, a lengthy questionnaire entitled SECURITY INVESTIGA-
TION DATA FOR SENSITIVE POSITIONS, and also signed a new
waiver for access to his tax records for 1982–86. But the FBI director
decreed, "An interview of Judge Scalia should not be needed."

Indeed, rather than find and interrogate everyone the nominee had
known since 1949, as in the previous dragnets, "major data banks were
searched" and Scalia was asked to name five peers not on the D.C.
Circuit and five individuals "with whom he interacts but do not share
his views." Even a member of the latter group credited Scalia: "a person
who is always genuinely searching for the truth...excellent demeanor
and temperament.... His loyalty and integrity were above reproach."[11]

*   *   *

At William Rehnquist's first confirmation hearing, back in 1971,
his testimony had filled all of forty-two pages of transcript. But it had
been rough stuff, the dawn of a new and uglier era.

The Democrats had charged that Rehnquist, as a poll monitor in
Arizona in the early 1960s, had intimidated Black and Hispanic voters.
They also cited a memo Rehnquist had written while clerking for Justice
Jackson that characterized *Plessy v. Ferguson*—the infamous ruling
upholding "separate but equal" facilities for the races—as correctly
decided. Rehnquist denied intimidating voters; the 1952 memo, he said,
had summarized Jackson's views.

"No black man," testified Clarence Mitchell of the NAACP, "could
believe that Mr. Rehnquist would give fair and impartial consideration
to any legal question involving race."

In December 1971, the Senate had confirmed Rehnquist over
unusually high opposition: sixty-eight to twenty-six.

On July 29, 1986, older and grayer, still Ichabod Crane–like thin
and dryly unflappable, Rehnquist returned to the Judiciary Committee.

As Thurmond cracked the gavel, the witness surveyed a minority panel loaded for bear. Ted Kennedy, who had participated in the 1971 hearings, had already declared Rehnquist "appalling" on race, "too extreme" for confirmation.

Two days earlier, the committee had announced it had found two *new* witnesses to Rehnquist's polling-site activities of the early '60s, both Democrats, including one who recalled scuffling with him. Additionally, the latest FBI background check had uncovered racial covenants in the deeds of two of Justice's Rehnquist's homes over the years, barring sale, respectively, to Blacks and Jews. The new witnesses were "mistaken," Rehnquist testified; as for the racial covenants, he, too, had learned of them from the FBI, and pledged to strike them. The Republicans also produced a witness: the Democratic Party chairman in the Arizona county where Rehnquist was alleged to have intimidated voters, who testified that the conduct ascribed to Rehnquist would have been brought to his attention immediately—and never was.

As an additional thrust, the Democrats demanded access to classified memoranda Rehnquist had written in the Nixon administration. Seven categories of interest were identified: surveillance of radical and antiwar groups, national security leak investigations, judicial nominations, Kent State, the May Day protests, and the Pentagon Papers. John Bolton, assistant attorney general for legislative affairs, appeared as a witness to invoke executive privilege and reject the Democrats' demands for the Nixon-era documents. When two Republicans—Charles Mathias of Maryland and the ever-prickly Specter—joined the Democrats' threat to subpoena the papers, the White House caved, making available a total of twenty-five Rehnquist memos from 1969 to 1971, covering all seven subjects.

This time, Rehnquist testified for *two days*, generating 287 pages of transcript. "Liberal Democrats pounded away," the *New York Times* reported, "at what they called Justice Rehnquist's insensitivity to minorities and the poor and questions about his truthfulness." Senator Hatch, freshman from Utah, "raised his voice to an angry shout" against the charges of racism.

Behold the Rehnquisition!

Poor Rehnquist. He was painfully shy, bookish by nature, and here he was, at the center of this…*ugly*…*undignified*…spectacle. Even so, his dry Midwestern wit prevailed. When Hatch noted that Rehnquist's "extremist" legal views were held by a majority of the lawmakers on the committee, the beleaguered justice deadpanned: "We're all extremists together."[12]

CHAPTER XVII

Justice Scalia

There is not a whole lot of use in being an ethnic, unless you're running for office or perhaps going through a confirmation hearing.

—Antonin Scalia, 1988

A t 11:02 a.m. on August 5, 1986, Chairman Thurmond gaveled the Scalia hearings to order in Room SD-106 of the Dirksen Senate Office Building. It was the nominee's second appearance before the Judiciary Committee in a little over four years; calm, ever professorial, Nino puffed on his pipe. "Judge Scalia is now cast in the role of a symbol," Thurmond declared, "proof of the vitality of the American Dream."

The chairman welcomed Maureen. "I believe eight of your nine children are here, are they not?"

"I do not know what happened to the ninth," Scalia said. He looked again. "They are all here, Senator. I have a full house." The family's size also figured in the introduction offered by Senator John Warner, Republican from the Scalias' adopted Virginia. "He has the ability to successfully manage, with his lovely wife, a family of nine children," Warner quipped. "That indicates something about his temperament."

D'Amato, a visitor to the committee, entered Scalia's official biography into the record, then waxed poetic about Salvatore Scalia's passage, like "so many millions of our ancestors," through Ellis Island. Only with the benefit of Fred McClure's recollection of how Scalia had spent his time in D'Amato's office can we understand the private joke the senator made: "Mama D'Amato, judge, sends her best."

Next came Biden, then in his third term. Chatty and digressive, the Delawarean said Scalia's rulings on administrative law had been "very important" but did not present a full range of issues. Therefore, Biden placed a premium on Scalia's "discussing with us, as freely and as openly as you have a reputation for doing, your judicial philosophy.... What do you mean by the notion that the Court should not create new rights under the Constitution unless a societal consensus—if I read your writings correctly—exists for that new right? What would this have meant to the Court that wrote *Brown v. the Board* or *Baker v. Carr* [the 1962 ruling affirming citizens' standing to challenge the apportionment of state representatives] or any number of other decisions? And what should it mean to a Court that is going to face reconsideration of *Roe v. Wade*?"

Two more visitors were welcomed, including Pete Domenici, Republican of New Mexico, another son of Italy. "If this establishes a precedent," joked Kennedy, "I want the chair to understand we have thirty-two Irishmen in the Senate."

"Italian Americans are Americans first and last," Domenici said, "and it is because we are Americans that we applaud a fellow Italian American's achievement of the American Dream."

The next visitor, Daniel Patrick Moynihan of New York, the former United Nations ambassador and polymathic Irish wit, well known to *Il Matador*, noted the high expectations of "another ethnic group in our country...academics." The last professor named to the Court had been Felix Frankfurter: "Forty-seven years between law professors is long enough."

Now Kennedy returned. The panel's most ruthless Democrat, heir to Camelot, had led the charge during the *Rehnquisition*. He knew Scalia personally, though; they had collaborated on legislation a decade earlier. The lion stilled his roar. "From the investigation carried out so far," Kennedy said, "as a scholar, public official, and federal judge, Mr. Scalia has demonstrated a brilliant legal intellect and earned the respect and affection of colleagues whose personal philosophies are far different." He found it "difficult" to declare Scalia "outside of the mainstream": "On the available record, I disagree with Judge Scalia on women's rights.... His position on this issue seems as insensitive as Justice Rehnquist's.... Should he be confirmed as a justice, I would hope that, as a result of these hearings and his new rank, he will look with greater sensitivity...on race discrimination, the right of women to escape their second-class status under the law and to share fully in the protections of the Constitution."

Howard Metzenbaum, a Democrat, was Scalia's tennis partner. "You know personally of your own area of bad judgment...whipping me on the court," the sixty-nine-year-old Ohioan joked. "It was a case of my integrity overcoming my judgment, Senator," Scalia countered, to audience laughter. Metzenbaum noted the Democrats' demand for memoranda Scalia had written in the Ford era. "I sincerely hope that the president will not choose to assert a claim of executive privilege," Metzenbaum said.

The blood lust was back.

Praising Scalia as "a lawyer's lawyer...a judge's judge," Orrin Hatch cited Scalia's extraordinary record on the Court of Appeals: "He has written eighty-six majority opinions and only nine of them have been accompanied by a dissenting opinion. In other words, Judge Scalia has won unanimous approval for his views in nearly 90 percent of his written opinions. Another 90 percent measure of success is found in the rate at which Judge Scalia's positions have been sustained on appeal.

The Supreme Court has adopted his view six of the seven times his cases have been reviewed on appeal."

Dennis DeConcini of Arizona urged his exhausted fellow Democrats to give Scalia's nomination hearing their "full energy and attention." Yet even the Italian-American lawmaker, himself the son of a judge, predicted Scalia "will serve this country well." While many observers considered Scalia a beneficiary, the embodiment, of the American Dream—limitless opportunity for enterprising individuals of modest means and foreign birth—only DeConcini mentioned the flip side: "The rapid assimilation of immigrants pumps strength and vitality into this great nation."

Alan Simpson, Republican of Wyoming, denounced the Rehnquisition. "Welcome to the pit," he told Scalia and his "fine family." There was no need to rehash Scalia's qualifications or opinions. "It is marvelous—the way you have that ability to bring that remarkable brilliance to a form where the common person can understand. That is what the law is all about. What good are we as lawyers or judges if the things we do for a client, or for a case, cannot even be understood? . . .

> We certainly washed all the laundry on Bill Rehnquist. I assume we will do that with you. And yet not one of us, not one of us up here, would want to sit right there at that table. We could not pass the test. We could not stand the heat. It is easier up here. Here we can brag and bluster and blather, almost like a comic book character you could invent, Captain Bombast: Pull the cape around the shoulders and shout the magic words, "Get him!" and rise above it all in a blast of hot air. . . . It is funny, but it really is not very funny at all. Human beings are involved, real families, and real hurt.

"Keep your fine humor," Simpson concluded. "Tell them you did play the piano, and they will likely ask you where, and when, and whether the place was properly licensed, or were there girls there. But through all the heavy guff...just, just recall that all of us—every single one of us right here, sitting here now, or outside, and me, too, who are your inquisitors—have already flunked the real test...America knows it and they are galled by it."

Through all this, Scalia—the rare nominee who *could* survive the strictest scrutiny, the devout Catholic who *had* lived an exemplary life—sat silent. Pat Leahy offered a respite. "My mother's family came here from Italy," he disclosed while making an overture to Maureen. "I would assume, in reading Mrs. Scalia's maiden name, that your children have really the best of all possible worlds—an Italian parent and an Irish parent." He offered the tired Scalia children a break in his office.

Jeremiah Denton, the Alabama Republican who had been a prisoner of war in Vietnam, also viewed Scalia through the prism of the Rehnquisition. "I believe that you will, on television, prohibit the disporting of you. I think you have enough toughness, enough intelligence, enough qualities that will not permit your being defeated here."

Jeremiah Denton knew toughness when he saw it.

He, too, believed Americans had been galled by the attacks on Rehnquist, and he predicted a "national backlash." Uniquely, Denton envisioned Scalia not as a builder of consensus on the Court but as a justice whose influence would be felt in dissent. The lawmaker quoted an unspecified colleague telling him Scalia's style "will rally the troops even if it never commands a majority."

The opening act was winding down. Howell Heflin, an Alabama Democrat, large, slow, and all drawl, could not resist a jab at the prominence of ethnicity in the proceedings thus far. "Almost every senator that has an Italian-American connection has come forward to welcome you...I would be remiss if I did not mention the fact that my great-great-grandfather—"

The crowd, and Scalia, burst into laughter.

"—married a *widduh*—"

More laughter, but Scalia was composing himself, leaning back, forefinger to nose.

"—who was married first to an Italian-American."

Again, the crowd, and Scalia, roaring in laughter!

"Let's get quiet," Thurmond said softly.

"It's not gonna get you in the club, pal," Leahy told Heflin.

With the lawmakers ignoring the chairman's barely audible injunction, it fell to Scalia to intervene: to reciprocate the levity while steering the hearing back on track.

"Senator, I've been to Alabama several times, too," Scalia said.

But Heflin wasn't done.

"So Judge *Scuh—Scuh-lee-uh*, it is with *pri-iiiii-ide* that *ahh* welcome *yeww* on behalf uh the *foh'thous'n'*, three-*huhhnn'rid* and twenty-two Italian-Americans in Alabama!"

Among the last to speak was a veteran of Main Justice: Mitch McConnell, freshman Republican from Kentucky. A graduate of the University of Kentucky College of Law, McConnell had served as deputy assistant attorney general for DOJ's Office of Legislative Affairs in 1974–75, and remembered Scalia well from those days.

"Everyone within the department, without exception, felt that you were not only the brightest lawyer that we had, but had the best sense of humor," McConnell told the nominee. "And of course those were days when we needed a good sense of humor. I never will forget, one morning, at a staff meeting, we all had to suffer through the embarrassment of the morning *Washington Post*, which revealed, that on the day before, two illegal aliens had been arrested working for the Immigration and Naturalization Service. So we had to maintain a good sense of humor, and you were clearly the one who made those meetings entertaining as well as informative."

In his closing remarks, McConnell—destined to become one of the all-time masters of the Senate, and a dominant force in the reshaping of the federal judiciary—zeroed in, with singular prescience, on a facet of Scalia's personality theretofore unmentioned: his *independence*. The lawmaker cited *Synar*, which had struck down the Gramm–Rudman deficit-reduction law as an unconstitutional delegation of authority to the Congress over the executive.

"This holding came as a blow to political conservatives interested in effectively reining in a runaway deficit," McConnell said. "Yet there was no hesitation on the part of Judge Scalia to strike it down." True judicial conservatism such as Scalia's, the senator concluded, "rejects judicial activism either of the left or of the right."[1]

*   *   *

After lunch recess, the witness was sworn. "Judge Scalia, if you will come around, please," Thurmond said. "Hold up your hand and be sworn."

> **THURMOND:** Will the testimony you give in this hearing
> be the truth, the whole truth, and nothing but the truth, so
> help you God?
> **SCALIA:** It will.

Scalia introduced Maureen and the kids, pausing to note of the youngest, Meg: "Her real name is Margaret but she said I should introduce her as Meg, because when she is called Margaret, she is usually in trouble."

With his first question, Chairman Thurmond sought Scalia's views on a technical issue: the differences between the roles of circuit court judges and Supreme Court justices. Scalia emphasized the finality of the high Court's rulings, but said appellate judges mastered "a much vaster body of law." In this, his first answer, Scalia moved pre-emptively to blunt expected questioning about when he would be obligated to respect Court precedent and when he would feel free, or compelled, to overturn it. "The Supreme Court is bound to its earlier decisions by the doctrine of *stare decisis*," he declared, "in which I strongly believe." Asked what made the Constitution a success, Scalia cited separation of powers.

> Most of the questions today will probably be about that portion of the Constitution that is called the Bill of Rights.... But if you had to put your finger on what has made our Constitution so enduring, I think it is the original document.... The amendments, by themselves, do not do anything. The Russian constitution probably has better, or at least as good, guarantees of personal freedom as our document does. What makes it work, what assures that those words are not just hollow promises, is the structure of government that the original Constitution established, the checks and balances among the three branches, in particular.

Thurmond gave Scalia a chance to rebut the label slapped on him by William Safire: the worst enemy of freedom of speech in America. "I have to say, it must be a misunderstanding," Scalia said. "I do not know of anything in my opinions, or my writings, that would display anything other than a high regard [for], and a desire to implement to the utmost, the requirements of the First Amendment.... I have spent my life in the field that the First Amendment is most designed to protect. In addition to having been a scholar, and a writer as a scholar, I think

I am one of the few Supreme Court nominees that has ever been the editor of a magazine."

Finally, the chairman pre-empted Specter. "Do you agree that *Marbury* requires the president and the Congress to always adhere to the Court's interpretation of the Constitution?"

Asked about *Marbury* at his murder board session, the nominee had decreed: "I'm not going to admit to anything as settled law." Now came his moment of truth.

"*Marbury* is of course one of the great pillars of American law," Scalia answered. "To the extent that you think a nominee would be so foolish, or so extreme, as to kick over one of the pillars of the Constitution, I suppose you should not confirm him. But I do not think I should answer questions regarding any specific Supreme Court opinion, even one as fundamental as *Marbury v. Madison.* If you could conclude from anything I have written or anything I have said that I would ignore *Marbury* v. *Madison,* I would, too, be in trouble, without your asking me specifically my views on *Marbury v. Madison.*"[2]

It was the kid from Queens telling the Senate: *Get real.*

*   *   *

"Judge Scalia," began Ted Kennedy, "if you were confirmed, do you expect to overrule *Roe v. Wade?*"

"Senator, I do not think it would be proper for me to answer." Thurmond interjected, but the witness kept going. "I think it is quite a thing [for future advocates on abortion law] to be arguing to somebody who you know has made a representation in the course of his confirmation hearings—and, that is, by way of *condition* to his being confirmed—that he will do this or do that. I think I would be in a very bad position to adjudicate the case without being accused of having a less than impartial view."

If he couldn't get an answer on overturning *Roe* specifically, Kennedy wanted Scalia to speak generally about his respect for precedent.

Here was the liberal lion of Camelot, in the center of the ring with *Il Matador*.

> **KENNEDY:** What is it going to take to overrule an existing Supreme Court decision?
> **SCALIA:** As you know, Senator, they are sometimes overruled.
> **KENNEDY:** I am interested in your view.
> **SCALIA:** My view is that they are sometimes overruled. And I think that—
> **KENNEDY:** But what weight do you give them?
> **SCALIA:** I will not say that I will never overrule prior Supreme Court precedent.
> **KENNEDY:** Well, what weight do you give the precedents of the Supreme Court? Are they given any weight? Are they given some weight? Are they given a lot of weight? Or does it depend on your view—
> **SCALIA:** It does not depend on my view. It depends on the nature of the precedent, the nature of the issue.... Government, even at the Supreme Court level, is a practical exercise. There are some things that are done, and when they are done, they are done and you move on. Now, which of those you think are so woven in the fabric of law that mistakes made are too late to correct, and which are not, that is a difficult question to answer. It can only be answered in the context of a particular case, and I do not think that I should answer anything in the context of a particular case.

KENNEDY: Well, do I understand that your answer with regard to Supreme Court decisions is that some of them are more powerful, more significant, than others in terms of how you would view in overruling them or overturning them?

SCALIA: Yes, I think so, Senator. May I supplement—

KENNEDY: And you are not prepared, on this issue [*Roe*], to say where that decision comes out, as I understand it?

SCALIA: That is right, Senator. And maybe I can be a little more forthcoming in response to your first question. As you followed it up, you said that some thought that [*Roe*] is why I was going onto the Court. I assure you, I have no agenda. I am not going onto the Court with a list of things that I want to do. My only agenda is to be a good judge.

"I gather from your answer that [*stare decisis*] is kind of a variable, that some [decisions] have stronger standing than others," Kennedy said. "You are not prepared to indicate, at least in that case—in the *Roe v. Wade* case—where you come out, as to whether you feel that that is a strong precedent or a weak precedent."

"That is right, sir. And nobody arguing that case before me should think that he is arguing to somebody who has his mind made up either way."

KENNEDY: Well, then, what is the relevance of the previous decision? Does that have any weight in your mind?

SCALIA: Of course.

KENNEDY: Well, could you tell us how much?

SCALIA: That is the question you asked earlier, Senator. And that is precisely the question—

KENNEDY: I know it. Well, let me go to another kind of question.

A retreat by the lion! In his next question, Kennedy misstated the reasoning in *Synar* and asked how the ruling would affect regulatory structure. "I don't think it affects it all, Senator," Scalia said. The judge had to explain the substance of the decision.

Scalia had *failed* students for less ineptitude.

"Let me back up a little bit," Kennedy said. He cited a Scalia article from *Regulation,* and again the witness schooled him: "I think you read it incorrectly.... It displayed quite the opposite view."

The lion was no match for *Il Matador!*

*   *   *

Charles Mathias, liberal Republican Marylander, returned to *Roe,* incredulous at Scalia's claim not to have made up his mind on the case. "I believe you have expressed doubts about that decision, both on moral as well as jurisprudential grounds."

"I may have criticized the decision, but I do not recall passing moral judgment on the issue. But I agree...that one of the primary qualifications for a judge is to set aside personal views."

MATHIAS: What does a judge do about a very deeply held personal position, a personal moral conviction, which may be pertinent to a matter before the Court?

SCALIA: Well, Senator, one of the moral obligations that a judge has is the obligation to live in a democratic society and to be bound by the determinations of that democratic society. If he feels that he cannot be, then he should not be sitting as a judge. There are doubtless laws on the books apart from abortion that I might not agree with, that I might think are misguided, perhaps some that I might even think in, the largest sense, are immoral in the results that they produce. In no way would I let that influence my determination of how they apply. And if indeed I felt that I could not separate my repugnance for the law from my impartial judgment of what the Constitution permits the society to do, I would recuse myself.

Now came Biden. He had read all of Scalia's speeches, he said. "And I find a very interesting—and I mean that sincerely—analysis of the newfound, newly enunciated, doctrine of original intent.... I cannot tell—and I am not being smart when I say this—whether your analysis of original meaning was one you meant, or whether it was done with tongue in cheek." Biden was referring to Scalia's remarks at the Meese conference, two months earlier, when the judge had confessed his fondness, as a professor, of provoking students with contrarian arguments.

> **SCALIA:** I am trying to fight against that inclination here.
> **BIDEN:** Well, let yourself go. Because it is pretty boring so far. [laughter]...And we may get a chance to see who you are a little bit more.

For all of Biden's verbosity, his loose, non-linear style and ceaseless reminders that he meant it, that he wasn't being a wise guy, wasn't joking, the Delawarean raised an important subject: he asked if Scalia believed in "a living Constitution."

"The Constitution is obviously not meant to be evolvable so easily that, in effect, a court of nine judges can treat it as though it is a bring-along-with-me statute and fill it up with whatever content the current times seem to require," Scalia replied. "To a large degree, it is intended to be an insulation against the current times, against the passions of the moment that may cause individual liberties to be disregarded, and it has served that function valuably very often. So I would never use the phrase 'living Constitution.'

"Now, there is within that phrase," he continued, "the notion that a certain amount of development of constitutional doctrine occurs, and I think there is room for that.... The strict original intentist, I think, would say that even such a clause as the cruel and unusual punishment clause [of the Eighth Amendment] would have to mean precisely the same thing today that it meant in 1789 ... that if lashing was fine then, lashing would be fine now. I am not sure I agree with that. I think that there are some provisions of the Constitution that may have a certain amount of evolutionary content."

> BIDEN: I am not being smart when I say, Judge, I do not suspect you of anything; I mean, truly.
> SCALIA: I did not mean it that way.
> BIDEN: ... I can read your speeches as saying you are being a devil's advocate and being a provocateur, on the one hand. I just hope you do not mean it. I am serious when I say that. For example, if you mean—if you subscribe to the view that you articulate as to what "original meaning" means, then I have real problems voting for a judge who holds that view. But the way you just explained it, it seems as though you are not totally wedded to that view; that you lean that way, but for example, in the area of cruel and unusual punishment, you see room for evolution. I assume you would argue the same regarding the Fourteenth Amendment. I assume you would say you could have gotten from *Plessy* to *Brown*, I hope.

SCALIA: I have always had trouble with lashing, Senator. I have always had trouble thinking that that is constitutional. And if I have trouble with that—

BIDEN: Are you being serious or being a wise guy?

SCALIA: I am being serious.

Biden chose to make his stand on *Watt*, the case where Scalia had demolished the notion of sleep as speech. Biden, like Kennedy before him, received a schooling from the master.

BIDEN: How do you define speech, Judge?

SCALIA: I define speech as any communicative activity.

BIDEN: Can it be nonverbal?

SCALIA: Yes.

BIDEN: Can it be nonverbal and also not written?

SCALIA: Yes.

BIDEN: So freedom of speech can encompass physical actions?

SCALIA: Yes, sir.

BIDEN: Good. That is a relief, because as I read your case, what I viewed as your dissent in the *Watt* case, I wondered...

SCALIA: *Watt* was a case in which what was at issue was sleeping as communicative activity.

BIDEN: Yes.

SCALIA: I did not say in the separate opinion that I wrote in that case, and that opinion was a dissent—

BIDEN: Correct.

SCALIA: —of our court. That dissent was vindicated by the Supreme Court, as far as the outcome was concerned.

BIDEN: But a different rationale.
SCALIA: Not the rationale.

Even a hearing of unrestricted length could not accommodate the correction of all of Biden's misstatements. But Scalia could not allow his opinions to be misrepresented.

> **SCALIA:** I did not say that one could prohibit sleeping merely for the purpose of eliminating the communicative aspect of sleeping, if there is any.... If they passed a law that allows all other sleeping but only prohibits sleeping where it is intended to communicate, then it would be invalidated.
> **BIDEN:** ... Let us say you take a physical action like sitting down to protest a law that has nothing to do with preventing people from sitting. It has to do with whether or not Black folk can be served in restaurants. And they say, "No, you cannot." So you sit out there on the sidewalk.... Does that situation require a heightened standard [to be protected speech]?
> **SCALIA:** I think not, Senator. In fact, it seems to me it happens all the time.... If you want to protest as a means of civil disobedience and take the penalty that is fine. But if the law is not itself directed against demonstrations or against communication, I do not think it is the kind of law that in and of itself requires the heightened scrutiny. That was the only point I was making in—
> **BIDEN:** That is very helpful to me. I am not being smart when I say that.

Biden was done—but he wanted credit for his labors. Only he, with his penetrating questions, had saved Scalia from appearing at odds with the civil rights movement! "You understand how, without that explanation, that it is possible someone could read a more restrictive application [from your opinion in *Watt*]?" Biden asked.

"I will have to write longer opinions," Scalia deadpanned.

*   *   *

The next challenges came from Republicans. Senator Chuck Grassley, a homespun and stubborn freshman, had served in the Iowa House from 1959 to 1975, then in the U.S. House until 1981. The former farmer and factory worker took offense at the "pretty doggone strong language" Scalia had used against legislative history. Scalia countered that he respected the practice and had sometimes incorporated it into his own opinions: "The trouble with legislative history, Senator, is figuring out what is reliable and what is not."

> **GRASSLEY:** Well, I want to tell you, as one who has served in Congress for twelve years, legislative history is very important to those of us here who want further detailed expression of that legislative intent, all right? You are not suggesting that for committee reports to have any meaning, that they must be actually written, rather than merely approved, by members of Congress? Are you suggesting that?
> **SCALIA:** I do not want to pin myself down to a commitment to use any particular type of legislative history or not to use any particular type of legislative history.... Congress does not act in committee reports. I will say that flat out. Congress acts by passing a law.

Pat Leahy, destined to serve another four decades with McConnell and Grassley, posed ineffectual questions about Scalia's consulting for

AT&T and secured a recusal promise for a particular case. Howell Heflin probed the nominee's 1979 declaration, in "The Disease as Cure," that he supported affirmative action programs for the poor and disadvantaged. Specter, not satisfied by Strom Thurmond's coverage of *Marbury*, asked if Scalia considered it a "settled issue."

"I do not want to say that anything is a 'settled issue.' If somebody wants to come in and challenge *Marbury v. Madison*, I will listen to that person," Scalia said. "Whether I would be likely to kick away *Marbury v. Madison*, given not only what I have just said, but also what I have said concerning my respect for the principle of *stare decisis*, I think you will have to judge on the basis of my record as a judge in the Court of Appeals, and your judgment as to whether I am, I suppose, on that issue sufficiently intemperate or extreme."

> **SPECTER:** Do you consider yourself a moderate judge?
> **SCALIA:** I suppose everybody considers himself a moderate, Senator; I do.
> **SPECTER:** ...I have not asked you to go very far...I am basing this on *Marbury v. Madison*.... How does a senator make a judgment on what a Supreme Court nominee is going to do if we do not get really categorical answers to fundamental questions like that?
> **SCALIA:** I think it is very hard, Senator, when you are dealing with someone that does not have a track record.... In my case, you have four years of that; you have extensive writings on administrative law and constitutional law from the years when I was a professor; you have testimony and statements that I made when I was in the executive branch. I am as sympathetic to your problem as you said you are to mine.... It is not a slippery slope; it is a precipice. *Marbury v. Madison* we all agree about, jurisdiction of the court; it

goes from one to the next.... *Plessy v. Ferguson* might have been considered a settled question at one time, but a litigant should have been able to come in and say, "It is wrong" and get a judge who has not committed himself to a committee, as a condition of his confirmation, to adhering to it.

SPECTER:... Will you let somebody litigate, after you are on the Supreme Court, the question of whether you have an obligation, under your oath, to uphold the Constitution?

SCALIA: I think you have finally gone over the edge of absurdity....

Howard Metzenbaum wanted to know if Scalia objected to the panel's seeing his memoranda from the Ford era. No, not personally, Scalia shrugged; but the demand violated separation of powers.

Paul Simon, a bow tie–sporting Illinois Democrat, read from a staff analysis of Scalia's rulings: "He will interpret civil rights statutes narrowly. In cases of race discrimination, the plaintiff will have a very difficult time proving his case because of the high standards Scalia imposes on race cases. The same will be true with gender discrimination.... The Court will have an ardent enemy of affirmative action."

Scalia, veteran performer, knew the moment required more than a dry defense of his academic writings; he needed to confront head on, dramatically, as Rehnquist had not, the core charge of *racism*. "Animosity toward racial minorities, in my case, would be a form of self-hate," he said. "I am a member of a racial minority myself, suffered, I expect, some minor discrimination in my years; nothing compared to what other racial groups have suffered.

"My wife's mother remembers the days—she is a Fitzgerald from Boston; I wish Senator Kennedy were here to know that—but she remembers the days when there were signs in Boston that said: NO IRISH NEED APPLY. I find all of that terribly offensive."

"I am a product of the melting pot in New York, grew up with people of all religious and ethnic backgrounds. When I lived in your state, Senator, I did not live in a monochrome suburb, but I lived in Hyde Park, and my kids went to a school that was at least 40 percent, maybe more than that, Black.... My kids socialized with, and dated, people of all races. I have absolutely no racial prejudices."

*   *   *

Finally, a rematch with Biden. Already laying ground for his 1988 presidential campaign, the senator returned to a subject earlier dispensed with: Scalia's membership, from 1971 to 1985, in Washington's Cosmos Club, then all male. Biden was unsatisfied with Scalia's explanation that the institution did not practice "invidious discrimination."

> **BIDEN:** Could it be invidious if in fact the effect of keeping women out was to have a detrimental impact upon their ability to do business, if they were businesswomen, or participate in sport, if they were sportswomen?
> **SCALIA:** I can see that, Senator, yes.
> **BIDEN:** In what context would you place those clubs which would discriminate based upon nationality?
> **SCALIA:** Well, you know, there is sort of affirmative and negative discrimination, I suppose. I have been a member of Italian-American clubs, members who share a common heritage. The exclusion of others is not an invidious exclusion at all. And likewise religious clubs, Knights of Columbus.... They exclude people of other religions not invidiously but just because they get together to celebrate what they have in common.

BIDEN: If in fact there was a club or organization that included not one group, but a group of people who shared nothing in common other than the fact they didn't like the Irish or the Italians—

SCALIA: Yes, I think that would be invidious.

The waste of time! Minutes after telling the nominee, "You've had a long day, Mr. Justice [*sic*]," Biden dragged the committee and spectators through these pointless, artless hypotheticals, fully aware that no other lawmaker considered the Cosmos Club membership important.

Now Biden wanted a final shot at *Roe*. His chosen route was the Ninth Amendment, which guarantees that the enumeration of certain rights in the Constitution cannot be construed as abridging other inherent rights. *Roe* had identified the Ninth Amendment as one of several sources in the Constitution from which emanated a right to privacy, unenumerated but inviolable, that encompassed a woman's choice to abort before viability.

BIDEN: [Do] you believe that implicit in the Ninth Amendment is a recognition of a right called the right of privacy...that there is such a thing as the right to privacy?

SCALIA: I think that's in effect asking me to rule on cases. I can say that the Supreme Court has held that there is such a thing as a right of privacy. But they haven't tied it to the Ninth Amendment. As far as I know, there is no Supreme Court holding that rests any right exclusively on the Ninth Amendment. They may include the Ninth in a litany of amendments from which various penumbras emanate....

BIDEN: Do you believe that there is such a thing as a constitutional right to privacy? Not delineating whether, for example, the right to terminate a pregnancy relates to the right to privacy, or the right to engage in homosexual activities in your home is a right to privacy, or the right to use contraceptives in your home is a right, but in a philosophic sense: Is there such a thing as a constitutionally protected right to privacy?

SCALIA: I don't think I could answer that, Senator, without violating the line I've tried to hold.... I do not want to be put in the position of having to tell [future litigants], you know, "I'm sorry, I believe in the right of privacy because I told the committee, in connection with considering my nomination, that I believe in it."

BIDEN: Well, the fact that you believe in the right to privacy doesn't mean that a case before you in fact rises to the level of being protected by that right. I think you are being a little bit disingenuous with me here.

This was the sharpest remark in the hearing, the only rebuke of Scalia.

BIDEN: If in fact you conclude that there is an existing right to privacy, that in no way predisposes you to have to rule one way or the other about whether or not a claimed right is encompassed by the provision.

SCALIA: Senator, I beg to differ. There have been scholarly criticisms of the whole notion of right to privacy.

BIDEN: Oh, I agree.

SCALIA: And it's not at all inconceivable that that criticism will be reflected in a brief before the Supreme Court.

Now Biden came unglued.

BIDEN: That may very well be, but it doesn't—in other words, if the right to privacy exists, if you believe the right to privacy exists—and I believe you have stated in—excuse me one moment.

[consults with staff]

BIDEN: I believe, and I can't pin down where you said it—it is in an article?

SCALIA: I don't think you'll find it in—

BIDEN: In the [article], didn't you say that the right to privacy is one of the deepest and most profoundly held beliefs in our society?

SCALIA: I don't recall having said that, Senator.

BIDEN: I'm sorry, I misspoke.

Il Matador—vittorioso!

But Biden was indefatigable. He asked one more time whether Scalia doubted that the right to privacy was a "deeply and profoundly held view" of American society. To prod him, Biden let fly with a first in the annals of Congress and the Court: "Forget the Constitution—let's just talk politics here, you and me."

It was precisely the opposite of what judges, and judicial nominees, are supposed to do, or be urged by lawmakers to do: *forget the Constitution...talk politics.*

"I can't answer that question without knowing what you mean by the right of privacy," Scalia countered. Now both beat a strategic retreat.

BIDEN: True.... Let's just start over again, clean the slate. Do you believe that Americans as a whole believe that that they have inherent right to privacy—that they think they have a right to privacy?...Do you have any doubt that Americans believe it?

SCALIA: No. I'll give you that, Senator.

BIDEN: Good man. I tell you, we're getting there.... If it is a long-held societal view that has been in effect recognized through constitutional interpretation, case law, Supreme Court cases, then you would be very reluctant to overturn it. Do I read that correctly, or am I putting words in your mouth?

SCALIA: No. Yes, I think that's a fair statement.

BIDEN: Now, the irony of all ironies is that the people who are concerned about you...pro-choice women's groups... worry you will use that rationale to overturn *Roe v. Wade*. Ironically, it seems to me, you could read your view as saying that if that hangs in the law another ten or fifteen years, it would be awful hard—you would, by your own test, have trouble overruling *Roe v. Wade*. So I guess what I am asking, without asking about *Roe v. Wade*, is whether there is a time frame?

SCALIA:...I agree with the statement that longstanding cases are more difficult to overrule than recent cases.

Here Biden, broken clock, told accurate time. His exchange with Scalia on the durability of *Roe* would prove prescient.

*   *   *

Mathias closed the questioning by returning to the nominee's suspicion of legislative history, particularly committee reports. "It is the distinctive threat with relationship to the judicial process of our time," Scalia warned, the "one failing perhaps in our entire governmental process bearing upon the relationship among the three branches."

> I think that one is bound by the meaning of the Constitution to the society to which it was promulgated. And if somebody should discover that the secret intent of the Framers was quite different from what the words seem to connote, it would not make any difference.... The starting point, in any case, is the text of the document and what it meant to the society that adopted it. I think it is part of my whole philosophy—which is essentially a democratic philosophy—that even the Constitution is, at bottom, at bottom, a democratic document. It was adopted by the people's acceptance of it, by their voting for it, and its legitimacy depends upon democratic adoption at the time it was enacted. Now, some of its provisions may have envisioned varying application with varying circumstances. That is a subject of some dispute and a point on which I am quite wishy-washy. But I am clear on the fact that the original meaning is the starting point and the beginning of wisdom.

Mathias wanted to hear more about the "wishy-washy" part: how original meaning could be reconciled with modern circumstances unforeseen by the Framers.

"On these types of issues, Senator, when the law has to be applied to circumstances that just did not exist at the time, you obviously have to decide as a judge what resolution would most comport with the application of that clause to the circumstances that did exist at the time and try to make it fit."

Thurmond praised the nominee, and the hearing was adjourned. Scalia had testified for seven and a half hours. It was a *tour de force*:

the most intellectually rigorous articulation of judicial restraint ever heard by the Senate Judiciary Committee. Even during the mad rushes of Kennedy and Biden, easily disposed of by *Il Matador*, the nominee had remained composed, erudite, charming, the kid from Queens, the immigrant's son with the Ivy League credentials and winning way with words.[3]

*   *   *

President Reagan watched the hearings sporadically. At times he was disgusted. He resented the "political posturing" of the Rehnquisition—the "lynch mob" led by Kennedy and Biden, with their "hysterical charges of coverup and stonewalling." Reagan thought his nominees had "emerged unscathed," saying in his weekly radio address that "I was especially delighted...because Judge Scalia is the first Italian-American in history to be named to the Supreme Court."[4]

Reagan's aides were also delighted. Not only had Scalia secured his confirmation with a masterful performance; in his triumph they saw an opening to reclaim some ground the executive had lost to Congress in the Rehnquisition. The morning after Scalia testified, White House counsel Peter Wallison reminded the president in a three-page memorandum, previously unpublished, that with the production of the twenty-five Rehnquist memos from 1969 to 1971, "we established a precedent that a Senate committee engaged in the confirmation process may have access to the files of a nominee who was an official of this or a former administration.... The Scalia nomination provides an ideal opportunity to assert executive privilege [to] limit substantially the scope of the precedent established.... Almost all of the Rehnquist papers we released relate to alleged 'abuses' of civil liberties or civil rights during the Nixon administration. The Scalia papers do not relate to any alleged wrongdoing. Thus, we could draw the line by saying that the president waived executive privilege for the Rehnquist documents because they were requested to clear the air concerning Watergate-related abuses, but that this issue is not present in the case of the Scalia documents."

Turning from law to politics, Wallison noted that Scalia was "a much more sympathetic figure than Rehnquist" and, "perhaps most important," that Scalia was backed by a "major constituency group [that] would react with dismay and anger if it appeared that the Senate committee was holding up his nomination because of a dispute with the president over a few documents."

The president agreed and asserted the privilege. The Democrats caved. No Scalia memoranda were made available.[5]

*   *   *

"First Day of Questioning Leaves Scalia Unscathed" —*Washington Post*

"Scalia Returns Soft Answers to Questions" —*New York Times*

"Scalia Questioned on Rights, Abortion" —*Philadelphia Inquirer*

"Scalia Declines to Say How He'd Vote on Abortion" —*Washington Times*

"Antonin Scalia Meshes Strong Intellect, Charm" —*Post-Star*

Gone was the hostile arena of the Rehnquisition, replaced by the "light sparring" and "far less rancorous" atmosphere of the Scalia hearing. The senators praised the nominee for his brilliance and humor, though a few Democrats, such as Heflin, felt Scalia had been "elusive, evasive...did not answer things I thought he should have answered."

"Scalia was direct and seemed confident in his answers," reported the *Post*. "There was little criticism and much praise of Scalia," the *Wall Street Journal* observed. The *Inquirer* saw the judge "breezing toward an expected easy Senate confirmation." One columnist noted, "The Italian community is understandably proud."

Where most observers saw a *bravura* performance, a deft and thoughtful exposition by a nominee supremely well qualified, critics in the media saw a broken system. While she conceded the nominee "may well be approved unanimously" by the eighteen senators on the Judiciary Committee, the *New York Times*' Linda Greenhouse dismissed the Rehnquist-Scalia hearings as "so unenlightening as to raise questions about how the Senate discharges its constitutional obligation to advise and consent to judicial nominations."

> By the time Judge Scalia came before the committee, the senators seemed worn out and distracted. The fifty-year-old former law professor is one of the country's leading conservative legal theorists. His intellectual force, strongly held views, and pungent manner of expression will make him a powerful figure on the Court. Yet the questioning was perfunctory and the answers were uninformative.... Some of Justice Rehnquist's strongest opponents, including Senator Kennedy, seemed to bend over to assure Judge Scalia that legal philosophy would not be the deciding factor when the time comes to vote.

Joan Biskupic wrote disapprovingly of the nominee's "breezy superiority" with his questioners, whom she portrayed as belonging to "the cozy good-old boy world of Washington, where Scalia had been welcomed."[6]

*   *   *

On August 6 the committee heard, individually and in panels, from seventeen expert witnesses: eleven in support of Scalia, six in opposition.

The supporters included Robert B. Fiske, Jr., head of the American Bar Association panel that had rated the nominee "well qualified" (later the first independent counsel in the Whitewater case), joined by two

ABA officials who had interviewed Scalia for the project; Carla Hills, a colleague of Scalia's from the Administrative Conference and Justice (later a HUD secretary and U.S. Trade Representative); attorney Lloyd Cutler (White House counsel to Presidents Carter and Clinton); Sally Katzen, also of the ABA; Bruce Fein, a former DOJ official and FCC general counsel; Jack Fuller, editorial page editor of the *Chicago Tribune* (formerly special assistant to Attorney General Levi); and Beverly LaHaye, founder of Concerned Women for America, the pro-life organization, 560,000 strong, that billed itself as the nation's largest non-partisan activist women's group.

The opposing witnesses were a Who's Who of 1980s left-wing activism: Eleanor Smeal, then in her third non-consecutive term, almost a household name, as president of the National Organization for Women, national membership around 135,000; Joseph L. Rauh, Jr., a former clerk to Justices Cardozo and Frankfurter and a legendary civil rights lawyer, representing the Leadership Conference on Civil Rights and Americans for Democratic Action; Washington-based attorney Audrey Feinberg of Paul, Weiss, appearing on behalf of The Nation Institute to present a scathing report on Scalia's jurisprudence she had been compiling over the last *year*; and officers from the Center for Constitutional Rights and Americans United for the Separation of Church and State.

"I find it very difficult to sit here in opposition to the nomination of the first Italian-American," said Smeal, a daughter of immigrants. "Justice Scalia's views by no means represent a consensus in the ethnic community which we have in common."

Citing Scalia's rulings and academic writings, particularly "The Disease as Cure," his critics conjured the specter of an authoritarian, majoritarian monster under whose jurisprudential tyranny Americans' constitutional rights would be trampled by rabid mobs in Congress and state legislatures—all while the monster pursued a paradoxical "agenda" to neuter the legislature in favor of the executive. The play-book was in use.

"A review of Judge Scalia's decisions reveals a record that is far removed from mainstream judicial thought," Audrey Feinberg testified. "Judge Scalia's decisions reveal a remarkably consistent record of failure to support civil rights and civil liberties. In case after case, Judge Scalia has shown a closed mind and a relentless insensitivity to the needs of women, minorities, and the poor, and he has slammed the courthouse doors in the faces of the disadvantaged.... He has a political agenda that is incompatible with the impartiality required of Supreme Court justices.... There must be a conscience in the confirmation process."

"Judge Scalia," agreed Laurence Gold, AFL-CIO general counsel, "takes an extremely skeptical view of judicial enforcement of the basic guarantees of the Bill of Rights." Gold worried that Scalia "would hobble Congress and aggrandize executive power." For all the nominee's paeans to *original meaning*, Scalia's rulings were "not the product of the doctrine of judicial restraint but of his own social and political views."

"Judge Scalia has ice water in his veins," Rauh testified. "He makes jokes about things we believe in deeply.... How do we remedy past wrongs that have been done women and Blacks and Hispanics? That is a serious problem. Judge Scalia, as a professor, laughed at that problem." Observations about icy veins aside, Rauh brushed aside personal attributes—and professional qualifications—as immaterial. "He is a great writer, he gets everything exactly right, he is the most articulate man in America," Rauh recited sarcastically. "There was testimony about this great affability and great charm. You do not build a consensus from one end; you build it from some more moderate position."

But it was Smeal, "appalled" by Scalia's views on abortion, affirmative action, and anti-discrimination law, who emerged as the panel's most searing witness. In written and spoken testimony, she denounced the nominee, his writings, and his rulings, as "extreme," "frightening," "unconscionable," "illogical," "cruel," marked by "total contempt for the jury system" and "opposition to constitutionally guaranteed rights." Scalia's confirmation, she argued, "would be a disaster...undoing, literally, the gains of the last twenty-five years for women's rights under the law.... He is blatantly contemptuous of the present Supreme Court for its ruling on the legality of abortion.... We are struck by his penchant to ridicule and to trivialize not just the remedies themselves but the very notion that those who have suffered from discrimination should in any way be given special consideration.... There is a lot ridicule and hostility...a lot of joking around about the remedial solutions...I think it is more demeaning when you joke."

Carla Hills testified that she had "known, admired, and been enriched by the wisdom of Antonin Scalia" since 1972, that she had seen him operate up close, even among those with a "divergence of views," and that he had always conducted himself "with intellectual precision, unfailing humor, and relentless fairness." Sally Katzen told the panel Scalia "never demonstrated any bias against or insensitivity to women."

> He solicited and listened to my views, notwithstanding that we often disagreed.... He related or responded to the other women in the section with the same courtesy and respect, treating us no differently than our male colleagues. In fact, it is my clear impression that he actively encouraged women to participate in the work of the section. As chairman-elect, he appointed six women as chairs of committees, and sixteen as vice-chairs of committees, which had the responsibility for selecting the next year's officers and council members.... Judge Scalia was very enthusiastic about women in leadership roles.

Feinberg's claim that Scalia would slam courthouse doors on the disadvantaged drew a challenge from a Democratic senator.

> **METZENBAUM:** He's a family man. He seems to be a very sensitive individual, and yet the harshness of that decision with respect to dismissing the case [*Trakas v. Quality Brands, Inc.*] because a woman didn't have the money, after she had been fired, in order to travel from Missouri to Washington to present her case—it's just somewhat difficult for me to comprehend.
>
> **FEINBERG:** I think perhaps it cannot be reconciled with his personal attributes. I think this committee has heard [about] his affability, his congeniality, his integrity. But those are not the only qualities that this committee should be looking over. You have to look at his record and his decisions. And his decisions paint a very different picture of who he is and what he stands for.[7]

The senators were unmoved. Even Democrats like DeConcini, who had complained of Scalia's "evasiveness," said they intended to confirm him. "He is a conservative, not an extremist," said Kennedy. "I disagree with him," declared Biden, "but his views are within the legitimate parameters of debate." Biden's analysis was surprisingly inept for the ranking member of the Judiciary Committee. "I do not find him significantly more conservative than Chief Justice Burger," he said of Scalia: an assessment contrary to the view expressed by every scholar and expert who had been quoted in the press over the preceding two months.

"Judge Scalia's philosophy is not my philosophy," said Leahy. "It is the philosophy of Ronald Reagan.... We should respect the mandate the president has earned." Metzenbaum counted Scalia's hostility to affirmative action a problem, along with his rulings against the press, but added: "I cannot conclude that he will pursue a course of constitutional extremism."

On August 15, the committee voted to advance Rehnquist's nomination to the Senate floor by a vote of thirteen to five; Scalia's, unanimously. "Justice Rehnquist and Judge Scalia will be confirmed by the Senate," vowed Majority Leader Dole, "by big numbers."[8]

On September 17, 1986, the hundred and ninety-ninth anniversary of the date the Constitution was passed out of the Convention in Philadelphia, the Senate approved Rehnquist as the nation's sixteenth chief justice, sixty-five to thirty-three; and Antonin Scalia as the hundred and sixth justice, ninety-eight to none. The vote on Rehnquist followed five days of debate on the Senate floor—the misery ended, at last, when sixteen Democrats joined in shutting it down. The debate on Scalia lasted seven minutes.[9]

*   *   *

Once again, the schedule left little room for celebration. The start of the Court's fall term was less than three weeks away. Scalia needed to wrap up his work at the D.C. Circuit and relocate his chambers: the computer gear; his library of books and papers; the family photos; the plaque, a gift from last year's clerks, that read: IT'S HARD TO GET IT RIGHT. It was a phrase Scalia's clerks heard often, "never in anger, never in rebuke," as one recalled, "but always as a reminder...often accompanied by a wry smile."

"I remember when we literally moved from his office at the D.C. Circuit to the Supreme Court. He drove me and Roy over in his car," recalled Pat Schiltz. Roy W. McLeese III, a graduate of Harvard University and NYU Law, served on Scalia's last roster of clerks on the D.C. Circuit Court and on his first at the Marble Temple, a distinction only he and Schiltz shared: *Knights Templar of the clerkorati*. The three men rode the judges' elevator to the basement garage where Scalia's car was parked. "Well, we had a good run here," Shiltz recalled the justice-designate saying as the elevator descended. "He was very relaxed, in a very good humor. . . . It was like it was the most natural thing in the world. He was very confident in his ability to do the job and he was very excited to have the job. I don't remember him doing any pondering or looking off into the distance or being the slightest bit intimidated by it."

On September 17, the day the Senate confirmed Scalia, the D.C. Circuit released his latest opinion. Joined by Mikva and the court's newest addition, Judge James Buckley, the conservative former senator from New York, Scalia wrote for a unanimous panel in *Parker v. U.S.*, rejecting the appeal of a Washington, D.C., man convicted on federal bank robbery and firearm charges. Floyd Parker contended the government's failure to produce the firearm, and witnesses' vague descriptions of it, meant prosecutors had failed to establish that the object was a "firearm" under the relevant statute, which had added five years onto his sentence. Scalia held the government had "presented sufficient evidence to permit a reasonable jury to infer that the object carried by Parker was a 'firearm.'"

The following day brought another unanimous Scalia opinion. With Mikva and Wright, he ruled in *Thomas v. New York* that the Environmental Protection Agency was not obligated to take action to curb "acid rain" under a finding—issued without notice, public comment, or publication in the *Federal Register*—signed by the agency's outgoing administrator one week before the end of the Carter administration. The absence of proper notice, Scalia wrote, meant the finding "cannot be the basis for . . . judicial relief."[10]

*　　*　　*

All the judges on the D.C. Circuit congratulated Scalia on his ascension to what Ruth Bader Ginsburg called the "higher region." Privately, they probably all wondered: *Will it ever happen for me?*

At least one of them moved immediately to make clear to Scalia that the deference he would receive, in the event of confirmation, would be limited. "Nino, Congratulations! I was delighted to hear the good news—you have earned the honor," wrote Harry Edwards in a postcard from Vancouver, British Columbia, Canada. "But, understand that I still plan to whip you on the squash court when my leg heals. Love to 'Mo.' Harry."[11]

A week before the Senate voted, Chief Judge Wald sent the clerk of the court a memo captioned: "Reassignment of Judge Scalia's Cases." Ginsburg got stuck with an unfinished opinion, which she sarcastically termed "my inheritance from AS." It was a "FERC" case, involving the Federal Energy Regulatory Commission: the kind that all the judges, even Scalia, dreaded as the driest and dreariest that the dismal field of administrative law could deliver. The chief enjoyed no immunity. "I am taking one and maybe two of the other Scalia left-behinds," Wald told RBG.[12]

From Scalia's four-year tenure on the D.C. Circuit, the most positive outcome, in personal terms, was the blossoming of his friendship with Ruth Ginsburg. Their correspondence in those years, scattered among the 223 boxes of Ginsburg's files at the Library of Congress, was the warmest, most affectionate, between any two judges on the court at that time—perhaps on any court at any time. Brilliant expositions of law and logic, unimpeachable evidence of a friendship in embryo, the RBG-Nino Papers, previously unpublished, captured the jurists' intellects, honesty, religiosity, filial devotion, ethnicity, and love of languages, criticism, debate, and wit.

From the outset Ginsburg exhibited an almost maternal attitude toward Scalia, repeatedly, and needlessly, expressing concern about the weight of his workload. Her summary of a conference among the judges in April 1983, six months after Scalia joined the bench, recorded: "RBG offered to trade if AS finds himself too loaded to manage the case." Three months later, in a separate matter, she wrote him privately: "Sorry about the headache this case is giving you." "Sorry to have put you through this labor," she wrote again, in ink, across another memo. "You had much the harder of the cases," she lamented in a 1985 exchange, "grappling with this sticky statute."[13]

Before Scalia had even completed his first year on the bench, RBG was sending him playful notes in memo form. After reviewing his draft in *Association of Data Processing v. Board of Governors* (1984), in which Scalia limned two sections of the Administrative Procedure Act that authorized judicial review of agency decisions, she congratulated him:

> Three puntas after this for any judge who writes that, under APA, the "substantial evidence" rein is tighter than the "arbitrary and capricious" one.... Also marked, proofreading errors spotted at the swimming pool.
>
> R.B.G.

Would Scalia get her puntas reference? RBG must have wondered. *What if he didn't?* So she sent the memo to his chambers a second time, annotated with her asterisk and scribbled citation, *Lafcadio's Adventures*, the 1914 novel by French laureate André Gide: an example of just the kind of literary arcana Scalia loved.

The two *kvelled* over each other. "Just right. I concur," she wrote on Scalia's draft in *Affiliated Communications v. FCC* (1985). "Beautifully done. I concur," she scrawled on another, two months later. In sending Nino her own drafts, Ginsburg reverently solicited "your careful reading and comments"; after receiving them she invariably found herself "borrowing liberally" from Scalia's thinking, "making the change Judge Scalia recommended," confiding she had "altered p. 7 precisely as you suggested." Soon after Scalia joined the panel, RBG felt close enough to him to write disparagingly about the court's other female judge, Pat Wald: "PMW is least effective when she attempts to build a case for her own interpretation."[14]

Scalia, for his part, heaped praise on RBG so superlative it was probably unknown even to his brightest students and clerks, possibly to his children. "A superb job," he wrote on Ginsburg's memo of January 24, 1985, attaching her latest draft opinion. "Just right. I could suggest no improvements. AS." "Excellent as usual," he scribbled, later that year, on her opinion in *Noxell Corp. v. Firehouse No. 1 Bar-B-Que Restaurant*.

With Ruth, Nino could let up in argument, let down his hair. When she encouraged him, in *Weil v. Markowitz*, to "change your vote on the first question [so] we can be unanimous," he capitulated the next day, writing in black ink on her memo: "Let's be unanimous. AS." He once apologized for his delay in delivering a difficult opinion, "sloth that I am." He could even admit error: "I am grateful for your insight regarding the impropriety of the agency's reliance upon § 402(h)," he wrote to Wald and RBG during consideration of *Eastern Carolina Broadcasting Co. v. FCC* (1985). "I had not seen that clearly, and you are unquestionably correct."

He admitted to RBG when his insight was based on nothing more than "my (blind luck) assumption." His tone was utterly unguarded. "The only real issue, then, is whether costs should be assessed just against Columbia or divided in some fashion among all the intervenors," he wrote in a FERC case. "I do not think we should waste a lot of our time on this sort of determination; and Columbia notably refrained from making any suggestion regarding an equitable apportionment. Let them pay."

"I concur," RBG scribbled. Even when copied on Nino's memoranda to others, she was always his primary audience. "Unlike Judge Ginsburg, I am not a connoisseur of this statute," he wrote McGowan, "but I add my less-informed praise to hers."

Scalia's trust in his new friend was total. In *Maryland People's Counsel v. FERC* (1985), he invested extraordinary authority in RBG: "I would be inclined to change my vote on the point if Judge Ginsburg (who at this stage of the matter, I understand, agrees with me) is persuaded to change hers. She has my proxy for that purpose.... Again, since Judge Ginsburg and I have discussed these matters and appear to see eye to eye, I will be content to have her cast my vote on the basis of her judgment as to whether the assurances from [the appellant] are adequate."

Among the final entries in the RBG-Nino Papers that are yet open to scholars—the first tranche, covering the D.C. Circuit years—is a handwritten note Ginsburg dashed off to her cherished friend, by then ensconced in the "higher region," in January 1987. She wanted Nino to see her draft in the FERC case she had inherited from him. That this note was meaningful to Ginsburg was manifest in her decision to place a photocopy of it in the case file for *Associated Gas Distributors v. FERC.*

"To Justice Scalia," she wrote, in her neat, understated cursive. "Nevermore shall I have cause to think of you in the dismal context of a FERC-y case!...Regards, Ruth."[15]

✳   ✳   ✳

On June 18, 1986, the day after Reagan's announcement, at least two justices sent messages of congratulation to their future colleague. In chambers, Justice John Paul Stevens, a Chicago native and graduate of the University of Chicago, penned a handwritten note, previously unpublished.

> Dear Judge Scalia,
>
> The next time I write to you I am sure I will address you as "Nino," but a little formality seems appropriate on this occasion. I am delighted that the President showed such excellent judgment and know that I will enjoy working with you and getting to know you better.
>
> If I can be helpful in any way during the transition, please let me know. In the meantime, I congratulate you and assure you that you will, indeed, be most welcome.
>
> Sincerely,
John

As a Ford appointee, Stevens had much in common with Scalia—though not jurisprudence. In the 1985–86 term, Stevens voted with the Court's leading liberal, William J. Brennan, 62 percent of the time, third behind Thurgood Marshall and Harry Blackmun.

Responding more warily were those justices who had felt the lash of Scalia's pen during his time as an academic. While Justice Lewis F. Powell's typed letter of June 18, also previously unpublished, conformed to convention, its emphasis on the tone used in the drafting of dissenting opinions, and their impact on the relationships between the justices, suggested Scalia's "sharp language" in the wake of *Bakke*, the landmark affirmative action case, had not gone unnoticed. Professor Scalia had argued that Justice Powell's "delightful compromise was drafted precisely to achieve" the same results Harvard Law had produced when the admissions office quietly winnowed the school's Jewish population.

Now Powell seemed intent on drawing close a potential adversary.

> PERSONAL
> Dear Nino:
>
> Warmest congratulations on your nomination to serve as an Associate Justice of this Court.
>
> Although you have the ordeal ahead of the Senate judiciary Committee hearings, in view of your distinguished record as a scholar and jurist I have no doubt as to your confirmation. You will be warmly welcomed here, and despite the sharp language that often appears in dissenting opinions—you will find (as the Chief Justice said) that the level of civility among the justices is high. This is a pleasant as well as a stimulating place to work, and to serve our country and profession.
>
> My wife Jo and I enjoyed visiting with you and Maureen when we were together at the Whites' dinner. We look forward to having you both as members of the Court's family.
>
> Sincerely,
[signed] Lewis

Most circumspect was Justice Blackmun. As the author of the majority opinion in *Roe*, the wiry Minnesotan had been the target of another of Scalia's harshest attacks—on national television. What's more, Scalia's scathing law review essay, "The Disease as Cure," had mockingly borrowed Blackmun's tag-line from *Bakke* ("In order to get beyond racism, we must first take account of race") as its subtitle.

At the time Blackmun had said nothing. Now the justice, nearing seventy-nine, so short his legs dangled high off the ground whenever he sat on the long wooden table in the chief's conference room, lay in wait for the newcomer he had dismissed ten years earlier, on first sight, as "plump, dark."

"I'm told... he is most dangerous when most ingratiating, and that he has a great ability to persuade one to his point of view," Blackmun told a conference of judges in the summer of 1986.

"Well, we'll see."[16]

*   *   *

All kinds of characters came out of the woodwork.

Scalia's papers at the Harvard Law School Library from this time, the period from nomination to confirmation, contain outreach from friends close and distant, former professors and colleagues—even the odd frenemy.

Frank Michelman, Scalia's former co-editor on the *Harvard Law Review*, a professor at the law school since 1963—more recently observed adopting an exaggerated Italian accent, in a Chicago hotel lobby, to shout "Hey, Fat Tony!" at the former assistant attorney general—sent the nominee a handwritten letter on Harvard stationery. In the justice's archive of correspondence, the Michelman letter, simultaneously self-absorbed and explicitly skeptical of Scalia, stands out.

> Dear Nino,
>
> I don't know why *I* should feel honored, but I do.
>
> I also, of course, feel pleased and excited for your sake. Trying to imagine how *you* must feel is beyond my powers.
>
> Ability, character, conviction, warmth, humanity, cheer, a love of argument, a respect for reason—all of these qualities [are] apt to serve the Court and the country, and you bring them (I feel in a position to know—1960 seems like yesterday) in abundance.

(Will I come to wonder about "conviction"? Well, perhaps now and then some gnashing of teeth—or even profound and passionate disagreement. But I confidently expect
you always to have—and to give—reasons.) . . . [emphases
in the original]

As ever,
Frank[17]

*   *   *

At 10:45 a.m. on September 26, a brilliantly sunny day in
Washington, with the temperature nearing eighty, the outgoing chief
justice, the confirmed nominees, and their wives gathered in the Blue
Room of the White House. Greeting them, all smiles, were Regan,
Wallison, and Meese: the winning team behind this day. The Burgers
and the Rehnquists had been here before; for Maureen and Nino,
however, the excitement was new, far beyond his investiture on the
Court of Appeals. This was more like First Communion or
Confirmation in the Catholic Church: the day Antonin Scalia
became, forevermore, Justice Scalia.

Ten minutes later the Reagans took their cue to "descend from the
living quarters" to the Blue Room. At the stroke of eleven, the group
entered the East Room. The 216 attendees, including Scalia's beloved
Aunts Eva and Lenora, rose in standing ovation. First onstage was
Maureen, trim and reserved in turquoise jacket and skirt with white
blouse, her short hair coiffed like Nancy Reagan's. Nino, in grey suit
and red tie, followed, trailed by Bill and Nan Rehnquist, and, as the
applause continued, the president.

"This ceremony is the culmination of our constitutional process
which involves each of the three branches of government," Reagan
began. He summoned Burger. The chief justice called it an honor and

personal privilege to administer the constitutional oath to Rehnquist, "a warm friend for fifteen years," and Scalia, "with whom I have worked on extrajudicial activities."

With his wife holding the Bible, Rehnquist took the oath. When it was over, amid sustained applause, he kissed Nan on the lips and removed from his pocket a short prepared statement. "Mr. President, I am grateful beyond measure to you for affording me the opportunity to serve the Court and to serve my country.... And I pray that God will grant me the patience, the wisdom, and the fortitude to worthily follow in the footsteps of my illustrious predecessors."

Now Burger summoned Scalia, who had forgotten to button his suit jacket. "If Mrs. Scalia will hold the Bible, place your left hand on the Bible, raising your right hand, and repeat after me." The room was silent save for Burger's stentorian Midwest intonation and Scalia's Jersey-Queens accent.

BURGER: I, Anne-toe-neen Scuh-lee-yuh—
SCALIA: I, Ant'nin Scalia—

It continued:

—do solemnly swear that I will support and defend the Constitution of the United States against all enemies foreign and domestic, that I will bear true faith and allegiance to the same, that I take this obligation freely and without any mental reservation or purpose of evasion, and that I will well and faithfully discharge the duties of the office on which I am about to enter, so help me God.

"My congratulations to you," Burger said. The applause lasted thirty seconds, during which Scalia shook hands with Burger and the president, accepted a kiss on his left cheek from Maureen, and waited for the ovation to recede. He shook his head and sported a closed-lipped smile, almost a grimace, as if entertaining—for the first time—a measure of disbelief at where he stood, what he had become. He made mischievous eye contact with someone on the right of the room, possibly his Aunt Lenora, put hand to forehead, and mouthed the words "my speech," as the applause abated.

"This is an occasion for *thank yous*," he said, speaking without notes. "It's very easy to know where to begin; it's very hard to know where to end. I'd begin, of course, with President Reagan, who has chosen to think me worthy of this appointment for which I'm very grateful; and [I] will do my best to live up to his confidence. I have to thank my wife, Maureen, who's an extraordinary woman and without whom I wouldn't be here—or if I were here, it wouldn't have been as much fun along the way."

For the first time, laughter filled the East Room. Reagan smiled broadly and looked over at Maureen. "I have to thank a lot of other people," Scalia said, waving his hand: acknowledgment that all who deserved his thanks would not receive them here. "Going way back to teachers in Public School 13 in Queens, Xavier High School in Manhattan, up to my colleagues on the court on which I presently serve who are here today." With his final words, Scalia sought to convey respect for his new colleagues, the other justices, all seated before him: "In the course of my last tour of duty on the Court of Appeals for the District of Columbia Circuit, I have come to know in one way or another all of the current justices on the Supreme Court. I have an enormous respect for that institution, and I have an enormous personal regard for each of them. I look forward to working with them in our common enterprise for many years to come. Thank you all very much."

In closing remarks, President Reagan noted that Scalia had distinguished himself "for his integrity and independence and for the force of his intellect." Of the administration's campaign to shift the Court's ideological balance to the right, to roll back the excesses of the Warren era, the chief executive made no mention; instead, he invoked the perils, anticipated at the Framing, of the courts' "making laws rather than interpreting them." It was one of Reagan's finest speeches: "The Founding Fathers gave careful thought to the role of the Supreme Court.... They settled on a judiciary that would be independent and strong, but one whose power would also, they believed, be confined within the boundaries of a written constitution and laws.... They knew that the courts, like the Constitution itself, must not be liberal or conservative. The question was and is, 'Will we have government by the people?'"

The Scalias were the last off stage as the audience applauded once more, and the Reagans and Burgers led the group into the White House Cross Hall for a reception with refreshments.[18]

*   *   *

Article VI of the Constitution requires all federal employees to take a *constitutional* oath; but federal statute also requires federal judges to take a *judicial* oath. After mounting the most systematic successful Supreme Court confirmation campaign in history, supporting two nominees, the Reagan team, at this penultimate hour, committed their only misstep. The White House told Tim Flannigan, Chief Justice Burger's special assistant, that "we want the combined constitutional and judicial oath to be administered at the White House ceremony." Burger—*sentinel to the end*—sent word back: the judicial oaths will be administered at the Court.[19]

That afternoon, Rehnquist and Scalia and their families gathered on the Court's famous marble steps to pose for photographers and TV cameras. Surrounded by buoyant wives and children, some grown, the two shook hands. "Both men," the Associated Press reported, "smiled broadly in the stifling heat."

"How happy are you?" a reporter shouted at Scalia.

"Moderately happy!"

Once inside, the Scalias posed for more photographs in Nino's new chambers. Sandra Day O'Connor, the junior justice since 1981, had taken Rehnquist's chambers; Rehnquist, naturally took Burger's. So Scalia inherited the chambers vacated after the death, ten months earlier, of retired Justice Potter Stewart. Now the nine justices donned their robes to pose in the chief's conference room. In the Court's new lineup—helmed by Rehnquist at center, Scalia at his far left, O'Connor at far right—Scalia, at fifty, was the youngest justice.

At 4:00 p.m. the ornate courtroom swelled with four hundred attendees. Maureen and the kids "occupied almost the entire front row." As his predecessors had done, Scalia sat in a nineteenth-century wooden chair, formerly used by Chief Justice John Marshall, in the well of the courtroom. In attendance were Arthur Goldberg, the only living former justice, and the widows of Justices Black and Douglas. Also present were Mary Ellen and Bob Bork.

In opening remarks, Burger heralded the Marble Temple, a symbol, he said, of the "constitutional division of powers and...supremacy of the law."

> Changes in the Court do not alter the basic continuity of the spirit that activates the Court as an institution under the Constitution. Many times each year the meaning of that grant document is debated at this very lectern, and this confirms John Marshall's description of the Constitution as a living document.

Burger closed by recalling what Earl Warren had said at Burger's investiture in 1969, the last such passing of the torch: "It is not likely ever for nine justices always to agree. If it ever comes to pass...the

Court will have lost its strength and will no longer be a real force in the affairs of our country." Seated in the Marshall chair, Scalia—apostle of judicial restraint, avowed enemy of the imperial judiciary—can only have bristled at Burger's reference to a "living" Constitution.

Now Attorney General Meese, formally attired, presented the official commissions for Rehnquist and Scalia, signed by Reagan and himself, to Court clerk Joseph Spaniol. "Know Ye," the commission instructed, that the president, "reposing special trust and confidence in the Wisdom, Uprightness, and Learning of Antonin Scalia," had nominated him and, with the advice and consent of the Senate, hereby appointed him associate justice.

All rose as Burger, in his last official act, summoned Rehnquist to the center of the bench. The justice placed his left hand on a Bible and raised his right. When it was over, Burger declared: "It is my privilege to present the new chief justice of the United States."

After the applause subsided, Chief Justice Rehnquist, in his first official act, summoned the chief deputy clerk to escort Scalia from the well. Fifteen years Rehnquist and Scalia had known each other, their fates bound at critical junctures; it was fitting that the hand that brought Scalia onto the Court, welcomed him to its elite ranks, was Rehnquist's.

"Judge Scalia," said Rehnquist—the last person to address Scalia that way—"are you prepared to take the oath?"

"I am," Scalia said. The Scalia kids "exchanged smiles" as their dad repeated after Rehnquist:

> I, Antonin Scalia, do solemnly swear that I will administer
> justice without respect to persons, and do equal right to the
> poor and to the rich, and that I will faithfully and impartially
> discharge and perform all the duties incumbent upon me as
> associate justice of the United States, according to the best of
> my abilities and understanding, agreeably to the Constitution

and laws of the United States; that I will support and defend
the Constitution of the United States against all enemies, foreign and domestic; that I will bear true faith and allegiance to
the same; that I take this obligation freely, without any mental
reservation or purpose of evasion; and that I will well and
faithfully discharge the duties of the office of which I am about
to enter. So help me God.

"Justice Scalia," said Rehnquist—the first person to address Scalia
that way—"on behalf of all the members of the Court and Chief Justice
Burger, it is a pleasure to extend to you a very warm welcome...and to
wish for you...a long and happy career in our common calling."

Thus Scalia became the only justice to take oaths from two different
chief justices on the same day. Applause filled the courtroom as the new
chief and associate justice took their places on the mahogany bench.[20]

Acknowledgments

This book originated in my high school years, when I first saw Justice Scalia on PBS's *The Constitution: That Delicate Balance.* He was immediately and unmistakably different from the other panelists, by turns trenchant and humorous, clever and compelling. By the time I became a Washington correspondent, in 1999, I had read his Princeton lectures, collected in *A Matter of Interpretation: Federal Courts and the Law* (1997).

Upon arriving in the capital, I wrote to the justice seeking an interview. Our correspondence over the next two years, humorous and revealing, and the pair of one-on-one lunches we shared at his beloved AV Ristorante—vinous, unforgettable, and off the record—convinced me I would write about him someday. Excerpts from our correspondence will appear in *Scalia: Supreme Court Years, 1986–2016.* Though I was never a Supreme Court correspondent *per se*, my work on a previous book about Watergate, my journalism career, and my work on this project have enabled me to cover numerous oral arguments at the Supreme Court and to interview six justices and one future justice, listed in the appendix.

I am inexpressibly grateful to my wife, Sara, love of my life, to her family, to whom this book is dedicated, to our sons, Aaron and Gray, and to my own family for the love they have all shown me in good times and bad, in sickness and in health, for richer or for richer. *Nunc quid sit amor.*

Over several years of research, one benefits from so many acts of kindness and diligence they cannot all be acknowledged or even recalled; my apologies for those omitted here. Any errors, of course, were my own.

My primary debt is to Justice Scalia: not just for his extraordinary generosity to a young reporter a quarter century ago, but for the exemplary life he led, inspiring and humbling, and for his multifaceted legacy.

Four of the Scalia children—Eugene, Father Paul, Christopher, and Meg—graciously allowed me, not long after their father's death, to interview them at length. Maureen Scalia kindly consented, at a Metropolitan Club event in Washington, to answer a few questions about her engagement, recounted nowhere else; she also provided clarification on a detail here and there and assistance with photograph captions. Eugene Scalia, former secretary of labor, opened many doors for me; made available many of the photographs used here, several previously unpublished; and helped me secure access to his father's P.S. 13 report card. The Scalias are an extraordinary family, and exposure to them, in any measure, is equally inspiring and humbling.

To all the interviewees, who opened their hearts and memories in the interests of a more accurate record of history and the Scalia legacy, I owe a special debt. The same is true for the blurbists, a distinguished group whose words of praise for this book, and its author, mean more to me than I can say.

At the Supreme Court, the Public Information Office staff, including Kathy Arberg, Ella Hunter, Patricia McCabe, Sarah Woessner, and their colleagues—the finest public servants a reporter could hope to encounter—helped arrange interviews; supplied photographs, documents, and information; and assisted me during oral arguments and on other occasions. Interviewed in chambers, Justice Clarence Thomas was exceedingly generous with his time and insight. The late Judge Laurence Silberman and his executive assistant Diane Champagne, at the Court of Appeals for the District of Columbia Circuit, assisted in ways large and small. Steve Pollak, Mark Langer, and Margie Gaines of the D.C. Circuit Historical Society helped me navigate the society's invaluable archives.

Reuniting with the team at Regnery was another blessing. Publisher Tom Spence invested in this project, and in me, and saw the merits of a two-volume work. Elizabeth Kantor and Laura Spence Swain, brilliant editors both, strengthened the manuscript and ensured it adhered to standards. John Caruso designed a compelling jacket. Harry Crocker looked out for me.

My literary agent, Keith Urbahn of Javelin, is the embodiment of a loyal friend. My last three books, and large chunks of my soul, would not exist without him. Special thanks also to co-founder Matt Latimer, Matt Carlini, and the whole team supporting Javelin's unrivaled roster of authors.

Christopher Ruddy, founder and CEO of Newsmax, is a great boss and supporter. Thanks also to Elliot Jacobson, Chris Wallace, Valeria Riccioli, Maurice Rosenberg, Alicia Kelly, Chris Knowles, Guillermo Garcia, Juan Silva, Jordan Clifford, Alex Heredia, Jake Pollack, Dan Susskind, Cole Charvet, Anna Laudiero, Katie Armstrong, Andrea Clarke, J. T. Trylch, Shannon Speight, Jessie D'Angelo, Renee Baldwin, Khan Ahmadzai, Isagani Valenzuela, and all the great anchors, correspondents, and other TV news professionals there.

Leonard Leo, Lee Liberman Otis, and Dean Reuter of the Federalist Society each helped in critical ways. Leonard arranged for attorney Andrea Picciotti-Bayer and legal-policy veteran Dan Casey to provide their expert research assistance and acumen, pro bono; I also treasure their kindness. Lee provided an important interview, documents, background guidance, a blurb, and other invaluable assistance. Dean opened many doors and offered insight as a legal ace and acclaimed historian.

Kristen Woychowski of the New York City Department of Education helped me secure access to the future justice's report card from P.S. 13 in Queens. Xavier High School in Manhattan enlisted professional photographers to take new images of old yearbook photographs for publication here. Deep thanks to Xavier communications director Shawna Gallagher Vega and photographer Michael Marmora.

Scalia's Xavier classmate Thomas Campion sent me dozens of documents and identified bygone classmates in photographs. Another Xavier classmate, Father Robert Connor, one of the book's most important interviewees, provided entrée to other members of Opus Dei who knew Justice Scalia, as well as photo caption information. Ed Whelan provided me with correspondence between Tom Campion and Maureen Scalia on which Whelan was copied.

Sarah Wharton, Lesley Schoenfeld, and Ed Moloy, archival custodians of the Antonin Scalia Papers at the Harvard Law School Library, responded cheerfully to countless requests for documents and photographs. The justice's archival legacy could not be in better hands.

At the University of Virginia School of Law, Jonathan Ashley and Loren Moulds helped secure archival photographs, including the cover image. At the University of Chicago Law School, Marsha Ferziger Nagorsky did the same. Many of these images were unseen for decades or previously unpublished.

At the Gerald R. Ford Presidential Library, rock star supervisory archivist Geir Gundersen steered me to dozens of documents, including declassified materials never published elsewhere. Elizabeth Druga helped me obtain previously unpublished photographs of President Ford and Assistant Attorney General Scalia. James Wilderotter, who served at the White House and Justice Department in the Ford era, supplied photographs and scans of his contemporaneous ID badges.

At the Ronald Reagan Presidential Library, Daniel Guttierez arranged for me to receive 1,600 pages of declassified documents. Ray Wilson fielded follow-up questions; Michael Pinckney helped me locate and publish previously unseen images of President Reagan and Judge Scalia.

Alex Lange of the National Archives and Records Administration's Still Picture Reference division found a clean copy of the 1974 "class photo" of DOJ leadership. Dorothy Alexander of NARA's Center for Legislative Archives helped me navigate the *Congressional Record* to research Scalia's appointments and confirmations. Stephen Saltzburg of the George Washington University Law School arranged for my researcher to have access to the school's library.

Loretta Deaver and Bruce Kirby and other professionals at the Library of Congress helped me to access the papers of Robert Bork, Ruth Bader Ginsburg, and other judges from the D.C. Circuit. Connie Cartledge helped decipher John Paul Stevens's 1986 note to Scalia.

Laura Poll of the Trenton Free Public Library tracked down the *Trenton Evening Times* article that contained the only interview ever granted by Scalia's father. Albert Rhodes, chief of the Ewing, New Jersey, Police Department, helped me research a traffic accident involving Scalia's parents. Felicity Democko of the Eastman School of Music provided information about Salvatore Eugene Scalia's enrollment there in the 1920s. Sarah Piccini of the Lackawanna Historical Society helped me search, though in vain, for surviving copies of the Italian-language newspaper that the justice's father published in Scranton, Pennsylvania. Colleen White of the Villa Victoria Academy confirmed little Nino's enrollment there in first grade.

Andrew Jay Schwartzman sent me materials from Scalia's service at the White House Office of Telecommunications Policy. Margaret Whitehead, the widow of Clay Whitehead, created the online archive of her husband's OTP papers that was central to my portrait of Scalia at the agency. Margaret also sent me photographs and provided tender encouragement. Brian Lamb and Henry Goldberg also fielded queries.

At the American Enterprise Institute, Karlyn Bowman showed great patience with my ceaseless requests for information, documents, and photographs. Thanks also to Anthony Wojtkowiak, Jennifer

Morretta, and Michael Turner for providing me with AEI videos, images, and transcripts.

Peter Robinson helped me secure access to the papers of former attorney general Ed Meese at the Hoover Institution Library and Archives, as did Chris Marino of Stanford University and attorney Christopher Hage of the Federalist Society, who volunteered his ace research services. Carol Leadenham of Stanford University sent me helpful newspaper clippings. Dean Reuter, all-star ally, put me in touch with Chris Hage. John Malcolm, director of the Meese Center and a vice president at the Heritage Foundation, helped me secure my inter-views with Attorney General Meese. Julia Dudley and Julia Chapman of the Syracuse University Libraries combed the papers of William Safire. My dear friend Kevin Leonard, who oversees the archive of my papers and tapes at Northwestern University, located my correspon-dence with Justice Scalia.

Mary Ellen Bork discussed sensitive personal matters and gener-ously loaned me her and Robert Bork's wedding album for reproduction of the photograph of that event that appears here. Robert Bork, Jr., answered numerous questions, large and small, about his father's friendship with Scalia, and enlisted the kind assistance of Judge Frank Easterbrook in researching Scalia's appearance before the Supreme Court.

Chuck Cooper introduced me to the incredible professionals at Alderson/Trustpoint One, the court reporting service that transcribed my recorded interviews. The folks there know how grateful I am to them. Charlie Savage of the *New York Times* made available an impor-tant recording of Justice Scalia, which Alderson/Trustpoint transcribed. Billy Brawner invited me to the Metropolitan Club event where I con-versed with Maureen Scalia.

Margaret Brennan, Elizabeth Campbell, and Hugo Rojas of CBS News helped me search old *Face the Nation* transcripts; former CBS

News political director Caitlin Conant put me in touch with Hugo Rojas. Andrea Mitchell of NBC News, Nina Totenberg of National Public Radio, and Sam Donaldson, formerly of ABC News, kindly listened to audio clips to identify bygone reporters, justices, and other speakers heard on official recordings. NPR's Scott Simon put me in touch with Nina Totenberg; Brian Karem of Slate put me in touch with Sam Donaldson. Phil Mattingly and Lisa Webster of CNN helped me research the network's coverage on the days of Scalia's nomination, confirmation hearing, and swearings-in.

Martin Swoverland of C-SPAN provided the image from Scalia's confirmation hearing. Greta Brawner has helped me in innumerable ways. Brian Lamb was my C-SPAN angel, Howard Mortman, my rabbi.

Ben Florance and Dominique Johnson extracted and organized information from dozens of previous books about the Supreme Court. I stand on the shoulders of all of the daily deadline reporters whose coverage of Scalia and the Court appear in my footnotes; equal thanks to all the historians, biographers, and other authors who preceded me to the subject.

Tricia Paoletta, Jim Steen, and Dean Reuter reviewed selected chapters. Mark Paoletta opened doors and provided wise counsel, personal and professional. Tom Feddo, Dan Miller, R. N., Scott Stossel, and Cal Thomas extended themselves in extraordinary ways.

Deep thanks also to: Marilyn and Neal Adams, Saori and Josh Adams, Matt Alvarez, Sakura Amend, Keith Appell, Dr. Larry Arnn, Sharyl Attkisson, Mary Barket, Stu Basinger, Geovana and Vince Benedetto, Scott Berger, Chartese Berry, Chris Berry, Tom Bevan, Jeffrey Birnbaum, John Bolton, Betsy Brawner, Greta and Billy Brawner, Shannon Bream, Christopher Buckley, Elisabeth Bumiller and Steve Weisman, Scott Berger, Tim Burger, Elliot Berke, Jim Byron, Carl Cannon, Tucker Carlson, Amy and Eric Carmen, Chris (Fab) Carter,

Chris Cassidy, Kim Caviness, Lyn Vaus, and Bob Vaus, Francesca Chambers, Shaun Chang, Dwight Chapin, Bronwyn and David Clark, Michael Clemente, Catherine Clinton, Scott Cohen, Dr. Jim Comerford, Sandy and Len Colodny, Alex Conant, Cece Connolly and Manuel Roig-Franzia, Mark Corallo, Kevin Corke, Bob Costas, John Crosset, Cory Crowley, Kelly and Jared Cutler, Debbie and Jack Dattisman, Ron Dermer, Tom DiNanno, Ashok Divecha, Ben Domenech, Kim Dontas, Maureen Dowd, Jennifer and Peter Dugas, Rich Edson, Keiko Ellis, Suzanne and Mark Einstein, Ahtra Elnashar, Mike Emanuel, Susan Ferrechio and Doug McKelway, Jory and Chris Fisher, Robin and Ronnie Fithian, Kenny Fletcher, Jonny Fluger, Rainey Foster, Kristine Frazao, Ashley and Hugh Gallagher, Bryan Garner, Josh Gerstein, Tim Goldsmith, Dr. Jesus Gonzalez, Philip Glass, Bob Greene, Abe Greenwald, Bryan Griffin, Hugo Gurdon, Lee Habib, Brian Haley, Vicki Hart, Chris Hartline, Rob Hartnett, Patty and Chip Heaps, Jacob Heilbrunn, Laura and Denny Herrmann, John Herzberg, Steve Hess, Hugh Hewitt, Connie and Chris Hillman, Rick Hohlt, Tish and Hal Hopkins, Carolyn and Joe Horter, Jim Hougan, Elodie and Austin Hunt, Heather and Derek Hunter, Will Hurd, Jay Jacobs, Alirezah Jafarzadeh, Ashley Jester and Chan, David Johns, Michelle and David Joubron, Nick Kalman, Glenn Kessler, Ron Kessler, Suhail Khan, Rear Admiral John Kirby (U.S. Navy, Retired), Erik Kirschbaum, Valerie Kiser and Dave Bosley, Phill Kline, Lara and Josh Knights, Marta Kumer, Jack Langer, Chris Lapetina, Kathy Lash and Joe Trippi, Matt Lee, Laura and Kevin Leonard, Steve Levingston, Matt Lloyd, Beth Lynch, Ray Locker, Mark London, Rich Lowry, Judge Jimmy Lynn, Tony Makris, Tom Mallon and Bill Bodenschatz, Manny Maris, Jonathan Martin, Greg Massoni, Mike McCloud, Kel McClanahan, Mary McElwee, Katie and Revan McQueen, Jay McMichael, the Honorable Dan Meuser, Frank Morano, Jefferson Morley, Jonathan Movroydis, Mark Moyar, Greg Mueller, Ramola and Michael Musante,

Vida and Rob Myers, Sophia Narrett and Dan Lippman, Andrew Napolitano, Chuck Nash, Graham Nash, Heather Nauert, Luke Nichter, Monica Notzon, Larry O'Connor, Kelly O'Donnell, Joan Ohayon, Morgan Ortagus, Shane O'Sullivan, Neil Patel, Jared Payne, Will Pearson, Laura Petito and David Jump, Joe Piscopo, Chris Plante, John Podhoretz, the Honorable Mike Pompeo, Matt Pottinger, Bonny Rafel, Johnna Miller Raskin, Katy Ricalde and Ed Buckley, Michelle Rice and John Hamilton, Joanne and Jim Rich, Daniel Rosen, Simon Rosenberg, Peter Rough, Norman Roule, Kristin and David Roush, Larry Sabato, Becky and Ryan Samuel, Julie and Will Schrot, Greg Schuckman, Arlen Schumer, H. Andrew Schwartz, Cindy and Ryan Schwarz, Geoff Shepard, Jeff Shesol, Erik Smith, Juli and David Smith, Laura Smith, Nancy Willis Smith, Jay Solomon, Rose and James Sprankle, John Stansfield, Alison Starling and Peter Alexander, Kate Starr, the Staten Island crew, now far-flung, and their progeny, Elad Strohmeyer, Beth Sworobuk and the entire Sworobuk family, Monica Tegeder, Roy Thomas, John Tichy, Sarah Tinsley, Eric Trager, Netanya and Michael Trimboli, Tevi Troy, Jen, Frank, William, and Sarah Truskolaski, Eve-Lyn and Brian Turmail, Denise and Vince Vitollo, Leland Vittert, Michael Von Sas, Ildi and Mory Watkins, John B. Williams, Brian Wilson, Sheila and Tom Wolfe, and Matt Yurus.

And it was the indomitable Rainey Foster who told me what I needed to hear, when I most needed to hear it: "You finish that book!"

James Rosen
Chesapeake Bay, Maryland
November 2022

List of Interviewees

Asterisks denote interviews conducted prior to the commencement of this project, but which informed the author's work on it.

Arkes, Hadley, via telephone, Washington, D.C., July 2, 2021.

Baker, John, via telephone, Amelia Island, Florida, September 15, 2021.

Barkow, Rachel, via telephone, New York, New York, July 20, 2017.

Bennett, Bill, via telephone, Southport, NC, August 4, 2017.

Bolton, John, Washington, D.C., May 2, 2017.

Bowman, Karlyn, via telephone, Washington, D.C., September 1, 2021.

Bork, Mary Ellen, via telephone, McLean, Virginia, February 5, 2021.

———, via telephone, McLean, Virginia, May 25, 2022.

Bork, Robert, McLean, Virginia, March 6, 2007.*

Bryce, Meg Scalia, via telephone, Charlottesville, Virginia, August 2, 2017.

———, via telephone, Charlottesville, Virginia, August 11, 2017.

Burger, Warren, Arlington, Virginia, August 25, 1994.*

Campion, Thomas, via telephone, McLean, Virginia, March 26, 2021.

Cappuccio, Paul, via telephone, New York, New York, June 6, 2017.

Cheney, Dick, via telephone, Jackson Hole, Wyoming, September 26, 2017.

Colby, William, via telephone, Washington, D.C., January 20, 1995.*

Coleman, Richard, via telephone, Malibu, California, October 6, 2017.

——, via telephone, Malibu, California, October 9, 2017.

Conerly, Helen, via telephone, Alpharetta, Georgia, July 22, 2017.

Connor, Robert, via telephone, South Orange, New Jersey, December 17, 2020.

——, via telephone, South Orange, New Jersey, December 29, 2020.

Coverdale, John, via telephone, South Orange, New Jersey, December 7, 2020.

Davis, Steve, via telephone, Century City, California, September 12, 2017.

Donato, Brian, via telephone, Earlysville, Virginia, November 7, 2017.

——, via telephone, Earlysville, Virginia, November 8, 2017.

Dormer, Robert, via telephone, Washington, D.C., November 8, 2017.

Epstein, Richard, via telephone, Norwalk, Connecticut, October 25, 2021.

Feil, Ralph, via telephone, Charlottesville, Virginia, November 8, 2017.

Feldman, Martin, via telephone, New Orleans, Louisiana, December 8, 2017.

Ferate, Anthony, ["A.J."], via telephone, Edmond, Oklahoma, October 16, 2021.

Ford, Gerald, New York, New York, January 25, 1994.*

Funk, William, via telephone, Portland, Oregon, December 13, 2017.

——, via telephone, Portland, Oregon, December 14, 2017.

Goeglein, Tim, via telephone, Washington, D.C., June 5, 2017.

Goldberg, Henry, via telephone, Bremen, Maine, June 27, 2017.

Graefe, Fred, via telephone, Washington, D.C., August 31, 2017.

Joshi, Sopan, via telephone, Chicago, Illinois, July 5, 2017.

——, via telephone, Chicago, Illinois, August 30, 2017.

Kennedy, Malcolm, Washington, D.C., January 5, 2021.

Lamb, Brian, Washington, D.C., May 10, 2017.

Leo, Leonard, Washington, D.C., August 28, 2017.

Lessig, Lawrence, via telephone, Cambridge, Massachusetts, August 8, 2017.

Levin, Daniel, via telephone, Washington, D.C., August 23, 2022

Lewin, Nathan, via telephone, Jerusalem, Israel, September 14, 2017.

Liberman [Otis], Lee, Washington, D.C., June 29, 2017.

———, via telephone, Washington, D.C., April 4, 2022.

———, via telephone, Washington, D.C., April 12, 2022.

Linsley, Kristin, via telephone, Kensington, California, July 7, 2017.

Lynn, James Murray, via correspondence, June 18, 2020.

McClure, Fred, via telephone, College Station, Texas, May 5, 2022.

Meese, Edwin M. III, via telephone, McLean, Virginia, February 2, 2021.

———, via telephone, McLean, Virginia, April 27, 2022.

Michelman, Frank, via telephone, Lexington, Massachusetts, October 3, 2017.

Napolitano, Andrew, via telephone, New York, New York, July 19, 2017.

———, via telephone, New York, New York, October 13, 2017.

———, via telephone, New York, New York, October 20, 2017.

North, Oliver, Washington, D.C., September 14, 2017.

Nussbaum, Bernard, via telephone, New York, New York, February 19, 2021.

Rehnquist, William H., via correspondence, June 29, 1993.*

———, Washington, D.C., October 20, 1993.*

———, Washington, D.C., May 21, 2001.*

Olson, Walter, via telephone, New Market, Maryland, April 30, 2020.

Phillips, Carter, via telephone, Arlington, Virginia, September 5, 2019.

Pogue, Richard, via telephone, Cleveland, Ohio, November 6, 2017.

Randolph, Raymond, via telephone, Bethesda, Maryland, August 3, 2021.

Raul, Alan C., via telephone, Washington, D.C., March 28, 2022.

Robinson, Ken, via telephone, Arlington, Virginia, July 23, 2017.

Rose, Tony and Meg, via telephone, Cheyenne, Wyoming, February 4, 2021.

Ross, Wilbur, via telephone, Washington, D.C., October 19, 2017.

Rossum, Ralph, via telephone, Dana Point, California, June 26, 2017.

———, via telephone, Dana Point, California, June 27, 2017.

Scalia, Antonin, Washington, D.C., November 11, 1999.*

———, Washington, D.C., [undated; Fall Term, 2001].*

Scalia, Christopher, Washington, D.C., October 17, 2017.

Scalia, Eugene, Washington, D.C., August 22, 2017.

———, Washington, D.C., September 8, 2017.

———, via telephone, Fairfax, Virginia, August 5, 2022.

Scalia, Paul, Arlington, Virginia, May 30, 2017.

Schiltz, Patrick, via telephone, Minneapolis, Minnesota, June 28, 2017.

———, via telephone, Minneapolis, Minnesota, June 29, 2017.

Schwab, Arthur, via telephone, Pittsburgh, Pennsylvania, November 8, 2017.

Schwartzman, Andrew, Washington, D.C., September 27, 2017.

Silberman, Laurence, Washington, D.C., May 22, 2017.

———, Washington, D.C., April 14, 2022.

———, via telephone, Washington, D.C., August 23, 2022.

Snyder, Anne, via telephone, McLean, Virginia, June 2, 2022.

Sotomayor, Sonia, New York, New York, October 7, 1998.*

Strauss, Peter, via telephone, New York, New York, December 10, 2017.

Swanson, James, via telephone, Washington, D.C., May 17, 2022.

Thomas, Clarence, Washington, D.C., July 6, 2017.

Thurmond, Strom, via telephone, Washington, D.C., April 3, 1996.*

Whelan, Ed, Washington, D.C., May 15, 2017.

Wilderotter, Jim, via telephone, Williamsburg, Virginia, February 18, 2021.

———, via telephone, Williamsburg, Virginia, March 2, 2021.

Notes

Chapter I: Little Nino

Epigraph: "College Education," commencement address at Catholic University, May 15, 1999, in Antonin Scalia, *Scalia Speaks: Reflections on Law, Faith, and Life Well Lived*, eds. Christopher J. Scalia and Edward Whelan (New York City: Crown Forum, 2017), 80.

1. William F. Buckley, Jr., "The Senate and the William Rehnquisition," *New York Daily News*, August 8, 1986.
2. Robert P. Hey, "Judge Scalia Seen as Major Force on Supreme Court," *Christian Science Monitor*, June 19, 1986.
3. John Bolton, interview by the author, Washington, D.C., May 2, 2017; Patrick Shiltz, interview by the author, June 28, 2017.
4. John Bolton, interview by the author, Washington, D.C., May 2, 2017; Linda Greenhouse, "Senate, 65 to 33, Votes to Confirm Rehnquist as 16th Chief Justice," *New York Times*, September 18, 1986; Anne Q. Hoy, "Goldwater Weary; Left before Vote," *Arizona Republic*, September 19, 1986. The imperfection of the vote bothered Scalia forever. "The two missing were Barry Goldwater and Jake Garn," he said in 2005. "So make it a hundred!"; "Constitutional Interpretation," C-SPAN, March 14, 2005.
5. Scalia, *Scalia Speaks*, 149; David R. Palombi, "Trenton Native Likely Candidate for Spot on U.S. Supreme Court," *Trenton Times*, November 4, 1985 (excelled, gifted).* Scalia once said of a boss who never revised Scalia's work: "I was always very proud, because he really [was] a perfectionist in all things"; "Justice Antonin Scalia," interview by Judith R. Hope, Oral History Project, The Historical Society of the District of Columbia Circuit, December 5, 1992, https://dcchs.org/wp-content/uploads/2019/03/Scalia-Complete-Oral-History-1.pdf, 24. Scalia expected people to act "honestly and perfectly," with "uncompromisable standards." Scalia, *Scalia Speaks*, 152, 345. *Where notes include multiple citations, key words are provided in parentheses to correlate passages from the main text to their respective source material.
6. Eugene Scalia, interview by the author, August 5, 2022; "Charlie Rose Show," PBS, June 2, 2008 (spoiled); Jeffrey S. Sutton, "Antonin Scalia—A Justice in Full," *National Review*, March 14, 2016 (reason); "Justice Antonin Scalia," Oral History, 2–3 (sulfur, Mohicans). All accounts of Scalia's early years are indebted to Joan Biskupic, *American Original: The Life and Constitution of Supreme Court Justice Antonin Scalia* (New York City: Sarah Crichton, 2010, paperback ed.), for which the justice granted twelve interviews, and Bruce Allen Murphy, *Scalia: A Court of One* (New York City: Simon & Schuster, 2015, paperback ed.). Despite receiving no cooperation from the Scalias, Murphy impressively documented their ancestry. Yet both books were unabashed in their contempt for Scalia's jurisprudence and conduct; each major event and phase of his career is treated in the most tendentious light. A Scalia clerk dismissed *Court of*

One as "cartoonish and incompetent." See Ed Whelan, "Murphy's Law," *National Review,* July 7, 2014, and Paul E. Peterson and Michael W. McConnell, eds., *Scalia's Constitution: Essays on Law and Education* (London: Palgrave Macmillan, 2017). Kristin Linsley, who clerked for Scalia in 1989–90, observed Biskupic "trashing Justice Scalia's jurisprudence category by category…a simplistic, non-legal, very badly done analysis." Reached in early 2017, Biskupic was warm and encouraging, agreeing to share the transcripts of her interviews of Scalia; contacted three months later, as requested, she ignored multiple messages. The remaining literature is largely academic. An exception is Bryan A. Garner's *Nino and Me: My Unusual Friendship with Justice Antonin Scalia* (New York City: Threshold Editions, 2018), an intimate memoir by Scalia's co-author and lecture partner. *The Unexpected Scalia: A Conservative Justice's Liberal Opinions* (Cambridge University Press: 2017) offered a curious hybrid of memoir and legal analysis by David Dorsen, a liberal acquaintance. *Scalia Speaks: Reflections on Law, Faith, and Life Well Lived* (New York City: Crown Forum, 2017), a collection of the justice's speeches edited by Christopher Scalia and Ed Whelan, is quoted frequently here. The two also edited *On Faith: Lessons from an American Believer* (New York City: Crown Forum, 2019), a collection of the justice's religious writings. Two former clerks, Jeffrey Sutton and the ubiquitous Whelan, compiled *The Essential Scalia: On the Constitution, the Courts, and the Rule of Law* (New York City: Crown Forum, 2020). The volume you are reading is the first biography since Scalia's death and the first to make use of a wealth of materials, including his oral history and FBI files, that were unavailable to previous writers.

7.   FBI report of Special Agent [redacted], "Antonin Scalia," April 6, 1982, and FBI teletype from Chicago to Director, April 7, 1982, both in the Scalia FBI files (parents' dates and places of birth); Murphy, *Scalia,* 7–10 (height, $400, languages); Scalia, *Scalia Speaks,* 16 (four characteristics).

8.   Eugene Scalia, interview by the author, Washington, D.C., August 22, 2017; FBI report of Special Agent [redacted], "Antonin Gregory Scalia," Newark field office, July 1, 1974 (loyal, excellent); FBI airtel from Director, FBI to SAC, Newark, June 27, 1974, Scalia FBI files (searches). Bruce Allen Murphy disclosed that Salvatore had served time in Italy for socialist agitation, but Murphy had the incarceration occurring once, "for a few hours," not the "night or two" Scalia recounted to Gene. Murphy, *Scalia,* 7. And *Court of One* is silent on the family's motivations for emigrating.

9.   "Justice Antonin Scalia," Oral History Project (Naples); Erasmo S. Ciccolella, *Vibrant Life, 1886–1942: Trenton's Italian Americans* (New York City: Center for Migration Studies, 1986, paperback ed.), 81; 1940. Census data at www .1940census.archives.gov.

10.   "Monument School to Be Entertained," *Trenton Evening Times,* December 19, 1913 (Santa); "Monument School Pupils Win Honor," *Trenton Evening Times,* January 8, 1915; "Monument School Nov. Honor Roll," *Trenton Evening Times,* December 10, 1915; "Justice Antonin Scalia," Oral History Project, 1, 2 (Little Italy, piano).

11.   Biskupic, *American Original,* 11–12, 366n4 (sturdy, pinned). Pasquale left Maria for another woman in New York but returned to the family for intervals when the children were grown. Scalia told Biskupic he was a teenager when he first met Pasquale. On Vincent Panaro's political career, see Ruth Marcus and Susan Schmidt, "Scalia Tenacious after Staking Out a Position," *Washington Post,* June 22, 1986.

12. FBI teletype from Chicago to Director, April 7, 1982 (2290037M) and FBI teletype from Newark to Director, April 8, 1982 (naturalized), both in the Scalia FBI files. An FBI report of April 9, 1982, states that the county clerk's office had located records from Salvatore's citizenship ceremony at the Mercer County Court House in Trenton, New Jersey. Mercer County Court House, volume 31, petition 6963.

13. "Justice Antonin Scalia," Oral History Project, 3 (tenor); Felicity Democko (of the Eastman School of Music), email to the author, September 13, 2017; Sarah Piccini (of the Lackawanna Historical Society), emails to the author, September 12, 2017. No libraries or historical associations in the Scranton area could locate any editions of *Il Minatore*.

14. "Justice Antonin Scalia," Oral History Project, 3; "Dr. S. Eugene Scalia," *New York Times*, January 7, 1986.

15. Scalia, *Scalia Speaks*, 26, 85, 147 (committed, face, terrific); Eugene Scalia, interview, August 22, 2017 (success story); "Q&A with Antonin Scalia," C-SPAN, May 2, 2008.

16. Thomas Campion, interview by the author, March 26, 2021 (willed, Dante); Biskupic, *American Original*, 15–20 (severe, shame, A+, wasn't all); Richard M. Coleman, "Antonin Scalia—Sui Generis—Part I," ireallymissreagan.com, April 15, 2016 (Latin, Greek); "Q&A with Antonin Scalia" (subjunctive); Eugene Scalia, interview by the author, August 22, 2017 (mean, letters from grandchildren), Meg Scalia Bryce, interview by the author, August 2, 2017; Paul Scalia, interview by the author, Arlington, Virginia, May 30, 2017, Arlington, Virginia; Jimmy Breslin, "This Queens Neighborhood Is Supreme," *New York Daily News*, June 20, 1986 (liberal man).

17. Eugene Scalia, interview by the author, August 22, 2017 (kinder); "America and the Courts: Interview with Judge Antonin Scalia," C-SPAN, April 1, 1986.

18. "Q&A with Antonin Scalia" (only); Scalia, *Scalia Speaks*, 147, 380, 395 (courtliness, brains). The "brains" remark recurs in *Scalia Speaks* and elsewhere, with minor variations. Scalia stated that "on one occasion he told me this (I have never forgotten it)." Scalia, *Scalia Speaks*; but elsewhere the justice said Salvatore "used to tell me" the line, suggesting repetition. Ibid., 147. But elsewhere the justice said Salvatore "used to tell me" the line, suggesting repetition. Ibid., 395. Biskupic quoted the justice using the phrase, and attributing it to his father, at a 2006 luncheon for the National Italian American Foundation on Capitol Hill. Biskupic, *American Original*, 17, 366n21.

19. Scalia, "The Disease as Cure: 'In Order to Get Beyond Racism, We Must First Take Account of Race,'" *Washington University Law Review* (1979) (teenager); Biskupic, *American Original*, 160 (Powells).

20. Kevin Shea, "Trenton Bishop Remembers Supreme Court Justice Scalia," *Trenton Times*, February 20, 2016 (baptized); "Parish History," *Cathedral of Saint Mary of the Assumption*, http://www.saintmaryscathedral-trenton.org/parish-history/; Nicholas G. Katsarelis, "Nominee: The Little 'Nino' of Trenton's Italian Neighborhood," Associated Press, June 18, 1986 (Eva); Biskupic, *American Original*, 20 (Lenora); Franklin Fisher and Brian Kates, "They Judged Him Back Then," *New York Daily News*, June 19, 1986 (word).

21. Scalia, *Scalia Speaks*, 16 (legendary); Tim Goeglein, interview by the author, June 5, 2017. A law school dean recalled accompanying Scalia—on a Friday evening in the

early 1990s, after an exhausting day of public appearances—to a rental car station so the justice could then embark on the lengthy drive from northern New Jersey "to the tip of Long Island" to visit his aunt. "I immediately offered to drive him myself," Riccio said, "or have the school provide transportation. But he insisted on renting a car and paying for it himself.... He said he wasn't looking forward to the drive, but wanted to visit his elderly aunt...who helped raise him and whom he hadn't seen in awhile." Ronald J. Riccio, "Remembering Antonin G. Scalia," Seton Hall Law, February 2016, https://law.shu.edu/About/news.cfm?customel_datapageid_6255=455836.

22. Biskupic, *American Original*, 14 (hated); Breslin, "This Queens Neighborhood" (garden); Antonin Scalia, "Childhood in New York: Antonin Scalia, Supreme Court Justice, b. 1936," *New York*, March 31, 2013 (wonderful, Greeks); "Justice Antonin Scalia," Oral History Project, 1 (two-time); Palombi, "Trenton Native" (two years); Associated Press, "Nominee Native of Trenton with Italian Heritage," *Camden Courier Post*, June 18, 1986; Colleen White of Villa Victoria Academy, email to the author, March 11, 2021 (first grade). On one occasion, Justice Scalia described his background as "lower-middle-class," then corrected himself: "Well, middle-class." "Supreme Court Justice Perspective," C-SPAN, April 9, 2008; Scalia, *Scalia Speaks*, 385. Biskupic reported that the Scalias moved to Queens when Scalia was six. Biskupic, *American Original*, 17. In *Scalia: A Court of One*, Murphy reported that the move occurred in 1939, when Nino was three. Murphy, *Scalia*, 10. Both were inaccurate. In his 1992 oral history for the Court of Appeals, Justice Scalia said "we moved to New York when I was five." "Justice Antonin Scalia," Oral History Project, 2. In addition, after Scalia's death, a Queens newspaper cited entries for "Dr. S. Eugene Scalia" in tax records and telephone directories that placed the move in 1941, when Nino was five. Ron Marzlock, "Justice Scalia's House," *Queens Chronicle*, February 18, 2016. Neither Biskupic nor Murphy noted the two-year separation between Catherine and Nino in Trenton and Sam in Elmhurst—the unspoken reason little Nino "hated" Trenton.

23. "Supreme Court Justice Perspective," C-SPAN (not organized, didn't drive); Scalia, *Scalia Speaks*, 52–55 (Packard, homework).

24. "Justice Antonin Scalia," Oral History Project, 5 (stickball, hoop); "Supreme Court Justice Perspective," C-SPAN (Boy Scout camp); Breslin, "This Queens Neighborhood" (Methodist, climber); Fisher and Kates, "They Judged Him" (jovial); Scalia, "Childhood in New York" (good-looking); Scalia, *Scalia Speaks*, 26, 52–55, 61, 118, 148 (wonderful, quintessential, Popeye, fair, hunting).

25. Scalia, "Childhood in New York" (McGee); Murphy, *Scalia*, 13 (released); Scalia, *Scalia Speaks*, 20, 117–129 (ethnics, strange, fish, invariable, released); Bryce, August 2, 2017. "You're not everybody else. You're a Scalia," Catherine Scalia Courtney quoted her brother Matthew saying, in mimicry of their parents. Remarks of Catherine Scalia Courtney, "Justice Scalia Memorial Service," C-SPAN, March 1, 2016.

26. "Justice Antonin Scalia," Oral History Project, 7 (silver). Scalia's P.S. 13 report card shows that of the forty-five grades recorded in nine subjects, Nino posted forty As, with five lonely Bs arising in four subjects (composition, geography, history and civics, sewing), swiftly redressed, in every case, with an A; Board of Education, City of New York, "Pupil's Duplicate Record: Scalia, Antonin," June 1946, in email to the author

from Kristin Woychowski, Office of the General Counsel, New York City Department of Education, October 27, 2022.

27. Interview with Applicant, April 5, 1982, and FBI report of Special Agent [redacted], "Antonin Scalia," May 6, 1982, both in the Scalia FBI files. "Gregory" appeared on some important documents, including the Scalias' 1960 wedding invitation. Christopher Scalia, email to the author, March 17, 2021 (attaching photograph of invitation).

28. Robert Connor, interview by the author, December 17, 2020 (loathe); Biskupic, *American Original*, 20–21 (diverse).

29. Antonin Scalia, answers to Department of Justice questionnaire, June 1, 1986, in Folder 4, Box 14287, Peter J. Wallison Files, Supreme Court—Scalia, Ronald Reagan Presidential Library; Scalia, *Scalia Speaks*, 307–17.

30. Ibid., 21 (substantially, patron). Photographs of Father Matthews appeared in the 1953 edition of *Evening Parade*, the Xavier yearbook. Scalia's patron saint was St. Antoninus, a fifteenth-century Dominican friar and archbishop of Florence known for his erudition. See Scalia, *Scalia Speaks*, 148.

31. Ibid., 243 (no-nonsense); Connor, interview by the author, December 17, 2020. Connor insisted Matthews was "avuncular with all of us" and used the term "affectionately," not as an ethnic slur; but it had to have been bracing for thirteen-year-old Nino to be addressed thusly in a "substantially Irish" school. Scalia got used to people mispronouncing, even mistaking, his name. "Actually, I'm not sure how it should be pronounced," he once joked. "For the record," son Christopher J. Scalia wrote in the introduction to *Scalia Speaks*, "he pronounced it 'ANT-uh-nin.'" Scalia, *Scalia Speaks*, 2, 22.

32. "Justice Antonin Scalia," Oral History Project (wonderful); "Q&A with Antonin Scalia; Scalia, *Scalia Speaks*, 244.

33. Biskupic, *American Original*, 18 (basement); Murphy, *Scalia*, 8–9 (dissertation, thesis, literalness, poem); Paul Scalia, interview by the author (*traduttore*).

34. "Justice Antonin Scalia Funeral Mass," C-SPAN, February 20, 2016. Justice Scalia recoiled from latter-day translations of the Bible that would reduce "Be not deceived, God is not mocked" to "Make no mistake about it—God is not made a fool of." See Hanna Rosin, "The Partisan," *GQ*, May 2001.

35. "Justice Antonin Scalia," Oral History Project, 4.

36. Margaret Talbot, "Supreme Confidence," *New Yorker*, March 28, 2005 (Michigan); "America and the Courts"; Jennifer Senior, "In Conversation: Antonin Scalia," *New York*, October 6, 2013; Paul Scalia, interview by the author.

37. "Justice Antonin Scalia," Oral History Project, 6 (pianistic).

38. Thomas F. Campion, "Presenting," *Xavier Review*, November 7, 1952, attached to a letter from Thomas Campion to Maureen Scalia, May 26, 2017, cc'd to Ed Whelan, and provided to the author by Whelan via email, January 29, 2021 (president, sterling, magazine, club, major); Connor, interview by the author, December 17, 2020 (favorite, not that well); Scalia, *Scalia Speaks*, 20, 69, 311 (debate, Mass, 69th, MacArthur); *Evening Parade: 1953 Xavier Yearbook* (Sodality, sparked, Macbeth, ability); "Supreme Court Justice Perspective," C-SPAN (lines). According to Robert Connor, some classmates at Xavier, including Connor himself at the time, addressed Scalia as "Tony." In remarks at Xavier in 2011, Scalia recalled having graduated with the rank of lieutenant colonel in the marching band. Scalia, *Scalia Speaks*, 307. But

Campion's 1952 article noted Scalia's "outstanding ability to lead won for him the command of that group and the rank of major."

39. Paul Scalia, interview by the author. In a 1984 speech, Judge Scalia identified "a compulsive precision" as the first characteristic of lawyers; Scalia, *Scalia Speaks*, 90.

40. Campion, interview by the author (dominant); Connor, interview by the author, December 17, 2020 (demanding); Robert A. Connor, "Antonin Scalia—A Justice in Full," *National Review*, March 14, 2016 (relentlessly). See also "The Rev. Morton Hill; Led Pornography Foes," *New York Times*, November 6, 1985.

41. Campion, "Presenting." "I think that may have been the peak of my favorable press coverage," Justice Scalia joked. Scalia, *Scalia Speaks*, 307–8.

42. Campion, "Presenting"; "Girls Debate Boys on Election Issues," *New York Times*, October 20, 1952; "A Conversation with Antonin Scalia," interview by Nina Totenberg, Smithsonian Associates, February 12, 2013 (Algonquin); Connor, interview by the author, December 17, 2020; Biskupic, *American Original*, 22–23 (dolt).

43. Campion, "Presenting."

44. "Supreme Court Justice Perspective," C-SPAN, April 9, 2008 (grind); Eugene Scalia, interview by the author, August 22, 2017.

45. Fisher and Kates, "They Judged Him" (no time); Irvin Molotsky, "Man in the News: Judge with Tenacity and Charm," *New York Times*, June 18, 1986 (Curia). The Roman Curia is "the ensemble of administrative and judicial offices through which the Pope directs the operations of the Catholic Church." "Curia, Roman," *Catholic Dictionary*, www.catholicculture.org.

46. Scalia, *Scalia Speaks*, 317 (emphasis in the original).

47. Murphy, *Scalia*, 17.

48. Connor, interview by the author, December 17, 2020.

Chapter II: The Incarnation

Epigraph: Antonin Scalia, *Scalia Speaks: Reflections on Law, Faith, and Life Well Lived*, eds. Christopher J. Scalia and Edward Whelan (New York City: Crown Forum, 2017), 145.

1. Ruth Marcus and Susan Schmidt, "Scalia Tenacious after Staking Out a Position," *Washington Post*, June 22, 1986; Franklin Fisher and Brian Kates, "They Judged Him Back Then," *New York Daily News*, June 19, 1986; Richard Stengel, "Warm Spirits, Cold Logic," *Time*, July 20, 1986.

2. Scalia, *Scalia Speaks*, 145 (soul, heck); "60 Minutes," CBS News, April 27, 2008 (calling); Joan Biskupic, *American Original: The Life and Constitution of Supreme Court Justice Antonin Scalia* (New York: Sarah Crichton, paperback ed., 2010), 22 (part).

3. "Two from Diocese Win 22 Honors at Xavier," *Brooklyn Tablet*, July 4, 1953.

4. "Justice Antonin Scalia," interview by Judith R. Hope, Oral History Project, The Historical Society of the District of Columbia Circuit, December 5, 1992, https://dcchs.org/wp-content/uploads/2019/03/Scalia-Complete-Oral-History-1.pdf, 8 (spatial, Princetonians). See also Scalia's interview with Stanley Pottinger, "Beyond Politics," PLUM TV, July 2006, quoted in Bruce Allen Murphy, *Scalia: A Court of*

One (New York City: Simon & Schuster, paperback ed. 2015), 20; and Biskupic, *American Original*, 23.

5. Scalia, *Scalia Speaks*, 145–46 (crushing).

6. Eugene Scalia, interview by the author, August 22, 2017. Father Paul Scalia, likewise, told me he never heard his father discuss ethnic prejudice but recalled Maureen's telling him about signs she had seen as a girl that read "HELP WANTED/IRISH NEED NOT APPLY." Paul Scalia, interview by the author, Arlington, Virginia, May 30, 2017. Justice Scalia, addressing Georgetown graduates in 1998, mused that Princeton's rejection had been a blessing: "I am sure I am a different person, and a better person, than I would have been if *my* will had been done" [emphasis in the original]. Scalia, *Scalia Speaks*, 146.

7. Antonin Scalia, answers to Department of Justice questionnaire, June 1, 1986, in Peter J. Wallison files, folder 2, Ronald Reagan Presidential Library; "Justice Antonin Scalia," Oral History Project, 7 (scholarship). Scalia once said Georgetown, prior to his time there, had been "pretty much a rich kids' school." See Scalia, *Scalia Speaks*, 380.

8. *Ye Domesday Booke Nineteen Fifty-Four* (Washington, D.C.: Georgetown University, 1954) (Holy Ghost); Richard M. Coleman, "Antonin Scalia—Sui Generis—Part I," ireallymissreagan.com, April 15, 2016 (finest); *Ye Domesday Booke 1955* (skills, exigencies).

9. Coleman, "Antonin Scalia—Sui Generis." Coleman's 3,300-word online essay offers the most detailed account of Scalia's Georgetown years. With their similar backgrounds—both had attended Jesuit high schools in New York City—the two became roommates and debate partners at Georgetown, then attended Harvard Law together. Their relationship lapsed after graduation but resumed in the 1970s and included vacations with their wives; Richard Coleman, interview by the author, October 9, 2017. The FBI's 1974 background investigation into Scalia found he had "associated with a good crowd in college"; see FBI teletype from Springfield to Director: Antonin Gregory Scalia, DAPLI, Special Candidate, Office of the Deputy Attorney General, June 28, 1974, Scalia FBI files.

10. Scalia, *Scalia Speaks*, 103.

11. Ibid., 59.

12. "Justice Antonin Scalia," Oral History Project, 9 (history major, philosophy minor); Coleman, "Antonin Scalia—Sui Generis." Recounting Scalia's Georgetown debating years, Bruce Allen Murphy made plain his hostility to his subject: "College debaters become a special breed, developing a verbally aggressive, almost narcissistically arrogant personality." Murphy, *Scalia*, 23.

13. David Margolick, "A Lawyer Vanishes, Leaving a Trail of Fraud Charges," *New York Times*, May 12, 1989, https://www.nytimes.com/1989/05/12/nyregion/a-lawyer-vanishes-leaving-a-trail-of-fraud-charges.html.

14. Richard Coleman, interview by the author, October 6, 2017; Margolick, "A Lawyer Vanishes" (handsome); *Ye Domesday Booke 1955*.

15. *Ye Domesday Booke Nineteen Fifty-Four* and *Ye Domesday Booke 1955* (ably, Brennan, Tony). Mask and Bauble viewed the Catholic University drama club with "intense envy," Scalia joked, "the same feelings…the teams of the American League had toward the Damn Yankees." See Scalia, *Scalia Speaks*, 125.

16. Coleman, "Antonin Scalia—Sui Generis."

17. Coleman, interview by the author, October 6, 2017.

18. Biskupic, *Amerian Original*, 25. Bruce Allen Murphy reported the Fribourg group was admitted to two general audiences with Pope Pius XII, who remained one of Scalia's favorite popes. Murphy, *Scalia*, 26. The justice once led a toast, only half in jest, "To Pio Dodicesimo [Pius XII], the greatest pope ever to reign over us." Andrew Napolitano, interview by the author, October 13, 2017.

19. "Supreme Court Justice Perspective" (Scalia's remarks at the Supreme Court to students from Thomas Jefferson High School in Alexandria, Virginia), C-SPAN, April 9, 2008 (Frenchmen); Scalia, *Scalia Speaks*, 78 (Anglo-Saxon, humility).

20. Murphy, *Scalia*, 27.

21. Scalia, *Scalia Speaks*, 146; Murphy, *Scalia,* 25 (sad); Timothy Goeglein, interview by the author, June 5, 2017 (bat).

22. Antonin Scalia, "Cohonguroton Address," Georgetown University, June 9, 1957, reprinted in "In Memory of Antonin Scalia (1936–2016): Two Speeches from the Associate Justice of the Supreme Court," *Utraque Unum* 9, no. 1 (Spring 2016): 85–87; Biskupic, *American Original*, 25–26; Murphy, *Scalia*, 26; Biskupic betrayed her hostility to her subject with a caustic critique of the young Scalia's "excessive but revealing" address: "His education, his Catholicism, and his first-in-the-class honor all led him to feel superior. This became the scaffolding of the public Antonin Scalia."

23. "Supreme Court Justice Perspective," C-SPAN, April 9, 2008. Scalia's father told a reporter his son had dreamed of being a lawyer since he was seven ("I don't think he ever considered anything else"). See David R. Palombi, "Trenton Native Likely Candidate for Spot on U.S. Supreme Court," *Trenton Times*, November 4, 1985.

24. "Justice Antonin Scalia," Oral History Project, 9 (reputation). Morality "has to be taught early in life," Scalia told an interviewer in 1975. "If a person hasn't formed his character…by the time he gets into law school, it is too late." See Arthur Ciervo, "Profiles: Antonin Scalia (C '57)," *Georgetown Today*, September 1975.

Chapter III: All Seasons

Epigraph: "America and the Courts: Interview with Judge Antonin Scalia," C-SPAN, April 1, 1986; Brian Lamb, interview by the author, Washington, D.C., May 10, 2017.

1. Dick Coleman, interview by the author, October 6, 2017 (scary, relieve); Lee Liberman, interview by the author, Washington, D.C., June 29, 2017 (passenger). "I'm sure he dated," Coleman said. "He was certainly not monastic"; Dick Coleman, interview by the author, October 9, 2017. Robert Connor told me Scalia brought girls to dances at Xavier and even introduced Connor to a girl he dated briefly; Robert Connor, interview by the author, December 17, 2020.

2. FBI form completed by Antonin Scalia, June 1986, attached to Scalia letter to [redacted], Office of the Deputy Attorney General, June 20, 1986, Scalia FBI files; "Hikes Penalties for Contempt," *Central New Jersey Home News*, August 21, 1956. In 2011, when he was seventy-five, Scalia plowed his car into the vehicle in front of him in morning traffic on the George Washington Parkway, triggering a four-car accident from which his vehicle had to be towed. He was fined $70; see "Scalia Cited in Traffic Accident," *Miami Herald*, March 30, 2011.

3. Arthur Ciervo, "Profiles: Antonin Scalia (C '57)," *Georgetown Today*, September 1975 (studies).

4. Antonin Scalia, *Scalia Speaks: Reflections on Law, Faith, and Life Well Lived*, eds. Christopher J. Scalia and Edward Whelan (New York City: Crown Forum, 2017), 174 (life-changing).

5. Dick Coleman, "Antonin Scalia—Sui Generis—Part I," ireallymissreagan.com, April 15, 2016; Stephen J. Adler, "Live Wire on the DC Circuit," *American Lawyer*, March 1985 (comical, gregariousness); Edward Lazarus, *Closed Chambers: The Rise, Fall, and Future of the Modern Supreme Court* (New York City: Penguin, paperback ed., 2005), 192 (superior); "Justice Antonin Scalia," Oral History Project, 3 (scholar, exciting, advance).

6. Laurence Silberman, interview by the author, Washington, D.C., May 22, 2017.

7. Margaret Talbot, "Supreme Confidence," *New Yorker*, March 28, 2005.

8. Herbert Wechsler, "Toward Neutral Principles of Constitutional Law," *Harvard Law Review* 73, no. 1 (November 1959): 1–35.

9. Joan Biskupic, *American Original: The Life and Constitution of Supreme Court Justice Antonin Scalia* (New York City: Sarah Crichton, paperback ed., 2010), 27–28; Bruce Allen Murphy, *Scalia: A Court of One* (New York City: Simon & Schuster, paperback ed., 2015), 38. "[Wechsler's] position meshed with Scalia's outlook, and he has developed it into an unswervingly narrow judicial philosophy." Douglas Frantz, "Scalia Embodies President's Hope for Court's Future," *Chicago Tribune*, August 3, 1986.

10. Frank I. Michelman, *Brennan and Democracy* (Princeton, New Jersey: Princeton University Press, 1999); Adler, "Live Wire" (chiding); Biskupic, *American Original*, 28 (bouts, cannoli).

11. Frank Michelman, interview by the author, October 3, 2017.

12. "He in later years, I think, wasn't especially pleased if he saw me on the verge of telling" the Fat Tony story, Michelman added—an inadvertent admission that, despite his claim to have "complied" with Scalia's request in the hotel lobby that the name be retired, Michelman on subsequent occasions, before other groups of people, malevolently threatened to resurface Fat Tony, provoking scowls from Scalia. Michelman's recollections also contained some inconsistencies. He recalled to a previous writer that Scalia had "chid[ed]" Adlai Stevenson supporters at Harvard. Adler, "Live Wire." Yet when I asked if Scalia's conservatism was evident in law school, Michelman replied, "To the best I've ever been able to [recall]…no. I knew he was smart. I knew he was Catholic and earnestly so, but nothing in the journal work that we did together, nothing in the sidebar conversations we would have as two people who were sitting with desks at opposite ends of the room, facing each other for many hours a day, sometimes [eating] our suppers together, and in a friendly relationship—I didn't catch it." Frank Michelman, interview by the author, October 3, 2017. Informed of the Fat Tony incident, one of Scalia's children told me that the justice, while averse to identity politics, certainly would have regarded the nickname as an ethnic slur.

13. Scalia, *Scalia Speaks*, 387–88.

14. "Justice Antonin Scalia," Oral History Project, 11 (tragedy); Eugene Scalia, interview by the author, Washington, D.C., August 22, 2017; Meg Scalia Bryce, interview by the author, August 11, 2017; Meg Scalia Bryce, email to the author, September 14,

2017; Maureen Scalia, conversation with the author, Metropolitan Club, Washington, D.C., April 5, 2018; Biskupic, *American Original*, 31 (too bad).

15. "Justice Antonin Scalia," Oral History Project, 11 (immersed); Maureen Scalia, conversation with the author; Nathan Lewin, "The Supreme Court's Jewish Gentile: My Memories of Justice Scalia," *Jewish Telegraphic Agency*, February 15, 2016; Coleman, "Antonin Scalia—Sui Generis."

16. Eugene Scalia, interview by the author, August 22, 2017; (sharp, O'Brien, bourbon); Meg Scalia Bryce, interview, August 2, 2017 (burglary).

17. Ibid., (stand); Biskupic, *American Original*, 30–31; Lamb, interview by the author. Judge Andrew Napolitano, a friend of the Scalias for decades, told me, "Maureen is a liberal Catholic, at least by Nino and my standards. She would accuse me of goading him…to say these strange traditionalist things," such as Nino's toast to Pope Pius XII. "Maureen rolled her eyes and accused me of putting him up to this…. I did use to goad him into those more extreme traditionalist Catholic statements in an environment in which I knew he would be comfortable making them." Andrew Napolitano, interview by the author, October 13, 2017.

18. "60 Minutes," CBS, April 27, 2008 (law and order, jail); Talbot, "Supreme Confidence" (weirdos, eggs); Paul Scalia, interview by the author. The flag-burning case was *Texas v. Johnson* 491 U.S. 397 (1989).

19. Eugene Scalia, interview by the author, August 22, 2017; Bryce, interview by the author, August 2, 2017.

20. Scalia, *Scalia Speaks*, 86, 267 (gaps, Brazil). Sopan Joshi, interview by the author, August 30, 2017 (bankruptcy).

21. "Justice Antonin Scalia," Oral History Project, 11 (bright); Scalia, *Scalia Speaks*, 60 (rings); David R. Palombi, "Trenton Native Likely Candidate for Spot on U.S. Supreme Court," *Trenton Times*, November 4, 1985 (top five); Michelman, interview by the author; Frank Michelman, email to the author, July 22, 2022 (Hiss).

22. Maureen Scalia, conversation with the author.

23. Thomas Campion, interview by the author, March 26, 2021.

24. "Mr. Scalia, Bride on European Tour," *Boston Sunday Globe*, September 25, 1960; Christopher Scalia, email to the author, March 17, 2021 (photograph of invitation). Tom Campion told me Nino "didn't strike me as being nervous." Campion, interview by the author.

25. Adler, "Live Wire" (perturbed).

26. "Justice Antonin Scalia," Oral History Project, 13; Scalia, *Scalia Speaks*, 343 (Auschwitz).

27. Paul Scalia, interview by the author, Arlington, Virginia, May 30, 2017; Ciervo, "Profiles: Antonin Scalia"; "Justice Antonin Scalia," Oral History Project (button); Bryce, email to the author (Frankfurt); FBI teletype from Chicago to Director, April 7, 1982, Scalia FBI files (itinerary). A black-and-white photograph Nino took on the Isle of Skye, juxtaposing a bus with nearby castle ruins, hung in the Scalias' home for the rest of their fifty-five years together. Christopher Scalia, interview by the author, Washington, D.C., October 17, 2017.

28. Scalia, *Scalia Speaks*, 95 (spy), 107 (significance); Robert Bolt, *A Man for All Seasons* (New York City: Vintage Books, paperback ed., 1962), 37–38; "Charlie Rose Show," PBS, June 20, 2008 (silly). A student in the first class Scalia ever taught, at UVA in

1967–68, recalled his reciting this scene with theatrical flair; Robert Dormer, interview by the author, November 8, 2017.

29. Nathan Lewin, interview by the author, September 14, 2017; Richard Pogue, interview by the author, November 6, 2017; Murphy, *Scalia: A Court of One*, 40–41 (sweat); "Charlie Rose Show," (jaw, ambition); Robert L. Jackson and Ronald J. Ostrow, "He Has Own Style of Conservatism: Scalia's Independent Past Suggests Future Surprises," *Los Angeles Times*, July 6, 1986 (3:00 a.m.); FBI report of Special Agent [redacted], Antonin Scalia, Washington, D.C., field office, April 19, 1982, containing summary of April 7, 1982 interview with [redacted], Scalia FBI files (spirited). That the interviewee was Lynn is revealed by this passage: "[Redacted] advised…that he recruited the applicant from law school." See also Albert Borowitz, *Jones, Day, Reavis & Pogue: The First Century* (Jones Day, 1993), 371. The partners agreed to defer Scalia's start until after the Sheldon Fellowship. Christopher Scalia has written that Scalia chose Jones Day because he worried that "legal practice in New York City was not compatible with family life"; Scalia, *Scalia Speaks*, 91.

30. Antonin Scalia, answers to Department of Justice questionnaire, June 1, 1986, in Folder 4, Box 14287, Peter J. Wallison Files, Supreme Court—Scalia, Ronald Reagan Presidential Library (Supreme Court of Ohio, interrogatories); "Justice Antonin Scalia," Oral History Project, 16 (enjoyed).

31. Adler, "Live Wire" (Hansell); Jackson and Ostrow, "He Has His Own Style" (never appeared); Scalia, answers to Department of Justice questionnaire (court appearances); "Justice Antonin Scalia," Oral History Project (advantages). Scalia made two court appearances in 1976: oral argument at the Supreme Court in *Dunhill v. Cuba* (see Chapter IX) and representing himself in District of Columbia Small Claims Court. Maureen was driving their Volkswagen bus into a D.C. parking garage and struck a pipe hanging below the clearance sign. The incident damaged the vehicle. The garage refused to pay for repairs, which were under $500, so Scalia sued in small claims court and won; FBI form completed by Antonin Scalia, June 1986, attached to Scalia letter to [redacted], Office of the Deputy Attorney General, June 20, 1986, Scalia FBI files.

32. Scalia, answers to Department of Justice questionnaire.

33. Pogue, interview by the author (dominated); Borowitz, *Jones, Day, Reavis & Pogue*, 115, 372 (genius); Murphy, *Scalia*, 46 (clients, Sears case); Adler, "Live Wire" (Goldwater, Buckley-type). Years later, when the Reagan administration was evaluating Scalia's "confirmability" for the Supreme Court, an aide listed the fact that Scalia was "a fan of Bill Buckley and the *National Review*" as a plus; see White House memo for Peter J. Wallison from Alan Charles Raul, Subject: Summary Information Regarding Certain Judges, June 5, 1986, Peter J. Wallison Files, Supreme Court—Rehnquist/Scalia Notebook II—Candidates, Ronald Reagan Presidential Library.

34. Scalia, *Scalia Speaks*, 329 (1994); Dan Wakefield, "William F. Buckley, Jr.: Portrait of a Complainer," *Esquire*, January 1961. Buckley revered Scalia as "the aphorist of the Court," saying of one opinion, "It's wonderful to be alive when such sentences are written." See "The Court Refranchises the States," Universal Press Syndicate, June 25, 1999.

35. "60 Minutes" (overachievers, roulette).

36. Pogue, interview (Laddy); Adler, "Live Wire" (prominent, hammer).

37. "Charlie Rose Show." Gene Scalia told me Catherine's refusal to leave Trenton was thought to have impeded Sam's career, and that Maureen Scalia, mindful of this, resolved to accept the burden of relocation whenever it supported Nino's professional advancement. Eugene Scalia, interview by the author, August 22, 2017.

38. "Justice Antonin Scalia," Oral History Project (enjoyed); Ciervo, "Profiles: Antonin Scalia (scale); Biskupic, *American Original*, 37.

39. "Q&A with Antonin Scalia"; Ibid., 64; Murphy, *Scalia*, 79.

40. "Remarks on the Resignation of Supreme Court Chief Justice Warren E. Burger and the Nominations of William H. Rehnquist to Be Chief Justice and Antonin Scalia to Be an Associate Justice, June 17, 1986," The American Presidency Project, U.C. Santa Barbara.

41. Robert A. Connor, "Antonin Scalia—A Justice in Full," *National Review*, March 14, 2016.

42. Connor, interview by the author, December 17, 2020; Robert Connor, email to the author, December 27, 2020. In later years, Connor told me, he occasionally "trotted out" the "I will rise" story to needle the justice, who would reply by harrumphing, "Oh, I couldn't have said that"; but Father Connor's recollection is vivid and was closely held from 1959 onward, offered only when Connor was contacted by this reporter. His account is bolstered by Justice Scalia's independent recollection that Jones Day at the time employed "about sixty lawyers in Cleveland and I think three lawyers in Washington." "Justice Antonin Scalia," Oral History Project, 13 (three lawyers).

43. Adler, "Live Wire" (glad).

44. Brian Donato, interview by the author, November 8, 2017.

45. Scalia, *Scalia Speaks*, 397–98.

46. Eugene Scalia, interview by the author, September 8, 2017.

47. Scalia, *Scalia Speaks*, 58.

48. Arthur Schwab, interview by the author, November 8, 2017.

49. Donato, interview by the author, November 8, 2017 (rolls, Halloween); Dormer, interview; Ralph Feil, interview by the author, November 8, 2017; Schwab, interview by the author. Catherine Scalia Courtney remarks, "Justice Scalia Memorial Service," March 1, 2016 (juicy). A former clerk told me Scalia admired the teaching style of Harvard Law professor Clark Byse. "I remember him talking about how Byse made Socratic questioning look so easy, and it was much harder when you actually had to do it yourself"; Patrick Schiltz, interview by the author, June 28, 2017. Donato recalled a female student's challenging Scalia on women's liberation and the professor's employing sophistry: "You want to be more like the men? And yet you wanted to criticize us for not succeeding in what we're doing, and doing it badly? So what you want is to not succeed and do it badly?" Donato, interview by the author, November 8, 2017. Ken Robinson, a colleague at the White House Office of Telecommunications Policy, Scalia's next place of employment, told me: "There wasn't a trace of racial or ethnic prejudice there, but, boy, he sure didn't like women's liberation.... He thought that women really ought to have a family-oriented career and focus.... I don't think he was openly prejudiced against anybody, but it was just pretty obvious that Nino [thought] men were preferable in the workplace." Robinson interview by the author, July 23, 2017.

50. Scalia, *Scalia Speaks*, 95, 313–14 (brook, regiment, contempt); "Protest at the University of Virginia," Univeristy of Virginia, explore.lib.virginia.edu; Kristin Jensen, "May 5, 1970—Protest on the Rotunda," University of Virginia, archives. law.virginia.edu; Donato, interview by the author, November 8, 2017 (SDS); oral argument in *Madsen v. Women's Health Center, Inc.* 512 U.S. 753 (1994), www.oyez.org; Linda Greenhouse, "Justices Appear Sympathetic to Anti-Abortion Protesters," *New York Times*, April 29, 1994 (quoting Scalia inaccurately).

Chapter IV: Open Skies

Epigraph: Freedom of the Press: Hearing before the Subcommittee on Constitutional Rights of the Committee on the Judiciary United States Senate.... September 28, 29, 30, October 12, 13, 14, 19 and 20, 1971 and February 1, 2, 8, 16 and 17, 1972.... (Washington, D.C.: U.S. Government Printing Office, 1972), tinyurl.com/mr42zcmm, 471.

1. Whitehead's biography and many OTP documents can be found in "The Papers of Clay T. Whitehead: White House Official, Industry Executive, and Telecom Pioneer" in the Library of Congress, available online at claytwhitehead.com; "Message to the Congress Transmitting Reorganization Plan 1 of 1970 to Establish an Office of Telecommunications Policy," February 1, 1970, The American Presidency Project, U.C. Santa Barbara.

2. OTP letter from Clay T. Whitehead to Robert Hampton [drafted by Scalia], February 1, 1971 in "The Papers of Clay T. Whitehead: White House Official, Industry Executive and Telecom Pioneer," Box 26, Civil Service Commission, 1971, Library of Congress, claytwhitehead.com (segments); Joan Biskupic, *American Original: The Life and Constitution of Supreme Court Justice Antonin Scalia* (New York City: Sarah Crichton, paperback ed., 2010), 38; Bruce Allen Murphy, *Scalia: A Court of One* (Simon & Schuster, paperback ed., 2015), 49; Stephen J. Adler, "Live Wire on the DC Circuit," *American Lawyer*, March 1985 (Lynn); Richard Vigilante, "Beyond the Burger Court," *Policy Review* (Spring 1984): 20–26. (monster); Henry Goldberg, interview by the author, June 27, 2017; Brian Lamb, interview by the author, Washington, D.C., May 10, 2017; Ken Robinson, interview by the author, July 23, 2017. Biskupic reported that Whitehead's hiring of Scalia was "prompted by" Jonathan Rose, a prominent Republican lawyer, even though Whitehead was already on record, in 1985, crediting Lynn.

3. OTP log (12/3/70–12/30/70) in "The Papers of Clay T. Whitehead: White House Official, Industry Executive and Telecom Pioneer," Box 31, List of OTP Activities and Correspondence (1 of 3), 1969–1973, Library of Congress, claytwhitehead.com (Mansur); OTP memo from Whitehead to Nino Scalia, January 5, 1971, in "The Papers of Clay T. Whitehead: White House Official, Industry Executive and Telecom Pioneer," Box 26, Congressional 1971, 1971–1974, Library of Congress, claytwhitehead.com; "Papers of Clay T. (Tom) Whitehead," C-SPAN, January 11, 2013 (ticket).

4. Goldberg, interview by the author.

5. From June to September 1970, Scalia was a "summer faculty member" at the U.S. Civil Service Commission. FBI teletype from St. Louis to Director, [Subject:] Antonin Scalia, DAPLI, U.S. Circuit Court Judge, District of Columbia, April 30, 1982, Scalia FBI files; Goldberg, interview by the author (sheltered); "Justice Antonin Scalia,"

interview by Judith R. Hope, Oral History Project, The Historical Society of the District of Columbia Circuit, December 5, 1992, 17, https://dcchs.org/wp-content /uploads/2019/03/Scalia-Complete-Oral-History-1.pdf (exposure).

6. FBI teletype (clearance); OTP log [6/22/71–9/18/71] in "The Papers of Clay T. Whitehead: White House Official, Industry Executive and Telecom Pioneer," Box 31, List of OTP Activities and Correspondence, 1969–1973, Library of Congress, claytwhitehead.com (Colson).

7. Adler, "Live Wire" (illegal); Robert L. Jackson and Ronald J. Ostrow, "He Has Own Style of Conservatism: Scalia's Independent Past Suggests Future Surprises," *Los Angeles Times*, July 6, 1986 (reruns).

8. OTP Personnel Qualification Evaluation form [undated; spring 1971] in "The Papers of Clay T. Whitehead: White House Official, Industry Executive and Telecom Pioneer," Box 26, Congressional 1971, 1971–1974, Library of Congress, claytwhitehead.com (mobile); OTP memo from Linda Smith to Mr. Whitehead, Re: Invitation to Speak to Georgia Radio/TV Institute, September 17, 1971 in "The Papers of Clay T. Whitehead: White House Official, Industry Executive and Telecom Pioneer," Box 41, Speech—Athens, Georgia, January 27, 1972, Library of Congress, claytwhitehead.com (shared); OTP draft testimony by Antonin Scalia, 5-3-71 in "The Papers of Clay T. Whitehead: White House Official, Industry Executive and Telecom Pioneer," Box 47, Testimony—Appropriations, May 13, 1971, Library of Congress, claytwhitehead.com (AUTODIN).

9. OTP draft testimony by AScalia, 5-3-71 in "The Papers of Clay T. Whitehead." Whitehead changed "Computer Society" to "Computer Economy."

10. OTP draft memorandum to the President, August 11, 1971, in "The Papers of Clay T. Whitehead: White House Official, Industry Executive and Telecom Pioneer," Box 24, Aerosat September 1970–December 1971, 1970–1973, Library of Congress, claytwhitehead.com.

11. Dennis Hevesi, "Clay T. Whitehead, Guide of Policy That Helped Cable TV, Is Dead at 69," *New York Times*, July 31, 2008.

12. Henry Goldberg, "Scalia's Contribution to Telecommunications Law," remarks at Federalist Society panel, November 18, 2016 (formative); OTP memo to Mr. Scalia, January 27, 1971, in "The Papers of Clay T. Whitehead: White House Official, Industry Executive and Telecom Pioneer," Box 26, Congressional 1971, 1971–1974, Library of Congress, claytwhitehead.com (enemy); OTP memo from Antonin Scalia to Mr. Whitehead, Subject: FTC Memo and Price Commission Matter, February 9, 1972 in "The Papers of Clay T. Whitehead: White House Official, Industry Executive and Telecom Pioneer," Box 29, Federal Trade Commission, 1972, Library of Congress, claytwhitehead.com (classmate); OTP memo from Antonin Scalia to Messrs. Dean, Hinchman et al., January 26, 1972 in "The Papers of Clay T. Whitehead: White House Official, Industry Executive and Telecom Pioneer," Box 27, CTW Letter to Speaker Albert, 1972–1973, Library of Congress, claytwhitehead.com (unfriendly); OTP memo from Antonin Scalia to Messrs. Whitehead, Dean, et al., June 19, 1972 in "The Papers of Clay T. Whitehead: White House Official, Industry Executive and Telecom Pioneer," Box 26, Commerce, 1972–1973, Library of Congress, claytwhitehead.com (Friday, risk); OTP memo from Bruce [Owen] to Walt

[Hinchman], Subject: The April NAB Speech, March 14, 1972 in "The Papers of Clay T. Whitehead: White House Official, Industry Executive and Telecom Pioneer," "The Papers of Clay T. Whitehead: White House Official, Industry Executive and Telecom Pioneer," Box 41, Speech—50th Annual Convention of NAB, April 10, 1972, Library of Congress, claytwhitehead.com (implications); OTP memo from Antonin Scalia to Don Baker et al., [no subject], September 1, 1971 in "The Papers of Clay T. Whitehead: White House Official, Industry Executive and Telecom Pioneer," Box 41, CTW Speeches, Talks, Testimonies, 1970–71, Library of Congress, claytwhitehead.com (charm).

13. OTP memo from Antonin Scalia to Mr. Whitehead, Subject: NAB Convention, February 11, 1972 in "The Papers of Clay T. Whitehead: White House Official, Industry Executive and Telecom Pioneer," Box 41, Speech—50th Annual Convention of NAB, April 10, 1972, Library of Congress, claytwhitehead.com (corridor); OTP memo August 13, 1971, in "The Papers of Clay T. Whitehead: White House Official, Industry Executive and Telecom Pioneer," Box 37, State Department, 1970–1973, Library of Congress, claytwhitehead.com (belligerent); Scalia annotation on OTP memo from Tom to Nino, May 31, 1972 in "The Papers of Clay T. Whitehead: White House Official, Industry Executive and Telecom Pioneer," Box 32, Network Antitrust Suits Memoranda, 1972, Library of Congress, claytwhitehead.com (reconsider). At other points Whitehead embraced Scalia's pugnacity. The director signed without revision a Scalia draft that pointedly accused a cabinet secretary of abrogating an agreement. OTP letter from Clay T. Whitehead to Maurice H. Stans, June 1, 1971, in "The Papers of Clay T. Whitehead: White House Official, Industry Executive and Telecom Pioneer," Box 35, OTP Work with Department of Commerce, 1971, Library of Congress, claytwhitehead.com.

14. Goldberg, "Scalia's Contribution to Telecommunications Law" (wiles); Adler, "Live Wire" (mix); Goldberg, interview by the author; OTP log [January 21, 1971–March 15, 1971] in "The Papers of Clay T. Whitehead: White House Official, Industry Executive and Telecom Pioneer," Box 31, List of OTP Activities and Correspondence, 1969–1973 (Valenti), Library of Congress, claytwhitehead.com.

15. Goldberg, "Scalia's Contribution to Telecommunications Law."

16. OTP memo from Antonin Scalia, re: UNESCO Draft Declaration of Guiding Principles for Space Broadcasting and USSR Request for a Convention on Direct Television Broadcasting, August 18, 1972, "The Papers of Clay T. Whitehead: White House Official, Industry Executive and Telecom Pioneer," Box 28, European Post-Apollo Cooperation, Library of Congress, claytwhitehead.com; OTP letter from Clay T. Whitehead to Samuel DePalma [drafted by "NScalia"], August 18, 1972 in "The Papers of Clay T. Whitehead: White House Official, Industry Executive and Telecom Pioneer," Box 37, State Department, 1970–1973, Library of Congress, claytwhitehead.com.

17. OTP memo from Antonin Scalia to Bruce Owen, Subject: Memorandum for Peter Flanigan, February 4, 1971, "The Papers of Clay T. Whitehead: White House Official, Industry Executive and Telecom Pioneer," Box 37, Spectrum Allocation, 1970–73, Library of Congress, claytwhitehead.com.

18. "Justice Antonin Scalia," Oral History, 17–18 (trenches, induce).

19. OTP memo from Helen C. Hall to The Staff, September 26, 1972, and OTP document entitled "Farewell party for Judy and Mr. Scalia———," "The Papers of Clay T. Whitehead: White House Official, Industry Executive and Telecom Pioneer," Box 27, CTW Social, 1969–1974, Library of Congress, claytwhitehead.com.

20. DOJ letter from Rehnquist to Scalia, October 15, 1971, October 15, 1971, "The Papers of Clay T. Whitehead: White House Official, Industry Executive and Telecom Pioneer," Box 24, Aerosat September 1970–December 1971, 1970–1973; James M. Naughton, "Nixon Names 2 to Supreme Court," *New York Times*, October 22, 1971.

Chapter V: Mr. Chairman

Epigraph: Administrative Conference of the United States: Hearing before the Subcommittee on Commercial and Administrative Law of the Committee on the Judiciary House of Representatives . . . May 20, 2010. . . . (Washington, D.C.: U.S. Government Printing Office, 2010), tinyurl.com/mtnk4afm, 32.

1. Laurence Silberman, interview by the author, Washington, D.C., May 22, 2017 (chubby); Henry Goldberg, interview by the author, June 27, 2017. Ken Robinson recalled Scalia's once returning to OTP with a tape measure, peeved that his old desk would not fit into his new office; Ken Robinson, interview by the author, July 23, 2017.

2. "Justice Antonin Scalia," interview by Judith R. Hope, Oral History Project, The Historical Society of the District of Columbia Circuit, December 5, 1992, https://dcchs.org/wp-content/uploads/2019/03/Scalia-Complete-Oral-History-1.pdf, 19 (love). For a 1975 photo of Cramton and Ruth Bader Ginsburg, see Cornell Law Library (@Cornell_Lawlib), "Way Back Wednesday: Then Columbia Law Prof. Ruth Bader Ginsburg with Dean Roger Cramton. . . .," Twitter, September 17, 2014, 10:44 a.m., https://twitter.com/Cornell_Lawlib/status/512250775003594752/photo/1.

3. "Justice Antonin Scalia," Oral History Project, 18. The official oral history transcript mistakenly used "root" for "route," "Crampton" for "Cramton."

4. Antonin Scalia, *Scalia Speaks: Reflections on Law, Faith, and Life Well Lived*, eds. Christopher J. Scalia and Edward Whelan (New York City: Crown Forum, 2017), 391.

5. Associated Press, "Chairman," *Reno Evening Gazette*, August 15, 1972; FBI memo from [redacted] to [redacted], Subject: Antonin Gregory Scalia, Departmental Applicant, Special Candidate, Office of the Deputy Attorney General, July 11, 1974, Scalia FBI files (referencing 1972 background investigation).

6. *Administrative Conference of the United States: Hearing* (Gaul, frankly, worried, kiss); *The Freedom of Information Act: Hearings before a Subcommittee of the Committee on Government Operations House of Representatives…May 2, 7, 8, 10 and 16, 1973….* (Washington, D.C.: U.S. Government Printing Office, 1973), https://tinyurl.com/3xth2nuv (60 percent); Scalia FBI files; FBI interview with [redacted], June 28, 1974, Scalia FBI files (convened); FBI teletype from St. Louis to Director, [Subject:] Antonin Scalia, DAPLI, U.S. Circuit Court Judge, District of Columbia, April 30, 1982, FBI files (eleven-day); FBI report by Special Agent [redacted], Detroit Field Office, Title: Antonin Gregory Scalia, June 28, 1974 (consultant, temperate, administrator), Scalia FBI files; FBI report by Special Agent [redacted], Washington

Field Office, Title: Antonin Gregory Scalia, June 28, 1974, Scalia FBI files (highly regarded); *Nomination of Judge Antonin Scalia: Hearings before the Committee on the Judiciary United States Senate…August 5 and 6, 1986….* (U.S. Government Printing Office, 1987), https://www.govinfo.gov/content/pkg/GPO-CHRG-SCALIA/pdf/GPO-CHRG-SCALIA.pdf (unfailing); David Burnham, "Inquiry to Focus on I.R.S. Policies," *New York Times,* May 18, 1974 (budget, dozen); David Burnham, "Regulatory Agencies Scored on Delays," *New York Times,* June 15, 1974 (delays); Brian Lamb, interview by the author, Washington D.C., May 10, 2017.

7. Joan Biskupic, *American Original: The Life and Constitution of Supreme Court Justice Antonin Scalia* (New York City: Sarah Crichton, paperback ed., 2010), 34; Bruce Allen Murphy, *Scalia: A Court of One* (Simon & Schuster, paperback ed., 2015), 56.

8. Ken Robinson, interview by the author, July 23, 2017. In suggesting I interview Robinson, Brian Lamb cautioned that Robinson held a "very calculating view of the world" and "a different view on Scalia." This proved true. For example, Robinson told me Scalia calculatingly took up tennis because President Nixon's top aides played the game; in fact, Scalia started playing the sport in Cleveland in the early '60s. "Justice Antonin Scalia," Oral History Project, 5.

9. Eugene Scalia, interview by the author, September 8, 2017.

10. Glenn Fowler, "Panel Splits on Whether Press Is Periled by Federal Criticism," *New York Times,* March 14, 1973.

Chapter VI: Main Justice

Epigraph: William F. Buckley, Jr., *Saving the Queen* (New York City: Doubleday, 1976), 1.

1. Robert H. Bork, *Saving Justice: Watergate, the Saturday Night Massacre, and Other Adventures of a Solicitor General* (New York City: Encounter, 2013); James Rosen, "Bork's Watergate," *Commentary,* May 2013; Robert H. Bork, "Why I Am for Nixon," *New Republic,* June 1, 1968.

2. Eugene Scalia, interview by the author, Washington, D.C., September 8, 2017; William Funk, interview by the author, December 13, 2017 (nobody); Jim Wilderotter, interview by the author, February 18, 2021 (meaner); "Honorable Laurence H. Silberman," interview by Raymond S. Rasenberger, Oral History Project, The Historical Society of the District of Columbia Circuit, December 13, 2001 (minefield).

3. Stephen J. Adler, "Live Wire on the DC Circuit," *American Lawyer,* March 1985 (imperative); Bruce Allen Murphy, *Scalia: A Court of One* (New York City: Simon & Schuster, paperback ed., 2015), 59 (president's legal adviser); Laurence Silberman, interview by the author, Washington, D.C., May 22, 2017 (single), Jim Wilderotter, interview by the author, March 2, 2021 (general counsel), Eugene Scalia, interview by the author, September 8, 2017 (president's lawyer's lawyer); Arthur Ciervo, "Profiles: Antonin Scalia (C '57)," *Georgetown Today,* September 1975 (government lawyers' lawyer).

4. FBI teletype from Savannah to Director, [Subject:] Antonin Gregory Scalia, DAPLI, Special Candidate, Office of Attorney General, June 28, 1974, Scalia FBI Files (ultimatum); "Justice Antonin Scalia," interview by Judith R. Hope, Oral History Project, The Historical Society of the District of Columbia Circuit, December 5,

1992, https://dcchs.org/wp-content/uploads/2019/03/Scalia-Complete-Oral
-History-1.pdf, 19 (began moving, Attila).

5. Edward W. Knappman, ed., *Watergate and the White House, Volume 1: June 1972–July 1973* (Facts on File, 1974); Evan Drossman, Edward Knappman, and Mary Clifford, eds., *Watergate and the White House, Volume 2: July–December 1973* (Facts on File, 1974); and Knappman, ed., *Watergate and the White House, Volume 3: January–September 1974* (New York City: Facts on File, 1974); James Rosen, *The Strong Man: John Mitchell and the Secrets of Watergate* (New York City: Doubleday, 2008); Jennifer Senior, "In Conversation: Antonin Scalia," *New York*, October 6, 2013 (sad, *Post*).

6. Silberman, interview by the author, May 22, 2017; Adler, "Live Wire" (Rose); Joan Biskupic, *American Original: The Life and Constitution of Supreme Court Justice Antonin Scalia* (New York City: Sarah Crichton, paperback ed., 2010), 33–39; Bruce Allen Murphy, *Scalia: A Court of One* (Simon & Schuster, paperback ed., 2015), 58–59; Robert L. Jackson and Ronald J. Ostrow, "He Has Own Style of Conservatism: Scalia's Independent Past Suggests Future Surprises," *Los Angeles Times*, July 6, 1986 (several thousand).

7. Eugene Scalia, interview by the author, Washington, D.C., August 22, 2017; Brian Donato, interview by the author, November 18, 2017 (wonderful); Silberman, interview by the author, May 22, 2017 (anytime); Remarks by Catherine Scalia Courtney, "Justice Scalia Memorial Service," C-SPAN, March 1, 2016 (Froggy, Grimm).

8. FBI airtel from Director, FBI to Special Agent in Charge, New York, [Subject:] Antonin Gregory Scalia, Departmental Applicant, Special Candidate, Office of the Deputy Attorney General, June 27, 1974, Scalia FBI files (1949); FBI report of Special Agent [redacted], Title: Antonin Gregory Scalia, Washington, D.C. field office, June 28, 1974, Scalia FBI files (higher character, position of trust, very brilliant); FBI teletype from Springfield to Director, [Subject:] Antonin Gregory Scalia, DAPLI, Special Candidate, Office of the Deputy attorney General, June 28, 1974, Scalia FBI files (caliber); FBI teletype from Savannah to Director, [Subject:] Antonin Gregory Scalia, DAPLI, Special Candidate, Office of Attorney General, June 28, 1974, Scalia FBI files (temperament); FBI report of Special Agent [redacted], Title: Antonin Gregory Scalia, Richmond field office, June 28, 1974, Scalia FBI files (professors); FBI report of [redacted], Title: Antonin Scalia, New York field office, June 28, 1974, Scalia FBI files (flawless).

9. FBI memo [unsigned], [Subject:] Antonin Gregory Scalia, Departmental Applicant, Special Candidate, June 20, 1974, Scalia FBI files (no adverse); FBI memorandum from [redacted] to [redacted], Subject: Antonin Gregory Scalia, Departmental Applicant, Special Candidate, Office of the Deputy Attorney General, July 11, 1974, Scalia FBI files (favorable, outstanding).

10. "Justice Antonin Scalia," Oral History (collector's); WH letter from President Ford to Antonin Scalia, September 10, 1974, White House Central Files/Subject Files, Box 2796, National Archives and Records Administration. Scalia's August 13 confirmation hearing before the Judiciary Committee also included Richard Velde, nominee to lead the Law Enforcement Assistance Administration. Senator Hugh

Scott of Virginia, Republican minority leader, introduced them; the Senate confirmed both without objection. See "Congressional Record, SENATE," August 22, 1974, https://www.congress.gov/bound-congressional-record/1974/08/22/senate-section, 29776, 29778, 30024.

11. "Justice Antonin Scalia," Oral History Project, 24–25 (siege, exertion); Antonin Scalia, remarks at the International Conference on the Administration of Justice and National Security in Democracies, Ottawa, Canada, June 12, 2007 (scant). This quotation is taken from a professional transcription of a partial recording provided to the author by reporter Charlie Savage of the *New York Times*. Charlie Savage, email to the author, February 23, 2021. Savage first published portions of the remarks in *Takeover: The Return of the Imperial Presidency and the Subversion of American Democracy* (Boston: Little, Brown, 2007). Fifteen years before the Ottawa speech, Scalia described the Situation Room meetings in nearly identical language. "Justice Antonin Scalia," Oral History Project, 24.

12. Antonin Scalia, *Scalia Speaks: Reflections on Law, Faith, and Life Well Lived*, eds. Christopher J. Scalia and Edward Whelan (New York City: Crown Forum, 2017), 216 (extravagant); Dick Cheney, interview by the author, September 26, 2017; James Rosen, *Cheney One on One: A Candid Conversation with America's Most Controversial Statesman* (Washington, D.C.: Regnery, 2015).

13. "Justice Antonin Scalia," Oral History Project (tendentious, proud); FBI report of Special Agent [redacted], Washington, D.C. field office, to [redacted; FBI headquarters], Subject: Antonin Scalia, April 19, 1982, Scalia FBI files (objective).

14. Scalia, *Scalia Speaks*, 389–92 (eulogy). Scalia's supreme regard for Lawton was evidenced by the phrase "a public servant for all administrations," an allusion to his hero, Sir Thomas More.

15. White House Central Files Name File, Scalia, Antonin, Box 2796, Gerald R. Ford Presidential Library (audience).

16. H. R. Haldeman, "The Nixon White House Tapes: The Decision to Record Presidential Conversations," *Prologue* 20 (Summer 1980): 79–87.

17. White House memo from Benton L. Becker to Philip Buchen, Subject: Presidential Tapes and Ehrlichman/Haldeman/Dean/Colson/Krogh Papers, August 13, 1974 [8:00 PM], Philip Buchen Files, Gerald R. Ford Presidential Library (TSD); White House memo from Benton Becker for Phil Buchen, Subject: H.R. Haldeman's counsel's informal request to review tapes and logs from June 20, 21, and 22, 1972, [dated] August 20, 1974, Philip Buchen Files, Gerald R. Ford Presidential Library. Becker's August 20 memo related a greater volume of total recordings, "approximately 950 reels of six[-]hour tapes." Becker's August 13 memo erroneously stated that Nixon aides H. R. Haldeman, John Ehrlichman, and John Dean had left the White House staff on July 18, 1973, an error Biskupic, without attribution, repeated. Biskupic, *American Original*, 370n35. The actual date was April 30, 1973.

18. White House memo from Benton Becker for Phil Buchen; White House memo from Bill Casselman to Phil Buchen, [no subject], August 18, 1974, Philip Buchen Files, Gerald R. Ford Presidential Library (Zone); White House memo from Benton L. Becker to Philip W. Buchen, Subject: Whereabouts of Presidential Papers of the Nixon Administration, August 29, 1974, Philip Buchen Files, Gerald R. Ford Presidential

(Safe-Zone); White House memo from Philip W. Buchen to the file, [no subject], August 14, 1974, Gerald R. Ford Presidential Library (packing).

19. The supervisory archivist at the Ford Presidential Library could find no vote tally on Scalia's nomination to AAG/OLC, and said that, based on entries in the *Congressional Record*, "it appears he was confirmed by unanimous consent"; Geir Gundersen to the author, March 10, 2021.

20. Unsigned White House memo, Subject: Draft 8/22/74, August 22, 1974, Philip Buchen Files, Gerald R. Ford Presidential Library (draft); White House letter from Gerald R. Ford to William B. Saxbe, August 22, 1974, Philip Buchen Files, Gerald R. Ford Presidential Library (advice). Ahead of Scalia's opinion, the tapes were relocated to the custody of the General Services Administration.

21. William Funk, interview by the author, December 13, 2017.

22. Biskupic, *American Original*, 370n41 (quickly); White House memo from Benton Becker for Phil Buchen (owner); John M. Crewdson, "White House Says Tapes Are Nixon's Own Property," *New York Times*, August 15, 1974.

23. Public Citizen letter from Arthur L. Fox II and Reuben B. Robertson III to Arthur F. Sampson, August 14, 1974, Philip Buchen Files, Gerald R. Ford Presidential Library; GSA letter from [unsigned; Sampson] to Arthur L. Fox II, Esq., and Reuben B. Robertson III, Esq., [undated, ca. August 23, 1974], Philip Buchen Files, Gerald R. Ford Presidential Library.

24. Funk, interview by the author, December 13, 2017; Paul Marcotte, "New Kid on the Block: Scalia Seen as a Charming Conservative with Ability to Effect Compromises," *American Bar Association Journal*, August 1, 1986 (baptism); Wilderotter, interview by the author, March 2, 2021 (ballistic); Scalia draft [undated; ca. September 3, 1974], Philip Buchen Files, Gerald R. Ford Presidential Library; Department of Justice letter from Attorney General Saxbe to the president, September 6, 1974 [final version], Philip Buchen Files, Gerald R. Ford Presidential Library. Bruce Allen Murphy reported erroneously that Saxbe sent the opinion to Ford "on the day that he pardoned Nixon," September 8. Murphy, *Scalia: A Court of One*, 62. Telephone logs show Scalia alerted Silberman on the evening of September 3 that the opinion was ready; see Laurence H. Silberman Papers, Box 48, Folder 3, Hoover Institution Library and Archives.

25. "Text of Saxbe's Opinion Issued as Guide to Ford," *St. Louis Post-Dispatch*, September 9, 1974; Gerald R. Ford, "Proclamation 4311—Granting Pardon to Richard Nixon," September 8, 1974, The American Presidency Project, UC Santa Barbara; Carol R. Richards, "Byrd Eyes Ownership of Tapes," *Pensacola News Journal*, September 13, 1974; Ronald J. Ostrow, "Nixon Control of Tapes Assailed by Some Justice Dept. Experts," *Los Angeles Times*, September 18, 1974.

26. For the iterations and chronological progress of PRMPA, see "S.4016—Presidential Recordings Preservation Act," Congress.gov, https://www.congress.gov/bill/93rd-congress/senate-bill/4016; Associated Press, "Court Says Nixon Must Be Compensated for Tapes," *New York Times*, November 18, 1992; Christopher Marquis, "Government Agrees to Pay Nixon Estate," *New York Times*, June 13, 2000. "I was happy to see that," Scalia said of the D.C. Circuit Court ruling, noting that Judge Ruth Bader Ginsburg had participated; see "Justice Antonin Scalia," Oral History Project, 21. In their treatments of the Nixon tapes case, neither Biskupic nor

Murphy reported the appellate court's decision in Nixon's favor, nor the Justice Department's massive settlement with the Nixon estate.

27. Laurence Silberman remarks, "Justice Scalia Memorial Service," C-SPAN, March 1, 2016.
28. Murphy, *Scalia: A Court of One*, 57–62; Biskupic, *American Original*, 43, 64.
29. "Justice Antonin Scalia," Oral History Project, 21; Ostrow, "Nixon Control of Tapes Assailed."

Chapter VII: Blood Lust

Epigraph: "Justice Antonin Scalia," interview by Judith R. Hope, Oral History Project, The Historical Society of the District of Columbia Circuit, December 5, 1992, https://dcchs.org/wp-content/uploads/2019/03/Scalia-Complete-Oral-History-1.pdf.

1. Jim Wilderotter, interview by the author, February 18, 2021; photographs of Wilderotter and Scalia and Wilderotter's White House photo ID in Jim Wilderotter, email to the author, March 6, 2021.
2. Joan Biskupic, *American Original: The Life and Constitution of Supreme Court Justice Antonin Scalia* (New York City: Sarah Crichton, paperback ed., 2010), 51 (authoritarian), 64 (game); Bruce Allen Murphy, *Scalia: A Court of One* (New York City: Simon & Schuster, paperback ed., 2015) 63–65, (stripes, secrecy, stonewall).
3. Arthur M. Schlesinger, Jr., *The Imperial Presidency* (Boston: Houghton Mifflin, 1973).
4. White House note from P.A. [Phillip Areeda] to P.B. [Philip Buchen], [no subject; undated; February 26, 1975], in Kenneth A. Lazarus Files, Box 25, Gerald R. Ford Presidential Library ("I agree with Nino"); White House memo for Antonin Scalia from Philip W. Buchen, Subject: *WEINBERGER v. WEISENFELD*, March 21, 1975, White House Central Files/Subject Files, Box 2796, National Archives and Records Administration, Box 2796; NSC memo for Maria Downs from Jeanne W. Davis, Subject: Acceptance of Gifts from Private Parties for Foreign Dignitaries, May 13, 1976, White House Central Files/Subject Files, Box 2796, National Archives and Records Administration, Box 2796 (referencing "a recent memorandum from Nino Scalia"); DOJ letter to the President from Antonin Scalia, October 1, 1976, Sarah C. Massengale Files, Box 23, Gerald R. Ford Presidential Library (fitness); White House memo for Phil Buchen from Dudley Chapman, Subject: Proposed exemption of U.S. flag tankers from oil import fee, March 21, 1975, Box 52, Philip Buchen Files, Gerald R. Ford Presidential Library ("Nino Scalia does not see a problem"); Antonin Scalia, answers to Department of Justice questionnaire, June 1, 1986, in Folder 4, Box 14287, Peter J. Wallison Files, Supreme Court—Scalia, Ronald Reagan Presidential Library; "Justice Antonin Scalia," Oral History Project (whale) [Scalia ruled against GSA, pleasing environmentalists]; White House Decision Memorandum, Subject: Submission of Amendment to Bankruptcy Act to Facilitate Filing by New York City, [undated; October 4, 1975] L. William Seidman Files, Box 78, Gerald R. Ford Presidential Library (noting "Rod Hills and Nino Scalia have drafted such legislation…[Scalia] believes that such legislation is necessary"); White House memo for Phil Buchen from Barry Roth, [no subject], June 1, 1976, Barry M. Roth Files, Box 31, Gerald R. Ford Presidential Library (nominees); DOJ memo [to] Rudolph W. Giuliani [from] Antonin Scalia, [no subject], June 16, 1976, Barry M. Roth Files, Box 31, Gerald R. Ford Presidential Library. In 1975, Scalia developed the

administration's legislative package to address New York City's fiscal default. He testified before the Senate that it was designed to prevent Gotham from "paying some of its existing debts" only to "return to its old ways." Scalia also noted that the city's default "might seriously disrupt banking, financial and commercial activities nationwide." See Associated Press, "House Panel OKs Backing of $7 Billion in Loans to NYC," *Fort Worth Star-Telegram*, November 1, 1975. On Scalia's work on sovereign immunity, including his collaboration with Senator Kennedy on legislation passed by Congress, see Kathryn E. Kovacs, "Scalia's Bargain," *Ohio State Law Journal* 77, no. 6 (May 31, 2016): 1155–94.

5. H.R.12471—A bill to amend section 552 of title 5, United States Code, known as the Freedom of Information Act, 93rd Congress (1973–1974), Congress.gov, https://www.congress.gov/bill/93rd-congress/house-bill/12471; S.2543, A bill to amend section 552 of title 5, United States Code, commonly known as the Freedom of Information Act, Congress.gov, https://www.congress.gov/bill/93rd-congress/senate-bill/2543?q=%7B%22search%22%3A%5B%22S.+2543+1974%22%2C%22S.%22%2C%222543%22%2C%221974%22%5D%7D&s=1&r=75; Richard L. Madden, "Senate Votes to Ease Access to Federal Documents," New York Times, May 31, 1974; Office of Management and Budget memo from Roy L. Ash for the president, Subject: Enrolled Bill H.R. 12471—Freedom of Information Act amendments, October 16, 1974, White House Records Office: Legislation Case Files, Box 9, Gerald R. Ford Presidential Library.

6. Letter from Albrecht to Ash, October 10, 1974, White House Records Office, Legislation Case Files, Gerald R. Ford Presidential Library.; DOD letter from Hoffman to Roy L. Ash, October 11, 1974, White House Records Office, Legislation Case Files, Gerald R. Ford Presidential Library; DOS memo from Aldrich for Geoffrey Shepard, Subject: Veto of Freedom of Information Act Amendments, October 9, 1974, White House Records Office, Legislation Case Files, Gerald R. Ford Presidential Library; Veterans Administration letter from Richard L. Roudebush to Roy L. Ash, October 18, 1974, White House Records Office, Legislation Case Files, Gerald R. Ford Presidential Library.

7. First CIA letter from W. E. Colby to the President, September 26, 1974, Philip Buchen Files, Box 26, National Security Chronological File, Gerald R. Ford Presidential Library; CIA memo for Mr. Warner from [redacted], Subject: Veto Action on H.R. 12471, September 23, 1974, in Russ Kick, "Supreme Court Justice Scalia Fought against the Freedom of Information Act," TheMemoryHole, April 6, 2004, memoryhole.org; DOJ memo for Philip W. Buchen from Antonin Scalia, Re: Applicability of the Freedom of Information Act to the White House Office, February 26, 1975, Lazarus Papers, Box 25, Gerald R. Ford Presidential Library (FIA).

8. Administrative Conference of the United States: Hearing (Gaul, frankly, worried, kiss); The Freedom of Information Act: Hearings before a Subcommittee of the Committee on Government Operations House of Representatives…May 2, 7, 8, 10 and 16, 1973.… (U.S. Government Printing Office, 1973), https://tinyurl.com/bdkznum2.

9. Tim Weiner, "William E. Colby, 76, Head of C.I.A. in a Time of Upheaval," *New York Times*, May 7, 1996 (disks); William E. Colby, *Honorable Men: My Life in the CIA* (Simon & Schuster, 1978); Felix Belair, Jr., "U.S. Aide Defends Pacification Program in Vietnam Despite Killings of Civilians," *New York Times*, July 20, 1971;

William Colby, interview by the author, January 20, 1995, James S. Rosen Papers, Northwestern University.

10. James Rosen, "CIA Report Reveals Mole among Watergate Burglars—Cuban Exile Eugenio Martinez," Fox News, September 1, 2016, https://www.foxnews.com/world/cia-report-reveals-mole-among-watergate-burglars-cuban-exile-eugenio-martinez.

11. Biskupic, *American Original*, 45–46; Murphy, *Scalia: A Court of One*, 65–66; White House memo from Ken Cole to the President, October 16, 1974, White House Records Office, Legislation Case Files, Gerald R. Ford Presidential Library; CIA memo for Mr. Warner from [redacted], September 23, 1974, in Kick, "Supreme Court Justice Scalia Fought."

12. CIA memo for the Record by John S. Warner, Subject: DCI's Meeting with Attorney General Saxbe, September 26, 1974, CIA Reading Room; Kick, "Supreme Court Justice Scalia Fought."

13. CIA Journal—Office of Legislative Counsel, Friday—21 June 1974, CIA Reading Room; CIA memo for Mr. Warner, September 23, 1974, in Kick, "Supreme Court Justice Scalia Fought."

14. DOJ memo for the Attorney General from Antonin Scalia, Re: Use of Warrantless Trespassory Microphones in Foreign Intelligence Matters, September 17, 1974, National Security Adviser's Presidential Agency Files, Gerald R. Ford Presidential Library; DOJ letter to the President from Attorney General Saxbe, September 18, 1974, Gerald R. Ford Presidential Library. The two-page Saxbe letter to Ford remains classified but its existence and length were confirmed by the Ford library. Geir Gundersen, email to the author April 30, 2021. Though Scalia's September 17 memo was declassified in 2009, it went unmentioned by Biskupic and Murphy. The first public reference came in a paper by scholar Peter Roady, who cited the opinion in a footnote but nowhere quoted from it, and who elsewhere dated it, incorrectly, to 1973. Peter Roady, "The Ford Administration, the National Security Agency, and the 'Year of Intelligence': Constructing a New Legal Framework for Intelligence," *Journal of Policy History* 32, no. 3 (July 2020): 325–59. Also notable about the September 17 opinion was its jaundiced view of the Watergate special prosecutors, with language anticipating the justice's famous dissent in *Morrison v. Olson* (1988). "The nature of the regulations creating the Watergate Special Prosecution Force provides an unusual degree of independence from the rest of the [Justice] Department," Scalia observed in the memo. He noted that the special prosecutors had argued in court, against DOJ policy, that a sitting president could be indicted. "This," he snapped, "is consistent with the fact that, as we understand it, the Special Prosecutor's briefs are not reviewed in the Department." He concluded that OLC was not bound to "the positions adopted by the Special Prosecutor."

15. Second CIA letter to The President from W. E. Colby, September 26, 1974, Philip Buchen Files, Gerald R. Ford Presidential Library; White House memo for General Scowcroft from Philip Buchen, [no subject], October 3, 1974, Philip Buchen Files, Gerald R. Ford Presidential Library; White House memo for The File from Philip Buchen, Subject: Meeting of the President and the Attorney General 10/10/74, October 10, 1974, Philip Buchen Files, Gerald R. Ford Presidential Library. After

their harrowing experience with Colby, Scalia admired Saxbe. He later wrote of Saxbe's "homespun wit" and what he called the Saxbe Hypothesis, which was "the proposition that the basic goal of the Republican Party is not to govern but to prevent the Democrats from doing so." Antonin Scalia, "Regulatory Reform: The Game Has Changed," *Regulation* 5, no. 1 (January–February 1981): 13–15.

16. DOJ memo for Geoffrey Shepard, Re: Proposed Veto Message to the Freedom of Information Act amendments, October 3, 1974, White House Records Office: Legislative Case Files, Gerald R. Ford Presidential Library; [Scalia's unsigned] DOJ memo [no addressee], [Subject:] Amendments to Freedom of Information Act/Draft Veto Message, [undated; ca. October 3, 1974], Gerald R. Ford Presidential Library.

17. White House letter to the House of Representatives from Gerald R. Ford, Veto of Freedom of Information Act Amendments, October 17, 1974, The American Presidency Project, UC Santa Barbara; "All Actions H.R.12471—93rd Congress (1973–1974), Congress.gov, https://www.congress.gov/bill/93rd-congress/house-bill/12471/all-actions?overview=closed#tabs; Biskupic, *American Original*, 47.

18. Charlie Savage, *Takeover: The Return of the Imperial Presidency and the Subversion of American Democracy* (Boston: Little, Brown, 2007).

19. Murphy reported that in 2007, William McNitt, a Ford library archivist, helped him uncover a set of documents from 1976. These included a Scalia opinion, adopted by President Ford, justifying continued covert funding for an anti-communist tribe in Laos, despite the fact that federal law required—and the administration had not provided—a presidential "finding" and congressional briefings. Murphy, *Scalia: A Court of One*, 71–72. Contacted in 2021, Geir Gundersen, supervisory archivist, told me, "I did not locate anything in our processed/open collections dealing with the meetings involving Antonin Scalia mentioned in Professor Murphy's book.... I was unable to verify Mr. McNitt's findings on behalf of Professor Murphy." Geir Gunderson, email to the author, March 18, 2021.

20. William Funk, interview by the author, December 13, 2017; Antonin Scalia, Remarks at the International Conference on the Administration of Justice and National Security in Democracies, Ottawa, Canada, June 12, 2007 (My God); Scalia answers on Justice Department questionnaire. "With respect to assassinations," a CIA memo said, "Nino Scalia...stated they were content to go with the draft bill contained in the Church report." Morning Meeting Participants from John S. Warner, [no subject], February 5, 1976, CIA Reading Room.

21. Antonin Scalia, *Scalia Speaks: Reflections on Law, Faith, and Life Well Lived*, eds. Christopher J. Scalia and Edward Whelan (New York City: Crown Forum, 2017), 393; Antonin Scalia, remarks at the International Conference on the Administration of Justice and National Security in Democracies. At the Ottawa conference, Scalia suggested that some of the 1970s reforms might have contributed to the intelligence failures that preceded the terrorist attacks of September 11, 2001.

Chapter VIII: Wonderfully Intimate

Epigraph: Antonin Scalia, *Scalia Speaks: Reflections on Law, Faith, and Life Well Lived*, eds. Christopher J. Scalia and Edward Whelan (New York City: Crown Forum, 2017), 379.

1. "'Nonpolitician' Levi Approved as Attorney General," *New York Times*, February 6, 1975; Neil A. Lewis, "Edward H. Levi, Attorney General Credited with Restoring Order after Watergate, Dies at 88," *New York Times*, March 8, 2000.

2. "Honorable Laurence H. Silberman," interview by Raymond S. Rasenberger, Oral History Project, The Historical Society of the District of Columbia Circuit, December 13, 2001; Laurence Silberman, interview by the author, Washington, D.C., May 22, 2017; Antonin Scalia, remarks at the International Conference on the Administration of Justice and National Security in Democracies (risk); *U.S. v. Ehrlichman* (546 F.2d 910 (D.C. Cir. 1976); Hugo F. Sonneschein et al., "In Memoriam: Edward H. Levi (1912–2000)," *University of Chicago Law Review* 67, no. 4 (Autumn 2000): 967–93; Robert H. Bork, "The Greatest Lawyer of His Time," *Wall Street Journal*, March 13, 2000.

3. Ethan Bronner, "Robert H. Bork, 1927–2012: A Conservative Whose Supreme Court Bid Set the Senate Afire," *New York Times*, December 19, 2012 (bear); DOJ memo for the President by Edward H. Levi, [no subject; "Robert H. Bork," 7], November 10, 1975, Richard B. Cheney files, Box 11, Gerald R. Ford Presidential Library (New York, Kirkland); Robert Bork, "Civil Rights—A Challenge," *New Republic*, August 31, 1963; Robert H. Bork, "Neutral Principles and Some First Amendment Problems," *Indiana Law Journal* 47, no. 1 (1971): 1–35, at 7; Robert H. Bork, Jr., "Joe Biden's Antitrust Paradox," *Wall Street Journal*, July 12, 2021 (Kents).

4. Antonin Scalia, Steven G. Calabresi, John Harrison, and William Bradford Reynolds, "In Memoriam: Robert H. Bork," *Harvard Journal of Law and Public Policy* 36, no. 3 (Summer 2013): 1231, 1233–43, 1245–56.

5. "Office of the Solicitor General," Justice.gov, www.justice.gov/osg; Scalia, Calabresi, Harrison, and Reynolds, "In Memoriam"; Robert H. Bork, *Saving Justice: Watergate, the Saturday Night Massacre, and Other Adventures of a Solicitor General* (New York City: Encounter, 2013); Eugene Scalia, interview by the author, Washington, D.C., September 8, 2017. Bork was actually nine years older than Scalia.

6. Sonneschein et al., "In Memoriam: Edward H. Levi"; "Friends of Nino" panel, Washington, D.C., April 29, 2016, https://jameswilsoninstitute.org/events/show/friends-of-nino-panel.

7. Scalia, *Scalia Speaks*, 246; *Church of the Holy Trinity v. United States*, 143 U.S. 457 (1892).

8. "Honorable Laurence H. Silberman," Oral History Project; Silberman, interview by Raymond S. Rasenberger, May 22, 2017 (mad); Silberman interview by the author, August 23, 2022 (Marlboro); William Funk told me Silberman and Scalia sometimes grew "testy" with each other. William Funk, interview by the author, December 13, 2017 (testy).

9. Supreme Court document, "Judge Scalia's Immediate Family", September 22, 1986, in Social Affairs, Office of: Records, 09/26/1986, Swearing-In Ceremony for Chief Justice Rehnquist and Justice Scalia, Box 14249, Ronald Reagan Presidential Library (annotated with the dates of birth of the nine Scalia children); Richard Stengel, "Warm Spirits, Cold Logic," *Time*, July 20, 1986 (baseball).

10. Hanna Rosin, "The Partisan," *GQ*, May 2001 (locked, drove); Arthur Ciervo, "Profiles: Antonin Scalia (C '57)," *Georgetown Today*, September 1975; "Judicial

Issues," C-SPAN, November 16, 2006 (dullard); "Justice Scalia," *60 Minutes*, CBS News, April 27, 2008; "Friends of Nino," (love children).

11. Catherine Scalia Courtney and Eugene Scalia (quoting Maureen on "pay less") remarks, "Justice Scalia Memorial Service," C-SPAN, March 1, 2016; "Justice Antonin Scalia," interview by Judith R. Hope, Oral History Project, The Historical Society of the District of Columbia Circuit, December 5, 1992, https://dcchs.org /wp-content/uploads/2019/03/Scalia-Complete-Oral-History-1.pdf, 12 (hands-on); Eugene Scalia, interview by the author, Washington, D.C., August 22, 2017 (amazing); Paul Scalia, interview by the author, May 30, 2017; Robert L. Jackson and Ronald J. Ostrow, "He Has Own Style of Conservatism: Scalia's Independent Past Suggests Future Surprises," *Los Angeles Times*, July 6, 1986 (disregard, fig).

12. Funk, interview, December 13, 2017. Scalia's foreign travel required National Security Council (NSC) approval, which was invariably granted. NSC memo from Jeanne W. Davis to Warren Rustand, January 3, 1975, White House Central Files/ Subject Files, National Archives and Records Administration, Box 91, FG 17-15/A, Gerald R. Ford Presidential Library (Mexico); NSC memo from Davis through Sally Quenneville to Warren S. Rustand, July 21, 1975, White House Central Files/Name Files, National Archives and Records Administration, Scalia, Box 2796, Gerald R. Ford Presidential Library (Canada); NSC memo from Nancy Gemmell to William Nicholson, May 10, 1976, White House Central Files/Subject Files, National Archives and Records Administration, Box 91, FG 17-15/A Legal Counsel, Office of Appointments, Gerald R. Ford Presidential Library (Italy); NSC memo from Davis through Gemmell to Nicholson, June 17, 1976, White House Central Files/Name Files, National Archives and Records Administration, Scalia, Box 2796, Gerald R. Ford Presidential Library (U.K.); NSC memo from Davis through Gemmell to Nicholson, July 8, 1976, White House Central Files/Name Files, National Archives and Records Administration, Scalia, Box 2796, Gerald R. Ford Presidential Library (West Germany). See also FBI teletype from Chicago field office to Director, April 7, 1982 (listing Scalia's foreign travel), Scalia FBI Files.

13. Scalia, *Scalia Speaks*, 65 (elite); "Friends of Nino" (Baker); William Funk, interview by the author, December 14, 2017.

14. "Friends of Nino" (Uhlmann). "He knew how phony the committee reports were," Silberman told me. Laurence Silberman, interview by Raymond S. Rasenberger, May 22, 2017.

15. Scalia testimony, May 10, 1973, *op cit.*; Scalia, *Scalia Speaks*, 242 (incunabula). Father Scalia suggested an earlier epiphany, citing the scene in *A Man for All Seasons* in which More's daughter says of an oath, "We don't need to know the wording—we know what it will mean!" and More replies, "It will mean what the words say!" Paul Scalia, interview by the author. Bolt, *A Man for All Seasons*, 47.

Chapter IX: *Il Matador*

Epigraph: House Committee (Pike Committee), State Department and NSC Subpoenas— Testimony: Scalia, Antonin, November 20, 1975, Box 51, John Marsh Files, Gerald R. Ford Presidential Library.

1. White House memo for the President from Philip Buchen, Subject: Chairman of the Federal Trade Commission, February 3, 1976, Richard B. Cheney Files, Box 5,

Gerald R. Ford Presidential Library. Previously unreported is the fact that the president's aides also considered poaching Scalia, requesting a copy of his FBI background check because he "is being considered for [a] White House Staff Position." White House memo to [redacted] FBI from Jane Dannenhauer, Subject: FBI Investigations, May 5, 1975, Scalia FBI Files.

2. DOJ memo for the President [from] Edward H. Levi, [no subject], November 10, 1975, Cheney Files, Box 11, Gerald R. Ford Presidential Library.

3. Scalia used this metaphor in administrative law. "He called it a bull fight sometimes," recalled Walter Olson, Scalia's colleague at the American Enterprise Institute, "both in agencies asserting powers and being reined in by other branches of government, White House–versus-agency conflicts, review of agency action in courts." Walter Olson, interview by the author, April 30, 2020.

4. The Freedom of Information Act: Hearings before a Subcommittee of the Committee on Government Operations House of Representatives…May 2, 7, 8, 10 and 16, 1973…. (Washington, D.C.: U.S. Government Printing Office, 1973), https://tinyurl.com/yckd5zrz.

5. *Newsmen's Privilege: Hearings before the Subcommittee on Courts, Civil Liberties, and the Administration of Justice of the Committee on the Judiciary House of Representatives…April 23 and 25, 1975….* (Washington, D.C.: U.S. Government Printing Office, 1976).

6. Scalia was correct: "Reporters Subpoenaed," *Boston Globe*, March 22, 1883; "Newsman Subpoenaed in Kavanaugh Inquiry," *Herald News* [Passaic, New Jersey], July 14, 1967.

7. "Freedom of the Press," American Enterprise Institute, July 29–30, 1975, transcript by the author. Tom Whitehead appeared on the second panel.

8. Antonin Scalia, remarks at the International Conference on the Administration of Justice and National Security in Democracies, Ottawa, Canada, June 12, 2007 (scant), quotation taken from professional transcription of a partial recording provided to the author by reporter Charlie Savage of the *New York Times*. Charlie Savage, email to the author, February 23, 2021. When the Pike Committee's work was completed, its own report leaked to CBS News correspondent Daniel Schorr. When he could not get CBS News to publish it, he gave the document to the *Village Voice*, which did, triggering subpoenas for Schorr and other prominent newsmen of the era. Richard D. Lyons, "Schorr and 21 Subpoenaed In Release of Pike Report; House Ethics Panel Subpoenas Schorr and Others in Investigation of Release of the Pike Intelligence Report," *New York Times*, August 8, 1976, https://www.nytimes.com/1976/08/26/archives/schorr-and-21-subpoenaed-in-release-of-pike-report-house-ethics.html?searchResultPosition=1.

9. "Justice Antonin Scalia," interview by Judith R. Hope, Oral History Project, The Historical Society of the District of Columbia Circuit, December 5, 1992, 25–26, https://dcchs.org/wp-content/uploads/2019/03/Scalia-Complete-Oral-History-1.pdf.

10. William Funk, interview by the author, December 13, 2017. Eugene Scalia told me, "My mom does mention that at certain points during the Ford administration, he was stuck over at the White House and…had to sleep on a couch." Eugene Scalia, interview by the author, Washington, D.C., September 8, 2017.

11. David Wise, "The Secret Committee Called '40'," *New York Times*, January 19, 1975.

12. John M. Crewdson, "House Unit Seeks Contempt Order against Kissinger," *New York Times*, November 15, 1975; White House memo to Brent Scowcroft from Jack Marsh, Phil Buchen, Larry Eagleburger, William Hyland, Subject: State Department Subpoena, [undated; ca. November 15, 1975], National Security Adviser's Trip Cables of Brent Scowcroft, Box 1, Gerald R. Ford Presidential Library (pressure): "Our information is that [Pike] is determined to force a vote [by the full Congress] and go down fighting," the group wrote. "Thus, all of us (Jack Marsh, Phil Buchen, Larry Eagleburger, Nino Scalia and Bill Hyland) believe that an offer should be made.... We also recommend reaffirming the president's assertion of executive privilege although this would alienate some members."

13. U.S. Intelligence Agencies and Activities: Committee Proceedings: Proceedings of the Select Committee on Intelligence U.S. House of Representatives...September 10, 29, October 1, November 4, 6, 13, 14, and 20, 1975.... (U.S. Government Printing Office, 1976). After a private White House briefing, Pike acknowledged the administration's "substantial compliance" and withdrew the contempt citation amid applause on the House floor. See David E. Rosenbaum, "House Committee Drops Charge against Kissinger," *New York Times*, December 11, 1975; Myron S. Waldman, "Pike Committee Settles for Paraphrased Data," *Newsday*, December 11, 1975. Asked if Kissinger ever thanked Scalia for his testimony in defense of the secretary, Funk doubted it. "Levi and Kissinger had butted heads...with President Ford supporting Levi. Henry did not take it well." William Funk, email to the author, March 10, 2021. In early 1976, Scalia drafted an opinion, approved by President Ford, that asserted executive privilege in response to a similarly broad set of subpoenas providing a similarly short compliance window. Representative Bella Abzug, the pugnacious New York Democrat who chaired the Government Operations Committee, demanded the NSA and FBI, among other agencies, produce *within eight working days* "all records concerning communications interceptions for use by any department or agency of the U.S. government which have taken place since January 1, 1947." "The information sought is extremely sensitive," Scalia warned, noting it included "decrypted and plaintext messages...descriptions of code-breaking techniques...[identities of] individuals serving as double agents on behalf of the United States [and] individuals identified...as agents of foreign powers." Scalia drafted a letter for Ford to send Abzug rejecting the subpoena and invoking executive privilege, but Buchen arranged instead for the attorney general and the defense secretary to invoke the privilege. On the need to do so, however, Levi, Buchen, Scowcroft, and Rumsfeld all agreed with Scalia. DOJ memo for Philip W. Buchen [from] Antonin Scalia, Subject: Claim of Executive Privilege with Respect to Materials Subpoenaed by the Committee on Governmental Operations, House of Representatives, February 17, 1976, Presidential Handwriting Files, Box 31, Gerald R. Ford Presidential Library; White House memo from Philip Buchen to the President, Subject: Subpoena for NSA and FBI Records of Communications Interceptions, February 17, 1976, Presidential Handwriting Files, Box 31, Gerald R. Ford Presidential Library; White House memo from Jim Connor to the President,

Subject: Subpoena for NSA and FBI Records of Communications Intercepts, February 17, 1976, Presidential Handwriting Files, Box 31, Gerald R. Ford Presidential Library; Hearing on the Interception of Non-Verbal Communications by the FBI and the National Security Agency, Subcommittee on Government Information and Individual Rights, February 25, 1976, in Loen and Leppert Files, Box 15 (Rumsfeld et al.), Gerald R. Ford Presidential Library.

14. *Executive Privilege—Secrecy in Government: Hearings before the Subcommittee on Government Operations United State Senate...September 29 and October 23, 1975....* (Washington, D.C.: U.S. Government Printing Office, 1976). Scalia's testimony was on October 23. Joan Biskupic, *American Original: The Life and Constitution of Supreme Court Justice Antonin Scalia* (New York City: Sarah Crichton, paperback ed., 2010), 49–51; Bruce Allen Murphy, *Scalia: A Court of One* (Simon & Schuster, paperback ed., 2015), 73–78. Scalia was once persuaded to tone down his testimony in advance. "The portions...bracketed on pp. 22–24 were deleted from the final text which I delivered," he notified a colleague. "I finally agreed with OMB that they were true but impolitic"; DOJ memo for Roderick Hills from Nino Scalia, May 18, 1975, CIA Reading Room.

15. Antonin Scalia, "Guadalajara! A Case Study in Regulation by Munificence," *Regulation* 2, no. 2 (March–April 1978): 23–29 (human); Remarks of the Honorable Jeffrey S. Sutton, *Proceedings of the Bar and Officers of the Supreme Court of the United States,* November 4, 2016 (chess).

16. *Alfred Dunhill of London, Inc. v. Republic of Cuba,* 425 U.S. 682 (1976); Ed Kitch, email to the author, August 26, 2021 (custom); Robert H. Bork, Jr., email to the author, forwarding email from Frank Easterbrook to Bork, both August 30, 2021. Scalia was admitted to the Supreme Court on January 12, one week before his appearance in *Dunhill.* Antonin Scalia, answers to Department of Justice questionnaire, June 1, 1986, in Folder 4, Box 14287, Peter J. Wallison Files, Supreme Court—Scalia, Ronald Reagan Presidential Library.

17. Supreme Court audio recording, oral reargument, *Alfred Dunhill of London, Inc. v. Republic of Cuba,* January 19, 1976, at https://www.oyez.org/cases/1974/73-1288; "Argument Audio," at https://www.supremecourt.gov/oral_arguments /argument_audio/2020 (1955). All quotations here from oral argument in *Dunhill* are based on the Court's official recording. The Court's official transcript was frequently inaccurate, as is the alternative version posted on lawaspect.com and oyez. com. Since no recordings of Scalia's appearances on TV and radio in the 1950s appear to have survived, since no "home videos" or other privately held films or tapes of him have surfaced, since no university appears to have filmed any of the debate tournaments he dominated in college, and since no television or radio outlets appear to have covered any of the occasions when he testified before Congress, the earliest known recording of Scalia is the videotape of the American Enterprise Institute panel discussion in July 1975, leaving the Court's *Dunhill* tape the second-oldest.

18. Bryan A. Garner, "Hon. Antonin Scalia, Associate Justice, Part 1," YouTube, December 25, 2014, https://www.youtube.com/watch?v=aWHhesqi1OQ.

19. *Banco Nacional de Cuba v. Sabbatino,* 376 U.S. 398 (1964).

Chapter X: Growing Oaks

Epigraph: Quoted in "Antonin Scalia, U.S. Supreme Court Justice and Former UChicago Law Professor, 1936–2016," February 24, 2016, https://www.law.uchicago.edu /news/antonin-scalia-us-supreme-court-justice-and-former-uchicago-law-professor -1936-2016.

1. Eulogizing Scalia, Chief Justice Roberts quipped that *Dunhill* established for Scalia "a perfect record at the Court"; "Bench Statement by the Chief Justice," February 22, 2016, https://pdfserver.amlaw.com/nlj/02-22-16%20Justice%20Scalia%20Bench%20 Statement.pdf. Scalia later complained the complex ruling in *Dunhill* was "frequently misdescribed"; Antonin Scalia, answers to Department of Justice questionnaire, June 1, 1986, in Folder 4, Box 14287, Peter J. Wallison Files, Supreme Court—Scalia, Ronald Reagan Presidential Library.

2. Bryan A. Garner, "Hon. Antonin Scalia, Associate Justice, Part 1," YouTube video, December 25, 2014, https://www.youtube.com/watch?v=aWHhesqi1OQ; Antonin Scalia and Bryan Garner, *Making Your Case: The Art of Persuading Judges* (Eagan, Minnesota: Thomson West, 2008), 26.

3. Joan Biskupic, *American Original: The Life and Constitution of Supreme Court Justice Antonin Scalia* (Sarah Crichton, paperback ed., 2010), 63. For Blackmun's notes—giving Scalia a grade of 85, lower than the other attorneys, and describing him as "plump, dark"—see Tony Mauro, "Scalia's One and Only Supreme Court Argument," Law.com, February 24, 2016, https://www.law.com/supremecourtbrief /almID/1202750561106 /scalias-one-and-only-supreme-court-argument/. In the same chapter Biskupic devoted four pages (57–61) to the life and career of William O. Douglas.

4. "Once more," Murphy wrote ruefully, "a lucky star seemed to hang over Scalia's career." Biskupic, *American Original*, 88.

5. "Justice Antonin Scalia," interview by Judith R. Hope, Oral History Project, The Historical Society of the District of Columbia Circuit, December 5, 1992, 24, 27, https://dcchs.org/wp-content/uploads/2019/03/Scalia-Complete-Oral-History-1.pdf (threw).

6. "Justice Antonin Scalia," Oral History Project, 27. Elsewhere Scalia recalled he "accompanied my former boss, Attorney General Ed Levi, on his return [to Chicago] after the people threw us out." Antonin Scalia, *Scalia Speaks: Reflections on Law, Faith, and Life Well Lived*, eds. Christopher J. Scalia and Edward Whelan (New York City: Crown Forum, 2017), 393.

7. Letter to Committee on the Judiciary from Edward H. Levi, July 30, 1986, Boxes 35 Folder 2, Edward H. Levi Papers (awe); Associated Press, "Ford Aides Checking Job Market," *Arizona Republic*, January 6, 1977; "Robert Heron Bork," Justice.gov, https://www.justice.gov/osg/bio/robert-h-bork. Georgetown's law school dean, "impressed" by Scalia's performance as an adjunct professor, offered him a full-time faculty position before Scalia chose Chicago. See FBI report of Special Agent [redacted], Washington, D.C. Field Office, to [redacted; FBI headquarters], Subject: Antonin Scalia, April 19, 1982, Scalia FBI Files.

8. Tamar Honig, "Scalia Began Career in Federal Judiciary as Law School Professor," *Chicago Maroon* [student newspaper], February 16, 2016; Larry Martz with Ann McDaniel and Maggie Malone, "A Pair for the Court: Rehnquist and Scalia Seem to

Be Two of a Tory Kind," *Newsweek*, June 30, 1986; Stephen J. Adler, "Live Wire on the DC Circuit," *American Lawyer*, March 1985 (imperative); Bruce Allen Murphy, *Scalia: A Court of One* (New York City: Simon & Schuster, paperback ed., 2015) (Howard); Eugene Scalia, interview by the author, Washington, D.C., September 8, 2017. During Scalia's Chicago tenure, only Anne and Eugene reached college age. One account suggests Chicago covered "half the private school tuition costs" for children of faculty. Robert L. Jackson and Ronald J. Ostrow, "He Has Own Style of Conservatism: Scalia's Independent Past Suggests Future Surprises," *Los Angeles Times*, July 6, 1986. Scalia joked: "In a big family, the first child is kind of like the first pancake. If it's not perfect, that's okay, there are a lot more coming along."

9. Richard A. Epstein, "Antonin Scalia: A Most Memorable Friend," Hoover Institution, February 15, 2016, https://www.hoover.org/research/antonin-scalia-most-memorable-friend; Carol Felsenthal, "Chicago Colleagues Recall Scalia's Poker Games and D.C. Ambitions," *Chicago*, February 16, 2016 (impression).

10. DOJ letter to the President from Antonin Scalia, January 14, 1976 [sic; 1977], White House Central Files/Subject Files, Gerald R. Ford Presidential Library; White House letter to Antonin Scalia, January 18, 1977, White House Central Files/Subject Files, National Archives and Records Administration. Scalia would have been mortified to learn his resignation letter was misdated. Silberman confirmed the president was aware of Scalia's work: "I did talk to Jerry Ford about it. It was a very important position." Quoted in Adler, "Live Wire."

11. Karlyn Bowman, "AEI: An Introduction," [unpublished, undated manuscript; ca. 2019]; Karlyn Bowman, email to the author, September 7, 2021; Karlyn Bowman, "Association to Institute: AEI through Four Presidencies" in Donald E. Abelson and Christopher J. Rastrick, eds., *Handbook on Think Tanks in Public Policy* (Northampton, Massachusetts: Edward Elgar, 2021); Biskupic, *American Original*, 72.

12. Antonin Scalia, answers to Department of Justice questionnaire, June 1, 1986, in Folder 4, Box 14287, Peter J. Wallison Files, Supreme Court—Scalia, Ronald Reagan Presidential Library (aspects); "About This Journal," *Regulation* 1, no. 1, (July/August 1977): 2 (foster); Richard Vigilante, "Beyond the Burger Court," *Policy Review*, spring 1984, 20–26 (sprightly); Joel Richardson, "Judge Criticizes Trend to Rights of Individuals," *Washington Post*, December 7, 1984 (1964); "Competition of Ideas," AEI brochure, [undated; ca. 1977], CIA Reading Room, https://www.cia.gov/readingroom/docs/CIA-RDP88-01315R000100180001-7.pdf.

13. Eugene Scalia, interview by the author, Washington, D.C., August 22, 2017; Christopher Scalia, interview by the author, Washington, D.C., October 17, 2017.

14. Felsenthal, "Chicago Colleagues" (world); Robin I. Mordfin and Marsha Ferziger Nagorsky, "Chicago and Law and Economics: A History," October 11, 2011, The University of Chicago: The Law School, https://www.law.uchicago.edu/news/chicago-and-law-and-economics-history; Murphy, *Scalia: A Court of One*, 81 (courses); remarks of the Honorable Bradford Clark, *Proceedings of the Bar and Officers of the Supreme Court of the United States*, November 4, 2016.

15. Jackson and Ostrow, "He Has Own Style" (hat); Geoffrey R. Stone, "Tough, Brilliant, and Kind: The Antonin Scalia I Knew," *Daily Beast*, February 14, 2016 (forehead). Stone's public claim in 2007 that Scalia's Catholicism influenced his

jurisprudence caused a major rift between Stone and Scalia; they reconciled in 2012. Paris Schutz, "University of Chicago Reflects on Justice Scalia's Death," WTTW, February 15, 2016, https://news.wttw.com/2016/02/15/university-chicago-reflects-justice-antonin-scalias-death.

16. Emily Sinovic, "Justice Antonin Scalia's Oregon Friends Remember His Wit, Warmth," KATU News, February 15, 2016, https://katu.com/news/local/justice-antonin-scalias-oregon-friends-remember-his-wit-warmth (Dulcich); "Thomas Vincent Dulcich," Oregon Live (*The Oregonian*) July 13–15, 2018, https://obits.oregonlive.com/us/obituaries/oregon/name/thomas-dulcich-obituary?pid=189585387; Lee Liberman, interview by the author, Washington, D.C., June 29, 2017.

17. FBI interview with [redacted], University of Chicago Law School, April 30, 1982, Scalia FBI Files; Felsenthal, "Chicago Colleagues" (inner); Laurence Silberman, interview by the author, Washington, D.C., May 22, 2017; confidential sources (fiddle, chiefly).

18. Adler, "Live Wire" (prepared); Jackson and Ostrow, "He Has His Own Style" (Becker).

19. Confidential source, interview by the author; Martz with McDaniel and Malone, "A Pair for the Court"; Murphy, *Scalia: A Court of One*, 82–83 (Pippins). After Scalia's death, a few African-American graduates from the University of Chicago Law School alleged that Scalia had exhibited "indisputable" hostility to Black students and discriminated in grading. See Evelyn Diaz, "Scalia's Former Students Drop Shocking Claims of Classroom Racism," Black Entertainment Television, February 29, 2016, https://www.bet.com/article/exfr23/scalia-s-former-students-drop-claims-of-classroom-racism. For a critical examination of these claims, see Ed Whelan, "The Parade of Posthumous Defamers of Scalia Continues," *National Review*, March 1, 2016, https://www.nationalreview.com/bench-memos/scalia-gawker-racial-charges/.

20. Chris DeMuth, remarks at American Enterprise Institute dinner, C-SPAN, December 6, 1989 (gently); Anne Brunsdale, remarks at American Enterprise Institute dinner, in "Judicial Address," C-SPAN, December 6, 1989 (spark); Walter Olson, interview by the author, April 30, 2020 (integral); "Anne Brunsdale, 82, ex-ITC Chairwoman," *Washington Times*, February 20, 2006.

21. Brunsdale, remarks at American Enterprise Institute dinner.

22. Scalia, "The Judicialization of Standardless Rulemaking: Two Wrongs Make a Right," *Regulation* 1, no. 1 (July–August 1977): 38–41; Brunsdale, remarks at American Enterprise Institute dinner.

23. Antonin Scalia, "Guadalajara! A Case Study in Regulation by Munificence," *Regulation* 2, no. 2 (March–April 1978): 23–29.

24. Associated Press, "Carter Aide Launches Reorganization Effort," *Tampa Tribune*, February 9, 1977; United Press International, "Congress Pay Raise 'Passed,'" *Desert Sun*, February 18, 1977; John Dillin, "Reorganization Targets Named," *Albuquerque Journal*, March 11, 1977 (bluff); "Reorganization Needed," *Fort Worth Star-Telegram*, April 6, 1977 (enable); Edward Walsh, "Carter Signs Bill Allowing Reorganization," *Washington Post*, April 7, 1977.

25. Tuition Tax Relief Bills: Hearings before the Subcommittee on Taxation and Debt Management Generally, Senate Finance Committee.... (Washington, D.C.: U.S. Government Printing Office, 1978), https://tinyurl.com/2uc94v9f; Jack Fuller, "Church Schools and Taxes: A Constitutional Enigma," *Chicago Tribune*, April 6, 1978 (Hungary). One writer quipped that the Scalias' having nine children was "the reason his first involvement in politics was in a fight for tuition tax credits." See Vigilante, "Beyond the Burger Court." In fact, the issue was hardly the occasion of Scalia's first political engagement, and his involvement in it owed to law and philosophy, not his family finances.

26. Olson, interview by the author; Walter Olson, "This Is What Antonin Scalia Taught Me," *Daily Beast*, February 16, 2016 (naïve, awful). A DOJ colleague of Scalia's told the FBI he was a "compulsive editor...tended to edit the work of subordinates for style"; See FBI report of Special Agent [redacted], Washington, D.C. Field Office, to [redacted; FBI headquarters], Subject: Antonin Scalia, April 19, 1982, Scalia FBI Files.

27. *The Advocates*, WGBH-TV, May 11, 1978, www.openvault.wgbh.org. Scalia's second appearance, a year later, also focused on education. Staged at Ohio State University, the episode was moderated by Scalia's Harvard classmate Michael Dukakis, then between terms as Massachusetts governor. While the opposing advocate began by thanking "Governor Dukakis," Scalia opened with "Thank you, Mike"; *The Advocates*," WGBH-TV, May 20, 1979, https://openvault.wgbh.org. No recordings could be located of Scalia's 1978 appearance on *Perspectives*, a Chicago-based TV show on which he discussed "The Crisis of Watergate" with faculty colleague Philip Kurland, nor of Scalia's 1979 turn on *From the Midway*, a University of Chicago–produced radio show, broadcast in markets as far away as Albany, for which he and colleague Franklin Zimring addressed "Criminal Justice: Individual Rights vs. Society's Needs"; "Friday's TV Talk," *Chicago Tribune*, May 5, 1978; "Public FM Radio," *Berkshire Eagle*, July 26, 1979.

28. The original AEI transcript, published in booklet form as *An Imperial Judiciary: Fact or Myth?* (Washington, D.C.: AEI, 1979), was unreliable; AEI.org now provides the video and a more accurate transcription. Biskupic's account of this debate—the only AEI event she covered in her book—used the faulty transcript and accordingly misquoted Scalia. Biskupic, *American Original*, 68.

29. Calvin R. Trice, "Scalia Gives Lecture at W&L," *Richmond Times-Dispatch*, April 16, 2005; Scalia, answers to DOJ questionnaire (Maureen); Harvard law student Cecil Yongo reviewed some of Justice Scalia's papers at the Harvard Law School Library in February 2020, shortly after the first release of materials and just before the coronavirus pandemic shuttered the library for more than a year. Yongo's online reporting on the papers' contents, while impossible to verify, appeared credible. Cecil Yongo, Twitter direct message exchange with the author, September 20–October 3, 2021. An archivist confirmed that Yongo had inspected the papers but provided no additional information. Ed Moloy, email correspondence with the author, September 30, 2021. Cecil Yongo "Between 1972 and 1982, Scalia turns down offers. . .," Twitter, February 20, 2020, https://twitter.com/cecilyongo/status/1230592810048344064 (Montana).

30. Silberman, interview by the author, May 22, 2017.

31. Eugene Scalia, interview by the author, August 22, 2017.

32. Meg Scalia Bryce, interview by the author, August 2, 2017; John H. Schapiro, "Antonin Scalia: A Personal Reminiscence," Kleinbard LLC, February 22, 2016, http://www.kleinbard.com/antonin-scalia-a-personal-reminiscence/; Antonin Scalia, "The Christian as Cretin" in Scalia, *Scalia Speaks*, 107–16; Biskupic, *American Original*, 76 (lonely, weirdo).

33. After marrying Federalist Society co-founder William Otis in 1993, Lee has been known as Lee Liberman Otis. Following originalist practice, the name she used at the time is used here.

34. Liberman, interview by the author, June 29, 2017; Leonard Leo, interview by the author, Washington, D.C., August 28, 2017; Biskupic, *American Original*, 77–80; Steven M. Teles, *The Rise of the Conservative Legal Movement: The Battle for Control of the Law* (Princeton, New Jersey: Princeton University Press, 2008), 137–42; Stephen Goode, "The Society That Has Liberals Talking Scared," *Washington Times*, July 14, 1986.

35. Steven Calabresi, remarks at Federalist Society gala, C-SPAN, November 15, 2007; Associated Press, "US Judge Attacks High Court 'Trend,'" *Fort Worth Star-Telegram*, April 25, 1982; Marcia Chambers, "Yale Is a Host to 2 Meetings about Politics," *New York Times*, May 2, 1982.

36. Murphy, *Scalia: A Court of One*, 84–88; Michael Avery and Danielle McLaughlin, *The Federalist Society: How Conservatives Took the Law Back from Liberals* (Nashville, Tennessee: Vanderbilt University Press, 2013), 1–3; "Leonard A. Leo," The Federalist Society, https://fedsoc.org/contributors/leonard-leo; "Federalist Society for Law & Public Policy Studies, ProPublica Nonprofit Explorer, https://projects.propublica.org/nonprofits/organizations/363235550 (2019); Rebecca R. Ruiz, Robert Gebeloff, Steve Eder, and Ben Protess, "A Conservative Agenda Unleashed on the Federal Courts," *New York Times*, March 14, 2020 (Trump); Antonin Scalia remarks in "Federalist Society Anniversary Dinner," C-SPAN, November 15, 2007, *ibid*. For an account of how the Society gave back to Scalia, in the form of scholarship and opinions cited in his jurisprudence, see Amanda Hollis-Brusky, *Ideas with Consequences: The Federalist Society and the Conservative Counterrevolution* (Oxford, England: Oxford University Press, paperback ed., 2019).

Chapter XI: Bitterly Disappointed

Epigraph: Tom Petty, "The Waiting," © Gone Gator Music, 1981.

1. The event was held May 23, 1979, but aired on PBS stations in December (competing in the Orlando market against *Star Trek* and *Carol Burnett and Friends*); *Orlando Sentinel Star*, December 9. The video and an updated transcript are available at AEI.org. A few months later Scalia revisited his theme of powerlessness: "There is abroad in our land the feeling that we no longer control our government, but it controls us, through thousands of law-making functionaries in every field of life.... That feeling, I am sorry to tell you, is well-founded.... I am in the greatest sympathy with the objective of revivifying what appears to be a failing system of self-government in the United States." See Antonin Scalia, "The Legislative Veto: A False Remedy for System Overload," *Regulation* 3, no. 6 (November–December 1979): 19–26.

2. Richard Epstein, "Antonin Scalia: A Most Memorable Friend," Hoover Institution, February 15, 2016, https://www.hoover.org/research/antonin-scalia-most -memorable-friend (hedges).

3. "Judge Silberman Interview," Energy Bar Association, January 2020, https://www .eba-net.org/assets/1/6/EBAAuthoredArticle_SIlberman_Interview_Jan2020.pdf (co-chair); "Honorable Laurence H. Silberman," interview by Raymond S. Rasenberger, Oral History Project, The Historical Society of the District of Columbia Circuit, December 13, 2001, https://dcchs.org/sb_pdf/complete-oral-history-laurence-silberman/ (every).

4. Epstein, "Antonin Scalia: A Most Memorable Friend." To Scalia, Epstein was a kind of frenemy. There was mutual fondness, but they clashed publicly after Scalia became a judge, and Epstein ultimately eulogized his friend with a mix of admiration and censure. "Good luck," Epstein wrote me. "Nino was a bundle of contradictions." Richard Epstein, email to the author, September 4, 2021.

5. Antonin Scalia, "Federal Trade Commission," *Regulation* 4, no. 6 (November–December 1980), 18–20.

6. Peter Behr and Merrill Brown, "Reagan Task Force Proposes One-Year Freeze on New U.S. Rules," *Louisville Courier-Journal*, November 9, 1980; United Press International, "Take Ax to Regulations, Experts' Panel Advises," *Berkshire Eagle*, December 10, 1980; Tim Wheeler, "Reagan's Regulatory Reform Plan May Take Longer Than Expected," *Tampa Tribune*, December 12, 1980.

7. Scalia, "Federal Trade Commission" (vied, average); Antonin Scalia, "The Disease as Cure: 'In Order to Get Beyond Racism, We Must First Take Account of Race,'" *Washington University Law Review* 147, no. 1 (1979): 147–57 (fancy); DOJ memo for Geoffrey Shepard, Re: Proposed Veto Message to the Freedom of Information Act amendments, October 3, 1974, White House Records Office: Legislative Case Files, Gerald R. Ford Presidential Library (readily); FBI report of Special Agent [redacted], Washington, D.C. Field Office, April 19, 1982, Scalia FBI Files (achieve); FBI report of Special Agent [redacted], New York Field Office, to [redacted; FBI headquarters], [undated; ca. April 9, 1982] (field), Scalia FBI Files; Antonin Scalia and Graham C. Lilly, "Appellate Justice: A Crisis in Virginia?," *Virginia Law Review* 57 (1971): 3–64; "Asymmetry Is an Unbalanced View," *Center* (May–June 1973): 38–39; Antonin Scalia, "Don't Go Near the Water," *Federal Communications Bar Journal* 25, no. 2 (1972–1973): 111–20. For a bibliography of Scalia's early published works, see "Scalia, Antonin," University of Virginia School of Law Library, Our History, Former Faculty, https://libguides.law.virginia.edu/faculty/scalia.

8. Antonin Scalia, "Guadalajara! A Case Study in Regulation by Munificence," *Regulation* 2, no. 2 (March–April 1978): 23–29; Scalia "The Legislative Veto"; Antonin Scalia, "Support Your Local Professor of Administrative Law," *Administrative Law Review* 34, no. 2 (Spring 1982): xvii–xxi, at xvii; "The Freedom of Information [Act] Has No Clothes," *Regulation* 7, no. 2 (March–April 1982); "Conference on Intelligence Legislation," American Bar Association, June 26–28, 1980, CIA Reading Room. Scalia's Notre Dame speech included sharp criticism of Justice White. In *Committee for Public Education and Religious Liberty v. Regan* (1980), White held that lacking "a single, more-encompassing construction of the

Establishment Clause," the Court's church-state jurisprudence "sacrifices clarity and predictability for flexibility." Scalia had argued as much, on television, for two years. "A stunning admission in a majority opinion," he snapped, "but indeed, as one might expect, somewhat understating the case." Antonin Scalia, "On Making It Look Easy by Doing It Wrong: A Critical View of the Justice Department," in Edward McGlynn Gaffney, Jr., ed., *Private Schools and the Public Good: Policy Alternatives for the Eighties* (South Bend, Indiana: University of Notre Dame Press, 1981), 173–85.

9. Antonin Scalia, "Vermont Yankee: The APA, the D.C. Circuit, and the Supreme Court," *The Supreme Court Review* (1978): 345–409, http://www.jstor.org/stable /3109536. One scholar has suggested Scalia was "the first conservative to give expression to the relationship between procedure and power" in administrative law. See Morton J. Horwitz, *The Transformation of American Law, 1870–1960: The Crisis of Legal Orthodoxy* (Oxford, England: Oxford University Press, 1992), 244.

10. Scalia, "The Disease as Cure"; Murphy declared the essay "hyperbolic." Bruce Allen Murphy, *Scalia: A Court of One* (New York City: Simon & Schuster, paperback ed., 2015), 92; Biskupic called it "a lesson in ethnic resentment." Joan Biskupic, *American Original: The Life and Constitution of Supreme Court Justice Antonin Scalia* (New York City: Sarah Crichton, paperback ed., 2010), 70. "Scalia's defense of his father is misplaced," another scholar charged. Bryan Keith Fair, "Been in the Storm Too Long, without Redemption: What We Must Do Next," *Southern University Law Review* 25, no. 1 (1997): 121–40.

11. Remarks of the Honorable Bradford Clark, *Proceedings of the Bar and Officers of the Supreme Court of the United States*, November 4, 2016.

12. Richard D. Lyons, "William French Smith Dies at 73; Reagan's First Attorney General," *New York Times*, October 30, 1990 (model, cool, private); Biskupic, *American Original*, 73–74 (went well). Scalia served on the Brigham Young Law School advisory board from 1979 to 1981; Antonin Scalia, answers to Department of Justice questionnaire, June 1, 1986, in Folder 4, Box 14287, Peter J. Wallison Files, Supreme Court—Scalia, Ronald Reagan Presidential Library. Following his interview with Attorney General Smith and his deputy, Scalia wrote a follow-up letter on Stanford Law stationery dated March 28, 1981, and reprinted in Paul Sabin, "In a 1981 Letter, Scalia Lists His Bona Fides," Slate, October 7, 2013, https://slate.com/ human-interest/2013/10/antonin-scalia-a-1981-letter-in-which-he-lists-his-commitments-to-the-gop.html. On the campaign by Italian-American groups on Scalia's behalf, see chapter 12.

13. William French Smith, *Law and Justice in the Reagan Administration: Memoirs of An Attorney General* (Stanford, California: Hoover Institution Press, 1991), 23; Biskupic, *American Original*, 74 (wept). In a 1998 speech, Scalia said Lee's appointment was "a bitter and unexpected disappointment." Antonin Scalia, *Scalia Speaks: Reflections on Law, Faith, and Life Well Lived*, eds. Christopher J. Scalia and Edward Whelan (New York City: Crown Forum, 2017), 146.

14. "Nomination of Edward C. Schmults to Be Deputy Attorney General," January 23, 1981, The American Presidency Project, U.C. Santa Barbara; Laurence Silberman, interview by the author, Washington, D.C., May 22, 2017.

15. Raymond Randolph, interview by the author, August 3, 2021 (angry). Scalia called the decision "a really bad call" by Smith. Scalia, *Scalia Speaks*, 146.

16. Robert S. Boyd, "No History, but a Nation's Little Wheels Must Also Turn," *Miami Herald*, September 29, 1973; David S. Broder, "Birch Bayh: The Great Amender," *Ithaca Journal*, March 1, 1975; Tony Mauro, "Scalia's One and Only Supreme Court Argument," Law.com, February 24, 2016, https://www.law.com /supremecourtbrief/almID/1202750561106/scalias-one-and-only-supreme-court -argument/ (dark); Jim Wilderotter, interview by the author, March 2, 2021 (bocce); Frank Michelman, interview by the author, October 3, 2017.

17. Antonin Scalia, "Regulatory Reform—the Game Has Changed," *Regulation* 5, no. 1 (January–February 1981): 13–15; Executive Order No. 12291—Federal Regulation, February 17, 1981, The American Presidency Project, U.C. Santa Barbara; Thomas Oliphant, "White House Review of US Regulations Turns to Hiring, Pay," *Boston Globe*, March 27, 1981.

18. Antonin Scalia, "An Interview on the New Executive Order with Murray Weidenbaum and James C. Miller III," American Enterprise Institute, April 11, 1981, https://www.aei.org/articles/an-interview-on-the-new-executive-order-with-murray-l-weidenbaum-and-james-c-miller-iii/; Robert D. Hershey, Jr., "Murray L. Weidenbaum, Reagan Economist, Dies at 87," *New York Times*, March 21, 2014 (undo); James M. Miller, "Biographical Sketch," jimmiller.org; Antonin Scalia, "Back to Basics: Making Law without Making Rules," *Regulation* 5, no. 4 (July–August 1981): 25–28 (jubilation); Antonin Scalia, "Regulatory Review and Management," *Regulation* 6, no. 1 (January–February 1982): 19–21 (mirage); Antonin Scalia, "Reagulation [*sic*]-The First Year: Regulatory Review and Management," American Enterprise Institute, February 11, 1982, https://www.aei.org/articles/reagulation-the-first-year-regulatory-review-and-management/; Irvin Molotsky, "Man in the News: Judge with Tenacity and Charm," *New York Times*, June 18, 1986 (shut).

19. "Search Spreads for Reagan's Justice," [Binghamton, New York,] *Press and Sun-Bulletin*, June 19, 1981 (Bork and Scalia); Steven R. Weisman, "Reagan Nominating Woman, an Arizona Appeals Judge, to Serve on Supreme Court," *New York Times*, July 8, 1981.

20. "Bork Held to Be Choice for Court," *New York Times*, August 13, 1981; Stuart Taylor, "Bork, A Former Solicitor General, Named to Key Appeals Court Post," *New York Times*, December 8, 1981. "My understanding," Gene Scalia told me, "is that the Reagan administration was initially talking to Judge Bork about the Second Circuit, which made more sense for him, in some respects, because his expertise was more in the area of anti-trust and business law, which is the Second Circuit docket.... At some point it was communicated to Bork by the White House that he'd be better positioned for the Supreme Court coming from the D.C. Circuit.... My father had been in discussions about the D.C. Circuit; but when Bork got interested, my dad was no longer in play for that seat." Eugene Scalia, interview by the author, Washington, D.C., September 8, 2017.

21. In August–September 1980, FTC retained Scalia again, to advise the agency on rule-making authority; on Scalia's consultancy and appellate work, see Scalia, Answers to DOJ Questionnaire.

22. "S.E.C.'s Dresser Inquiry Upheld; Procedures and Process Cited," *New York Times*, November 18, 1980. For the Indonesia-U.S. Business Committee, Scalia drafted *amicus* briefs in a case involving a union lawsuit against OPEC, the Arab oil cartel.

A New Jersey firm hired Scalia in a class action suit brought by women claiming that drug manufacturers' use of diethylstilbestrol (DES), prescribed to prevent miscarriages, had caused vaginal cancer and other abnormalities. Since most plaintiffs could not identify which drug caused their injuries, their attorneys pressed the theory, known as "market-share liability," that companies could be assessed damages based on their standing in the relevant industry. Representing Merck in the case was Scalia's Xavier classmate Tom Campion, who retained Scalia to draft briefs challenging the constitutionality of market-share liability.

23. *INS v. Chadha*, 462 U.S. 919 (1983); Linda Greenhouse, "Supreme Court, 7–2, Restricts Congress's Right to Overrule Actions by Executive Branch," *New York Times*, June 24, 1983; Associated Press, "Alien's Deportation Fight Led to Landmark Decision," *New York Times*, June 25, 1983; Scalia, "The Legislative Veto: A False Remedy" (threat); Scalia, Answers to DOJ Questionnaire. In 1982 an interest group hired Scalia to assess a proposed constitutional amendment mandating balanced budgets; Scalia, *Constitutional Aspects of SJR 58/HJR 350: The Tax Limitation/Balanced Budget Amendment*, Tax Limitation Research Foundation, 1982.

24. The Stanford student described Scalia's death as "a sad loss for the country, his family, and me personally," in the comments to Epstein, "Antonin Scalia: A Most Memorable Friend."

25. Confidential source, interview by the author (politicking); Mike Brody, quoted in Jade Hernandez, "Justice Scalia Remembered in Chicago," WLS-TV, February 14, 2016, www.abc7chicago.com. Despite Brody's appearing for the interview in "blue jeans with a hole in them and a red t-shirt," Scalia hired him for the 1983–84 term.

26. Scalia's rejection of the Seventh Circuit judgeship was disclosed in 1986, in Larry Martz with Ann McDaniel and Maggie Malone's "A Pair for the Court: Rehnquist and Scalia Seem to Be Two of a Tory Kind," *Newsweek*, June 30, 1986; James F. Simon, *The Center Holds: The Power Struggle inside the Rehnquist Court* (New York City: Simon & Schuster, 1992), 140; Biskupic, *American Original*, 80 (wait).

Chapter XII: Judge Scalia

Epigraph: "America and the Courts," C-SPAN, April 1, 1986. Ten months later, Justice Scalia told a New Orleans audience "I had the unrealistic ambition of being a federal judge back in 1960." Remarks before the Fellows of the American Bar Foundation and the National Conference of Bar Presidents, February 15, 1987, Box 77, Folder 16-17, Antonin Scalia Papers, Harvard School of Law Library.

1. "Roger Robb," Historical Society of the District of Columbia Circuit, https://dcchs.org/judges/roger-robb/; Marjorie Hunter, "Judge J. Skelly Wright, Segregation Foe, Dies at 77," *New York Times*, August 8, 1988 (second, most liberal).

2. Laurence Silberman, interview by the author, Washington, D.C., May 22, 2017.

3. Memo from Julian O. von Kalinowski to William French Smith, December 16, 1980, Counsel to the President: Judicial Selection Files, Scalia, Antonin, Box 2, Ronald Reagan Presidential Library; Letter from Donald E. Santarelli to Edwin Meese, December 19, 1980; Letter from Carla A. Hills to Tim McNamar[a], December 22, 1980, Counsel to the President: Judicial Selection Files, Scalia, Antonin, Box 2, Ronald Reagan Presidential Library; Letter from Frank D. Stella to Red Cavaney, March 19,

1981, Counsel to the President: Judicial Selection Files, Scalia, Antonin, Box 2, Ronald Reagan Presidential Library; Letter from Jeno F. Paulucci and Stella to President Reagan, June 22, 1981, Counsel to the President: Judicial Selection Files, Scalia, Antonin, Box 2, Ronald Reagan Presidential Library; Letter from Stella to Reagan, July 21, 1981; Memo from Saloschin to Fielding, July 27, 1981, Counsel to the President: Judicial Selection Files, Scalia, Antonin, Box 2, Ronald Reagan Presidential Library; White House letter from Fielding to Stella, August 3, 1981, Counsel to the President: Judicial Selection Files, Scalia, Antonin, Box 2, Ronald Reagan Presidential Library (merits); White House memo from Burgess to Fielding, Subject: Nino Scalia, August 4, 1981, Counsel to the President: Judicial Selection Files, Scalia, Antonin, Box 2, Ronald Reagan Presidential Library; White House letter from Fielding to Mark S. Fowler, August 18, 1981, Counsel to the President: Judicial Selection Files, Scalia, Antonin, Box 2, Ronald Reagan Presidential Library (frankly); White House letter from Fielding to Saloschin, August 24, 1981, Counsel to the President: Judicial Selection Files, Scalia, Antonin, Box 2, Ronald Reagan Presidential Library; White House letter from Fielding to Pete V. Domenici, August 31, 1981, Counsel to the President: Judicial Selection Files, Scalia, Antonin, Box 2, Ronald Reagan Presidential Library.

4. Laura A. Kiernan and Fred Barbash, "Appeals Judge Plans to Leave U.S. Court Here," *Washington Post*, April 2, 1982; DOJ memo from William R. Robie to Director, FBI, March 24, 1982 (position), Scalia FBI Files; FBI report of Special Agent [redacted], San Francisco Field Office to [redacted; FBI headquarters], April 5, 1982 (capacity) , Scalia FBI Files; FBI report of Special Agent [redacted], Newark [New Jersey] Field Office, April 9, 1982 (smartest, qualified), Scalia FBI Files; FBI report of Special Agent [redacted], Richmond Field Office, to [redacted; FBI headquarters], April 8, 1982 (contrary); FBI report of Special Agent [redacted], Cleveland Field Office, to [redacted], Scalia FBI Files; FBI headquarters, April 8, 1982, Scalia FBI Files (interfere); FBI report of Special Agent [redacted], Tampa Field Office, April 9, 1982, Scalia FBI Files, (model); FBI report of Special Agent [redacted], Boston Field Office, to [redacted; FBI headquarters], April 9, 1982, Scalia FBI Files, (better); FBI report of Special Agent [redacted], New York Field Office, to [redacted; FBI headquarters], [undated; ca. April 9, 1982], Scalia FBI Files; FBI report of Special Agent [redacted], Washington, D.C. Field Office, April 19, 1982, Scalia FBI Files (OLC, arrogance, equal); FBI report of Special Agent [redacted], Alexandria, Virginia, Field Office, to [redacted; FBI headquarters], April 21, 1982, Scalia FBI Files (church-going); FBI report of Special Agent [redacted], Chicago Field Office, to [redacted; FBI headquarters], May 6, 1982, Scalia FBI Files (with Scalia's interview and Tax Check Waiver form of April 5 attached).

5. Raymond Randolph, interview by the author, August 3, 2021; "A. Raymond Randolph," United States Court of Appeals: District of Columbia Circuit, https://www.cadc.uscourts.gov/internet/home.nsf/content/VL+-+Judges+-+ARR.

6. DOJ letter from Smith to Reagan, July 6, 1982 Ronald Reagan Presidential Library; White House memo from Fielding to Reagan, Subject: Nomination of Antonin Scalia to be United States Circuit Judge for the District of Columbia Circuit, July 9, 1982 Ronald Reagan Presidential Library; [unsigned] White House memo for the President, Subject: Recommended Telephone Call/To: Antonin Scalia, July 13, 1982; White

House press release, July 14, 1982, Counsel to the President: Judicial Selection Files, Ronald Reagan Presidential Library. On July 16, Fielding sent a congratulatory "Dear Nino" letter to the Scalias' Chicago home, appending the press releases.

7. David R. Palombi, "Trenton Native Likely Candidate for Spot on U.S. Supreme Court," *Trenton Times*, November 4, 1985.

8. FBI report of Special Agent [redacted], Washington, D.C. Field Office, April 19, 1982, Scalia FBI Files (weekends).

9. Eugene Scalia, interview by the author, Washington, D.C., September 8, 2017.

10. Stephen J. Adler, "Live Wire on the DC Circuit," *American Lawyer*, March 1985 (celebrating); Anne Brunsdale, remarks at American Enterprise Institute dinner, in "Judicial Address," C-SPAN, December 6, 1989.

11. Robert Connor, interview by the author, December 17, 2020.

12. Court of Appeals for the District of Columbia Circuit letter from Scalia to Edward Allen Tamm, August 11, 1983 [with enclosures], Peter J. Wallison Files, Supreme Court—Scalia, Box 14287, Ronald Reagan Presidential Library (1982 financial disclosure); Dave Boyer, "Antonin Scalia's Candor, Humor Recalled Ahead of Supreme Court Justice's Funeral," *Washington Times*, February 18, 2016 (beer). The FBI determined in April 1982 that the Scalias owed $64,849 on the $75,000 mortgage on their Chicago home "The loan has never been delinquent, and [Scalia] is considered to have a very good credit standing." FBI report of Special Agent [redacted], May 6, 1982, Scalia FBI Files. Bruce Allen Murphy skillfully used FOIA to obtain hundreds of documents from the Reagan Presidential Library, including the financial disclosure form referenced here, but he misreported Scalia's Chicago salary as "nearly $50,000" when the document listed it as $32,972 and misreported Scalia's judicial salary as $77,300 when the documents listed it as $74,300. Cf. Murphy, *Scalia: A Court of One*, 97, and "Antonin Scalia," Counsel to the President: Judicial Selection Files, Scalia, Antonin, Box 2, Ronald Reagan Presidential Library.

13. Eugene Scalia, interview by the author, September 8, 2017 (Catherine).

14. Adler, "Live Wire" (obvious, list, substantial); White House memo for Peter J. Wallison from Alan Charles Raul, Subject: Summary Information Regarding Certain Judges, June 5, 1986, Peter J. Wallison Files, Supreme Court—Rehnquist/Scalia Notebook II—Candidates, Ronald Reagan Presidential Library.

15. Confirmation of Federal Judges: Hearings before the Committee on the Judiciary United States Senate...May 26, 27; June 16, 23; July 14, 21; August 4, 11, 18; September 15, 22, 29; December 1, 6, and 8, 1982.... (Washington, D.C.: U.S. Government Printing Office, 1983), 81–93, https://tinyurl.com/2ya567k4.

16. *Congressional Record, SENATE—August 5, 1982,* 19630; "Antonin Scalia," Historical Society of the District of Columbia Circuit, https://dcchs.org/judges/scalia-antonin/; 28 U.S. Code Title 28—JUDICIARY AND JUDICIAL PROCEDURE, § 453, Oaths of Justices and Judges.

Chapter XIII: Particularly Dangerous

Epigraph: Antonin Scalia, *Scalia Speaks: Reflections on Law, Faith, and Life Well Lived*, eds. Christopher J. Scalia and Edward Whelan (New York City: Crown Forum, 2017), 43.

1. Antonin Scalia, remarks at "Portrait Presentation Ceremony: Ruth Bader Ginsburg," November 3, 2000, United States Court of Appeals for the District of Columbia Circuit, https://dcchs.org/wp-content/uploads/2019/02/Ruth-Bader-Ginsburg-Portrait-Transcript.pdf.

2. Richard Vigilante, "Beyond the Burger Court," *Policy Review* (Spring 1984): 20–26; Stephen J. Adler, "Live Wire on the DC Circuit," *American Lawyer* (March 1985).

3. Nomination of Judge Antonin Scalia: Hearings before the Committee on the Judiciary United States Senate…August 5 and 6, 1986…. (Washington, D.C.: U.S. Government Printing Office, 1987) (ponderous); America and the Courts," C-SPAN, April 1, 1986 (business).

4. Abner Mikva, quoted in Adler, "Live Wire"; "The Honorable Robert H. Bork," interview by Victoria L. Radd, March 13, 1992, Oral History Project, The Historical Society of the District of Columbia Circuit, https://dcchs.org/sb_pdf/complete-oral-history-bork/.

5. Joan Biskupic, *American Original: The Life and Constitution of Supreme Court Justice Antonin Scalia* (New York City: Sarah Crichton, paperback ed., 2010), 88.

6. "The Honorable Oliver Gasch," interviews by Stuart H. Newberger, December 2, 9, and 19, 1991, and January 19 and March 2, 1992, Oral History Project, The Historical Society of the District of Columbia Circuit. Samples of Scalia's stationery can be found in the archives of contemporaries, such as Bork, whose papers have been released to the public.

7. Ralph A. Rossum, *Antonin Scalia's Jurisprudence: Text and Tradition* (Lawrence, Kansas: University Press of Kansas, paperback ed., 2016), 4. See also Ralph A. Rossum, "The Wit and Wisdom of Justice Scalia," *Claremont Review of Books* (Summer 2005).

8. *Washington Post Co. v. United States Department of State*, 685 F. 2d 698 (1982).

9. Remarks by Hadley Arkes in "Friends of Nino" panel, Washington, D.C., April 29, 2016, https://jameswilsoninstitute.org/events/show/friends-of-nino-panel (regrettable).

10. "America and the Courts" (surprised); "Circuit Judge to Speak on Regulatory Reform," *Morning Call* [Allentown, Pennsylvania], September 12, 1982; Anne White, "Judge Scalia Lectures on Regulatory Reform," *Brown and White* [Lehigh student newspaper] 94, no. 6 (September 17, 1982).

11. *Community for Creative Non-Violence v. Watt*, 670 F. 2d 1213 (1982); *Clark v. Community for Creative Non-Violence*, 468 U.S. 288 (1984); Court of Appeals for the District of Columbia Circuit memo to All Active Judges from Judge Wilkey, Re No. 82-2445 *CCNV v. Watt*, January 27, 1983, JSWP, Box 141, Library of Congress (divergence); Leslie Maitland, "Sleep Protected? Court Asked to Rule," *Dayton* [Ohio] *Daily News*, December 29, 1982 (Kanter).

12. *Chaney v. Heckler*, 718 F.2d 1174 (1983); *Heckler v. Chaney*, 470 U.S. 821 (1985); Adler, "Live Wire" (farfetched). Displeased at the court's denial of *en banc* review, Scalia penned a dissent to that decision. Gently informed by chief deputy clerk Robert A. Bonner that such statements "are ordinarily not published, and that it is customary to advise the court of a different intent," Scalia told his colleagues, in a previously unpublished memo: "I apologize for my ignorance on both counts, and trouble you

again to advise that my statement in *Chaney*, attached, will be published." See Court of Appeals for the District of Columbia Circuit memo to Chief Judge Robinson [et al.] from Judge Scalia, Re: *Larry Leon CHANEY, et al. v. Heckler, Secretary of HHS*, No. 82-2321, January 4, 1984, J. Skelley Wright Papers, Box 148, Library of Congress; Court of Appeals for the District of Columbia Circuit Order, *Gary L. Ryan v. Bureau of Alcohol, Tobacco and Firearms*, 715 F.2d 644 (1983), filed November 8 (Bonner).

13. Marjorie Hunter, "Judge J. Skelly Wright, Segregation Foe, Dies at 77," *New York Times*, August 8, 1988; *Calvert Cliffs' Coordinating Committee v. Atomic Energy Commission*, 449 F.2d 1109 (1971).

14. Patrick Schiltz, interview by the author, June 28, 2017. "Skelly Wright was really old and somewhat out of it by that time," Lee Liberman, who also clerked for Scalia on the Circuit Court and Supreme Court, told me. "That was a tricky problem." Lee Liberman, interview by the author, Washington, D.C., June 29, 2017.

15. Adler, "Live Wire" (bench memos); Gary Lawson, "On Getting It Right: Remembering Justice Antonin Scalia," *Boston University Law Review* 96, no. 2 (March 2016): 299–302 (cart); Schiltz, interview, June 28, 2017; Jade Hernandez, "Justice Scalia Remembered in Chicago," WLS-TV, February 14, 2016, www .abc7chicago.com. For a rare example of a bench memo by a Scalia clerk, see Court of Appeals for the District of Columbia Circuit memo to Judge Scalia from [unsigned by clerk], Re: *Associated Gas Distributors, et al. v. FERC*, No. 84-1454, [undated; November 1985]; Court of Appeals for the District of Columbia Circuit memo to Chief Judge Wald from Judge Ginsburg, Re: *Associated Gas Distributors v. FERC*, No. 84-1454, September 22, 1986 (referencing "the Scalia chambers bench memo"); and Court of Appeals for the District of Columbia Circuit memo to Judge Ruth Bader Ginsburg from [Wright clerk] John Walsh, Re: *Associated Gas Distributors v. FERC*, No. 84-1454, December 23, 1986 (referencing "the Scalia chambers memo"), all in Box 89, Folder 8, Ruth Bader Ginsburg Papers, Library of Congress.

16. Brian Lamb, interview by the author, Washington, D.C., May 10, 2017; Henry Goldberg, interview by the author, June 27, 2017.

17. *United Presbyterian Church in the U.S.A. v. Reagan*, 738 F.2d 1375 (1984).

18. *Moore v. U.S. House of Representatives*, 733 F.2d 946 (1984) (properly limited); Antonin Scalia, "The Doctrine of Standing as an Essential Element of the Separation of Powers," *Suffolk University Law Review* 17 (1983): 881–99.

19. Remarks by Michael Uhlmann in "Conference on Intelligence Legislation," American Bar Association, June 26–28, 1980, CIA Reading Room.

20. "Claire Bork, Wife of Former Attorney General, Dies at 50," *Chicago Tribune*, December 10, 1980; Mike Capuzzo, "On the Comeback Trail: Robert Bork Takes His Constitutional Ideas on the Road," *Philadelphia Inquirer*, March 6, 1990 (beams); Tim Drake, "Judge Bork Converts to the Catholic Faith," Catholic Education Resource Center, [undated; ca. July 2003], https://www.catholiceducation.org/en/faith-and-character/faith-and-character/judge-bork-converts-to-the-catholic-faith.html (priests); Al Kamen and Matt Schudel, "Robert H. Bork, 1927–2012: Conservative Judicial Icon Dies at 85," *Miami Herald*, December 20, 2012 (partner, Yale); Mary Ellen Bork, interview by the author, February 5, 2021; Mary Ellen Bork, email to the author, March 7, 2021.

21. *Ollman v. Evans and Novak*, 750 F.2d 970 (1984); Court of Appeals for the District of Columbia Circuit memo from Judge Scalia to the Court, Re: 79-2265—*Bertell Ollman v. Evans & Novak*, August 27, 1984, Folder 2, Box 216, Robert H. Bork Papers, Library of Congress; Robert H. Bork, *The Tempting of America: The Political Seduction of the Law* (New York City: Touchstone, paperback ed., 1990), 167–70. Among the first to learn of Scalia's displeasure with the majority ruling in *Ollman* was its author, Ken Starr, who notified Bork, in a previously unpublished memo, about an "extended conversation late Friday with Nino…. Like you, Nino expressed no particular fondness for multipart tests which judges are quick these days to dream up. I fully share that view. But we have not indulged here in a bout of judicial creativity. The process in this case has been much more of a common-law codification exercise…into how we can go about this process of calling balls and strikes other than on the basis of who happens to be on the panel of the day"; see Court of Appeals for the District of Columbia Circuit memo to Judge Bork from Judge Starr, Re: No. 79-2265, *Bertell Ollman v. Rowland Evans, Robert Novak*, July 17, 1984, Robert H. Bork Papers, Library of Congress.

22. Court of Appeals for the District of Columbia Circuit memo from Judge Ginsburg to Judge Scalia [cc: Judge Bork], Re: No. 79-2265—*Ollman v. Evans*, August 23, 1984, Box 216, Folder 2, Robert H. Bork Papers, Library of Congress; Court of Appeals for the District of Columbia Circuit memo from Judge Scalia to Judge Ginsburg [cc: Judge Bork], Re: *Ollman v. Evans and Novak*, No. 79-2265, Box 216, Folder 2, Robert H. Bork Papers, Library of Congress; Court of Appeals for the District of Columbia Circuit memo from Judge Ginsburg to Judge Bork, Re: *Ollman v. Evans and Novak*—No. 79-2265, November 26, 1984, Box 216, Folder 2, Robert H. Bork Papers, Library of Congress.

23. Court of Appeals for the District of Columbia Circuit memo to All Active Judges from Judge Wilkey, Re: Nos. 82-2445 & 82-2477 *Community for Creative Non-Violence, et al. v. James G. Watt, et al.*, February 1, 1983, Box 141, J. Skelley Wright Papers, Library of Congress; Court of Appeals for the District of Columbia Circuit memo to Chief Judge Robinson [et al.] from Judge Edwards, Re: *CCNV v. Watt*, Nos. 82-2445 & 82-2477, February 2, 1983, Box 141, J. Skelley Wright Papers, Library of Congress.

24. Harry Edwards, quoted in Adler, "Live Wire."

25. Court of Appeals for the District of Columbia Circuit memo to Chief Judge Robinson and Judge Ginsburg from Judge Scalia, Re: Oral Argument, Tuesday, March 26, 1985, Box 77, Folder 7, Ruth Bader Ginsburg Papers, Library of Congress (running order); Court of Appeals for the District of Columbia Circuit conference memo by R.B.G., No. 82-20092, *Gary L. Ryan v. Bureau of Alcohol, Tobacco and Firearms*, April 21, 1983, Box 73, Folder 1, Ruth Bader Ginsburg Papers, Library of Congress (dangerous); Court of Appeals for the District of Columbia Circuit conference memo by R.B.G., No. 82-1910/82-2108, *Assoc. of Data Processing Service Organ,. Inc., et al. v. Bd. of Governors of Federal Reserve System*, April 26, 1983, Box 76, Folder 7, Ruth Bader Ginsburg Papers, Library of Congress (attracted).

26. Court of Appeals for the District of Columbia Circuit conference memo by R.B.G., No. 82-20092, *Gary L. Ryan v. Bureau of Alcohol, Tobacco and Firearms*, April 21,

1983, Ruth Bader Ginsburg Papers, Library of Congress (dangerous); Court of Appeals for the District of Columbia Circuit memo to Judge Scalia from Judge Ginsburg, Re: No 82-20292, *Ryan v. Bureau of Alcohol, Tobacco and Firearms*, July 11, 1983 (*Goodrich*); Court of Appeals for the District of Columbia Circuit memo to Judge Ginsburg and Judge Scalia [cc: Mr. Fisher] from Judge Tamm, Re: No. 83-1981, *James Hayes v. Allstate Ins. Co.*, June 6, 1984, Ruth Bader Ginsburg Papers, Library of Congress (herewith); Court of Appeals for the District of Columbia Circuit memo to Judge Ginsburg and Judge Scalia from Judge Mikva, Re: *Maryland People's Counsel v. FERC*, No. 84-1019, argued January 22, 1985, [dated] January 22, 1985, Box 82, Folder 12, Ruth Bader Ginsburg Papers, Library of Congress (pertinent); Court of Appeals for the District of Columbia Circuit memo to Judge Wald and Judge Scalia from Judge Ginsburg, Re: *Noxell v. Firehouse No. 1*, Nos. 84-5167/5196, April 2, 1985, Box 85, Folder 12, Ruth Bader Ginsburg Papers, Library of Congress (ambiguous); Court of Appeals for the District of Columbia Circuit memo to Judge Mikva and Judge Scalia from Judge Ginsburg, Re: *Maryland People's Counsel v. FERC*, April 26, 1985, Box 82 Folder 12, Ruth Bader Ginsburg Papers, Library of Congress (liberally); Court of Appeals for the District of Columbia Circuit memo to Judge Scalia [cc: Judge Ginsburg] from Judge Wald, Re: *Eastern Carolinas Broadcasting Co. v. FCC*, No. 84-1174, May 6, 1985, Box 79, Folder 8, Ruth Bader Ginsburg Papers, Library of Congress (deleted, fully incorporated); Court of Appeals for the District of Columbia Circuit memo to Judge McGowan [cc: Judge Scalia] from Judge Ginsburg, Re: No. 83-2298, *General Medical Company v. FDA*, July 25, 1985, Box 78, Folder 13, Ruth Bader Ginsburg Papers, Library of Congress (fine with me); Court of Appeals for the District of Columbia Circuit memo to Judge Ginsburg and Judge Scalia from Judge McGowan, Re: No. 83-2298, *General Medical Company v. FDA & Heckler, Secy. of HHS*, July 29, 1985, Box 78, Folder 13, Ruth Bader Ginsburg Papers, Library of Congress (printer); Court of Appeals for the District of Columbia Circuit memo to Judge Scalia [cc: Judge Wald] from Judge Ginsburg, Re: *Noxell Corp. v. Firehouse No. 1 Bar-B-Que Restaurant*, Nos. 84-5167, 84-5196, August 6, 1985, Ruth Bader Ginsburg Papers, Library of Congress (altered p. 7); Court of Appeals for the District of Columbia Circuit memo to Judge Mikva and Judge Scalia from Judge Ginsburg, Re: No. 84-1019, etc., *Maryland People's Counsel v. FERC*, October 31, 1985, Box 82, Folder 11, Ruth Bader Ginsburg Papers, Library of Congress (suggested clarifications).

27. "Honorable Abner J. Mikva," interviews by Stephen J. Pollak, October 28, 1997, Oral History Project, The Historical Society of the District of Columbia Circuit, https://dcchs.org/judges/mikva-abner-j/?portfolioCats=11.

28. Vigilante, "Beyond the Burger Court," (imposing); "Local Programs," *St. Louis Post-Dispatch*, April 7, 1986 (television); Adler, "Live Wire" (leader, Edwards, outshining, uninterested, prepared, bored, knife, delighted, dangerous); Aric Press with Ann McDaniel, "Free-Market Jurist," *Newsweek*, June 10, 1985. A White House staff lawyer described Bork as the "godfather of the original intent school…the academic proselytizer of judicial restraint," and called Bork's pioneering study *The Antitrust Paradox: A Policy at War with Itself* (Basic Books, 1978) "the Bible of the legal side of the Chicago school movement." See White House memo to Peter J.

Wallison from Alan Charles Raul, Subject: Robert H. Bork, [undated; ca. June 1986], Peter J. Wallison Files, Ronald Reagan Presidential Library.

Chapter XIV: Inevitable Hour

Epigraph: "Supreme Court Justice Perspective," C-SPAN, April 9, 2008.

1. *Illinois Commerce Commission v. Interstate Commerce Commission*, 749 F.2d 875.
2. *Gott v. Walters*, 756 F.2d 902 (1985).
3. *Hirschey v. Federal Energy Regulatory Commission* (FERC), 777 F.2d 1 (1985). When colleagues persisted with legislative history, Scalia offered pointers. "It would be a more valid use of legislative history to rephrase the analysis somewhat as follows," he told Ruth Bader Ginsburg. Court of Appeals for the District of Columbia Circuit memo to Judge Ginsburg [cc: Judge Wald] from Judge Scalia, August 5, 1985.
4. Speaking Engagements and Events, 1982–2016, Boxes 74–75, Antonin Scalia Papers, Harvard Law School Library; "UD Law Grads to Hear Judge," *Dayton Daily News*, May 19, 1984; Antonin Scalia, "The Legal Profession," in *Scalia Speaks: Reflections on Law, Faith, and Life Well Lived*, eds. Christopher J. Scalia and Edward Whelan (New York City: Crown Forum, 2017), 89–96 (Dayton); Remarks by Antonin Scalia and Richard A. Epstein, Cato Institute, October 26, 1984; Antonin Scalia, "Economic Affairs as Human Affairs" *Cato Journal* 4, no. 3 (Winter 1985): 703–9; Richard A. Epstein, "Judicial Review: Reckoning on Two Kinds of Error," *Cato Journal* 4, no. 3 (Winter 1985): 711–18; *Scalia v. Epstein: Two Views on Judicial Activism* (Washington, D.C.: Cato Institute, 1985).
5. William Safire, "Office Pool," *New York Times*, December 31, 1984; William Safire, "*Free Speech v. Scalia*," *New York Times*, April 29, 1985; *Safir v. Dole*, 718 F.2d 475 (1983); *Safir v. United States Lines, Inc.*, 616 F. Supp. 613 (1985); *Marshall P. Safir, Plaintiff-appellant, v. United States Lines Inc.* [et al.] 792 F.2d 19 (1986); In re American President Lines, Ltd., 804 F.2d 1307 (1986); "Marshall Safire, 75, Shipping Executive," *New York Times*, March 30, 1995.
6. Joan Biskupic, *American Original: The Life and Constitution of Supreme Court Justice Antonin Scalia* (New York City: Sarah Crichton, paperback ed., 2010), 122–23; "Dr. S. Eugene Scalia," *New York Times*, January 7, 1986; Find a Grave, https://www.findagrave.com/memorial/158139419/catherine-scalia; Margaret Talbot, "Supreme Confidence," *New Yorker*, March 28, 2005 (Michigan); Thomas Gray, "Elegy Written in a Country Churchyard," *The English Poems* (Hebden Bridge, England: Shearsman Books, paperback ed., 2014); David R. Palombi, "Trenton Native Likely Candidate for Spot on U.S. Supreme Court," *Trenton Times*, November 4, 1985 (gifted); "Justice Antonin Scalia," interview by Judith R. Hope, December 5, 1992, Oral History Project, The Historical Society of the District of Columbia Circuit, https://dcchs.org/wp-content/uploads/2019/03/Scalia-Complete-Oral-History-1.pdf.
7. "UT Notes," *Austin American-Statesman*, January 18, 1986; *In re Reporters Committee for Freedom of Press*, 773 F.2d 1325 (1985).
8. *Synar v. United States*, 626 F. Supp. 1374 (D.D.C. 1986); Ralph A. Rossum, *Antonin Scalia's Jurisprudence: Text and Tradition* (Lawrence, Kansas: University Press of Kansas, paperback ed., 2016), 17 (fingerprints); "Statement on Signing the Bill

Increasing the Public Debt Limit and Enacting the Balanced Budget and Emergency Deficit Control Act of 1985," December 12, 1985, The American Presidency Project, U.C. Santa Barbara; Lyle Denniston [*Baltimore Sun* Service], "Judge Spars with Gramm-Rudman Foes," *Sacramento Bee*, January 11, 1986 (dominated, jousted, sharpest); Tony Mauro [Gannett News Service], "Congressmen Challenge Budget Law," *Pensacola News Journal*, January 11, 1986 (hard, unimpressed); Associated Press, "District Court Case: Gramm-Rudman Act Blasted," *Daily News* [Lebanon, Pennsylvania], January 11, 1986 (Nixon); Robert Pear, "Court Hears Impassioned Debate over Legality of New Budget Law," *New York Times*, January 11, 1986; *Bowsher v. Synar*, 478 US 714 (1986).

9. Donald T. Regan, *For the Record: From Wall Street to Washington* (New York City: St. Martin's Press, paperback ed., 1989), 368–71; White House memo to the File by Peter J. Wallison, August 29, 1986, Supreme Court—Rehnquist/Scalia, General Selection Scenario 1–3, Peter J. Wallison Files, Ronald Reagan Presidential Library.

10. White House memo for Donald T. Regan from Peter J. Wallison, Subject: Philosophical Directions of the Supreme Court Justices, May 30, 1986, Supreme Court—Rehnquist/Scalia Notebook II Candidates 1–3, Peter J. Wallison Files, Ronald Reagan Presidential Library (seventy-five); White House memo to the File by Peter J. Wallison, August 29, 1986, Supreme Court—Rehnquist/Scalia, General Selection Scenario 1–3, Peter J. Wallison Files, Ronald Reagan Presidential Library (several, certain, minimize, leading, tired); White House document entitled "POTENTIAL LIST," [undated; ca. May 1986], attached to Wallison memo, Peter J. Wallison Files, Ronald Reagan Presidential Library (eighteen); Department of Justice memo from Steve A. Matthews to Special Project Committee, Subject: Judge Anthony M. Kennedy, May 23, 1986, Supreme Court—Rehnquist/Scalia Notebook I Candidates, Peter J. Wallison Files, Ronald Reagan Presidential Library; Edwin Meese III, interview by the author, February 2, 2021.

11. White House memo to Peter J. Wallison from Alan Charles Raul, Subject: Summary Information Regarding Certain Judges, June 5, 1986, Peter J. Wallison Files, Supreme Court—Rehnquist/Scalia Notebook II—Candidates, Ronald Reagan Presidential Library; White House memo to Peter J. Wallison from Alan Charles Raul, Subject: Robert H. Bork, [undated; ca. June 1986], Peter J. Wallison Files, Ronald Reagan Presidential Library. The decision upholding the right of an anti-Reagan protester to purchase subway advertising space, authored by Bork and joined by Scalia, was *Lebron v. Washington Metropolitan Area Transit Authority*, 749 F.2d 893 (1983). See also April 10, 1986, *States News Service* quoted in [DOJ] memo, Robert H. Bork: Biographical Information, Peter Wallison Files, Supreme Court/Rehnquist/Scalia Notebook I—Candidates, Ronald Reagan Presidential Library (radical).

12. Lee Liberman, interview by the author, Washington, D.C., June 29, 2017; Unsigned, undated, unaddressed Department of Justice memo [ca. June 1986], Supreme Court—Rehnquist/Scalia Notebook I—Candidates, Peter J. Wallison Files, Ronald Reagan Presidential Library. Liberman did not compare Bork and Scalia, and she downplayed their dispute in *Ollman*, saying "there is less to this disagreement than meets the eye."

13. Ronald Reagan, *The Reagan Diaries*, ed. Douglas Brinkley (New York City: Harper, 2007), 419; John Bolton, interview by the author, Washington, D.C., May 2, 2017; Regan, *For the Record*; Meese, interview by the author, February 2, 2021; Alan C.

Raul, interview by the author, March 28, 2022; Edwin Meese, *With Reagan: The Inside Story* (Washington, D.C.: Regnery, 1992), 318; Peter J. Wallison, *Ronald Reagan: The Power of Conviction and the Success of His Presidency* (New York City: Basic Books, paperback ed., 2004), 151–54; Presidential schedules for May–June 1986, Ronald Reagan Presidential Library; White House memo for the President from Peter J. Wallison, Subject: Questions for Prospective Supreme Court Nominees, June 11, 1986, Ronald Reagan Presidential Library ("Scalia is also a candidate for Chief Justice"); Interview with Peter Wallison, Charlottesville, Virginia, October 28–29, 2003, Ronald Reagan Oral History Project, Miller Center, UVA. White House Interview Program, Interview with Peter Wallison, Martha Joynt Kumar, Washington, D.C., January 27, 2000. Wallison's 1986 memo to the file listed June 12, a Thursday, as a Tuesday, and misidentified the date of the Reagan-Scalia meeting of June 16 as May 16. Judge Silberman told me, "Scalia got chosen first because he was younger, he was more charming, and Reagan liked him…. Reagan liked Scalia much better than Bork." A "senior Reagan adviser" was quoted as saying Reagan found Scalia "warm and personable"; See Gerald M. Boyd, "Meeting 3 Weeks Ago Set Off Search, a Well-Kept Secret," *New York Times*, June 18, 1986. Raul told me that when he ran into Justice Scalia near the end of his life and mentioned how close Reagan had come to nominating him as chief, a stunned Scalia said he had never heard that before.

Chapter XV: The Culmination
Epigraph: "America and the Courts," C-SPAN, April 1, 1986.

1. Wayne King and Warren Weaver, Jr., "Whom to Appoint?" *New York Times*, May 21, 1986 (ballots); Philip Shenon, "Shift Gives Reagan D.C. Circuit Majority," *New York Times*, May 24, 1986; Philip Shenon, "Reagan Is as Intent as Ever on Making Over the Courts," *New York Times*, June 1, 1986, "Injudicious Judicial Choice," *Pittsburgh Post-Gazette*, June 3, 1986; *Boston Globe* Service, "Opportunity Waning for Reagan to Appoint Court Justices," *News Tribune* [Tacoma, Washington], June 12, 1986.

2. James L. Swanson, interview by the author, May 17, 2022; James L. Swanson, email to the author, May 16, 2022; James L. Swanson, UCLA letter to Antonin Scalia, August 23, 1985; Antonin Scalia, Court of Appeals for the District of Columbia Circuit letter to James L. Swanson, September 18, 1985; Court of Appeals for the District of Columbia Circuit itinerary of Judge Antonin Scalia, November 15–17, 1986 [*sic*, for 1985], all in Box 76, Folder 11, ASP/HLSL; "Judge Scalia Visits UCLAW; Lectures on Legislative Intent," *The Docket*, February 21, 1986.

3. Joan Biskupic, *American Original: The Life and Constitution of Supreme Court Justice Antonin Scalia* (New York City: Sarah Crichton, paperback ed., 2010), 108 (Maureen, floating). Biskupic reported erroneously that Meese telephoned Scalia to arrange the meeting with the president. Program for Attorney General's Conference on Economic Liberties, Washington, D.C., June 14, 1986, in Folders 10 and 11, Box 590, Edwin Meese Papers, Hoover Institution Archives; Gerald M. Boyd, "Meeting 3 Weeks Ago Set Off Search, a Well-Kept Secret," *New York Times*, June 18, 1986 (twenty-one).

4. Antonin Scalia, Address before the Attorney General's Conference on Economic Liberties in Washington, D.C., June 14, 1986, Box 76, Folder 32, Antonin Scalia Papers, Harvard School of Law Library.

5.   Richard A. Epstein, "Antonin Scalia: A Most Memorable Friend," February 15, 2016, https://www.hoover.org/research/antonin-scalia-most-memorable-friend; Richard Epstein, interview by the author, October 25, 2021; Richard Epstein, email to the author, September 4, 2021.

6.   White House memo to the File by Peter J. Wallison, August 29, 1986, Supreme Court—Rehnquist/Scalia, General Selection Scenario 1–3, Peter J. Wallison Files, Ronald Reagan Presidential Library (came, choice); Wallison 2003 oral history (ceremony, accepted, delighted). One contemporary account depicted Reagan and Scalia "trading a few anecdotes…about old judges." Evan Thomas, "Reagan's Mr. Right," *Time*, June 30, 1986. Reagan's diary noted: "A meeting with Judge Scalia—he will be my appointee to Sup. Ct. as Rehnquist moves up to chief. We'll announce the whole pckg. Tomorrow"; Reagan, *The Reagan Diaries*, 419.

7.   Eugene Scalia, interview by the author, Washington, D.C., September 8, 2017 (circus); Patrick Schiltz, interview by the author, June 29, 2017.

8.   Laurence Silberman, interview by the author, May 22, 2017; Eugene Scalia, interview by the author, September 8, 2017; confidential source, interview by the author (Harry).

9.   Peter J. Wallison, *Ronald Reagan: The Power of Conviction and the Success of His Presidency* (New York City: Basic Books, paperback ed., 2004), 153–54 (11:45, lit up); Biskupic, *American Original*, 106–9 (urged, pumped).

10. Biskupic, *American Original*, 109 (copies); Presidential schedules for May–June 1986, Ronald Reagan Presidential Library; Remarks on the Resignation of Supreme Court Chief Justice Warren E. Burger, The American Presidency Project, U.C. Santa Barbara; Partial video of Burger-Rehnquist-Scalia event, Master Tape #551, Ronald Reagan Presidential Library (See "Press Availability. President Reagan's Remarks Regarding the Retirement of Chief Justice Warren Burger and Nomination of Justice William Rehnquist for Chief Justice and Antonin Scalia as Associate Justice. Justice Burger's Remarks. Press Room," June 17, 1986, Reagan Presidential Library, https://www.reaganlibrary.gov/archives/video/press-availability-president-reagans-remarks-regarding-retirement-chief-justice); "Remarks by President Ronald Reagan during Announcement of Resignation of Chief Justice Warren Burger" (complete audio), National Archives and Records Administration, https://catalog.archives.gov/id/161351542.

11. Eugene Scalia, interview by the author, September 8, 2017. Scalia first disclosed Rehnquist's comment in a Federalist Society course that Scalia co-taught annually with Georgetown professor John Baker. At a panel on Scalia's legacy, held at the University Club in April 2016, Professor Baker disclosed—without naming Rehnquist—that one of Scalia's Republican colleagues on the Supreme Court had told him: "Nino, don't worry so much about the reasoning, just get the right result." "Friends of Nino" panel, transcribed by the author, Washington, D.C., April 29, 2016, https://jameswilsoninstitute.org/events/show/friends-of-nino-panel. Anthony Ferate, an Oklahoma lawyer who attended the Scalia-Baker course in August 2013, in Park City, Utah, and again in August 2015, in Vail, Colorado, and who kept the materials Scalia distributed as well as his own notes, confirmed to me that Scalia related this anecdote at the 2015 session and identified Rehnquist as the justice who had said this to him. "Scalia: Care abt. reasoning/Rehnquist only looked @ outcome,"

Ferate's notes recorded. Anthony Ferate, interview by the author, October 16, 2021; Anthony Ferate, emails to the author (with attached materials and notes), October 18, 2021. Baker stated at the "Friends of Nino" panel event that Rehnquist had made this remark to Scalia shortly after the latter joined the Supreme Court; however, Ferate was firm in his recollection that Scalia had stated explicitly that he was still on the D.C. Circuit when Rehnquist made the remark. Asked about this discrepancy, Baker deferred to Ferate's recollection.

Chapter XVI: The Nominee

Epigraph: George F. Will, "The Court: These Two Will Have Impact," *Washington Post*, June 19, 1986.

1. Aric Press, "Reagan Justice," *Newsweek*, June 30, 1986; Stephen Wermiel, "Changes on High Court Are Likely to Increase Conservatives' Clout," *Wall Street Journal*, June 18, 1986 (significant).

2. Irvin Molotsky, "Man in the News: Judge with Tenacity and Charm," *New York Times*, June 18, 1986; Robert L. Jackson and Ronald J. Ostrow, "He Has Own Style of Conservatism: Scalia's Independent Past Suggests Future Surprises," *Los Angeles Times*, July 6, 1986; Edward Walsh, "Confirmation of Justices Predicted by End of Year," *Washington Post*, June 18, 1986; Jon Margolis, "Chief Justice Burger Resigns," *Chicago Tribune*, June 19, 1986; Richard Stengel, "Warm Spirits, Cold Logic," *Time*, July 20, 1986; Robert P. Hey, "Judge Scalia Seen as Major Force on Supreme Court," *Christian Science Monitor*, June 19, 1986; Ruth Marcus, "Judge a Favorite with Conservative Lawyers, Activists," *Washington Post*, June 18, 1986; Evan Thomas, "Reagan's Mr. Right: Rehnquist Is Picked for the Court's Top Job," *Time*, June 30, 1986; Paul Duggan, "Columnist Jimmy Breslin, Bard of the New York Streets, Dies at 88," *Washington Post*, March 19, 2017, https://www.washingtonpost.com/national/columnist-jimmy-breslin-bard-of-the-new-york-streets-dies-at-88/2017/03/19/51540cbe-0cae-11e7-9d5a-a83e627dc120_story.html; Brian McDonald, "Jimmy Breslin: The Tabloid Bard," *Politico*, December 28, 2017, https://www.politico.com/magazine/story/2017/12/28/jimmy-breslin-obituary-216196/; Jimmy Breslin, "This Queens Neighborhood Is Supreme," *New York Daily News*, June 20, 1986; "The Next Supreme Court," *Wall Street Journal*, June 18, 1986; "Burger, Rehnquist and Scalia," *Baltimore Sun*, June 18, 1986.

3. Democratic Congressman Don Edwards of California, quoted in Karen Tumulty and Bob Secter, "Senate Republicans Praise Choices," *Los Angeles Times*, June 18, 1986 (hard-liner, league); Democratic Congressman Pat Schroeder of Colorado, quoted in Tom Diaz, "Rehnquist Chosen to Lead Court," *Washington Times*, June 18, 1986 (frightening); Walsh, "Confirmation of Justices Predicted" (open question); Hey, "Judge Scalia Seen as Major Force" (delightful); Marcus, "Judge a Favorite" (uproarious, dialogue); Steven V. Roberts, "Selection Praised by G.O.P. Senators," *New York Times*, June 18, 1986 (mute); Ted Gest, "Reagan's Court: Two Steps to the Right," *U.S. News & World Report*, June 30, 1986 (Leahy, sail).

4. American Bar Association letter to Strom Thurmond from Robert B. Fiske, Jr., August 5, 1986; Statement of Senator James T. Broyhill, Senate Judiciary Committee Transcript, August 5, 1986 (exhaustive).

5.   Gest, "Reagan's Court" (Dershowitz); Ed Rogers, "Bell Opposes Opening of
      Rehnquist's Files," *Washington Times*, August 4, 1986 (Smeal); Douglas Frantz,
      "Scalia Embodies President's Hope for Court's Future," *Chicago Tribune*, August
      3, 1986 (Tribe, Neas); Al Kamen, "Burger Quits, Rehnquist Chosen to Lead Court,"
      Washington Post, June 18, 1986 (distinguished, affability); Stuart Taylor, Jr.,
      "Liberals Portray Scalia as Threat But Bar Group Sees Him as Open," *New York
      Times*, August 7, 1986.
6.   Pellegrino D'Acierno, ed., *The Italian American Heritage: A Companion to
      Literature and Arts* (Oxfordshire, England: Routledge, 1998); Charles Porcelli, letter
      to Ronald Reagan, June 19, 1986, Supreme Court nominations, Rehnquist/Scalia
      responses, Peter J. Wallison Files, Ronald Reagan Presidential Library; Bruno
      Giuffrida, letter to Ronald Reagan, June 19, 1986, Supreme Court nominations,
      Rehnquist/Scalia responses, Peter J. Wallison Files, Ronald Reagan Presidential
      Library; Joseph L. Andreis, letter to Ronald Reagan, June 26, 1986, Supreme Court
      nominations, Rehnquist/Scalia responses, Peter J. Wallison Files, Ronald Reagan
      Presidential Library; Frank Montemuro, letter to Reagan, June 24, 1986; Sarubbi
      letter to Reagan, June 30, 1986, Supreme Court nominations, Rehnquist/Scalia
      responses, Peter J. Wallison Files, Ronald Reagan Presidential Library.
7.   White House memo for Mari Maseng from Charlotte Demoss, Subject: Status of
      Scalia Photo Request, June 26, 1986, Box OA 17968, Carl A. Anderson Files, Ronald
      Reagan Presidential Library; White House memo for the president from Mari Maseng,
      Subject: Photo-Op with Antonin Scalia, July 3, 1986, Box OA 17968, Carl A.
      Anderson Files, Ronald Reagan Presidential Library; White House memo for Maseng
      from LK [Linas Kojelis], undated [ca. July 3, 1986], Subject: Suggestions for Italian
      American Outreach, Box OA 17968, Carl A. Anderson Files, Ronald Reagan
      Presidential Library.
8.   Joseph Volz, "Scalia Beat Bork for Post," *New York Daily News*, June 19, 1986;
      Ronald J. Ostrow and Philip Hager, "Court Nominees Face Ideology Issue," *Los
      Angeles Times*, June 19, 1986; Ronald J. Ostrow, "Style and Personality Called
      Contagious: Scalia Described as Persuasive, Affable," *Los Angeles Times*, June 18,
      1986 (robust, smokes); Marcus, "Judge a Favorite" (vigor); James Reston, "Hear Ye
      in the Court," *New York Times*, June 18, 1986; Eugene Scalia, interview by the
      author, Washington, D.C., September 8, 2017; Laurence Silberman, interview by the
      author, Washington, D.C., May 22, 2017. Bork's annotated pocket diaries recorded
      the Borks' dining at the Scalias' home periodically in these years. Mary Ellen said
      Bob was not upset when Reagan chose Scalia. "He was glad that Nino was there
      because of his ability," she told me. "Their record on the Court of Appeals was almost
      identical." Bruce Allen Murphy also attributed Scalia's nomination to ethnicity,
      calling him "a *de facto* affirmative action choice." Bruce Allen Murphy, *Scalia: A
      Court of One* (New York City: Simon & Schuster, paperback ed., 2015), 124.
9.   White House memo to Judge Antonin Scalia from William L. Ball III, Subject:
      Confirmation Process, June 20, 1986, OA 18180—Department of Justice/Scalia,
      Peter J. Wallison Files, Ronald Reagan Presidential Library; White House memo
      from Pam Turner, Nancy Kennedy, and Fred McClure to William L. Ball, Subject:
      Subjects for Discussion with Judge Scalia, June 19, 1986, OA 18180—Department
      of Justice/Scalia, Peter J. Wallison Files, Ronald Reagan Presidential Library; White

House letter from Peter J. Wallison to Antonin Scalia, June 23, 1986, enclosing DOJ memo from Theodore B. Olson to Robert A. McConnell, Subject: Appropriate Limitations on Responses by Nominees to the Supreme Court in the Course of Confirmation Hearings, March 1, 1982, OA 14287, Department of Justice/Scalia, Peter J. Wallison Files, Ronald Reagan Presidential Library; Unsigned [Turner, Kennedy, and McClure], unaddressed [Ball] White House memos, Subject: Meetings for Judge Scalia, July [*sic*, for June] 15 and June 25, 1986, Supreme Court—Scalia, OA 14287, Peter J. Wallison Files, Ronald Reagan Presidential Library; Fred McClure, interview by the author, May 5, 2002.

10. Silberman, interview by the author, May 22, 2017; McClure, interview by the author, May 5, 2022 (admit); Patrick Schiltz, interview by the author, June 28, 2017.

11. FBI airtel from Director FBI (77-131275) to All FBI Field Offices, June 18, 1986, Scalia FBI Files (considering); FBI Message Form from Director FBI to FBI Field Offices in Washington, D.C., [et al.], June 20, 1986, Scalia FBI Files (Form 86, waiver, interview, interacts); Court of Appeals letter to [redacted], Office of the Deputy Attorney General, from Antonin Scalia, June 20, 1986, Scalia FBI Files (completed forms); FBI airtel from Special Agent in Charge, San Juan to Director, FBI, June 26, 1986 (data banks), Scalia FBI Files; FBI report of [redacted], New York Field Office to [redacted; FBI headquarters], June 27, 1986, Scalia FBI Files (reproach). Scalia's financial disclosure form listed equal assets and liabilities: $612,596 ($1.65 million today). From his parents' estate Nino had inherited under $300,000, against which he had borrowed nearly $32,000.

12. Nominations of William H. Rehnquist, of Arizona, and Lewis F. Powell, Jr., of Virginia, to Be Associate Justices of the Supreme Court of the United States: Hearings before the Committee on the Judiciary, United States Senate…November 3, 4, 8, 9, and 10, 1971…. (Washington, D.C.: U.S. Government Printing Office, 1971), https://www.govinfo.gov/content/pkg/GPO-CHRG-REHNQUIST-POWELL/pdf/GPO-CHRG-REHNQUIST-POWELL.pdf; Nomination of Justice William Hubbs Rehnquist: Hearings before the Committee on the Judiciary, United States Senate…July 29, 30, 31, and August 1, 1986…. (Washington, D.C.: U.S. Government Printing Office, 1987), https://www.govinfo.gov/content/pkg/GPO-CHRG-REHNQUIST/pdf/GPO-CHRG-REHNQUIST.pdf; Stuart Taylor, Jr., "Opposition to Rehnquist Nomination Hardens as 2 New Witnesses Emerge," *New York Times*, July 27, 1986; Stuart Taylor, Jr., "Senate Opens Rehnquist Hearing, and the Battle Lines Are Drawn," *New York Times*, July 30, 1986; Stuart Taylor, Jr., "Rehnquist Says He Didn't Deter Voters in 60's," *New York Times*, July 31, 1986; Stuart Taylor, Jr., "President Asserts He Will Withhold Rehnquist Memos," *New York Times*, August 1, 1986; Linda Greenhouse, "Gentle or Prosecutorial Persistence: Questioners Take on Range of Roles," *New York Times*, August 1, 1986 (extremists); Stuart Taylor, Jr., "4 Rebut Testimony of Rehnquist on Challenging of Voters in 60's," *New York Times*, August 2, 1986; Linda Greenhouse, "Rehnquist Memos from Nixon Years Studied by Panel," *New York Times*, August 7, 1986.

Chapter XVII: Justice Scalia

Epigraph: Antonin Scalia, *Scalia Speaks: Reflections on Law, Faith, and Life Well Lived*, eds. Christopher J. Scalia and Edward Whelan (New York City: Crown Forum, 2017), 21.

1. Nomination of Judge Antonin Scalia: Hearings before the Committee on the Judiciary, United States Senate...August 5 and 6, 1986.... (Washington, D.C.: U.S. Printing Office, 1987), https://www.govinfo.gov/content/pkg/GPO-CHRG -SCALIA/pdf/GPO-CHRG-SCALIA.pdf; "McConnell, Mitch, 1942, Person Authority Record," National Archives and Records Administration, https://catalog .archives.gov/id/177146503.

2. Biskupic opens *American Original* with a scene from the Federalist Society gala at the Mayflower Hotel, in 2008, when Justice Scalia solicited the final question from the audience with an exhortation to "make it easy...like Strom Thurmond's first question to me when I was up for my confirmation." As can be seen in the video of the justice's remarks posted online, Scalia told the audience about the 1986 hearing: "The first question he asks me, he says, [mimics Thurmond's drawl], 'Now, Judge *Skull-ee-yuh*, what do *yeww* think of judicial activism?'" The crowd roared. Biskupic explained to her readers: "Thurmond had opened with a question that played right into Scalia's view that judges were wrongly going beyond the letter of the law to solve society's larger problems." Scalia drew more laughter when he reared back like a baseball batter and said, all smiles: "Lemme have that one, Senator!...I'm ready for that pitch!" In leading with this scene, Biskupic framed the justice as humorous, larger than life, reveling in partisanship. In fact, Thurmond's opening question was not about judicial activism; it focused on the differing roles of appellate judges and Supreme Court justices. Biskupic apparently never reviewed the transcript, which showed the justice's recollection was mistaken. None of the twelve questions Thurmond posed at the 1986 hearing—nor any of the five he posed during Scalia's 1982 hearing, where Thurmond was the sole questioner—related to judicial activism. At the 1986 hearing, only two senators used the term: McConnell, near the end of opening statements, and Charles Mathias, in the final round of questioning. While the biographer's error may have been a case where animus prevailed over due diligence, Scalia's faulty memory is more difficult to explain. Rather than conclude that he invented the remark from Thurmond, which would have been out of character and of no benefit to himself, we are left to infer that Scalia must have conflated the hearing with one of his private talks with the chairman. See Joan Biskupic, *American Original: The Life and Constitution of Supreme Court Justice Antonin Scalia* (New York City: Sarah Crichton, paperback ed., 2010), 3; "Role of the Judiciary," C-SPAN, November 22, 2008 (gala); Confirmation of Federal Judges: Hearings before the Committee on the Judiciary United States Senate...May 26, 27; June 16, 23; July 14, 21; August 4, 11, 18; September 15, 22, 29; December 1, 6, and 8, 1982.... (Washington, D.C.: U.S. Government Printing Office, 1983), 81–93, https://tinyurl.com/3m9xesmb.

3. Nomination of Judge Antonin Scalia: Hearings before the Committee on the Judiciary United States Senate...August 5 and 6, 1986.... (Washington, D.C.: U.S. Government Printing Office, 1987).

4. "Radio Address to the Nation on the United States Supreme Court Nominations," August 9, 1986, The American Presidency Project, U.C. Santa Barbara; Al Kamen, "For Rehnquist, Aftermath of Confirmation Is Routine," *Washington Post*, September 19, 1986 (mob).

5. White House memo for the President from Peter J. Wallison, Subject: Executive Privilege, August 6, 1986, White House Office of Records Management Subject Files, Ronald Reagan Presidential Library. Wallison's reference to Watergate was misplaced; Rehnquist left DOJ for the Supreme Court five months before the ill-fated break-in and surveillance operation began. Biskupic and Murphy made no mention of the clash over executive privilege in the Scalia nomination.

6. Aaron Epstein, "Scalia Questioned on Rights, Abortion as Hearings Open," *Philadelphia Inquirer*, August 6, 1986 (breezing); Theo Stamos, "Scalia Declines to Say How He'd Vote on Abortion," *Washington Times*, August 6, 1986 (hostile); Stuart Taylor, Jr., "Scalia Returns Soft Answers to Senators," *New York Times*, August 6, 1986; Douglas Frantz, "Antonin Scalia Meshes Strong Intellect, Charm," *Post-Star* [Glens Falls, New York], August 6, 1986; Al Kamen and Howard Kurtz, "First Day of Questioning Leaves Scalia Unscathed," *Washington Post*, August 6, 1986 (sparring, rancorous, direct); Senate Judiciary Committee Transcript, August 5, 1986 (Heflin); Linda Greenhouse, "Advice, or Consent? The Court, the Congress and the White House," *New York Times*, August 10, 1986; Donald Kaul, "Justice Italian Style," *Cedar Rapids Gazette*, August 11, 1986 (proud); Stephen Wermiel, "Rehnquist Nomination as Chief Justice to Go to Senate; Panel Also Clears Scalia," *Wall Street Journal*, August 15, 1986 (much praise); Biskupic, *American Original*, 117.

7. Senate Judiciary Committee Transcript; Doug Struck, "NOW, 20 Years Old, Is Hoping to Grow," Baltimore Sun, June 16, 1986 (135,000).

8. Senate Judiciary Committee Transcript (DeConcini/confirm); Linda Greenhouse, "Senate Unit Backs Rehnquist, 13–5," *New York Times*, August 15, 1986 (DeConcini/evasive, Kennedy, parameters, unanimously); Howard Kurtz, "Senate Panel Approves Rehnquist, 13 to 5," *Washington Post*, August 15, 1986 (significantly, mandate, extremism); Miranda S. Spivack, "Rehnquist, Scalia Appear Headed for Easy Confirmation by Senate," *Hartford Courant*, September 12, 1986 (Dole).

9. Linda Greenhouse, "Senate, 65 to 33, Votes to Confirm Rehnquist as 16th Justice," *New York Times*, September 18, 1986 (five days); Al Kamen, "Rehnquist Confirmed in 65–33 Vote," *Washington Post*, September 18, 1986 (seven minutes). For the official certificate of Scalia's confirmation, dated September 17 and signed by Senate secretary Jo-Anne Coe, see Box Oversize, Folder 1, Antonin Scalia Papers, Harvard Law School Library.

10. Gary Lawson, "On Getting It Right: Remembering Justice Antonin Scalia," *Boston University Law Review*, March 2016 (plaque); *Floyd D. Parker v. U.S.*, 801 F.2d 1382 (1986); Lee M. Thomas, Administrator, *United States Environmental Protection Agency, and Alabama Power Company, et al. v. State of New York, et al.*, 802 F.2d 1443 (1986).

11. Postcard to Hon. Antonin Scalia from Harry [Edwards], [undated; postmarked June 17, 1986], Antonin Scalia Papers, Harvard Law School Library.

12. Court of Appeals for the District of Columbia Circuit memo to Chief Judge Wald from Judge Ginsburg, Re: *Associated Gas Distributors v. FERC*, No. 84-1454, September 22, 1986, Box 89, Folder 8, Ruth Bader Ginsburg Papers, Library of Congress (region); Court of Appeals for the District of Columbia Circuit memo to Mr. [George A.] Fisher [cc: Judges Ginsburg, Scalia, Starr] from Judge Wald, Reassignment of Judge Scalia's Cases, September 10, 1986, Box 89, Folder 8, Ruth Bader Ginsburg Papers, Library of Congress; Court of Appeals for the District of Columbia Circuit memo to Judge Ruth Bader Ginsburg from Judge Wald, Re: *Associated Gas Distributors v. FERC*, No. 84-1454, September 23, 1986, Box 89, Folder 8, Ruth Bader Ginsburg Papers, Library of Congress (FERC, left-behinds); Court of Appeals for the District of Columbia Circuit handwritten note to Susan Williams from RBG, January 30, 1987, Box 89, Folder 8, Ruth Bader Ginsburg Papers, Library of Congress (inheritance).

13. Court of Appeals for the District of Columbia Circuit conference memo by R.B.G., No. 82-1910/82-2108—*Assoc. of Data Processing Service Organ., Inc., et al. v. Bd. Of Governors of Federal Reserve System*, April 26, 1983, Box 76, Folder 7 (trade), Ruth Bader Ginsburg Papers, Library of Congress; Court of Appeals for the District of Columbia Circuit memo to Judge Scalia from Judge Ginsburg, Re: No. 82-2092, *Ryan v. Bureau of Alcohol, Tobacco and Firearms*, July 11, 1983, Box 73, Folder 1, Ruth Bader Ginsburg Papers, Library of Congress (headache); Ginsburg annotation on Court of Appeals for the District of Columbia Circuit memo to Judge Ginsburg [cc: Judge Mikva] from Judge Scalia, Re: No. 84-1019—*Maryland People's Counsel v. FERC*, October 2, 1985, Box 82, Folder 12, Ruth Bader Ginsburg Papers, Library of Congress (labor); Court of Appeals for the District of Columbia Circuit memo to Judge McGowan [cc: Judge Scalia] from Judge Ginsburg, Re: No. 83-2298—*General Medical Company v. FDA & Heckler, Secy. Of HHS*, July 3, 1985, Box 78, Folder 13, Ruth Bader Ginsburg Papers, Library of Congress (grappling).

14. Ruth Bader Ginsburg annotation on Court of Appeals for the District of Columbia Circuit memo to Judge Scalia from Judge Ginsburg, Re: *Ass'n of Data Processing, etc. v. Board of Governors*—Nos. 82-1910 & 82-2108, September 4, 1984, Box 76, Folder 7, Ruth Bader Ginsburg Papers, Library of Congress (Gide); Ruth Bader Ginsburg annotation on Court of Appeals for the District of Columbia Circuit memo to Chief Judge Robinson and Judge Ginsburg from Judge Scalia, Re Nos. 83-1686, 83-1871—Affiliated Communications Corp. v. FCC & USA, April 9, 1985, Box 77, Folder 7, Ruth Bader Ginsburg Papers, Library of Congress (just right); Ginsburg annotation on Court of Appeals for the District of Columbia Circuit memo to Judge Ginsburg and Judge McGowan from Judge Scalia, Re: No. 84-5377—*USA v. George Vernon Hansen*, August 12, 1985, Box 82, Folder 10, Ruth Bader Ginsburg Papers, Library of Congress (beautifully done); Court of Appeals for the District of Columbia Circuit memo to Judge Scalia from Judge Ginsburg, July 11, 1983 (appreciate, PMW); Court of Appeals for the District of Columbia Circuit memo to Judge Mikva and Judge Scalia from Judge Ginsburg, Re: *Maryland People's Counsel v. FERC*, No. 84-1090, April 26, 1985, Box 82, Folder 12, Ruth Bader Ginsburg Papers, Library of Congress (liberally); Court of Appeals for the District of Columbia Circuit memo to Judge Wald and Judge Scalia from Judge Ginsburg, Re: *Noxell v. Firehouse No. 1*, Nos. 84-5167/5196, April 2, 1985, Box 84, Folder 4, Ruth Bader Ginsburg Papers,

Library of Congress (recommended); Court of Appeals for the District of Columbia Circuit memo to Judge Scalia [cc: Judge Wald] from Judge Ginsburg, Re: *Noxell Corp. v. Firehouse No. 1 Bar-B-Que Restaurant*, No. 84-5167, August 6, 1985, Box 84, Folder 4, Ruth Bader Ginsburg Papers, Library of Congress (altered); Court of Appeals for the District of Columbia Circuit Conference Memo by R.B.G., No. 84-1074—*Aero Service Division, Western Geophysical Co. of America v. FAA*, March 26, 1985, Box 79, Folder 3 Ruth Bader Ginsburg Papers, Library of Congress (indulge).

15. Scalia annotation on Court of Appeals for the District of Columbia Circuit memo to Judge Tamm and Judge Scalia from Judge Ginsburg, Re: No. 84-1091—*Guard v. Nuclear Regulatory Commission*, January 24, 1985, Box 79, Folder 5, Ruth Bader Ginsburg Papers, Library of Congress (superb); Scalia annotation on Court of Appeals for the District of Columbia Circuit memo to Judge Scalia [cc: Judge Wald] from Judge Ginsburg, Re: *Noxell Corp. v. Firehouse No. 1 Bar-B-Que Restaurant*, No. 84-5167, August 6, 1985, Box 84, Folder 4, Ruth Bader Ginsburg Papers, Library of Congress (excellent); Scalia annotation on Court of Appeals for the District of Columbia Circuit memo to Judge Scalia [cc: Judge Tamm] from Judge Ginsburg, Re: No. 84-5096, *Weil v. Markowitz*, March 11, 1985, Box 80, Folder 3, Ruth Bader Ginsburg Papers, Library of Congress (unanimous); Court of Appeals for the District of Columbia Circuit memo to Judge Ginsburg [cc: Judge Mikva] from Judge Scalia, Re: No. 84-5167—*Noxell Corp. v. Firehouse No. 1 Bar-B-Que Restaurant*, June 17, 1985, Box 84, Folder 4, Ruth Bader Ginsburg Papers, Library of Congress (sloth); Court of Appeals for the District of Columbia Circuit memo to Judge Wald and Judge Ginsburg from Judge Scalia, Re: *Eastern Carolina Broadcasting Co. v. FCC*, No. 84-1174, May 3, 1985, Box 79, Folder 8, Ruth Bader Ginsburg Papers, Library of Congress (insight); Ginsburg annotation on Court of Appeals for the District of Columbia Circuit memo to Judge Ginsburg [cc: Judge Mikva] from Judge Scalia, Re: No. 84-1019—*Maryland People's Counsel v. FERC*, October 2, 1985, Box 82, Folder 12, Ruth Bader Ginsburg Papers, Library of Congress (blind, intervenors); Court of Appeals for the District of Columbia Circuit memo to Judge McGowan [cc: Judge Ginsburg] from Judge Scalia, Re: No. 83-2298—*General Medical Company v. FDA & Heckler, Secy. of HHS*, July 19, 1985, Box 78, Folder 13, Ruth Bader Ginsburg Papers, Library of Congress (connoisseur); Court of Appeals for the District of Columbia Circuit memo to Judge Mikva and Judge Ginsburg from Judge Scalia, Re: No. 84-1090—*Maryland People's Counsel v. FERC*, June 20, 1985, Box 82, Folder 11, Ruth Bader Ginsburg Papers, Library of Congress (proxy); Handwritten Court of Appeals for the District of Columbia Circuit note to Justice Scalia from Judge Ginsburg, Re: *Associated Gas*, January 30, 1987, Box 89, Folder 8, Ruth Bader Ginsburg Papers, Library of Congress (FERC-y).

16. United States Supreme Court note to Judge Scalia from John [Paul Stevens] and United States Supreme Court letter to Nino [Scalia] from Lewis [Powell], both June 18, 1986, Box 24, Folder 7, Antonin Scalia Papers, Harvard Law School Library; Stuart Taylor, Jr., "High Court's 1985–86 Term: Mixed Results for President," *New York Times*, July 10, 1986 (62 percent); Cover photograph, *Smithsonian*, January 1977 (dangled); Stuart Taylor, Jr., "The Morning Line on the Bench, as Revised," *New York Times*, September 25, 1986 (dangerous).

17. Handwritten note to Nino [Scalia] from Frank [Michelman], June 23, 1986, Box 24, Folder 3, Antonin Scalia Papers, Harvard Law School Library.

18. "Remarks at the Swearing-in Ceremony for William H. Rehnquist as Chief Justice and Antonin Scalia as Associate Justice of the Supreme Court of the United States," September 26, 1986, The American Presidency Project, U.C. Santa Barbara; video of Rehnquist-Scalia ceremony at the White House, Ronald Reagan Presidential Library, https://www.youtube.com/watch?v=3t3DQiMX8ao&t=494s; Stuart Taylor, Jr., "Rehnquist and Scalia Take Their Places on Court," *New York Times*, September 27, 1986.

19. White House memo to Peter J. Wallison from Alan Charles Raul, Subject: East Room Swearing-in Ceremony, September 24, 1986, Box 19157, Alan Charles Raul Files, Ronald Reagan Presidential Library; White House Schedule of Swearing-in Proceedings, September 26, 1986 [September 24], Box 19157, Alan Charles Raul Files, Ronald Reagan Presidential Library.

20. Richard Carelli, Asbury Park Press [AP], September 27, 1986 (cameras, stifling, wisdom); Associated Press Wirephoto captions, *The News* [Paterson, New Jersey], September 27, 1986 (Scalias, justices posing); Andrea Neal, "Scalia Now Must Learn the Ropes," *Tampa Bay Times* [UPI], September 27, 1986 (Stewart); Taylor, "Rehnquist and Scalia Take Their Places," (400, occupied); Tony Mauro, "Rehnquist, Scalia Join Supreme Court," *Herald Statesman* [Yonkers; Gannett News Service], September 27, 1986 (moderately); Ruth Marcus, "Rehnquist, Scalia Take Their Oaths," *Washington Post*, September 27, 1986 (well, Bork); Glen Elsasser, "Rehnquist Is Chief Justice," *Chicago Tribune* (antique, Spaniol, smiles, mahogany); *Supreme Court Journal*, October Term 1985, 887–93 (transcript of Supreme Court swearing-in proceedings), https://www.supremecourt.gov/pdfs/journals/scannedjournals/1985_journal.pdf.

Index